JORVIK

A Tale of the Last Viking

Sheelagh Kelly was born in York, where she still lives. When she left work as a book-keeper to bring up two daughters, her interest in genealogy and desire to trace her own ancestors resulted in her first book, *A Long Way from Heaven*. What she subsequently discovered led on to the highly successful and entertaining Feeney Saga, *For My Brother's Sins, Erin's Child* and *Dickie*.

Also in Arrow by Sheelagh Kelly

A Long Way from Heaven
For My Brother's Sins
Erin's Child
My Father, My Son
Dickie

JORVIK

A Tale of the Last Viking

Sheelagh Kelly

ARROW

First published by Arrow Books in 1993

1 3 5 7 9 10 8 6 4 2

First published in Great Britain by
Century in 1992

Arrow edition 1993
Random House, 20 Vauxhall Bridge Road, London SW1V 2SA

Random House Australia (Pty) Limited
20 Alfred Street, Milsons Point, Sydney,
New South Wales 2061, Australia

Random House New Zealand Limited
18 Poland Road, Glenfield
Auckland 10, New Zealand

Random House South Africa (Pty) Limited
PO Box 337, Bergvlei, South Africa

Random House UK Limited Reg. No. 954009

A CIP catalogue record for this book
is available from the British Library

ISBN 0 09 970570 2

Typeset by Pure Tech Corporation, Pondicherry, India
Printed and bound in Great Britain by
Cox & Wyman Ltd, Reading, Berkshire

For
James Andrew Robbins

Author's Note

Although Harald of Norway was not known by his nickname Hardrada until well after his death, I have used this name in order to more easily distinguish him from Harold of England. Similarly, I have employed the Old English title of ealdorman rather than the Danish eorl to avoid confusion with the higher rank of earl. Apart from Jorvik, most of the place names are in the Anglo-Saxon form.

Place Names

Ægelsburg	– Aylesbury, Bucks.
Assandun	– Ashingdon, Essex
Bathum	– Bath
Brytland	– Wales
Conyngstrete	– Coney Street, York
Corcaig	– Cork
Dyflinn	– Dublin
Dyflinnstein	– lost place in York, situated north of North Street
Earlsburh	– residence of the Northumbrian earls, on which site was later built St Mary's Abbey
Eochaill	– Youghal
Elrondyng	– the Multangular Tower
Fuleford	– Fulford
Gæignesburh	– Gainsborough, Lincs.
Gleawanceaster	– Gloucester
Grenewic	– Greenwich
Hedeby	– lost market town in Denmark, replaced by Schleswig
Humbre	– Humber
Jorvik	– York
Lindissi	– Lindsey, Lincs.
Nidaros	– Trondheim, Norway
Osboldewic	– Osbaldwick, York
Oxnaford	– Oxford
Richale	– Riccall, Yorks.
Sæfern	– Severn
Skarthaborg	– Scarborough

Stiklarstadir	–	Stiklestad, Norway
Stanfordbrycg	–	Stamford Bridge, Yorks.
Steinngata	–	Stonegate, York
Tathaceaster	–	Tadcaster, Yorks.
Temes	–	Thames
Treante	–	Trent
Use	–	Ouse
Varangian Sea	–	Baltic
Wæringwicumshire	–	Warwickshire
Walbegata	–	Walmgate, York
Weorgornaceaster	–	Worcester
Wintanceaster	–	Winchester

Glossary

The following list is a mixture of Old Norse, Old English and Irish terms

biarki	– little bear
brok	– breeches
bryd-guma	– bridegroom
carl or churl	– common man
drengr	– brave, worthy man
ealdorman	– king's representative acting between monarch and people
finn-gall	– fair foreigner
fostri	– foster father, foster son etc.
fyrd	– the King's militia
gemot	– meeting
hnefatafl	– board game
hersir	– a landed nobleman
jarl	– earl
kerling	– old woman
kotsetlan	– cottagers owing service to their lord
langskips	– longships
lochlannach	– men of the land of lakes and rivers
morgengyfu	– morning gift
nithing	– a man without honour
shire-reeve	– sheriff
skald	– poet
skoari	– cobbler
skyr	– porridge

sokemen	– superior landowning peasant
thegn	– nobleman owning more than five hides of land. A king's thegn owed duties to the monarch and might have thegns of his own
thrall	– slave
ves-heill!	– a salutation meaning 'Be in good health!'
wapentake (*vapnatak*)	– a subdivision of land, also the legal assembly of that subdivision
wealas	– foreigners
witan	– council

Chapter One

13 November A.D. *1002, St Brice's Day.*

None of them knew that they rode towards massacre. The whispers had not yet filtered into the northern lands from whence they came. They knew, of course, that all was not well in Ethelred's England; almost fifty years had elapsed since the fall of Eric Bloodaxe and the dissolution of the great Viking kingdom of Jorvik, but in the latter years the triumphant achievements of King Alfred's line had been despoiled by a monarch who was as cowardly as he was foolish. Encouraged by Ethelred's capricious reign, the Norsemen had reinstigated their plunder. Throughout the last two decades the king's ineffectual method of coping with the viking scourge was to pay them massive amounts of Danegeld. Now, even the most English of Englishmen had begun to wonder if life might be easier under the shrewd King Swein Forkbeard, rather than being bled to death by their own fitful monarch . . . These mutterings had reached the court. In fear for his life, Ethelred saw treachery even from those Danes who had served him well for years. This led to his rashest decision so far: he ordered a massacre of all the Danes in England.

However, the family who rode south on that St Brice's Day was not privy to these machinations. Ahead lay gaiety, several days' feasting and a comfortable bed. Since mooring their boat in the Treante when the water changed course, they had ridden for

1

days over tangled heath and moorland, wild marshy plains and sections of Roman road overgrown with weeds. In between these long stretches of isolation they would happen upon a stockaded town or village where Einar would blow his trumpet to warn of their coming. With luck, there would be another such haven before nightfall. The densely-forested route they travelled now was no place to camp; only the distant thud of a woodman's axe bespoke another human presence. They had not encountered a soul for the last twenty miles.

Einar, his wife Ragnhild and their three small children were on their way to a feast at the house of Ragnhild's sister, Estrid, in celebration of her first-born. Estrid and her husband had temporary residence in Wessex; they were amongst a group of hostages taken by Ethelred after the last payment of Danegeld with the aim of ensuring the cessation of Viking raids on the country. Forkbeard's sister and her husband were held captive, too. In keeping with Ethelred's past decisions this was met with contempt by Einar, who was one of those ready to accept Forkbeard on the English throne – even though he was a Dane. Einar, a Vestfolder by heritage, could not abide the Danes, and it made him furious when some ignorant oaf of an Englishman lumped all Scandinavians together under this same title; the Danes were a much inferior breed to the people of Norway. Even so, now that Forkbeard had won Norway from Olaf Tryggvason, and just as brothers might squabble amongst themselves yet become as one in times of family strife, so the bond of Norse tongue and cultural unity led Einar to accept the Danish king in favour of Ethelred.

Unlike his wife, who had emigrated from Norway with her family as a girl, Einar was the second generation to have been born at Jorvik. His parents were dead now, as were Ragnhild's, but the couple

2

kept links with Norway and often visited those siblings who had chosen to return to the fjords. Indeed, each considered their estate at Jorvik to be merely an extension of the family's Norwegian homeland. Nevertheless, they had assimilated well with the native population to build a thriving Anglo-Scandinavian centre of world trade.

However, the part of England into which they ventured now was like a foreign country, and Einar came well-armed into Wessex, keeping his horse near the wooden wagon that conveyed his family. In addition to his own axe and sword, he brought five sokemen who were well-equipped for danger, for although the hostages were permitted to go about their everyday affairs, they were under close watch and there would be Anglo-Saxons at the feasting. Only the thrall, or slave, who drove the wagon had no axe to protect himself, the law forbidding him to carry arms.

At thirty-five, Einar was ten years his wife's senior, though by no means past his prime. The voluminous cloak that draped not just his flanks but those of his mount, the density and richness of its cloth, the fur hat and neatly-trimmed beard, the array of weapons, all shouted nobility; 'twas a very rich man who carried a sword.

His wife, too, was swathed in tiers of luxury, only her round healthy face at the mercy of the weather. Ragnhild, heavily pregnant, had qualms about making the long trip beyond the safety of the Danelaw, and it was merely out of affection for her sister that she did so. With Einar the Short – a jocular title as he was six foot four – and his bodyguards to protect her, she had few fears about wild animals or outlaws, but what use would they be if the jolting cart encouraged her child to be born? She shifted in discomfort, rousing the sleeping infant whose head was on her lap. With tender hand she petted him back to slumber, gazing fondly at her other children, both of whom also slept, cushioned against the November frosts by a pile of hides and straw.

A chaffinch gave fluid call to warn his tribe of intruders. They rose as a cloud, but soon dropped back to the forest floor pecking for beechmast as the wagon rumbled on. Ragnhild's clear blue eyes rolled upwards through the branches, some completely bare, the oaks still well-clothed. This morning the sun had shone but now in the mid-afternoon the light was failing and the snatches of sky were grey. One of the cumbersome wooden wheels hit a tree root, jarring her yet again and setting the unborn child squirming. She prayed to Frigg, mother of the gods, to hold the child safe and make the journey over soon.

'Want to pee-wee!' A thin wail emerged from beneath the goatskins calling a halt to the journey.

Ragnhild sighed and donned a helpless expression. 'What a place to choose. Husband, can you . . . ?'

'Sling the pigling to me!' boomed Einar, but he was smiling as he threw back his cloak, dismounted and hoisted his three-year-old daughter from the cart. Still drowsy, she was held out to perform her task. 'With luck such as mine there will come a hundred outlaws screaming for blood when I have my hands thus full.' When nothing happened immediately, Einar began to whistle. Shortly, the pattering of droplets onto rotting leaves accompanied his tune and both were enveloped in steam.

Disturbed from their nap, the six-year-old boy and his younger sister examined their location whilst their mother gulped water from a kidskin. During those few moments whilst the horses rested, the intensity of the silence became unnerving. Ragnhild's flesh crawled and she wished herself somewhere less hostile. The thrall used this interlude to flex his muscles, tensed against the cold, but to little effect. Still aching, he hunched into his threadbare wrap and raked at a

4

fleabite with grimy nails. Of all the travellers he was the darkest. Whilst the sokemen varied in colouring, their lord's family was pure Nordic – five shades of blond ranging from Einar's dark yellow to the youngest's silver-white.

'Finished?' asked Einar. 'Shake off the drops then.' And he swung her back into the cart where the occupants made grumbles of complaint as a draught swept under the goatskin yet again. The thrall urged the horses into movement and once more the wagon-wheels crunched over beechmast and bark. 'By the gods, my arse aches!' Einar winced and shifted in his stirrups. 'I hope this feast is worth it.'

'Are we nearly there?' whined the boy, Ragnor.

'Ja, soon be there,' soothed his mother. 'Einar, tell them some riddles to entertain them.' With vociferous accord, the children became more animated.

'Hmm, let me see.' Einar took one hand from the reins to pull at his beard. 'What has skin but cannot hold water?' They failed to guess.

'Gunnhilde!' he told them. The little girl sulked at the laughter which her incontinence provoked and buried her head under the covers.

'I've got one and you won't guess it,' piped up her sister. 'What has teeth but cannot bite?'

'That's easy, ninny,' scoffed Ragnor. ''Tis a comb. I have a better one. What has a mouth but cannot speak?'

Einar rubbed his chin, swaying to the horse's gait. 'I cannot guess – you must tell me.'

'A river!' The boy was pleased at outwitting his father.

'But a river does speak,' objected Ragnhild, seeking to put the boy in his place for his cocksureness. 'It whispers, it argues, it roars . . .'

Her husband interjected: 'What stinks but is not a pig, can walk and run but cannot sit?'

After much puzzlement the children could only come up with, 'A cow?'

'No – a Dane with piles!' Einar's sokemen laughed heartily.

'What are pi . . .'

'Your father is a gowk!' Cuckoo, Ragnhild called him as she pruned the child's question. ''Tis best he gets his foolery over before we reach polite company.'

Einar forced his mouth into a serious angle. 'One last riddle. What cuts but cannot kill?'

'Mother's tongue!' laughed the children, who had heard this a dozen times before. Einar laughed too as his wife swung an arm at him. 'Methinks I should rest my own tongue now before it is ripped out.'

When they emerged from the forest they met with a party of southern Danes, also on their way to the feast, which gave Ragnhild new reason to be nervous. She whispered a warning for her husband to adopt his best behaviour and for the moment he reserved his wit, but she knew that when the horns brimmed with drink he would be unable to constrain his impishness. Already Ragnhild was rehearsing excuses to her hosts in order to leave the feast early and so miss the inevitable fight.

Night was falling and frost beginning to sparkle on the goatskins when, to her relief, they reached their destination. The merry sound of lute and pipe wavered out to meet them, but Einar was wary before entering the large timber house, first checking behind the door and then counting the number of Anglo-Saxons present. On establishing that there was insufficient number to offer threat, he relaxed. The guests were welcomed into the torchlit hall by the proud new parents with their baby son, given bowls of water and towels and treated with the utmost hospitality. The children were handed to the charge of a female slave who, after feeding them, put them to bed. Despite constant napping on the journey they were exhausted and were soon asleep.

Ragnhild was tired, too. Smoke from the central

fire billowed around the room seeking an outlet in the thatch. In no time at all her eyes became red, her chest tight. Far from soothing her, the music aggravated her headache. She had little appetite for the gargantuan meal of meat, fish and fowl laid out in the feasting hall. At home she ate frugally, and even Einar had a modest appetite for such a big man. Watching him now through the pall of smoke and flickering candlelight, his wife wished he would be as moderate in his liquid consumption. Einar imbibed freely of the horn which, by nature of its shape, was impossible to put down until drained.

Mead and wine flowed. Einar behaved abominably, unable to withhold his jokes even before the meal was over, but his neighbour seemed to find the big man uproariously entertaining – probably because he did not understand half of the Northern dialect. Would his reaction be the same when Einar began to joke at the expense of the English? Ragnhild did not wish to find out. Begging her sister's understanding, she excused herself and went to the sleeping quarters at the end of the hall. Before retiring, she examined her three children, all of whom slept. Shivering against the cold, she laid on the sleeping bench attached to the wall and pulled the eiderdowns over her head. But the moment she closed her eyes she was once again jarring up and down in the wagon, and each time she prepared to slip into unconsciousness, the roar of drunken men would jolt her awake. Her advanced state of pregnancy brought restlessness, too. The child was unusually active, grinding its head into her bladder. With a sigh, she heaved her bulk from the mattress and, trembling with cold, groped her way outside to relieve herself.

Whilst she fumbled and squatted in the pitch-black latrine, a stealthy procession of feet trod by. Preoccupied with cold and discomfort Ragnhild ignored it. The din from the hall increased; there was

7

pandemonium now. The ghastly screams warned Ragnhild this was more than drunken revelry. Clutching her belly she made an impulsive rush at the doorway and came upon a shambles.

Fuddled by drink and outnumbered, the Norsemen had had no time to unsheath their weapons. A score lay dead already while others struggled on, trying to wrest the swords from their attackers. Even Einar's bodyguards, ever alert for danger, had been lulled by the hospitality and were now battling for their lives. Heart thudding, Ragnhild searched wildly for her husband but could not see him. Her children! She wheeled towards the room in which they slept, just in time to see their assassin emerge with reddened sword. Her lips parted but nothing emerged. Too numbed to scream, she backed away, trying to escape the carnage, but the fighting engulfed her. Her passage through the flailing arms was clumsy; she tripped and continued her escape on all fours, balking as her hand encountered a bloody puddle but not daring to stop. Her only salvation lay in the hope that the attackers were too engrossed in their killing to look down and notice her. Sobbing, she reached the door, scrambled to her feet and lurched out into the night.

With the most casual of actions a passing soldier employed his sword. Too shocked to feel pain, Ragnhild instinctively protected her abdomen. The Englishman tugged his weapon from her left shoulder, crimson spouted, Ragnhild fell and knew no more.

It was a blessing. Unconscious and presumed dead, she was spared the sight of her children massacred in their beds, her husband with his arms hacked off as he tried to prevent the murder of his family, the rest of her kin dead too. When she came round the house was ablaze, the air thick with the stench of burning flesh, and the perpetrators gone. Using her last ounce of energy she dragged herself from the encroaching flames, before fainting again. Revived a second time, she found herself being carried away by those thralls who had hidden at the first sign of trouble, away to the house of a bondsman where, bawling in agony and grief, she was delivered of a son. The labour was mercifully short. Sapped by loss of blood from her wound, Ragnhild could not have endured a lengthy travail.

Now, watching the child suckle under her bandaged shoulder, she chose a name worthy of his victorious fight for life: Sigurd. In years to come this precious babe would be the one to exact blood-money from the English as payment for his family's slaughter; his mother would ensure that.

Vengeance did not have to wait on Sigurd's adulthood. Enraged by the death of his sister Gunnhilde and thousands of Scandinavian men, women and children at the hands of Ethelred, King Swein Forkbeard launched a punitive mission into Wessex and East Anglia, wreaking dreadful retribution. Until then, Ragnhild and her son had remained in hiding; ignorant over the extent of the butchery, she was too terrified of a return to Jorvik, convinced she would find similiar carnage there. Even when a pedlar brought news that the Danelaw was largely untouched, its Scandinavian populace too dense to incur attack from their English neighbours, she retained her obsession that it was just another plot. Besides, if the pedlar's other information were true then there was no reason for her to return: Ethelred had confiscated all Einar's property and had given it to one of his henchmen. On Swein's departure from the coast, Ragnhild and her baby son escaped with him, and with only her skills as a midwife to earn her a living, settled in the Vestfold region of Norway, the family homeland.

The small community in which they lived had once been a marketplace, but now the traders passed it by in search of more favourable ports. Nestled at the head of a small bay that formed a ready-made harbour, it was for the most extent protected from pirate raids by numerous islets amongst the shallow waters at its mouth, and by the mountain range behind. Between mountains and shore was a sloping meadow where the visiting traders had once camped, their ships laden with pelts of marten and bear, sealskins, walrus hide and ivory that had been bartered for silver and soapstone vessels hewn from the local rock. The folk who lived in the scattered buildings at the foot of the mountains still crafted their bowls and hammered out jewellery, but their main occupation was farming. It was here in this region of deep forests, secret lakes and lush vegetation that Ragnhild and her son led their bucolic existence.

Dispossessed, Ragnhild was permitted to live in the home of her brother Olaf and his wife, but it was a sad decline. From being the wife of a chieftain she was now reduced to peasantry, her hands red from menial work. For the first couple of years Olaf tried to persuade her to marry again; this annoyed her. 'It is a hard thing when my own brother wants to be rid of me!'

'You are only six and twenty and yet you act like a grandmother!' retorted Olaf, a dour and reserved man. 'Does it not make you crave for more children of your own when you deliver other women's?'

Ragnhild was fond of infants and loved her own son dearly, but as she said now, 'I would sacrifice the child I have if it would bring Einar back. I shall never, never find one who measures up to him – and I shall never marry again so if you want to be rid of me you must find some other method!'

Olaf matched her prickliness. 'I have no wish to be rid of you, woman! You are my sister – all I wish for is to see you happy.'

Ragnhild's brother could argue all he liked but he

still made her feel like a burden. To salve the pain of injustice and to keep the blood-feud alive she would tell Sigurd of his noble forebears and of their prosperous living in Jorvik, the metropolis of the northern world. Even from babyhood the graphic tale of the massacre was impressed upon him, so nurturing revenge.

The saga never lost its impact. At each telling Sigurd would be unable to rest, his mind alive with the picture of his father's death at the hands of cowards. Not for him the frivolous games of other boys, he must use his days for practising his sword-strokes in readiness for the English. When Uncle Olaf had carved him a set of farm animals out of bone his mother had flung them away and scolded his tears of disappointment. 'A man does not weep! Especially the man who is my hope for the future. One day when you are old enough you will avenge your father and your brother and sisters, and reclaim your position. Then I will be proud of you. The monster Ethelred shall rue the day he gave the order to spill our blood.'

Yet where had all this rhetoric led? Now, when Sigurd felt old enough to enact the role his mother had planned for him she and others held him back. Fired with such tremendous rage at the English king for his cruel deed, he grew impatient with those who told him he must wait until he was old enough. Where was this country called England in which he had been sired? What did years matter when one was capable of knocking the sword from one's teacher's hands and having him cry for mercy? Sigurd could do this . . . at least, he had managed it once. That he had earned a whipping afterwards for his dishonourable method of fighting did not count. He had done it – and for the sake of Odin, where did honour come into this? You were meant to kill your enemy, not furnish him with the chance to kill you. That was what came of all this Christian rubbish; his foster-father Uncle Olaf had, like most Norwegians, adopted this religion but Sigurd preferred the old gods favoured by his mother. What use was this Christ Who preached peace when what Sigurd needed was muscle and courage to avenge his father's murder? To this end he wore round his neck a silver amulet depicting Thor's mighty hammer which, one day, would crack the skull of the English king whom Sigurd had grown to loathe.

If only they would let him go! Why had his mother suddenly become so protective of him? Truth to tell, it was a rather nice feeling in one respect, for Sigurd had always been jealous of the affectionate way his mother indulged other young boys, contradicting every statement she had made to her own son about playing childish games. Not for Ragnhild the selflessness of motherhood. Any pride she might have in her child was conditional upon him winning back her own position. Indeed, Ragnhild was a paradox: she could be warm and maternal or downright vicious. The English blade might have maimed her shoulder, disallowing her to raise her left elbow above breast level, but that did not prevent her from using the other arm. If Sigurd upset her he could only hope that if she held ought in her hand it was a stick and not a club, for she would use either to beat him. She had a tongue on her like Loki, god of mischief, and was far more aggressive than some of the men. And yet at night, Sigurd would hear frightened little mews coming from her bed. For all her faults she was his mother and he loved her. It was good to know that under the disciplined crust she really cared for his well-being.

The boy might have been sobered to learn that it was not just out of fear for his personal safety that Ragnhild held him back, but fear that he would be defeated. If Sigurd died her future died with him. He must wait, achieve potency, or all her nurturing would be wiped out in one stroke.

King Swein had proved something of a disappointment to Sigurd's mother. The raids on England that had occurred over the last decade were little more than acts of piracy. Content to be bought off with thousands of pounds of English silver, the vikings would retire to their own lands, leaving the hated Ethelred still monarch. Sigurd himself did not mind this so much, for he wanted personal involvement in Ethelred's downfall, longed to be at him, pined for adventure of any kind. He noticed not the stupendous beauty of the Norwegian fjords and mountains, only the boredom of his pastoral life, the long dark winters soaked to the bone with rain and snow, chapped by howling winds, and the claustrophobic attentions of neighbours who knew more about him than he did himself. Oh, to meet a man he did not know!

Then, in 1013 when Sigurd was in his eleventh year, a strange phenomenon occurred; a host of warships appeared in the bay. Like eels they came, pulled as if by instinct to the sea. Every river, every fjord, disgorged their shoals of men, men drawn from peaceful occupations by the greater pull of war and the promise of wealth, for King Swein had decreed that England was once again ripe for attack. This was to be no lightning raid but a highly organized military operation. This time he would not be fobbed off with bribes but was intent on conquest and political power. With every day the fleet swelled, until now it was ready to sail for Aggersborg, one of the King's fortresses in the north of Denmark, where all would unite with other Scandinavians to make an awesome force.

The once-tranquil meadow came alive. People scurried back and forth to load the ships with weapons and food. How great was Sigurd's thrill at confronting all these strangers; his only quandary being which one he should talk to first. Their stations varied from thrall to farmer to mercenary. The latter he admired from a respectful distance, eager to engage them in conversation but kept far too busy by his Uncle Olaf who was making ready his own ship. Sigurd longed to be part of the expedition, but he had learnt from past experience that there was little point in asking . . . However, if one did not ask one could not be told No. The plan was as yet incomplete, but Sigurd's mind worked on it as he paused now to watch his mother baking in the open air – every sunbeam was utilized after the long dark winter holed up indoors. Ragnhild was part of the problem; how could he escape under her eagle eye in broad daylight?

He leaned on the timber wall of the house and made casual enquiry of her. 'Will you go to wish Uncle farewell when he sets sail?' Sigurd's voice was as yet at the opposite end of the scale to the deep guttural tone of his uncle, however hard he might try to sound manly.

'Hah!' Ragnhild barely glanced up from the wooden trough in which she pummelled dough. Moisture glistened on her temple. 'Where would I find the time with all this extra work to do?' There had been herrings to pickle, ale to brew and meat to cure ready for the voyage. 'And who will get the praise when the battle is won, eh? Not the womenfolk. I'd like to know where they'd be without us to feed them.' Like that of her son, her own voice danced up and down along the sentence, ending with an upwards inflection in the manner of Nordic speech. She gave a last angry thump at the dough then tore off a large fistful and began to shape it ready for baking. 'The ships will sink before they are out of the bay with all this food on board – and who would care?'

His mother was inclined to forthright views but Sigurd was puzzled by her attitude today of all days.

'Are you not glad that we . . .' He checked himself hurriedly, 'that Uncle is going at last to punish the dog Ethelred for the death of my father?'

Her expression was mean. 'Uncle – pff! He is not interested in avenging your father. All he cares about is his own gain. He says he'll win back our land for us, but you can be sure if he wins anything it will be for himself: You and I, he treats like slaves. My own brother! I am not a vindictive woman but sometimes I could cut out his lying tongue and stick it up his rear. "Come and live with me," he tells us. "I will take care of you." And this is the way he takes care of us!' Ragnhild banged floury hands at her bosom. 'Look at me in this sack, when his own wife wears cloth of gold!'

Sigurd thought there could be another reason for her anger. 'Does your shoulder hurt today, Mother?' The old wound still caused pain, showing itself in these bouts of irascibility; but this happened mainly in low temperatures. The weather was glorious today, not a cloud in the sky, the lambs were shorn and now grazed high on the slopes.

She rounded on him in an explosion of flour. 'Do I have to feel pain before I voice a grievance?' Then after an extended glare she sighed and dropped her chin to rest between the bronze oval brooches which held the shoulderstraps of her dress. 'Ja, ja . . . it hurts, even the sun cannot help now. I fear I shall not live to see the English rat defeated. You must pardon me if I do not share your joy, but I have seen it all before. Time after time our men sail away to England, and still he thrives while I grow old.'

The lines of annoyance had smoothed into a world-weary expression. Her frame was well-fed, with pads of fat upon her hips and breast, yet discomfort pinched her face, lending the illusion that she was under-nourished. The last decade had brought silver to her hair-roots; each year the gold diminished and each year Ragnhild felt even more devalued. Her shins were turning bandy from squatting by the fire. Though the latter were hidden by the long gown, Sigurd had to concede that she did look old, old and sad and worn. He wondered what she was thinking of now, for her mind was obviously far away. His mother often drifted off like this whilst he was speaking to her.

Ragnhild was thinking of Einar and her three dead infants. Even Sigurd, precious as he was, could never make up for their loss. For all her talk of vengeance, she knew in her heart that even when Ethelred was conquered it would not help the pain, would not stop the vivid nightmares from which she woke terrified and crying out loud. Often, whilst she toiled, she replayed her life with Einar, how she had met him, their first kiss . . .

Moved by her doleful expression, Sigurd wanted to put his arms round her but that would not have been masculine, would label him a child. Instead he injected his voice with a gruff affection. 'Old – nei! No one would guess you have a man for a son.'

Ragnhild laughed then, became a different person, squeezed his cheeks between floury hands and squashed her nose against his, before returning to her task. Placing the loaves on an iron plate she grasped its long handle and set it over the embers of the fire. 'Is this man to carry those herring barrels down to the ship or does he think they will walk there by themselves?'

Sigurd brushed the flour from his cheeks, hefted one of the barrels onto his shoulder and loped down the path to the jetty. Denuded of their figureheads lest they upset the good spirits of the land, the longships basked in the glittering waters like harmless ducks. Tomorrow, the ducks would metamorphose into dragons whose snarling teeth would rip into the very bowels of Ethelred's kingdom. Sigurd paused, barrel on shoulder. It was impossible to count the ships – the bay seemed crammed with them – and even more difficult to pinpoint his uncle's craft amongst the identical prows. Sigurd's deeply-set blue eyes narrowed further against the glare of sun on water. Ah! there was Uncle Olaf's pennant dangling at the top of his mast. He hefted the barrel and directed his gangling legs toward the far end of the stone jetty where he now noticed Uncle Olaf himself giving instructions to his crew; instructions, not orders, for Olaf had no following. Apart from his thralls the crew was made up with men of equal status who had merely banded together in their cause.

As he approached, Sigurd evaluated the man in a new light, remembering his mother's opinion. Would Olaf really steal what belonged to his kin? Honourable Uncle Olaf, who had taught Sigurd how to read the runes, had encouraged his natural talent for wood-carving and spent as much time with him in swordplay as he had with his own sons? Dour, unimaginative Olaf – did he really have such an ambitious spirit? Maybe . . . for why did he leave his sons in charge of the Vestfold estate instead of taking them along to fight? Unless perhaps Uncle Olaf had his eye on something better across the North Sea. Jorvik, perhaps?

No, Sigurd was not convinced. He had always been fond of his uncle and despite Ragnhild's grumbles she and her son were treated as part of this closely-knit family. His mother liked to grumble. It was also a habit of hers that she trusted no one – understandable after the horrors she had endured, but Sigurd felt that this mistrust should not extend to one's kin. Nevertheless, Olaf was a farmer, and were not farmers always hungry for land?

'Ah, *fostri*!' Olaf turned and caught sight of the boy with the barrel. 'What delicacies has your mother sent us?'

17

'Herrings.' The barrel was beginning to rub Sigurd's shoulder.

'And I'll wager she sent them with her blessing for a safe voyage.'

Sigurd grinned. Uncle Olaf was not the merriest of souls but his sarcasm did hold a ring of humour. Receiving instructions to put the barrel in the cargo hold, Sigurd stepped into the boat which was almost on an equal level with the jetty. Being a merchant craft it was bulkier than the warships, but retained a certain grace, its stem and stern rising in elegant curves out of the water. Between these two points stretched eighty feet of oak and pine. Amidships was an open cargo hold, with decking fore and aft where there were also four rowing benches. At present, its rectangular sail was hauled neatly into the yard. Sigurd deposited the barrel and paused to wipe the gloss from his brow.

'Tired after carrying just one?' teased Uncle Olaf. ''Tis fortunate we do not have to rely on your stamina to win England.' Sigurd gave an innocent smile and allowed his blond hair to be ruffled as he went on his way back to the house for another barrel. When he had transported half of them, Uncle Olaf said he deserved a short rest. In gratitude, he sagged to the deck and leaned against one of the rowing benches in the stern, one arm draped over the side. Hypnotized by the rippling azure waters, his mind drifted. Absent fingers picked at the tufts of tarred animal hair that caulked the grooves in the planking. The daydream wafted him to one of the warships, steered it through treacherous waters and sea-battles, to cleave in glory England's rivers.

His eyes perused the stack of weapons that his uncle's crew would use. With their lack of ornamentation, the spears and axes failed to inspire, for Uncle Olaf was less prosperous than his brother-in-law had been. Sigurd promised himself now that on retrieving his estate he would buy a sword with a silver hilt like his father would have owned, and a shield embossed with gold that would blind his enemies – perhaps, he decided affectionately, he would have one made for Uncle too, just to repay him for . . . Sigurd's eyes focused on his uncle's axe and his thoughts were instantly funnelled into the present. He stared at it, sucking on his necklace of blue beads. A plan took shape but, glancing about him, he decided there were too many folk around for him to enact it right now. That was the nub of the matter – there were always too many folk about – but the answer would surely come to one so determined. Jumping to his feet he leapt back onto the jetty and resumed work.

'Hey, frog's legs!' One of his neighbours, a tooth-less old man, hailed him with a wink. 'You are in fine leaping form today. I see a look in your eye that tells me you intend to sneak off with the fleet when it sails.'

Alarmed at being so easily read, Sigurd tried to assume melancholy. 'Alas, I must stay behind to take care of my mother.'

The elder bared his gums and delivered a crafty nudge. 'You cannot fool me! I was young once . . .'

'Er, my pardons, old friend!' Sigurd edged back-wards. 'I must not tarry for there is work to be done.' He spun and hurried on his way praying that Uncle Olaf had not overheard the old goat's comment. That was yet another disadvantage of this place; he could not tell any of these folk a thing they did not already know about him.

The following morning, when Ragnhild took ad-vantage of the climate and squatted outside the timber house to clean a hare, Sigurd hovered round her, showing particular concern for her well-being. 'Here, let me do that for you if your shoulder pains you.'

She did not look up, her fingers wrenching the skin

19

from the carcase. 'The day I cannot remove a hare's kirtle is the day I cannot lift my hand to your backside.'

Sigurd looked hurt and sank to the ground. 'I wanted but to help. I thought that now the food is loaded and Uncle about to leave you deserve a well-earned rest.'

His altruism was met by an outraged laugh. 'Rest? Look at those broks you wear!' In the way that he was seated with his knees drawn under his chin she could see a portion of buttock peeping through his yellow leggings. 'And your good aunt will no doubt have many a task for me when her husband is not around to curb her.' Ragnhild complained about Olaf treating her with disrespect but his wife, unchecked, could be a hundred times worse. 'As if it is not bad enough him creeping off just as haymaking is upon us – oh, quickly!' She wagged a blood-smeared finger at the milch cow which had lifted its tail to urinate.

Well-primed, Sigurd grabbed a bowl and, running to the cow's rear, held this out beneath the flow. The urine splashed up from the wooden surface into his face. Sigurd contorted his mouth but remained there dutifully to catch the rest. It was rather aggravating that his mother forbade him to waste his time on childish pursuits yet seemed not to regard this as trivial. Had he been in two minds over his plans before then this had nudged him into a decision: he was not going to stand here catching cow's piss for the rest of his life, even for his mother's sake.

When the beast finished he transported the bowl at arms' length to a vat and tipped in its contents which would be used for its ammoniac properties in the cleaning of clothes. Still wearing the look of distaste he then submerged his head into a barrel of water, sloshed it around vigorously, withdrew it and shook it like a dog.

His mother reared away under the cascade of droplets and laughed at his obvious disgust. 'Come, take those broks off and let me mend them while I have a spare moment to breathe.'

'Er . . . nei!' He pulled his kirtle down over the rip, backing away as he spoke. 'I promised Uncle I would help look after the farmstead while he is away. If you do not wish me to assist with the hare then I have many tasks to attend.'

Ragnhild cocked her scarved head in disbelieving manner. 'You think your mother is an addle-brain?' For a moment Sigurd feared she was wise to his plan, but was relieved when she smirked, 'You go to wave the ships off – and with your genitals hanging out! Such respect you show our heroes.'

Dropping his manly stance, he pleaded with her, face wreathed in earnest, 'Can the mending not wait until later, Mother? 'Twill be such a sight it would be cruel of you to make me miss it.'

She clubbed him with the skinned hare. 'Oh, I am such a cruel mother! Be gone then, if you must.'

Sigurd made as if to kiss her, paused and agonized for a moment, then after a quick look to make sure the act was unobserved he lunged a peck at her cheek and tore off across the flowered pasture, blond hair bobbing as he ran.

Ragnhild shook her head and waved after him, though he did not turn to see it.

Chapter Two

Sigurd was not so dimwitted as to hide on his uncle's ship. On discovery of the stowaway Olaf would have turned back whatever the outcome – and for his nephew the outcome would have been very painful. Instead, last night, he had chosen another vessel which carried a rowing boat in its belly, packed with leather sleeping bags and tents; the perfect hiding place for the broad-axe he had stolen from his uncle's ship. He would have preferred a sword, but these were all kept on their owner's person and at least the axe was a respectable weapon and not the usual tool of a farmer.

What a nerve-racking task it had been to accomplish his plan with no darkness to shroud him! When he crept from his bed an hour or so before midnight the sun was yet visible, turning the whole bay pink in its descent. It had required great pluck to tiptoe between those camped upon the meadow and down to the jetty, steal aboard his uncle's ship, transfer the axe to his appointed vessel and return to bed without anyone hearing. Now, in triumphant mood, he lay hugging the axe beneath a goatskin, listening to the swish of the water, the activity and cursing of the crew. The ship was a more lissome vessel than his uncle's, its red sail billowing to the wind and carrying it on the outer edges of the fleet across the Vik. Atop the bowed fore-stem a dragon curled its tongue at the air, tasting for salt. Sigurd did not know to whom the ship belonged and did not care. He was on his way to kill his enemy at last!

But as the protective breakwater of skerries gave way to open sea and the rampant prow began to heave and plunge, his exhilaration dwindled. The sun beat down, transforming his goatskin hideaway into an oven. Already, he sweated profusely. His leggings stuck to his limbs and worked their way into the cleft of his buttocks. He grew so hot and irritated that he feared his blood must boil dry. It had been his intention not to reveal his presence until the fleet was well on its way to Denmark, but whether it was safe or no he could not bear the heat a moment longer. Lifting a corner of the hide, he squinted against the cerulean glare.

'Spy!' A fist grabbed his tunic and hauled him into full view of fifty angry vikings who noisily agreed with the punishment. 'Over the side with him!'

Before he could shout anything more than, '*Nei!*' Sigurd was lifted off the deck and cast through the air. He had no time even to close his mouth as his body plummeted into deep water. When he bobbed to the surface, gasping, the ship had put a good length between them. In panic, Sigurd held up his arm, called, 'Hold!' and promptly sank again. Regaining his wits he began to paddle with arms and legs towards a nearer vessel but then, remembering his axe and unwilling to abandon it to those wretches, he felt compelled to swim after the ship from whence he had been flung.

The crew were laughing and pointing at his floundering efforts. When one of them finally extended an oar as a means of rescue he realized that they had only been making sport of him and anger flared. On being hauled aboard dripping, Sigurd took a few moments to recover then leapt for his uncle's axe and began to swing it at his tormentors. Whereupon they roared and whooped with glee, prodded him with swords and aimed their axes at his bare feet, making him dance. Driven to frenzy by their taunts, Sigurd

rotated the weapon above his head, but his only
accomplishment was to make them roar the louder
when he skidded on the wet deck and lost his balance. All belligerence was put aside to enjoy the
comic actions of this boy with the axe almost as big
as himself. The mercenaries clutched their bellies in
mirth – which perpetuated Sigurd's wrath and made
them laugh all the merrier.

Eventually, a brutish-looking Norseman wiped the
tears from his cicatriced face and begged him, 'Cease,
biarki, before you kill us with laughter. Oh! my gut
aches as if it has eaten rotten meat.' He spread his
tightly-breeched legs and inserted his thumbs into the
belt that held his kirtle in place. 'Tell me, what is the
name of this noble warrior who is to slay the English
for us?'

The boy showed resentment at being dubbed 'little
bear'. 'I am Sigurd, son of . . .'

'Sigurd Smallaxe!' interrupted a voice, causing
renewed merriment.

'Sigurd, son of Einar the Short!' retorted the boy,
puce with rage.

The mockery was now replaced by murmurs of
admiration, some fake, others genuine. Einar's size
and abilities were renowned, as was his cowardly
murder. The chieftain, Thorald, appraised the dripping boy whose chest rose and fell with sustained
temper. He was a tall lad with deeply-set eyes that
varied from light to dark blue with the intermittent
flashes of sunlight. He had also a fringe which even
when plastered with brine refused to lie down and
fell into two curls that kissed in the centre of his
brow. Despite the innocent looks and that ridiculous
axe there was conviction in his stance. Thorald began
to pay him more courtesy. 'So . . . you think you will
come and fight the English with us? Why, then, does
one so brave skulk like a rat?'

Sigurd merely glared at Thorald from beneath his

eyebrows, receiving an overall impression of hair. The viking's head was encompassed by matted straw-coloured locks that merged with his beard. His eyes, too, were almost obscured by overhanging brows, and it was impossible to tell through the tangled moustache whether Thorald had any teeth. Only his nose was clearly visible, obviously a frequent target, for its bridge had a pronounced dent in it. Notwithstanding the heavy distribution of gold jewellery around his body, it was evident that Thorald had achieved his rank through brute strength rather than birth; his manner and speech were exceedingly coarse.

At the boy's reticence, Thorald cast back his cloak to reveal bangled arms, placed one large foot on a rowing bench and leaned on it. 'I have heard it said that Einar's son was born on the day that he himself perished. If that is true then by my calculations you are too young to join us.'

The boy seethed. 'Everyone tells me I am too young! If I had asked my uncle to take me on his ship he would have made me stay behind; that is why I did not ask. I may not officially be a man,' this transition would not take place until he was twelve, 'but I am taller and stronger than boys three years older than I. There is not a youth within miles who is as skilled with the sword . . .'

'As skilled as with an axe?' teased Thorald.

'I have even beaten my uncle! I am grown weary of being treated like a child. I must avenge the murder of my father and my brother and sisters.'

The chieftain asked the name of Sigurd's uncle.

'Olaf Sweinsson. He is my mother's kin. He goes to win back our land stolen by the English.'

Thorald played with his grubby beard. The boy noticed that the outer finger of his right hand had been partly severed. The rest of his digits were calloused and scarred from battle. To Sigurd he represented experience, the type of experience that could

25

never be found in Uncle Olaf. What better ally to throw in with? For the moment he decided to over-look the recent mockery.

'Hmm . . . and where lies your land?'

'At Jorvik – but the task of winning it back should fall to me, not my uncle.'

Something flickered in Thorald's eyes. In his eager-ness to curry help, Sigurd misinterpreted the innate cunning for genuine interest. Thorald supported his elbow on his belly and tapped a thoughtful finger to his moustache, concealing all slyness. 'It shall be a fierce battle – are you not afraid to die?'

Sigurd looked indignant. 'A true warrior is afraid of nought. If I succeed in avenging my family's murder then I shall ride to Valhalla a happy man.'

The chieftain draped an arm round the boy's wet shoulders. 'My own brother was murdered by Ethelred also.'

Sigurd appeared even more keen. 'If that is so then we have much in common! You must let me join your force.'

'Have no fear, Sigurd Smallaxe,' the title was meant more kindly now but it continued to sting the boy's pride, 'this time there is no price the English can pay to escape our weapons. We will set our dragons at their throats, put our King on the throne and win back your father's land.' There was a unified roar of approval from the crew members who drifted back to their occupations.

Thorald's steely eyes had noted that his conversa-tion partner looked none too well. He pointed at Sigurd's green cheeks. 'Er, tell me, bold warrior, these are your fighting colours, ja?'

Whilst others guffawed Sigurd admitted that this was the first time, since he was a babe in arms, that he had actually been on a proper voyage and a mouthful of brine had exacerbated the sickness. Thor-ald groped through his rough outer layer to find a

26

note of comfort and said it would pass if the boy sucked a pebble, a few of which he kept for such a purpose. It then became evident that the wind had dropped. In this and neighbouring vessels men were beginning to haul in the huge rectangular sails and unstep the masts. Pine oars were taken down from their supports and the shutters removed from oar-holes. Thorald pushed the lad at one of the rowing benches which were more numerous than in his uncle's ship. 'Come! Shake yourself off, yellow-shanks, we have need of you after all. Share an oar with Ulf Bareface. He has only the muscle of half a man and you will help to balance the rowing power.'

Ulf, a young man with cropped neck and a fringe that almost tangled with his lashes, showed contempt of this unfair remark. What had the lack of a beard to do with ability? Thorald was well aware of his sensitivity in this area and his comments were merely designed to taunt, but Sigurd, appraising the rangy man with the watery blue eyes in their bony sockets, shallow jaw and only the faintest wisps of hair on his cheeks, took the comment literally. 'Move over!' He squelched onto the bench beside Ulf, tucked his axe underneath, and tried to grasp the oar; this was difficult, for Ulf had already leaned into his stroke. Surly of feature, he ignored the command, leaning to and fro, increasing the beat with each second. With Thorald's hugeness denying any form of backlash, Ulf would have to take reprisal on the boy who was far too arrogant by half.

Thorald grinned and relieved the helmsman. From his raised position in the stern he could catch a good view of the boy's comical attempts to pair up with Ulf. Finally achieving hold, Sigurd clamped the oar and leaned into the stroke, comparing his own arms with those of Ulf which he now noticed were not weak at all but knotted with muscle – too late! In that same instant he was catapulted by the violence

27

of Ulf's backwards lunge onto the feet of the man behind. Thorald hooted with laughter and almost lost control of the steerboard. The rear oarsman delivered a good-natured kick to the boy's head, whilst Ulf, still rowing, turned to issue derision from beneath his heavy fringe.

Irate at being humiliated by one so despised as Ulf, Sigurd made great drama out of retaking his position for another attempt. This time Ulf deliberately stopped rowing to allow the boy access to the oar, further advertising his scorn. By now Sigurd was well aware that he had made an enemy, though was not quite sure how that had come about; had he not been trying to help the weakling? No matter, Ulf was of little consequence when one remembered the task ahead. Grabbing the oar, he determined to keep tight hold of it ever after.

As the hour finally came to bed down for the night his blistered hands and chafing limbs had caused him to forget all about his seasickness. When Ulf Bareface made the unexpected gesture of kindness – 'Come, take my place and share Eric's sleeping bag tonight,' he was too tired to question this newfound generosity. Only when he was tucked up and unable to escape did he realise that Eric Fart had been well-named.

It took almost three days to reach North Jutland. Never once in that time did it occur to Sigurd just how frantic his mother would be at his disappearance. If he spared a thought for her at all it was to imagine how proud she would be of her son. Was not this what she had raised him to do?

Ragnhild held other opinions. 'That worthless, scheming little worm. If Ethelred does not kill him then I will!' Only when Sigurd had missed two meals and had failed to come home that night did she propound this theory to her sister-in-law. 'He has gone with Olaf and not a weapon to his name!'

Red with both anger and exertion she leaned on her pitchfork to snatch a well-earned break. Haymaking had begun early this morning. Olaf's wife had not permitted any of the workers nor Ragnhild to rest even though the sun was now at midheaven and unbearably hot. Across the meadows ranks of womenfolk and the occasional male scythed and raked the grass, tossed it this way and that then hung it over poles to dry. Ragnhild's shoulder groaned for mercy but she was not to receive it from her sister-in-law.

Olaf's wife Thora, as dour as her husband, dismissed the matter with a flick of her hand. 'The worthless child will be safe enough with his uncle. Back to work now or we shall not be done before nightfall.'

'Surely we could pause for a morsel to eat!' objected Ragnhild.

'It is not good to work on a full belly,' responded Thora, and made chivvying movements with her hands to urge Ragnhild on.

Ragnhild's temper was up and she slapped at the interfering hands. 'Stop that! I am not an ox to be goaded and worked till I drop. When you work as hard as I do then you can order me about.' Refusing to go further she threw aside her pitchfork and sat down with a bump amongst the sweet-smelling hay, ripped off her headscarf and used it to mop her face. 'You carry on if you want to. I shall rest – and do not dare to say my son is worthless!'

'You have just said as much yourself!' scoffed Thora.

'I am his mother. I can say what I like about him, you cannot! Besides, I repent of my words. They were only said out of anger because you treat me like a slave. When Sigurd wins back my estate I shall be gone from here in a flash.'

'Oh, there is gratitude for you!' Thora bumped the seated Ragnhild with a knee. 'Where would you have been without me when you were widowed and left with nought? I have fed you, clothed you . . .'

'Not you! Olaf!'

'Where is the difference?' demanded Thora. 'And do we get any return for our kindness? Nei, all we have for those years of sacrifice are constant moans and laziness!'

Ragnhild's mouth gaped at this slander, but to offer her instinctive retort would be to make a fool of herself. So, she simply clamped her lips together, and folded her arms until she could produce a suitable reply. 'I understand that you have always viewed me as a threat . . .'

Thora frowned. 'What foolery is this you spout?'

'Einar was much richer than Olaf, my clothes when I came here were much finer than yours, you felt envious – nei, nei!' She spoke over Thora's objection. 'I can quite understand your feelings. It must have been very difficult for you to live life in the shadows. It would not do to have a servant dressed more finely than her mistress.'

Thora gasped. 'We never treated you as a servant!'

But Ragnhild continued evenly, 'I suppose it was a little foolish of me to expect that I would be treated with the same respect I had in Jorvik. You as a country-dweller have not been privileged to learn the niceties of a lady's role – but I can assure you now, Thora,' her voice was oh, so sincere, 'that you do not need to worry much longer. The moment I have word that Sigurd has won our land back I shall cease to be a burden on you and will sail at once for England.'

Ragnhild's false generosity was more insulting than a curse. Thora grew spiteful. 'Hah! If Olaf allows you to!'

'Olaf has no say in the matter.'

'You do not think a bairn will be capable of doing as you say?'

'Sigurd shall succeed,' came the firm reply.

Such hauteur provoked Thora to cruelty. 'He may be dead already!' She flounced away across the shorn meadow to bully others who had started to flag.

Ragnhild remained firmly in her place, trying to feign triumph but at the same time unable to force Thora's words from her mind. No, he was not dead. 'Wait till I get my hands on you,' she warned him! Then: 'Oh where are you, son? Where are you?'

Aggersborg, a circular fortress with massive ramparts and towered gates, was the largest of the Danish strongholds, a huge pimple on the flat and featureless landscape around the Limfjord. Within its sphere the barrack houses, each over a hundred feet long, were placed in blocks of four so as to form a series of inner courtyards where the men of Swein's army polished their fighting techniques. During the time spent training here, Sigurd warmed to these rough men who with good humour had so far managed to shield him from his uncle's eye. Though conscious of the differences between the northern races, he had not inherited his father's aversion to Danes and treated all as welcome company – and such incredible tales they told him! For themselves, the men were endeared by his deadly serious air and attempts to look manly, and in their leisure hours would engage him in mock battles, though one or two were not so well-disposed when the weapon they had lent him drew their own blood. Especially intolerant was Ulf, for the boy provided Thorald with the constant excuse – as if he needed one – to compare the two beardless chins, tilting them this way and that and announcing, 'Ah, I do declare that Sigurd is sprouting fluff. Poor Ulf, he is still as bald as a girl-child's twat!'

With all these taunts, Ulf began to detest the boy's very existence. To deter comparison, he would take himself as far away as possible from whatever vicinity

Sigurd happened to be in. For this reason he had declined to join today's mock battle, and sat apart with his friend. Yet even here he could not escape; Eric Fart was laughing and gesticulating at the boy who wore a scabbard that was much too long and dragged along the ground as he paraded manfully about his business, finally becoming entangled with his legs and tripping him. Eric fell onto his back laughing.

Ulf fumed. 'What is so funny? The little runt, he is no better than my arsehole. I would dearly love to teach him some humility. He crows and struts too loudly, boasts that he is not afraid to die but first he should be made to look death in the face.' He was tired of others indulging Sigurd, allowing him to inflict wounds which, if caused by a man, would bring harsh punishment.

Eric sprawled upon the ground, paunch to the heavens, his vigour spent for the moment. Built like an Icelandic pony, with heavy body, short limbs, his face as dark and ugly as a troll, he too was often the butt of Thorald's jokes, hence he and Ulf shared a common bond. 'Why not teach him then, instead of moaning to me?' Expert in the art of conserving energy, he raised his shoulders just enough to extend a slothlike arm for a cup of ale.

Ulf grew angrier, watching the boy being permitted to win so often. 'Ja, indeed I will!' He jumped up, inserted his fingers into the handle of his shield, hefted the sword on loan from his leader and, with menace tensing his lips, advanced on his unwitting victim.

Breathless at yet another triumph, Sigurd was about to rest when Ulf's sword bore down on him. Only just in time he twisted his body and parried the blow with his shield, but its force knocked him into a sitting position. Expecting to be allowed to rise, Sigurd half-grinned, dropped his guard – and was appalled to see Ulf's blade lunging for his throat. He had no recourse but to collapse onto his back and hope that the point would stop short.

Ulf straddled him, exerting firm pressure on the hilt. Sigurd felt the tip bite through nerve and gasped. Appeased at having produced a look of fear, Ulf was about to grant mercy, but Sigurd could not afford to wait. Fearing that Ulf meant to kill him he panicked and with a haphazard swipe of his own weapon tried to knock Ulf's blade out of position.

Thorald heard the clang of iron and looked up, annoyed. 'Hey! Who mistreats my sword!' He bullocked his way through the onlookers, shouldered Ulf aside and, by means of a handful of tunic, dragged Sigurd to his feet. 'Doest not know how to treat a blade by now?' With weapons being extremely valuable it was a fool who crossed sword with sword; thrusts were always met by shield or flesh.

'I had no choice!' Sigurd clutched his throat and looked horrified when his fingers came away smeared with blood. 'He meant to kill me!'

Thorald grabbed the sword which he had lent the boy. 'I will kill you myself if you've ruined my life-quencher! You can keep to your own axe until you are competent.' He ran his frown along the blade looking for serrations – then without warning swung it at Ulf's head. The younger man parried with his shield but dared not make a retaliatory blow. The onlookers, including Sigurd, watched the two press against each other like sparring walruses, waited for Thorald's next move, but all that came were wounding words. 'Are you a suckling that you have learnt so little respect for your weapon?'

Livid, Ulf retorted through a grimace, ''Twas not I who struck metal!'

'So! The boy was right, your aim was for flesh?' Thorald growled into the younger man's face. 'Then take care, Bareface. I would not wish to see my young

33

friend harmed in any way.' He gave a hefty shove, dismissing Ulf, and when the other turned to go delivered a kick to his patched buttock.

Belittled, Ulf slunk off to moan to his friend. Sigurd took the opposite direction and went into the barrack house. The rapid change from sunlight to darkness blinded him for the moment. He groped for a bench, sat down, vision swimming. Quaking at how near he had come to death, he touched his throat again. The blood had begun to clot. Instead of wiping it away he left it there as a badge of initiation, and yet it continued to puzzle him why Ulf was so sullen and dangerous towards him, when they were about to face a common enemy.

Knowing his friend well, Eric was in no such state of confusion. He observed with languid eye, hiding a grin as Ulf threw shield and weapon on the ground and paced before him like one demented. Ulf did not like to lose at anything. Eric had known him come to violence over something as trivial as a board game.

At last Ulf's shallow jaw opened to articulate his displeasure. 'I can only imagine that Thorald has designs on the boy!'

'Then shouldst you not feel pity for him?' Eric rubbed his eye with a knuckle, each grubby finger adorned by a ring.

Ulf ranted and fumed a while longer, then finally acquiesced. 'Ja, in that you may be right.' He shook his cropped head. 'I will grant Smallaxe credit, he did not beg for mercy as I had thought.'

'*Hoped*,' corrected Eric, shuffling his body into a more comfortable position upon the hard-baked ground. 'I cannot see why you waste so much energy on fry like him. He is cocksure, ja, but he has done you no personal harm. For myself, I like him. 'Tis Thorald who has stirred your temper. He is too big for you so you vent your anger on the boy.'

'Look at you, pig in shit!' Ulf threw himself upon

his fat lazy friend and a wrestling match ensued, which ended as it always did with Ulf winning and his good humour restored. The two fell away from each other laughing, to find Sigurd looking down at them.

'And what crave you, pup?' Ulf tugged his red tunic into place but remained in his supine position alongside Eric.

'Take care!' jeered the ugly one. 'He may have come for revenge.'

Sigurd replied with dignity, 'I crave only answer; what harm have I done that you should want to kill me?'

'Fie!' Eric assumed a generous air. 'Cease this talk of murder and sit you down – take some ale, some cake, take anything you will.' His offer rebuffed, he shrugged, reached for a cake himself and popped it whole into his mouth.

Ulf sat up to retie one of his criss-crossed garters. 'Had I wished to kill you then you should not be standing here.'

It was hard to uphold a dignified profile in the face of such disdain. Sigurd wanted to kick him. 'I only stand here because I knocked your blade from my throat!'

Ulf sneered. 'And almost cut your head off into the bargain! Fool, I was set to release you when you acted so rash.'

'Even so, 'twas a good move,' donated Eric. Ulf gave his friend a dangerous look but Eric's eyes were closed.

Sigurd pressed for an answer. Always eager to make friends, he hated it when people snubbed him and was prepared to make numerous attempts before relegating them to his short list of enemies. 'I believe if Thorald had not intervened you would have killed me and . . .'

'Do not put great faith in Thorald,' cut in Ulf.

'. . . and I would know why!' finished Sigurd.

Garter tied, Ulf leaned back on his palms and looked mystified. 'But do you not tell everyone you are not afraid to die?'

'For a cause!' The deep-set eyes widened with boyish frustration. 'Not at the hands of a supposed friend.'

'You would gain more friends if you stopped crowing like a rooster,' returned Ulf. 'That was all I wished to teach you – that you are no more nor less than any man here, and that death is not something to be scoffed at.'

Eric endorsed this. 'You should really thank him, Smallaxe. It is the most useful lesson you have learnt here.'

Sigurd looked down at the recumbent goblin and pondered over his words. It had indeed been a dreadful shock and admittedly a good lesson, but he still felt the need to hit back at Ulf for his unprovoked savagery. Ulf's face reminded him of something – ah yes, that was it! Often the waves bored hollows in rocks at the water's edge, the ebb-tide leaving droplets of brine in each cup: that was what Ulf's face resembled. His jaw might be shallow but was chavelled from granite, obstinate, ungiving. Folding into a squat, he began to pare the chipped nail on his big toe and asked, 'How old are you?'

'Four and twenty.' Ulf used Eric's belly as a pillow.

'Then why have you no beard?'

Ulf shot upright, but Eric with the minimum of action held him back and told Sigurd, 'The gods think him too beautiful to hide under a matt of hair.'

Content to have pricked Ulf in this childish manner, Sigurd found the ability to grin and told Eric, 'They must consider you most ugly – they gave you double measure.'

The dark one responded with a cacophony of flatulence to show that he was not in the least offended and shut his eyes again. Disgusted, Ulf moved out of range.

Sigurd tried to put all ill-feeling behind him. 'I heard such an incredible tale from the man called Roric – his ship was bitten in two by Orca!' Amongst sailors, the killer whale was feared above all.

Ulf ignored him, but Eric replied, 'If it's tales you want you should have come to me. I could have told you that – but no, everyone thinks Eric is just a fart-box and knows nought.'

The boy, eager for another saga, asked, 'You have seen Orca?'

'Of course.' The black lashes never lifted.

'What colour was he – and how big?'

Eric's reply was shirty. 'Why should I waste my breath when you come to me last?'

'Oh, I beg you to tell me!'

'Well . . .' As the thud of footsteps signalled another's arrival, Eric opened one eye. 'Ah, here is Thorald, it will have to wait until later.'

A hulking Thorald joined the trio. 'Good! I see you have made friends.'

Sigurd glanced at Ulf then went back to fiddling with his toenail. He was performing more gingerly now, having tugged the loose part close to the nailbed. Thorald hunkered with them and shared their ale. For a time the talk was on the coming invasion, then in a lull, Sigurd asked, 'Did any of you know my father in person?'

Thorald splashed ale from the jug in his haste to dive in with an answer. 'I had that honour! Einar was the best friend a man could have. I have never known anyone to compare in strength nor courage. There was one time . . .' He went on to relate many anecdotes in which the two men had supposedly committed various deeds of valour, ending with the flattering comment, 'You are very like him.'

Sigurd, who had been leaning forward attentively,

37

now blushed with pride. Despite Thorald's rough veneer the boy had begun to regard him as a father figure. He was so very different to Uncle Olaf.

Ulf shared a knowing look with Eric. Now, each was certain Thorald had plans for the boy. After listening to the homily, Ulf examined his farmer's hands and mused, 'If he was so skilful, how is it that he is dead?'

Sigurd erupted, and the action caused him to rip the nail into flesh, increasing his ire. 'He was caught unawares by Ethelred's men!'

'That shows a certain lack of judgment,' goaded Ulf, yet privately marvelled at the way the boy contorted his toe up to his mouth and licked away the blood. 'A man should always keep his sword at hand.'

'And so he did!' Sigurd's toe throbbed; he sucked it and spat. 'But what use is one blade against a hundred!'

'He went unaccompanied amongst his enemy?' Ulf clicked his tongue and shook his head in woeful fashion.

Sigurd's voice rose to a yell. 'He had five men! He did not need an army!'

The more the boy shouted the calmer Ulf's response. 'It seems to me that he did.' The whiskerless mouth smirked at Eric. Sigurd, growing more and more heated, was about to throw himself upon his tormentor, but a commotion turned all heads.

'The King!' Thorald jumped to his feet. 'The time is nigh. Keep your energy for the English, Smallaxe – to the ships!'

Swein unleashed his fleet of wind-steeds upon the North Sea, the host of multi-coloured sails in contrast to the brilliant blue of the sky, two hundred craning necks with England in their sights. Inebriated by the magnificence, Sigurd gazed in awe at the might and beauty of the langskips, none so resplendent as that of the monarch who sailed at their midst, his prow and tiller embellished with gold.

The sea was kind, parting in sensuous swell to oaken breast and belly. With neither map nor compass the viking fleet navigated by means of sun and star, the feel of the wind, and centuries of experience by their forefathers. Sigurd daydreamed of these brave explorers who had left the legacy of their voyaging: how had they felt, sailing into the unknown? Had their hearts trembled with the same boyish worries as Sigurd's whilst on the outside remaining firm and resolute, that none might know their cowardice?

'Make yourself useful!' Ulf threw a bailing scoop which knocked the dreamy look from Sigurd's face.

The boy responded with a bad-tempered howl and rubbed his head. 'Why do you not take your turn?'

'Because I tell you to do it!' Ulf's face defied argument.

Grumbling, Sigurd knelt, lifted a plank and peered into the cavity. 'It is not worth bailing. There is hardly two inches of water.'

'I have known men drown in two inches of water.'

So threatening was Ulf's face that Sigurd had to do as he was told, but managed to flick at least one scoop in Ulf's direction before the hollow eyes warned him to desist.

The hours rolled by. Some craft travelled faster than the others, some ploughed on whilst others slept. The leaders covered over a hundred miles in that first twenty-four hours, and thus during the ensuing voyage the fleet began to thin out. Sigurd reckoned they had been at sea a week when at last, new land was sighted, a land very different from the mountainous fjords of home. Piloted by auk and gull the warships made for the coast of Kent where they dropped anchor to assess the situation and adjust the rudders to the shallower waters. In place of grassy banks there were long ribbons of shingled beach where the creamy tide rushed and whispered. Shields were displayed on a rail along the sides of the ships, their metal bosses catching the light to dazzle the group of fisherfolk on the shore. To these simple onlookers the gilded craft appeared as mythical beasts – their flanks studded with a hundred silver nipples, their gaping jaws invoking terror – and they fled to give warning.

Impatient at the delay, Sigurd turned to Ulf – Thorald had extracted much delight in forcing them into a rowing partnership. 'When are we to launch the attack?'

Ulf stretched his lithe bronze hands to the July sun and yawned. 'Why ask me? I am not an important warrior like you. I just follow orders.'

By now, Sigurd had come to understand that the lugubrious expression was not reserved for him alone but was Ulf's natural mien. Still, it was irritating, especially when in addition to this Ulf never gave a straight answer. He looked to Eric who provided sapient conjecture but no real explanation. The thin chest heaved with impatience. Why he endured the company of these two was hard to say; one stank, the other was gloomy and neither was in the least informed about their mission.

He called out his question to Thorald, who could always be relied upon, telling Sigurd, 'The King gives leave for us to refresh ourselves whilst the rest of the fleet catches up. He says it would be reckless to attack here where resistance is greatest. We shall sail north up the coast and be in the Humbre by tomorrow morn. I wonder what England will say when she wakes to find us in her back passage – a nice surprise, ja?'

'I cannot think of a more horrible shock than to wake and find you in my back passage,' muttered

Ulf. In the same breath he rose from the bench, stripped naked and dived overboard.

Others adopted this brazen romp, displaying to any English spectator just how confident they were of victory. The sea threshed as if with netted fish. Sigurd, too, peeled off his clothes and dived. Sunny though it was, this had no effect on the temperature of the waves. The impact sent him gasping upwards, tossing the freezing water from his hair and making rapid retreat to the launch. He had almost dragged his shivering haunches back on board when Eric shouted, 'Sigurd no-balls!' and grabbed his ankle to pull him back with a splash.

There was much horseplay, even from Ulf. No one seemed to be concerned about attack, only the effect of the icy water on their genitalia. When they clambered back on deck there was raucous laughter and comparison of parts.

After breakfasting on salted herrings, battle helmets were donned and full weaponry displayed. The mood remained merry. Swein Forkbeard led his awesome fleet northwards along an everchanging coastline, sailing as planned into the Humbre and from there up the Treante into the heart of the Danelaw, laying waste to both sides of the river so that by the time they reached Gæignesburh word of their viciousness preceded them and Earl Uhtred of Northumbria submitted almost without resistance. Shire by shire, they accepted Swein as overlord until all the land to the North of Watling Street, the old Roman boundary, was his.

Sigurd, primed for battle, suffered days of melancholia at this anti-climax. Turning his back on the city of Gæignesburh he slouched upon the riverbank, chin on palm, and gazed across the water at a flat landscape that covered miles and miles. Somewhere out there beyond the fields of blue flax, Jorvik beckoned.

Catching him so despondent, Thorald crouched beside him and offered a sup of ale that was an identical shade of brown to the river. When Sigurd refused he shook his head, jingling the elaborate earrings. 'I cannot understand you, Smallaxe. Are you not pleased at our success? Look! They give us aid freely.' There was great activity around the river-bank with locals delivering food and horses to the camp.

'It is no fun to take from cowards,' sulked the boy. 'I had expected some sort of fight.'

'And fight there will be when we meet Ethelred,' Thorald assured him. 'These men yield because they are of our blood. They know Swein will rule them better.'

'Then why does the King need to take hostages?' retorted Sigurd.

'Sad to say, one cannot always trust one's friends.' The brute looked pained, then grabbed a passerby and roughly divested him of the goat cheese he carried.

Sigurd watched the filthy fingers mangle the cheese. 'Now that the North has surrendered we should have little trouble at Jorvik. When shall we go?' He was nervous that his uncle might get there before him and then what would he do? He could hardly oppose the one who had given him succour for the past eleven years.

'First we must capture the rest of England.' A gap opened midst Thorald's beard and the cheese began to disappear into it.

Sigurd cheered up. 'And kill Ethelred? I cannot wait.'

Thorald stopped chewing and looked pensive. 'For what you will see of him mayhap you would be better placed looking after the ship until we return.'

The boy was horrified. 'And put all that training to waste?'

Thorald was patient, locking him in a sweaty embrace whilst making a disgusting noise in the consumption of the cheese. 'It is impossible for all of us to kill one man, Smallaxe – and if you fall in battle then who will retrieve your estate?' Seeing that he had introduced doubt to the boy's mind, Thorald went on, 'It will be no easy task to keep these hostages in order, but we trust you to do this and maintain the ship.'

So, whilst Thorald and his men marched off with the King to harry English Mercia, Sigurd was left to idle away the summer months on the banks of the Treante.

At least he was not the only one to miss the excitement: Swein's younger son, Cnut, had been put in command of the ships and hostages. Sigurd had only ever seen Cnut from afar, a tall and strong-limbed youth with long fair hair and sharp eyes, in most things very good-looking, apart from his nose which was like that of an eagle. He decided that this was the opportunity to take a closer look. In bold manner he approached the royal ship and without hesitation hopped aboard.

Cnut had isolated himself from his men and was hunched on the rowing bench nearest the prow. His pose was one of deep introspection which Sigurd mistook for boredom, and in the confidence that any attention would be well-received, he made his approach along the deck. Without asking permission, he sat down beside the King's son. What need was there for reverence – he was as good as any man. However, he did donate a wide smile. It would be folly to alienate such a well-placed friend.

The youth glanced up at the intrusion but did not question the boy's presence and immediately returned to his thoughts. Sigurd put his age at about eighteen, though he had an air of maturity. His tunic was russet trimmed with gold, making Sigurd conscious of his

43

own shabby garb. His yellow leggings were traversed with dirt and grass stains, and the rip had widened; thoughts of this drew absent fingers to his crotch which he fondled awhile as he thought of something to say. After a period of non-communication, he attempted to break the ice with a riddle. 'What has breath but cannot breathe?'

Cnut, being older, had heard this dozens of times before and sighed the answer. 'The wind. If you must intrude upon my thoughts you had best come up with something more amusing than that, child – and stop playing with your balls.'

Sigurd was peeved at being called child, but removed the offending hand. 'I could tell you about my estate at Jorvik if it would not bore you too greatly, *hersir*.' Cnut passed him a smile that spoke disbelief. 'Forsooth!' retorted Sigurd.

With no hope of being left to his dream, Cnut turned full attention on the interloper, his gold armlets catching the sun. 'Then why are you not on the estate attending to your affairs?'

'Because it was stolen from me by Ethelred, but when my friends return I shall have it back.'

Cnut realized that the boy was serious and now leaned closer, his odour that of any other man. 'Come then, tell me more.' He listened with interest whilst Sigurd related the entire saga, at the end of which he nodded in cognizance. 'You have as much right to hate Ethelred as I. My own kin were slain in that massacre.'

'Then do you not resent being banned from witnessing Ethelred's death?' asked Sigurd.

Cnut shrugged. 'It matters not who kills him so long as he is dead.' He noted the feverish desperation in Sigurd's eye. 'But you, I think, feel differently.'

The boy's answer was fervent. 'What I would give to be the one to wield the death-blow! That is all I have lived my life for.'

'It is a poor life woven around destruction,' opined Cnut. 'My intent is not to destroy men but to rally them to me. You think that brought face to face with Ethelred you could have defeated him?'

'Easily,' came the immodest reply. 'With Odin at my shoulder.'

Cnut was greatly amused by the lad's confidence which matched his own. 'I must have men such as you by me if I am ever called upon to rule – though for myself I would choose Christ to aid my battle axe.'

Sigurd lowered his voice to an urgent whisper. 'Let not the All-Father hear you!'

Cnut laughed again. 'Why? The Christian God is mightier by far.' He cocked his ear, then: 'Hark! Is that Thor who speaks? Nei, 'tis my growling stomach!' He laughed at Sigurd's jutting lip. 'I mock you not, my friend! Come, will you honour me by eating at my table, Sigurd Einarsson?'

Sigurd forgave the jibe and made graceful acceptance. 'The honour is mine, *hersir*.' He followed the King's son from the ship to a house.

At the merest signal from Cnut great activity began and soon trenchers of bream were being laid before them. As they ate, Cnut ventured; 'You are lonely in your friends' absence, ja?'

Sigurd crunched on the less sharp bones and thought about it, but was unable to find the word that described his frustration. 'Not lonely . . . buzzy.'

Cnut laughed, inhaled a particle of fish and endured a bout of choking. 'Buzzy!'

'I feel like a bee in a pot. I long for them to return so that we can go to Jorvik.' Sigurd glanced at Cnut who was now drinking from a silver goblet. 'Mayhap I do not have to wait if you would . . .'

'I regret, young friend,' Cnut wiped the moisture from his eyes and impaled another piece of fish on his knife, 'that my presence is required here.'

'But you have nought of real import to do here, have you?' Sigurd pointed out.

'Nought to do?' Cnut gave an astonished laugh. 'What would you like to see me do? Go around prodding arses with my sword just to show my power? Power lies in here, boy.' He tapped his breast. 'You can be sure that if I were to desert my post and go to Jorvik then you would quickly see what effect my absence has.' He soothed the boy's disappointment. 'Have patience. When the whole country is under my father's rule then you shall have your estate back. If you should have any trouble just come to your friend Cnut and he promises to help you.'

Sigurd grinned his thanks and decided that he liked Cnut more than anyone else he had met so far. The King's son hailed him as a friend before witnesses!

Cnut liked Sigurd, too. Not only was the boy amusing but he was ready to listen and learn. There were not many prepared to accept wisdom from an eighteen year old, be he royal or no.

As an aid to digestion, Cnut summoned one of the King's skalds to relax them with verse. After this cerebral sojourn, a leg-wrestling match took place. The lad was permitted to join in this, and all subsequent games that Cnut enjoyed throughout that summer. Battered but proud in this friendship, he even managed to forget about his estate at Jorvik for the time being.

Alas, it was inevitable that Cnut should grow bored with one so callow and yearn for more adult pursuits. One day a wagon bearing a young woman and her maidservant trundled towards the horse trough where the two friends slouched idle. Sigurd, prattling away in boyish vein, became aware that Cnut was inattentive and gave him a dig in his left kidney. 'Weave me a kirtle!'

Cnut grunted annoyance and rubbed his side. 'What nonsense do you spout, mustard shanks?'

46

'You were away gathering wool, were you not?'
Sigurd was cross. 'You must have gathered enough to
weave a kirtle whilst I have been wasting my breath.
How long have I been talking to myself?'

'Since one more interesting came into view.' Cnut
reverted to his moonstruck pose. 'Is she not the most
beautiful creature?'

Sigurd clamped his necklace between his teeth
and peered up and down the narrow street, but
could see only a cart with two plain-looking women
in it.

'I have made enquiries,' confided the youth as the
wagon drew level. 'The Saxons call her Aelgifu. She
has much in common with ourselves. Her father was
an ealdorman of Northumbria who was cruelly murdered by Ethelred.'

Sigurd might not pay credit to her looks but on
hearing this he immediately empathized . . . until faced
with Cnut's request. 'Friend Sigurd, run and ask her
if she would stop awhile.'

The boy spat out his beads. 'Why do not you go?'

'I, the son of the King?' Cnut feigned a regal air.
'It would be far beneath my dignity to run after a
wagon, and much it would impress her.'

'Oh, spare no thought for my dignity!' Sigurd looked
offended. 'And you said we were off to spear some
fish.' He mouthed his beads again and twiddled his
fringe.

'So we are,' grinned his older friend. 'Go! Before
she gets away or I will spear you.'

With bad grace, Sigurd unwound his legs and rose,
plucking at his yellow leggings. 'Which one is she?'

Cnut roared, 'You think I would waste my kisses on
the old crone?'

'They are both old,' came the artless reply, at which
Cnut lashed out with his feet and urged him to be
gone. The torn braid on his kirtle flapping up and
down, Sigurd pounded after the wagon which had

now gained some fifty yards on him. The two women on board heard his breathless pleas to stop but merely giggled. Eventually, when she glanced back and noticed that Sigurd was about to give up, Aelgifu ordered the driver to rein in and waited for the boy to come panting alongside.

Sigurd leaned heavily on the wagon, dust eddying around his bare feet, and spoke to the object of Cnut's desire. Close to, she was still no beauty. 'I bring greetings from my friend Cnut. He asks if you will tarry and speak with him awhile.'

Aelgifu looked down her nose at him. 'Why does he not come after me himself if he is so eager?'

'My lady, the King of England's son does not chase wagons like a dog. Am I to return and tell him you refuse his invitation?'

'When his gallant little dog has run so far to deliver it?' At the spark of mischief in her eyes Sigurd realized the foolishness of his last comment and, blushing with anger, spun away.

'Tell your master I will be there in the time that it takes my wagon to come around,' called Aelgifu good-naturedly.

Sigurd wheeled, 'Lady, I have no master!' and marched back along the dusty road in the direction of Cnut.

On seeing that the wagon moved on, Cnut met Sigurd's return with ill-temper. 'If she is lost to me because of you . . .'

Sigurd incised the threat. 'How shall the wagon turn in the narrow street? She has gone around the houses to get to you.'

Cnut turned and looked the other way to see Aelgifu's wagon appear from a side street. His amiability returned and he patted the boy's shoulder. 'Well done, friend.'

'You will not think so when you speak to her!' Sigurd looked grim as he sank to his haunches. 'She is the most disrespectful creature I have met.' He shoved his necklace into his mouth.

Cnut merely laughed, straightened his richly-adorned tunic and ran a quick comb through his hair. 'Then I shall not force you to remain in her company. Run along to your fishing now.'

Sigurd did not care for being dismissed in such a manner, lisping through the beads, 'You may well prefer the fish of my choosing after a few seconds in the company of that old trout.'

Cnut did not take his eyes off the woman, but Sigurd was left in no doubt as to his anger. 'Speak thus about Aelgifu again and it is not you who will be eating fish but they who shall be eating you.' Reassuming his smile he went to greet his lady love as her wagon made its trundling approach. The friendship mutually terminated, Sigurd loped off to the river, wondering how the war was progressing.

Faraway in Vestfold, Ragnhild wondered too. No word had come to tell if Sigurd was alive or dead. Corn-cutting month was over, the cattle and sheep had been rounded up and driven back down the mountains to the valleys, beasts were slaughtered and their meat dried for the winter. Ragnhild had contributed every effort to this but still she had been chivvied and pushed by her sister-in-law just as she had been for the past eleven years. And all her silent curses – just you wait! – counted for nothing. Now the outside work was almost over but with the doors shut firm against the coming winter there were hides to be worked into clothing and numerous other articles. The only thing to look forward to was the Yuletide feast and the hope that as the year ended news would come of Sigurd's fate. As Ragnhild sat here with the smell of the byre in her nostrils, fingers sore from driving a needle through leather, she wondered yet again how the mighty army progressed.

Swein's army, having won Oxnaford and Wintanceaster, now marched on Lunden where lurked Ethelred. But here there was firmer resistance. Ethelred's force was backed by that of Swein's former ally, Thorkell the Tall who, after a viking raid of earlier years, had seen how lucrative it was to be in the pouch of the English king and so had stayed behind to act as mercenary. With this combined force, plus that of its valiant citizens, Lunden stood resolute.

When a section of his army came to grief in the Temes, Swein decided not to waste further energy on an untenable Lunden. Instead he turned his force westwards to Bathum where, under his skilful campaign, the viking army conquered the last pockets of resistance. With her King and only effective army locked in Lunden, England was obliged to accept Swein as monarch. The vikings marched in triumph back to Gægignesburh where they took time to regroup and allowed Ethelred to stew. Sigurd considered this to be an apt accompaniment to his eleventh birthday, but hoped he would not be kept waiting here too long for it was now very cold and his ripped apparel was a poor shield against the November draughts. When offered a dead man's cloak he accepted with gratitude, though huddled inside its threadbare folds he vowed that once in Jorvik he would never again be so reduced.

Happily for Sigurd, Lunden could not maintain its lone fight, and finally came to terms. Swein's demands for tribute and supplies for his army during the winter were granted – yet even then the demons from the sea continued to harry. With the vikings thus preoccupied, Ethelred sent his wife and children across the Channel to safety, left his mercenaries to defend the city and spent some time prevaricating in his ship on the Temes until shortly after Christmas when he decided it would be more politic to retire to Normandy. Deserted by its king, Lunden surrendered completely. Thorkell, his force too inferior to take on Swein, slunk off to Grenewic.

There were celebrations with music, boat-racing and horsefights, feastings and fresh meat at Gæignesburh, carousing in the alehouses. Despite the funny diversions when Ulf lost his reserve under a glut of fruit wine and – dressed as a woman – slavered kisses over Thorald, and despite Eric's almost indecent generosity, all this was anticlimax to Sigurd who had expected the war to end in Ethelred's death. The festivities served only as obstacles to his main aim. He grew more impatient than ever to get to Jorvik, plagued by the certainty that he must bump into his uncle sooner or later, and it was a nuisance having to keep his eyes peeled for Olaf the entire time. The only helpful factor was that Olaf was not expecting him to be here, and amongst the thousands of men could quite easily pass by without noticing him. Still, Uncle would be making for Jorvik himself any day. Sigurd must be there before him. This he put to Thorald.

'So be it, my friend!' Thorald threw aside the bone on which he had been sucking, his beard slimy with grease. 'I give you my word that we will go this very day. Let me see . . .' The viking had amassed many weapons, shields and headgear after the fighting; now he pulled a conical helmet from the pile and rammed it on Sigurd's dome with a helpful thump. 'Here! This may come in useful.'

Sigurd adjusted the helmet which was far too big. 'The noseguard chafes.' He lifted it from his head.

'Does it? No matter, we will lop a bit off – come here.' Thorald grabbed the boy's neck and pretended to cut a piece off Sigurd's nose. Roaring with laughter, he slapped the boy's back fetching a grin to the mouths of his lice-ridden army. Sigurd did not care to be the butt of their merriment again and threw

51

the helmet back from whence it came. 'I will have one made when I get my estate back.'

'If your head is not cleaved in two first,' provided Ulf.

Sigurd was ignorant over the amount of resistance to expect, but as he now said to Thorald, 'With the backing of fifty men I cannot see failure.'

Thorald hawked up phlegm. 'True, but I do not intend to enlist such numbers, as the King has need of them here. Twelve of us should be sufficient to rout the usurper from your estate. I have been to Jorvik before – the people there are not fighters.'

Leaving the ship at anchor, they loaded food and weapons onto the captured horses and soon were on their way. Sigurd was going home at last.

Chapter Three

Eoforwic, or Jorvik as the Norsemen mispronounced it, was situated between two rivers, the larger tidal flow bisecting the heart of the city which was then rejoined by a wooden bridge; the other, a beck, curved around the stone walls and towers of the old Roman fortress, providing access for merchant vessels to the timber shacks of the suburbs. Much of the encircling land was very marshy. To the east of the metropolis lay a range of chalk hills; far to the west lay rugged mountains. Apart from the Saxon churches and Roman relics, it was a city built entirely of wood.

Sigurd was impressed by the grandiosity of Jorvik, the main part of which was protected by earthen ramparts topped with a wooden palisade – though many buildings existed outside these defences, too. On either bank of the river Use was a network of straw-littered alleys, so narrow that the eaves almost kissed. Many of the tightly-packed dwellings were fronted by stalls that displayed various commodities. Most were dark with age, but occasionally the line was relieved by the construction of a replacement building giving the streets the appearance of rows on a gaming board.

The majority of the townspeople seemed prosperous, and richly dressed, though Sigurd was taken aback by the way they and their dwellings stank; in the thinly-populated coastal area where he had lived, the wind would dispose of most objectionable smells.

Relief was to come as the men walked their horses across the wooden bridge; the stench of decaying refuse, excrement and rotting timber was overthrown by the more pleasant aroma of fish, for Jorvik was a busy fishing port, too. Along the wharfs, where patient mallards waddled and herring gulls dived and mewed and wheeled about the masts, festoons of nets hung out to dry, glittering with the remnants of their last haul. Sigurd's mouth began to water over baking bread and ale – and strangers! Not one person here knew so much as his name.

Many centuries ago his ancestor, an army officer, had been granted a tract of land in reward for good service to the King. This had been subdivided by the officer and each portion given to a man who had served under him and who might prefer domesticity to the harsh viking existence. The descendents of these men continued to live here; Sigurd wondered aloud over the total number of citizens.

'Mm . . . between eight and ten thousand, I would guess,' answered Thorald.

'Eight thousand!' Eight thousand strangers. Sigurd beamed and rode tall in his saddle, eyes missing nought as they neared their destination.

Armed with details from his mother as to where the family property lay, Sigurd and his band of helpers made for the shire called Peseholme, situated in the north-eastern corner of the city. To one side it was protected by ramparts, to the other lay the Fosse, so dispensing with the need for a defensive wall to repel invaders. But the Fosse itself was prone to invade the city – even when it kept within its banks the land around it was permanent marsh – and the inhabitants had protected themselves with a long floodbank, eight feet high by forty feet wide, made of clay and brushwood held down with rocks. Within these barricades the wooden houses were grouped around an open space of grass and trees, amongst them a stone church dedicated to St Cuthbert. Each building was fenced off from its neighbour by a wattle enclosure and had a ditch for drainage. One house was larger than the rest, a barnlike structure composed of wedge-shaped sections of tree trunk, with an acre plot and various outbuildings. Sigurd voiced the assumption that this surely must be his father's house.

Thorald sat astride his horse and weighed the view inside the open gates. All was tranquil, with fowl scratching in the dirt, slaves tending the vegetables in the garth, a cat curled up in a patch of winter sunlight. No one ventured to accost them as they urged their horses forward and into the enclosure, though the thralls did look inquisitive at the large number of visitors. A red kite scavenged a midden pile, flying off with a bone in its beak. The men dismounted and threw back their cloaks to give easy access to swords. A veiled woman came out of the house to greet them, but on seeing their demeanour her face lost its convivial air and she immediately fled, scattering hens.

Thorald donned an expression of mild offence and made comment to Eric, 'Cover your face, ugly one. The mistress obviously fears she is beset by demons.'

The men and Sigurd filed cautiously into the main hall of the house. Its walls were insulated with wattle and daub, skins and other hangings. Across the glassless windows, little more than slits, were stretched the membranes of animals in order to let in the light but not the cold; nevertheless it was dingy enough to require illumination and pottery lamps with liquid fat and floating wick were dotted about the room. The flooring to each side of the room was raised and upon these platforms were benches and stools. A tripod straddled the central hearth, and suspended from it by an iron hoop was a pot containing fish broth tended by a slavegirl. A look of panic rippled her dirt-smeared features, but Thorald reassured her with a casual flick of his hand. 'Worry not, 'tis that broth I am after . . . first.' He flopped his meaty buttocks upon a bench and sat with legs agape. 'Plenty of time for you later.'

Unsure of what to do in her mistress's absence, the girl served the men with wooden bowls containing broth. Sigurd marvelled at their casual air while his own gut churned in anticipation of attack. However, he was famished and not wishing to appear frightened, he accepted the soup. Whilst it was being consumed the master of the house, alerted by his wife, returned with several carls, all armed. The bowls were cast unceremoniously to the floor. In his shock Sigurd tipped the hot liquid over his knee and hopped about, thereupon being knocked aside in the mêlée. There was swift locking of weapons; jugs and vessels fell from shelves, furniture toppled, only the lamps remained anchored but flickered and spat dangerously as the men jostled. Sigurd gripped his axe and made ready for the first opportunity to use it but alas, the battle was brief. Their tactics and numbers much superior, Thorald's men soon had the advantage, with the carls lying dead upon the floor and their master held against the wall at swordpoint.

'What shall we do with him, my lord?' Thorald was looking at Sigurd, a devilish gleam to his eye. At the boy's look of astonishment he added, 'Is it not your right to decide his fate, and have you not been aching to put your weapon to good use? What better use than on the man who robbed you of your landright?'

Sigurd was hesitant now. He wanted to kill the man, not simply from revenge but also to learn how it felt to take human life. Had his enemy faced him with a weapon then he knew he would have been able to do it, but to raise his axe now . . .

Thorald's voice stirred him. 'What holds you, Sigurd? All these months you have been pestering to kill an Englishman, well, here is one before you . . .'

His expression became teasing. 'Do not tell me you are afraid?'

'I am not afraid!' Sigurd glared at the man and began to heft his axe, causing his intended victim to sweat more profusely. He had killed pigs and cattle without qualm, but it was one thing to provide food and another to use one's axe on a weaponless fellow. He began to imagine the impact of his axe on the man's skull. The man who a moment ago had been lord of his estate was now at his mercy. Delaying the moment, he said, 'You took my father's property. Can you give good reason why I should not take your life?'

His victim's eyes showed fear but he spoke bravely. 'I know nothing of your father. This land was granted to me by King Ethelred; it is rightfully mine.'

'Your king is vanquished,' retorted Sigurd. 'His boons are forfeit, and so will be your life lest you go peaceably and vow not to return and attack us.'

Before the man could reply, Thorald laughed aloud and embraced his soldiers in the joke. 'I begin to see that friend Smallaxe is less brave than he pretends.'

Sigurd blushed with anger.

Ulf offered a logical explanation, which was meant as jest but unwittingly aided the boy's predicament. 'Have you considered, Thorald, that you are standing very close? Mayhap Smallaxe doth hold the fear that he might strike off your head by mistake – his aim is not so good.'

Thorald guffawed in recognition and with much theatricality held the prisoner at arms' length.

Sigurd was furious at Ulf. He raised his axe, then lowered it. 'He is too tall! I cannot reach.'

'Fetch him a stool,' called Eric, who broke wind and then sat himself down.

Thorald groaned with impatience. 'Wouldst fetch him a stool in battle? For Frigg's sake get it done, boy!' He bullied the unfortunate man to his knees.

Sigurd looked around him. The assembled faces wore a uniform disregard for his plight. Death was commonplace to them. He rebelled in firm voice. 'Nei! I refuse to kill a man as I would a slave. He put up a good fight, let him go free.'

Thorald gave a dismissive swipe at the air. 'Oh, you disappoint me. The lion's roar hides a little mouse.'

Sigurd thrust out his chest. 'This is my house and I shall say who lives and dies here!'

Thorald shrugged and tapped the boy with his sword. 'You are a fool. He will creep back in the night and kill you.'

Sigurd locked eyes with his captive. 'If he returns it shall be he who dies – now go!'

The merchant moved warily through the knot of hostile men, his eyes flitting from one to the other until he reached the door. There, he turned tail, collected his weeping lady and ran.

'You should have killed him,' warned Thorald, though in light rather than heavy mood. 'He will be back if he has any spine – oh, look! The bastard spilt my soup. Let me run after him and cut off his ears.'

Jingling as he moved he cupped a huge hand to the boy's scalp. 'Christ, grant me the wisdom to understand you, Smallaxe. In play you inflict all manner of wounds upon your comrades and yet when I give you your enemy on a plate you touch not one hair of his beard!'

Eric came to the youngster's defence. 'Doest not remember the first time you killed an enemy, Thorald?'

The hairy face was split by a grin. 'Ah, I do indeed! What a fight that was.' Thorald proceeded to give all the glorious details.

'Then do you wonder that Sigurd spared the man?' asked Eric when the catalogue was finished. ''Tis no fun to kill an undefended opponent. Let him have something worthwhile to remember. Killing your first man is like having your first woman.'

The change of topic was welcomed by lewd ululations from the men and the proposal that they should go a-courting. Then one of them spotted the thrall who cowered in the murk and she was dragged before them. 'Did you ever see ought so skinny?' demanded Thorald. ''Tis like throwing a starving dog a meatless bone.' He turned to Sigurd and added to his education. 'My friend, there are three things a man needs after a battle: wine, meat and a fat woman ... but never mind, this one will do for now.' He tripped her and threw her to the floor.

Sigurd's mouth fell open as the chieftain dropped his breeches, pulled up the girl's threadbare dress and without ceremony raped her.

That the girl was accustomed to being used by her previous master did not lessen the indignity and her face showed distress. Sigurd watched with a combination of interest and revulsion. Afterwards, Thorald offered her to his men, four of whom accepted. Ulf and the rest seemed more concerned in salvaging what was left in the cauldron. 'And what of you, Smallaxe?' enquired Thorald. 'Is there any service the girl can provide for you?'

Sigurd hesitated, then with a flourish of bravado dropped his trousers and stepped out of them. 'She can mend this hole – and be quick about it!'

Thorald doubled over in laughter, then grabbed a bowl of broth from one of the others and gave it to Sigurd, patting him on the head in sympathy. 'Poor bairn, take this and build up your strength.'

Whilst they were eating, a nervous deputation arrived. Word of the new thegn had already reached the other occupants of Peseholme and now their representatives came with prudent gifts of meat and honey.

Later, when the light outside was failing and the shutters were closed against the hoary eve, the men sat drinking ale. One of them complained that it would take a long time to get merry on this weak brew and so it was jointly decided that they would go and purchase local wine. Some of the men took baths in order to impress the gentler womenfolk of Jorvik, for they had been without the fair sex too long. On returning from his own successful joinder, Thorald helped Sigurd with an inventory of his chattels, undertaking a thorough search of the house which produced two kists full of silver and gold. Despite all of this Thorald appeared somewhat disgruntled. 'I fear you have misled me as to the extent of your father's holdings, Sigurd. I had visioned more land.'

'I, too.' Sigurd looked perplexed, then paid homage to Thorald for his assistance. 'But I am greatly in your debt, *hersir*, and I would like to reward your services and those of your men.'

'Oh, there is no need,' Thorald was quick to reply, the ghost of a smile lifting his moustache. 'We acted as friends.'

'Then I most humbly thank you, but my friends must have some reward.' Sigurd adopted the fatherly air that made him so endearing. 'Afore you depart you shall all be my guests at a feast of celebration.'

Thorald shared a cunning grin with his men who had one by one returned. 'We will be honoured to be guests of Sigurd Smallaxe if that would not be too great an imposition.'

'You are welcome to remain for as long as you desire,' responded Sigurd, and was puzzled by the inexplicable burst of laughter that followed. When it died away he added, 'I wouldst bring my mother to live with me, but I am not sure how to . . .'

'Cease your worry, Smallaxe!' Thorald cut him off. 'There is bound to be a ship returning to Norway soon. I personally will arrange for your mother to be brought over.'

Sigurd voiced his gratitude, and was to reiterate

this when the deposed thegn put his case before the *vapnatak*, or local assembly, to argue that his estate had been taken by foul means. Too inexperienced to speak on his own behalf, the boy appointed Thorald to state his claim that the land was rightfully his and so eloquent was his defence that the twelve leading thegns of the wapentake reached their majority verdict: the land had indeed been wrongfully taken. Sigurd gave wholehearted praise to his supporters and once again fêted them, but when they were still his guests many days afterwards he became irritated by their obtrusion. Their depletion of his winter food stocks was nothing compared to their sniggers whenever he gave the thralls a command – in fact, they seemed to be laughing most of the time at some private joke. He was therefore relieved when Thorald announced that the threat of attack from the previous occupant was now unlikely and, along with his men, finally left for Gæignesburh.

Alone but for the servants, the boy began to stalk about the house, for the first time able to assume the role of master, although not entirely certain of his obligations in that quarter. Perhaps he should be out hawking or riding around his estate, but his estate was not so extensive as he had imagined from listening to his mother's tales. Had her memory and bitterness played tricks upon her, or was there yet more to discover? He squatted by one of the chests and opened it, playing with the shiny contents. There had been moments when he feared that Thorald might ride out of here taking the money with him, but here it still was, and Thorald had even been generous enough to leave him a horse too. He dropped the hasp, padlocked the chest and began to pace the hall again. He had already investigated most of the city, conversed with each of his neighbours and had bought himself a pair of boots, a hat, a sheepskin tunic and thicker breeches, for it had recently snowed. What could he do now? Bored, he reached up to a shelf and took down several clay pots to see whether they contained anything nice to eat. In doing this he came across two pieces of wood with a series of lines etched on them. Familiar with the runic alphabet thanks to his uncle, Sigurd was able to tell that these compiled a register of dues and tributes owed to the lord of this estate and prayers to the gods to protect them. But of much greater significance than this was the message cut at the foot of the list: *This was carved by Einar*. The simple thrill of holding something of his father's turned Sigurd's limbs a-wobble. He hugged the dusty pieces of bark to his breast and swore an oath that he would run this estate in a manner of which his father would be proud.

When his heart stopped racing, he perused the list again. Into Sigurd's government came a township called Osboldewic. Among its inhabitants were several freedmen, once slaves, of whom he could demand a few days' work per week and tenants who owed him rent. Thorald, unable to decipher the runes, had overlooked this important document, but Sigurd, eager to imprint his authority on those underlings acted upon it without delay.

Asking the way to Osboldewic, he was told that it was some two miles east of Jorvik and was directed under the old Anglo-Saxon Stonebow, across a narrow wooden bridge and onwards towards the Forest of Galtres, a mixture of densely-packed trees, flat marshes and scrubland. In all innocence he rode out alone, his only concern being the sharp bite of frost, unaware that the forest was a haven for outlaws, wild boar and wolves. Luck transported him safely to the other side. The first indication that he had arrived was a fence that marked the outer boundary. He dismounted at the gate, then led his horse through to the common grazing land. Riding on, he traversed a frozen meadow before finally coming to the garden plots that surrounded a collection of mean wattle shacks. The occupants, darned of breech and lank of hair, abandoned their various labours to assemble, shifty-eyed, around the visitor who from the platform of his horse introduced himself.

'I am Sigurd, lord of this estate. I am led to understand that certain men from this village owe me two days' work per week. To whom does this apply? Raise your hands.' When the chapped hands were held aloft he nodded and continued, 'In future, all dues will be paid to ... what are you laughing at?' He elevated himself in his stirrups and lanced a finger at one kotsetlan who was grinning. 'You dare to laugh at your master, dog!'

For some reason the other villagers found his attitude comical, too; his remark met with blatant laughter. 'Master!' came a derisive mutter. Sigurd rode his horse at the culprit who was forced to jump out of the way to avoid being mown down. 'You, keep a civil tongue in your head or I will cut it out!' His angry breath clung to the January air whilst his eyes toured the gathering. 'Which of you is the man Algrim?'

Lips creased in irony, Algrim raised his arm then bowed. 'It is I ... *my lord*.'

'I come to remind you that you owe me one lamb and two pence at Candlemas. I expect them to be paid on time.'

Algrim clasped his hands over the rope that knotted his mantle and cowered in a suitably inferior pose. 'Would my lord not prefer a nice fat ewe ... so's he can suckle from her teat when he misses his mother!'

The youngster wheeled his horse to rebuke those who sniggered at Algrim's taunt, but his horsemanship was none too adept; he unseated himself, falling heavily onto a frozen puddle and breaking the ice, whereupon the onlookers could not restrain their jollification.

The horse cantered off. Now that Sigurd was on the ground it was not so easy to be masterful; the men, though clods, were all so much bigger than he. One of them had the affront to hand him his axe which had fallen with him. He stood opposing them for long furious seconds, before turning on his heel and charging off to stalk his horse. Trying to deafen his ears to their remarks on his wet behind, he caught the rein, jumped into the saddle and, more carefully this time, drove the horse at them so that they had to scatter. 'You shall not laugh so loud on my return!'

Sigurd galloped back to his house where further humiliation was to come in the form of his uncle. His angry entrance was pulled up short at the sight of Olaf and two men eating from his table.

'Heill, Sigurd.' The atmosphere was even cooler than outside. Olaf had been unamused to learn from one of the thralls that his nephew had beaten him to Einar's estate – he had not had the slightest inkling that the boy was even in England.

Sigurd, red-cheeked from his exercise, lingered in the doorway. His uncle pushed aside the bowl of mussels and crooked a finger. 'Come you here.'

The boy pulled off his hat and approached warily, then flinched at the quick movement from his uncle's hand. But it was the axe that Olaf was aiming for.

'Mine, I think.' He pointed to the runic letters carved on the handle.

'Your pardon, Uncle.' Sigurd looked chastened. 'But I did not have a weapon worthy of . . .'

'You did not have any weapon at all so you stole mine!' Olaf thumped the axe's shaft at the floor. 'Do you know what the law does to thieves?'

Sigurd did not wish to know. 'I humbly beg your forgiveness, Uncle!'

'Humility is a trait you have not yet acquired, Sigurd!' Olaf put the axe aside. 'Your mother will be ashamed of you.'

'Not when she knows the reason. I only took it so I could win back my father's land!'

'You knew I had sworn to do that for her! Did you not trust me?'

'Ja, of course, but . . .'

'Silence!' Olaf glared him into submission, then continued in hurt tone to his friends, 'He does not trust me, when I have treated him as my own son for eleven years.'

'Please, Uncle, let me speak,' Sigurd urged. ''Twas not a matter of trusting you. I had to do it for myself, to revenge my father's honour and fight for what is mine. I do not want any man to risk his life on my behalf.'

Olaf glared at him for a while, then nodded his understanding and uttered less harshly, 'Well . . . in that at least you are to be admired.' He indicated for the boy to join him at the table.

Sigurd shuffled along a bench and rested clasped hands on the greasy wood. 'So you won't send me back to Norway?'

'Nei – but I am still angry with you for deceiving me!' Olaf became more avuncular then, leaning towards his nephew. 'Sigurd, you cannot possibly hope to run your father's estate . . . I am sorry, *your* estate, alone. You need help.'

'I have help.' Sigurd pointed at the thralls who hovered should there be any request from their masters.

Olaf smiled his condescension. 'Not of the right kind. It takes experience to run a place like this.' He brought his palm down on the table. 'Nei! I insist on giving you the benefit of my advice. My sister would never forgive me if I left you to the mercy of unscrupulous tenants who would shirk from paying their dues.'

'I know how to deal with them,' the boy assured him, heart sinking. He had just got rid of Thorald and now his uncle wanted to interfere.

Alas, no matter how he tried he could not persuade his uncle to leave. Life was even worse than when Thorald had been here, for at least then Sigurd had had some kind of freedom. There were times when he even considered riding to Gæignesburh to enlist the mercenaries' help. Every day he clutched the tiny hammer that hung around his neck and made secret offerings to Thor and Odin the All-Father for assistance. Then, one day, his prayers were heeded. At the sound of many visitors, Sigurd left his meal and ran outside. There was Thorald with what appeared to be his entire crew, most of them on foot though some were mounted, having travelled along the riverbank as the ship would not take the horses. The youngster beamed.

'Such hearty welcome, Smallaxe!' Thorald jumped down from his horse and delivered an affectionate cuff to the excited boy. 'I did not expect you would be so pleased to see . . .' His voice trailed off and his eyes narrowed as Olaf came out of the house with his two friends in attendance. 'And who have we here, Sigurd?'

''Tis I who should ask that of you,' replied Olaf, equally suspicious at the large number of men, a motley collection.

Sigurd explained quickly to Thorald, '*Hersir*, this is my uncle. Uncle, these are the friends who helped me win back the estate.'

'Ah, then I must thank you on behalf of my sister.' Olaf was courteous, but retained his guard. 'You have business in Jorvik, ja?'

Thorald shook his head, tinkling his earrings. 'We go north and merely dropped anchor so that we may pay our respects to friend Sigurd.'

'Then you must come and take meat with us.'

Olaf extended his arm as indication for the men to enter.

Whilst those on horseback gave custody of their mounts to the thralls and joined the rest inside, Sigurd held back and hissed to Thorald, 'I cannot rid myself of him! He insists that I am not old enough to run the place myself. Can you stay and help me?'

'Why, have we not always done so, *biarki*?' Thorald dropped his leonine head to conspire. 'Tell me, how many men does your uncle have?'

'Just the two you see with him.' Sigurd twiddled his unruly fringe. 'The rest remained to serve the King. I have tried every way to persuade him to go but he will not heed. Mayhap he wouldst listen to another man.'

Thorald winked and patted the boy's shoulder. 'It should be easy. Now, come before your uncle is more distrustful of us than he is already.' His great hand scooped Sigurd into the gloom of the house.

Beside the welcoming crackle of the fire, the men and the boy partook of a meal of fish and beer. After which, Thorald delivered a belch, performed an exaggerated stretch and announced to Olaf, 'Well . . . we would not wish to outstay our welcome, *hersir*. I thank you for your hospitality.' He tweezed a last morsel of pike from the wooden trencher, stuffed it into his beard and rose. 'Come, men, let us row whilst light prevails.'

Too astonished to object, Sigurd watched as his friends filed outside, mounted their horses and deserted him. He went to bed that night cursing them – but when he rose the next morning there was Thorald, Ulf and Eric and the rest of the dirty band eating breakfast!

The boy rubbed his eyes. 'Wha . . . I thought you had deserted me!'

'What a slur to cast upon one's bosom friends!'

scolded Thorald. 'You enlisted our help, did you
not?'

'Ja – but you spake not a word to Uncle, so I
thought . . .'

'We did not speak then for we had things to do,
but we returned later.' Thorald bit deep into a shive
of warm bread.

Sigurd peered around the room. 'Where is Uncle?'

Thorald projected surprise. 'Why, we persuaded
him to leave as you asked us to do. Here, eat some
of this loaf before Eric crams it all down his neck.'
He grabbed the flat loaf of barley bread from Eric's
hand and slammed it before the boy.

'But how?' Sigurd was delighted.

The bearded jaw chewed vigorously. 'Oh . . . we
simply explained to him that he is not the master
here.'

Sigurd could not believe that it had been accomplished so easily but was nevertheless grateful to
Thorald and sat between him and Eric to eat a bowl
of skyr brought by a thrall. 'I never heard a thing.'

'Ja, I notice you are a very sound sleeper.' Thorald's
eyes glittered.

'Where has he gone?'

'To Gaeignesburh, so he said.'

The boy's spoon paused halfway to his mouth. 'I
suppose he has taken my axe with him?' When Thorald nodded, he looked downcast at the loss, but not
for long. 'Ah well . . . I have enough money now to
buy one of my own.' He swallowed the porridge and
grinned. 'I did not have the chance to tell you last
night but I have discovered where the rest of my
father's land is.'

Thorald tried not to look too alert. 'Ja?'

'Alas, my tenants need to have sense knocked into
them. They refuse to pay their dues. Uncle was going
to attend to it . . .'

'Fear not, little brother!' Thorald seized the boy

under his armpits and hoisted him playfully from the bench, the spoon still in his mouth. 'Their geld will be in your coffers by noon.'

And so it was. Confronted by Thorald, the kotsetlan performed their obligations without a whimper. However, Sigurd himself had cause to complain when Thorald and his men showed no sign of leaving. Out of gratitude for their aid, he tolerated his guests' presence for a week before asking when they planned to row north as had been their spoken intent.

Thorald was stooped over a game of hnefatafl, his opponent Ulf. The others, replete from yet another meal at Sigurd's expense dozed about the golden shadows. Thorald's voice was vague as he tried to concentrate on his next move. 'Oh, you are so hospitable, Sigurd, that I have no plans to leave just yet. Besides, you will need us here if your uncle should return.' The fingers holding one of his chalk pieces hovered over which square to lay it on.

Sigurd was not to be detoured. 'It has been weeks. If he was planning to return he would have done so by now. I am grateful for your assistance in winning back my land, *hersir*, but my purse is not bottomless. I fear that when my mother comes from Norway there will be nought left for her.'

Thorald merely grunted and made his move. Ulf fingered his bare neck and studied the board from under his fringe. He had wagered a great deal of money on this game and Thorald's red pieces had his hnefi, or king, almost surrounded. He hesitated too long. Thorald began to torment him about his lack of skill, managing to equate this with his lack of manhood; an angry Ulf would relinquish the game more quickly.

Sigurd was annoyed both at Thorald's lack of attention to his query and to his insults to Ulf. Having no facial hair yet himself he sometimes wondered if Thorald's remarks were aimed at him, too.

He persisted with his interrogation. 'When does she come?'

'Soon,' mumbled Thorald. Ulf still dallied over where to deposit his white piece. 'Come, Bareface, get it over with. You know you must lose to a superior player.'

Sigurd persisted. 'But when does she come? You said . . .'

Thorald lost patience both with Sigurd and Ulf. 'I said soon! Now quiet your tongue – Ulf, make your move or the game is forfeit.'

Sigurd was furious. 'You dare bid me quiet in my own house!'

In a trice he found himself sprawled at Thorald's feet, his ear burning. 'Your house – hah!' Thorald reached down, grasped a handful of the sheepskin tunic and worried him like a rat. 'You live here by my grace only! Think you that I would waste my sword to get the land for a little fish like you? You can thank Christ I am a kindly man or you would not even have reached the coast of England! Now run outside and play with the other children!'

Sigurd fell again under the weight of his shove, but before Thorald could reseat himself the boy grabbed the man's own sword, propped close at hand, and lunged at him.

Only by an agile jerk of his hips did Thorald escape disembowelment. As the boy's swordarm brushed harmlessly against his flank he caught Sigurd and dealt a blow that sent him hurtling yet again to the floor with his nose bleeding. 'That is your first and last try, Smallaxe!' Enraged, he picked up the sword and wagged it at the boy.

'If you would stick that in me then you had better do it now!' retorted Sigurd, blood trickling down his upper lip. 'For I have not come here to let my land be taken from one rogue by another. The first chance I get to remove you I shall take it.' He glared defiantly at the man who towered over him.

'I do not soil this noble weapon with the blood of weanlings!' roared Thorald, and began to attack Sigurd with the hilt. His victim rolled up like a hedgehog but the blows did not stop.

The commotion woke even Eric who at first observed the beating with dozy eyes, but then became concerned at the ferocity of the attack and tried to intervene. 'Hey, Thorald, a bent sword will not serve you well in your next battle unless you aim to fight round corners!'

Things were looking desperate for Sigurd. Thorald seemed to have lost his reason. Handicapped by rage and the absence of his little finger, he would occasionally lose his grip and drop the sword, only to retrieve it and begin again. With everyone gathered round the event, Ulf took the opportunity to move one of Thorald's pieces backwards, then decided that he too must help the wretched boy. It took only three words. 'Your move, Thorald!'

The tense moment broken, Thorald looked up and after a few breathless seconds of indecision, leaned his weapon back against the bench. Face still livid, he picked Sigurd up, one hand at the scruff of his neck, the other at his breeches, carried him outside and hurled him into a midden pit. 'Go practise with your wooden sword before you are man enough to use a real one!' He went back to his seat and looked down at the board . . . then rolled a mistrustful eye at his opponent.

'Your move,' repeated the granite lips.

Face bloodied, seething with rage and frustration, the boy clawed his way from the putrid, maggot-ridden debris and stood there trembling, fighting tears. It was pointless trying to attack Thorald with only the small knife that hung from his belt. Instead, he worked out his anger on the boundary fence, stabbing at the timber, gouging and tearing with his blade, his

71

mind supplanting wood for flesh. 'I have a good mind to go and sink his shit-ridden boat!'

But when Ulf came upon him later he was in less defiant mood, huddled pathetically against a wattle hut. The young man paused. 'You are badly hurt?' His words hovered in a cloud then dissolved into the cold afternoon air.

Sigurd had always found Ulf detached and cold. The enquiry astonished him. He shook his head, looked up into the insipid eyes and offered hesitantly, 'I should thank you for preventing my death.'

Ulf brushed his part off. ''Twas only favour for favour; you did me service by interrupting the game. Thorald was cheating. When he was preoccupied with you it gave me a chance to even things out.' The shallow jaw gave hint that its owner was amused.

'Did you win?' Sigurd's nose was red. There was dried blood around his nostrils.

Ulf nodded, swaying from heel to toe as the cold ground permeated his boots. 'Ja, a good thing too. I had wagered all the money in my purse on that game.'

The boy adopted the role of a father. 'Was it not rash to wager all that you own against a cheat?'

Ulf countered, 'Is that not what you just did?'

Sigurd gave a rueful smile and touched his brow to see if it was still bleeding.

At the resulting wince, Ulf felt sorry for Thorald's victim and descended beside him, hugging his shaggy cloak around himself. 'I tried to warn you he was dangerous.'

Sigurd looked confused. 'I thought you were the dangerous one. He has always been so friendly.'

Ulf shrugged. 'He will probably be so again when he has slept off his temper.'

'He is no friend of mine.' Sigurd's eyes turned dark. 'And I shall prove it to him.'

'Take care, Sigurd.' Ulf did not call him Smallaxe

72

this time. 'Now that you have served your purpose and he knows the full extent of your landholding, Thorald can kill you at any time. But if you do not offend him you will be safe enough.'

'I am not af . . .' began Sigurd, then gave sheepish acquiescence.

'Ja,' cognized Ulf. 'You learn.'

After a pause, Sigurd asked, 'Why do you follow Thorald when he insults you so?'

'Everybody insults Ulf,' came the phlegmatic reply. 'I may just as well ride with one as another.'

Sigurd turned to him with new enthusiasm. 'Then ride with me and I will share my land with you!'

'You and I against Thorald!' Ulf laughed aloud at the combination, making Sigurd aware that he had never seen this young man so amused.

'Not just we two.' Sigurd kept his voice low. 'Your friend Eric will join us and the two of you could persuade the others.'

'Eric, ja it may be so, the others will refuse. They are totally bound to Thorald.' Ulf scrambled to his feet, dismissing the plan as boyish fantasy. 'I am going for a pee.'

In Ulf's absence, Sigurd thumped his body against the cold and mulled over the idea. When Ulf returned and asked if he was coming back into the house he shook his head. Ulf turned to go.

'If I was older would you ride with me?'

Ulf was moved to kindness by the wistful tone. 'Perchance, ja.'

Sigurd put conviction into his response. 'Then I shall call upon your help again some day.'

Ulf gave a curt nod, then after a second's thought dropped his mantle over Sigurd's head, plunging him into darkness. When the boy emerged Ulf had gone back inside the timber house.

Later, when Thorald had slept off his bad humour he came looking for his victim who totally ignored him. This helped to rekindle animosity. 'Oh, stop sulking! Are you not back in your father's house? And that is what you wanted, ja?'

Sigurd could not help but retort, 'I wanted to be master!'

'He who would be master should first learn how to act the part! Your uncle was right about you, you are just a silly child.' After a tense moment, Thorald managed to control his temper. 'Come, it does not befit a warrior to mope.' He held out his mutilated hand. 'Let us be friends – did I not help you be rid of your uncle?'

'Huh! You are twice as bad!' Sigurd gave a feisty tug at Ulf's cloak, huddling right into it, knees and all.

Patience waning, Thorald flourished his hand. 'I offer you one last chance to make the best of things.'

Sigurd beheld him with contempt. 'I think it is you who has the best of things. You have my land, my house, my food . . .'

'Go rot then!' Thorald turned his back on the boy and strode back to the house. 'If you do not want to be my friend you can bed down in the slaves' hut!'

'What do I care when you treat me like a slave already! Tell me where my uncle has gone and I will gladly fetch him back.'

Thorald gave a nasty laugh and slammed the door.

As the night grew even cooler so did the boy's blood. Shivering and bouncing up and down Sigurd realized he would indeed have to spend the night with the thralls or freeze to death. First, he visited the cesspit to empty his bladder. The stream of urine disturbed the contents, emitting a foul odour. Sigurd pulled his shirt down, came from behind the wattle fence and went towards the mean shack where he showed his contempt of the thralls by curling up amongst the dogs.

In the morning he extricated himself from the pile

of musky fur and visited the cesspit again. This time
he noticed something other than the smell. A lock of
blond hair floated amongst the green scum; it was
attached to someone's head. The boy gasped, then
knelt and peered closer. A pair of male legs came up
behind him. He swung round in alarm.

Thorald urinated calmly into the pit. 'Are you in
better mood this morn?'

'There's a fellow in there!' Sigurd jumped up and
pointed.

Thorald's eyebrows rose in surprise. 'Is there? Must
have come out for a piss in the dark and stumbled
right in – it is a treacherous place.' Unconcerned, he
turned away. 'Art coming in to breakfast?'

'It is my uncle!' There was horror in Sigurd's voice.

'What?' Thorald was still half-asleep. 'Nei, it cannot be. I saw him leave. That is just a bit of dog
hair.'

'You killed him!'

'Me?' Thorald's belly jutted with indignation. 'I
was not the one who wanted rid of him.'

Sigurd panicked. 'I did not want him dead!'

'Aha . . .' Thorald shook his head with a look of
reproof. 'You should be more cautious, young friend.
I and a dozen others heard you say, "I cannot get
rid of him".'

'But no one would believe . . .'

'Of course not.'

Sigurd's heart leapt. 'What of the two men who
were with him?'

'With whom?' Thorald overacted his role of innocence. 'There has been no one here but we friends.'
He put a finger over his lips. 'Have no care, your
secret is safe with me. I will tell no one how fond
you were of the axe he took from you.'

Sigurd's thoughts made him giddy. He wanted to
ask what Thorald had done with the axe – he would
never have cast such a valuable weapon into a cesspit

– but he had no time to utter a word for Thorald was laying an arm across his shoulders and drawing him towards the house. 'Now, have you yet decided if my friendship is preferable to that of the thralls?'

Dumbfounded, Sigurd looked up into the ursine face. It appeared to be friendly, but knowing what he knew now the boy was more respectful. Trying to hide his distaste of the word he murmured, 'Ja.'

'Goooood!' Thorald delivered a magnanimous slap to his back, aggravating a bruise. 'Then come and eat at my table.'

Unwilling to be completely dominated, Sigurd made a correction. '*My* table.'

Thorald had to laugh. 'Have it your way, little mule – *your* table. Now, wilt thou come and eat?'

Sigurd might have found his uncle irksome, but the bonds of family were irrevocable; he would not allow Olaf's death to go unpunished.

'I will eat,' he replied, then added the silent oath: *I'll eat at your table until I am old enough to make it my table, and then I shall kill you.*

Chapter Four

Sigurd was never to discover what had happened to
the other men nor to the axe, and he did not enquire
for fear of bringing Thorald's wrath down upon
himself. When the initial trauma receded he considered making application to the law over his uncle's
death, but decided that his word against Thorald's
was not a fair contest. His only recourse was to bide
his time and pretend fealty.

There were others in England more practised in
this art. Eadric Streona, ealdorman of West Mercia
and one of those responsible for Ethelred's unwise
decisions in the past, now came over to Swein offering to kill Ethelred's heirs in return for favours.
However, there was no time for him to carry this out,
for on Candlemas 1014, just five weeks after his
conquest of England, King Swein died. In the absence of his elder son who now ruled Denmark, the
throne fell to the eighteen-year-old Cnut, and thus
came the answer to Sigurd's problem. With Cnut in
Jorvik for his father's interment at St Peter's Minster,
all he had to do was get close to the monarch and
remind him of their summer friendship. No matter
that it had ended on a sour note, the young King
would remember the good times and, enacting the
promise he had made to Sigurd, would command
Thorald to leave.

Enlisted for help, Ulf said the boy should leave well
alone. 'Were I in your shoes I should consider myself
fortunate.'

'Fortunate? To be treated like a guest at my own table!'

'Wouldst rather be a meal on that table? Be enslaved or dead?' Ulf repeated his grim statement. 'Leave well alone, boy.'

Sigurd had glimpsed the inner Ulf now, knew that there was real human fellowship here if one could avoid the bouts of vindictiveness to which Ulf was prone – he and Eric were the only ones Sigurd could call genuine friends – but still he did not appreciate the advice. He hated relying on Thorald for food and clothing, but would not abandon what was rightfully his, even if there had been somewhere else to go. Thorald knew what was in Sigurd's heart but merely showed his contempt by turning his back on the boy, and as yet Sigurd did not dare to take advantage. But now perhaps he would not have to.

As the whole city prepared for the burial, Sigurd told Ulf: 'I need someone to keep Thorald out of the way whilst I speak with Cnut.'

'On first-name terms with our King, eh?' Ulf was using a whetstone to sharpen his knife. The sun was bright for February and both were taking every advantage of it, keeping their indoor work for a less clement day.

'We met at Gæignesburh whilst you and Thorald let Ethelred slip out of the country.' Sigurd could not help the taunt. 'He and I were great friends. I know that if I ask he'll command Thorald to be gone from my property.'

Ulf ran a light thumb down the blade. 'He can command all he likes but can he bring you back to life after Thorald has ripped out your lights? For this he will do if he hears of your plotting.'

Sigurd ruminated, eyeing the activity in the yard: a thrall mending hurdles, another employed with a besom, yet another carting dung. 'Mayhap 'twould be best if I ask Cnut to send him into exile.'

'Cnut, this! Cnut, that! It is the King you speak of – Eric! Where is that fat little fart? He is meant to be helping me.' Arms akimbo, Ulf swivelled his cropped head in search of Eric.

The boy was dismissive. 'Only a king, not a god, and he is my friend.'

'So was Thorald – once,' Ulf reminded him. 'Ah, there you are, loose buttocks!' Eric had appeared in the act of lacing his trousers. 'What was it, women or ale?'

Eric gawped, his short legs making no effort to rush. His mode of walk was very ungainly, chest puffing, head lolling from shoulder to shoulder, hands moving like turtle flippers. 'What?'

Ulf repeated the sarcasm. 'What was it that forced you into the laborious act of dropping your breeches, a woman or a surfeit of ale? If you have enough strength left could you perchance help me to butcher this horse?' He indicated the small, rough-coated animal tethered to a pole some yards away. For five years it had been put to work until ripe for slaughter, now it would provide a welcome change to the dried and salted flesh of winter fare.

Eric wiped the back of his hand over his nose and went to fetch ropes. The horse sensed what was to befall it and began to dance and buck; its executioners cursed and struggled over it. 'Hold the bastard down!' Ulf tried to grip his rope whilst the horse almost swung him off his feet. An audience of dogs yelped with drooling anticipation. 'Sit there, young one! Do not bother to exert yourself, we have everything under control!'

Sigurd watched unmoved as the horse was cornered, stunned by Ulf's axe and dropped like a boulder. 'You will not help me, why should I help you?'

'Help you do what?' asked Eric, relaxing into a yawn.

'He entreats me to occupy our hairy friend whilst

he petitions the King.' A black kitten had leapt onto Ulf's shoulder. Totally disregarding it, he beavered away at the steaming carcase whilst Eric appeared to be assisting but in fact did very little. 'He is a personal friend of Cnut, did you not know?'

'I am!' bawled Sigurd at Eric's disbelieving laugh. 'He will tell you so himself if you help me get close to him.'

Under Sigurd's constant pestering, Ulf finally gave in just to be rid of the whining voice. 'Stop! Stop! I agree to help. Though it will all be a dangerous waste of time. I doubt you will even snatch a glimpse of him.'

This last opinion was prophetic. Vast crowds lined the old Roman route of the *via principalis* as the royal bier was transported with reverence into St Peter's Minster. Behind the malodorous wall of bodies Sigurd could see little, but kept nudging Ulf into action. Irritated, Ulf nudged him back and knocked him into his neighbour who in return cuffed the boy. Sigurd changed tactics, gazing up at Ulf with childish accusation. Ulf, never loquacious, could not think of a topic that would engage Thorald long enough for the boy to slip away. Then he saw an old woman in the crowd and tugged at Thorald's sleeve. 'See the kerling over there? She has more hair on her chin than I!'

Thorald spotted the moustached grandmother and gave a rude laugh. ''Tis true – look, look, men!'

Ulf felt the boy slip away, using bodies to screen his escape, and kept a nervous eye on his passage through the crush until he lost track of him. The joke that he had instigated became a succession of jokes, all at his expense. He bit on his tongue. If this did not work he would murder Sigurd himself.

Well-distanced from the others, Sigurd waited impatiently for the ceremony to be over, never taking his eyes from the massive stone cathedral. With its arches and columns, vaulted roof and large windows it would make a fitting palace. One day, he would own a house like that. When Cnut eventually stepped through the great doors with his entourage of courtiers, the boy approached without awe, but long before he had reached his target the way was barred by soldiers. 'Let me pass! I wish to speak to Cnut.' No one heeded him except to issue an oath and shove him back into the crowd. Sigurd, jostled to the rear, was unable to fight his way back through and so began to run behind the wall of bodies, jumping up and down like a gazelle and shouting, 'Cnut!' but his voice was lost amid other cries of homage. The golden young king rode away without Sigurd coming within twenty yards of him.

'Damn them!' he complained angrily to Ulf later when they sat juxtaposed in the latrine. 'Why would they not let me near him?'

One of Ulf's hollowed eyes beheld him with spite. 'Clearly they were ignorant of your intimate relationship with the King.'

The boyish temper soared. 'You talk as if Cnut is a god! He is a man, our equal. You or I could be King if we wished.'

'You, maybe, not I.'

'You have no ambition, Ulf.'

'My ambition is to stay alive. Which will be a feat in itself if Thorald finds that I have conspired with you. All that ridicule for nought.' Shallow jaw morose, Ulf made use of a square of moss and tugged up his breeches.

Sigurd remained on the plank with the holes cut into it. Virtually every time he came here he had the same thought: what would my mother say if she knew I was doing this on my uncle – and even worse, that I am partly responsible for him being in there? Ulf was leaving. Sigurd, never keen to be left here alone, tried to delay his exit. 'Have you really no ambition?'

Ulf was outside the withy fence now. His stolid face appeared above it, looking down at the boy. 'A house and a piece of land is all I desire. That is what I came here for.'

'I too,' nodded Sigurd. 'And once I purge myself of that hairy-arsed villain I will have it.'

Ulf sighed and walked away.

With Cnut's return to Gaeignesburh, Sigurd was forced to continue life under Thorald and wait until he was old enough to carry out the eviction himself. But oh! The road to adulthood was so very tedious.

This thought had barely emerged when an uprising took place. The Danelaw might accept Cnut without question but in the south the councillors of the Witan were already scheming for the return of Ethelred, who must surely have learnt a valuable lesson during his brief exile. In this hope, they despatched a messenger to Normandy, offering their King a second chance if he would promise to rule them more justly in the future. In usual cowardly response, Ethelred sent one of his sons to test the ground first, saying that he would remedy their past complaints and would not retaliate for their lack of help in regard to Swein, if they pledged total allegiance to him. With both sides in agreement, came the declaration that never again would a Dane usurp the English throne.

On Shrove Tuesday, whilst Ragnhild was still hunched over the fire in her snowbound Norwegian cabin dreaming of her son, the Christian community of Jorvik ate up all their rich food in preparation for Lent. It was during the weeks of abstinence that the news came of Ethelred's landing in the south; this infuriated Sigurd who was immediately on the alert. 'Will you ask Thorald if I may come?' He worked alongside his friends Ulf and Eric in the yard, each at their separate occupations.

Ulf continued to repair his boot, stitching on a new flat sole. 'Come where?'

'Come with you when you go to fight Ethelred.'

Ulf snorted. 'I go nowhere. So long as he remains down south he can do whatsoever he likes.'

Sigurd found it hard to understand Ulf: he would fight violently if one of his friends upset him, yet when there was a real threat he acted with caution. 'I'll wager if Ethelred called you Bareface you would go.'

He ducked as Ulf lashed out, but the taunt made little difference to the outcome. Even when warning came that Ethelred was advancing upon Lindissi, Ulf did not seem to care as long as he himself was safe in the fortress of Jorvik. His attitude was typical amongst Thorald's men; only when a direct plea came from Cnut did they grudgingly rally to him.

'Can I come?' Sigurd jumped up and down as they prepared to travel to Gaeignesburh.

'Shall we let him?' teased Thorald, looking around at his partners, then dealt mean judgment. 'Nei, you are still too young for fighting and I would hate to see my little friend hurt. Bide here and guard the house.'

Idiot, thought Sigurd privately. How can I be old enough to protect the house and yet not old enough to fight for the King? But, left on the wharf to watch Thorald and his men row away he could not help a thrill of anticipation, cradling the hope that the great bear would be killed by the English, even if it would mean robbing Sigurd of that pleasure.

It had not occurred to Sigurd that Cnut could be defeated, and so he was greatly shocked when Thorald returned after Easter minus half his force. The remaining half was not without injury: Eric was badly slashed across the thigh and Ulf's brow was encrusted with blood. 'Do not fear,' Eric calmed the excited boy. ''Tis not fatal. Ulf sweats blood because he lost his purse in the skirmish.' Ulf was too tired to offer retaliation. Indeed, all looked exhausted.

The bearlike mercenary explained as he and his men took comfort in ale, their stench overpowering. 'Ethelred took us offguard in Lindissi, outnumbered us. When I saw him at the head of the army I knew – did I not say, Ulf?' Ulf was too tired even to nod. 'When I saw him leading his men I knew it was already written that we would lose. Ethelred never leads unless he is sure of victory – and by the gods, he was victorious that day!' Thorald took a clumsy swig of ale; some of his men had fallen asleep with their heads on the table. 'Burnt every living thing, all those good folk who had harboured us, little babes too, the butcher . . . And the one called Eadric Streona! I would surely love to meet him face to face – he left us in the lurch and went back to Ethelred!'

'Where is the King now?' asked Sigurd.

'Cnut?' Thorald drained his cup. 'Gone to sea.'

'But he still held hostages!' Sigurd referred to those given to King Swein during last year's victory. 'Why did he not bargain?'

'You think a devil like Ethelred could care about them?' Thorald's head began to droop. 'Cnut let them go to make room on the ships.'

'In one piece?' exclaimed Sigurd.

Thorald thumped the table. 'For pity's sake, boy, let me sleep! Nei, they did not go in one piece but four – he lopped off their hands and noses. Now, art thou sated?'

'And then he turned tail.' Sigurd showed contempt, viewing the decision to run and fight another day not as proof of maturity but cowardice. 'Could he not have rowed with you to Jorvik instead of leaving its loyal citizens at Ethelred's mercy?'

Thorald settled back, eyes closed, but defended the

action. 'He merely goes to Denmark to gather levies. He will return.'

'So why did you not go with him?' demanded the boy scornfully.

Thorald's chest rumbled with laughter, but his voice was drowsy. 'And leave you to your land, you mean. Cabbage head, do you believe you would be any better off if I did go? You think the English would let you live here as I do? They would flay you alive and nail your skin to the door. That is why Thorald stays in Jorvik – to protect his little friend. Now get you gone and let me sleep!'

In the south the Witan was already beginning to regret its decision to welcome Ethelred back, for he had returned to his old ways, paying Thorkell the Tall and his army at Grenewic twenty-one thousand pounds in the hope of keeping their services. Thorkell and his nine ships had now rowed out of Grenewic harbour: no one was privy to his whereabouts.

This uncertain state of affairs continued into the autumn when a flood-tide swept far inland destroying many homesteads and drowning a countless number of human beings. The vernal equinox brought no alleviation. Sigurd, now twelve and officially a man, waited for news of Cnut's return, but none came. In company with most of those inside the Danelaw, he knew little of what went on down in the south; it was a completely different world.

If Sigurd had but known it, the enemy had fallen into disarray. At the Great Council at Oxnaford, Ealdorman Eadric Streona had redeemed his folly of backing Cnut by murdering the leading thegns of the Danelaw, Siferth and Morcar who had given in so easily to Swein Forkbeard. Ethelred had been accessory to this by confiscating the dead men's properties and ordering Siferth's widow to be taken hostage to keep the Danelaw quiet. Out of the blue, Ethelred's son Edmund – perhaps with a thought to winning the affections of the people – rescued Siferth's widow, and not only had the audacity to marry her but grabbed all Siferth's and Morcar's property too. This might endear him to the folk of the Danelaw but not unexpectedly it alienated him from his father and also enraged Eadric. The might of the English army was gradually eroded by private feuds.

Messengers brought the news to the north. In Jorvik Sigurd and the rest of the population waited anxiously behind the wooden barricades to see what happened. What happened was that Edmund had enough strength behind him and was such a good general that by September, with his father laid low by illness he had captured most of the Danelaw. As the fall of Jorvik seemed unavoidable, Thorald held a council of his remaining men. Sigurd, eager to be involved, joined them at the table.

'We must weigh matters very carefully.' In the shadowy interior, Thorald played with one of the rings on his fingers, twisting it round and round. ''Tis all very well waiting for Cnut to return, but what sort of position does that place us in? If we make a stand – always assuming that we could find enough men to stand with us – and we fail, then even if Edmund does not kill us he will certainly confiscate all our property.'

My property, thought Sigurd childishly.

Thorald laid his palm firmly on the table. 'I say we should ride out and offer Edmund our services.'

Sigurd expressed shock at the disloyalty. 'But he is the son of Ethelred!'

This meant nothing to those who sold their allegiance to the highest bidder; most regarded him with derision. Only Ulf and Eric voted against the action, but even they agreed to fall in with the majority verdict.

'You cannot!' Sigurd thumped the table and glared at each one of them. 'Cnut is our rightful King.'

Thorald looked tired. 'But Cnut is not here.'

'He shall be!' Sigurd beat the table again, rattling spoons. 'And when he comes I shall inform him of your treachery!'

'He is a personal friend of Cnut,' was Ulf's dry explanation to Thorald.

The mountain of hair sighed. 'I knew I should live to regret permitting you to keep your life, Smallaxe. My heart has grown too fond of you. I hope you will not be so foolish as to pursue that intention for I would not enjoy killing you.'

I shall enjoy killing you, though, thought Sigurd as the motion was carried and the meeting broke up.

When the inevitable came and Jorvik fell, life was not so very different. Allied to Edmund, Thorald was allowed to keep all his property and Sigurd retained his precarious role. Then came the glorious news that Cnut had landed in the south bringing with him the vast experience of Jarl Eirik, Regent of Norway, his own brother Harald, and a massive army. It was also clear at last where Thorkell the Tall had crept off to all those months ago; familiar with Ethelred's penchant for leaving his mercenaries in the lurch, Thorkell had taken his money and had sailed to enlist with Cnut. There was little effective resistance to Cnut's army, for Ethelred lay wasting in his bed. Sigurd was quick to point out Thorald's mistake in bartering with Edmund; they should all ride out now and join the viking force.

Thorald seemed unconcerned, picking his teeth with a bone needle. 'You little schemer! Up to your tricks again – you persuade me to go in the hope that I am killed and then you can have your land back.'

'That is not so!' objected Sigurd. 'I want to go and fight too. We should support the King.'

Teeth cleared of meat, Thorald put the needle back into the hollow bird-bone that hung from his belt and explained as if to an infant: 'Smallaxe, as we speak there are three kings in England. I support whichever one is close at hand and at the moment that happens to be Edmund.'

There was another who saw the wisdom in this attitude. Eadric Streona despatched a messenger to Edmund, suggesting that they join forces. Edmund was well aware that most of his father's past difficulties had been because he had accepted poor advice from his councillors. He had also seen how treacherous Eadric could be. However, his own army was jaded from constant battle whilst Cnut's was fresh; reluctantly he agreed to meet Eadric. Afterwards, the ealdorman paid another call.

On this dreary evening, Sigurd and a group of Thorald's men were kicking an inflated pig's bladder around the yard, when a party of riders clattered through the gates.

'Attend the horses, boy!' A richly-dressed man alighted and threw his reins at Sigurd. The latter, startled into compliance, barely saw the visitor's face as he hurried through the dusk, but he brought with him an air of menace and the grammar was English.

Thorald's portly frame barred the doorway. 'Who comes?'

Jaundiced of mien, the boy poised with the reins in his hands, his ear cocked for the identity of the one who had insulted him.

'You are Thorald?' The voice was muffled by the restless jingling of harness. Sigurd tied the reins to a post and hurried towards the house but the door was barred to all save the host and his visitor whose own men were left standing in the dusk. Sigurd leaned towards Ulf and from the edge of his mouth asked, 'Doest know who he is?'

Ulf shrugged and viewed the newcomers with mistrust until the more gregarious Eric called for them to join the game. Undeterred at being barred, Sigurd unlatched the door and marched inside just in time to catch the announcement, 'I am Eadric of West Mercia, counsellor to King Ethelred.'

If Sigurd had held a weapon then he would have used it. 'A dog of Ethelred's in my house!' The words were uttered under his breath but Eadric glanced up at him sharply. His eyes were those of a predatory rodent. Punctual as a moulting stoat, Eadric would change his colours with autumn and spring. Like the stoat he might change hue, but he could not shed the black tip of his tail that marked his wicked nature.

Thorald looked up too and noted the boy's shiver. 'What ails thee, Smallaxe?'

Sigurd gathered his wits. 'I came to ask if your guest requires wine, *hersir*.'

By the glint in his eye, Thorald had seen through the politeness, but allowed the youngster to eavesdrop for the moment. Accepting the offer of wine he bade Eadric voice his business, discounting Sigurd's presence. 'Have no care for him, he is just a boy. So, my lord Eadric, I have long wished to meet you!'

Sigurd glanced at them as he went to pour the wine. With the room in darkness, apart from the immediate area around the fire, he saw only disembodied faces. The effect was one of evil.

Eadric drank from the wooden cup provided and spoke to his host. 'I am flattered.'

'Don't be,' replied Thorald.

A silence followed in which each man came to gauge a likemindedness in the other. From outside came the jeers and exhortations of those who played more innocent games. Eventually, it was Eadric who breeched the hiatus. 'I am given to understand that you are a man of some influence in this city.'

Taking a second or two to interpret the comment, Thorald gave a diffident shrug. 'There are some who listen to what I have to say.'

'You are a loyal subject of Edmund?'

The Norseman became more wary; his eyes glittered over the rim of the cup. 'But of course.'

Eadric regarded him for a while, then was blunt. 'Some say that you are an opportunist.'

'A lie!' Thorald looked wounded. 'Which man told you this? I will stick him on a skewer!'

Eadric showed disdain at his melodrama. 'I have come to ask, what price your loyalty?'

Thorald narrowed his eyes and placed different emphasis on the last comment. 'You come to ask can I be bought.'

Eadric took another gulp of wine. The way he moved his tongue against his palate showed he had drunk better. 'I make no offers yet, but should it happen that Edmund's men become disaffected and wish to return their allegiance to the rightful King . . .'

Thorald cut him off abruptly, deciding it was time for Sigurd to leave. 'More wine, my lord?' When Eadric shook his head his host turned to the boy. 'Leave us now, Smallaxe.'

Sigurd pressed his lips together at being so dismissed, but was forced to exit. However, he had caught the gist of the conversation: Thorald was being asked to fight with Ethelred – and after all they had been through to conquer him! Outside he sought the company of Ulf and Eric, drawing them away from the game, to tell them of the conspiracy.

'That man is one of Ethelred's counsellors!'

'I could have told you that,' drawled Eric.

'Then why did you not say?' demanded the boy.

'You did not ask.'

'What else do you know of him?'

Eric tried to look intelligent. 'Oh, there is a great deal I could say if I had the time, but hark! The others call me back to the game.'

Sigurd grabbed him. 'You knew that he was in there conspiring with Thorald to fight against our King?'

'Well . . .' Eric was saved by Ulf.

'Pay no heed to this bag of wind. Art certain what you heard in there?'

'Have I not ears?' Sigurd waggled a lobe. 'They intend to join Ethelred.'

Ulf pondered, nipping his weak chin. 'Then I fail to see what we can do.'

'We must ride and warn Cnut of this treachery!'

Eric shook his black mane. 'Oh, nei! The risk it is too great.'

Sigurd grew angry. 'You are both cowards!'

'We are fond of living,' amended Eric.

'Overfond! Look at your fat belly. Tell me, why did you fight for Swein and not his son? Why did you come to England in the first place? If all you wanted to do was sit on your arse why not sit at home?'

'Hush! Keep your voice down.' Eric looked over his shoulder then replied to the angry questions with logical calm. 'We fought for Swein because he was mighty. Cnut is only a stripling. We are not mercenaries like Thorald, but farmers. We came to England for land . . .'

'But you have no land!' argued Sigurd.

Eric had to agree and waved his flippers. 'Not yet, but Thorald permits us to . . .'

'Thorald has no land either! The land he holds is mine, and when Cnut triumphs it shall be so again!' Sigurd's voice turned crafty. 'But I could be persuaded to grant some of it to my friends.' He waited for a response. When none came immediately he spat at them, 'Well, I for one will not hang back and watch my father's murderer reclaim this country! I go to ride with Cnut.'

'Wait, wait!' Ulf dragged him back. 'You cannot go alone and you certainly cannot go now, for Thorald will guess at your absence and have one of us ride after you.' He thought for a while about the boy's offer, speaking his views aloud to Eric. 'We should not be so hasty to throw away this chance of land that the lad offers. Cnut is young, it is true, but he has men of vast experience as his shoulder-comrades – Jarl Eirik and Thorkell. 'Tis said he makes great headway in Wessex; with English loyalties split between father and son it is not impossible that Cnut could be victorious.' After the briefest of pauses Ulf made his decision. 'So be it, we will go with Sigurd.'

He looked taken aback by this himself, but no more than Eric who reeled in dismay. The surprise was not that the decision had been taken for him – it was always thus between the two of them – the question was, why did Ulf bother to appoint himself as Sigurd's protector? 'There is no need for the boy to go, Ulf, no one forces him.'

'Nei, but he is right about Cnut. We should not desert him. Besides, what have we to lose?'

'Our lives?' Eric spoke the obvious.

Ulf confirmed Sigurd's previous opinion. 'Thorald keeps promising to give us land but we see none.'

'The only land you will see is six feet of earth if you go creeping off with this headstrong fool.'

'Who said we must go now?' asked Ulf. 'We wait until tomorrow when Thorald goes hunting. He will think it odd if we decline to go with him but we can slip away in the forest.'

'In broad daylight?' Eric was stunned.

'Better than trying to sneak out after curfew.'

Eric gave a cynical laugh. 'Better to stay put altogether . . .' He glanced at Ulf and abandoned his argument. 'Oh, I see my mind has been made up for me! So be it, I go – but this little prick had better not be fooling us.'

Sigurd made dignified comment. 'I never lie to those I call friend; to them I am loyal unto death.'

'You are no good to me dead,' grumbled Eric. 'A dead man cannot give me land.'

'Then you will just have to ensure I stay alive.' Sigurd directed a pointed grin at Ulf.

The next morning, with the rough knowledge of where Cnut's army could be found, they gave Thorald the slip and rode for Wessex. One by one the horses went lame, forcing the trio to proceed on foot. Autumnal storms chased them over heath and marsh. Shoes burst, were repaired and burst again. Sigurd's feet throbbed as if on fire. 'By the gods, I wish I had eight legs like Sleipnir.' He spoke of Odin's horse as he limped along.

'I wish I had eight penises but no one will give me them.' Eric looked so deadly serious that the boy was forced to giggle.

Eric chuckled too, walking in his cumbersome fashion, flap, flap, flap, but Ulf could not see the joke. 'Christ, where is this damned King?' He stopped at a spring where a tin cup dangled on a pole, put there for the convenience of wayfarers. In the bottom was an inch of rainwater and an assortment of dead insects. Ulf tipped them out and ladled water from the spring. The others waited to make use of the cup too.

After drinking, Eric spat. 'If there is no alehouse soon I shall turn back.' He broke wind.

Ulf wafted with a hand. 'Well, you have put paid to our chances of finding the King today. If he was in the vicinity he will be miles away after getting a whiff of that.'

Sigurd was taking his turn when his deeply-set eyes were lit by a glimmer of recognition. Almost invisible against the banks of pewter cloud was a wisp of smoke from a campfire. Urging his friends on, he was relieved to see more tendrils of smoke and a large assembly of men and tents. This surely must be the

93

King. 'It is best if I approach alone,' he told the others. 'For Cnut knows my face.'

Ulf agreed and sat upon the ground, not caring that it was wet for his whole body ached. 'Ja, 'tis best. If he sees this ugly old fart he may kill us without quarter.'

Sigurd had no horn to blow in order to show that he came without subterfuge, but confident of his reception he marched openly across the pasture to where Cnut's army camped. No one took any notice as the boy wandered around the group of tents. Only when he saw a tent more splendid than the rest with the King's banner fluttering at its apex, did his approach give others cause for concern. Within feet of his target, he was seized by guards and treated as an enemy.

'I come as friend to see Cnut!' It was difficult to talk with the soldier's arm choking him.

'How did he get this near to the King without anyone stopping him?' demanded the furious Commander of the Guard, whilst his free hand pulled the knife from Sigurd's belt. 'This could now be embedded in Cnut's heart!'

'I come not to harm the King but to warn him!' croaked Sigurd, hands gripping the restrictive arm.

'Cut him down!' ordered the Commander and sent him tumbling.

A guard pulled his sword. About to die, the boy shrieked in horror, 'Cnut, my friend!'

The flap of the tent was pulled aside and there stood the King. 'Who calls upon my friendship?'

The executioner stayed his hand, giving Sigurd precious time to call out his identity. 'It is I, Sigurd Einarsson!' Unable to stand, his white face appealed.

'He came armed to your tent, my lord,' explained the Commander, holding up the knife.

'Stand!' Cnut was twenty-one now but had altered little since that meeting with Sigurd. The boy, on the other hand, had grown out of all recognition; the King did not know him. 'Who sent you?'

Sigurd was frantic. 'None, my lord! I alone come to serve you.'

The hawkish face showed rejection. 'Serve me with a knife in the back!'

'Nei! Upon my oath I am a loyal subject. Do you not remember? We passed a summer at Gæignesburh when your father laid siege to Lunden.' He enunciated his claim to friendship. 'Sigurd Einarsson!'

The King shook his head. Sigurd felt wretched that he should be so unmemorable, but was now forced to rush on in order to protect himself. 'I came here to warn you of treachery! Thorald of Jorvik who was your man now fights on the side of Eadric of Mercia. I came to offer my aid in his defeat.'

The golden young King looked accusing. 'An honest man would have warned of his coming, not crept in like a serpent.'

Perspiration oozed from the boy's armpits. 'Lord, I have no horn to blow! But I am ready to pledge my loyalty.'

'Why should I trust you?'

Sigurd could offer no reason. 'I can only give you my word that I hate Ethelred with all my heart and have promised vengeance on him and all his kin. If I lie you may cut off my tongue!'

The executioner poised on Cnut's decision, but the King was still trying to recall the boy. He played with his beard. 'You say we met at Gaeignesburh?'

'Ja, it is so, my lord! But I have grown since then. We would wrestle and go fishing together . . . until you found better sport in the Lady Aelgifu.' The boy prayed his artful comment would provoke recognition and could have cried with joy when Cnut turned his face to the sky in laughter.

'You were the one who ran after her wagon for me!'

Weak with relief, Sigurd performed a vigorous nod.

'Ja – your little dog.' Sweat trickled down his brow. A cool wind brought awareness of how damp his shirt had become.

'How couldst I forget?' Cnut signalled for the guard to release the prisoner. 'You were very angry with me, I think.'

Heart still beating fast, the boy delivered a sickly grin and with it a question: 'How fares the Lady Aelgifu, my lord king?' His voice tremored.

Cnut grinned back. 'She is most healthy, as is my son.' He nodded and studied the lad with the unruly fringe. 'So, you come to help me again, Sigurd . . . A pity there are not more like you.'

Sigurd was pricked by guilt and it showed in his face. 'In truth there are, oh noble one. I durst not say before, in fear that your guards would ride out and kill them, but I bring two friends with me. They are back there aways.' His arm came up to point. Having quickly outgrown the clothes provided by Thorald, the cuffs were halfway up his forearm. 'I came ahead to vouch for them.'

Cnut laughed. 'And almost got yourself killed.' He turned to one of his officers and commanded, 'Bring them here – gently.' The man rode off with a group to find Ulf and Eric, whose nervousness at being encircled by the King's men was soon blown away when they witnessed the boy seated alongside Cnut like some courtier. His expression was vain as they were brought into the King's tent to swear their allegiance. A hungry Eric licked his lips as the boy polished off the bread that had just acted as a trencher for his stew, and looked around hopefully. A meal was provided and as the newcomers ate, Cnut enquired, 'What is the mood of other Jorvik citizens?'

Much easier in spirit and voice, Sigurd replied for the three of them. 'My lord, we have listened to the gossip and believe most of the people are loyal to you. They do but wait for you to release them from the Englishman's yoke.'

'Then we must go forth and test their hospitality,' announced Cnut.

'Lord King, mine will be the first table you eat off when we arrive,' vouched Sigurd, and grinned in triumph at his two friends.

Chapter Five

During that autumn of 1015 Cnut's army ravaged Wessex. Sigurd was elated that the King adopted him as favourite but was dismayed when he found that all this qualified him to do was hang on Cnut's arm like a talisman. The King disallowed him to join the fighting, voicing the opinion that Sigurd was far too amusing to waste on battle; who would make him laugh if the boy died?

Then, one morning a sentinel gave word that there were ships massing off the coast. As Cnut prepared for attack, a messenger came and knelt before him.

'My lord, I come from Ealdorman Eadric of Mercia who offers his army to your bidding. He craves permission to speak with you.'

Upon short consultation with his officers, Cnut gave leave for Eadric to enter the camp. As the waiting party marched forward Sigurd recognized another of its number. 'Thorald!'

Ulf cuffed him. 'I thought you to say he plotted against Cnut! Have we gone against him just to feel his wrath?'

'I swear I did not mishear!' Sigurd mirrored his apprehension. 'Come, we must warn the King.'

Whilst Eric and Ulf grumbled at his stupidity, he ran to Cnut. 'Lord, these are the men of whom I spoke – Thorald who stole my land and Eadric the turncoat. I beg you, do not trust them!'

Cnut stilled the babble of concern with a raised hand. 'You must not presume to offer your King advice.'

The dangerous group moved nearer. Sigurd could barely contain his impatience. 'But I know Thorald! I heard him bargaining with Ethelred's man.'

'Then why do both come?'

Confused himself, Sigurd was unable to answer this but prattled away in a last attempt to prevent the influx of evil.

Cnut was indisposed to listen. 'We shall hear what they do say.'

As the group neared, Sigurd took a backwards step and placed himself behind the King, but Thorald could not fail to notice him at such close proximity, and with him Ulf and Eric. For a moment he faltered, his expression one of murder, but in the last remaining strides up to the King his quick mind found a solution. 'Ah! I see that my men arrived, lord. I despatched them ahead to bring tidings of my coming.' After bowing, he extended an arm to pat Sigurd who ducked away.

Cnut regarded him without passion. 'Come you to plight obedience?'

'It is so, my lord.' Eadric came out of his bow and though he spoke to Cnut he held the boy with cockatrice eye. 'King Ethelred is failing and in my view England would be a lesser place under his son.'

Cnut interpreted the situation a different way. 'Nei, you fear that Edmund will not reward you as I would.'

The stoat inclined his head. 'If it so pleases you to reward me for my loyalty I shall present no argument, my lord.'

'And what wouldst you consider apt reward for your bravery?'

Eadric pretended to think deeply. 'If you were to grant the title Earl of Mercia, I believe it would sit quite prettily upon these shoulders, my lord.' Sigurd had never known a grin to look so malicious.

'And what of you?' The king turned to Thorald.

'Oh, I have no such lofty ambitions, King.' The uncouth bear tried to appear servile. 'To follow you is my reward.'

'We have over forty ships at your disposal, my lord,' announced Eadric.

'Then I thank you, and accept your terms of allegiance,' replied Cnut. Sigurd could have thrashed him.

When Thorald and Eadric backed away from the King to make camp, Sigurd kept a sharp eye on their whereabouts, so too did Ulf and Eric. Bowing, the boy petitioned for leave to sleep within Cnut's own circle of guards. 'You may trust Thorald, lord, but I do not. Given half the chance he will kill us.'

Cnut granted the favour. 'But when did you hear me say I trusted him? I trust neither of them. Alas, if I am to win England I need all the help I can get, even that of rascals.'

Sigurd watched his shaggy antagonist's every move. 'Thorald may turn against you just as he turned against Edmund.'

'We shall see,' was all the young King replied, leaving Sigurd and his friends with the prospect of much insomnolence.

Contradicting all fears, the King's decision appeared to have been right, for by the arrival of winter the West Saxons had submitted to the greater force. Cnut, his brother Harald plus Eadric and the combined fleet crossed the Temes, took Mercia and during Christmas captured Wæringwicumshire, here outmatching any massacre that Ethelred had committed. Edmund tried to gather support but now men were refusing to assemble without the presence of Ethelred who languished in Lunden. In his absence they began to desert and return home. Edmund, pushed further and further north by Cnut's army, resorted to threats: any disaffection would invoke heavy penalty. Failed threats gave way to encouragement: if they held loyal he would do as they wished and ask his father to join forces with him.

But the invalid King, fearing a plot to betray him, decided at the last moment to stay in Lunden. Desperate, Edmund rode to Jorvik to enlist the help of Uhtred, the jarl or Earl of Northumbria. Well informed of this, Cnut prepared for another attack but it did not come. Spies returned with the news that Edmund had used Uhtred's support to take private retribution over Eadric's desertion! With his main opponent engrossed in destroying Eadric's lands, Cnut ordered the army to march on Northumbria.

Uhtred, learning of this, left Edmund to his private vengeance and sped home to Jorvik, but it was too late. Twenty thousand enemy soldiers converged on the prize and Uhtred was forced to yield.

For Sigurd it was a hollow triumph. His friends maintained their disbelief over what he had told them of the conspiracy between Eadric and Thorald no matter how he denied it. 'I promise you that I did not mishear!'

'You also promised us that we would each be rewarded with a share of your land.' Eric was huddled into his sheepskin cape, nose and cheeks red from the biting wind, fingers seemingly frozen around the reins, and his mood at odds with the victorious re-entry to Jorvik. 'Yet here we are back to where we started. We risked our lives . . .'

Sigurd made angry defence. 'How could I have known then that Thorald would keep changing his colours and get round Cnut?'

'Your argument is useless.' Ulf was suffering from a cold, making his expression even more surly than normal. Each word that he uttered rasped his throat and in consequence were kept to a minimum, but he was angry enough to make a contribution now, however painful. His nose streamed as he got down from his horse, elbowing aside the crowds of jubilant people in the marketplace and responded to their glad tidings by snorting the mucus indiscriminately from his nose. This provided more room for movement. 'You are still landless – Cnut is not about to dispossess Thorald when he needs his help. Nor can any of us even rely on Thorald's charity for a roof over our heads.'

'That is soon remedied. I will ask the King for protection.' A confident, pink-cheeked Sigurd kneed his horse.

'Do not be surprised if we are dead when you return!' called Eric, performing a theatrical look over his shoulder.

Sigurd laughed. 'Have no care. My eye has never left Thorald. He is ov . . . oh, he was there a moment ago.' He swivelled his head. A pall of white breath hung over the crowd of townsfolk who cheered the conquering army. With so many faces it was impossible even to pick out one so easily distinguishable as Thorald's. 'No matter, he will have headed for Peseholme.'

'That is not so far away that he cannot sneak back to issue vengeance!'

But Sigurd ignored Eric's comment and urged his tired horse along Conyngstrete, packed with joyous townsfolk, minstrels, beggars and vendors towards Earlsburh, the fortified quarters of the King and the Northumbrian earls.

Had he not been mounted it would have been almost impossible to forge a passage. The horse also offered another advantage. Why Sigurd turned to look back he could not say, perhaps it was from force of habit over these past months, but it was lucky that he did so for he saw Thorald with two henchmen not five yards behind him. The hair on his body rose. There were insects all over him, beneath his arms, creeping round in his groin and along his thighs.

Panic almost caused him to abandon his horse – maybe it would be easier for his thin body to slip through the crowd – but *no, you fool! Thorald would then run you down.* He kicked his mount. The horse grunted and lurched forward, harness jingling. The crowd parted on a note of disapproval. Sigurd flung a look over his shoulder. Thorald was still there.

'Go on! Go on!' He raised his heels and gave the horse a vicious kick in the flanks. It tossed back its head and set into a canter. 'Out of the way!' roared Sigurd. The crowd parted, women screamed, baskets of bread and fruit were knocked into the road and trampled in the mud, men lashed out as the horse threatened to trample them too. One after the other people jumped out of the way as a terrified Sigurd rode at them with Thorald in pursuit. He lashed and kicked the horse all the way along Conyngstrete, fighting the panic that threatened to send him out of control. The gates of Earlsburh were in sight. One last look over his shoulder. The flared nostrils of Thorald's mount were almost touching his own horse's rump! Thorald had a sword in his hand! Sigurd could not help the yell of fear, pressed himself flat to the horse's back as it galloped for the entrance. His mouth bled from contact with the wooden saddle bow as he crouched over it, but he was oblivious to all save his pursuer. He was through the gates! Guards came running to investigate the rude entry. The horse slewed around as its rider hauled on the reins. Sigurd was about to bawl for assistance against his attackers but as he turned to point he noticed that Thorald had remained on the other side of the gates – and was laughing heartily with his henchmen, all of them pointing at Sigurd.

Feeling an idiot, Sigurd uttered a glowering curse and turning away hauled his unfortunate horse after him. Cnut had only just dismounted from his own horse and did not appear pleased to see the young man, turning away with a look of weariness.

'My Lord!' Sigurd, hair plastered to his brow despite the cold, dropped the reins of his steaming nag and ran after the King.

Cnut paused, closed his eyes, then turned back with impatience. 'Do you never rest?'

Sigurd was still shaking from his mad dash, and his unpreparedness for this reaction caused him to falter. 'My lord, I beg your pardon if my presence tries you. I came only to ask for your protection from Thorald.' He crumpled his hat, looking downcast.

'Do you think I have nought else to worry me than this pretend feud you have with the great bear?'

'It is not pretend!' Sigurd looked aggrieved. 'He has just chased me down the street with sword in hand! If I had not possessed the faster horse he would have killed me for sure.'

Even though he regarded this to be an exaggeration, Cnut held onto his temper because of his liking for the lad. 'Sigurd, if it appears that I have no care for your welfare then you must forgive me, but I have just been greeted with the news that Olaf Haraldsson has taken the chance of my absence to kill Jarl Swein and make Norway his own!'

Sigurd bit his lip, aware that this was drastic. 'Oh . . . my lord, it is I who must ask forgiveness.' He did not know what else to add, other than, 'I will give you every help I can to win Norway back!'

Cnut shook his head. 'I cannot leave the greater prize yet.' He paused for thought, even now unable to accept the grim blow. Norway was not that important in itself, though the sea around it was, for it gave access to the Varangian Sea, and he had lost it. Then he glanced at Sigurd, who looked so earnest in his offer of help that he found the inclination to smile. 'But I thank you for your loyalty. When we are done with Edmund maybe then we will deal with

Olaf. Now, what did you ask of me?' He rubbed his eyes to show he was tired.

Sigurd came erect. 'All I ask is that I and my friends be allowed to camp here under your protection.'

'Then it is granted,' replied Cnut and immediately turned away, leaving a wary Sigurd to return to his friends in the marketplace and relate his hair-raising tale.

Henceforth, the three friends bivouacked with the King's housecarls at Earlsburh, ever on the alert for Thorald's sophistry. They were wise to do so, for even jarls now succumbed to foul play; when Uhtred of Northumbria came under safe conduct to pay homage he was set upon and murdered, his position given to Cnut's brother-in-law. No man was safe.

Cnut gathered more troops to his cause and marched south again, veering well clear of Edmund's savagery in Mercia. Before Easter 1016 they had arrived at their ships and rowed for Lunden. At last a shred of nous pierced Edmund's frenzy of destruction. Envisioning the crown of England on a Scandinavian head, he raced to Lunden to be reconciled with his father: together they would beat the viking menace. Alas, there was no time to put their union to the test. On St George's Day Ethelred's illness robbed Sigurd of any personal redress; his father's murderer was dead.

With Wessex fallen and Cnut's ships bearing down on Lunden, there was only one option for King Edmund. He took flight into the still loyal west country in the hope of raising an army. Meanwhile Cnut's men moved up the Temes until halted by Lunden Bridge. Whence, they set to digging a channel using this as a means to drag their ships around the obstacle and into the upper river. Once the fleet was through, the crews built earthworks around the walls of Lunden so that no one could get in or out and from where they attacked time after time. Though showered with arrows and bombarded with rocks the Lundeners held firm.

Throughout this period, Sigurd had been observing Thorald's every move, his method of fighting, his weaknesses, in preparation for the day that he himself would have to meet the foe in battle. Thorald knew that he was being watched but merely responded with that cunning smile of his, and called to his young adversary during a lull in the bombardment. 'You look tired, Smallaxe! Art losing sleep wondering when I will creep up on you? Well, you can watch and wait all you like, but you will not see the blow that kills you.'

Sigurd, coated in mud due to leaning against the massive earthworks, responded accordingly whilst making himself look alert, slapping mud on the barricade though there was no visible breech to mend. 'Who says I shall be the one killed? If you had any courage you would fight me now face to face.'

Thorald was not to be provoked, gesturing idly. 'Why spoil the fun? There are others who must be attended to first. Time enough to deal with small-fry when Edmund is conquered. Until then it pleases me to watch you sweat.'

Sigurd bared his teeth to offer more, but the exchange was halted by Ulf who had been to relieve himself and had overheard urgent news from down the line. 'Edmund is on the march again with a fresh army! The King has ordered Eadric to go on ahead and intercept him before he reaches Lunden.'

Thorald looked sharp and prepared to muster his troops to ride with Eadric. 'Then I go too – do you ride with us, Ulf?'

'Nay, I will stay and guard the barricades.'

'Look after the cub, you mean!' Thorald mocked. 'Then I will say my farewells and leave you to build mud-pies with Smallaxe.'

'And when you return I will make you eat them!' retorted Sigurd. 'If Edmund does not kill you first!'

Thorald departed on a laugh of confidence. 'He has as much chance as do you, Smallaxe! We shall have him thrashed within the week.'

But Edmund was not the indecisive weakling that his father had been. He was a hard fighter, easily rivalling Thorald and far superior to Eadric. Under the skilful deployment of his opponent's west-countrymen Eadric became disconcerted, and in his panic ordered a retreat, thus leaving Edmund to retrieve Wessex.

Even in the knowledge of this disaster Sigurd could not help but register a personal note of triumph, and when a disgraced Thorald returned, mangled and war-stained, the boy risked a jibe. 'Heill, Thorald! Men, do not stand there, drop to your knees for you are in the presence of a great hero – the fastest runner in Cnut's army!'

Thorald grabbed a dollop of mud from the earthworks and hurled it at his tormentor with great accuracy. 'I am also a champion mud-slinger! Thank the gods it is not an axe, wretch.' But still he sought to offer explanation to his comrades. 'Eadric ran! I had no choice but to follow or be massacred.' Then he dropped to the ground, too exhausted to care about scoring points over a child.

Sigurd clawed mud from his hair, his teasing not over yet. 'I'll wager you regret that you ever threw in with Eadric. Why, he has made you look an utter fool before the King.'

Ulf caught a handful of the boy's tunic, dragging him away. 'And you will be a dead fool if you insist on probing Thorald's wound! If you stopped to think beyond your own personal grievance you would see that there is no cause for laughter. This defeat means we will not be home for a good while yet!'

Indeed, Eadric's invertibrate handling of the affair

served to extend a war that Cnut had deemed already won. The summer and autumn of 1016 were devoured by constant battles with great slaughter on both sides, but Edmund Ironside as he had come to be known, was not to be defeated. After assembling fresh troops he marched on Lunden and lifted the siege, driving the enemy across the Temes and putting them to flight. While he paused to recruit and regroup, Cnut's men attacked Lunden again, but were unsuccessful and were forced to withdraw northwards into Mercia where they salved their defeat in plunder. For the first time Cnut envisaged failure. More and more men were rallying to the young Englishman's cause, chasing the viking army into Kent where yet another battle was fought at Ægelesburg.

The days became shorter. Rutting stags competed with the noise of battle, the crack of their antlers ringing out like sword on shield. Birds grew restless; Sigurd knew how they felt. As usual he had been left on the sidelines to look after the horses whilst fighting took place. It was not going well; Ironside was worthy of the nickname they gave him and his troops had debilitated much of Cnut's army. Sigurd wondered if Thorald was amongst the dead, for though he had tried to keep an eye on his foe's battle tactics he had soon lost him in the mêlée. Edmund's troops were pressing forward now; Sigurd jumped up and down in alarm while the horses rolled their eyes and danced. Sigurd uttered calming words – and then he saw a group of men break from the fighting and run towards Edmund's side, Eadric's standard fluttering alongside a white rag. As the boy watched in disbelief, others followed – and there was Thorald! His unmistakable figure lumbered after Eadric, his company too, all of them deserting their King. The fight collapsed into butchery. With his dead supporters forming a blanket at his feet, Cnut had no option but to retreat with Edmund's men in pursuit. Valour was displaced by flight. Sigurd, too, ran with hair streaming and feet pounding; he abandoned the horses and ran, ran for his life.

'Was I not right!' he yelled when the wave of violence ebbed and the bloody survivors lay panting on the ground. 'Did I not say to Cnut that Thorald was not to be trusted – but would he listen!' His relief at finding that Ulf and Eric had slipped through the bloodletting was short-lived. He cursed and chided them as a father might. 'And you accused me of inventing it all!'

'Then we most humbly crave your pardon!' panted Ulf, sweat and blood mingling on his face. 'Does that still qualify us for the land you promised or do we have to lick your feet?'

Without a word, Eric got up and lumbered away.

Sigurd banged at the ground. 'Those wretched turncoats, I hope Edmund castrates them!'

But Edmund was loth to waste the gesture, desperate for help from any source. He himself might be a doughty foe but his ill-trained men could not match the Danes on equal terms; their only hope lay in superiority of numbers.

After falling back and resting for a while to collect support, Cnut and his men embarked on another raid, anchoring in an Essex river and destroying all that had evaded them before. On their way back to the ships with their booty, however, they found that Edmund's army had overtaken them and were now, on this cool October evening, camped on Assandun Hill. Though one and a half miles stood between them, the fluttering banners of the enemy could clearly be seen; their numbers were alarming. Sigurd hung onto Cnut's every word as the King discussed the position with his generals.

'Any attempt to run for the ships shall meet with trouble.' Cnut was tired of battle; his twenty-two years hung more like forty on his weary face. 'There are but two choices: we can abandon our prizes and the ships and try to escape overland, or . . .' He looked into each grim face, 'we can stay and give battle.'

Another battle! A unified look of fatigue met his words, but the men remained loyal. 'Whatever your move we are with you, oh lord!' One of them spoke up for all.

Cnut made his decision. 'There is a time to run and a time to stand. If I am to die, better to have Edmund's sword in my breast than in my back. Let every able man follow me up yonder hill. 'Tis higher than theirs, so we can look down on them.' The eagle gave an encouraging smile.

Not one word of dissent was mumbled as the weary men dragged themselves up the hill at Canewdon. All would follow their King unto death, and none more eager than Sigurd. 'My lord, I beg you, allow me to fight on the morrow! Have you not said yourself that you need every able man? Give me the chance and I will prove that I am more than able.'

Cnut looked down at the boy. Sigurd was fourteen now; there was blond down upon his cheeks and his arms were sufficiently muscular to use a weapon for a few hours at least. Though reluctant to endanger his young friend, Cnut recognized the desperation and eventually granted Sigurd the chance to prove himself, if only to die. After a pause, he shouted orders to another. 'Fetch this man a shield and spear!'

Bloated with enthusiasm, Sigurd grasped the shield in his left hand and hefted the thrusting spear with his right. 'You can depend on me, my lord!'

'I doubt it not, *drengr*.' Cnut nodded kindly as the boy marched off to parade before his friends.

Later, as Sigurd reclined with Ulf and Eric by their campfire, gazing across at that other hillside dotted with the campfires of Edmund's army, he began to ponder more astutely on tomorrow's battle. With the darkness came the mystery of death. He experienced a sudden prick of fear in his belly, his limbs and bowels trembled and when his voice emerged it seemed to do so from the opposite end of a tunnel. 'I wonder at which of those fires Thorald warms his hands.'

Ulf huddled further inside his cloak and stared across at the twinkling fires. 'So long as he is over there and I am over here I care not.'

'What if you should meet him on the field tomorrow?' Sigurd plucked at his leggings, imploring his thudding heart be still.

Ulf groaned. 'Those are just the words of comfort to grant me a good night's slumber.' The thought of another bloodbath made him want to curl up and sleep forever.

'Nei, the question was a valid one.' Eric added to the gloom. 'Any man of us could face Thorald tomorrow.'

Ulf turned. The blackness hid his expression though not the acerbic tone. 'You talk as if Thorald is our only bane – are you blind to how many other campfires there are? We may never even see Thorald.'

Eric rubbed first a stocky thigh, then a black beard. 'That is true. If he gets the chance he will stab us in the back before we lay eyes on him.' It was delivered in cryptic vein but Ulf did not find it amusing. For Sigurd, too, the remark prevented sleep. Over and over in his mind he rehearsed his clash with Thorald. Only once in that rehearsal did the wrong person die; he forbade himself to think of that possibility again.

They breakfasted before the sun had fully risen, with nervous gut and bowel expelling more than was imbibed. There was much fidgeting, men squatting, stretching, limbering up for battle, windmilling arms, rotating shoulders. Some kneeled pensive, daubing their cheeks with red and blue, some wore vests of mail, whilst others like Ulf and Eric were forced to rely on thick leather jerkins. Sigurd wore no protection but his tunic. He perched upon one leg and gripped his other ankle, hopping and tottering for no reason other than to keep occupied. Eric took hold of him. 'Just stand you there, boy – no, right there.' He adjusted Sigurd's position and crouched behind him. 'That is excellent, now just keep in front of me as we walk down the hill.' He pushed his human shield before him until Sigurd recognized the jape and cursed him. There was matching badinage amongst the other men, and loud laughter, but their eyes were like glass.

When they were in position, churchmen toured the line with rood and incantation, stirring fervour in the men who shouted, 'In Christ! In Christ!' whilst Sigurd closed his eyes and prayed most zealously, 'Odin, All-Father, mightiest of warriors, give strength to my spear and pain to my enemies!'

Hard on the heels of the churchmen came the King, splendid in his golden crown, who wound them up into a frenzy until every breast pounded and every mouth bawled, 'To aaarms!' Behind his plain wooden shield, Sigurd's virgin fingers opened and closed upon the leather handle. In his highly charged state he hopped from foot to foot and tapped the shaft of his weapon at the ground. With king's standard and bishop's crozier aloft, the men hurled insults across the dewy pastures. The jibes were good-humoured; an innocent ear might never guess that they were about to kill each other. Lower down the line a warrior stepped forth, dropped his breeches and presented his buttocks to the enemy. Keyed for action of any type, Sigurd issued a yelping laugh, dropped his own breeches and jiggled his white behind. Enlivened by the consequent laughter, he repeated the performance. 'Take care, no-balls, lest arrows fly,' warned a laconic voice.

Ironside was the first to move, charging on foot down the hill at Assandun towards them. His army was split into three divisions, the centre contingent under his own command, Ulfcytel and the East Angles on his left and Eadric commanding the right flank. The sun was risen and shone a path to glory. Cnut's army of nobles, farmers, rogues and bishops advanced to meet them in a single line, crucifix replaced by sword. They did not run, for that would be to throw away the benefit of higher ground, but Sigurd found it nigh impossible to hold back. As they plodded down the hill, he uttered in heady breath, 'You like a wager, Ulf. What will you pay if I am the one to kill Thorald?'

'You are still in the land of dreams,' laughed Eric on his right, but it was a nervous laugh.

Ulf gave his reply as they marched, marched, marched forth unto death. 'If you kill Thorald then not only will I give you my finest brooch, but I will drink your health from his skull – provided he has not already killed me.' Self-preservation told his feet to walk the other way, but fear of being dubbed a coward pressed him onwards.

Eric stumbled, making his response impatient. 'I have told you, we will not even see him!' The advancing army was in range.

'I will seek him out,' vowed the boy from behind his shield.

Eric sighed. 'Then we had better keep close to him,' he told Ulf – upon which there came the murderous shower of spears and stones and arrows, thudding down upon the panoply of shields and luckless heads. Cnut's army returned the volley, raised a cheer as foes went down, then pressed on.

Edmund had begun to realize the foolishness of his brave but hasty dash; the ground before Assandun was uneven, causing his division and that of Ulfcytel to advance more rapidly than that of Eadric on the right. The gap between them had widened. Cnut's eagle eye was quick to see this. He urged his men into a charge. Sigurd tightened his grip on the spear and ran, heard the thunder of enemy feet as thousands hurled themselves towards him, saw the glittering points of lances, saw the hatred on their faces, calling death upon their foe, mouths agape in battle-cry, ten thousand tongues raised in one blood-curdling yell: '*To arrrrms!*'

Nearer, nearer charged Death – but lo! Eadric had halted his own division well to the rear of the others, saw and heard the deafening clash as shield met shield and sword met flesh. Stretched out in a line and finding no troops to their front, the Danish left swung inwards to envelop the unprotected English flank and the good luck that had so marked Cnut's campaign came to his aid again. Watching in horror, Eadric once more attended the voice of expedience in his ear and led the retreat from the field, leaving Edmund in the lurch.

From the corner of his eye Sigurd saw the mass withdrawal, but was too enmeshed in the fight to wonder whether Thorald was amongst it. The men before him snarled and gaped like rabid dogs. Flesh was rent and ripped and grazed, blood and brains dressed the green English pastures, friend killed friend in error . . . it was all more terrible than he had ever dreamed. A youth came at him with aimed sword. Balanced on the edge of panic Sigurd jabbed wildly with his spear, keeping the youth at bay but at the same time falling back to safer ranks. The youth was engulfed into the tangle of bodies and fell but not at Sigurd's hand. A farmer took his place, raised his hand-axe and swung it with great force at Sigurd's head; he raised his shield, the axeblade thudded into it, cleaving the wood in two and the impetus carrying Sigurd to the ground. Protection gone, he raised his spearpoint in defence, but his attacker, content at having dropped him, turned to seek another target. Sigurd felt pain now. Looking at his breast he saw red but had no time for close examination. In the brawl he was being stamped upon; men tripped over him and fell to their deaths. He dragged himself to his feet, encouraged that he could still do so; the wound was not life-threatening. Invincible of spirit, he relaunched himself into the fray.

They had vouched to fight side by side. Eric was protecting Sigurd's back, but Ulf had become parted from them. Right arm aching, Ulf hung the shield across his shoulder in order to employ his left. The muscles that wielded the sword with fresh vigour were caked with blood, his face too. His fringe was plastered to his skull, but the eyes below were sharp with concentration. Suddenly an unmistakable figure loomed before him. Ulf's bowels felt the tremor of impending death as Thorald's battleaxe swiped again and again at his head. He took a jumping step backwards to avoid the vicious arc of the blade, trod on someone and stumbled. The hairy face laughed and its owner pressed his attack, the flaring twelve-inch blade scything only inches away now, teasing, grazing. Ulf could not right himself, tottered, fell, but continued to jab at Thorald with his sword whilst attempting in vain to rise. Moisture trickled from Sigurd's fringe into his eyes. As he blinked and sloughed it off a window opened in the howling mass of carnage and he glimpsed his friend's predicament. Thorald hoisted his long-handled axe to inflict the deathblow but Ulf forbade it with a succession of frantic lunges. Open to injury, Sigurd performed an agile dance through the fracas, gyrating his hips to avoid the crimson blades. Ulf was tiring; his expression told his fate. He was ready to lie down and meet death. Sigurd barged even harder through the crush. He was almost there, Thorald had knocked the weapon from Ulf's hands, his axe was raised to cut Ulf's skull in two when Sigurd reached them. The youth's lips curled back to emit a full-throated roar. Valour, honour, fairplay were the furthest things from the boy's mind. Vengeance drove the point of his spear beneath Thorald's raised armpit through a rent in his mail and between his ribs.

It was a far cry from how he had imagined it – how easily the point slithered in, expending hardly any effort at all. Thorald stood impaled with a look of astonishment, but not for long. Ulf, reborn, dragged his own exhausted body from the ground and thrust his sword into Thorald's throat. The man gurgled and fell dead. Sigurd paused to stare down at him, but was punched into further action by Ulf; to contemplate another's death might bring about one's own. The fight raged on for hour after hour after hour. In the dwindling light a pall of steam hung over the once-green pasture, now a bloody morass. Although outflanked and outnumbered, the English endured the combat until late in the afternoon when, seeing no other way, Edmund fled with aching heart and the bloodied remnants of his army.

Now there was time to contemplate. The verdant fields groaned with wounded – earls, bishops, peasants, all equal in their plight. Scoured throats drank, deeply grateful, wounds were staunched, tired limbs granted rest, but sleep eluded brains so taut.

Given time to reflect on the killing of Thorald, Sigurd killed him ten times over. He languished beside Ulf, garments stiff with dried sweat, the reek of blood in his nostrils, watching the camp followers perform their dainty trek around the vast array of fallen to attend the wounds, and still his mind refused to cease its butchery.

In time, he looked around for Eric who had wandered off, probably for a pee he decided, and the thought made his own bladder sympathetic. He rose,

wincing as the material of his shirt pulled away from
his chest-wound, then put a considerate distance between himself and the others before relieving himself.
It was whilst he watered the bush that he heard
sobbing. Frowning, he completed his task then meandered in and out of the thicket for the source of the
woe.

Immediately he saw that it was Eric he jumped
back in shock, but not quickly enough, for the racking stopped dead and Eric whirled on him.

'I came only for a pee!' Sigurd looked embarrassed
and rubbed at his wound.

'Then piss and be gone!' Eric's dirty face bore
channels which he quickly dashed away with a hand.

Sigurd ran, and made no mention of this shameful
discovery to Ulf who would surely abandon the friendship if he knew of it. When Eric returned later no
explanation was given nor was it asked for. It was as
if Sigurd had dreamt the entire thing.

When they had recouped their energy, the friends
themselves performed a tour, not to tend the wounded
but to salvage valuables – weapons, helmets and
silver belt buckles, even damaged swords could be
bartered for new ones at the weaponsmiths. Sigurd
was partial to one with a whalebone handle and also
found its sheath which he buckled at his waist. But
he was looking for more than these. 'If Ulf is to keep
his promise we must find Thorald's body. I think it
fell somewhere over there.'

'You jest!' groaned Ulf, his face a mass of cuts and
one more fearsome gash upon his brow. 'How shall
we find him amongst thousands?'

'His evil odour shall mark him,' responded the
youth and, after many circuits, by some miracle finally led them to the grotesque hairy corpse.

Ulf grimaced. How small was man in death, how flat,
how shrunken. 'Will not the brooch suffice? The rest,
I confess, was mere boast.'

For answer Sigurd picked up a fallen axe, raised it and brought it down to cut through bone and gristle and sinew – at least, this was his intent had his green limbs been strong enough; the axe had to be employed twice more before the head was removed.

That night it was boiled in a cauldron over the fire until the flesh and hair floated off it and Sigurd held the cleaned skull upon his palm. The lower jaw had broken away from the top and was somewhere at the bottom of the cauldron. 'He does not look so dangerous like this.' Sigurd upturned the cranium, filled it with ale and handed it to Ulf.

Ulf took a deep breath. 'No one else would induce me to do this but my good friend Sigurd who today saved my life. I shall never forget.' So saying, he put the grisly cup to his lips, then passed it to Eric who drank too. The boy watched him closely for signs of hesitation, but there was none, which made him glad.

After living alongside these men for the past three years, and in particular after what they had gone through today, Sigurd felt overwhelmed by the sense of comradeship. His eyes burned with emotion as he toasted his dear friends. 'By this cup we three are bound together.' He tossed back his head to drink the last drop, then with no particular aim he flung Thorald's skull over his shoulder, away into the night.

It was difficult to wind down after a battle and the violence continued in the form of competitions and games. Despite the horrors he had faced, or perhaps because of them, Sigurd had the yen to snatch at a boyhood he had never really known, do the silly things that boys did if unencumbered by a mother such as Ragnhild. That evening as he sat by the campfire watching Ulf doze, a wicked thought came to mind and he whispered it to Eric. 'I wonder what Ulf would look like with a beard?' Eric, half-asleep himself, just grunted. The boy sprang up with impish face and temporarily left the group. When he returned he had a bunch of hair cut from his pony's tail; this he draped gently over the sleeping Ulf's chin.

Eric viewed the mischief through heavy lids and gave a word of caution. 'You sail close to the wind.'

Sigurd turned from his prank with a devil-may-care grin . . . a mistake, for Ulf was a light sleeper. The moment the hair tickled his chin he jumped up ready for attack. Sigurd rose too, laughing. 'Only a jest, my friend!'

Ulf clawed the threads of horsehair from his mouth, eyes like pools of acid.

'How soon doest thou forget!' mocked Sigurd. 'Did I not save your life?'

Ulf's fingers sought the last elusive hair on his lips. 'When you have saved my life ten times, then you can make jest! Until then . . .' The fingers at his mouth became a fist that aimed for Sigurd's jaw.

The boy was unconscious for ten minutes. He woke to hear concerned words from Eric. 'I think you have broken his skull.'

'Nei, it is too thick,' growled Ulf. 'See, the little bastard wakes.'

Sigurd looked up at Ulf with an expression of glazed bewilderment. Eric laughed. 'I think you will never play a joke on Ulf again, ja!'

Fully rested, Cnut's army trailed Edmund into Gleawanceastershire, but before any fresh engagement Eadric Streona came creeping back to ingratiate himself with Cnut, making out that his pretend partnership with Edmund and his flight from the field at Assandun had been deliberate policy in support of the young Dane. Sigurd began to think that perhaps

119

this man was a wizard, for just as Edmund had taken
him back without question, so Cnut appeared to
forgive his lapse. Eadric had come to offer advice:
despite the massive losses at Assandun, Edmund's
army remained devoted and an outright victory was
impossible. Would it not be better for all if Cnut
came to terms with Edmund?

Sigurd could gnash his teeth all he wanted at the
thought of Ethelred's line continuing in office, but
Cnut accepted the stoat's advice and decreed that to
protect lives he would come to an arrangement with
his brave and tenacious adversary. A meeting was
arranged on an island in the Sæfern where the two
kings exchanged gifts and drew up a charter that
divided the country thus: Cnut himself was to hold
the main body of England, but Edmund could have
Wessex.

Sigurd almost choked on his resentment when he
heard. 'That Ethelred's whelp is to have even an inch
of English soil is too much to bear! The King must
have lost his mind to listen to Eadric.'

'Hush, lest you lose your balls,' urged Eric.

But Sigurd was too angry to listen. 'Eadric must
have some reason of his own for suggesting this
arrangement, for he hath no love for Edmund.'

These suspicions were heightened the following
month when news came that Edmund had died unexpectedly at the age of just twenty-two. Rumours
were rife that Eadric was responsible, and Sigurd
thought so too. 'Hah! Watch closely now, Eadric will
jump into Edmund's shoes as if they were made for
him.' But for once he did not care if his predictions
were right. With the rest of Ethelred's sons in exile
and his line brought to a halt, as far as the crown of
England was concerned, Sigurd assumed his father's
honour to have been revenged.

Ergo, in 1017 Cnut succeeded to the throne of all
England, dividing it into four parts: himself retaining

Wessex, and giving East Anglia to Thorkell, Northumbria to Jarl Eirik and Mercia to Eadric.

Sigurd was pleased to find himself invited to follow the King to his palace at Wintanceaster, but was somewhat discomfited by the state of his clothes which, like those of his fellows, were gored and in tatters. There was even more of a contrast now that Cnut had changed out of his own stained garb. However, he was not to be on open display for the audience was held in private – an even greater honour in Sigurd's opinion, yet he was curious to know why this was so. Cnut bade his young friend to sit beside his throne, noticing that he had acquired a sword. Rank decreed that the spoils of war were his, but his fondness for Sigurd caused him to overlook the impertinence. 'You warned me of Thorald's treachery and I did not heed.'

Such noble confession brought generous response from the boy. 'Thorald had a way of winning people's affection, my lord. He duped me, too. When I think of the way I let him take my land . . .' He puffed out his lips. 'He has paid for that now.'

Cnut drank from a golden goblet. 'You killed him?'

'Ja – at the Battle of Assandun.' Sigurd rubbed at the carvings on the base of the throne.

Cnut leaned the back of his head against the timber and gazed into the past. 'Ah, I was too busy there myself to notice. Was it an honourable end?'

The boy hung his head, not certain what answer was expected.

'Good.' The King nodded thoughtfully and put down his goblet. 'There are others who deserve such an end, too.'

Sigurd wondered, during the thoughtful pause that followed, whether Cnut referred to Eadric. He made a tentative offer. 'Should ever you need my sword in achieving those ends, my lord, it is at your disposal.'

'Even for less glorious deeds than battle?' The

monarch appeared to read his mind and Sigurd in return deciphered his unspoken command.

'Whatever you ask of me I will do it,' he pledged, fully understanding now why the audience was in private.

Cnut nodded, still thoughtful, then a flashing smile transformed his hawkish face into one more handsome. 'As from now your land is returned to you.'

'I thank you, munificent one.' Sigurd thought it impolitic to reply that he had been going to claim it anyway.

The monarch called for one of his English clerks to put this in writing. 'And for your services you shall return to Jorvik bearing the rank of King's thegn. I will call upon you when I need help in building bridges. There is much rebuilding to be done both in land and hearts.'

Sigurd bowed in recognition of the honour, though he hoped that the title would not impinge too greatly on his time, for he had much work to do on his own behalf.

From the way Cnut was nodding, the audience was obviously at an end. Sigurd himself had more to say. 'I pay homage to your favour and your friendship, oh mighty King . . . There is just one matter I would air. Thorald was the owner of a longship . . .'

The palatial hall resounded to Cnut's laughter. 'The audacity of the lad! I honour him with titles and he would seize the prizes too! Are you not content with your sword – ja, I *know* it did not start the battle in your hand! Methinks I should hold fast to my crown.' He leaned forward as if to deliver rebuke, but his eyes were yet merry. 'Sigurd, if every man in my fyrd was to ask for a ship in reward . . .' He had no need to finish, point made.

But the boy was dogged. 'My lord, what is one less ship to you who hath a hundred? And have I not just promised you my sword? What is a sword without a ship? If you should ever have need of it I promise it, too, will be at your disposal.'

Cnut remained amused at the way Sigurd always tried to manipulate an extra favour. 'I am mad to listen but yes, if you can find Thorald's ship amongst those I have from Edmund's gesture of goodwill then you may take it. Now go, before I lose my throne to you!'

Inflated by self-importance, Sigurd went to tell Ulf and Eric. 'I go to Jorvik now. Will you come to claim the land I promised you? If so, you are welcome in my house until you choose to build your own.'

'*Your* house?' questioned Eric with a sly look at Ulf.

'*My* house, *my* land,' declared Sigurd. 'If you do not take the word of a king's thegn then ask the King himself.'

Both showed how impressed they were by making noises. 'King's thegn, eh?' breathed Ulf. 'Shall we dare speak to our noble lord?'

'I give you leave to speak when spoken to.' Sigurd grinned to show this was a jest – though only half a jest.

'Why, we are so honoured,' exclaimed the sober face. 'How shall we celebrate our master's good fortune?'

'Baptise him!' said Eric, and without further ado the two emptied their pots of ale over Sigurd's head.

He took the teasing well, though made sure he got his own back by drenching them with ale too.

The next day the three friends travelled on foot to the place where the captured ships were moored, and amongst them found Thorald's. As soon as they had hired a crew they rowed to Jorvik.

Grimy and aching for a bath though he was, the new thegn's first act was to go from chair to chair with a knife, carving runic marks in the wood. Curious,

123

Ulf asked for explanation. His young friend began to point. 'Sigurd's chair, Sigurd's table, Sigurd's stool . . .'

Ulf summoned Eric to look for himself. 'No man will cheat our young friend again, methinks.'

'We had better watch ourselves,' replied a droll Eric. 'Or he will be drinking ale from our skulls.'

Still carving, his tongue nipped in concentration, Sigurd answered the jocular doubts. 'Friends need never fear my wrath. To them I am loyal unto death. But those who break my trust, try to make mock of me . . . they are not so wise.' He sat back on his heels to brush the dust from the woodcuts. 'Today another such fool is to discover that.'

It had been three years since the incident between Sigurd and his tenants. Algrim, the main culprit, had wiped it from his mind and did not recognize the battle-stained youth who rode up to the group of men working in the field. Sigurd reined in his horse before Algrim and looked down from his platform. The man broke off working and squinted up at him. When Sigurd did not explain the object of his visit but continued to glare, Algrim frowned his puzzlement. 'Good day to you, friend.'

Sigurd did not return the greeting, upholding his rigidity. Algrim shrugged and was about to go back to his work when the youth broke his silence. 'What do you hear?'

The lines on the walnut face deepened as Algrim listened. 'I hear nought.'

'Then allow me to open your ear so that you may heed your master when next he speaks to you.' With a deftness of blade, Sigurd lopped off Algrim's left ear before he even had time to feel it.

The kotsetlan were at once angry and fearful, cowering in a horrified group around their mutilated friend whilst the blood trickled in rivulets between his fingers and down his breast.

The fourteen-year-old Sigurd held them with his cold, deeply-set eyes, then thrust his weapon back in its scabbard. 'Remember me,' he said, and rode home to eat at his own table.

Chapter Six

Cnut's reign was launched with a demand for tribute and a purge of all eminent Englishmen, upon whose banishment or execution their estates were given to Cnut's fellow Danes. His next action was to marry, not his consort Aelgifu of whom he was still very fond, but Ethelred's widow, either as a genuine gesture of harmony between the two cultures, or merely to show domination of the English. Ulf saw the move as even shrewder. When Sigurd voiced his incomprehension at such a choice – 'Why does he marry that old troll, she must be over thirty!' – he was given the likely explanation by his friend.

'By marrying the Duke of Normandy's sister, he reduces the risk of invasion from that quarter,' Ulf told him, and Sigurd had to concede to the ruler's mastery of a situation.

The union meant that Aelgifu's children would lose out to Cnut's legitimate heirs, but even so they fared better than Ethelred's descendants, some of whom were exiled into Europe, the other infant son packed off to the King of Sweden to be secretly disposed of. By Yuletide most obstacles in Cnut's way had been removed; only one remained. Nauseated by Eadric Streona's perfidy towards former allies, the King decided his time had come. Whilst those in Jorvik thought Sigurd was enjoying a merry Yule with Cnut in Lunden, he and two more of the King's trusted men were disposing of Eadric's body over the palace wall.

Sigurd was happy to do this for his friend, and admired Cnut's iron rule, for this was also his way – though after establishing that he was lord of his own estate he was proving to be a fair master, telling his retainers, 'You have the right to leave, but if you stay I shall protect you well so long as you are loyal.'

Things went smoothly until the following year when he was once again wont to question Cnut's judgment, and this time it was over matters more serious than marriage. Cnut had paid off his fleet and sent most of it back to Denmark, retaining only forty ships, but even more worrying, the Norse element in Cnut's entourage had begun to decrease in favour of Englishmen, one of these being the influential Archbishop Wulfstan of Jorvik. Included in Cnut's announcement that England would once again be ruled by the laws set down by King Edgar – which were judged to be fair ones – was the decree that his subjects must honour one God and keep the Christian faith. There was pressure upon those who were not yet baptised to rectify this immediately. Sigurd resisted, convinced that this total rejection of the gods would be his own downfall.

For those like himself who had interest in politics, there was also a new figure to watch, an Englishman called Godwin who had appeared from nowhere and risen to the rank of Earl in just one year. He too had great favour with the King; this irked Sigurd, who moaned to his friends, 'What has Godwin done that is so special? Nought out of the ordinary that I can see. What reward have I got for my loyal service? Little, except the return of what was rightfully mine – and in truth I won that for myself.'

'Some of us would be thankful to have the tributes paid to a King's thegn,' reproved Eric.

'Huh! I work hard for it. I doubt that you would take kindly to spending every third month at court,

127

on duty day and night. Oh, I am not ungrateful,'
Sigurd was condescending. 'But it is hardly com-
parable to an earldom, is it? I have nought against
Godwin save for the fact that he does not deserve
the prizes heaped upon him.'

It was fortunate that there were things to be done
at home to take his mind off such annoyances. One
of these – a most revolting task but one which could
not be shirked – was to exhume his uncle's body from
the cesspit. Naturally, there were thralls to do this,
but their lord must be present and the mere sight and
smell of the remains caused him to heave. With the
need to assuage himself of his part in Olaf's murder,
Sigurd paid deep thought to the type of burial his
uncle might have wanted and hence, though pagan
himself, had the body interred in the nearby church
of St Cuthbert's.

Thoughts of Uncle begat thoughts of Mother. Duty
decreed that he should have sent word to her long
before this and indeed he had pondered upon it many
times, but Sigurd had been out of her clutches for
too long, enjoyed being left to his own devices. Until
now he had fobbed off his conscience with the reply
that he must bring the estate back to its former glory
before his mother came to live here, but in truth it
was simply the knowledge that when Ragnhild did
come she would try to take over completely. Now,
though, there was no excuse: he was old enough to
resist her bullying. Perhaps the time had come for
their reunion. With a ship of his own he could have
gone for Ragnhild himself, but not wishing to face
the rest of Olaf's family, decided otherwise. Carving
his message on a twig, he gave it to the owner of a
vessel bound for Norway, and waited for his mother
to come.

At the very same moment as he carved his message,
Ragnhild was thinking also of him. Sigurd had been
away for five years, during which she had heard

nothing at all of his welfare. Of course there had been snippets of information about the viking army's progress, but of her son and brother – nothing. At least her sister-in-law was in the same boat; she did not know if Olaf had come through the fighting either. Their shared dilemma brought them a little closer. Thora's face might be as dour as ever, as she squinted over her lace-work in the dim candlelight whilst Ragnhild cooked supper for the ten people who sat around the hearth, but her voice showed genuine interest. 'I wonder what young Sigurd looks like now? After all this time it will be hard for you to recognize him.'

Ragnhild did not give acid retort on the stupidity of this comment as she might once have done: she knew that Thora must be as worried about Olaf as Ragnhild was about her son. 'When I think of him I see only Einar on our wedding day.' In this rare moment of intimacy with her sister-in-law, Ragnhild's smile was warm but sad. 'I cannot imagine him any other way. Oh, why does he not send word, Thora?' But Thora could only shrug and pretend to concentrate on her lace-making, otherwise she would cry.

Ragnhild would have been comforted in her loneliness to know that her son was indeed very much like his father. In his seventeenth year Sigurd was four inches taller than the average man, had overtaken Ulf's height and stood head and shoulders above Eric. His legs remained long and skinny but the upper half of his body had become more muscular from the use of heavy weapons. He was proud of his blond hair and had allowed it to grow very long – almost to his shoulder-blades. A silken covering of hair had developed on his cheeks too, but so fine that it could barely be seen.

As for every soldier returning from battle, life for the youth was an anticlimax. The first flush of victory at being his own master was now diluted by the stifling mundanity of life in Jorvik. For a time he had been content to perform his skills as a wood-carver, providing new furniture for his home, and to pass his leisure hours hunting; but enacted every day even the latter became just as monotonous as the table games Ulf loved so much. Restless by nature, Sigurd felt trapped, but could not explain what it was he wanted from life. As promised, he had marked out tracts of land for Ulf and Eric, but neither had come around to building themselves a house yet, simply allowing others to work it and drawing the dues. Both seemed content to remain here, if the melancholic Ulf could ever be deemed content. All they wanted was a roof over their heads, food, women and good hunting, each of which the now wealthy young noble could provide. According to his rank of king's thegn, he was dressed in blue knee-length tunic of finest quality wool, tightly-thonged trousers, flowing cloak, gold brooches and soft leather shoes. His armoury was well-stocked and to ward off boredom, Sigurd had been practising every day with all types of weapons, lately achieving the aim he had set himself, that of ambidexterity – a spear from either hand would now reach equal target. How frustrating, then, that aside from local competition there was no outlet for his wizardry. What was needed was an expedition.

'You mean a viking raid,' said Ulf when Sigurd made his proposal.

'Ja, it could be called that,' agreed Sigurd who, hunkered outside in the cloudless morn, was employed in carving himself a saddle bow. After a week of rain it was good to feel the warmth on one's back – even if it did amplify the stench of rotting offal. Around him echoed the sounds of Jorvik, the lowing of milch cows and cattle brought to slaughter, the methodic clanking and acrid whiff of molten lead from the smelting works, the honking of geese, the shouts of encouragement from man to horse when his wagon got bogged down in the unpaved road.

'On where?'

Sigurd mused. 'Ireland?'

Ulf began to sweep up the chips of wood with a handbrush. 'The King will not be pleased.' There had been peace in Ireland for some years and there had always been great links between Jorvik and Dyflinn. Cnut hoped to nurture those good relations.

'The King is not here.' Sigurd grinned and blew the dust from his handiwork. Cnut's brother King Harald had died childless and he had sailed to Denmark to assume sovereignty and also to ensure that no new viking raids could be launched on England. Sigurd had not been called upon to accompany him and, as the King was not there to require his duties, had also been excused from his month at court which left his summer free to do as he pleased. 'There will be women,' he added, seeking to offer inducement to Eric, who was quite degenerate in this regard. Sigurd himself had recently become more interested in females too, though he had not enjoyed any intimacy yet.

'Knowing you, there will also be fighting,' grumbled Eric.

'Fat old toad!' Sigurd tossed his blond hair, nose and upper lip coated in sawdust. 'How can you bear just to lounge there day after day after day? 'Tis hard to tell the difference between you and that dungheap. It drives me insane to watch you.' Outside the enclosure, the neighbour was still trying to remove his cart from the mud. Irritated by his exhortations, Sigurd leapt up and went out to offer aid. There were already five men pushing the cart, themselves bogged down to the ankles in mud. Further along the street lengths of duckboard had been laid out to avoid such an accident, but here there were none. Whilst two gossiping housewives leaned over a fence and watched with interest, Sigurd fetched some bits of wattle fencing that he kept for such a purpose and tucked them against the front wheels. Eventually, the timber wagon broke free with a slurping noise. Sigurd's neighbour thanked his assistants and went on his way. The women returned to gossiping, eyeing the young thegn and letting out an occasional giggle. Self-conscious of his thin legs, and feeling that the laughter was directed at him, Sigurd walked quickly to escape them. Large or small, he had reached the conclusion that communities were identical the world over – everyone was interested in everyone else's business; yet another reason to get away for a while.

When Sigurd came back he did not resume his carving but injected all energy into persuading his friends to join his expedition. 'You eat my food, drink my beer and yet you refuse to keep me company on a little trip!'

'In my experience you are very dangerous company, Sigurd. Little trips have big swords at the end of them.' Ulf proceeded to brush the chips of wood into a neat pile, then gave way with an air of resignation. 'But . . . if you choose to present us as leeches then we have little option.'

Sigurd grinned and punched his friend in the chest. 'Do not portray it as such a chore! We will have a merry old time. Now, we must make preparations . . .'

'First you need thirty or forty other fools such as us to crew the ship,' instructed Eric.

'I can already name a score who would jump at the chance, and the others will not be hard to find. But as to the route . . . I have asked around and a merchant tells me that the way to go is down the Use, up the east coast and into the fjords of Lothene and Straeclyd. There is only a narrow piece of land to cover – about twenty miles. He says we can save six hundred miles this way!'

'I could have told you that.' Eric finished making a ring from twisted strands of tin and leaned back against a wagonwheel. 'But you must waste your time listening to others.'

Sigurd was eager to share Eric's navigatory skills. 'So you have been to Ireland before?' Eric's shrug was noncommittal. 'Then tell us which way would you go? The man said the northern route is safer.'

'Oh, true, true!' Eric sounded knowledgable. 'For 'tis mainly by sea and you save six hundred miles.'

'But I wish to see more of southern England, and perhaps the land of the Wealas . . .'

'Ja, ja, that would be interesting . . .'

' . . . But this man said that the Wealas are savages.'

'And he is right!' Eric gave a sapient nod. 'You have never met men like them – in fact they are not men, but devils. I could have told you that.'

'So you do not advise it?' pressed Sigurd.

'Nei, the northern way is best.' Eric leaned forward and gave Sigurd the ring he had made. 'Here, take it, my fingers are laden.'

Sigurd thanked him and put the ring on his longest finger. It was his first such adornment; though the silver talisman remained on its thong, the blue beads had disappeared in battle. For more permanent decoration he had chosen to have dragons tattooed on his forearms.

Eric went off to the latrine. In his absence Sigurd paid dubious compliment. 'You would never guess to look at Eric that he possessed such wide knowledge. I'll wager he could answer questions on any topic that you put to him.'

'Ask him about the skurrahnefalskrim,' suggested Ulf without looking at him.

Sigurd had never heard of this and prodded Ulf to enlarge, but received only the laconic instruction, 'Ask Eric, he will know.'

133

When Eric returned, shuffling his breeches into place, Sigurd pestered for the answer to his question.

'Have I heard of the skurrahnefalskrim?' Eric sat down. 'Of course! Another of these men you keep meeting told you of it, I suppose – he will not know as much as I.'

'I know nothing at all,' replied the youth. ''Twas Ulf here who . . .'

Ulf jumped in. 'I said that you could probably tell him, for I have never heard of it.'

'Never heard of the skurrahnefalskrim? Well, I shall tell you. It is huge.' Eric spread his arms. 'Ten times the size of Orca.'

Sigurd gave an exclamation. Ulf made no murmur and kept his face averted.

'It has teeth like . . . like the points of that spear! Twenty rows of them. It can both swim and walk and fly. It has a mouth that could swallow ten houses . . .'

'And there is one behind you,' announced Ulf.

'*What!*' Eric swivelled.

Ulf turned to Sigurd. 'That is how knowledgeable he is – there is no such thing as a skurrahnefalskrim. It is a nonsense word.'

Sigurd collapsed into laughter at his own gullibility, and accused Eric, 'So you know nought of Ireland neither, you old rogue!'

'He is expert at nothing save how to fart,' denounced Ulf.

Eric shrugged off the laughter. 'I just misheard what you said, that is all! You may have invented the skurrahnefalskrim but believe me there is such a monster as I describe – its name escapes me for the moment. I just pray that we do not run into one for then you will not be laughing.'

The mustered crew totalled thirty-five, which was only just sufficient to man the oars with no relief in times of fatigue. Sigurd, eager to go, dismissed this, said they would have to place their trust in the wind and with a spirit of adventure he embarked for Ireland. The first leg of his journey down the east coast – which involved the inevitable bout of seasickness – was undertaken without delay for he had made this trip several times before. Much of the coast around the southern tip of England, though, was new territory and Sigurd chose to drop anchor here for a few days, not only from a yen to investigate the towns but to restock with food before continuing.

As they rounded the peninsula of Cornwall, Ulf and Eric shared the muttered hope that their young friend had forgotten about his desire to see the land of the Wealas; he had not.

'Had I wished to go straight to Ireland I would have taken the northern route,' he told them. 'Nei, I am eager to see if these Wealas are really as fierce as you say they are.' He ordered the helmsman to continue to follow the coast until they came to Brytland whence he gave instructions to haul into the first stretch of beach they encountered.

One by one the crew members hopped into the sea and dragged the boat ashore. Once landed, Sigurd vaulted from ship to beach and took up a demanding stance, arms akimbo, whilst the wavelets eddied round his feet. 'Where are all these devils you bragged of then, Eric?' Noticing that he was getting his feet wet he squelched his way through the shiny belt of wormcasts and seaweed to firmer ground. 'Why do none of them come out and attack us?'

'Let us hope it is because they have poor hearing,' suggested Ulf.

'Come! Let us go look for them.' Sigurd ordered a number of men to remain and guard the boat, then crunched purposefully across the bank of shingle, leading the expedition. Ulf and Eric reluctantly followed.

The blue sky and sea breeze made it a pleasant if

monotonous walk. Keeping to a coastal path they saw nothing for miles and were beginning to get hungry, when the outline of a town appeared on the horizon. Sigurd called a halt, took stock and advised the crew to approach with caution.

'As if we need to be told,' muttered Ulf.

Long before they reached the main town they came across a solitary house which, in their numbers, they felt safe enough to enter. There was no one at home. Sigurd opened a door onto a room that smelt of onion broth, which awaited the owner's return for dinner. There was no woman to tend it. A few of the men went in and sauntered around, picking up bread, apples, a cold fowl and consuming them there and then.

With no one to detain them they purloined everything of value and moved on to the town, where the relaxed atmosphere served to relax them also.

The discovery that it was a Norse settlement did not please Sigurd. 'Devils?' He rounded on Eric and mocked him for his alarmist conjecture. 'They are just like us.' It was for this very reason the young viking did not tarry. There was no excitement to be had here. After a leisurely afternoon amongst the locals they made their way back to the ship. It was still light as they passed the solitary house which they had rifled earlier. Again there was no sign of life. They did not stop this time but marched straight on for it was a long way to their ship.

The hour grew later. Darkness hindered their passage. Luckily there was not far to go now and shortly there appeared a beacon to guide them; the men whom they had left behind had lighted a fire on the beach, their dark shapes sprawled hither and thither around it.

'Lazy dogs,' muttered Sigurd, whose feet were aching now. 'Not even a look-out. We could kill them where they lay and they would know nought.' The words brought a glint to his eye. 'Hah! What a devilish plan. Gather you round, men, and listen. We will divide into groups and give them the fright of their lives. The day has been wasted up to now, so let us have a little sport. When I shout the signal we will charge upon them from different angles; they will not know whether to run or piss themselves.'

Eric did not think much of the plan. 'What if they do not recognize us and retaliate?'

'It is easy to recognize you even in darkness, fart-arse!' grumbled Sigurd. 'Why do you always have to spoil my games? If you move those fat legs fast enough the others will not have time to react. Come! Do as I say.'

Once in position he gave the signal and his men charged down the grassy embankment onto the beach screaming like lunatics and brandishing weapons. Thoroughly enjoying himself, Sigurd leapt astride the nearest victim, raised his axe and roared, 'You are dead!'

To his disappointment there was no scream of fright, in fact no reaction at all. He frowned, lowered his weapon and stooped quickly to peer at the man on the ground. The victim's eyes were open but he was already dead, congealed blood upon his neck. Sigurd shot upright in alarm, others did the same, but before a word was uttered the Wealas attacked, pouring in their dozens from rock and dune where they had been waiting for the rest of the viking crew to return, streaming across the beach, wielding the weapons they had taken from Sigurd's dead comrades whom they had massacred earlier.

Sigurd jumped round to face them but the attack was so sudden and so violent that he was carried backwards and almost lost his footing in the rush. After a brief and painful skirmish he saw that there was little merit in continuing the stand and had to concede that these foreigners were too savage even for a blooded veteran like himself. He gave one last wild defensive swipe with his axe and fled after his comrades to the ship. The pursuing Wealas continued to spear them as they desperately tried to lug their craft into the water, chased them right into the waves and even when they had successfully launched it, the rain of missiles and arrows followed them. When the frantic rowers had put a safe distance between themselves and the land, Sigurd looked back to see fifteen of his crew dead upon the beach.

A wild-eyed Ulf berated him, leaning vigorously into the oar and addressing his anger to Eric. 'This is the last time I let him talk us into his mad games! If you hear me agree to anything he proposes, just wrap me in chains!'

Eric was equally irate, black hair caked with sand and blood, though none of his wounds were serious. 'When have you ever listened to me? Nor him, neither – I warned him the Wealas were devils!'

Sigurd made lame excuses. 'They took us by surprise, that is all! Had I been prepared . . .'

'Shut up and prepare yourself now for hard work!' barked Ulf. 'I do not intend to set foot in Brytland ever again and with only twenty of us to man the oars it will be a long haul to Ireland – and Christ knows what you will get us into there! I shall deem myself lucky if I ever get home.'

After tempers had abated there followed a period of sensible discussion and it was decided that they should try to find a sheltered bay where they could anchor for the night and so recoup strength for the arduous journey ahead. In the morning luck smiled upon them, sending a wind that made the oars redundant for most of that first day of their journey. On the third morning, to the relief of the exhausted crew, land came into sight.

When the Norse had first invaded this emerald isle they came upon a country of petty kingships and warring tribes. Over the following centuries, internal battles raged between Irish and Norse, Irish and Irish, Norse and Norse . . . whilst during each tentative truce, native kings intermarried with Norse princesses and raised children of mixed race who were in turn attacked by outsiders of Scandinavian blood. Now, by the grace of Brian Boroimhe, Erin had been free of Norse domination for the past five years. Though terrible foes, the Irish were generous in victory and had allowed the Norse kings to remain in the great seaports they had built along the east coast, where the inhabitants had, in speech and religion, become almost Irish themselves.

Originally, the young viking had elected not to put in at any of these seaports, for his men would only waste their time drinking and looking for women. However, the ferocity of the coastline and the inadequacy of the crew changed his plans. More than once the ship almost fell foul of jagged rocks, thrown to and fro by the foaming white-tops, and so when a welcoming harbour came into sight he called for the helmsman to steer her inshore.

The Irish called this place Eochaill, on account of its surrounding hills being covered with yew trees. Here, the inhospitality of the coastline was not matched by the people whom Sigurd found warm and friendly, too friendly for his purposes; it was adventure he wanted, not ceilidhs. After a brief sojourn, much to the disgruntlement of his crew, he raised anchor and rowed inland up a skein of black water.

It was late afternoon. Oars flexed against the current, the serpent cleaved the darkly flowing waters, past wooded hills and ancient rocks where moss and fern and ivy vied for prominence and every fissure was probed by some green tendril seeking hospice. The land to either side varied with each contour of the river, from lush to barren, but always there was about it an air of mysticism born of the claustrophobic silence that pursued them. Enclaved by greenery, the viking craft slunk around each curve, feeling its way like an asp hunting prey, but no human did she see.

Towards evening, the waters became shallower. Between them, the vikings decided to make camp for the night and a fire was set on the bank in preparation for the salmon that were to be baked upon it. After the meal, Sigurd prescribed an observation on foot away from the river, but still no humanity could be found. The woods in which they trod began to adopt an aura that was not of this world. As darkness fell, the vikings placed talismen around the camp to ward off evil forces.

In the morning, whilst the mists still hovered round the treetops they relaunched the ship in the hope of catching out some lie-a-bed. Ulf, balanced in the prow, was the one to spot the tents, inducing a ripple of excitement from the crew. The land was more open now, requiring stealth. Mooring the ship, they proceeded on crouched tiptoe, inching forth to take a closer look. Like the wolf they loped in single file, each in the footsteps of the one before so as to present the smallest profile.

The sleepers in the tents were on a return journey from Waterford to Cork. By the number of horses and tents, Sigurd estimated that he was up against only a dozen men at most. If there were horses there would be silver, too. There was no look-out. Pausing, he turned to those behind and by gesture of hand urged the group to split and approach from different angles. The advance proceeded, great precision to each footfall. The lazy atmosphere of the morning took on a sharper edge. As the circle of strangers tightened around them, the horses became uneasy and snorted a warning to each other. From one of the tents emerged a drowsy face – becoming instantly awake as it saw the invaders.

Sigurd gave cry. He and his fellow vikings charged upon the tents, legs leaping high over the tussocks of grass and heather, hacking at the panicked occupants neath the canvas who squealed like piglets in a sack. Some managed to flee the tents before the vikings fell upon them and gave good battle, but most were killed where they lay. An accompanying monk called out to his Maker, but no Christ could protect him from Sigurd's pagan axe. Since the carnage of Assandun the killing of men, armed or unarmed, came easily. Women and children, wearing only their shifts, ran amok, looked in vain for hiding place, but found no tree to screen them from the awful vision of their men and boys being cut down. Panicked by the open country, their whinnies joined those of the terrified horses which wrenched and bucked against their hobbles.

The killing was over in minutes, terminating in a crescendo of shouting and whooping from the attackers. Fifteen women and young girls were rounded up to be paraded half-naked before the howling savages, poked and prodded in every vile manner. Exhilarated, Sigurd whipped his blond hair from his face and marched up and down the row of trembling females, passing over each sobbing wench until he came to one that he liked the look of. Her face was striking in its terror. She was not dark like many of the others but had wavy, light-brown hair that fell past her shoulders, and very fair skin. Her blue eyes were glazed with shock. She had a very distinct cupid's bow to her mouth, but this delicacy was at variance with the rest of her, for her bones were large; combined with good carriage this lent the impression of height, however on comparing her with the others Sigurd noted that she was if anything slightly shorter. His detailed examination told him also that her hands were strong and practical-looking, more like a youth's if they had not been so clasped in entreaty to her breast. Sigurd's eyes ran south and he was dismayed to notice the bulge of her abdomen.

All desire went. Una shrank as the youth's tattooed arm reached for her throat, but instead of strangling her he grasped a handful of tousled locks and dragged her forward. When she resisted he uttered guttural words, few of which she understood. The gulf between Norse and Irish was so great that the original invaders had long since dropped their own language to assimilate with the native population, but Norse words had survived and Una who had lived amongst the Ostmen for most of her sixteen years, had learnt to interpret them. However, this man's accent was very different.

Una's heart pumped terror through her veins, her whole body quivering under his grip. The other men were older than the one who had selected her. His height and bearing had misled her at first but now, looking at him, she saw that his face was that of a boy, his beard hardly more than fluff. He had a long narrow head, deeply-set eyes and a straight nose. Had she not just experienced his cruelty at first-hand, then the thinness of his lips would have been proof enough. He had the blond flowing locks of the other Lochlannach she had known – though much longer – held back with a band woven of red, blue and silver threads. He was quite slim, his hands and feet appearing too big for such a frame. In a mad sort of logic Una hoped that she would go to him for he would not rape her; the disgust in his eyes when he had noted her pregnancy had told her this.

But alas! Another man was trying to take possession of her. She cringed into her shift. The youth spoke in guttural tongue. His dark and swarthy opponent ignored the threat and pulled her towards him. The youth clamped his arm. It appeared that they were going to fight ... Then the older one backed down with a laughing shrug and chose a different woman. Sheer terror and incomprehension of the accent made it difficult for Una to grasp what was being said. At one point, judging from his authoritative posture, she had thought that the youth must be in command, but now she changed her mind as the savages began an undisciplined orgy of rapine. Their only master was Satan. Una stood rooted like a tree whilst all around her women and girls were violated. Sigurd dragged her off to some long grass, where he pulled her down. She screamed and resisted.

That look of disgust appeared again. 'Do you imagine I would touch you who looks and smells like a sow? Hold your noise and lie there until I tell you to move!' He formed his words in such a way that made it easy for Una to grasp the gist of them, but she was to frightened to respond to the insult.

Sigurd flopped over onto his belly and parted the grass with his hands in order to watch the proceedings. There was no compassion in his action towards her. Had she not been filled with child he would have raped her. Watching the orgy he grew hard but did not know what to do about it. He felt like rushing out and flinging himself on top of one of the women who lay spreadeagled and weeping, but he did not want an audience for his début. He had had no sexual dealings with women until now. What if he failed? Besides, he had discarded most of these women as too ugly, apart from the one who sat trembling like the grass nearby. He cast an eye over his shoulder, wondering whether he could force himself to overlook her belly. Her face was as white as that of a Scandinavian woman and the brush of her long hair against his skin when he had grasped her neck invigorated him more than any experience since battle. Whilst others enacted their lust, Sigurd made plans: now that he was a man he needed a wife. This woman was as good as any he had seen; after the child was born he would take her.

Una shivered in fear under his icy blue stare. Fear of him certainly, but fear, too, of her own powers. Yesterday she had witnessed all this as if it were real, seen the golden youth charging through the scrub, blond hair flying, seen the murder and rapine . . . It had not been a dream. She had been fully conscious and the night had been hours away. Transfixed, she had stood and watched it happen, whilst others tried without luck to shake her from her trance. When it was over she had fainted and on recovery had attempted to convince herself that it had been imagined, but it had not. Today's reality corroborated each fact.

It was not the first such happening, but was positively the most vivid. Una's grandmother had been similarly possessed, able to see these terrible things that no one else could see. It had been her death earlier this year which had marked the onset of Una's visions, as if they were bequeathed. Una had not wanted them, felt cursed, but knew that she was powerless to resist. Grandmother had predicted long ago that in the passage of time the Sight would be handed down to Una. Until then, she had said, Una must be content to gain her knowledge from the runes. By this source she had also foreseen that Una would suffer a loveless marriage, and it was at this point that Una began to doubt the authenticity of her grandmother's claims, for the Irish lord to whom she had been given last year in marriage was as noble and handsome a man as any maid could wish for . . . until the wedding night. Subjected to Eoghan O'Cellaigh's bestial appetite, Una prayed for escape. To lie beneath his body was an act of such abhorrence that each time her husband went to battle she hoped he would die . . . and now he was dead, leaving his child in her belly and his brains on the grass.

144

Una sneaked a look at her captor who was once more watching the violation. At first too terrified to care, the knowledge that he found her repellent now tacked hurt pride to her emotions. Who was this boy to uptilt his nose when he himself stunk of fish and beer and sweat? Wary of eye, she followed the line of his legs, his buttocks, his hard unyielding back, the painted arms and that yellow hair.

His lust unsated, Sigurd grew impatient and rolled over, his body knocking into hers. Una was quick to avert her eyes, but he just laid there, did not speak until the cries of the women had died.

There was much jocularity from the others when Sigurd rejoined them, dragging his captive after him.

'That was quick work,' quipped one of them, pointing at Una's belly.

Sigurd laughed and made a coarse response which Una did not understand, and pushed her at the less-fortunate huddle of women whilst he and others examined the rest of their loot – gold, silver, ivory and silks, goblets encrusted with precious stones; these latter were not to the vikings' aesthetic taste but would be useful as barter. The women's clothes were sorted out, the finer kept and the rest thrown back to cover their bruised bodies. Then goods, horses and women were divided up amongst the raiders. Some, like Ulf, preferred to take their quota in metal rather than flesh. Sigurd kept the girl Una and chose another strong-looking wench; Eric selected four.

Morning became noon. Despite the orgy of rape and killing, perhaps because of it, there remained a certain giddiness of manner in the group. Whilst Ulf and Sigurd argued with the others over how many each had killed, Eric pried metal inlay from the spine of a book. 'Did you see the way that bald one died? He was so fat that when I pricked him he exploded like a troll caught in the midnight sun – poof! I have never in my life seen anything like it.'

'Fat!' Ulf stopped arguing and beheld his friend with mockery. 'Have you never looked down? The gods help us if that were ever pierced.' He shoved a toe at Eric's belly. 'We would all be drowned in blubber – come! Let us take a dip, I badly need to cool off.' Leaving two of their number to keep an eye on the prizes, the vikings stripped off and pelted naked for the water, laughing and braying like children.

Ulf fought to arrive first, plunged in and began to splash around in circles. One by one bodies hit the water, crashing into each other. 'I propose a contest!' yelled Eric.

'To see who can make the most bubbles?' Sigurd eschewed the offer. 'You would win easily, fart-arse.' He pressed his sole into Eric's black beard and shoved him disparagingly. 'And that would not please Ulf who always has to win. Now, if we had a contest to see who has the smallest tool . . .'

Ulf dived for his friend, knocked him backwards and thrust his head under water. Sigurd tried to wriggle free but Ulf held on. He then tried lashing out with his feet but kicked only water. Above the boiling surface, Ulf clung onto his neck, grimacing with the effort. With no chance to fill his lungs before being pushed under Sigurd was now desperate for air. Expelling the last bubble through his lips he started to buck and thrash about. The dragons reached for life. Still Ulf held him under. Sigurd's head began to pound. He must breathe, he must . . . reflex forced him to inhale, water flooded into his belly and lungs, he began to drown . . . a warm black cloak descended over his eyebrows.

Una witnessed this accident from the bank, watched in grave concern as the youth's limp body was dragged from the water and his friends started to pump his back. The concern was for herself, not Sigurd; if he died she had lost her protection from the others.

Sigurd barked and hawked, buttocks lifting from the ground as his retching body vomited water. Eric cackled and Ulf delivered one of his rare grins. 'Methinks you win the bubble contest, Sig!'

Una realized with a jolt that it was not an accident at all, it was a game! These men were truly mad. She continued to watch as the young viking aimed a vicious foot at the one with the cropped hair. 'Bastard! I will not play your games again.' He barked, coughed, then rubbed his gut.

'Here!' Still naked, Eric made a generous offer. 'I caught this fish this morn, you can take it.'

'Fish! I have probably swallowed half the river.' Sigurd got to his feet, coughed loudly and shook the water from his limbs as if nought untoward had occurred. 'Nei, I go hunting. I have a fancy for something on four legs.'

Eric passed a look of disgust to Ulf who was now dressing. 'By Christ, this man will shag anything. If you are tired of your little girl already will you not loan her to me whilst you are away?'

Una was heartened to get the gist of her captor's remark, 'Touch one hair and you die, fatman,' though all the while he was away she felt at risk. Relief at seeing his blond head bobbing across the heath with his fellows was sullied with what occurred next.

'Not a thing!' railed Sigurd. 'No so much as a blackbird in this wretched countryside – we walked for miles! Well, I am sick of dried meat. I am determined to have fresh fayre even if it means having to kill one of the horses.' With this he sized up the captured nags, selected one and ordered his men to despatch it, whilst Una looked on in disgust.

Her loathing was to be compounded when the horse had been skinned. Sigurd hacked off a piece of its rump and threw it at the captives, spattering them with blood. 'Here! You shall cook this, then maybe we will give you a bite.'

'I have something they could take a bite of,' offered Eric, ever generous.

'Filthy pig,' muttered Una, and interpreted the lewd suggestion to those who did not understand. A few of the women complied with Sigurd's order whilst others dumbly refused to budge. By some hand or another the meal was served and consumed – though not by the prisoners, whose stomachs were too bilious with torment.

The afternoon was passed mainly in rest. Towards evening, the vikings drank heavily from the barrels they had brought from their ship and at sunset were once again playing dangerous games. The large bonfire provided more fun. 'I wager three of my women to your girl that you cannot walk through flames,' slurred Eric, addressing Sigurd.

Una tensed, but the youth was contemptuous. 'They are all hags – if you put up ten marks of silver I might consider it.'

'Done!' Eric thumped the ground. 'Let us see you.'

The glowing embers were poked and tossed about to form a smouldering carpet. Sigurd, the worse for drink, teetered on the edge of the fire, eager for an opportunity to show off in front of the girl.

'Oh, ja, very good!' sneered Eric. 'Anyone can do it with boots on! I do not pay ten marks to cheats. Take them off.'

'Off! Off!' chanted the drunken horde.

Sigurd objected loudly, but in the end unlaced his boots, threw them at Eric then belched and primed himself. The flattened fire could not be more than three yards wide; it should be easy. He hesitated . . . then performed the wager in one swift rush. 'Aah, ooh, shite!' He was only into the middle, his legs working faster and faster as his soles began to burn, he hopped and jumped the last portion and fell over to great appreciation from the onlookers, whence he rolled about nursing his badly blistered soles. After much theatrical display, he hobbled bandy-legged on the edges of his feet to collect his money from Eric. 'As my mother would say, "I am not a vindictive person, Eric, but I hope your balls drop off".' He dropped his impersonation of Ragnhild and spoke in a normal voice to negate Eric's offer of the women. 'Nei, you can use the old hags for now, I will have them for labour when we go home.' He flopped heavily beside Una to drink more ale and bawl lewd songs. Occasionally he put his hand inside her dress when he knew he had an audience, though it was done more from bravado than lust; she hummed worse than a goat.

Una permitted this indignity, having endured much worse at the hands of her dead husband. Besides, to remain serene under such childish molestation helped to elevate her above his heathen level. As the youth grew drunker she took from a knotted corner of her shift a collection of stones marked with runes and put them down before Sigurd.

'You want me to throw them, ja?' He made a drunken gesture. She nodded. In exaggerated manner he took the pebbles one by one into his fist then scattered them at her dirty feet and joked, 'Will I die the morrow?'

Catching his drift, she scrutinized the runes for a moment, then replied in her own tongue, 'Ye'll live to be an old man, *finn-gall*.'

He understood the term of address – 'fair-foreigner', having heard it in Eochaill, but the rest was gibberish. He shook his head to show incomprehension. With the headband gone astray, his hair tumbled about his bleary face. Una could have pretended ignorance, need not have spoken to him at all, but something compelled her to repeat her statement in halting Norse, 'You shall live to be an old man, very old.'

It was sufficiently competent for him to grasp. He gave a clumsy nod of recognition. 'So, you do understand me after all.'

'A little, if you speak slowly,' she replied.

'Where did you learn to speak with northmen?'

'There are many of your kind in the place where I come from.'

His face was thoughtful for a while, then he took a lump of horsemeat that had been cooking in the embers and thrust it at her. 'Eat!'

She looked revolted. 'I am a Christian. It is forbidden to eat horseflesh.'

Insulted at this rebuff, he stared at her with narrowed eyes for another moment, then tossed the meat aside and turned back to the runes as if nothing had happened. 'So, you say I shall live to be a very old man?' A groan passed his lips. 'Oh, do not tell me I shall die in my bed!'

Una was studying the runes again. 'I see a battle, I see many battles, but 'tis a woman who'll bring about your death.'

'Shit!' Sigurd laughed loudly for the benefit of his friends who were taking notice. 'The only way a woman could kill me is if she fucked me to death.'

Una ignored the ribaldry and concentrated on the stones. 'There is a man . . . A man whom you love will betray ye, but 'tis the woman who will cause your death.'

With a roar of contempt Sigurd grabbed a book that the dead monk had carried and used it to fuel the fire. It dropped open, its exquisite illuminated pages turning brown.

Una remained outwardly calm, though she abhorred such ignorant destruction. ''Tis true, *finn-gall*.'

He turned on her, swaying. 'Know my name! It is Sigurd – your master!'

The girl held him with that unnerving stare, half fear, half contempt. 'And I am Una.'

Sigurd felt that she was mocking him. He was furious, but pretended he did not care. 'Eric, I have changed my mind. I will make use of one of those women!' He grabbed the female hand which Eric offered. 'And let us see which one of us is still alive in the morning!' Barely able to stand, he dragged her off to his tent, helped on his way by bawdy comments.

Una watched him vanish under canvas, then darted wary eyes at the others, fearing that his absence could mean rape by one of them. Inside the tent Sigurd threw the woman on the ground and covered her. Still in deep shock from the butchery she had witnessed, she yielded without protest whilst he made futile stabs at penetration. Eventually he accepted defeat, rolled off and threatened to kill her if she told anyone. On closing his eyes he found himself thinking of the girl by the camp fire. Then he passed out.

He woke to a crapulence of mouth and a vague feeling that he had made a fool of himself last night. Further thought produced the nightmarish memory of sexual failure. He hardly dared turn his head to look at the woman, but when he did it was to find that she had sneaked from the tent whilst he snored. He half-hoped she had escaped completely so that he would not have to look at her – that is, if he could remember which one she was. Anticipating mockery from his comrades he spent a while longer here before, head pounding and eyes bloodshot, he crawled from the tent.

His friends were too worn out from their own debauchery to offer comment – not even a good morning – and so he was left in peace to wash the foul taste from his mouth and try to bring himself back to life. He glanced over at the knot of slavewomen who had made a feckless attempt to escape last night but had been hauled back and put under guard. He paid them much thought. Later in the morning when Sigurd had eaten and his head no longer pounded he decided he must make another attempt to lose his virginity. It took a great deal of nerve to march up to the group of women, wondering as he approached had the one from last night told the others? Would he be able to accomplish the act this time? What if there was something wrong with him? But he had to know now for he could not wait for Una to give birth only to make a thorough fool of himself.

Without leave he grabbed a woman, the first that came to hand, and dragged her back to his tent. She fought and scratched, drawing blood from his cheeks, but it did her no good. The rape was short-lived but effective; he was now a man in every sense and when the time came he could prove it to Una. Leaving the distressed woman behind him he emerged from the tent and strutted over to the other captives to prove himself again, this time in full view of everyone. His activities inflamed his comrades and they too advanced on the group, panicked them into mass flight, caught them and used them.

To struggle led to more injury, so after a few days the women gave up trying to oppose their captors and accepted their fate with stoicism – why make life even harder? However, there was much discord between the prisoners themselves, especially between Una and another of the girls in Sigurd's possession who was dubbed Black Mary, for her youth was lost beneath a countenance that was as black and bitter as a sloe. He neither knew nor cared of the relationship between them, neither was he particularly conscious of any rift. What he was extremely sensitive to was the magnetic lure of Una, from whom he found it impossible to stay away.

Had he bothered to ask, he would have learned that Mary was Una's sister-in-law; close to her brother, Eoghan, she had always resented being displaced in his affections by one of inferior birth and to see Una now talking with his murderer gave her double reason for hate. Until now Mary, being a couple of years older, had been accustomed to taking precedence over Una ... but now they were on a par, both were slaves, and Una would be bullied no longer, at least not by this girl.

Black Mary watched the young viking speak to the object of his lust, detestation of both filling every corner of her body. The moment Sigurd had passed out of earshot she swooped like a pterodactyl on Una, nipping tender flesh and yanking hair, luring the other women into her feud.

'Will ye look at her fawning like a vixen on heat around my brother's murderer!' Her eyes were blacker than ever in this mood.

''Twas not I talking to him,' corrected Una, wrenching her hair from Mary's fingers and returning to her washing which she pounded on the riverbank. ''Twas him talking to me. I do not welcome his attention. Besides, Sigurd did not murder Eoghan. 'Twas the dark one, Eric.'

'Hark!' Black Mary wheeled in triumph on the others. 'Doesn't she know their names already!' With their muttered agreement, she turned back to Una, hatred in her face, which like her manner was coarse. 'What does it matter which head of the serpent struck the blow. He's dead, is he not? And you cavortin' with them like a whore, my dear brother's child in your belly.'

'Have a care,' one of the others warned Mary, 'lest she turns her magic on us.'

'She has no magic!' scoffed Mary.

'What about the visions? Didn't she tell us something like this was going to happen?'

'I'll grant she can peer into the future, but can she do anything about it?' The dark woman looked crafty. 'She cannot! She's powerless like the rest of us. I've tested her so-called magic, 'tis harmless. D'ye think I'd still be alive if it wasn't? Hasn't she always hated me!'

''Tis a mean mouth ye have on ye, Mary. I tried my best to be friends but ye'd have none of it.' Una wrung out her garment and stood with dripping hands to move away but the women, convinced as to her impotence, formed a ring around her. She grew alarmed at their hostility. 'Will ye let me pass!'

'What's the password?' Black Mary hissed into her face and knocked the clean garment from her hands.

'She should know that,' said one who did not know Una very well but shared Mary's dislike of the way she curried favour with the viking. ''Tis harlot! Harlot, harlot!' The others began to chant with her.

'Let me go, I've done nothing wrong!' Una clenched her wet fists and tried to forge a way through but the circle tightened on her.

'What is amiss here?' Sigurd had returned.

Black Mary checked her attack, but did not cower and retreat as did the others. She turned upon him with lips stretched taut across her teeth. 'Come, sisters! Let us give the young hog a smile.' The others sucked in their breath, expecting punishment, but Mary did not flinch. 'To be sure, he doesn't understand a word, do ye, my noble lord?' She bowed her head to Sigurd, wearing an expression of total subservience. 'Ye can say what the devil ye like so long as ye wear your best smile, he'll not understand a word of it. Listen.' She clasped her hands to her breast and gazed entreatingly at Sigurd. 'We were just keeping your little whore hot for ye, master. Will ye look at her cheeks all red and glowing.'

Sigurd's nostrils flared. 'What do you say? You must learn to abandon your words in favour of mine.'

Black Mary continued to smile. 'Sure, he'd look more like a woman than a man with all that hair if he didn't stink so foul. Come, Una,' she pulled the girl into a falsely affectionate embrace. 'Ye say ye don't like your man's attention, then prove it. Call him what ye will.'

Una hesitated, then muttered into her breast, 'Ye've a face on ye like a pig's pezzle.' No hand came out to smite her. The other women dared to relax now. Una set the previous antagonism aside for the moment, to enjoy this newfound game. 'An' your breath stinks like a rotting carcase,' she added sweetly.

The women tittered. The young viking began to suspect a plot. He looked from one grimy face to another.

Black Mary spoke again. 'Oh, son of Satan's whore . . .' She was instantly felled by a blow. All but herself and Una fled in disorder. Sigurd left the black crumpled figure to be tended by the fair one. A rueful Mary sat up, testing her jaw which felt broken and was already beginning to swell. ''Tis obvious he's been called that before.' Realizing it was Una at her elbow, she knocked away the helping hand and rose to her feet unaided. 'Away with ye, bitch!'

Una stood her ground. 'An' what right have you to call me names? You who ate at my table, who danced and sang with me . . .'

'For my brother's sake!' came the hot response, blood and saliva dribbling from the lopsided jaw. 'Now he's dead I'll pretend no more. An' I warn ye,' Black Mary took the hand from her jaw and wagged a finger, 'ye'll have no friend while you're the viking's harlot.'

'I am not his nor any man's harlot!' Una stooped to retrieve the garment she had washed, now a muddy rag. 'But if that's what all of ye think then be damned to your friendship! None of ye can give me my freedom, but Sigurd can, an' if I have to dance naked to his whistle then by God I will – to Hell with the lot o' yese!'

Chapter Seven

The vikings spent the best of the summer in Ireland, making other lightning raids on monasteries and small colonies, their poorly-clad slaves at the mercy of Irish downpours and coastal winds. The ship would not take the horses they had captured and these were sold, but they were left with prizes aplenty for their families back home. Towards autumn they made their last port of call at Dyflinn to stock up with food and hire more crew, then returned to Jorvik by the northern passage, their ship low in the water under its ballast of loot.

On the second day of the voyage, Una felt the onset of labour. At first she had been uncertain, but by nightfall when the waves of pain launched themselves as strongly as those against the prow, she was forced to swallow her pride and ask the other women for help. One by one they turned their backs. Una panicked. Helpless as a doe with the baying of wolves in its ears, she began to totter about the deck between the rowers. Harsh male voices demanded that she make herself scarce, but locked in her distress she knew not where she trod and kept pacing, pacing . . . A corner, she must find a quiet corner! But there were no corners on a ship. Una vomited. Another male voice split the darkness. 'Agh! Some bastard has thrown up over my back!' Una staggered away from the angry voice and back to the group of women, begging, pleading, but met with excommunication.

Terrorized by pain, she huddled into the darkness

and prayed. Each time the spasms came she rammed a knot of her dress into her mouth and bit on it so hard that she feared her teeth would crack, and in time it went away. But the waves of agony became too powerful to conceal and she began to moan out loud.

Sigurd had decided that they would row throughout the night so that their land journey might be accomplished more safely in daylight. Whilst others took their turn at the oars, he and the relief crew slept, but now an inhuman howl rent his dream. Roused, he lifted his head, wondering if the ship was being attacked, but the rhythmic creak of the oars soothed him back towards oblivion. Another scream brought him crashing into consciousness, and prompt as an echo came another.

'Have we devils aboard?' Rousing Ulf who shared his sleeping bag, he got to his feet, pressed a hand to his brow and looked for the source of the noise. For a moment only the sound of rowing pierced the darkness, then it came again. His brain latched on to who was responsible. 'Those . . . wretched women! They are more trouble than they are worth. Quiet, back there!' He made for the stern. 'Another peep and you will all be in the sea!'

But no threat could halt nature's mischief. Sigurd cursed again and hopped along the deck, almost tripping over Una whose distorted face gleamed up at him, white as the moon. It was all too evident then what was happening.

'Oh . . .' Sigurd backed away. 'You had better get on with it.' About to go, he noticed that no one was assisting her, the other women all curled up apparently asleep. Disgusted, he kicked the nearest one, Black Mary. 'Why do none of you give her help?'

'To be sure, she never asked for it . . . master,' sulked the drowsy woman. By necessity and beatings the prisoners had learnt their captors' tongue but Sigurd did not like the tone.

'If she dies, you all die, ja? Now, keep her quiet!'

Racked by pain, Una was glad of any help, even the rough handling of her sister-in-law. When the labour changed course and she was gripped by the urge to expel whatever was inside her, two of the women held her under the arms whilst she squatted and strained and tried her best not to yell. Like many of her countrywomen, her pubic bone had been broken at birth by the midwife and the gap prevented from knitting so as to allow the adult woman to be delivered more easily. It did not help. Una felt that she was dying, prayed indeed that she would die and be spared this dreadful agony. Eventually, in a flesh-splitting rush of gore, the child was ejected from the darkness of its mother's body into the darkness of life.

''Tis a boy.' Kneeling, Black Mary laid the infant on her lap whilst another woman delivered the after-birth, then with the tiny knife that also prepared food she cut the umbilicus and wrapped the baby in a piece cut from Una's smock, for there were no bands to swaddle his green limbs.

Though her innards felt ragged and her limbs trembled from labour, joy and exhilaration crept into Una's voice. 'Is he fit?'

'And what do you care?' was her sister-in-law's hurtful riposte. 'Ye cared nought for his poor father.'

Una made no comment on the latter, saying only, 'He is my child.'

'And ye don't deserve him!'

For one heart-stopping moment Una feared she was to be deprived of her son then, grudgingly, Black Mary surrendered the bundle to her arms. Una gazed over every inch of him. From the time of his conception she had wondered whether or not she would hate him when he was born, but now she drowned beneath a floodtide of love and an urge to protect.

One of the women pulled the crude shawl away

159

from the baby's face, her words more amicable than Una had come to expect. 'How will ye be knowing him?'

'She'll not be calling him anything!' Mary incised before Una had the time even to think. ''Tis I who'll give him his name. He'll be known as Murtagh – seaman – and by the Virgin he'll make a greater man by far than any of this viking scum.' She turned to pass a murderous look along the deck at the shape that was her captor.

Hair fluttering in the night wind, Sigurd perched forward. Looking out over the waves, deeply involved with his thoughts, he took a moment to heed the call that summoned him to his turn at the oar. When he answered he noticed too that the banshee wailing had stopped and out of curiosity went to investigate. 'Is it male or female?' He looked at the bundle in Una's arms.

''Tis a boy,' announced Black Mary.

Sigurd looked pleased and called out through the darkness, 'Friends, witness this!' Rude hands took the bundle from Una's arms and held it aloft. 'My first male slave!'

Oh, the thoughtlessness, the injustice! Una was plunged from the crest of euphoria into the very pit of despair. Her mind screamed in unison with the mouth of her son – Mother of Mercy, have I gone through all this just for him to be a slave? Help me, sweet Jesus, help me!

Sigurd dumped the puling infant back at her. Her arms enveloped him like a hawk shrouds its kill, face crumpling. Not a word, not a care for my health . . .

Una was mistaken. He did have thoughts of her, though he spoke them only to himself: Good Freyja, heal her with your kiss, mend her quickly, so that her sweet flesh might soon be locked round mine.

Navigation of the strip of land between the firths of

Clyde and Forth proved arduous for all. To carry the boat they slotted the oars through the oarholes and hoisted the weight on to their shoulders, all the while tensed in anticipation of attack. They took constant rests. Without these Una felt that she would have died, her body still raw from its travails.

Sigurd's vainglorious entrance to Jorvik coincided with the appearance of an unfamiliar woman in his yard. Burdened with implements, he held her with shrewd eye, believing her to be another claimant on his property. The woman did not flinch – then almost simultaneously each hailed their recognition, '*Mother!*' '*Son!*'

Throwing down his baggage, Sigurd came to meet Ragnhild who beheld him with happiness. Though their meeting was inhibited by a natural reserve, affection still shone in both pairs of eyes. 'How you have changed!' Maternal hands stroked his lightly-bearded chin, running over every inch of a face tanned from its voyage. 'And so tall – not so tall as your father by a long way, but oh . . . !'

In the way he shook his head, Sigurd displayed that he too could not credit the transformation of his mother. It had been only . . . six years! He had thought her old before but now . . . oh, she must be over forty!

After the endearments came the rebukes, his mother using her good arm to deal a hefty cuff to his head. 'Tut! Look at your hair! It is almost to your knees.' From the brooch on her right shoulder hung a chain laden with scissors, purse, needles, keys, which tinkled as she smote him. 'And I still have to punish you for running away like that! Why did you take so long to send for me? You cannot imagine how I suffered under your aunt – still, there was fun to be had when your message came. I certainly told her what to do with her orders. But no thanks to you, unruly boy!'

161

Sigurd tried to look amused but could not hide his embarrassment at being treated as if he were still ten years old. 'Mother, that is grand reward for the part I took in destroying my father's murderer and winning our land back!'

Her round face pouted. 'Winning it back for what? I arrive to find the thralls lying idle, my son a-viking and the house falling to bits! Look, look at this!' She kicked at the timber walls and seized the chip of rotten timber that came away. 'Riddled with worm!'

Sigurd glanced uncomfortably at his friends who were obviously enjoying this.

Ragnhild threw down the piece of wood and wagged a finger. 'What you need is a wife to keep you in order.'

'Ah!' Sigurd managed to interpose at last. 'See what I bring from my travels!'

Ragnhild appraised the pathetic group of women with mild interest, before grasping his meaning. 'One of those? Brainless, you cannot marry a slave!'

He countered with a hurt scowl. 'Nei! They are only slaves because I made them so. The clothes we took from them show they were quite wealthy.' He reached for Una who clung to her baby and drew her away from the others. 'What about this one? She is very good-looking, ja?'

'So is that horse over there but I doubt you would marry that. Talk sense, boy!' Ragnhild slipped into an air of efficiency. 'Your mother is here just in time. I shall find you a suitable bride.' She shooed Una and the other women towards a grass-roofed outhouse then turned her attention to the rest of her son's booty, missing his look of dismay. 'Come, let us see what other worthless rubbish you have brought home.'

Eric nudged Ulf with a grin. 'The mighty warrior returns . . . to a skelping from his mother!'

Ragnhild bridled at their obvious amusement. 'And

who are these fine fellows?' By the tone of the remark it was not a compliment. Under her disapproving eye each examined his grubby apparel and proceeded to shrink into it.

Sigurd took refuge in their shared humiliation. 'These are my loyal friends, Eric and Ulf. We have fought side by side – and often with each other,' he grinned at them, 'ever since we came to England.'

'It certainly smells like it.' Ragnhild was expert at disparagement. 'Do their houses not have baths?'

'They live here,' explained Sigurd. 'I thought as there was plenty of room . . .'

'Wouldst you turn your father's house into the biggest pigsty in Jorvik?' she interrupted. 'Look at this one!' Eric gasped under her punch. Ulf prepared himself for a similar blow. Much as he might object that the lack of a beard did not affect his own virility and much as he might try to prove this by his hearty participation in the rapine that often followed battle, Ulf was nevertheless very conscious of his shortcoming when dealing with females on a social basis. There was always the fear that women would laugh at his naked chin, hence the reason he had never tried to find a wife. This shyness was evident in his pose, as if he were trying to hide beneath his fringe. Far from being repelled, Ragnhild was charmed and began to cluck over his torn clothes. 'Oh well, I suppose you cannot help it with no woman in the house. Do not worry, I shall take you in hand.' It was obvious which one she preferred; her words for Eric were less matronly. 'Go and bathe immediately whilst I have private words with my son! If you are clean I may allow you to continue living here, but only until Sigurd is wed, then you will each have to build your own house.' As they slunk away, she proceeded with her investigation of the booty, holding up a roll of silk interwoven with gold thread. 'Ah! This is better. At least now I will have something to wear for your wedding – though of course it is not so good as I wore in the old days. You have a long way to go before you equal your father in wealth. Come! Fetch the rest of it inside and spread it out. Then you too will take a bath. Ay, ay, Jorvik is not the place it was; everyone seems to live like oxen.'

Chasing away the house slaves, which left just the two of them in the room, Ragnhild hugged him for the first time. 'Oh, what a fine son I have!'

'Apart from my bad odour.' Sigurd allowed himself to be crushed against her breast.

'We will let that pass. I am so pleased to see you!' She held him at arms' length to marvel again at how he had matured. 'When I think of the totty boy who left me . . . and how I rejoice to hear that the pig Ethelred rots in his grave! Tell me, did his sons die also?'

'One of them. The others are driven from the land.'

'Ja, ja, that is what the folk round here are telling me but I would hear it from the lips of a man who was there.'

''Tis true,' confirmed Sigurd.

'Good, good. I am not a vindictive woman but I pray to Freyja to rot their balls so that the devil's seed is ended.'

Sigurd remembered then. 'Hark to my good fortune! The King has appointed me his thegn.'

His mother reeled back in admiration. 'How so?' She pulled two stools close together, planted her bottom on one of them and tapped the other. 'Come, come! I must hear every word.'

Sigurd told her of his relationship with the King, and for the first time his mother seemed truly impressed. Then she spoilt the effect by enquiring in dubious tone, 'And is that all that has happened since you crept away like a thief? Come, I demand to know it all.'

He emitted a boyish groan, pulled off his woven

164

band and gave his head a good scratch. 'There's too much to tell at once. First, oh kind little mother, won't you feed the grumbling trolls in my belly?'

'Kind little mother!' scoffed Ragnhild. 'I thought you had changed but you are still the scheming flatterer who ran away and left me. Before a crumb passes those lips I would at least have news of your uncle. It has been weeks since I arrived and I have seen nor heard nothing of him. I assumed he was with your expedition.'

Sigurd had forgotten all about his uncle and the shock of remembrance was mirrored in his expression. Ragnhild could not fail to decipher it. Instead of asking what was wrong she waited for him to tell her.

Sigurd was blunt. 'My uncle is dead.'

His mother put both plump hands up to cover her mouth as he disclosed all that had occurred with Thorald, excluding only his own desire to be rid of his uncle. 'But you will be glad to know that I killed Thorald for his treachery,' came the hasty addendum.

Still shocked, Ragnhild whispered, 'And what of poor Olaf now? Is he still in the cesspit?'

Sigurd grasped her hands and shook them, looking into her face. 'Mother, what do you take me for? As soon as ever I could I gave him a decent burial.' His mind recalled the gruesome task, then thrust it aside. 'You will see the stone I have erected to his memory in the kirk across the way.'

'I will go there, leave my offering for the gods to take care of him. We must send word to his wife. Oh, my poor brother . . .'

'This I shall do – but come, let us not dwell on sad affairs, there is nought more we can do for Uncle. Take a proper look at all the riches I bring you.' He undid one of the bundles, then began to place one ornament after another upon her body – wrists, arms, fingers, neck, hair, all were adorned with jewels until her smile returned and she pealed with laughter. 'Enough! Before I sink into the earth under the weight of all this.'

'Now will you admit you are proud of me?' Sigurd was laughing too.

His mother delivered a push that almost unseated him. 'Your head is obviously swollen enough without my praise. Away, stinkhorn, and take your bath while I see if there is ought decent to eat in this hovel.'

Black Mary's words virtually echoed Ragnhild's: 'Holy Mother, is there nought fit to eat in this hovel?' She stared around the bleak walls.

Una rocked and shushed her crying infant, eyes transcribing Mary's horror. She coughed as, instead of the welcoming smell of peat, woodsmoke filled her lungs. 'I'll have to feed Murtagh.' She squatted where she stood, put the child to her breast, then re-examined her grim suroundings – though there was little to see. The walls were ten feet long at most and at the edges of the room where the roof came down to meet them it was impossible for a person to stand upright. Along two of the walls were earth-filled benches covered in rags where the lucky ones slept; the rest would curl up by the central hearth on the earthen floor. Apart from a few artifacts that hung from nails embedded in the walls there were only shadows cast by the one tiny rushlight anchored to a beam. Una bent her head and wept in desolation.

Black Mary cursed her weakness. 'For God's sake is it not bad enough! We're here, there is nought we can do and must make the best of it.' At her words the others crowded round the fire. The slave who had been in occupation when they arrived, introduced herself and offered to share the ingredients of her cooking pot. Black Mary sniffed in distaste and enquired what it was.

'Sheep,' replied the other. 'And if you turn your nose up like that you can do without. There's plenty more of us who'll be glad of it.'

'How many?' Una sniffed and wiped her eyes.

'Five.'

Una displayed yet more shock. 'Mercy, that makes eleven all living here!'

'Oh, she can add up!' The thrall had a low opinion of the Irish. 'You might help the master when it comes to granting us rations, lest he thinks he can feed eleven of us with the same that served five. At least the extra bodies will keep us warm through the winter.'

Una and her fellow captives came to vouch for the truth of these words, welcoming anything that offered warmth. One of the English thralls donated the bits of fleece she had collected, to prevent baby Murtagh dying from the cold, but there was not enough to clothe eleven adults, whose only insulation was provided by the dungpile on the outside wall and the rotting matter on the floor. As for food, the master was not so parsimonious as feared and doubled the corn ration, though the meat was restricted to a single sheep between all. When this was almost gone and what was left was rancid, they eked out their rations with plantains, dandelion leaves and hibernating hedgehogs. It was remarkable that only two of their number died.

There was no sympathy from their captors. The Lady Ragnhild addressed them only when she had orders to impart and by now the thralls knew their role well enough for her to leave them to it. At first, she had been a figure of fun when she had called the newcomers before her to impress all her rules and regulations. They had sniggered and mimicked her accent. 'You must tell me if any of you get viz child, ja? And I shall not hef you sneaking off to gif yourself abortions. Any bairn is the property of mine son. It is also important zat you tell me each month ven you are unclean so that you do not contaminate my food, ja?'

Una had the temerity to ask a question, clutching her new babe. 'May it please my lady, I have not yet been purified after my deliverance; could I be allowed to see the priest?'

Ragnhild thought on this. There were many things an unpurified slave could not do. She granted leave. 'So be it – and when your menses return you must inform me.'

This Una was glad to do, for each menstruation saved her from having to work in the big house where the thegn's eyes ravished her. What should have been a monthly event began to take place every fifteen days, supplemented by a dabble of sheep's blood on her clothes and granting her five days' rest from any cooking or association with foodstuffs and worktools that might turn rusty.

Una grinned to herself as she hid in the latrine with a cloth saturated in fresh sheep's blood and dabbed it onto the back of her dress for the second time this month. Then, with the 'evidence' upon her clothes, she went to see Ragnhild, telling her, 'My lady, I am unclean and unable to dig vegetables today.'

'Very well, you can . . .' Ragnhild frowned and made mental calculation. 'It seems like only two weeks ago that you were indisposed. There must be some malady . . .'

'No, my lady!' Una was quick to correct her. ''Twas not me.'

Ragnhild looked at her. 'I could have sworn it was. Well, there are plenty of other tasks.' Giving Una instructions, she watched her walk away.

Una congratulated herself on managing to outsmart her captors yet again and, the next day, went to the latrine to keep up the pretence. Unfortunately, she did not realize that she was being watched. Ragnhild crept as softly as she could up to the wattle fence, peeped around it and caught Una in the act.

'Why, you sly vixen! You think you can outwit me?' Ragnhild's hand shot out and grabbed Una, causing the slave to yell in fright. 'Like blood, do you? Well, I shall give you plenty!' And she laid into Una so brutally with a stick that blood oozed from the weals it inflicted. 'There! Have some more!' Ragnhild continued to hit the slave until she was too tired to lift her arm, but she had not finished the punishment yet. 'And for your deception you will work in the fields for the rest of the month!'

In future, when Una claimed unfitness she knew that it meant extra hard labour in the cold, and thus her cycle became more regular.

Throughout the winter nights when they weren't being worked and beaten by Ragnhild, the survivors told tales around the fire and made themselves candles from rushes and mutton fat. There were sagas in the big house too, but life here was worlds apart, as the more fortunate houseslaves could testify. Instead of stringy bits of rancid ewe there was a whole sheep roasting on the spit and cabbage and fresh bread. Instead of tallow rushlights the room shone with beeswax candles robbed from an Irish monastery. There were skins on the walls and eiderdown quilts on the beds.

Ragnhild, swathed in warm clothing, basked in the glow of a roaring fire, laughing and feasting with Sigurd and his two friends – whom she had begun to treat as her own sons, especially Ulf with his youthful face. Some things had not changed; she remained the obsessive grumbler, but despite her chastisements Sigurd could tell that his mother delighted in her regained status, rejoiced in being mistress of Peseholme. In this he was glad, for it might just cause her to rethink her policy about finding him a wife to whom she would have to relinquish her superiority as queen of the household. This gave him leave to pursue the Irish girl, Una, from whom it was impossible to keep his mind. If he assumed his mother was in ignorance of the latter then he was wrong. Ragnhild had by no means abandoned her aim of finding him a wife, but had merely decided to wait a year whilst he indulged his callow lust. He was, for all his boastful exploits, still a youth. Better that he should tire of the slave of his own accord, for only then would he settle down and be an industrious husband.

Hitherto Sigurd had managed to content himself with fantasizing about Una, deterred from physical contact by the infant slung across her breast. But now the ice had melted, new life burgeoned all around him and his own untested juices sizzled with urgency. When the thralls trouped out to fulfil this morning's tasks, Una was not amongst them. Impulse propelled Sigurd towards the hut where a cow devoured its grass roof; the beast lumbered away as he neared.

Inside the dark lair Black Mary spun wool with distaff and spindle, humming and twisting the yarn through work-hardened fingers. When her master's outline robbed her of the only source of light, she looked up but did not stop, humming all the louder when she saw who it was, breaking into merry Irish song: 'Oh-oh, cross your legs or you're in for a shock. 'Tis the devil himself with his ugly big tra-la-la-la!'

The young Norseman squinted into the gloom, assailed by the foisty smell. Una was hunkered on the earthen floor, having just fed her babe. She had her face bent over him, talking and smiling in a maternal fashion, kissing his soft cheeks. Her long hair tumbled over one shoulder to form a protective curtain, as if shielding the child from the terrible world into which he had been plunged. Totally involved with Murtagh, she was oblivious to Sigurd's presence. Sigurd, blind to her dirty state, thought how radiant she looked and wished those eyes would shine upon him so fondly.

Lips still curved, Una tossed her hair away from her face to question Mary about the rude ditty, only now catching sight of him in the doorway. Her expression underwent vast change, the bloom draining from her cheeks. Once again she was the slave he had made her.

On attracting such a display, Sigurd showed pique. 'Give the child to her!' He jabbed an abrupt thumb at Black Mary and came right into the hovel beneath the apex of its roof which was the only place he could stand upright. 'There is something I wish you to do.'

Una glanced at her sister-in-law, and retained her acquisitive crouch over the child, but for once Black Mary jumped to Sigurd's command, welcoming each and every opportunity to hold her nephew. She might hate its mother but the child himself was of her own kin and she loved him dearly. Unwilling to part with her son, but lacking option, Una rose and handed charge of the babe to Mary.

'Take it out,' ordered Sigurd, then stepped back so that Black Mary did not soil his clothes as she passed. Never once did he stop to imagine what it must be like for the people who had to live in this cramped environment.

Una's anxious eyes followed the woman's exit, rationale telling her there was no threat to the child whilst her maternal instincts screamed the opposite. She was still craning her neck when his gartered legs took a step towards her. Una herself took a pace back. Sigurd postponed his action for a moment, resting his head to one side to ask a question that had suddenly occurred to him. 'Tell me, why have I never seen you weep for your dead husband?'

Her voice emerged from the shadows on that musical lilt he found so captivating in its foreignness. 'He meant nought to me.'

171

This appeared to boost the youth's confidence and he took another step. Again she moved away, taking herself to the limits of the room where she eyed him warily.

The sight of her, pressed so defensively against the gabled wall ignited his rancour. 'You know that I have the right to take you any time I wish?'

'Then do it,' she challenged, trying to appear calm whilst beneath the grimy skirts her knees trembled. 'But take warning, there'll be no second time.'

He frowned disbelief. 'You would take your own life rather than have my pleasure?'

A scornful laugh rent the shadows. 'Not my life! The last man who took his pleasure on me is dead.'

For the moment he was interested enough to forgive the threat. 'You speak of your husband, ja?'

'He was no more husband than you are! A husband is one who takes care of his wife and loves her. O'Cellaigh used me as he would a piece of meat.' Una turned sly. 'But he did not know that I can do magic.'

Sigurd crossed his arms over his blue tunic and laughed.

'He's dead, is he not?' retorted Una. 'Who do ye think is accountable?'

'My friends and I!' laughed Sigurd.

Una stood firm, the whites of her eyes glittering through the murk. 'But you were a stranger. Why did ye come to that particular place on that particular day? Because I asked Jesus to set me free.'

'But you are not free!' Highly amused, Sigurd unfolded his arms, raised a hand to one of the roof beams and leaned on it.

'Not yet . . . but I shall be.' It was said with great confidence. Una had never before realized her proclivity for acting.

Enjoying himself, Sigurd indulged her. 'And the runes told you this?'

She shook her head. 'The runes are only one of my talents. Besides, I never see my own fate there, only that of others.'

'Ah, yes!' mocked Sigurd. 'I remember you told me, I shall live to be a very old man. So . . . how are you certain that you shall be freed?'

'That truth was brought to me by greater magic,' revealed Una. 'Magic that rules you also. 'Tis already written that you will give me my freedom.'

The listener spluttered. 'Oh, will I? Do I go to the trouble of winning slaves just to set them free?'

'Mayhap it shall not be today, nor tomorrow, but it shall come. I trust the Lord.' And she added an opinion of her own: 'When you're a man ye'll learn 'tis wrong to own people.'

'When I am a man?' Amusement turned to wrath. The youth took a last swaggering step forwards and shoved his face into hers. 'Doest know how many men I have killed?'

Pressed tight against the rotting wall with only words at her disposal, Una countered bravely, 'That doesn't make you a man. A true man wins people with kindness and gentleness, not the edge of his sword.'

He was close enough to kiss her – could have shown her all the kindness and gentleness she craved – but instead he scoffed: 'No wonder the Christian men are so easily beaten if those are their teachings.'

In return her eyes belittled him. 'One day ye'll accept the power of the true God. Jesus'll make ye set me free. Ye cannot change what is written.'

His hands came up to shake her, only one thought keeping them at bay: what if she really could do magic?

This doubt relayed itself to Una. Using his lack of maturity to aid her bluff, she pressed the dart of superstition home. 'Remember what I told you on that night ye came: 'twill be a woman who destroys ye.'

He placed his hands on the timber to either side of her face and leaned on them. His whole body trembled to repay such insolence, but her words had conjured such an air of sorcery that it became as effective as a wall between them. He hung there, hypnotized and quite furious. 'I could kill you at my whim!'

'Then why don't ye?'

He spoke through his teeth. 'Because a slave is worth money and I do not dispose of wealth so freely! Be thankful you have escaped me for today.'

'I have no wish to escape.'

Sigurd cursed her ambiguity aloud. 'You say if I touch you you will call upon your magic and have me killed, you say you want your freedom but now you say you have no wish to escape! In the name of Odin what do you want?' Wrenching free of her mesmerizing gaze, he spun away.

Una remained hugging the wall. 'If I escape, your men will hunt me down and kill me. The Lord knoweth, I do want my freedom but not at the price of my life. I accept that I must wait for it to come from you.'

'Then you shall wait forever!' Sigurd grew tired of her incoherent prating and headed for daylight. 'Back to work with you!'

Alone, Una sagged, half in relief, half regret. He was overbearing, a young tyrant, too adept at casual violence . . . but from the moment she had faced him on that Irish heath, she had felt something very odd happening inside her.

Chapter Eight

Frustrated, mocked, rejected, Sigurd became a torment to all those forced to live with him, though none were conversant with the true source of the problem and he was disinclined to enlighten them. What a laughing stock he would be if they knew – his advances rebuffed by one so low!

The air between himself and Una became even more electric. Blighted hopes gave way to drastic intent: I shall take her, he decided, watching her now sowing beans and planting woad. Whatever her tricks she will fend me off no longer. She is mine and I shall have her.

All that day his leaden loins hovered on the verge of explosion. Una felt him watching her every move and played on such overt lust, taunting with her body as she carried pails back and forth from well to house. *Oh, and don't ye hunger for me! But 'tis not time yet, my lord and master.* Una had decided to use his appetite as a weapon to gain her own freedom and that of her son. She would give in to him – eventually – but it must be at the right moment. Too soon, and she might lose this valuable hold over him. Make him wait too long, and he would tire of the game.

This strategy was not something she chose to reveal to any of her fellow prisoners, especially Black Mary. Crammed together in the hut she and the latter had been compelled to form a truce. It was impossible to spend twenty-four hours of the day at each other's throats, but they could never be bosom friends and by force of nature Mary had ensured that Una found no confidante amongst the others, either. Una did not care; the less folk who knew her tactics the better. Soon she would be freed and they would still be thralls . . . if she could just manage to hold him off until the time was right; his expression today was very dangerous.

Behind Sigurd's dark look were darker thoughts: *Oh ja, you little bitch* – his eyes touched the places that his hands could not – *I know just what you are at but beware, for tonight I shall pay you another visit.*

Little did either of them guess that by evening he would be as far away from Una as ever. That afternoon Ulf came to find him.

'The Lady Ragnhild shouts for you.'

Sigurd was alert. 'What does she hold in her hand?'

Ulf allayed the worry. 'She does not seek to punish you for ought, there is a messenger arrived from the King.'

'Cnut!' Sigurd came alive, pulled a comb from his pouch and ran it through his hair. 'I wonder if he comes – I should dearly love to see him again.' Long strides carried him to the house where the King's messenger had already been given refreshment and now with Sigurd's arrival imparted the news.

'*Hersir*, a great council is to be held at Cirenceaster at Eastertide. My lord the King commands your presence.'

Ragnhild clasped her hands in anticipation of more honour for her son and immediately organized provisions for his trip. Eric and Ulf would act as company.

As interesting as the diversion might be, it had not disposed of Sigurd's baser urges. When he and Una crossed the yard together, he to visit the bathhouse, she to load his victuals, he caught her elbow and walked alongside her for a few yards, making her heart beat faster. 'When I come back . . .' His eyes finished the threat. Released, Una hurried away.

Later, amidst an air of adventure, the three friends shouted goodbyes to Ragnhild, directing their horses at the gates. Sigurd could not prevent his eyes from looking for Una. His belly flipped over. There she was, plucking a goose. The goose honked its outrage. Fingers ripping, Una stared not at her work but at Sigurd. How much more resplendent he looked than his hooded counterparts. His horse, a heavy-limbed chestnut with feathered legs, glowed as if it had been polished. Every buckle of its harness was ornamented, its bridle adorned with silver studs, its collar harness mounted with bronze and its iron stirrups inlaid with copper. As the horse ambled past, Sigurd turned his head and purposefully locked eyes with her. Each tried to outstare the other till the gate blocked their view, and odd as it might seem for one so markedly afraid of him, Una felt the painful chill of loneliness.

Cleansed of dust from their journey, the three men entered Court. 'One day I shall have a room like this,' promised Sigurd, admiring the decorative weaponry upon the walls – hundreds of swords and axes arranged in burnished symmetry, shields painted with dragons of red, blue and gold, huge drinking horns with silver mounts. He moved with the ease of one who knows his own importance, nodding to the gilded ranks of noblemen assembled there and proceeding to the throne where he bowed to his friend the King. Cnut acknowledged him, but there was a cool edge to his mouth that served to temper Sigurd's blitheness.

'Stay!' Sigurd had been about to retreat from the throne with his friends, but the King's voice held him there.

'Come forth, Sigurd Einarsson, so that you do not mishear what I have to say.' If the King's original message had incubated hopes of favour then these were fast becoming sterile; the face beneath the crown was not that of an old friend.

'I called upon your presence,' announced Cnut, 'for I have received word that in my absence you instigated a viking raid upon Ireland. What have you to say on this?'

Sigurd, taken offguard, could think of no response. Behind him, Eric and Ulf shuffled with unease.

The King twitched a golden eyebrow. 'Didst think that far away in Denmark I would not hear of it?' He lifted his chin. 'Well, let me tell you that a king has many ears . . .'

I'll wager you have one in your arse, too, thought Sigurd, wondering angrily who had informed on him. It could be any one of a dozen northern thegns who were jealous of his relationship with the monarch.

'. . . and though I be far away those ears are listening. Your digressions will not be tolerated!' Cnut's voice was increasingly harsh. 'Didst think that the title I bestowed upon you gave leave to further your own greed for wealth?'

'Nei, my lord.' Sigurd looked at his feet. Rebuked thus before all the nobles of England he felt like a naughty child, and at this moment hated his former friend. How could the King humiliate him in front of Englishmen? He who had helped Cnut vanquish these people! Feeling himself to be the object of derision, and mistakenly attributing the mockery to Godwin who was seated close to the King, he raised defiant eyes to glare at his audience. Why had this one man, a man not much older than himself, earned such favour and was now adorned with the grand title, Earl of the West Saxons? It seemed that he could do no wrong and Sigurd no right.

But the rebuke was not exclusive to Sigurd. Cnut had turned away to envelop Thorkell the Tall in his ire. Thorkell, in Cnut's absence, had acted as Regent but had apparently enjoyed the role too much and upset many people who had wasted no time in complaining to the King. 'There are others here present who are of like mind, motivated by personal gain. That is why I gather you here, that you might bear joint witness to this warning: such errant behaviour will not be suffered. Those who cross me will pay heavy debt. Have I not just had a bellyful of squabbles in Denmark? I do not wish to return and be told that my subjects cause havoc at home!' Once again his eagle eyes were upon Sigurd. 'How can I promise my people order and justice when my thegns run wild upon their property? We must have unity or all that we have won shall shrivel to nought.' Pinching the bridge of his aquiline nose as if to contain exasperation, he paused, then turned back to Sigurd. 'Pope Benedict entreats me to use my power in the service of peace, and as God is my judge that is what I fully intend to do. I shall start by building a kirk at Assandun for the souls of those who perished there in battle. You, Sigurd Einarsson, and your two good friends shall help to lift the stones, then might you know Christ's greatness.'

Sigurd was apprehensive. 'Does my lord ask that I forsake the old gods and follow this Christ?'

'Thou wouldst be a fool not to.' Cnut softened. 'But I shall not force it.'

Sigurd posed a last relevant question. 'King of kings, if next year a new god is born, one who proves more powerful than your Christ – what then?'

'Then I should support him, of course,' replied the monarch with customary shrewdness. 'But be assured it shall never happen. Now, go in peace and do God's will.'

During the time spent in the construction of the shrine, Sigurd chewed over these last words and began to see the political expedience of his own baptism; it might help him with Una, too. He wondered what course his life would take now that the King had forbidden him to go viking. Primary malice had been washed away by the sweat of toil and he had come to the decision that the King was right about consolidating one's gains; it was foolish to waste his efforts for a little fun, better by far to channel that exuberance into securing a wedge of Cnut's great nation. It might not happen as quickly as he would like, for while some people had things handed to them on a platter, Sigurd had learnt by experience that he was not of Godwin's ilk; he had always had to work and fight for everything he had achieved, but triumph was all the more acute after a long wait. Excitement spurred his adze. He chipped and sliced and with each sculpted timber made his plans; after his baptism in the new kirk he would go on to make himself an important citizen of Jorvik, make his voice heard at the council, send its echoes down to Lunden and win the King's respect . . . but that was all to come. First, there was another conquest.

The separation, almost nine months, had only worked to heighten Sigurd's feelings for Una. She was the thing most upon his mind as he and his friends rode the last miles to Jorvik that Christmas Eve. That it was Christmas needed no proclamation; even outside the city ramparts in the ploughswain's street joyous voices could be heard from within. Micklegata rang to the sound of the Waits, candlelit processions chanted their way through the dark and narrow lanes to the religious houses where they would hold their vigils, but such holiness was far from Sigurd's thoughts. His entire body burnt with such longing . . .

'Art gone deaf?' Ulf's voice was testy, his inner things chafed from the saddle. 'I ask my question three times and still you do not answer.'

'Forgive me, I am ready for my bed.' Sigurd took

a gauntlet from the reins and scratched his back. 'What did you ask of me?'

'I ask what gift you bring the Lady Ragnhild from your travels.'

Sigurd gawped. 'Aiee! She will have my balls, I never gave it a thought. Stop, stop! We must find a merchant or silversmith, a shoemaker! Anything will do! I durst not go home empty-handed. Oh, thanks be to the gods!' He pointed to a sign, reined in his horse and prepared to go inside the house of the silversmith, hoping that the man would put trade before lawful observance of a holy day.

Ulf and Eric dismounted too, rubbing their posteriors and bending their legs. After a long time Sigurd emerged with a tiny leather pouch and took from it a ring that he brandished in triumph.

Eric sucked his teeth. 'All that wait for such a paltry thing!'

'It cost enough!' Sigurd was hurt.

'I dare say it did, and I meant no offence.' Tis proof of your courage that you take her so small a gift but will it not be dwarfed by mine?' Eric patted the box strapped to the packhorse. 'I know how the dame oft berates your offerings.'

Sigurd frowned. It was the first time he had noticed the box. 'You have a gift for my mother?'

'Ja – but do not be shamed by its size. It is from both of us, is it not, Ulf? I am sure Ragnhild would understand.'

'What is it?'

'I would show you but 'twould only delay your own search . . .'

'No matter.' The size of the box was evidence enough for Sigurd. 'Wait here! I shall go buy something else to go with this.'

'Why do you torment him so,' grumbled Ulf, acquainted with Eric's joke. ''Tis too cold to stand here all night while you play games.' Eric simply chuckled.

Sigurd returned with a bolt of fine quality wool. Unfortunately Eric's gift had also increased in size.

'I too had second thoughts,' said his ugly friend, patting the huge box that he was trying to load onto the horse. ''Twas mean to buy her a gift between two of us. This cost me the earth, but nothing is too good for our dear Ragnhild.'

Sigurd was livid. 'Swine! You do this a-purpose to shame me before my mother!' He wagged a threatening finger. 'I will buy one last gift and do not dare to better me again!'

'Nei, enough, enough!' Ulf grabbed a handful of the blond hair and dragged Sigurd back. 'I shall tarry here no longer and freeze my plums off. Can you not see this wretch has you for a fool – the box is empty, he borrowed it from that house over there.'

'It is not empty!' An indignant Eric forestalled Sigurd's attack. 'Heed!' Supporting the box on one knee he lifted a corner of the lid and at the same time broke noisy wind. 'Oh! That is why I did not want to show you what was in it! My gift to Ragnhild has escaped.' He looked dolefully at Sigurd who dealt a laughing punch.

'I do not think my mother wouldst appreciate a fart in a box. Eric, look out! Behind you is a skur-rahnefalskrim!' As Eric spun the youth leapt at him and dealt retribution to his ears.

Ulf sighed at their playful tussles. 'Get thee to a mad-house, I am gone home.'

Remembering Una, Sigurd vaulted onto his horse and begat a gallop along Micklegata that erupted into mayhem as Ulf strove for supremacy. The members of the religious procession on the bridge were forced to jump or be trampled to death, their candles fast extinguished in the Use.

Ulf careered through the gates only seconds before the others, all three horses churning up mud in their whinnying skid. Pink-faced, Sigurd laughed and dismounted, calling breathlessly for aid. In those few moments of handing the reins to another he gazed across at the slaves' hut barred against the cold, and wondered what was taking place behind that door. The maddening itch returned . . .

'Sigurd, where have you been?!' Ragnhild, hearing the din, had emerged to greet her son, her head and neck heavily veiled against the cold. 'No word nor sign! Did the King grant favour?'

Sigurd tore his eyes from Una's hovel to share a rueful glance with Ulf. 'It might be classed as favour by some.' He laughed and rubbed his glowing face.

'Good!' She tugged off Ulf's hood and nipped his cheek affectionately. 'Then come inside and tell me all about it. I have a splendid Yule log burning in the hearth and food to fill your belly – even enough for yours, Bearface.' Ulf winced, then realized she was talking to Eric with his heavy black growth.

Sigurd laughed to himself and followed the others into the welcoming light of the house where the timber walls were festooned with greenery. The conquest of Una would have to wait until the festivities were past.

Perforce, it had to wait much longer for another reason than wassailing: Una herself. The girl was as intransigent as ever. Any other master would have raped her, but this was too easy an option; he must win her spirit, too. In an attempt to forget about her he paid recourse to the other females at his disposal – what an unresponsive bunch they were! Lying like blocks of wood, pretending not to be impressed . . . he had quickly lost interest, allowing Ulf and Eric to use them as they wished. Due to their efforts, two of the women had given birth, with Ragnhild as midwife, thus providing Sigurd with more slaves . . . but he wanted only one. Una must indeed be in possession of magic, for what other girl of eighteen was so expert a manipulator?

Day by day, Sigurd weakened to her ploy. By the time another spring came round he had become totally infatuated. He confided in no one – how could he say to men next to whom he had fought, "I feel as though a thousand elvers swim around my belly." But everyone knew, from his friends to the lowest thrall, and could see it from the way he behaved towards her.

The other slavewomen began to tease Una. 'How will you like that old sow Ragnhild for your mother-in-law?'

'Why, how can ye talk about her so,' cried Black Mary in false reproach. 'To be sure, isn't she the loveliest woman y'ever met. Can't ye just see those tears in her eyes when she's forced to ask us to muck out the pigs.' She mimicked Ragnhild's accent. 'It breaks mine poor heart to verk you so hard, jaaa!'

Even Una had to laugh, carving squares of moss for use in the latrine and holding one up for inspection. 'D'ye think this'll be big enough for her ladyship's backside?'

Black Mary eyed it. 'Mayhap – but is it soft enough?'

Una rubbed a thumb over the dark green filaments. 'Not quite.' Full of glee, she ran over to a briar, nipped off a thorn and embedded it in the square of moss to accompanying giggles.

'Make sure ye put Ragnhild's name on it,' warned Black Mary, raking together some fluffy seed-heads of coltsfoot for use in her own mattress. 'If I get that up my bottom you'll know about it.'

One of their number had found a supply of peat. Glad to have detoured conversation from Sigurd, Una seized a turf and put it to her face, inhaling deeply. 'Ooh, God, will ye just smell that! Come, away to the house and burn some and let's all have a good cry and think of home.'

'Crying, is it?' said Black Mary. 'Sure, you wouldn't

leave here if ye had the chance now. Ye have life too good, what with all the privileges himself gives ye.'

Una shrugged this off. ''Tis nought so sure as I'll be back home afore you,' she told Mary, and flounced away.

Ragnhild had begun to regret her own laxity in not selling Una whilst her son was away down south; his relationship with the thrall was unhealthy. It was imperative that she resurrect her plan to find him a wife, and the sooner the better. This she told him. 'It will prevent you from making a complete jackass of yourself.'

Sigurd, eating his last mouthful of breakfast, played dumb. 'Jackass? What do you mean by that?'

'One of these things!' Ragnhild formed a donkey's ears with her hands and brayed. 'You know very well what I mean! You and that Irish mare, between you you shall breed a mule! Doest believe nobody notices the way you are always sniffing round her with your tongue hanging out? You are the laughing stock.'

Her son turned grim and rose from the table. 'Show me which man has laughed and I will kill him!'

'You would need many blades to stop all who laugh – and would you kill your friends over a wench? Tsk! Even the servants talk about you.'

'They shall soon regret it. I am master here and I will do as I like.' He bent over and started to run a comb through his long hair towards the ground, yanking at resistant knots.

His mother's attitude was unaffected. 'Nobody denied you the right to bed which slave you want, but when you fall in love . . . that is another matter.'

'Love?' Still bending, Sigurd gasped and hoped that his hair would mask his crimson face.

'You do not fool your mother!' Ragnhild leaned over and whacked his bottom with her spoon. 'I have known you too long.' She became more constructive.

'Be warned, son, there is something weird about that one. She has bewitched you. You would be wise to sell her.'

Sigurd pulled a ball of hair from his comb and threw it on the fire; it sizzled. 'Why should I want to get rid of a perfectly good wench?'

'Huh! Good for some things.' His mother turned her back on him.

This was Eric's opinion, too. 'She must be very good at love.' He leaned in sly manner towards Ulf when the three were taking a midday break together. 'Wouldst Sigurd lend her to his old friend for a few days' entertainment?'

Though annoyed at his teasing, Sigurd was relieved that no one had guessed the truly embarrassing fact of the relationship: its celibate nature. A droll look upon his face, he replied to Eric's question, 'Your idea of entertaining a woman would be to organize a farting contest. You have not the vigour to cope with that one there.'

Una sat outside the thralls' hut grinding flour with a quernstone, knowing from their lascivious grins that the men were discussing her. She looked hard at Sigurd, trying to make him feel uncomfortable and succeeding. He was the first to look away. Damn her! She was an odd one.

'You speak of vigour – you, too, will need some for this wife your mother promises to bring you,' opined Eric.

Sigurd grimaced and drained his cup. 'I wish that she would leave me be. I am not ready for a wife yet.'

Ulf agreed. 'Nor I. 'Tis wiser to make use of slavewomen, for they do all your bidding and will not answer back.'

'And if only he could grow a pair of tits himself he would not need them at all,' mocked Eric.

Whilst the two bandied insults Sigurd had barely

taken his eyes off Una, watching those male hands grip the quernstone – what ecstasy to feel them gripped around his own throbbing flesh. He imagined their coolness on him . . . His buttocks clenched.

'But if your mother has her mind set on finding you a wife,' continued Ulf, 'I would give you good advice: you must dominate her from the start, show her who is master.'

A cry from the house caused Sigurd to laugh. 'The same way that you dominate my mother? Hark! The old she-wolf is calling to her cub.' He threw back his head and mimicked a wolf's howl. 'Oolf! Oolf! You had better run and see what she wants before she sinks her teeth into you.' Eric's belly shook as Ulf jumped to his feet with a growl.

'Your mother is worse than any wife! I am at her beck and call every moment of the day.'

'You must show her who is master, Ulf,' teased Sigurd and rubbed at his crotch.

'I shall!'

'Ulf – ah, there you are!' Ragnhild summoned him briskly. 'Did you not hear me calling? Come, if you have finished quaffing I will cut that hair of yours afore it sends you blind.' She went back into the house without waiting for response.

'Coming, Ragnhild!' Scowling at the others' laughter, Ulf was forced to obey.

'Oh, thou spake with real conviction, Ulf!' Pleased that Ulf's misfortune had detracted from his own, Sigurd proceeded to torment his friend when they met again an hour later. 'Well, didst show Ragnhild who is master?'

Ulf replied from beneath a savaged fringe. 'Ja – that is why I look like a monk!'

A scream of abuse emerged from the direction of the latrine. Both men looked up startled, then went back to their conversation, Ulf resuming his complaint. 'Those shears of hers are more murderous than any axe! I did not dare to move. Why should you escape?' He tugged at Sigurd's abundant mane.

The blond man laughed. 'She will have to catch me napping.'

Ulf's cavernous eyes took on a humorous glint. 'Mayhap that is what she intends to do. She has asked me to take her on a little trip.'

Sigurd's first reaction was to give Ulf a playful nudge. 'I think I have mistaken her fondness for you! Might I soon be calling you Father? Where goest the pair of you – on a love tryst?'

Ulf examined the sky. 'Mm, she would not tell. It is a secret.'

'A secret wedding!' But the joke froze on Sigurd's lips. 'Shite . . . I do believe she is going to find me a wife.' Rushing to the house, he accosted his mother, but her secrecy could not be pierced. He dithered whilst she, clad in her finest, ordered the thrall to load food onto a wagon – enough for a year, commented her son. 'And what have you in that bag?' From the way Ragnhild clutched it to her bosom when he mentioned it, the bag obviously contained valuables.

But he was not to see. 'Just a few bits and pieces!' Ragnhild slapped away his hand. 'Why the look of worry? Do you think I run away with your money?'

'Nei, nei! Just tell me where Ulf takes you.' The finery, the loaded wagon, the bag of valuables answered the question for him. 'You go to barter for a bride!'

Ragnhild looked smug. 'You shall find out when I return. Oolf! Time to go, my pretty one.'

'Mother, I told you I do not want . . .' Sigurd's objection was lost as the wagon pulled away.

'If I were you I would put Ragnhild's absence to good use.' Eric had limped up to stand behind him, rubbing his injured bottom. 'Let us invite some friends around for an ale-drinking contest. If this wife of yours is ought like Ragnhild then we must enjoy ourselves whilst we can.'

Sigurd was thinking once more of Una. 'I agree, but for me to enjoy myself does not involve the pursuits you have in mind.' He took Eric's arm. 'My friend, I would ask you a favour.' The other man immediately reached for his purse. 'Nei, 'tis not money. Whilst my mother is away, get you gone also. Visit your drinking cronies and sup yourself crazy. Go hunting, fishing . . . do what you will.'

'So long as I leave you in peace with your little goddess of love.' The black beard gaped in laughter.

Sigurd laughed too. 'You will do this for me?'

'Ja, of course! Am I not your dearest friend?'

'Nei.' Sigurd feigned bemusement.

Eric dealt a playful thump and repeated his earlier comment. 'She must surely be very good. After all this time are you not bored of tupping her? Come, do not be shy, tell me some of the things she does to you.'

Sigurd fielded the question and offered to give Eric two barrels of ale to take with him. The instant his friend limped off he himself went to the bathhouse, which was a stone-floored building where could be taken either steambaths or a warm tub. Today, he chose the latter.

Whilst he sat with the perfumed water lapping round his hips it struck him as ridiculous that he went to this trouble for one who had not bathed in months. In his pursuit of Una he had tried everything – threats, confrontation, he had even tried ignoring her – and now he fell upon his last resort: he would humble himself by taking her a gift. With his hair still dribbling down his back, he marched confidently to the slaves' hut where he found her alone, boiling up the dried roots of madder plants to obtain a red dye.

Una's hand paused over the cauldron as he entered.

189

Sigurd watched her anxious eyes flick towards the shadows where he now noticed the sleeping child. For the moment he tolerated the brat's presence; now that it was past drawing sustenance from that coveted breast, he did not resent it quite so much. 'Leave that. You will go and take a bath.'

'A bath!' Una could not stop the exclamation. The last proper bath she had taken was on her wedding night; did this herald a similiar consequence? Panic fluttered in her belly. 'The Lady Ragnhild, 'tis angry she'll be if I leave my work.'

'The lady is not here.' There was a significant gleam to his eye. 'Go now. I will return later.'

Leaving Murtagh asleep, Una wandered across to the bathhouse and plunged her body in the lukewarm water that Sigurd had used, having to admit to herself that it did feel good. Not daring to remain as long as she would have liked, she wrung out her hair, and stepped from the tub to dry herself. The master had left his own towel on the floor; it was damp but was still an unaccustomed luxury to Una. Redonning her filthy clothes, she went back to her duties. The master had apparently been waiting for her; she had barely knelt down at the cauldron when he returned, his own long hair still as damp as hers.

'I bring you this.' In the centre of his palm was a small crucifix from one of the Irish raids.

It appeared that at last the gods were on his side; her face mellowed and she actually smiled at him. Alas, due to the foibles of his mother, Sigurd found it hard to donate a gift graciously for fear that it would be reduced in value as it had so many times by Ragnhild – 'It is not as good as your father would have given, but never mind!' It had become his habit to make the receiver think they were doing him a favour by taking it off his hands. Hence in callow fashion he spoilt his chances now. 'You may have it, 'tis of no use to me. I was only going to take it to the silversmith to be melted down, but the size of it would hardly make it worth the trouble.'

Una's smile turned cynical. 'I don't need to ask what you expect in return – give me not baths and trinkets but milk for Murtagh!'

The blond Norseman upbraided her in his foreign, undulating speech. 'Vat is dis you call Murtagh?'

Una returned the fury. 'He has been here nigh eighteen months and ye don't even know his name! He is my son!'

With equal vehemence, he grabbed the crucifix, droplets of water from his hair pattering on to her sleeve. 'You do not want it? That is fine! What does it matter to me?' And he flung it on the fire and stalked off, leaving her to gaze in regret at the embers.

Simultaneously, Murtagh woke and began to grizzle. Torn two ways, Una chose her child, lifting him from his bed of rags to pacify him. Whilst she delivered her reassuring cuddle, Black Mary entered.

'Hm, gone at last, has he? Sure, I dursn't come in lest he's waving his jiggling bone around.'

Una was cool. 'Stop all that dirty talk in front of Murtagh.'

'Oh, so pure now!' Black Mary gave a bitter laugh. 'And after what the poor wee fellow has just been forced to watch.'

'There was nought to see!'

Mary eyed Una's wet hair in disbelief. 'He gives baths to all his slaves, does he?' She diverted her amusement to another matter for a moment. 'Hah! Did ye hear the yell? Fat Eric found your thorn. Sure, I hope it ripped him to pieces.' Then she gave her attention to the crying child and took him from his mother. 'My poor wee darling! Come to the one that loves ye best.' Murtagh went happily to her embrace. 'Did that lustful wretch come and make ye cry?'

Watching the immediate cessation of tears, Una felt a twinge of spite towards her child and went back to mixing the dye. Black Mary was acting now as if she and the boy were alone, nuzzling and cooing at him. 'Will my wee one come plant some seeds in the garth with his aunt? Or have ye watched enough seed-planting in here?'

Una scolded again, but Mary had words only for her nephew. 'Away with me then, Murty-wurty.' The black-haired child locked puny arms round her neck and the pair went out into the March sun.

The moment she was alone, Una grabbed a stick and raked frantically amongst the embers, but the tiny crucifix was lost. Angry both at this and the usurpation of her child, she collapsed into a defeated squat, head in hands. When she looked up again it was to see that her master had returned.

'Why are you so like a mule?' mumbled the youth from the doorway. 'I feed you well, do I not?'

With his back to the light it was difficult for Una to see his expression, but the mood of self-pity was evident. 'Well enough.'

'And I do not beat you.'

Una pretended that the dye needed attention and bobbed down beside the cauldron. 'It matters not. I am still the thrall and you the master.'

Sigurd bounded in to chastise. 'No man would think so! You have made me the fool amongst everyone. My mother tells me I should sell you.' He drew compensation from the look that flickered in her eyes. 'You would not like that, I think?'

Una proceeded to stir, but glanced up at him. 'I would not.'

Her honesty encouraged him, converting his bombastic approach to one that was almost pleading. 'Then what would you really like? You may speak as freely as you wish for the moment.'

Una could have laughed. 'And that's the nub! I do not wish to speak freely just for this moment, but forever and ay.'

Sigurd readopted his demanding tone. 'You want that I should make an ass of myself in front of everyone just so that I might lie with you, when I could do that any time I like? You think you are that special?'

Una turned sullen, paying all her attention to the dye now, mixing and stirring. ''Tis not I who ask ye to lie in my bed, *finn-gall*. All I desire is my freedom.'

'All! You ask a great deal.' After the burst of thunder, Sigurd prevaricated, watching her red-stained fingers do their work. 'If I freed you . . . then you would come to me willingly?'

Una suppressed the excitement that rose in her breast. 'If you also free my child.'

Her master's response was sardonic. 'Your child? You mean the one gotten by the man you profess to have hated? What is this bairn to you?' Jealousy began to gnaw again.

The stick paused in its rotation, Una's face wistful. 'Before he was born I thought I'd hate him too . . . but I don't. He is the most precious thing in the world to me. I could never accept my freedom and abandon him to slavery.'

Sigurd burst into laughter that had a tinge of resentment at this 'precious' child. 'I see where this leads us! If I agree to free the two of you, then you will say "but you must also free Mary, for I could not go without her . . ." and so on and so forth until I had no slaves left at all.'

Una shook her head, partly in wonder that he could be so unobservant of the animosity between the two women. ''Tis for you to do what ye choose with the others.'

'It is most kind of you to grant me this!' Sigurd bent from the waist to bring his head closer to her squatting figure. 'Well, let me tell you that it is for me to do as I choose with any of you!' Her rash admittance of love for the child had provided him

193

with new grist. 'And now it is my turn to barter.' His fingers picked the wet hair from her cheeks and tucked it behind her ear so that she might better heed him. 'If you do not yield then I will sell your son and you shall never hold him again. What have you to say on that?'

Her plan scuttled, Una gulped and fixed her eyes to the bubbling dye. Oh, the devil! How could she have hoped to bargain with such a one? Tapping the stick against the cauldron to remove the drips of red, she laid it aside, pulse racing. 'I cannot stop ye.'

'That is right!' Elevated now, he nodded down at her.

Mouth dry, Una raised her body in sacrificial pose. 'Then I pray ye, master, take what ye want and get it over with.'

'I do not want it that way!' Sigurd gave a violent kick at the door, plunging the hovel into darkness but for the firelight. At the slamming of the flimsy piece of wattle, Mary looked up from tending the earth, her nostrils pinched in disgust. Inside, Sigurd took hold of the girl and shook her. 'Look at me! Even in defeat you rule me! What is wrong with me, woman? Am I so ugly? Why cannot you even call me by my name, Sigurd?'

Una was moved by his emotion but would not give in, saying calmly, 'I call ye by the name you've taught me, Master. I submit to ye. What more can you ask?'

'I ask that you love me!'

'By force?'

'Nei!' Sigurd shook his head with the hasty reply. 'I retract what I said about the brat. I promise I will never sell him.'

Still, this was not enough for Una. 'Will ye free him?'

'Ja, ja!' His lower half was now a-blaze.

'You lie, master.' What had dared her to say it!

Frustration made him bellow at her, 'Ja, I lie! I

shall not free him because if I did I would have to free his mother and then she would leave me!' He bent his knees in order to bring his face level, squashed her cheeks between his palms. 'Una,' he crooned her name, 'doest not know I love thee?' Passion seethed in eye and loin, his whole body engorged with blood. Whilst Una trembled he slid his fingers up into her hair and dragged her skull towards his mouth, leaving her just time to catch her breath before his mouth pressed down on hers.

Una hated her body for the way it responded to his kiss, hated the way her arms held him when she told them not to, hated the way her belly thrilled and her groin pressed itself eagerly at his . . . Such irony that she who had never known desire now found it in her captor.

Sigurd had imagined her body through her clothes. Unbound, her breasts were heavier than he had assumed. Excited, he fell on them, crushing his face between them, rubbing his mouth and tongue around their globes. Una's head fell back, eyes half-closed, palms on either side of his head, raking her fingers through his hair, pressing down onto his shoulders, sweeping the muscles of his back, pulling him closer, bringing her head forward now to lay against his moist perfumed skin. *Why do you let him treat you like this, running his hands over you as if he is buying a horse?* She wrenched herself away to confront him with anger, breathing heavily.

Sigurd withdrew his fervid lips only to pant, 'Do not stop, oh mercy, do not stop me,' then pressed them back into the curve of her neck to suck and nibble. Una shivered and gave up all resistance as his face moved around her body. There were no rough bristles as there had been on her husband's jaw, just a soft, youthful beard. Oh, that such a cruel mouth could glide so tenderly on her skin . . .

Then, what little control he might have had vanished

and so did Una's. He writhed and squirmed and ground himself right up into her whilst his mouth bit and kissed and ate her and Una moaned and locked her heels around his back, shouted arousal into his hair, tried to get closer and closer to stop him slipping out of her for his movements had become so frantic, clung and kissed and plunged together, two gripping beasts . . .

Sigurd gave one almighty heave, she heaved with him, he left her, came back, filled her with his seed, Una arched in one last gigantic thrust of passion, lifting his body . . . then fell back. Both sore and soothed, their panting bodies cleaved together, rising, falling with each breath till passion waned to sweat-drenched languor and neither one was slave nor master but both were one.

Without disengagement of their union, merely a short rest, Sigurd began to move again, less hurriedly this time. He hoisted his body onto his elbows and tried to read her face while his belly caressed her. Una lay beneath him, limbs spreadeagled. No longer did her arms embrace him. Sigurd paused, looked into her eyes. 'You have grown bored of me already?'

With languid murmur, she draped her wrists around his back. 'You are so lusty ye've sapped me of strength.'

He made a joke. 'Ah, this is so you can get out of work afterwards.' When she laughed, he told her, 'Then hang onto me and I will do all the work.' He scooped his arms beneath her, buried his face in her hair and began to glide towards another climax.

And afterwards he proved to her by shows of tenderness that his words of love had not been simply to deceive, touched gentle lips upon her shoulder, eased wisps of hair from brow and neck, adorning each with kisses, laid his palm upon her chest to feel each rib, traced gentle fingertips around a breast, raising goosebumps. Una shivered. Thinking she was cold, he reached around their bodies seeking the ends of his cloak which he tugged up to cover both of them. Abruptly, she started to cry.

Sigurd beheld the display with mild horror. 'Do you hate me so much?'

She hid her face. 'I do not hate you at all, that is why I weep!'

He laughed his gratitude and snuggled his belly into her side.

God, I should hate him, she agonized. Why don't I? Her tear-stained face warned him, 'I must not lie like this all day.'

He grinned, licked the salt from her cheek and massaged her shin with his foot. 'Why, will your master beat you?'

Plunged back to loathsome earth, she did not return the humour. 'There are other slaves who live here, and it will make life very difficult for me if they find us like this.'

Oh, we will make life difficult for you, whore. Black Mary took her ear from the chink in the timbers and hurried to intercept Murtagh, who was eating soil. *You can be sure of that.*

Chapter Nine

Hunting, carving, swimming, carousing – all took second place to that which he had found with Una. Dawn saw him loitering once more at her threshold. Any fears of wrecked fantasies had been dispelled; love with her was as marvellous as he had imagined – better. Even when his body was apart from Una his mind was inside her; he loved her thirty, forty, fifty times a day! Only one hurdle remained: even those two days of intimacy could not persuade her to react to him as a lover. She lay there now, smiling yes, but as distant as ever.

After enjoying a sensual moment or two, he fell on to his back and muttered rebuke. 'You do not touch me.'

Previously engaged in thought, Una wore a look of confusion, then brought a palm up to his chest, avoiding the heathen amulet that dangled there. 'I touch ye now.'

Looking down at those almost male hands against his body, he received a weird thrill. Swallowing his passion, he murmured, 'I did not mean there.'

Offence withdrew her fingers, remembering how Eoghan would force her hand between his legs. She could never touch the neck of a plucked goose but that she thought of him. ''Tis not right!'

He turned his head and kissed her shoulder. 'Not right for lovers to touch?'

'You are not my lover but my master.'

'Oh fie! I thought that we had dealt with all that.'

Una turned on to her side to entreat him. 'If you free us I swear, I swear we'll not leave. How could we when I have no barter?'

'No barter save your body.' Sigurd was not to be duped. 'Methinks you use me.'

She became wheedling, appealing to his status. 'Would my lord not rather make love to a free woman?'

'The instant you were free you would go back from whence you came, by whatever method.' In one quick jerk he was sitting in a posture of aggression.

Una's eyes picked out the muscles on his naked back for a while, as confused in her emotions as Sigurd was about his own. In two days she had received more tenderness from this savage than from a whole year with Eoghan. She did have feeling for him, but how could it be termed love when this man had robbed her of everything, including liberty? Was it just the sense of danger that produced this thrill? One moment he could be so fond, yet Una knew he was capable of great violence. Despite his oaths of love she could never be quite sure . . .

Her locks had wrapped themselves around her arms. Disentangling herself, she rose to her knees, put her hands over his shoulders and began to pick the blond hair from his face, combing it behind his neck and gathering it into a pony's tail. Holding it thus, she kissed his nape and pushed her breasts into his shoulder-blades, her left hand sneaking under his arm, round his waist and pressing itself into his belly. Sigurd closed his eyes to her ministrations, leaning back on the cushion of her mounds. Her warm breath whispered Irish endearments in his ear. He made a noise of pleasure in his throat and rubbed the back of his head against her shoulder. 'I sit here tame as a hound whilst you may call me all the loathsome names you can think of.'

'I call you only loved one.' Was it just to trick her

master that she said it? Una did not know. Perhaps the deception was working too well.

'I shall have to believe you, for I love you also.' A large hand came up to stroke her hair and in doing so caught her nose with an elbow.

She laughed, 'Indeed, 'tis only a lover would break a girl's nose,' and forgave him with a kiss.

'You must teach me this tongue of yours so that I might know if the others plot against me.'

Una moved her chin on his shoulder. ''Twill be hard for a Norseman to master.'

He gave a playful jerk of his shoulder, clattering her teeth together. 'This Norseman can master ought.'

'Ye think so?' Una's hands became teasing; fingers crept down his belly then fluttered away just as he expected touch. He growled. Una laughed and tickled him again. Sigurd drew his knees up, pinning the tormenting hand between his belly and thigh. Letting go of his hair she used her free hand to grope under his buttocks.

'Ow! Take care, wench.' He sucked in his breath.

'Did ye not want me to touch ye!' Una gave a lilting laugh. '*Begged* me.'

In a trice she was on her back and being tickled to the point of hysteria. They rolled around like puppies, biting and grasping any appendage that came into reach, ending in tears of laughter. Their union was rudely broken by the jingle of harness from the yard. Sigurd groaned into her chest. 'The Lady Ragnhild returns. I am to be robbed of my pleasure so soon.' Already he could hear his name being called.

Outside, Eric was trying to protect his young friend. 'Er, Ragnhild, will you not come into the house and taste this fruit wine? It is very good.'

She looked inside the house then shoved the dark-haired obstacle aside. 'Out of my way, pisspot! I can tell without tasting it that it's good, just by looking at your face. Now, where is that son of mine? Sigurd!'

200

Eric collared Ulf, hissing, 'He's in there with the slavegirl! Try to divert Ragnhild.'

Ulf refused. 'I owe that little bastard a favour for his disrespect. Ragnhild – he is in there!' He wagged a finger at the slave hut.

Una heard the woman's approach and threw the tattooed dragon off her waist. 'Do not let her catch us, I beg you!'

Sigurd was undaunted, but released her body from his, reaching between his shoulder-blades to brush off irritating fragments of refuse from contact with the floor.

Una showed more expedience, grabbing her clothes, but before either had the chance to dress they were framed in a shaft of light.

Ragnhild stood in the doorway with a wise nodding of head. 'Did I not guess I would find you here?' There was a disgusted interval during which Sigurd awaited more rebuke; it came beneath a thin veil of sarcasm. 'If you intend to keep the wench from her work could you perchance lay some grain beneath her back so that we might at least have benefit of flour from your grindings? Come! I have matters of import to discuss – and you!' She jabbed a thumb at Una. 'To work. We have much to prepare.'

'Prepare for what?' Sigurd hopped into his breeches.

'For your wedding.' Ragnhild enjoyed the jolt it gave them both. 'That is what I have been doing these past days, negotiating your bonding settlements – and a task it was, too. I had to promise all manner of things. No matter, you shall consider all well worth it when you see her.' She turned and went outside.

An anguished Una turned to Sigurd, but the attentive lover had vanished. 'Mother!' Blind to Una's distress, he grabbed his shirt and with his other hand grasping the waistband of his breeches, followed Ragnhild. The sun's warmth had lured the honey bees out to look for water. Clumsy from its winter idleness one of the black creatures hummed around Sigurd's ear; a testy hand swiped it.

'She is absolutely beautiful!' laughed his mother in glee. 'And her family very wealthy.' Both these things had been important factors, but Ragnhild also liked the girl's persona; she looked strong, and Sigurd needed a strong wife.

'Did you have to announce it thus?' Voice waspish, Sigurd gripped the shirt under his chin whilst fumbling for the belt of his trousers.

'Why so?' Ragnhild began to walk towards the big house.

'Because . . . because I would like a say in the type of woman I wed before you have told it to the world!'

'Nonsense!' The beekeeper was knelt preparing a new skep in which to rear this year's swarm; instead of walking round him Ragnhild kicked him out of the way. 'You have no idea of what makes a good wife, you are too busy nosing around that Irish slut. Well, wait until the morrow and you will praise my wisdom.'

'Tomorrow!' Sigurd tugged the belt through its buckle.

'Ja!' Ragnhild stopped, whipped the shirt from under his chin and gave it a flourish before draping it over his head. 'That is why we must make haste. Oh, not for the wedding.' She laughed as his panicked face emerged through the neck of the garment and helped him to insert his arms as if he were still a baby. 'Tomorrow is just for Estorhild and her family to come and meet you, but we must waste no time in arranging the union. When you see her I know you will agree.'

Contrary to his dislike of being manipulated, Sigurd did agree: he could not help but do so. Only a fool would throw away the chance of attaining such a breathtaking wife. Estorhild was sixteen. Topped by a silken snood, her hair fell to her waist and was so blonde as to be almost white. Every feature of her face was perfect, her complexion clear and healthy. She had tiny hands and feet but the rest of her body looked stout enough to accomplish a wife's daily tasks. She was high-breasted, elegant of limb and sleek of hip. 'Mannish hips,' Ragnhild had termed them, her only cause for concern – they might spell trouble in childbirth – but if this was her only quibble then it was a job well done. Estorhild's family was of Anglo-Norse descent, very well-placed in society, owning several ploughlands in the North Riding of Eoforwicshire, and from the manner in which her parents addressed Sigurd they must be equally pleased with him.

Fighting shyness, Estorhild inched forth to meet her prospective husband. In movement she lost a little of her grace, rolling from side to side like a peasant woman, but it was not a thing Sigurd would notice when his current female waddled like a duck, thought Ragnhild, and was delighted by the way her son looked upon her choice. It had not been so difficult to take his mind from the slave. The other men present were equally impressed. Everyone, including the slaves, had been assembled in the yard to greet the bride and her entourage. Estorhild felt like a cow being offered for sale under the examining eye of the groom's friends and decided she did not care for them. The one with the heavy fringe looked surly whilst his shaggy black partner was almost licking his lips.

'Where did my lady find such a beauty?' Eric murmured. 'And can she find one for me?'

'I am glad you are at last considering taking a wife,' said a prim Ragnhild, leading him and Ulf aside, 'for you will need one to run this new house of yours.'

The black eyebrows descended. 'What house?'

'Ja, *what* house!' Ragnhild speared him with a direct gaze. 'Didst I not warn you that when my son was wed you would have to leave? I see no expedience in your pose.'

'Er, we had not forgotten.' Eric spoke for both himself and Ulf. 'Indeed, we were discussing it only the other day . . .'

'Discussion does not build houses!'

'We begin tomorrow, dear widow. Ulf, who is a confirmed bachelor, shall live with me and my wife, when I find one, and we shall share the work.'

Ragnhild laughed to show her opinion of this arrangement.

Eric sighed. 'But my quest for a bride has been fruitless so far.'

'It surprises me not.' Ragnhild poked the fat belly. 'Any candidate would first have to be divested of her nose.'

'So, as I said before . . . ' Eric made a flourish at Sigurd's betrothed.

'I shall find you one,' vouched Ragnhild. 'But do not expect miracles.'

'I realize that you must have had to travel far and wide to find one such as Estorhild,' granted Eric.

'In truth, not far at all.' Ragnhild's search had not been totally at random. She had made enquiries beforehand as to where eligible maids might be found, and Estorhild came from a township not far from the Jorvik boundary. 'But I fear I may have to travel many a mile to find a girl willing to partner one so ugly.'

'Such thoughtfulness is touching,' muttered Eric.

But Ragnhild had turned her attention to Ulf, encircling the rangy body with a crushing arm. 'And is my other fine son positive that I cannot do him similar favour?'

Ulf cringed; throughout the hunt for Sigurd's bride Ragnhild had tried to coerce him into matrimony too. He was half glad that he would be leaving soon; such attention could oft be tiresome. But one could not

204

thump a woman and Ulf had to rely on curtness to make his point. 'I thank you, Ragnhild, nei.'

'Oh, he thinks too much of his foster-mother to share his little bag of sweetmeats with another!' Ragnhild's hand swooped between his buttocks making him jump on tiptoe, much to the amusement of Eric who doubled over. 'Methinks I shall miss you too . . . but hold! There is no need for both of you to go. You, Ulf, could remain with . . .'

Hands protecting genitals, Ulf cut in hastily, 'That would be unfair to Estorhild! See the way she beholds my friend, they should be given the chance to be alone together.'

'But they will not be alone. Shall I myself not still be living here?' Ragnhild made a final attempt to coax, then gave up and looked at Estorhild. 'I have to agree that she does find my son acceptable – and who indeed would not?'

Another viewed the introduction with less enthusiasm. Every cell of Una's body felt dead. Her arms hung loose at her sides as if attached with heavy weights. Her eyelids drooped, but she could not tear her eyes from her rival. Without looking down she bent to the child who tugged at her skirt and sat him astride her hip, still watching. But Sigurd did not look at her, his mind too full of other things – *cannot take his eyes away from the white-haired beauty*. Why? Why had he pestered and coaxed and begged all those months if now she was to be so easily discarded? *Because he has had what he wanted*, her mind answered. *You gave in to him; you do not excite him any more. Now you will never be free.*

Black Mary edged up to gloat. 'Ah dear, look at him,' she sighed. 'Smitten indeed – an' can ye blame him? There's not a woman around here to compare with that maid.' Damage inflicted, she minced away.

Una tightened her jaw and put a hand under

205

Murtagh's dress to rub the apple-like buttocks, reminding herself of more important bonds. 'What do we care for him?' She kissed the child's dark head and swayed her body, while Murtagh played with the thong at her neck and laughed as if he saw the lie.

The guests stayed overnight and left the following afternoon, by which time an agreement had been sealed: the wedding was planned for November when the harvest would be in and the beasts killed for the winter. Unprompted, Sigurd was glad to offer a hefty bride-price for the privilege of welding his own family to another so rich, and Estorhild in turn would bring with her a substantial dowry.

Putting the last hours of daylight to good use, Una was working in a quiet corner of the garth when Sigurd appeared as if no interval had occurred in his love affair.

There was no sweet greeting from Una who used her hoe to such violence that she dislodged plants as well as weeds. 'I cannot believe that ye stand here as if nought has happened!'

Sigurd beheld her with confusion as plant after plant fell to her anger. 'But . . . nought has happened. I still feel the same way about you as I did yesterday.'

'You were not with me yesterday! You were with herself!'

'Estorhild? So I make arrangements for wedlock, what has that to do with us?'

Una's reply verged on a scream. 'You could not take your eyes from her!'

He had the audacity to laugh. 'But naturally! You saw her too, did you not? Such a beauty – hold! Where do you go?' Una had thrown down her implement and was now tearing across the enclosure. The beanstalk legs ran after her and caught her at the gate.

She turned on him. 'Fret you not! I make no bid for freedom, I'm off to fetch the kine from the green.'

Still he clung on to her. Una's blue eyes were hard. 'Will ye let me go, master?'

Snorting, he dropped her hand and watched her march over the duckboard that bridged the muddy road and on to the grass that formed the nucleus of Peseholme. Equally irate now, he followed her, overtook her and instead of laying himself open to the prying observations of neighbours he dragged her under a group of gnarled oaks. 'You think that because I have found a wife it means I do not love you?'

Una fought to dismantle his grip. 'I'd like to know what else it can mean!'

Sigurd pushed her up against the trunk of a tree with his body. 'Feel! Feel how I want you!'

Assaulted from both behind and in front, she wriggled. 'Only until your bride comes!'

'Oh foolish woman!' His blond hair took off in all directions. 'You think because she is so fair that I will scorn you? She is a beauty, ja, but I prize her no more than I would one of those horses which the Arabs breed.'

Pinioned by greater strength, Una's resistance waned into feminine tears. 'Ye make such a fine couple,' she replied in a small voice.

'So do you and I.' Sigurd took her tears between his lips, attempted to make love to her, but again she wriggled.

'There is a difference! Estorhild will be the one who sits beside your fire, who sleeps in your bed, who has your children! The one whom you converse with. You are not truly interested in me.' Sobbing, she glared into his face. 'Only the games that you can play upon my body.'

'You malign me!' Sigurd frowned, but ceased his groping.

'I speak the truth! Ye never ask me of my life in Corcaig, who my father and mother were, do I have

207

brothers, sisters, uncles, do I like to sing, do I dance
– you never talk to me as ye would your wife, as if
ye really loved me!'

He backed off, subdued, and looked across the
green to where some thatchers worked on a neighbour's roof. 'The reason I do not ask you these things
is because I do not wish to hear about your life in
Ireland . . .' Regressing into boyhood, he wound a
lock of blond hair round his finger. 'I fear that you
yearn to be back there with those you love better
than me.' He fell quiet, then gave a small laugh.
When Una looked angry again he explained, 'I do
not laugh at you: one of the thatchers has just fallen
from the roof and is dangling from a beam by his
fingernails.'

Una craned a look, but felt unable to smile at the
man's misfortune.

Sigurd unloosed the hair from his finger and returned to her with more kindly approach. 'You wouldst
not want me to speak of Estorhild when I am making
love to you, and neither do I wish to hear of other
lives. If you would talk then there is much else that
we can say to each other. I know enough about you,
I do not need to ask.' He breathed seduction in her
ear. 'Let me love you, Una. I will even give you milk
instead of whey for that brat of yours.'

Subservience and longing conspired against her.
When he led she followed meekly. Until November
he was hers alone.

The clemency of autumn spelt a glorious wedding
feast. Rubicund forest yielded stag and wild boar, the
Use teemed with pike and roach and trout, branches
hung low neath the weight of apples, plums, black-
berries, raspberries, the hives dripped with honey, the
stores bulged with wheat, rye, barley and oats, and
there was good German wine to be had from the
ships. All of these, plus a roast swan as centrepiece,

were displayed to great effect in the living-hall where the panpipes trilled merry and the folk of Jorvik danced in bright array.

A few weeks earlier, Sigurd had despatched an invitation to the King, partly to impress his mother. Ulf thought him mad, 'He will never come! He has too much to concern him at court.'

'You mean Thorkell?' News had filtered up from the south that Thorkell the Tall had been outlawed.

'Ja.' Ulf's watery blue eye held a glint of warning. 'That is what comes of being over-ambitious.'

Sigurd disagreed. 'A man can never be too ambitious. Look at Godwin.'

'Ah, I see.' Ulf nodded. 'You think that an invitation to your wedding will encourage the King to grant you Thorkell's old position.'

'And what is wrong with that?' asked Sigurd. 'A man must grasp each chance as it comes – which puts me in mind of something that I meant to ask. Now that I am to take a wife, I shall have less time to run my estate: how wouldst you like to be my reeve?'

'Nei!' Ulf backed off as if presented with some horrible task. 'Nei, ask Eric.'

Sigurd laughed down his nose. 'Are you mad! He would believe every sad tale that my tenants would try in order not to pay their dues. He is so generous he would probably pay them to live upon my land and have us ruined in a twelvemonth. Nei, you are as my brother and I wish you to accept the honour.'

'I am unworthy! It is beyond my capabilities.'

Sigurd argued, 'But you have ridden around with me for four years helping to run the place . . .'

'Nei, nei!' Ulf was adamant. 'I have the land you gave me and that is enough responsibility. You may crave the stars but I do not.'

Sigurd looked displeased. 'I would prefer it to go to one I can trust, but if you do not want it . . .'

Ulf realized he had insulted his friend and put a

hand to the taller man's shoulder. 'Sig, I am honoured, but it is not for me. I am a simple man.'

The young lord nodded his understanding. 'Then you will not wish to sit beside the King at my wedding?' He grinned now.

Ulf looked pessimistic. 'My friend, I fear that you will be disappointed.'

Sigurd's confidence was unshaken. 'The King shall come.'

Looking around the hall now he regretted his over-optimism. The King had deigned neither to attend his wedding nor grant him favour. Godwin had taken over Thorkell's privileged rank. However, Cnut had sent his regrets plus a valuable gift, allowing Sigurd to keep face with his neighbours, and the reception did not lack its distinguished guests: the presence of Jarl Eirik of Northumbria was enough to illustrate Sigurd's esteem, and placate his mother over the King's non-appearance.

Ragnhild was seated on the groom's left, her mood at odds with the gay occasion. Invariably, she felt nervous at any large gathering, a legacy of the massacre nineteen years ago. Tapping his foot to the music, Sigurd leaned over the arm of his settle to ask if she were happy. 'This brings back memories, ja, Mother?'

A fraction of her abstract gaze remained. 'It is a wonderful wedding, my son. Ja, wonderful.' She appeared to come to her senses then. 'Of course, it cannot compare with the feasts we had in your father's day. Oh, they were gigantic!' Sigurd gave a false laugh and wondered if he would ever live up to his father's memory. To compensate, he renewed examination of the bride who shared his seat. Her hair had been combed back to display her face and was tied in a knot at the nape from where it hung freely, intermingled with ribbons. The style drew his attention to something he had not spotted on the earlier meeting – her jaw was very square; he hoped it did not spell obstinacy. No matter, her husband would tame her.

Husband! He congratulated himself on the title, admiring Estorhild's garb – a silken cap, trailing robe edged with golden braid, the ubiquitous shoulder-brooches linked with festoons of silver chains, a long flowing cloak pinned with another golden brooch and flung back over her shoulders.

His overt gaze upon her breasts unnerved her. To look away provided no comfort. If she looked across the hearth at the jarl in his place of honour between the richly-carved pillars that held the roof, she found him staring back. If she looked along the rows of benches, there too she found ogling males. One of them had made an awful stink.

Unable to reach Eric with his foot, Sigurd threw him a rebuking glare – what if Estorhild thought he was responsible? It was all very well for the black one, who had been first of the friends to marry and now lived on his own land with his bride of two months and Ulf; all three were here for the wedding. Ragnhild's choice was poles apart from today's beauteous bride, though more handsome than the ugly Eric had a right to expect. She had already, during their short partnership, managed to curtail his over-generosity towards strangers and his shyness of work – if not his foul habits. Sigurd wondered how she could bear to sleep with him, then turned his eyes back to more lovely features.

Estorhild blushed and fluttered a quick glance, her voice and attitude girlish. 'I beg you, husband, do not stare so!'

Upon realizing what he had been doing, he smiled. 'I crave my lady wife's pardon. After the summer's absence I feared that my memory of your beauty might be false, but on second meeting I find you even more desirable.'

211

Estorhild's flush was born not just from his close-
ness but from empathy with the uttered sentiment.
Throughout the summer she too had wondered if he
could possibly be as splendid as she had thought at
their first meeting. How could one pine so fervently
for a man one had met only once? But Estorhild had,
and could not have been more avid of the choice of
husband had she made it for herself. Though shy,
she had been well instructed in social intercourse and
now paid graceful thanks to his compliment. 'If I
may make so bold, my lord is in fine fettle himself.'
Sigurd's apparel was of equal richness to her own,
adorned with bells and bangles; he wore pendulous
rings in his ears, new shoes of calfskin with the hair
left on for warmth, and looked more noble than the
jarl.

'So you will not balk at sharing my bed this eve?'
He covered her hand, uttered an emollient laugh, then
in crafty manner lifted his goblet in toast to the priest
who had officiated. *You pious lick-trencher! I saw
your eyes upon my wife whilst you spouted the words
of your Lord Almighty.* Caught out, the priest gave a
lecherous nod and stuffed his mouth full of cake.

Waiting by to serve the rowdy guests, Una damned
her lover, challenged him. *Look not at her but over
here at the one who holds your seed still damp between
her legs!* But he did not notice her, or did not want
to, last night's passion vanished from his mind.

Black Mary nudged Una from her thoughts. 'The
groom calls out for bridal ale.' When Una glared at
her, she donned surprise. 'Are ye not always keen to
do your master's bidding?'

Resentment burning in her breast, Una went to
serve the couple with the ceremonial ale, a bonding
ritual of the Norsefolk that had long preceded Christianity, though Una was unaware of the heathen
implications. She stood before the table and leaned
across to pour.

212

Sigurd was forced to look at her then. Their eyes met briefly as he held his cup neath the flow from her pitcher. His face showed not one jot of emotion. Throughout the junketing and dancing, the oratories from Ulf and Eric and other friends, he did not look at her again.

It took no supernatural vision to inform Una that she would be the one called upon to prepare the bride for the marriage bed. Whether Black Mary had volunteered her name or whether 'twas a cruel jest by the Lady Ragnhild – who loathed her son's concubine – it did not really matter. It was as gross a humiliation as could be heaped upon her. Una swore never to forgive Sigurd for allowing it.

Disrobed by the thralls, Estorhild stood in her fine woollen undergarments, totally naive to the identity of the one combing her hair. Black Mary shook the creases from her lady's marriage gown and folded it away in a chest, enjoying every minute of her sister-in-law's downfall. Una raked an antler comb through the blonde waves, came to a knot and vented her spleen.

'Agh! You are too rough.' Estorhild turned sharply and cuffed the slave. 'Change places or I shall be bald before I meet my husband.'

Stupid wee girlie, Una raged inside but, passionless of feature, she handed the long-toothed comb to her sister-in-law who caressed the golden tresses so gently that Estorhild shut her eyes and mouthed pleasure. So soothing was Mary's comb, it induced confidence from the recipient. 'Oh, that helps to quiet my breast . . . I feel as if I have a sparrow in there. I know so little of my husband.'

'Nor I, my lady.' Black Mary passed a crafty look at Una over her lady's shoulder. 'Mayhap Una can tell ye more.'

Unwitting to the look that passed between the

slaves, Estorhild was eager for information. 'You have been with your master a long time?'

'Two years, my lady.' Eyes averted, Una lifted a pitcher and filled a bowl with warm water.

'And he is a kind master to you?'

Una's nostrils flared. 'As kind as a master can be.'

Estorhild was ignorant of the double meaning and met the comment with approval. 'Then if he is kind to slaves he will surely be kind to his wife.'

Black Mary's comb whispered ever so lightly upon her scalp. 'With hair as beautiful as yours, my lady, the master cannot fail to love ye.'

Una poised with the bowl, aching to tip it over her rival. 'May it please my lady?'

'Yea, but be as gentle as your friend.' Estorhild allowed Una to sponge her which she did without incurring another blow. The three years between their ages could have been trebled, for Estorhild was as a child beside one who had suffered like Una.

Mary was bent on persecution. 'Should ye want to know what your wedding holds for ye, milady, Una is gifted in the runes.'

Una passed her a murderous look, but their mistress gave haughty reply. 'I have no use for such heathen practise. It is unwise to know the future.' But whilst the thrall continued to sponge her body, Estorhild wished that she did know what lay ahead.

When it was done, the bride looked nervously at the attendants and took a deep breath. 'You may go tell them I am ready.'

With Una encumbered by the bowl and towels, her assistant put aside the comb and beat her to the door. 'I will go, my lady!' It was not an act of pity: if Una was allowed to leave the room she could slip away and avoid the final ceremony. Black Mary wanted her to sup her poisoned chalice to the dregs.

There was no need to go far to deliver the message. Hardly was the door closed on Black Mary than it

214

burst open again to admit a noisy host of revellers who hauled a disrobed bryd-guma at their midst, and oh so joyful did he look. Una attempted to creep around the bawdy throng but one of its number almost elbowed the bowl of water from her hands, forcing her to step back. Estorhild, flushed and virginal, was tugged not unwillingly to lie upon the marriage bed, whence a laughing Sigurd, wearing only his dragons, tumbled in beside her.

Una was compelled to stand amongst her fellow witnesses and watch the body she loved lie upon foreign territory. *And he does not even see me.*

But he did. 'Twas Sigurd, not discretion, who bade the merry crowd withdraw before the maidenhead was pierced, turning an ale-happy face upon the watchers and crying, 'Be gone!' so that those Irish eyes might be spared. Content at doling out this act of mercy, he turned about and performed different service on his wife, whilst his pathetic little concubine vilified him in her thoughts and told him that he would do greater kindness by poking out her eyes.

The sun rose unseen through autumn mist. Sigurd woke from habit and prepared his body to leave its comfortable bed . . . his marriage bed. He turned to examine Estorhild's sleeping face, but the room was too dark and he looked away to pick at his eyelashes.

Her drowsy voice emerged from beneath the eiderdown. 'I hope I did not wake you? I have laid here all night unable to sleep.'

'Forgive me.' Sigurd rolled over and took her in his arms. 'I am told I make noises like a pig.'

She kissed his shoulder. ''Twas not you but excitement which churns my breast. You made no sound.'

'That is a relief. I always knew that Ulf lied. When we shared a bed together in our fighting days he would complain that I woke him whilst it was still night.'

'You must have been dreaming of your fighting days just now, before waking.' Estorhild nuzzled him, voice loving. 'You leapt about as though in battle.'

'Did I speak?' He tensed, but his young wife was not yet familiar enough to notice.

'Nay.' She patted him, then smoothed her hand over his chest and pushed her body into his.

Sigurd threw the eiderdown aside and put one foot to the floor. 'Well . . . there is work a-waiting.'

Estorhild uttered disbelief. 'Work – when we are just wed?'

'There is still an estate to be run. I shall only be gone until breakfast, then the celebration shall proceed.' The feasting would probably continue for days.

The girlish voice invited, half-bashful, half-provocative: 'If you want me I am willing.'

She had felt his erection and assumed it was for her. Did he tell her that he woke with this bull's horn even when he slept alone? Nei. Pulling the covers back over himself, he put it to good use.

Afterwards, he left her without a backwards glance. Estorhild dressed and opened the window shutters, but did not leave the bed-closet, troubled over what she could have done wrong between last night and this morning – Sigurd had been almost cool towards her. Hence the reason that when Ragnhild came looking for her daughter-in-law it was to find her weeping.

'What is this? You have wedding guests who wait in the great hall to be entertained. Where is your husband?'

'I am afraid I have displeased him!' sobbed Estorhild.

'Impossible.' Ragnhild peeped into the hall to check that the thralls were providing for the guests, especially the bride's family, who had slept on the floor.

'Then why has he bestowed no *morgengyfu*?' This

crucial morning gift was meant to show that a bride had pleased her husband. 'Because I am not worthy!'

Ragnhild was unsympathetic. 'If you are fishing for compliments you have chosen the wrong ear.' She pulled the girl to her feet and began to plait the lustrous blonde hair. 'Come! Stop feeling sorry for yourself and tell me what the problem is.'

'I know not!' Estorhild dabbed her eyes. 'But something troubles my husband and he was perfectly all right yesterday.'

Fingers halfway down the braid, Ragnhild cogitated for a while, then narrowed her eyes. By Thor, if it wasn't that Irish cow! Had she not warned her son that Una would bewitch him? And now she was proved right, for what else but magic could distract his mind from this virtuous pearl? Ragnhild felt sorry for her daughter-in-law now, and though her words and fingers remained brusque her intention was kinder. 'Stop snivelling and listen.' Fumbling in her attempts to tie a ribbon on the plait she threw it over Estorhild's shoulder. 'Oh, here, do it yourself! Now, heed: you have not displeased him, it is simply that my son is backwards in these matters. The gift has probably slipped his mind, that is all.'

Estorhild tied the red ribbon. 'But he barely spoke to me . . .'

'If you want conversation you have me! Now, heed. When he asks what you wish for your morning gift, tell him you need a handmaiden.'

'But . . .'

Ragnhild ignored the interruption and continued firmly, 'Not just any handmaiden, but a particular girl. You know the two who prepared you for your wedding eve? 'Tis not the dark one but the other you will ask for.'

'I do not care for her,' said Estorhild. 'I would not trust her to use a comb on . . .'

'Will you stop butting in when I am trying to help

217

you!' One of Ragnhild's brooches clattered to the floor. 'Oh, does nought go right today? Pick that up for me and pin it on, my fingers are more than useless these days.' She held out deformed knuckles. 'Look at them! This is probably her doing as well.'

Estorhild fastened the brooch to the older woman's left breast. 'Whose?'

'I would tell you if you would listen! The slave, Una. You said you did not trust her and you would be right, but it is not only your comb which you should keep away from her.'

Estorhild's innocence did not extend to stupidity; she remembered now the exchange between Black Mary and Una last night, and guessed that there must be some relationship between her husband and the slave. Her comely brow descended in a frown. 'You are telling me that . . .'

'She is Sigurd's concubine, ja.'

Estorhild put her hands to her face. Oh, how humiliating to be told this by her mother-in-law! 'Then how can you do me the disservice to propose that I bring her to my house?'

Ragnhild's braids dangled over her impatient bosom. 'Because I am wiser than you! When she is in your possession then you can do what you like with her – sell her, and her magic will be broken.' From a length of gauze she fashioned a veil for Estorhild like the one which she herself wore, plucking it this way and that around the distraught face. 'Now you are decent, art going to act the mistress of the house and serve breakfast to your husband when he comes in from his duties?'

By no accident Ragnhild was in the mist-dampened yard when at eight o'clock her son returned from delegating the morning's work on his estate. She caught his bridle, staggered backwards under the lunge of the horse and gave it a clout for its impudence.

218

'Have care, little mother!' Sigurd was almost dislodged as his mount answered with a testy display of its own. 'The nag will have me on my arse.'

'It must wait its turn! Get down, I have words for you, and quickly. What do you mean by insulting your bride and by that same token your mother who chose her?'

'It is too early for riddles.' Sigurd dismounted, his hair and face jewelled with droplets.

'You left her weeping! She thinks she is a failure as a wife.'

Her reproofs met only bafflement.

'You gave her no gift, ninny! What was she to think?'

He cursed his forgetfulness out loud, and was doubly irked that it had to be his mother who reminded him of his obligation.

'Your mind on other things, no doubt.' Sour-faced, Ragnhild moved aside as a thrall took charge of the horse.

Sigurd could not refute the accusation. Estorhild had done her duty as a wife, had denied him not one perfect inch of her, but when he lay there afterwards it was not his wife he thought of. He snapped into life. 'I had best go and make amends, take her a gift of money.'

Ragnhild hurried after him. 'Oh, that my son is such a dullard! That will just confirm to her that you have forgotten; had you intended to give her money you could have given it to her without delay.' Her wrinkled face conspired. 'I have smoothed the ground for you. Tell her instead that you have been racking your brains for something that would be worthy of such a bride but have as yet failed and so thought it best that she make her own choice of gift. I will wait in the hall with your guests so that you may make your peace with her – and while you are at it, give her a bairn!'

Ignorant of any collusion between his wife and mother, Sigurd laughed, ''Twill be my pleasure!' and went directly to Estorhild in the bower.

She asked immediately, 'Where have you been?' imagining him with the Irishwoman.

'Why, I have been at my duties as I said I would.' He took off his cloak and laid it over the bed. 'I truly beg your pardon for leaving you so rudely after you pleased me so well last night.'

Estorhild watched as the ends of his hair dripped onto his breast, then gave a tentative smile. 'I did?'

'Ja!' he nodded warmly. 'And I have been racking my brains how to reward you. Of course, I should be happy to bestow a gift of money too, but is there ought special you desire, ought at all?'

Estorhild pretended to think carefully. 'You are most gracious, but I want for nought. I have all I need in my husband.' She enveloped him in a charming smile of forgiveness. 'However . . . I have no wish to offend by refusing your gift. Perhaps a wench?'

Sigurd thought this an odd choice. 'There are many wenches around the place and they are all at your disposal.'

Estorhild clasped her hands to her perfect breast. 'They are needed for other chores. I had in mind one who could attend to my personal requirements – a handmaid to make me look attractive for my husband.'

'She would have difficulty improving on what the gods hath bestowed.' Sigurd considered it remarkable that she could still appear so chaste after the deeds that he had performed upon her.

Estorhild was used to being pampered at home and getting what she asked for. Her lower lip jutted. 'You say I may have ought, but that which I ask for you deny me.'

'Nei, if that is all you require you may have a wench with pleasure. I will send one of them over.'

'Oh, may I choose?' Her response was hasty. 'I must have a woman with the right temperament to suit my own . . . and you have still to discover much about that.'

Sigurd's mouth curled. 'I have already discovered one thing about you: that you like to make love in the morning.' He peeled the veil from around her neck. 'I can see that I shall get no work done at all.' And Estorhild yielded to him in the hope that her enthusiasm would prevent him from seeking pleasure elsewhere.

Before they went in to join their guests, she asked again if, after the celebrations were over, she might go to the slaves' quarters and choose a woman. Her persistence brought mistrust. Sigurd had the uneasy feeling that he already knew which one she would choose, and that his mother had a hand in all this. He studied his bride carefully, but saw only love in her eyes and duly shrugged his permission. What matter if it was Una? With such a beautiful wife he should not have cared what a slave girl would think . . . but he did.

Chapter Ten

With the guests departed and her husband's concubine standing before her, Estorhild was indecisive.
It was all very well for her mother-in-law to supply
the plan but Estorhild was certain that she did not
want this woman as her slave, loathed the thought of
those fingers plaiting her hair and washing her body.
Alas, only by possession of the slave could she sell
her. Rumination brought forth choice: would it not
be better to put Una to work – hard work – so that
she became less attractive to Sigurd? Though what he
saw in her now could scarcely be guessed. Estorhild
looked her rival up and down, dismissed her hair as
nondescript and her nose as piggish. A blush rose as
she remembered how she had bared her soul to this
woman on her wedding night, this woman who probably knew Sigurd's body better than she did herself.
Her mother-in-law had told of magic and the thought
unsettled Estorhild. What if the slave should put a
spell on her?

Una kept her own gaze aptly servile, but deep
inside frustration boiled. How she longed to meet
Sigurd's wife on equal ground, to say to her, 'He
loves me best . . .' but then she began to puzzle over
the close examination being paid to her. The lady
said nothing, just stared and stared. Una risked an
upwards glance and met a gaze akin to hatred. Why
. . . Estorhild knew! Someone had informed her of
Una's position. Sigurd? No, he wanted the best of
both worlds, he would not have told her. It must have

been the Lady Ragnhild, but to what purpose Una could not guess, for why would she wish to hurt her daughter-in-law so blatantly? Fear pursued the revelation, fear made worse by the look in Estorhild's eyes. Her mistress could kill her right now if she so wished; a thrall's life was worthless.

Estorhild saw her dread, and was startled that such response could be produced without utterance of threat. Had it been any other girl standing before her she would have immediately put them at their ease, but for Una there was to be no quarter. She held herself erect, boasting her finery and informed Una of her reason for being here. 'You are to be my new house slave. You shall eat and sleep here, tend the fire, the cooking, cleaning, the washing of clothes and other household duties.'

Una was startled herself, now – the wife inviting her husband's concubine into her home! But she reacted dutifully. 'So be it, my lady, and what of my son?'

Estorhild froze, hardly daring to ask. 'Your son? Who is the father?'

Grasping this one tiny dart, Una aimed it long enough to give her mistress a fright, before admitting, 'He is dead.'

Estorhild concealed her relief. 'Well, the child cannot live here. You must leave him in the care of one of the other women.'

'Shall I not be permitted to see him at all?'

'Not if you persist in your insolence.' Una dropped her eyes and Estorhild relented. 'When I have no use for you then I may allow it.'

And when will she not have use for me, thought Una, bowed beneath the massive load of work inflicted on her throughout the day. 'Sweep the ashes, wash the clothes, tend the fire, comb my hair – gently, fool! Fetch some logs, heat the stones for the oven, fetch water from the well, the vegetable garth needs

223

attention, make a poultice for the Lady Ragnhild's shoulder – idiot, that is too hot!'

If it were not the young mistress dictating orders it was the old one. 'Go fetch a skeel of fish from the market,' said Ragnhild.

Una found it hard to catch what the woman said. 'A what, my lady?'

'A skeel, a skeel!' Ragnhild threw a wooden pail at her. 'Are you so stupid that you do not know what a skeel is?'

I must be, thought Una as she made for the fish market. Stupid to think I could win freedom this way.

'Would ye be fillin' that with the silver fellas.' She handed her bucket to the fishwife. Whilst awaiting her purchase, she gazed across the Use at Dyflinnstein where the Irish ships berthed, and dreamed of her homeland. It was the only tranquil moment of the day. When she lugged the heavy pail almost a mile back to Peseholme there was an endless round of slap and punch and shove and work and toil until Una was ready to collapse. And Sigurd had allowed it.

Ragnhild sat by the hearth with her daughter-in-law awaiting Sigurd's homecoming from the local witan, murmuring of Una, 'You understand that I am not a vindictive woman, Estorhild, but even I would not blame you if you worked her until she drops after the mischief she has wrought. Her magic is surely weakened now.'

Estorhild had embarked on a tapestry; it was eight inches deep and would eventually span each wall. She had intended it to be deeper but her mother-in-law said that anything over a foot would be a waste of time, concealed by the pall of smoke that hung over their heads. Estorhild felt she had a lot to learn. Threading new wool, she chanced a peep at Una who was now in the delicate act of transferring hot pebbles from the fire to the stone oven that was built into the wall. These in place, she inserted the fish wrapped in grass, then placed more hot stones on top, burning her hands in the process. Her hair was lank from the heat of her task, her face smudged in ash, her whole demeanour one of bedragglement. Estorhild relaxed in her own superiority and praised Ragnhild. 'I was right to listen to you, Mother.'

But when Sigurd came home to find Una waiting on him at table and Estorhild saw the look that passed between them, she knew she had made the wrong decision.

Una was hurt. He did not have to look at her to know this. Hurt oozed out of her, poisoning his meal. Sigurd was furious at being trapped in this position by his wife, though he controlled it well. Between each mouthful of baked fish Estorhild snatched glances at him, sensing his discomfort. Her shoulder in agony today, Ragnhild winced at the simple act of breaking bread, and tried to join husband and wife in conversation, but the atmosphere remained bleak.

Una peeled the remnants of a candle from a pricket on the wall and attached a fresh one, ramming it down securely, for the threat of conflagration was ever-present in these timber houses. In every move she kept her back to Sigurd.

Her master's actions were taut as he cut and ate the fish. He had eaten only half of it when, abruptly, he put down his knife, wiped his mouth and made for the door.

'What ails my husband?' called Estorhild.

Sigurd did not turn. 'I have no appetite. I go to work at my lathe.'

His wife and mother exchanged worried looks as the door banged shut, then each berated Una.

'See what a fine cook you are?' Estorhild deliberately tipped her husband's trencher at the floor, consigning the meal to a small dog that was her pet. 'You shall do better tomorrow or you shall find

yourself in worse trouble! I will have the master beat
you.' She turned away and resumed her tapestry in
an attempt to steady her nerves. Ragnhild plodded
after her, both turning their backs on Una.

'What should I do now?' the young wife beseeched
the old one. 'He is so angry with me. I should not
have tricked him.'

Ragnhild tried to knead the pain from her shoulder.
'A little frown, you call that anger? He will cool down
after an hour with his lathe. I have seen it all before.'

Una cursed them, wanting to shout, *You don't know
him like I do! I know a side of him that you have never
seen nor would you ever wish to see it.*

Restless, Estorhild put aside her tapestry and went
to rummage about in a chest, fetching out a parcel
of linen so exquisitely fine that when she unrolled it
for Ragnhild's inspection her hand was clearly visible
through it. 'If I were to sew some garment for my
husband with this . . .'

'Ja, ja, do what you will.' Ragnhild had grown tired
of the girlish insecurities. 'I must have some balm for
my shoulder. Una, fetch me . . .' She gaped at the
vacant place, then looked askance at her daughter-
in-law. As if by magic, Una had gone.

The group of thralls, both male and female, hugged
their fire, work over apart from the odd summons to
the big house. Engrossed in the tale which Black
Mary wove so well, none shifted to make room at
Una's entrance. Ignoring them too, she clambered
past and went to Murtagh's bed.

'Don't be waking him!' Black Mary left her tale in
mid-air to give warning. 'He's had the devil in him all
day, I've just got him to sleep.' Away from Norse ears
they often lapsed into Irish, which Mary did now.

Una hesitated over the mawkish child, arms aching.
''Tis only holding him I need to be.'

'Sure, and isn't there another ye could be holding?'

226

Black Mary winked at the circle of brutish faces who were all aware of her meaning and leered. 'You being so much closer to him now.'

'I don't need your twisted talk after the day I've had!' snapped Una. 'Ye know well enough 'twas the young mistress who ordered me there.'

Black Mary showed mirth. 'A body ought to tell the poor lady what a fool she's making of herself.'

'A body has been kind enough to do that already.' Una's eyes pierced those of her sister-in-law. 'Isn't that why she worked me near to death?'

The cackling laugh came again.

Una knelt and pulled the fusty blankets over the little bare arm, the touch of Murtagh's skin only heightening the pain of segregation. 'Did he ask for me at all?'

'Murtagh? Not once.' Black Mary gripped her knees to her chest and rested her chin on them. 'He said all sorts of other things, though. New words an' the like.'

One of the other women begged, 'Oh, do not torment us like this, Mary, get on with your tale.' And Black Mary resumed her ghostly saga whilst the listeners hung on every word.

Shunned, Una sat by the child for a moment, then brushing his forehead with the lightest of kisses, she left the hut.

Black Mary's voice became more and more demonic, the circle around her tightening in anticipation of the climax. She did not let them down. As they reeled away in horror and admiration, Black Mary got to her feet. 'To be sure, ye've a wonderful way with ye, Mary,' said one. 'Won't ye tell us more?'

'Not now.' Mary opened the door and watched Una creep across the yard to enter her master's workroom. 'But I may have a fancier tale to tell on my return.'

*

He knew that she would follow him. When someone entered his carpentry room, annexed to the house but reached only by an outer door, he did not need to look up, but continued planing a length of chestnut, blond hair flapping around his shoulders. Una reflected his taciturnity. Under her accusing glare he finally tossed down the plane to rally, 'I do not know what the difference is! What matter who owns you?'

'So ye readily confess that ye gave me to her!' Una advanced like a rampant goose.

Sigurd's chest heaved. 'She asked for a handmaiden – I did not know she would choose . . .'

'Handmaiden! D'ye know what she has had me do today?'

He spread his tattooed arms. 'She had you cook supper, ja?'

'*Ja*! A supper that you would not eat and so earned me more rebuke!'

'I am sorry.' Face no longer hard, he touched her arm. 'I was taken unawares to find you in my house, and with the pair of them hovering like hawks for my reaction . . . I had no appetite.'

'Nor I! For I am worked near to death.'

He groaned and enveloped her. 'I would not have sanctioned this. You know me better.'

Una leaned on him. 'Ye must have words with your wife.'

Sigurd was uneasy. He did not wish for confrontation so early in his marriage. Perhaps the two women could be persuaded to meet halfway. ''Twill be difficult. I have transferred your ownership to Estorhild.' An idea came to him of a way round the problem. 'But she did state that she wanted you as handmaid. If I remind her of this your work will be lighter.'

Una shoved him away, hissing, 'I'll not work for her at all!'

He lost his temper. 'A slave does not dictate for whom she works!'

She reacted as though he had slapped her. Sorry at once, he tried to hold her again but she pushed him off. His face was earnest. 'Does she treat you so badly?'

'That she does!' Una screeched her exasperation at him. 'But 'twouldn't matter if she showered me with kisses! She is your *wife*. Do ye not see, oh fool of fools? I want to be your wife!'

How long ago had the yearning for freedom been overtaken by a different urge? What could liberty bring to a young widow with no house, no belongings and a son to care for? But marriage to one so rich and influential, one whose body had become an addiction with her, what a marvellous life that would be . . . *would* have been.

He moaned her name. 'Una, my heart longs for it to be, but you know that we can never wed, even if you were free. I must have a wife who is of the right class.'

'And I am just a slave!'

'You are more to me than that.'

Devoid of animation, she mumbled, 'Tell me what I am, then, for I no longer know.'

'You are . . .' Sigurd could not find the answer, too confused himself.

'I shall tell you what I am.' Una squared up to him. 'I'm the mother of your child.'

He stared at her.

Crouched outside the slit that passed for a window, Black Mary opened her mouth and awaited the master's reaction. Sigurd did not know how to react. He had taken it for granted that any children would come from his legitimate partner.

Una wrung her hands and waited for him to respond, eyes anxious. When he continued to gape, she offered droll comment. 'Your wife'll not be pleased.' The sentence ended on a bitter laugh.

Sigurd looked down at her, wondering how he

could feel so differently about two women. Estorhild was beautiful, desirable, an advertisement of his status and a perfect vessel for his sons; he did feel affection for her . . . but the passion inspired by Una, this he could never feel for his wife. He folded her in his arms and rested his chin on her head. 'You are right, she will not.' At her sigh, he bent his face to hers, the thin lips graced by a smile. 'But I am.'

With a gasp of relief, Una dropped her brow to his chest. He lifted her chin to deliver a long, loving kiss. She drew breath and leaned on him again, aching for sleep, but there was a question unanswered. 'Tell me, my lord, will your child be born to slavery?'

His hands ceased rubbing her back. This was obviously not a possibility he had considered; he did so very carefully now, his hands resuming their circular movement round her back whilst he deliberated. After much ponderance he spoke, not to her face but to the wall behind her. 'I cannot free you now, for you belong to Estorhild. It is not done to take back a gift.'

Una showed great resentment at being dubbed a chattel. 'You are her master too! Ye can persuade her.' She looked into his face and saw the truth. 'But ye do not wish to free me. Ye still think I'd leave ye.'

'And so you would!' He wrapped his fingers in her hair.

'Not I!'

'You say that! But how do I know it is not trickery designed to make me free you?'

Una sighed and recognized the futility of argument. 'Whatever I say ye'll not believe me. I and the child, *your* child, must accept whatever you demand.' She clutched his blue tunic. 'But if I'm forced to work for your wife I beg ye to spare me one thing . . .'

He interrupted. 'I have sworn I will make it easier for you.'

''Tis not just that.' Una took a breath and clarified her plea. 'Don't force me to sleep in your house. I couldn't bear to listen to ye making love to her.'

Sigurd nodded his understanding. 'This I can grant you. Tonight you shall sleep in your usual place.'

Anticipating Una's exit, Mary scuttled away like a black beetle, though Sigurd was to delay his concubine, placing his hand on her belly and murmuring in her ear, 'I wish to love you, but will it harm the child?'

How unpredictable he could be. In the one breath he refused to give her freedom, in the next he worried over a slave that was as yet unborn. She said that it would be all right, but her voice lacked enthusiasm.

'You are tired. I will not force you.' Sigurd made do with an embrace. 'Go to your bed now and dream of me, as I will dream of you.' He opened the door and both stepped into the cold.

Estorhild, holding a lamp to the night in search of her errant husband, saw him take leave of his concubine. Before he noticed her, she backed into the house, venting her distress on Ragnhild. 'So that is what he calls working at his lathe!'

The older woman was ready for bed and spoke through a yawn. 'Well, after all is said and done, he is a man.' She had no need to ask what Estorhild had seen. 'You must expect him to have concubines. Even my dear husband went astray. Keep her working hard and in a few days your problem shall be gone.'

Estorhild was about to retort when Sigurd came in. Though there were only three years difference in their ages he seemed much more authoritative than she could ever imagine herself to be, and gave both women a look that told more than words. 'I have sent Una back to the slave-house. She will return in the morn, as a handmaiden. Is there ought either of you wish to say on this?' His threat was answered by silence. 'Good, then I am off to bed. Come, wife.'

Estorhild went with him, and once in bed made reparation for her wrongdoing. She came to him wifely-warm and Sigurd accepted all she offered. Whereas he felt that there was a part of Una he would never have, however deeply he infiltrated her flesh, Estorhild gave herself completely. Why then, was it so uninspiring?

Afterwards, whilst her husband fell to instant sleep, Estorhild lay awake, still angered by her mother-in-law's light dismissal of the affair and by the prescribed remedy: bringing the girl here had only exacerbated matters. She would not stand Una's company for another hour, let alone days. Tomorrow, her rival would be sold.

Una waited until Sigurd had left his house before presenting herself for duty. It was at once apparent that the master had been firm, for her duties were very different today. This was fortunate, for Una felt nauseous and still ached from yesterday's toil. Her first task was to plait her mistress's hair.

'Let me see if you have improved since the last time you attended me,' said Estorhild.

Una stood behind her and combed so gently that Estorhild was robbed of the excuse to complain. After this, she was told to attend Ragnhild, helping her to wash and dress and combing her hair too. All morning Estorhild appeared to be waiting for something, but not until Una was employed as sempstress did she discover what that was.

Estorhild kept appearing at Una's shoulder every few minutes to examine her work, but waited until her rival had run her needle through an entire length of cloth before she asked her to hold it up for inspection.

'Wanton!' She snatched the material and brandished it before her mother-in-law. 'See how she has ruined the fine cloth with the size of her stitches?' It was thrust back under Una's nose. 'Doest think you make a tent?'

If I did, thought Una, I'd shove you in it and stitch up the flap.

Whilst Ragnhild tut-tutted, her son's wife assumed charge of the task. 'You are skilled for nought! Get you gone and saddle my horse, then return here – in a more comely manner than you are now, or I shall never be able to sell such a poor-looking creature.'

'Sell?' Una was poleaxed.

'That is what I said! I am weary of your incompetence.' Estorhild draped a veil round her head and neck. 'I shall take you to the marketplace and hope I can charm some fool to take you off my hands.'

'I know why you are really doing this!' yelled Una, with no care for her safety. ''Tis because of Sigurd!'

Ragnhild gasped outrage. 'Such discourtesy! Let me get my hands on her!' She looked for a weapon.

Estorhild pursed her lips and advanced on the slavegirl. Una backed away. 'Ye cannot sell me! I am a Christian, the church disallows it.'

Estorhild knew that there was truth in this; although the church turned a blind eye to the ownership of Christian slaves it expressly forbade the selling of them. But as she retorted now, 'I care not! Besides, who is to know if I sell you to one of the merchant ships sailing for the Orient?'

'No!' Una dodged her mistress's grasp and with frantic eye ran outside to find a saviour. Estorhild and her cohort watched their victim running in circles like a headless chicken, before the hopelessness of her predicament hit her and, totally dispirited, she stood there, panting.

'I must get my son!' She reared away as Estorhild took hold of her.

Ragnhild advised her daughter-in-law against including Murtagh in the sale. 'You cannot sell your husband's property.'

'He is no one's property, he is my son!' Una fell to her knees. 'Please, my lady, I beg you, if you have any mercy do not part us. He's only a babe!'

The young girl bit her lip. For all that Estorhild hated her rival, cruelty was not a facet of her nature.

'Please, please, I beg ye!' Every ounce of effort was injected into Una's supplication.

Her mistress looked at Ragnhild who flapped the air as if washing her hands of the matter and shuffled inside the house, for it was cold. 'So be it.' Estorhild showed compunction. 'But hide him 'neath your cloak as we go.'

Shut up in the hovel, Black Mary had missed the drama taking place outside. Her attempts to spin wool were hindered by little Murtagh who kept grasping the spindle-whorl that dangled at his aunt's feet as she moved across the room. 'Murtagh, will ye give that up at once, ye naughty wee boy! Ye don't help at all.' Distaff pinned beneath her left arm, she leaned over to extract the spindle from baby hands. 'Oh, look now! Isn't this your mother.' Una had entered. 'Go see what she wants.'

Oblivious to the odd lack of sarcasm, Una responded, 'I have come for himself.'

Too busy unravelling the yarn to notice the waxen expression, Black Mary exclaimed, 'Sure and 'tis welcome y'are! The wee mite has mischief tipping out of his ears the day. Have ye not?' She pretended to bite her nephew's nose. Murtagh giggled and fell over. 'Una, come in or out but close the door, won't ye!'

Without further ado, Una picked Murtagh up and left, giving Mary no chance to realize that her darling boy was being taken. With fear quaking her belly, she followed her mistress's horse towards her new life.

Sigurd had been to visit his friends Ulf and Eric and did not return until the eve. The three had been hunting in the forest, a merry expedition and most rewarding, as witnessed by the hart with lolling tongue draped over his horse. Sigurd hoped that there would not be any unpleasantness at home to mar the day, and was therefore much relieved when his wife was the one to dish out supper. Voicing appreciation, he wasted no time in eating. Estorhild served herself and Ragnhild, then sat down. Her husband noticed that she kept looking at him and felt that she was waiting for him to make comment, so he told her of his day with Ulf and Eric.

'Doest like my new gown?' asked Estorhild with anxious smile when he failed to remark upon the light blue robe with its golden girdle.

'Ja, it is er . . . it is most comely.' Sigurd made a gesture with his knife.

'I thought when you said nought that you did not like it.'

'If I said nought 'twas because you look good in everything you wear.'

Her insecurity assuaged, Estorhild turned rosy with pleasure.

'It does not do to be so vain,' scolded her mother-in-law. 'You would do well to pay more heed to wifely duties, at which you need practice.'

Unsure in her role, Estorhild cast her eyes to the floor and wished that her mother-in-law would take herself off to bed. Ragnhild must have read her thoughts, for shortly after eating she left the two alone. The house thrall was packed off to a dark corner, to all intents and purposes gone from the room. Relaxed from the meal and the loving attentions of his wife, Sigurd felt too lazy to visit Una just yet, but he would. He had confided in Ulf and Eric about the child and bored them with his proud ambitions for its future; his son might well be born of a thrall, but Sigurd would ensure that he was well looked after. He was not, he boasted to his friends, one of those who went around impregnating women and caring nought for the outcome; the birth of his child was an event to be welcomed.

Estorhild tried to pet him into making love to her by tickling his nose with the end of her braid, but he offered a vague smile and a kiss on the cheek. When she persisted, he left his chair. 'I am bloody from my hunting. Perchance after I have bathed . . . Have I clean clothes?'

Estorhild scurried round collecting them, then held her breath as he made for the door, knowing where his legs took him. 'I will send for hot water!' Her voice was rather shrill.

'Nei, sit you there, I shall not be long.' Sigurd went directly to the thralls' hut and threw open the door. 'Hot water for my bath – and quickly!' Looking beyond the action he had stirred, he asked, 'Where be Una?'

Black Mary came alert. 'Isn't she at your house, master?'

'Hm!' He swung out of the hut and looked around the enclosure. A white moon shed its beams into every corner; it was almost as clear as daylight. Perhaps Una waited in his carpentry room. Sigurd went there, found no one, and lingered amid the wood-shavings breathing in one of his favourite perfumes. Outside a gaggle of slaves transported water for his bath. He accosted one of them. 'Find the woman Una. I wish to see her here when I come out.'

By the time hot water licked his waist, Sigurd had begun to worry over her disappearance. Had Estorhild disobeyed him and worked her too hard, causing her to run away? The idea was unbearable. Using his hands as a bowl he scooped water over his head and neck, gave a cursory massage of his body then dried himself and slipped into fresh underbreeches. His towelling was inefficient and the garment clung to his buttocks. Rubbing away the small irritation, he finished dressing, lashed a comb through his hair, then went to meet Una.

She was not to be found. Sigurd roared for all to hear, 'Una! Una! Out with you now!'

'Hark to him bellowing like a rutting stag.' Black Mary enjoyed the show at first, but then came a twinge of alarm. Nimble of foot, she moved outside and waited for Una to appear.

Sigurd put both hands to his damp head in an attitude of uncertainty. He caught the black-haired slave's eye and shouted, 'Is Una's brat in there?'

Mary's knees buckled. 'He is not, master . . . she came to take him this morning. I have seen neither of them since.' *The bitch, the bitch! She's run away with Murtagh*! Fighting the vomit that rose to her throat she watched Sigurd run to the main door of the house.

Estorhild flinched as her husband burst in and lifted her bodily from her seat. 'What have you done with her?'

'Why, Sigurd, you hurt me!' Eyes bulging, she tried to unlock his fingers from her arm. 'If you speak of Una then I have sold her – she was clumsy and totally unsuited to my needs. Your mother will vouch for my complaint!' The words came rushing out, fending off the assault that threatened in his eyes.

He worried her like a dog with a rat. 'I demand that you tell me the name of the buyer!'

'I know not!' she burst into childish tears. 'He was just a man! I did not ask his name.'

'What did he look like?' The ruddiness of Sigurd's face was heightened by his blond hair.

'I do not remember.'

'You shall remember!' The threat intensified.

Estorhild's face was mottled. She balked and trembled. 'Why are you so angry? They are but slaves.'

'She belongs to me!' He paid no heed to Murtagh's fate.

'No! You gave the woman to me.'

Corrected thus, he searched for justification of his wrath. 'You had no right to dispose of her without telling me! If you were aggrieved with my morning gift you had only to say and I would have given you another.'

'I hoped to spare your feelings!' wept Estorhild.

''Twas greater insult to go behind my back!' His headband felt ready to snap, so turbulent were his thoughts.

'You make no mention of the child I sold with her! Only the woman. Speak plain to me, husband, and tell me what she means to you.'

'What she means to me is none of your concern!'

'I am your wife!' Estorhild stopped shrilling and fell upon his chest, to whimper, 'Do I not please you?'

'Of course you do!' There was irritation. 'Have I not showed it often enough?'

'Then why must you always creep off to pleasure yourself with a slave?'

'All husbands have concubines!'

'But none so special as this one! Why is she so important to you?'

'She carries my child!' he roared. 'There! Is that enough for you? Now will you tell me where I can find her?'

Browbeaten into submission, Estorhild told him. 'I sold her to a merchant on the Staith. I do not know his name, but he has a deep wound across his brow.'

'So I must peer into the face of every man in Jorvik until I find him?' Sigurd threw a cloak round his shoulders.

His wife clasped nervous hands, wondering whether to tell him. He saw the doubt. 'What is it? Speak!'

'The merchant was a Dane . . . set for Hedeby this afternoon – if you strike me I shall leave!' She threw up her arms as rage suffused his eye.

He held back and glowered, whilst in the next room

his mother snuggled under her quilt, deaf to all. Reining his temper, he used a gold pin to fasten his cloak. 'I go now and in my absence may you ponder on this: you are my wife and I respect you, one day we will have children, what I have is yours . . . but you do not own me. Now, I go to find Una. I cannot say when I will return, but when I do Una shall be with me. I will build her a house away from this one so that you do not have to look upon her, but I will see her whenever I wish.'

Too impatient to wait for a mount to be harnessed, Sigurd ran from Peseholme, through the blood-stench of Marketshire where the crude framework of staves were yet displaying wares by torchlight, and directly along Usegata to the wharf where he found several merchant ships laden with goods they had bartered in Jorvik; two of them were bound for Hedeby in Denmark. Encouraged, Sigurd enquired after the man with the scarred forehead. At once he was told, 'Ah, you must mean Yngvarr Split-head! No, this is not his ship, he sailed just after noon.'

Sigurd groaned and swore. There was no time to hire a crew for his own longboat. 'When do you yourselves sail?'

His informant grunted under the weight of a bale. 'On the next tide – if I do not bust my gut first.' He tottered up to the ship with his burden.

'Will you take me? I need to see this man.'

'Did he owe you money?' The bale was dropped into the arms of another man to a sound of relief.

'Nei, but my wife . . . well, you know what women are!' Sigurd gave a bluff gesture. 'She sold him one of my best concubines and I wish to buy her back.'

'Did she have a child with her?' Receiving an eager nod, the informant laughed. 'Ho, you do not need to go so far! No sooner had Yngvarr bought them than he sold them again to a local man. She was like a

239

fish – kept trying to jump overboard. If she did this at open sea he would lose his money so he palmed her off on to another, the name of whom I cannot say.'

Thanking him, Sigurd turned to look up and down the Staith. Though relieved to hear that Una was still in Jorvik, finding her remained a problem. There were eight thousand people in the city; where did he begin? Stamping his feet to aid decision, he opted for method and headed for the building nearest to the wooden bridge over the Use; from here he would work his way along the wharf. He would visit every domicile in Jorvik if he had to, but he would find her.

For three hours he travelled the cold damp alleys rapping on doors, then had to postpone his search until the morning. He did not go home but took accommodation in an ale-house, confirming his threat to Estorhild that he would not go home without Una.

Over the next day he visited every place of industry, never stopping even to eat until night-time. It had been dark for some hours when he began to look outside the city boundary in Walbegata, though trade continued by torchflare: silversmiths, coiners, wood-carvers, shieldmakers, stonecarvers, metalworkers – none had made recent purchase of a thrall and her child. Sigurd grew so accustomed to hearing the word 'Nay', that when an affirmative response came he did not react fittingly.

The room would have been pitch-black but for the oil-lamps which were dotted amongst the stacks of tanned hide. The man, isolated in a pool of such light, peered up from his work when his inquisitor continued to stare at him gormlessly. 'Yea, I bought a slavewoman yesterday. For what reason do you ask?' Having just used an awl to puncture holes in a tiny flat sole – obviously a baby's shoe – he began to stitch the pieces together on a last.

240

Sigurd cleared his throat and inhaled the smell of leather. 'Because, if it is the one, my wife parted with her in error and I would like to buy her back. Could I see her, *skoari*?'

'That you may. Just allow me to finish this.' Accompanied by much squinting, the final linen thread was inserted and the shoe turned the right way out. 'There! Fit for a king's son. Have you a child, *hersir*? No? Ah, well.' The shoemaker, a twig of a man, rose and picked his way through the dim light between stacks of hides and cut-out patterns, eventually calling into the yard at the rear.

A woman came, her face illuminated by the lamp she held aloft. On seeing the customer her eyes, hitherto dull, lit in recognition. Sigurd looked upon Una with undisguised pleasure. 'That is the one! Would you allow me to buy her back?'

The shoemaker stroked his beard and held Sigurd's narrow face with a cagey look on his own. 'If I give her to you then I shall be without help until I can find another.'

Sigurd chuckled at being fool enough to show his keenness to have her. 'Tell me what you paid and I will pay double – for her and the child,' he added hastily.

The man's reticence was wiped away by magnanimity. 'Then you may certainly take her! Would that I made such a profit on everything I sold. I paid two marks of silver for the pair. Double the price that will be be four marks . . . and of course there is the purchase tax of fourpence that I shall have to pay on selling her.'

Sigurd's response showed that the price was exorbitant, but if he wanted Una he would have to accept the man's word. Una dared not even blink while the bargain was being fixed. The shoemaker, sitting cross-legged on the floor, brought out a pair of tiny scales and dropped a weight onto one of the pans.

His fingertips were discoloured and marked with old cuts from his leatherwork. Sigurd bent over, long hair tumbling for the other man's amazed inspection, and dropped first three arm-rings, the equivalent of three marks, then silver coins into the higher pan until a balance was achieved. There was infuriating delay when a coin had to be nipped in half to bring the pans level before Una changed hands.

'Well, what are you waiting for?' demanded her previous owner. 'Go and collect your child.'

'Er, one moment!' Sigurd kept his purse open. 'Could I impose upon your good nature once more and hire a bed for the night? I hear the curfew bell and fear I cannot reach the city gates before they are barred against me.' It was a lie but would grant him a peaceful night with Una.

The shoemaker looked bemused. 'I must be going deaf – but of course you must stay. No! I would not take payment.' He waved aside the further offer of money. 'You shall be my guest. Woman, fetch the *hersir* some ale and meat. Oh, I beg your pardon, here am I giving orders when she is your slave now!'

Sigurd refused the food. 'My thanks, I have eaten. I would just be grateful for a place to sleep for myself . . . and the woman.'

The manner in which this was conveyed explained much to the shoemaker. 'Ah! I see.' No wonder the man had been willing to pay such an inflated price – she was his concubine! He viewed her with new eyes, but still did not find her attractive himself. His voice dropped to a conspiratorial whisper. 'I have a little room that should meet your purpose.' He gave instructions to Una as to where to take the guest and chuckled to himself as he went back to his leatherwork.

The moment they were alone – not counting Murtagh who slept on the floor – Una's stoicism collapsed. She put down the lamp and fell against her rescuer, weeping. He held onto her tightly. 'Didst think I would let you go as easily as that?'

She sniffed and rubbed her tears on to his kirtle, voice catching with emotion. 'I knew ye'd come.' When he laughed warmly she added, 'But whether ye'd find me, that was another matter. Oh, Sigurd, I was nigh packed off across the world! 'Twas only because the man who bought me thought I was mad that I was saved.'

'I know.' He caught the trailing ends of his cloak, stretching them out like wings, and wrapped them round their two bodies. 'But even if you had gone to Hedeby I would still have come after you, if only to hear you say what you have just said.'

Una did not understand.

'You called me Sigurd, for the first time.' He tilted her chin with a forefinger and gave thanks with his eyes.

Una sniffed and sighed. 'And the last if your wife has ought to do with it.'

'Hush.' He laid a hand over her mouth; it had the combined trace of silver, horse and leather. 'Speak not of Estorhild tonight.' And he made love to her whilst the babe slept on.

In the morning, as they passed through the bridge-gate on Fossegata, Sigurd told Una of his intention to build her a house of her own.

Startled, she looked up at him. 'Does this mean . . .'

'You know better than to ask that.' He quashed all notions of freedom.

Una hefted Murtagh into a more comfortable position. 'I wasn't thinking to be free, I'm asking what position I'm to have.'

'How shall you be called?' Sigurd mused. 'Hmm, you cannot be my lawful wife for I already have one, but you can be my heart-wife.'

Una snorted. 'No better than a concubine to be

ordered about as usual. What will Lady Estorhild have to say?'

'She knows of my intention already. Our houses will be far enough apart for her not to have to look on you . . . but near enough to save my legs the journey.' He smiled as they entered the gates to the city.

'And what of my duties?'

'They shall be light and will not take you to Estorhild's house. You will soon have enough burden to carry with our child – the Lady Estorhild knows about this, also.' The mention of children brought him to the one she carried in her arms. 'I ask only one thing of you: whenever I come to visit, I do not wish to see him.'

Una noted the dismissive gesture and gave mute affirmation. They took a right turn and went a few dozen paces without exchanging words until they had almost reached Peseholme Green.

'Whilst the house is built we must have somewhere that we may meet without interference. Every noon you will go in that direction,' Sigurd pointed directly ahead, 'and walk until you come to a Roman milestone. There you will wait for me to return from my duties, when I will set you a personal task.' His deep-set eyes glittered.

''Twill be no task.' Una's eyes returned the warmth, but soon disposed of it as they turned right into the compound. Trepidation in her heart, she went with her son back to the thralls' hut, Sigurd to his own house.

Having learnt that Murtagh had been sold along with his mother, Black Mary had suffered real anguish. The two days of near bereavement were worse than any physical pain that was inflicted by Ragnhild when she caught her idle and vacant. On Una's return, Mary almost tore the child from her arms, weeping with relief. 'How could you allow my brother's son to be sold! I'll kill you, ye bitch!'

244

'Did you expect me to leave him behind?' Tired, Una dropped to the floor.

'Better here with one who loves him!' accused Black Mary. 'In your selfish possession did ye not stop to think where he was headed? Ye did not! Ye just wanted to take him away from me.' She hugged Murtagh, daring Una to grab him again. *And when the time is right you are going to know just what that feels like, bitch!*

Una stared impassively into the black eyes and for the time being allowed her sister-in-law free access to Murtagh; soon she and her child would be away from this interference.

Chapter Eleven

The new house was erected in the southernmost corner of the acre enclosure. Just before this point there was a group of trees and a gentle curve in the boundary so that anything happening beyond could not be seen from the main house. It could, however, be observed from the slaves' hut. Like everyone else, Black Mary had witnessed cartloads of timber being transported through the gates and knew that building work was in progress but, ignorant of its purpose, she took little heed. She was far too busy even to think of the bastard that Una carried, for there was so much to do at this time of year – or at any time of year, for a slave. With November frosts nipping the last blades of pasture, the kine that were to live through the winter were brought into the byre attached to the house, the walls daubed with mud and insulated with skins and the doors kept firmly shuttered. Only the slaves ventured out when they did not have to, but today was a day of comparative rest for most of them. Black Mary and Una were outside finishing a light wash, eager to join the others who roosted on the hearth with their dinner of broth. It was sunny but cold. Red hands squeezed the garments out and hung them from a tree branch.

Black Mary chuckled as Sigurd's horse tripped and almost threw him. Her master dealt a blow to the one who had left the obstacle in its path. 'Will ye ever listen to that. Not a shred of humour in his breast, and him so funny to look at with his woman's hair.'

Una defended her lover. 'Amongst friends he can be quite the joker.'

'And you'd know all about that, I suppose.' Black Mary dismissed the claim. 'Vikings don't make jokes – they just cut throats.'

Una paid no heed, having more on her mind to worry about. This morning there had been a vision but so hazy that she was unable to interpret its meaning. For a period of no more than five seconds, she had found herself looking down on the bodies of two dead children, and was attacked by a feeling of evil. Then it was gone. Concerned for the child within and also for Murtagh, she still puzzled now over what it could mean.

Just one garment remained in the tub, a pair of Sigurd's underbreeches. Black Mary squeezed these too and shook them out. Though she could not abide such base chores she was unable to resist poking fun at Una, and slipped her hand into the garment.

'Will ye look at the cut o' these his wife has made for him. Isn't she the excellent sempstress – the cloth's so fine ye can see right through it.'

Worried over the vision, Una rose to the bait. 'Where's the sense of breeches that don't cover your backside?' With a violent jerk she emptied the contents of the tub, left it to seep across the yard and went inside to lamplight and shadows. Black Mary was quick to follow. Both elbowed their way into the circle and set upon warming their insides with broth, though their naked feet were dead to all stimulus. Amid desultory chatter, the door opened and all gave inward groans as the master poked his head in.

But the summons was for Una. 'Come, the house is ready.' He withdrew and waited outside, leaving the door open and the cold washing over their red feet.

247

Mary took her face from the soup-bowl as Una abandoned hers and went to collect her child plus a bundle of worktools. 'And where is it you'll be off to?'

Child in one arm, bundle in the other, Una returned the level stare. 'Away from here – is that not what all of ye wished for?' She included the others in her look of defiance and was about to move on when Black Mary, out of concern for Murtagh, leapt up and stayed her exit.

'Where to?'

'Did ye not see the new house being built? 'Tis mine.' Una could not prevent the smugness.

The listeners gawped, then shared an exclamation. Mary showed first disbelief then disgust, but both gave way to a more important factor. 'You're not taking himself.' She made a grab for Murtagh.

But Una swivelled her body away. 'He is my son and he comes with me.'

'You care for him as much as ye did his father!' accused Black Mary. 'Leave him to someone who does love him.' She was intent on wresting the child from its mother's arms but at this point Sigurd's narrow face reappeared, barked, 'Hurry, Una!' and Mary shrank back to watch the child she loved being taken from her, rooted there by helpless fury.

Another shared this same emotion, with no power of redress at her fingertips. 'How blatantly he doth parade his concubine,' said Estorhild, peeping from a window with Ragnhild as Sigurd and Una walked off together.

The older woman tried to make light of it. 'You must get yourself with child, ja? Then he will not want to know her.' She pulled Estorhild back towards the warmth of the hearth. Both women wore cloaks and veils, for even with the fire it was chilly.

Steeped in misery, the young girl played with the

end of her plait, using it as a brush on her cheek. 'But hers will be born afore mine.'

Ragnhild showed renewed pique at her son's crass behaviour. 'All he wants is to build up his stock of thralls. The child will have no rank. And as I keep telling you, if the gods grant you a virile man then you must expect him to have concubines.'

'But not to love them above his wife!'

'Oh, for pity's sake!' November was always a bad time for Ragnhild.

Curtailing further dialogue, a swarthy face appeared in the doorway. Estorhild could not help a sickened exclamation and even though it was under her breath the guests heard it.

'Do not treat your husband's friends so badly!' chastised Ragnhild, and beckoned to Eric and Ulf. 'Come in, come in, put the wood in its place! Take no heed of this one, she is but cross at her husband who neglects her.'

Eric came to the hearth, wearing the uncertain smile of an unwelcome guest, Ulf with his usual dour approach. Both kept their cloaks on and huddled over the hearth until the heat interfused their cold limbs.

'Where is our lord and master?' asked Eric, looking round.

'I will let you guess.' Ragnhild cocked her head at him.

'Ah . . .' Eric gave a sidelong grin at Ulf which further annoyed Estorhild. He saw the expression on her face and looked abashed.

Ragnhild told them about the new house. 'But then I'll wager you already knew about it.'

'Nei!' said both innocently.

'You men!' Ragnhild was not to be gulled. 'You are all the same, protecting each other.'

Eric asked where the new domicile was and when told, said, 'I shall go and root him out.'

Ulf allowed him to get to the door then swiftly prevented his exit. 'Nei, I shall go!' Concealing his face from the women, in whose company he was never easy, he hissed, 'Sit you down! I forbid you to leave me with those two – one would ravish me and the other cut my balls off from the look in her eye.'

'I shall only take two minutes to look for Sig...'

'And probably dip your wick into the bargain! I know you. If you find him at it you will join in. Two minutes can mean two hours – get you back to the fire.' He slammed the door behind him.

Sigurd did not appreciate being disturbed in his lovemaking and left Ulf in no doubt as to this by a volley of insults.

'You grow to be as bad as Eric,' responded Ulf as the two of them left Una and went back to the main house. 'It shall wither away and drop off.'

'Nei, it is only disuse that rots it, Ulf.'

Ulf ignored the insinuation. 'And such a house for a concubine!'

'You do not know what you talk about.' The younger man was shirty. 'Una is special to me. I would not have her living amongst those miserable beasts when she carries my child.'

'I think you are touched with madness,' said Ulf. 'I am no judge of women but to neglect the beauty you have at home...'

'Ja! It is because you are no judge of women that you do not fully understand, Ulf.' Sigurd's expression became intense. 'Una, she... she takes me to the sky! Estorhild, well, yes she is sweet and guileless, but when I touch her I feel nought. I have but to think of Una and...' His eyes conveyed euphoria.

Ulf was unmoved. 'There are other qualities in a wife besides that.'

'Oh, you...' Sigurd clammed up, annoyed that his friend did not side with him. But then as he mentally compared Estorhild's attributes to Una's, a mischievous thought occurred to him; there was one thing at which his wife was very expert. His mood changed. 'Come, do not let us fall out.' One of his arms found Ulf's shoulder as they reached the house. 'Have a bite to eat then we shall tell some tales and perhaps enjoy a game. Una is not about to disappear, she will keep till the morrow.'

Inside, while Sigurd caught up on the news from his friends, Estorhild hissed to her mother-in-law, 'You tell me I should get with child, but how am I to do that with so many rivals for his company? If it is not the wench it is those two. How I hate their stupid faces.'

'You cannot expect your husband to give up his friends for you,' Ragnhild hissed back.

'I would not mind but they exclude me from their chat. Oh no!' She slapped a hand to her brow as a game of hnefatafl was set up. 'I might as well take myself to bed.'

But before she could rise, Sigurd called to her, 'Do not sit so quiet over there. Come and have a game with Ulf.'

Both Ulf and Estorhild enquired with their eyes, but Sigurd insisted. 'Come! I would have you two be friends, and what better way to get to know each other?'

As the two reluctantly sat down to play, Sigurd nudged Eric and waited for the fun to begin. He had challenged Estorhild before and she had beat him easily; this ploy was designed to get revenge on Ulf for being so mean about Una.

As the game progressed Ulf's face became darker and darker. When finally his hnefi was surrounded by Estorhild's men he continued to glare down at the board, as if unable to believe that he was beaten.

Sigurd and Eric were creased with mirth as Estorhild said tentatively, 'I think I have won.'

Ulf heard the splutter and glared at the conspirators. Beaten by a woman, their laughter said! How they howled at the restrained violence on his face. Estorhild too did not like it and, jumping to her feet, rushed off to her bed-closet. The moment she was gone Ulf dived for Sigurd whilst Eric tried to hold him off, laughter still on both tongues.

Ragnhild beat them all with a long-handled pan until they cowered like small boys. 'Call yourselves men! Look what you have done to that poor girl.'

'We were not teasing her!' Sigurd defended his head while his mother aimed blows. 'It was this old misery. I sought to put him in his place for despoiling my fun by his rude visit.'

'That is all you ever think about!' roared his mother. 'Well, you had better start thinking about your wife or you will not have one.'

'Oh, she is so touchy.' As his mother backed off, a red-faced Sigurd picked up a fallen chair and banged it into place. 'If she tried to share my humour she would fare better.' He warded off another of his mother's accusations. 'Ja, ja! I will be more careful what I say to her in future. Go fetch her and let me play the good husband.'

Ragnhild found it hard to persuade the tearful girl to emerge from the bed-closet and began to share Sigurd's impatience. He had his faults but none were so bad as this spoilt brat wanted to paint them. 'You do not know how lucky you are to have a husband at all. Stop whining and come out. He does not love her. I told you, it is the magic.'

The reply was spirited if tearful. 'You said also that if I got rid of her the magic would be broken, but look! She is back and her magic is as strong as ever. The house he has built for her is almost as fine as this.' Estorhild lay on the bed clutching a handful of eiderdown. Sometimes she felt so lonely, longed to be at home with her mother or sisters to talk to. It was no use telling Ragnhild of her worries; she would get no condolence from that icy breast.

'Such exaggeration!' Ragnhild pointed around the room. 'Look, look at the finery. No slave ever had tapestries on her walls, nor silk upon her back. Look at the golden rings upon your arms and in your ears – she has none of those.'

'No, but she has my husband's love and she has his child.' Estorhild buried her face and mumbled through the quilt. 'And there is nought that I can do about it.'

Black Mary was less defeatist. She had accrued few belongings during her years of enslavement, except for those she had managed to filch from the big house. Most of these she shared with her fellow unfortunates, except for that which she had most recently acquired. So precious was this oil of rue that she had hidden it away to keep for her own use, for with rape a constant threat one never quite knew when one might have to purge one's belly of a devil's child. Precious, yes, but now she was about to share it with the one whom she despised. She cradled the phial in her dirty palm, pondering how to sneak it into Una's food. There would be no chance this eve, with the boar most likely rutting with his sow, but in the morning she would visit under pretext of seeing Murtagh and the outcome would serve Una well for her robbing ways.

It was no coincidence that Black Mary arrived as Una was about to eat breakfast; they were well informed as to each other's habits. At the tap on her door Una delayed her meal of porridge and went to answer it, showing disdain when she saw who her visitor was.

''Tis my nephew I would see before I begin my duties.' Black Mary clutched a tattered cloak under her chin. 'I'll not get another chance before nightfall and then he'll be a-bed. Is he woken?'

'He is.' Una shivered and moved aside. 'Ye'd best come in.'

Entry was met by the smell of new timber. Black Mary's jaw dropped – the house had a wooden floor!

Murtagh was beside the fire, already eating his porridge. Without comment on the house Black Mary went straight to him and dropped to her haunches. Una interrupted the greeting between aunt and nephew. 'I have a proposition to put to you.'

Black Mary rolled an arrogant eye, but waited to hear what the proposition was.

'Much as there's no love lost between the pair of us, I'm ready to admit that Murtagh has a fondness for ye. If ye've a mind I'd be willing for him to spend his evenings with you and the daytime with me.'

The hard face yielded for the merest second, then Mary gave that cynical laugh of hers. ''Tis not for Murtagh's sake nor my own that you relent! Can't I see that my lord and master omitted to add a separate closet to his love bower and the child disturbs his lechery!'

Una flushed at the accuracy of the guess. After weeks of chilly passion on wild uncultivated heath, both had looked forward to their first night of love in the new house, but Murtagh had almost ruined it by crying out every few minutes. He had slept at last, but not before Sigurd had come close to leaving.

'Worry not!' Black Mary was quite amused. 'The child is ever welcome in my house if not in his own. Ye know I'd willingly keep him if I could.'

Una was dignified. 'That is not necessary while he has a mother who loves him.' She was about to return to her porridge, but felt uncomfortable with her sister-in-law watching. 'Will you eat with us?'

A look of wonder met her generosity. Black Mary seemed more approachable this morning and there was genuine thanks in her eye as she accepted. Una went to fetch another bowl, having a little further to travel than normal for the area was half as big again as that of the slaves' hut; if it were bare at present it would not be for long; Sigurd had promised to equip her with all the items she needed.

She returned with the bowl which she filled with porridge from the cauldron and gave to her sister-in-law. All three ate. Black Mary passed as much time as she dared with Murtagh then, reverting to her bitter self, went off to work.

Very soon afterwards, Una began to feel queasy. It came as rude surprise for she had thought herself done with morning sickness weeks ago. Despite the low temperature she felt abnormally hot and was experiencing some dizziness; but there was no respite for a slave, even a favoured one such as Una. Thankfully, her duties were not too physical and she was able to perform them sitting down. With Murtagh in obedient mood, she went on carding wool for another hour until her brow and underarms began to sweat so profusely that she could not go on. In the pause her vision blurred. She was attacked so suddenly by retching that she was unable to reach the door and vomited upon the fragrant timber. Murtagh came to observe as his mother made gurgling noises, shivered right down to her feet and retched in agony. When, simultaneously, her bowels poured forth their contents, he ran outside to his aunt.

Black Mary crouched attentively over the babbling child, knowing full well what ailed him but feigning ignorance. 'Has Murtagh come to help his aunt? Why, 'tis a good boy he is today! Away then, take this wee tool and do some digging. If your mother doesn't want ye then ye can stay with me all day an' all night too.' With Murtagh so easily distracted from his mother's plight, she returned to her work happily confident.

Clamped by spasm, Una fell to her knees, pressed her brow into the planking, strings of saliva dangling from her mouth, hands trying to knead the pain from back and belly. Whether hours went by or only seconds, she could not tell, could only lie there while the pain twisted her in its grasp until she was utterly exausted, totally drained, drained of everything.

By evening, Una was back on her feet, however unsteadily. The floor was sluiced and fresh haulm upon it, but the stench of her affliction clung in the air to twitch the lord's nostrils as he entered. Despite her weak state, she experienced anger; the hours of pain, the loss of her child and all he could do was complain about the smell.

He laughed. 'Why do you look so outraged?'

She became aware of the scowl on her face and relaxed her brow to answer, 'I have been ill. Forgive me if I offend your nose.' Tottering, she placed one hand in the small of her back and with the other reached up to shake the bunches of dried lavender that hung from a beam in an effort to perfume the room.

Fondness in his eyes, he reached for her. 'No matter, I shall make you forget about your illness.'

'Sigurd.' Eyes half-closed, she laid a hand upon his chest. 'I cannot lie with ye tonight.' Pre-empting his groan of annoyance, she indicated a bundle of rags. 'See there.'

Frowning in confusion, Sigurd bent and pulled aside the folds of cloth that held a minutely perfect babe.

Una could not have imagined his reaction. He was devastated. As she moved to the bed and eased her aching body onto it, he could do nothing but stare at his child, totally at a loss for words.

Una's voice was wan. ''Tis sorry I am that ye'll not have another slave.' The sarcasm was reckless. She

cringed as he whirled with bunched fist. In the realization that she had grossly misjudged him – he had
wanted this child because it was theirs – her face
crumpled and she began to sob.

Sigurd went to her bedside and dropped his head
on her breast, trying to comfort both her and himself.
Her distress racked his body. Never had he felt such
pain. When her tears subsided, he asked, 'What occurred to make him born so early?'

Her voice shuddered. 'I know not. Could it be that
I stood too long in the moonlight?'

'He is no moonchild, he is perfect.' Sigurd would
never forget the dead babe so long as he lived. His
blond hair fell across her breasts as he pressed tender
lips to hers. 'How fares your health now?'

'I am weak.' Self-pity brought another bout of
tears. 'My whole body aches and I need medicine for
the bleeding.'

There was no hesitation. 'I will bring a physician.'

After a gap of half an hour he returned with help.
Whilst the physician worked on her Sigurd took the
body outside and interred it near the boundary fence,
his thoughts conflicting with uttered sentiments. Once
Una's treatment was completed he left her to sleep
and went back to the marital house, deeply despondent and harbouring the resentful thought that Una
had failed him.

The atmosphere at home was very different, the
hall ablaze with lamp and candle, meat roasting on
a spit over the fire with a thrall constantly turning
it, and Estorhild to bring him ale the moment he was
through the door. As had become her habit, she
pretended that he had been at his lathe, acting her
role of wife to the full and never once paying reference to his concubine in word nor deed. Sulking and
crying had done not the slightest good, as Ragnhild
had been quick to point out. The only way to win
him was by being a good wife. Whilst Ragnhild

grumbled about the cold making her joints ache, the young beauty watched her husband eating. Instead of sitting beside her he balanced on a stool, his mind elsewhere. There was nothing new in that, but tonight she had the feeling that his thoughts were not happy ones. This was an encouraging sign! If the concubine was making him unhappy then his wife must use the evening to reverse that process.

Ragnhild grew tired of waiting for Sigurd to finish his meal and went off to bed. When his bowl was empty, Sigurd remained hunched over it, face reflective. The thrall slunk around the table, collected the bowls and melted into the background. Estorhild came behind her husband, massaging his temples.

'Mm, that is good.' He leaned back against her and closed his eyes, then opened one of them to squint up over the shelf of her bosom. 'You are very quiet this eve.' She smiled at the inverted face, but said nothing. Something about the curve of her lips replaced his lazy expression with one of interest. Head still tilted, he pursed his moustached lips inviting her kiss. Her braids dangled over his chest as she leaned forward and touched her mouth to his, still smiling. Intrigued, Sigurd pulled her round onto his lap. She rested a hand on his shoulder, retaining her happy mien and causing his own smile to broaden by the second until he was laughing. Estorhild seemed to have a magic of her own tonight, her beauty amplified by the memory of Una's gaunt face. He shoved all thoughts of the latter aside. 'Come! Tell me then – you have a secret.'

His wife's response was coy. 'It is no secret. I am to have a child.' The look on her husband's face came as reward for all the weeks of hurt. In boyish fashion he crowed his delight to the roof, delighting her further and waking Ragnhild.

Both fell to chuckling as she bawled, 'Has someone

258

let a cockerel into the house?' and Sigurd responded, 'Ja! And a fine lusty cockerel he is too!'

As the laughter petered out, a cloud passed over her face. Sigurd asked immediately what was amiss.

'It is nought . . .'

He reared in mock severity. 'The father of your child insists that you tell him!'

Her eyes were warm as she tweaked his young beard. 'I am overjoyed to be having your child, if only another did not share that privilege.'

He smarted and looked away, remembering Una white and wretched, that tiny perfect mite. 'You are the only one. Una has lost her child.'

Despite his change of mood, she wanted to cry her own joy, and with her fervent kisses soon brought the happiness back to his eye. At this moment she felt she could ask anything of him and he would grant it. After one more intense kiss, she did so. 'My husband, you know I have no wish to anger you especially on a night as wonderful as this, but now that we are to have a babe . . . could we not spend more time together?'

Will you give up your concubine, that was what she really asked. Sigurd paused to review the contrasting events of the day. A short while ago he had felt like a dead man; now his wife had brought him alive. His wife, not Una. He looked at this child-mother, so beautiful, so willing to please, and began to feel for her the tenderness she deserved. Taking a ring from his finger and slipping it over one of hers, he cupped her face, kissed her, and gave her diplomatic question a straight answer. 'I will not see her again.'

It was only a small diversion from the truth. What kind of man would abandon Una without first making sure she was well? When he entered the cabin around midday he was glad to find the objectionable odour had gone, replaced by pine and lavender. He was less pleased to see Murtagh.

Una began to rise from her pallet. 'I did not expect you at this hour.'

He bade her remain where she was, she looked so drawn. Reclining, she spoke to the boy. 'Murtagh, find Aunt Mary.' His aunt had brought him back this morning before she started work. Seeing Una indisposed had apparently not come as any news, but she had been good enough – if goodness was her aim – to ask if Una wanted her to look after the boy until she was well. Una had refused, the loss of her baby making her only child more valuable than ever, but now it looked as if she would have to grovel.

Murtagh came to her for protection from the man whom he had learnt to fear. His mother spoke harshly to him. 'Away with ye now!'

Sigurd totally ignored the child, who understood what was required of him but was unable to open the door and stood waiting for aid.

'Could you . . . ?' Una indicated the problem.

Making it clear that this act was beneath him, Sigurd nevertheless opened the door for the black-haired child to toddle out, then closed it without bothering to see whether Murtagh went in the right direction. 'I have brought gifts to aid your recovery.' He came to lay them on the floor beside her bed, gesturing awkwardly. 'There is food, some winter shoes, cloth that you can make into a robe when you are better, and this to keep you warm.' He unrolled the martenskin coverlet and spread it over her.

She did not remark on the luxuriance of the gifts, but murmured, 'I am sorry that I lost your child.'

He did not appear to hear her. 'Some leggings.' He shook these out to display them.

'I said . . .'

'I hear.' He cut her off, proceeding with his inventory. 'Some hareskin gloves, and what else?' He poked

260

amongst the array of gifts. 'Oh ja, a brooch to fasten your cloak.' He held it to her gaze. It was of Celtic style adorned with the gaudy jewels she liked so well.

Una gave up all mention of the lost child, knowing that he was deaf by choice.

After a moment he stood. 'I shall leave you now.'

Her eyes showed regret. 'So soon? Will ye return tonight, for I must ask Mary to . . .'

'Nei, I shall not be here tonight.' He exhibited unwillingness to look at her when he said it. 'You must have time to recover your health.'

She was touched by his thoughtfulness. 'I thank my lord, and hope to be more favourable to his eye when next he comes to visit.'

Sigurd nodded and opened the door. *If I do not see her, if I can just keep away then I will stay true to Estorhild.* Looking as she did now it was not hard to find Una undesirable. Why then did it hurt so much to leave?

Though still wobbly of leg and pale of feature, Una was on her feet the next day and waiting outside the church for the priest to emerge from mass. When he came out she knelt on a bed of fallen leaves and kissed the hem of his robe, was in turn given a candle and led to the altar for purification. Now that she was clean in the eyes of both God and Lord Sigurd, she went home and waited for her lover to come to her.

She waited in vain. Yuletide was upon them and still he had not been. He must know that she was fully recovered for he had seen her working in the yard, but he gave no look nor sign that he noticed her. She was to learn the reason from Black Mary – of course.

'Did ye not hear?' The black eyebrows lifted like rook wings. 'His wife is with child!' How great the thrill to be had from Una's expression. 'Now that

261

you're out of favour, I wonder if he'll allow ye to stay in the house?'

Una struck back. 'Well, if he's not to visit I'll have no need o' your services, will I? Murtagh can spend more time with his mother!' She stalked away.

With all the work that Christmas inflicted there was no time to dwell on loneliness, but work did not rob her of other emotions: grief, a sense of betrayal and injustice. One day he had sworn to go to the ends of the earth in pursuit of his love, the next he bought her off with tawdry gifts. He had not even loved her enough to be honest.

But then were you honest, she asked herself. Were you not guilty of using him as a means towards freedom? At first, maybe, she argued, but not after he had lain with me. I loved him – *love him*. I cannot help it.

One ray of hope shone through the heartache: now that she no longer mattered, would he free her? For had the vision not said that freedom would come by his hand? At this moment it lacked importance.

In contrast, Estorhild could not have been happier, directing servants, overseeing the baking of the bread, the brewing, preserving, spinning and weaving. The keys to the storeroom and coffers jingled from the girdle-hangers at her waist. So benevolent was her husband with his gifts of foreign oils and perfumes that she had to have more shelves built to hold them, shelves which Sigurd erected with his practical hands. How she adored him! They talked as they had never talked before, confided to each other their hopes and dreams. Estorhild learnt of her husband's ambitions and promised to help him all she could in their achievement. As for her own dream, she had that already in her loving husband.

In the months before Estorhild's gestation became so obvious as to prohibit her from society, Sigurd came to realize just how great an asset she was. The King, here in Jorvik on business, had honoured his thegn with a visit. So attentive a hostess was Estorhild that Cnut had barely taken his eyes off her, obviously ignorant that her radiance stemmed from pregnancy. The host felt quite superfluous, but at the end of the evening was to be compensated: the King announced himself so pleased with the hospitality provided by his thegn's wife that he felt obliged to offer promotion. Sigurd was now a shire-reeve, responsible for collecting tolls, checking that there was no Sunday trading, keeping an eye on the moneyers and handing out fines.

Yet the old discontent at Godwin's meteoric rise was there to override his pleasure. 'What is a reeve compared to a jarl?' he would grumble to his wife.

And Estorhild was always there to soothe him. 'One day you too will have such power. I am certain of it.' And she kissed and nuzzled him back to confidence.

'You are right.' He gave a determined nod. 'I shall let no one stand in my way.'

Not even his wife, thought Estorhild, as she helped her husband prepare for his journey to Lunden on the King's errand, the second time this month.

'It is good that the King honours you, but I wish your duties did not take you away so often. 'Twould not be so hard if I could go too.'

'I go to work, not to play,' replied Sigurd, packing essentials into the leather bags that hung from his saddle.

'I am sure the King would find a little space in the palace for me,' she wheedled.

'No doubt he would. Much as I trust Cnut with my life I would not trust him with my wife – besides, 'twould have to be more than a little space.' He patted her belly. 'Get you back into the house lest you meet ought that would harm the child.'

Her radiance was marred by grumpiness. 'I cannot go out for fear of harming the bairn, I cannot have visitors for fear that my bulging belly offends them – what is there left for me? I am too ugly. How glad you must be to get away.'

Sigurd gave a carefree laugh and buckled the panniers. 'You look fine to me.'

Ragnhild had emerged to see him off. 'Oh, is this one fishing for compliments again?'

'Who would praise me in this loathsome state?' Estorhild cast a miserable look over her abdomen.

The day was hot and her husband grew vexed at constantly having to reassure her. 'For the last time, you are not loathsome! What woman expects her belly to be flat when it holds a child?' Kissing her, he mounted and rode off to join with Ulf and Eric who were to accompany him to the capital, leaving his wife to mope.

Being cooped up in such hot weather with only her mother-in-law for company was frustrating to one who enjoyed the high life. If he wasn't on some battlefield with the King's militia he was off with his friends or talking to strangers, anything to avoid the onerous company of his wife. When Sigurd returned from Lunden her first sentence was a twin to her last. 'Oh, husband, I wish it were a more pretty sight to greet you.'

Caked in dust, he eased his leg across the horse's back. 'All I wish for is a bath and a good meal. Here, my pretty little bedfellow, mayhap this gift will lift your spirits. Is Mother in the house?'

Estorhild nodded and admired the bracelet he had put upon her wrist. 'Have you bought her one also?' When he showed her the hair decoration, she approved. 'Your mother cannot fail to like it.'

Sigurd looked glum. 'Well, they do say that Easter is a time of miracles.'

Both went into the house.

Out of the sun it was cooler. Sigurd gave Ragnhild her gift and collapsed into a chair. His mother greeted it with the usual mild enthusiasm and asked for news. After he had supplied a few details he rose and went to the door.

Using the chair to lever herself up, Estorhild stood too. 'Where goest thou?'

He gave an impatient laugh, 'I go to the latrine, if I have your grace.'

When he came back, Estorhild beheld him with suspicion. 'You have been a long time there.'

'Oh, I beg my lady's pardon. I did not know the relief of my bowels was of such import or I should have taken her with me as witness.' Sigurd returned to his chair and picked up a goblet. 'I go for my bath after I have supped this.' He looked her in the face. 'I inform you of this so that you can keep a check on my movements.'

''Tis only because I miss you.' She sounded pathetic.

He ceased being flippant and rubbed her hand. 'I know. I missed you also.'

Ragnhild asked then, 'How are Ulf and Eric?'

'Hah! Eric gets fatter than ever. His horse walks bandy-legged.'

Estorhild took this to heart. When Sigurd next looked at her quiet tears trickled down the rosy cheeks. He groaned in exasperation. ''Twas not a jibe at you, silly wench!' With an entreating gesture at his mother he complained, 'Each and every time I open my mouth I say the wrong thing. What is the matter with this woman?'

'It is hard for one so vain as Estorhild to accept the loss of her beauty,' explained his mother.

Estorhild wept fresh tears that neither of them understood her insecurity, did not realize how she worried over Sigurd's absences for fear that these would harm the marriage she had nurtured so well. Only one thing boosted her spirits about the trips abroad: at least they kept him out of the clutches of the sorceress.

She could not help it. All the time he was in the bathhouse she peeped through the window to check that no one else went in there. His ablutions seemed to take longer than usual. When he came back she lumbered to her chair pretending she had been there all the time, but once he cut into his meal her whines and moans began again.

'Do you expect me to pay compliment every five minutes?' Sigurd's demand fought its way through a mouthful of bread. 'You are my beautiful wife, you bear my child, I would not have it any other way – now can I finish my meal in peace?'

You might have made it more sincere, thought Estorhild, eyes brimming with tears, but allowed him to eat in silence.

And in that silence he began to think of other things.

Five months had passed since Una had talked with her lover; she had given up expecting him now. There had been great pain at first, but now that had eased and the separation was not without its delights, for she was able to devote more time to Murtagh who had been badly neglected during the affair. The boy was almost three years old now and a joy to be with, the one light in her dreary existence.

Her master's work over for the day, Una was attending to her own, perched upon the threshold in the warm evening, stitching clothes for Murtagh out of the cloth which Sigurd had given her before their estrangement. Behind her in the house Murtagh was having a conversation with a doll his mother had made from rags. She laughed at the childish prattle, broke the thread with her teeth and called him over in order to hold the garment against him. 'Won't you look the grand man in this?'

Murtagh seemed to agree, galloping around the room like a colt. There was no furniture to obstruct his wild play; Sigurd's promise to make her some had died with her baby.

She turned back to the yard, imbibing the last few breaths of fresh air before twilight turned to dark. Someone was approaching. Murtagh immediately ran to his mother and pointed a stubby finger. 'Man!'

Una, still seated, put an arm round him. It was obvious that Sigurd expected the child to be dismissed. Reluctant to do this, but without choice, she kissed the boy who clung to her and pushed him in the direction of the thralls' hut. 'Murtagh, go see Aunt Mary.'

The words had become engraved on his brain. Giving the man one last fearful glance, Murtagh ran across the garth.

Una remained as she was, gazing not at him but at the sky, and said eventually, 'Look at the moon.'

Sigurd raised his eyes. The planet was orange against the deep blue of the sky, but from the look he gave Una, he failed to share her wonder.

'Ye'll want to come in.' She stood by the door waiting for him to pass. Once inside she lit a rushlight.

Sigurd looked around the cabin, noting few differences since last he had been here. Una waited for him to speak; at last he did so, a mite uncomfortably she noted. 'You wish to know why I have not been.'

'I need no explanation.'

He gave a bitter laugh and looked at his feet. 'Ah, the runes told you all about it.'

Una retained her level gaze. In fact, she had recently been visited by one of her dreams but would not divulge its contents to her master; he would see for himself in time. 'I meant that you owe me no explanation. I am but a slave.'

She did not speak as if she were only a slave. Sigurd's moustache twitched in pique. He had known she would make it difficult for him. 'Are you fully healed?'

'Well enough for your purposes,' was her cold retort.

'I did not come here simply to bed you.'

'Then your visit has nought to do with the fact that your wife's belly is out to here?'

'Nei! I can slake my lust anywhere.' He fought down his anger to offer awkwardly, 'I missed you, Una.' When she responded with derision, he threw another tantrum. 'Say if you wish me to go!'

Una risked a mocking curl of lip. 'The slave giving her master orders?'

He grabbed the impudent face between his hands and screwed his bearded mouth around hers. Her belly leapt, resistance was lost.

Afterwards, while she lay pensive on her bed and he with cheek pressed to her shoulder, Sigurd murmured: 'I am most truly sorry about the child. 'Twas bad for me, too. I welcomed its birth.'

Una stared up into the rafters, felt the goosebumps rise as his moustache tickled her breast. 'Is that why ye wouldn't let me speak of it?'

He nodded; she would not wish to hear the whole reason, how in his mind he had blamed her, called her a failure – but he was over that bitterness now. 'When Estorhild told me that she was with child I could not risk distressing her and have the same thing happening as did to you . . . so I promised I would not see you again.'

'But now her belly prevents you from making love to her you remember Una.'

He did not lift his head. 'Would that it were so

simple. I did not lie when I said I had missed you – did I not just prove it?'

She touched a light finger to his nose. In truth their lovemaking had been as good as ever. Una despised her own weakness. 'You treat me like one of the kine.'

He tried to charm her then, reaching up to tweak her lobe. 'I see no notches in your ear.' When she failed to be amused he himself became more serious, propping himself on an elbow. 'You must understand that things are very different now. Estorhild is my wife – a good wife – and I must try to keep her happy even though it will be hard to stay away from you. But just because I do not see so much of you does not mean I love you less.' Desire washed over his face once more.

'If I hadn't lost the child things would still be the same between us.' Una sounded wistful.

He turned over and kissed her with the promise, 'We will have more.'

And out of fear that she would lose his love completely, she did not have the heart to tell him they would not.

'He is going with his Irish mare again.' Estorhild sat with her husband's mother, tablet-weaving a length of braid for the gown she would wear after the child was born. The finished portion coiled around her domed abdomen and under the seat, providing a game for two kittens. Her fingers twisted the antler plaques as she worked, so as to alter the warp thread and produce the intricate pattern, but in her mind she twisted Una's neck.

'It is understandable.' Ragnhild made slow progress on the sock she was knitting. 'Your belly is too big to accommodate him. As soon as the child is born all will be well. You have his heart, I know.'

'He has told you?' Trapped by her body inside the

house whilst others enjoyed the sun, powerless to keep Sigurd from his mare, the young wife's insecurity thrived. 'He never tells me.'

'Pff! You don't expect a man to speak of such things. Nei, he does not have to tell me. Her magic is becoming weaker. Did he not manage to evade her spell for five long months? Soon he will tire of her. She is looking worn.' Ragnhild grinned conspiratorially at the younger woman. 'I give her plenty of work to do.'

Estorhild paused in her weaving, but still used the square plates of antler as a toy for worried fingers, clicking them together. 'You are good to me, Mother. How fortunate I am to have you with me for the birth. I am so frightened . . .' She bit her lip.

Ragnhild was as unsympathetic as ever. 'What have you to be afraid of? Pampered by your husband, no work to do – if you had given birth as I did to Sigurd you would have a right to be afraid.' She shook her head grimly. 'I shall never forget that day, never. . . . To have my husband and children butchered, almost to die myself before giving Sigurd life . . . you do not know what suffering is.'

At the height of her labour, Estorhild remembered these words, using them in an effort to block her screams, but it did no good. Under her mother-in-law's recriminations, she felt shamed by her lack of control, but continued to yell regardless. Her agony echoed round the enclosure for all to hear. Under Ragnhild's command, there was a number of women in attendance, all jammed into the sealed room. A couple walked Estorhild up and down as far as the crowd would allow, others rubbed and massaged her. She felt stifled by the press of bodies, the June heat and the women's constant bickering about how things should be done.

Some time ago Ragnhild had delved into her bag of midwife's potions and given a dose of ergot to speed up the labour, after which the pain had become excruciating. All Estorhild wanted to do was to lie down and sleep forever, but the horrendous contractions kept jolting her awake.

In the main hall a kettle of water heated over the fire. Sigurd watched it boil, feeling excluded from this women's festival. He had been with Una, about to make love, when the horrible screams curtailed passion. He had left her at once, excited at the thought of his child being born – but that had been this morning. It was evening now – why did it take so long? His wife yelled again.

Ragnhild sighed, plugged her ears with rags and tried to continue with her knitting. The birth was taking longer than was good for all and the child had as yet been unable to puncture the bag of fluid. With the aid of supportive arms, Estorhild squatted over her bed of straw, juddered and threw herself into another wailing contraction.

'Lay her back.' Ragnhild put aside her knitting and, lowering herself with some difficulty from the chair, inserted a finger into the pain-racked body, wiggling its long nail about. Adjacent to Estorhild's cry came a trickle of fluid. 'There! That will help him to crawl out.' Ragnhild dipped her hand into a pot of grease and smeared the birth canal. Wiping her fingers on a rag, she allowed the other women to attend to Estorhild and went back to her knitting.

Black Mary hovered unobtrusively, waiting to clear away the mess. The waiting did not bother her; the longer she stood here the less work she would have to do. As Estorhild's suffering went on Mary began to hum, partly to alleviate the boredom but mainly from devilment.

Una had not been permitted to come anywhere near the birthplace lest she cast a spell on the child, and was at this moment collecting bee-bread from her hive. She took no pleasure from Estorhild's caterwauling, was even moved enough to try and help the birth along by loosening every tight place she could find – every locked door, every window, every knot, in order that the birth proceed unrestricted.

Through her agony Estorhild felt a change take place. There began an eternal sequence of pushing and straining, face contorted, sinews bulging in her neck. Whilst the women took turns to jack up Estorhild's perspiring body, the grandmother-to-be blithely continued to knit, even when informed that the child's crown had begun to show.

'Hold out your hands, Mother!' A sweating Estorhild gasped between contractions. 'You must be ready to catch it.'

'What?' Ragnhild saw that her daughter-in-law's lips were moving and took the obstruction from one of her ears.

'Your hands!' shrieked Estorhild. 'You must keep them free!'

'Pooh! You think I have not done this before?' Ragnhild's fingers worked in conjunction with the single needle.

'I beg you! Hold your hands ready, or his head will crash onto the ground!' Estorhild's beauty was lost neath a prunelike distortion as another pain threatened to split her wide open. She gritted her teeth and strained and pushed and heaved . . .

Sigurd's daughter was born on a tide of blood and mucus, snortling and grunting like a red piglet. With expert timing, Ragnhild put aside her knitting and caught the tiny skull, her fingers drenched with the birth waters. Estorhild hung there, panting, while her mother-in-law poked straws up the baby's nostrils and issued a terse command to another woman who had taken hold of the umbilical cord. 'Be sharp or the afterbirth will float up to her heart and kill her!'

The woman tugged hard at the cord. 'It won't come.'

Ragnhild groaned at the incompetence. 'If you allow the womb to contract we will never get it out!' Succeeding in clearing the baby's airways, she gave a sharp yank on the cord, making Estorhild yell. The afterbirth plopped onto the straw. Ragnhild held her breath for the crimson fountain that might accompany it, but to Estorhild's great fortune there came only birth fluid. Everyone relaxed. Estorhild flopped back onto the straw and for all her exhaustion was strong enough to enquire after her child.

'Is she well?' The mother ran anxious eyes over every digit, cursing Ragnhild's ineptitude as her old fingers dithered over the severing of the cord. How she wished her own mother were here. Ragnhild would surely kill the babe with her tight bandaging of its limbs.

'Ja, ja, all is well. Oh, what a little beauty!' Ragnhild grinned, delivered a smacking kiss to the wizened face and began to rock the child so vigorously that its mother held her breath. 'Hup, hup, hup!' The infant bounced up and down in Ragnhild's arms. 'My first grandchild! No matter that it is not a son, you will do better next time.' After kissing the swaddled babe once more she placed her in Estorhild's arms.

'Your father will be pleased with you, I think,' whispered mother to child, then broke down with the emotion of deliverance.

'Ay, ay, ay!' Ragnhild bustled happily to the door. 'We had better let Sigurd in to see what he has made.'

Sigurd had been waiting anxiously outside the room. When beckoned, he entered like an awkward boy and on presentation of his daughter he could think of nothing appropriate to say. His first response was to laugh. Chuckling like an idiot, he took the baby from his wife. Concerned at his ginger handling, Estorhild put out a hand, but he soothed her anxiety. 'I only take her to see the world!'

'The sun has gone down, she will freeze to death!'

objected the new mother. But Sigurd laughed, went through the hall and out of doors where he held his newborn in the air and shouted aloud for all inside to hear, 'World! Here is my daughter!'

And Una, hearing that cry, ruffled her own child's black hair, then went back to work.

Chapter Twelve

The weeks following the birth were given to decontaminating the house and those who had assisted, holy water being splashed over all. Estorhild was allowed back into the kirk to undergo her own purification, and only then deemed fit to mix once again in society. However, Estorhild was too consumed with her babe to want to entertain Sigurd's guests. Only when Ragnhild pointed out the dangers of this did she begin to take more care of her attitude and her appearance when in Sigurd's company.

She need not have worried; Sigurd was too captivated by his new daughter to bother with Una. His time was spent in organizing a feast to mark her name-giving, inviting neighbours, the Jarl of Northumbria and other influential citizens of Jorvik, and of course his old friends Ulf and Eric.

Now the father of a baby girl himself, Eric shared the new parents' enthusiasm. 'Why, she has more hair than Ulf!'

When Ulf made to grab him, Sigurd warned, 'Avast! Or I shall fine the pair of you for brawling in the presence of your noble lord.'

Ulf showed he was unimpressed by thumping Sigurd, whilst Eric turned to the new mother. 'See how he treats his friends! I'll wager this ogre even beats his child.'

'Nei, he is the perfect father.' Estorhild linked her free arm with that of her husband.

Sigurd himself purveyed an air of mystery, though

whispering loud enough for his wife to hear. 'Alas, I harbour doubts that I am the true father. The babe has characteristics that I vaguely recall in another man but his name escapes me for the moment. The noises she makes . . .' He shook his head, perplexed.

Estorhild administered a chiding nudge, but smiled at the confused friends. 'You will see in time what my husband means.'

Eric paid compliment to her appearance. 'That is a fine blue robe you wear, the colour becomes you.'

'Trust a man!' laughed Estorhild, her face radiantly happy below the gold circlet. ''Tis not blue but purple – but I thank you anyway.' She patted his swarthy cheek. Whatever had happened to her? Only months ago she detested Sigurd's friends and now felt genuine warmth towards them. Perhaps it was because Eric, however repulsive his looks, was always quick to offer the compliment forgotten by her husband.

There was a brief ceremony in which the babe's head was annointed with water. Sigurd had already performed this act on the night his child was born. It had been the custom long before the Christians took hold of the idea.

Prior to the celebratory feast, the child herself was fed. 'Hark!' Sigurd elbowed Ulf. 'There is the strange noise I told you of earlier.' Bloated with milk, the tiny parcel was expelling her flatulence from both ends. Sigurd cocked his head. 'Tell me, where have I heard that sound before?'

Ulf and Eric had begun to chuckle.

'Why, 'twas you!' Sigurd seized his dark-haired friend and pretended to throttle him. 'You are the true father – I will kill you!'

The friends broke up, laughing. Eric stooped over the baby on Estorhild's lap. 'I like this child! She is a woman after my own heart.'

'I think the word you seek is fart,' corrected Ulf, then to Sigurd, 'She shall not be hard to name, my friend.' When the other laughed and moved away to mingle with his guests, Ulf bent towards Estorhild and muttered self-consciously, 'I am most glad to see the pair of you so happy.' That was all, but Estorhild knew what he meant and bowed her gracious head.

'Come, my friends!' Sigurd called the assembly to order. His long hair was bleached by the sun, his face tanned and happy. 'Eat at my table and join me in celebrating the finest daughter a man could have.'

He and Estorhild took to their settle between the ornate high-seat pillars. Facing them in the other place of honour sat the Jarl and his lady. The remainder of the guests jostled for the superior seats closest to the hearth. Normally, Ragnhild took the other settle but she did not mind relinquishing this to the Jarl for today, and if she fought for a place it was only to ensure she was next to Ulf. She patted his knee as the tables were carried in. 'You do not come to see me so often as I would like.'

'Blame this one.' Ulf pointed at Eric. 'He is too busy fathering children to do any work and leaves it all to me.'

Ragnhild craned her head around Ulf to ask, 'And how is your daughter, Eric?'

'Oh, she thrives.' Eric balanced a mountain of food on his trencher. 'My good wife sends her apologies that she cannot be here but she is fat with child again. It embarrasses me that I am so fruitful.' He sank his teeth into a chicken leg, obviously relishing the chance to overindulge, which his wife would curb were she present. She was a loving soul but almost as bossy as Sigurd's mother.

Ragnhild turned a crabbed face to Ulf. 'Who would have thought that anybody would sleep with him? And what of you, Ulf? Does not living amongst such fruitfulness tempt you to wed?' Her hand slid up his thigh.

'Nei, I am content to be an uncle.' Ulf crossed his legs and, eager to change the subject, delayed carving his lump of venison to reach into the purse at his waistband. 'Here, Sigurd, I almost forgot. I bring a gift for your daughter.' It was a silver bangle. 'I regret it is too large at present.'

'No matter, she will wear it on her wedding day.' Sigurd handed the gift to his wife who, unable to place it on the baby's swaddled arm, added it to those already on a ribbon around Gytha's neck. She was laden with such tributes.

Ulf almost choked on his meat. 'She is just born and you speak of weddings!'

'But ja! I have it all arranged.' Sigurd was looking directly at the Jarl, a twinkle in his eye.

'He is serious too,' Ulf muttered to Eric.

When no more could be eaten, the tables were folded away and the women and menfolk drifted into groups of their own sex. Amongst the men, conversation veered away from the child and on to hunting and other male pursuits. Ulf raised his horn. 'Ves heill, Father.'

'Drink-hail, my friend.' Sigurd drank too.

'Tell me,' came Ulf's casual enquiry. 'Do you still see Una?' He had noticed that at no time had the woman been present.

Sigurd did not answer immediately, showing annoyance that Ulf had raised the affair at such a time. He took another drink from his horn. 'I see her, but not so often. I am a family man now.'

And this was the way he fully intended it to stay. Estorhild had forbidden Una to serve at the feast and he had declined to argue. He had not lain with his concubine for some weeks.

Weeks, months . . . the visits grew further apart. Estorhild had appointed a nurse so that she could devote her full time to her husband and the achievement of his ambitions, though it was not so much she who kept him from wandering, but Gytha. Never had a man been so besotted with a child.

'It is just the newness of fatherhood,' replied Ragnhild to her daughter-in-law's rather jealous observation that Sigurd spent more time with Gytha than with her. 'He will not be so enamoured when he has three or four under his feet.'

Estorhild winced. 'I cannot face another such ordeal just yet.'

'Oh, a few months and it will soon be forgotten,' Ragnhild assured her. 'And the next one will be easier.'

Estorhild was unconvinced. 'It will be a long time before I endure such pain again – if ever. I have just won Sigurd from his concubine and I refuse to drive him back to her by growing fat and ugly again!' Besides, there were other factors which she chose not to divulge to Ragnhild: if she were big with child that would mean an end to the social life that she had come to expect, travelling around England, being entertained by those under Sigurd's rule, the trips to Lunden when Sigurd was asked to serve on the witan. Much as Estorhild loved Gytha she had no wish to sacrifice all that for motherhood. 'That is why I seek your help, my lady.' She became wheedling. 'Surely one so skilled in midwifery can offer me advice on how I might prevent it happening.'

'You would deny your husband his sons?'

'Not deny!' Estorhild was beseeching. 'Just postpone until I can be sure that he has finished with Una. You know what happened the last time.'

Ragnhild was thoughtful. 'Yes . . . perhaps you are right. He is very fickle.' She looked at her daughter-in-law who showed apprehension. 'There are ways I can help you . . .'

'Oh, please, anything!' cried Estorhild.

'But only until Sigurd asks why you do not conceive!' Ragnhild was firm. 'Then you must do your duty.'

One year passed. Sigurd was far too happy in his present role to think it odd that his wife had not yet conceived again. He had a beautiful daughter and a wife who was committed to helping him achieve his aims. What more could a man ask for? There were also plenty of outside influences to keep him occupied: Cnut, plagued by news of Thorkell the Tall's mischief in Scandinavia, decided that the outlaw was better to have as a friend than an enemy and so went to Denmark where a reconciliation took place. As a safeguard they exchanged sons and Thorkell now governed Denmark in Cnut's name. Sigurd had been asked to join the fleet as a precaution, but his warrior's skills had not been needed this time and he was eager to return home to Jorvik, not just to his family but for another reason. Jarl Eirik had died and a new incumbent had been appointed. Unlike Cnut, Jarl Siward was not a statesman but a ferocious warrior with primitive methods of controlling his subjects. He and Sigurd were old brothers-in-arms, understood each other and the people of the North. Here, then, was the ideal chance for Sigurd to further his ambitions. All of these things, plus his dear daughter, helped to relegate Una to memory. Only occasionally did her magic pierce his contentment and lure him back to her. Estorhild knew of this and however much she might hate to compromise she had to be grateful that the visits were very rare.

Another summer passed and still Gytha was Sigurd's only child. As happy as Estorhild was with the situation she knew that it could not go on forever; he was bound to question his wife's infertility some time.

Ragnhild, too, was beginning to question, saying

that it was high time for an addition to the family, 'It is two years since you gave birth to Gytha! I said I would help you but this is ridiculous.'

But whenever the subject was mooted Estorhild managed to give some excuse or another. She became increasingly nervous that her mother-in-law would draw Sigurd's attention to her barren state. Paradoxically, it was this nervousness rather than any interference from Ragnhild which brought about the question she had been dreading. 'I cannot help but wonder,' Sigurd told his wife one winter's eve as they sat beside the fire after Ragnhild and Gytha had gone to bed, 'if all is well with your health.'

Her flesh prickled. 'I am perfectly well, husband. Do I not look it?'

'Indeed you do,' he replied with a smile. 'But you are worried about something. I think I know what that might be. Is it not a little odd that you have not yet produced a brother or sister for our dear girl? I have wondered myself . . .'

'It is not so unusual,' said his wife hurriedly. 'Her birth was a difficult one. It takes time for the body to recover.'

He gave a suggestive laugh and reached for her. 'There does not appear to be anything wrong with your body that I can see.'

Desperate to change the subject, she allowed him to take liberties with her, interspersing her words with kisses. 'It is not for want of trying that I fail to conceive, oh dear one.'

He laughed again and spoke kindly. 'If you are worried on my behalf then do not be. I can wait for my son. It will happen some time – mayhap tonight.' And he led her to bed.

Sigurd might laugh but underneath he was concerned about his wife, so much so that he consulted with his mother. Ragnhild did not think there was much of a problem. 'Let me treat Estorhild,' she told her son. 'And before a six-month is out you will be a father again.'

Ignorant that he had been duped, Sigurd was happy to leave such matters to the women. Immediately she had spoken to him Ragnhild went to her daughter-in-law and told her there would be no more preventative measures.

'Oh, but . . .'

'I told you I would help only until your husband began to question,' cut in Ragnhild. 'Now he thinks there is something wrong with you. I have told him you will get with child within six months and by the gods you will!'

For most of that prophesied six-month, luck kept pregnancy at bay. But when the summer came it brought with it news that the Lady Estorhild was with child. Sigurd was in turns enraptured and puzzled when Estorhild, who had just divulged her secret, broke down in tears. 'My dear wife, what is wrong?' He ran his eyes over her body then back to her face as if looking for signs of illness.

Estorhild continued to sob for a while, then blew her nose and gave an unconvincing laugh. 'Oh, I am just too silly!'

'Nay, what is it, tell me?'

'I am afraid!'

He tried to comfort her in his rough way. 'I would be afraid too if I had to bear a child, but you have done it before so surely it will not be so bad?'

'Nay, it is not that.' She eyed him then looked away. He begged her again to tell him and eventually she blurted it out. 'I would be happy to carry your child but I am afraid that when I am fat you will go to her again!'

'Una?' He saw that even the name made her cringe. 'Why, I have not been there for a long time.'

'It is two months – nay, I do not keep a check on you!' She saw the hard edge come to his mouth and tried to repair the damage. 'Because I love you I have accepted that she is part of your life and you must see her from time to time . . . but oh, Sigurd, I am so afraid that when I am no longer attractive to you then you will go more often and then it will become a habit again and I will lose you and . . .'

'Stop, stop!' He shook his head and hugged her. 'You are distraught. There is no danger of that happening, you are far too valuable to me.'

Too valuable! Not too beloved or too dear, but too valuable, too useful. Estorhild burst into a fresh bout of tears but this time did not bother to explain them. Fear was displaced by resentment.

'I promise you here and now,' vowed Sigurd. 'Come look at me!' He tilted her brine-streaked face. 'Upon my oath, while you carry my child you will be as beautiful to me as ever you were and I will pay court to no other.'

Liar! thought Estorhild, but dared not voice it. You can say that now when my belly is still flat, but I know. Time will be my witness.

But the time which Estorhild feared did not arrive. Her belly swelled to huge proportions and still her husband kept his word and did not visit Una once. That the knowledge was based on intuition rather than fact did not matter, Estorhild had had plenty of experience of Sigurd's dalliances to know when he was lying or not and she was sure of his fidelity. With this feeling of security, the child inside her ceased to be a threat and she came to love and want it.

Black Mary should have been pleased that Una had been virtually deserted, and so she was, but it was a perverse kind of satisfaction. The fact that the master rarely paid his visits meant that there was no need for Murtagh to be shoved off to his aunt's; Mary did not see half so much of him as she would have liked. Perhaps the worst thing of all was to see the man who had effectively destroyed her life so happy in his own, the nucleus of that happiness being the child, Gytha. Three years after her birth the squalling red-faced piglet had evolved into a cherub: blonde, blue-eyed and indulged by master and slave alike – even the dour Ulf bent to her whims. Forced to pretend liking or invite suspicion, Black Mary could not afford the latter – life was hard enough – and so she acted with the crowd.

This autumn eve, she watched the master ride through the gates carrying Gytha on the front of his saddle, a common sight but one which never failed to arouse resentment. Where was *her* child, the one whom she could sit upon *her* saddle and teach *her* way of life, the one she had never been allowed to have, for all prospects of marriage to one of her own class had died on that fateful day in Erin.

A heavily-pregnant Estorhild came a short way out of the house with a neighbour of similar age and condition. As her friend took her leave, Estorhild reached up maternal arms and lifted Gytha down from the horse, ignoring Sigurd with whom she was peeved. He had only yesterday returned from the King's palace and was clearly bent on spending as much time as he could with his daughter.

But when he unloosed his boots from the stirrups, jumped down and gave her a hearty kiss, her frosti-ness melted and she relented to ask, 'How went your visit?' He had been to see Jarl Siward.

'Good, good! I told you 'twould be a clever ploy to take Gytha along. She had the Jarl in the palm of her hand.'

'And so would your wife if you had chosen to take her,' came the petty reply. 'There was a time when I won you favours, but now that I am ugly you do not need me any more.'

Sigurd issued a mental sigh. Even in motherhood Estorhild could be childish. What did she want of him? He could understand her being jealous of Una – though he had kept his promise to stay away, even though it had been damned hard – but it was as if she were jealous of her own daughter. She was beginning to annoy him again, but he fought the tendency and lowered his head to kiss and reassure her.

Black Mary watched him stoop to whisper in his wife's ear, bringing all three golden heads together, a tableau of intimacy. She pictured those three heads split assunder by an axe. So consuming was her hatred of them that it frightened her. She forced herself to concentrate on her work until the mood receded, fearing that one day this hate would destroy her, but, she hoped not before it had destroyed him.

Gytha voiced complaint that her parents were ignoring her. Sigurd responded with cajolery. 'I have a gift for you in my workroom. If you are good and eat up all your supper I will let you have it.' The three went into the house to join Ragnhild. All sat down to the meal, which Gytha did not fully consume but received her gift anyway.

'The child does as she likes with you,' chivvied Ragnhild as Sigurd brought in the miniature longship he had carved so painstakingly.

'Oh, that is most humorous coming from your lips,' laughed Sigurd.

'What can you mean?' Ragnhild manufactured innocence.

'You think I do not know why you got rid of the nurse? Have I not witnessed all the sly cuddling and petting and feeding her with plums?'

'Nei! That is just to fatten her up. She is such a skinny little chick.'

'Blatherer!' Sigurd turned to his wife. 'I should be most envious of the treatment she gives my daughter. If ever I received a pat from Mother as a child 'twas usually with a shovel.' When Ragnhild swiped at him he laughed again – 'Doest see?' – and held up the ship for his daughter's approval. 'What think you to this, my pretty one?'

A smile lit up the angelic face. 'Duck.'

'Duck!' Ego deflated, Sigurd appraised the ship for only seconds before consigning it to the fire.

'Goose!' With a kind laugh, Estorhild leaned over her belly to touch his arm. Despite her sometimes childish outpourings, motherhood had brought a maturity to her face that added to her beauty. 'She does not know the word for ship, that is all. To destroy your work so wantonly . . .'

'Nei, she is right.' His reply was terse. 'It was like a duck – I shall go and carve another!'

'Sigurd, you have been out all day! Can you not grant your faithful wife a little of your time? You could spend all week carving a ship fit for a king and she still would call it a duck because she is three years old.' Her husband was such a perfectionist in his work. 'Come, sit with us, do. You promised to tell us your news from the south and still we have not heard it.'

Sigurd reseated himself beside his wife, telling her and Ragnhild of his conversations with his friend the King and of the honours heaped upon Godwin his rival since last they had met. 'Sometimes I think Cnut forgets about his friends in the North.'

His mother unconsciously rubbed salt in the wound. 'Hmm. So the King did not think you worthy of promotion this time? You are still just a shire-reeve.'

'Ja, just a shire-reeve, Mother. I am sorry to disappoint you.' Sigurd grimaced at Estorhild, and a period of silence followed. During the lull he stared into the fire, remembering all the occasions when he had brought his mother gifts or made announcements and none had been good enough for her. He remembered each and every one, and as he mentally listed them he came to the time when he had returned triumphant from Ireland and received not congratulations for winning back his father's land, but chastisement. From there his mind went off at a tangent, remembering Una as she had been then and how she was now. In his mind he made love to her. It had been difficult to stay away so long, but she had been understanding. Una, like Estorhild, had learnt to compromise. He looked at his wife who looked back at him. He smiled, but felt no more than fondness and soon went back to thoughts of Una. Ragnhild had dropped her knitting needle and was groping under her seat. Gytha toddled over, picked it up and began to run around waving it. 'Nei! Do not run with that needle in your hand!' called her grandmother. 'I once knew a little girl who did that – she fell over and the needle went right through her eye.'

Sigurd came out of his dream. 'Gytha, fetch it here!' But the child defied even her father, bending over and peeping at him through her legs. With a roar Sigurd leapt on her, flung her upside down and vibrated his lips with a trumpeting sound on her bottom. It tickled and made her drop the needle. Giggling, she was hurled up and down in her father's arms.

'Do not treat her as if she were a sack of grain!' With great difficulty, Estorhild retrieved the tool. 'Throwing her about like that after she has just eaten, you shall make her sick.'

'You will be sorry when the other one comes,' promised Ragnhild, taking the bone needle from her daughter-in-law. 'She will not like to share all this attention with a brother or sister.'

'Your mother is right.' Estorhild tried to be stern. 'Come, let me calm her or she will be too excited for bed. I have this potion to put on. She has been scratch, scratch, scratch all week.'

'Oh, they are wicked women, tearing us apart!' Sigurd gave his child one last tickle then passed her to his wife and once again relaxed with his thoughts.

287

Estorhild lowered herself back onto the settle and tried to make Gytha stand before her, but the child kept hopping about and falling over. 'Be still or I will not allow you to go riding with your father again. Tell her, Sigurd – Sigurd!'

'Mm?' Sigurd wrenched himself away from Una. 'Oh, ja, do as your mother tells you, child.'

Estorhild showed pique. 'Why should she listen to me when her father does not!'

'I do listen to you!'

With one ear, thought Estorhild. While your mouth speaks your mind thinks of the slave. She voiced her objection. 'No one listens to Estorhild now that she is just a fat lump!'

'Oh, not that again!' cried Ragnhild and Sigurd in unison, then laughed.

Subdued, Estorhild took a comb from a case attached to her brooch and chased lice from Gytha's fine blonde hair, then commanded the thrall to fetch the potion – hemlock and wormwood boiled in butter.

'Oh, look who is come!' Ragnhild beamed as Ulf entered, closely followed by Eric. 'What do you here, night-hawks?'

'A nice welcome!' Eric picked up Gytha who had run to him and tossed her over his shoulder. 'So we need an invitation to come see our lady-love?'

'Not if you are gentle!' A more cheery Estorhild abandoned the lousing and came to pour the guests wine. 'You are as bad as this one, throwing her about. What manner of woman will she grow up to be? No man will want her she will be so rough.'

'This man will take her!' Eric sat the child on his lap, their heads contrasting.

Ulf sat nearby and offered the ribbon he had brought. 'She is already promised to me, are you not, Gytha?'

'Oh well, I shall have to have the next one,' sighed

Eric, and handed the girl to Ulf. 'Estorhild, you look more lovely than ever.'

The host rolled his eyes. 'I cannot remain here and listen to these two seducing my womenfolk. Have your lechery over when I return.' He pulled at his drooping breeches. 'I shall not be long but I must go and carve another ship for this ungrateful little wench – and if you call this one duck,' he warned Gytha playfully, 'I shall throw you upon the fire.'

Estorhild glanced at her mother-in-law then at the menfolk as the door closed on Sigurd. Without a word being said, all knew he was not going to his lathe.

Una, having eaten her evening meal, was now making cheese for herself, six-year-old Murtagh assisting. Whilst scraping the curds from the whey she told him a folk-tale that was to be pruned by Sigurd's arrival. It had been months since his last visit and she had not been expecting him, but her face shone a welcome. She wiped her hands on a rag. 'Murtagh, run and see Aunt Mary.'

The little boy, a mouse of a creature, eyed the man who had ruined his enjoyment, then wiped his own hands down his garment – a square of woollen material with a hole cut in for the head and tied with a cord. At the door he turned and looked back into the room. His mother and the man were looking at each other, not at him. Disconsolate, he left.

Aunt Mary was pleased to see him as always, though she grasped the chance to slander his mother. 'Got her lord and master there again, has she? Too busy for her own son. Never care, my darling, your aunt loves the skin of ye.' She drew him into the human circle by the fire and gave him a titbit. 'You're more my son than hers. God'll punish her for neglecting you so.'

Murtagh was too young to feel such embitterment. He loved his mother, she was the centre of his life, but he was all too aware that every time the Man came to visit he himself was shooed out of the way, and he did not like it. Aunt Mary never banished him, was always sad to see him leave. He allowed himself to be crushed against her breast and listened thumb in mouth as she began one of her tales, one he loved well.

Aunt Mary told how his father was the son of a chieftain who, if he had not been taken offguard, would have killed every one of his attackers single-handedly, for was he not the son of Tadhg Mor O'Cellaigh who had served with Brian Boroimhe at the Battle of Clontarf and had not the ferocity of his sword helped to shatter the Norse chains from Erin's neck forever? 'When you are grown,' Mary finished, 'ye'll be as brave and strong as your father and worthy of the name O'Cellaigh.'

And Murtagh in childish lisp boasted that he would. If only he were not so very frightened of the Man.

The following afternoon, Sigurd was with Una again when a thrall brought word from the main house. He was to come at once: the Lady Estorhild was ill.

'How did she know I would be here?' he muttered to his mistress, anticipating the argument that would greet his infidelity.

'Blessed Virgin, 'tis still the innocent y'are where women are concerned! Ye think she does not know every single time ye make love to me, just as I know when ye make love to her?' The cupid's bow turned petulant. 'This sickness is a device.'

But Sigurd was already dressing. 'Nei, she complained of feeling unwell this morning. I must go and see.' Delivering a preoccupied kiss he left. Had the discovery that he had broken his word caused his wife's illness? She had made no accusation but had been subdued since his return last night. He felt wretched for breaking his promise, but had she not driven him to it with her moaning?

When he arrived at the big house his mother told him, 'Estorhild has begun her labour. It is before time and the child is too weak to crawl out. He is wedged across her belly. I am not strong enough to shift him. You must fetch the physician. Take Gytha with you – I need her out of the way.'

She hurried back to tend the stricken woman. Jiggling Gytha up and down as he ran, Sigurd went to fetch help, ignorant that his son was already dead.

For the next few days he grieved with his wife, still wondering if his renewed visits to Una were to blame, for nothing had been said. For this reason he remained at Estorhild's side to comfort her with the promise that their next child would be a son.

But no one could grieve forever and Estorhild had begun to act very oddly towards him, being nicer to Ulf and Eric than she was to her husband. When he returned from his duties she would still be where he had left her working at her tapestry, yet seemed to have made little progress on it. It was the same this evening. The look on his face when he entered the hall showed that he was losing patience with her. He threw down his gloves and warmed his hands at the fire. 'Must I get my own ale again?'

'Hush! I will get it for you.' His mother waddled towards the pitcher, delivering a cuff in passing. 'Sit you down and stop your grousing.'

Sigurd's eyes burned. On the battlefield he was supreme, but in his own house he was full of inadequacies, trapped between a domineering mother and a frigid wife and wondering what he had done to deserve either.

Lowering her voice, Ragnhild warned, 'You must not be so impatient with her.'

'How do you expect me to react when every night

I come home and I no longer have a wife but a woman of stone?'

'And how do you expect her to react when she has just witnessed her child come from her belly in pieces?' hissed Ragnhild. The physician had been forced to dismember the babe in the womb or risk losing the mother.

Sigurd's face showed nausea at the horrendous image, but retorted, 'I have lost a child, too! It grieves me deeply, but it is of no benefit to mope when there is an estate to be run. She leaves everything to you.'

Ragnhild said she could cope.

'That has nought to do with it, Mother! She cannot expect just to sit there, she must earn her keep. Instead of wasting her thoughts on a dead child why does she not lavish her affection on the one she already has?' He pointed at Gytha who sat on the floor in a pose of neglect and lifted her on to his lap. 'And some for her husband would not go amiss. Did she not complain loud enough when I once neglected her?'

'Oh, you men, you understand nought! I know what she is going through, remember? It will take more than a few weeks for her to recover – indeed, she will never fully get over it.'

Sigurd projected horror. 'You mean Gytha and I will have to put up with this forever?'

Estorhild sat and listened to them harping at each other, but could not have cared about either, her head full of black clouds.

Ragnhild gave him a shove. 'Gowk! She will be well enough if she gets the help she deserves. She has put up with a lot from you – and you know what I am talking about! If you want to vilify anyone for this situation you need look no further than your Irish witch.'

'She is no witch,' Sigurd's moustache bristled in

derision, but then he noticed that his wife's eyes had focused on him and was unsettled by her gaze.

Ragnhild sat down. 'Nei? Then why am I always receiving complaints from our neighbours about her magicking their bees to her own hive? And milk going sour when it has barely left the udder? If she can do that then she can put a spell on your child.'

'I order you to cease this foolish talk!'

Gytha lifted an apprehensive face from his chest; rarely had she heard her father raise his voice in anger. For her sake and for the ominous manner in which his wife was looking at him Sigurd controlled his ire. 'Come, let us eat before we kill each other. Wife, sit by me and tell me of your day.' He put Gytha from his knee and motioned for the servants to bring the meal forth.

'I am not hungry.' Estorhild turned her face away.

Sigurd made clumsy attempts to bridge the gulf between them, but when Estorhild finally looked at him again there was spite in her eyes. 'What do you here anyway? Should you not be riding your Irish mare?'

He tried to remain calm. 'I am here, am I not? With my wife.'

Estorhild replied bitterly, 'What use is a wife who cannot bear sons?'

He tried to comfort. 'There will be others.'

'I wanted this one!' She glared at him, then turned away.

Sigurd could not understand her rejection of him. 'It is as if you blame me that our son was born dead.'

'And so I do!' Her eyes swam. 'Your mother is right; it is that Irish mare of yours working her magic. That Loki-in-a-dress! She is jealous that she does not have your child. She cast her spell on me so that I lost mine!' Oh, the agony of that loss.

'You are deranged! She did not cast a spell on Gytha, did she?'

'How would you know?' Estorhild looked quite mad in her tirade, blue eyes distended as if they might burst from their sockets. 'You are too blinded by lust to see ought! And you swore that you would not go to her! You lied! You lied and now we must suffer, Gytha and I!'

He grew tired of being harangued. 'Enough! If anyone would harm our daughter then it is you with your shrewish outburst.'

Estorhild noticed the effect on her child and immediately burst into tears. Ragnhild threw up her hands in despair. Sigurd was unmoved. 'I shall take Gytha outside whilst you control your madness. I would wish to see you recovered when we return.'

'Do not bother to return!' Estorhild screamed after him. 'For I shall never speak to you again!'

With the city and his wife's heart encased in ice, Sigurd turned to Una for warmth. This day saw them descend with hordes of other citizens upon the frozen rivers to make merry with skates and sledges. Una had never worn such things on her feet and had difficulty keeping upright on the bone skates. Clumsily, she shuffled alongside Sigurd on the ice, grasping the rod that was to propel her along and shrieking when every few seconds she lost her balance. Teeth gritted, she concentrated on every move.

'You can skate and talk at the same time,' laughed Sigurd, gliding expertly along. Besides several layers of clothing, fur gloves and boots, he wore a pointed hat with a complete marten skin sewn around its rim, so that the animal's mask sat between his eyebrows.

'A know-it-all such as you might be able to, I cannot.' Una hung on to the pole as if it were a lifeline.

'There! Have you not just proved my point?' Coming back to her, Sigurd took her head in his hands and jerked it so that she was looking into the marten's sightless eyes. 'Look up at where you go, not down at your feet.' He laughed as she tottered again, and helped to right her.

Eventually, Una grasped the idea. Their poles moved in unison, if a little slowly.

'Now you are matching my rhythm.' His deeply-set eyes teased seduction.

She reproved him – 'Even the ice does not cool your blood!' – but his words immediately transported her to a warm and passionate bed, sending a wave of pleasure through her body. 'I always thought that the men of the north were passionless but five years with you has taught me different.'

He raised a red-gold eyebrow. 'Is that how long it has been?'

She nodded with a puff of silvery air. 'And more.'

'Five years.' He sounded disbelieving. 'And you have never tried to run away from me.'

'As I promised at the outset, but ye chose not to believe me then.'

Sigurd was thoughtful. 'Do you dream of your old life still?'

Una slipped, gave a little shriek, then laughed and answered him. 'Of course. D'ye not think of your life before you came to this country?'

His response emerged on a sardonic cloud. 'Ja, I remember how I could not wait to get away from it.'

'What was it like? Ye've never told me about it.'

'A few trees, a little water . . .' Sigurd shrugged. 'And neighbours who knew all your business before you knew it yourself.'

Her blue eyes sparkled. 'The same as this place, then.'

Sigurd had to agree. 'Let us leave them all behind today – come, I race you!' Using the pole to good effect, he punted away down the solidified river.

Una struck out, and fell on all fours. Luckily she was well-padded with clothing. Sigurd looked over his back to see where she was, cannoned into someone, twizzled another five yards on his rear and lay flat on the ice laughing until Una skated over to join him.

At a more careful pace they moved along the frozen river, away from the city where trees and countryside were enveloped in icy calm and there was no one to spy on their kisses. By the time they returned to the Staith Una's teeth were chattering. 'Mother of God, these skates are frozen to my feet!'

Exhilarated by her cheerful presence, Sigurd voiced his remedy. 'Let us see what the merchants have on their ships to warm you!' He and Una headed towards the craft that had been left high and dry on icy mudbanks when the river had frozen at ebb-tide. Removing their skates, they vaulted on board. No one accosted them, the merchant being off in some alehouse.

Sigurd ignored Una's warnings and yanked a tarpaulin aside. 'Ah, what have we here?' He began to examine the bundle of pelts.

Una sucked in her breath as he uncovered a polar bear hide. 'Oh, Sigurd!' She touched a reverent hand to the creamy fur, rippling the upper layer to expose the soft white down beneath. 'Never have I seen a thing so beautiful.'

'That is only because you have never seen yourself,' flattered her lover. 'Here, try it on.' Hefting the skin, he wrapped it around her.

A gasp hit the cold air as she hugged her bedizened form. 'What if someone should see?'

'Let them – let them all see!' He flung his arms wide. 'Ho there! Merchant, show yourself!'

Hurriedly, Una removed the heavy pelt and bundled it up. Sigurd grabbed it. 'Put it back! It is yours.'

She gasped again. 'Ye cannot . . .'

'Do not tell me that I cannot!' Sigurd jumped onto the wharf and bawled, 'Merchant! If you do not come now we shall leave without payment.'

Una was infected by his exhilaration. 'Sigurd, you are touched with madness today!'

'Then it must be from living with Estorhild for she is so crazed these days.' If his wife spoke to him at all it was to issue abuse. 'Now put it back on! I do not care if folk think me mad. I am tired of looking at mournful women.'

The merchant finally came, his expression one of panic at seeing his valuable skin being purloined; this soon turned to one of unction when he realized he had a buyer.

The polar bear skin probably cost as much as all the others sewn together, but Sigurd was feeling reckless today and did not even haggle. Much as her head soared at being clothed in such luxury, Una felt so conspicuous that she wanted to take the fur off before entering the compound. 'For the love of God, I cannot go in prancing like a queen!'

Sigurd refused, his ebullience giving way to firm command. 'Nei, let them look if they wish to.' He grasped handfuls of the white fur and pulled it right up to her chin, using it to bring her face close to his. 'You are the only woman who has made me happy, truly happy, and I would have them all know that.' He clamped his mouth to hers and his kiss was returned most heartily.

A solitary slave worked in the yard, but that was all it took to distribute the word of Una's acquisition; by nightfall everyone knew.

'I don't believe it!' pouted Black Mary when a fellow slave passed on the news.

'Then ask Aldred – he has seen it with his own eyes! A white fur down to her feet, says he!'

'A skin fit for a queen,' breathed Mary when

eventually she caught a glimpse of it. 'And me with no shoes to my feet.'

Estorhild confronted Sigurd when he deigned to come home for supper. 'How dare you humiliate me like this! Parading your wench like an empress!'

He unpinned his cloak and threw it over a chair. 'You are upsetting Gytha with your shrieking, woman.' Looking around for something to distract the child he saw only his helmet and gave her that.

'Damn Gytha!'

Hearing her name issued like a curse the little girl's mouth trembled and the blue eyes welled tears. Helmet jammed tight, she stretched her arms to her father. Ragnhild covered her ears, which was as well, for her daughter-in-law had not finished. 'And do not call me woman – I am your wife!'

'Oh, she has remembered!' Sigurd jeered at his mother as he picked up the crying child and lifted the helmet from over her eyes. 'I thought it must have escaped your mind, the way you have been treating me for the last six months.'

'If I have forgotten that I am your wife that is because my husband holds me second to his whore!'

'I will not stand for this!'

'Then be seated!' parried Estorhild, as Sigurd left the house taking his daughter with him.

Una was taken aback when he appeared carrying Gytha; never had he done this before. He was obviously in a foul mood and so apart from the initial greeting she said nothing, allowing him to play on the floor with his child until he cooled down. She compared Gytha's bandy legs with the straight ones of her son and wondered how this could be when she herself had been unable to provide swaddling rags at the time when his limbs had needed them. Black Mary would say this was an illustration of how God took care of His own.

Murtagh had now learned to leave without being

told whenever the master came in. He did so now, resentful at the infant who was permitted to remain and coveting the helmet that she played with; had they been alone he would have taken it from her.

Gytha had found a stick on the floor and was using it to beat her father's helmet like a drum. In a fit of boyishness Sigurd put it on his head, allowed her to continue beating it and looked up to laugh at Una, but her mind was elsewhere. 'What ails you?'

She blinked and changed her weight to her other hip. 'I am trying to equate this tender man with the one who brought me from Erin, the one who cut down young boys, children, as if they were blades of grass.'

Sigurd beheld her as if she were mad. 'Did you expect me to treat my own child like that?'

'What difference? Those you killed were someone else's bairns. They bleed just the same.'

He dismissed her sentimentality, removing the helmet for the blows were beginning to jar. 'When you kill the father it is wise to kill the son or one day he will come after you.'

Una was quiet for a time, thinking of her own son. How fortunate that he had not been born earlier, or he too might have perished that day. Her lover did not appear to realize the significance of what he had said. She asked him, 'Remember when ye brought me back after your wife sold me? Ye said that when ye came to visit me ye didn't wish Murtagh to be here, and I've always respected your desire because I love ye. Yet ye never stop to think how much it hurts for me to see your child, the one I should have borne.'

Sigurd was thoughtful, watching his daughter using the helmet as a bucket now and the stick to mix the imaginary contents. 'Do you ask me not to bring her again?'

Una nodded. ''Tis a beautiful flower she is, but each time I look at her I'm reminded I can never bear your child myself.'

He showed unfamiliar sensitivity, reaching over the infant to touch Una's cheek. 'There is time yet.' She shook her head. 'Why are you so sure? Did the runes tell you so?' A smile played about his lips.

'You should not tease me.' She hung her head.

'And you should not believe a handful of stones.'

'I do not need the runes to tell me. Besides, I've told ye I never see my own fate there. If there was going to be another child there would have been one by now.' She looked at him from under her lashes. 'D'ye mind very much?'

Sigurd looked distant, then as Gytha twisted in his lap to look up at him, he smiled again. 'How could I mind with this precious jewel to give me all the love I need.' He pretended to bite a chunk from his daughter's neck. She squeaked and dropped the helmet which rolled across the wooden floor.

Jealous of Gytha's role in his life, Una added, 'I didn't tell ye before for fear that I would lose you altogether. 'Tis bad enough having to share ye.'

Sigurd rested his chin on Gytha's head whilst she squirmed to get away. 'You have not had to share me for some time. My wife . . . I think she is frozen with the river.'

No, but I have still to share you with that one, thought Una, envying the child in his embrace. Then she patted him. 'Have cheer, 'tis with me y'are now. Let me fetch my master some refreshment.' Along with ale she gave him and his daughter a piece of flat cake made from honey and crammed with dried fruits.

The memory of its taste must have lingered on the child's tongue, for when spring came and the doors were thrown open to the light Gytha returned to Una's house, toddling in on her own.

'What're you doing here?' Una bent over, hands on knees. 'Your mother'll be angry with ye for coming.'

'I come for cake,' said Gytha expectantly, and made grasping motions with her fingers.

Una clicked her tongue and shooed out a butterfly whom the sun had lured from hibernation. ''Tis lucky y'are that I happen to have just made one.' She gave the child a wedge of the cake she had so enjoyed. Feeling a surge of possessiveness, Murtagh came to hug his mother's hips and demanded the same.

'Don't worry, son, she'll not be stopping today.' Una smiled fondly at the boy, broke off a piece of cake for him and steered Gytha to the door. 'Away now and run along home.' She had just taken the little girl outside when Estorhild burst upon them, saw Gytha about to bite into the cake and slapped it from her hand.

'You took my husband's love and now you try to lure my child away too!' She attacked Una, slapping and screaming. 'Bitch! Harlot!'

Gytha, already stung to tears by her mother's blow, now wailed louder. Murtagh cried too, afraid of the woman who was hitting his mother.

Trying to escape the blows, Una gave an impulsive yell. 'Sure, I don't want your brat!'

Black Mary, working the soil, watched and sniggered along with other thralls as Estorhild hoisted her daughter and left Una battered and shaken. But when the laughter died an idea was born; the most vicious and cunning idea that would destroy each of her enemies with one blow, and later Black Mary was to wander past Una's house, eyes to the ground. Gytha's cake still lay where it had fallen, as yet unseen by dog or bird. Performing a hasty dip, Mary picked it up and walked on.

Sigurd was not to hear of the incident from either

party: Estorhild did not speak to him at all when he came home for supper and Una had no wish to spoil a pleasant evening when he came to see her later. The evening was not to remain pleasant. Sigurd had made love to her and had gone home, and Una was about to close her eyes when out of the blue she was visited by the dreadful power she had thought to have escaped, so long had it been since her last vision. The things she saw were so horrible that she cried out, bringing Murtagh running. Transfixed, she was not even conscious of his presence as he shook her in fear. When the vision cleared the terror remained in her eyes. At long last she was imbued with the truth of how her freedom was to come.

She saw her distressed child then and clutched him to her. Her instincts were to run, but there was no use running. Neither was there ought to be gained from warning the other participants. She knew of old that there was nothing she could do to avert the terrible consequences.

She did not sleep that night but lay cuddling her son's thin body. At first light she went to the church of St Cuthbert where she prayed for courage. Afterwards she went home and waited for Murtagh to awake, never once letting him out of her sight. The day was long.

Black Mary could not have guessed that her aim would be achieved so easily. The child wandered voluntarily to her own destruction. Sigurd had as usual risen early and had gone to attend his duties before breakfast. Ragnhild was yet a-bed. Estorhild, still bereaved over the loss of her unborn son, was weaving, her mind far away; to all intents and purposes, Gytha was playing by the doorway.

With no one to check her adventurous spirit, the child wandered around the enclosure. Most of the slaves were occupied indoors cooking breakfast or away in the fields. Black Mary, feeding the hens, was the only one about when Gytha came up, pointed at the fowl and said, 'I will do that.'

Without a word, Mary gave the child the pot of grain and supervised her clumsy attempts to feed the hens. Still no one came. Mary's heart began to thump. She crossed herself. Oh, Lord grant me the courage to do it! Any moment now the tranquil garth could be transformed into a marketplace. What if someone were to see her leading Gytha away? But who would suspect – everyone loved the golden-haired child, did they not? What onlooker, if onlooker there be, would imagine that Mary could be intent on harm?

She bent low over the golden head, keeping her eyes peeled for danger. 'I have a cake for ye. Will ye come with me to have it?'

Immediately, the child dropped the bowl, grasped the woman's hand and allowed herself to be led away. Still no one came.

'Gytha! Gytha!' The child's mother toured the enclosure, calling. When Estorhild had last looked up, Gytha had been playing by the doorway; on her next examination, the jambs framed emptiness. 'Gytha!' The call grew more urgent. If the child had wandered out of the enclosure she was in danger from all manner of things. Ragnhild, looking like a sackful of piglets, shuffled from her bed yawning and scratching her wobbly rump. One of her plaits had come undone in the night and dangled in a tousled matt over her breast. 'What is the din?' When informed of the problem she began to call too.

Estorhild ran from house to shippen to pigsty. No one had seen Gytha. She burst into the slave hut. 'Have you seen my daughter?'

Skirts tied around hips, the women stood in a washtub, treading clothes. They peered at her through the shroud of steam, hair plastered to cheeks, thighs

pink and gleaming. Black Mary tilted her head as if
in thought. 'I have not, my lady . . . not for some
time. The last I saw of her she was with Una.'

Estorhild almost collapsed, wasted no time in pelting off to Una's house and lurched inside screaming,
'Where is she?'

Both Una and her son jumped at the hysterical
demand. 'Who?'

Estorhild came over and shook her forcefully. 'You
know, you witch! My daughter!'

'I've not seen . . .'

'Liar!' Estorhild slapped her. Murtagh cowered.
'Where is she, where?'

Una rubbed her cheek and held out her hand to
the boy who seized it. 'My lady, ye can see for
yourself she is not here!'

It was quite obvious that there was nowhere the
child could be hidden. Estorhild stormed out and
careered around the back of the house. Her search
yielded a tiny shoe. With a moan she pounced on it.
'Oh, my bairn! My bairn!'

Stunned, Una watched her tear away. Fear swirled
around her body. There was nowhere to run. Instead,
she clung to her own child. 'Oh, Murtagh! I love ye,
son! I love ye!'

Ragnhild grabbed and shook her daughter-in-law
who was by now thoroughly distraught and incoherent. 'What have you discovered?'

For answer, Estorhild gulped in lungfuls of air and
held up the shoe.

The older woman moaned in distress. 'Oh, nei!
Where didst you find it?'

Unable to speak, Estorhild sobbed and gulped and
gasped, flinging her arm towards Una's house.

Her mother-in-law shook her again. 'Is that all you
found?'

Estorhild nodded and sagged.

'Then we must search again.' Ragnhild called for

help. Everyone hurried to assist including Black Mary. The search widened to neighbouring properties but turned up nothing. Mary was frustrated; only she knew the spot where Gytha lay but she could not lead them there lest she should incriminate herself.

When Sigurd returned to break his fast there was pandemonium. Immediately, he ordered everyone to search again.

'We do not need to search!' His enraged mother grabbed handfuls of his tunic. 'Your Irish mare knows where she is! Look!' She brandished the shoe. 'Look what your wife found outside her house – and look what your bewitchment has done to us all!'

Whilst Sigurd fell dumb, his wife found her voice. 'I told you she was jealous, warned you that she might harm Gytha out of venom, but you would not listen! Yesterday I found her trying to lure Gytha with cake! She has taken her, I know she has!'

Sigurd came to life and charged over to Una's house, concern for his child overriding all bonds. He read the terror on her face as guilt. 'Where is she, Una?'

She pushed Murtagh into the background and came towards the man, hands appeasing. 'Sigurd, ye must listen to me. I swear . . .'

'Where!'

She shrank back. ''Twas not me!'

'Where?'

Tears streaming down her face, Una surrendered to the inevitable. 'I swear, I swear by the Holy Virgin that I would never harm her.'

'For the last time – where?!'

'Ye'll find her body near an oak tree.' Oh dear God, what had made her say that!

Equally aghast, Sigurd backed away then tore off to instigate another hunt.

Eventually he found Gytha, hidden in the foul and rotting matter of a refuse pile. Nearby was an oak tree. At first it looked as if she was just asleep but when Sigurd grasped her she did not wake. Her fingers were curled around something; a lump of cake. Sigurd gave a roar of anguish, seized his child and shook her. But Estorhild's eyes were glued to the damning evidence. 'Your Irish mare.' The words could hardly get past the lump in her throat. 'That is the cake I knocked from Gytha's hand but the witch's magic was too strong . . .' She fell in a faint.

Sigurd's eyes were red with emotion and fury. Very gently, he laid the child down, then, crazed by grief, raced back to Una's house. She saw him coming, pressed a fervent kiss to Murtagh's cheek. 'Quick! Before he comes, run to Aunt Mary!'

But Murtagh had no time to leave before Sigurd came upon them in a fury, knocking the child out of the way. Murtagh scrambled to his feet and ran outside. His mother faced Sigurd who glared back at her, breathing heavily. She saw the hatred in his eyes. 'That first night,' he panted. 'You told me . . . you said a woman would bring about my death. You have tried to destroy me by killing my child and all because I wouldst not free you.'

'Beloved, you are wrong!' she moaned, pleading, whilst all the time knowing that the plea was useless.

He turned away, giving her a second's reprieve. She heard a sob. The sob became a roar. He wheeled around and in that same movement drew his blade and sliced clean through her neck, freeing her from this life of drudgery. Her head fell to the floor.

Heaving, Sigurd watched the blood spurt, then charged outside, ran blindly, leapt onto the nearest horse and rode at full gallop out of the enclosure, he knew not where.

Murtagh watched the man ride away and decided it was safe to go home. Concerned over his mother's welfare, he had disobeyed her order to go to Aunt Mary's and hidden nearby, but what he saw inside the house now sent him fleeing to his aunt. He tried to tell her but could not speak. Carrying the terror-stricken child, Black Mary went to see for herself, covering her mouth in revulsion at the discovery, whilst at the same instant triumph filled her heart. She had destroyed both the boar and his sow. Now she had Murtagh all to herself. Pressing his face into her breast, she went home.

Sigurd drove the horse and himself to exhaustion before hauling viciously on the reins and throwing his body at the ground. He lay there fists clenched, pummelling the earth, his mind crammed with unassuaged violence, and wanting to turn that violence upon himself. Amid the suicidal rage that seared his brain came echoes from the past: she had prophesied on that first night that a woman would be responsible for his death. Much as he hated to give credence to her magic he had to recognize it now for he was as near to death as he had ever been.

In that hour of torment the voice of logic tried to argue against despair; she also told you that you will live to be a very old man. You will not die from this pain, Sigurd Einarsson. And then he would slip back. No! That was just to pacify me until she had the chance to carry out her revenge for my enslavement of her – and what terrible revenge she had chosen! She knew that a woman would be the one to destroy me because she was that woman.

Well, she had come very close to achieving her aim, but he had destroyed her first. Had she always hated him, he wondered? Whilst her hands caressed his flesh did they seek out his veins? He thought of his little girl, cringed into his grief and banged his fist again and again at the ground, sending up dust. He felt so close to ending his life, but if he did then Una would have won, her prophesy would have come true. He was going to live, and for as long as he did live he was never going to trust any woman other than his mother. Yes, he would live, but he would never be the same inside.

Chapter Thirteen

Sigurd did not return until nightfall. He delayed his entry to the house not wishing to face Estorhild; she would scourge him with abuse... but then it could be no worse than he laid upon himself. He had thought her crazed when she accused Una, but he was the one deranged to have been so blind. Oh, that so sweet a breast could harbour such venom!

Crushed by shock, Estorhild did not turn to look at him, even when he unbuckled his sword and dropped it, clattering, onto the floor. The thrall who was pressing pleats – such a normal occupation amid this carnage – mishandled her flattened ball of glass in alarm and leapt to retrieve it.

'Begone!' Ragnhild dismissed her and came to put a hand on Sigurd's arm, the mark of tears on her ashen face. 'You dealt with her, then.' It was not a question. Ragnhild had seen the result of his wrath. Sigurd looked down at her. So bitter, so dangerous was his face, that his mother dropped her hold on him and retreated. 'Well, you know me, son, I am not a vindictive person but I praise your action. I would have done the same myself.' Her mouth crumpled and she turned away to dab at her eyes. 'Oh, my poor grandbairn!'

A noise emerged from Estorhild, a small whimpering animal sound. Sigurd noticed then the little dress on her lap. As he watched, she folded the arms of the garment neatly across its breast, then hugged it as if the child were still inside. Something inside his breast felt ready to explode. He turned, went outside, grabbed a flaming torch and marched purposefully to Una's house. Torch aloft, he stared for a moment through the open doorway at the black form of her decapitated body which lay just as he had left it, then flung the burning brand inside, watched whilst it took hold and soon the whole place was ablaze.

Sparks began to dance against the night sky, coming dangerously close to neighbouring thatches. Plants and saplings blackened, writhed like he himself writhed. Alerted by the smoke that wafted into their houses, folk dashed out, saw the madman doing nothing and ran to douse the fire themselves. He roared at them not to meddle in his affairs and the tone of his voice brooked no opposition. Their only recourse was to toss bucketfuls of water upon their own thatches and pray that they did not ignite.

By morning there was only a pile of smouldering ashes to remind him. Slaves were ordered to dig these into the ground and in time when cabbages began to sprout it was impossible to tell there had ever been a house here.

There was one living reminder of Una, but so terrified was he of the master that Sigurd was rarely forced to look upon him. Nor did he have to listen to his voice, for Murtagh had never spoken since that dreadful day. To add to this misfortune, his left eye had turned inwards, raising much superstition amongst the inhabitants of Peseholme.

'You should have killed that child when you killed its mother!' Ragnhild would quote at her son. 'She has left the mark of the witch upon him. When he looks at you with that skellied eye ... by the gods, it makes me shiver! Mark my words, you will live to regret sparing him.'

'You think I showed mercy in not killing him?'

demanded Sigurd. 'Nei, that would have been too easy a death. I will never kill him, for that would be to free him. Murtagh shall be a slave for the rest of his life. I would see her child suffer, as she made mine to suffer.'

And so, Murtagh lived amongst the other captives with his Aunt Mary who smothered him with the maternal love that slavery had denied her. Without the facilities bestowed on his mother the child was now more poorly dressed, though his aunt sacrificed her own meagre comforts to clothe him as best she could. She would remind him over and over again what a famous clan he was descended from, how his father had been the son of a great warrior. This was all Murtagh O'Cellaigh had to cling to as he performed his base chores – battering rats and mice with a lump of wood, picking weevils out of the grain – for he knew in his heart that he would never have the bravery to stand up to the man who had murdered his mother.

After the anger came melancholy. If Sigurd ever had any youth then it was vanished now. His beard concealed the lines of bitterness and misery around his mouth but these emotions still showed in his eyes. The red tunic that had once hung so well on him, now became the portent used by other wild creatures, warning lesser breeds to keep away. Whilst Estorhild passed her long days at a shrine praying to be healed, her husband spent even more time travelling about his various estates which he ruled with merciless precision. Neither Sigurd nor Estorhild spoke of the child buried in St Cuthbert's churchyard, rarely spoke at all to each other. Throughout the spring and early summer this continued. Whenever they happened to be at home together Estorhild would devote her attention to tapestries and vestments, he to the repair of weapons. Ragnhild placed herself between them as a buffer, speaking first to the one on her right, then to the one on her left; but right never spoke to left, nor left to right.

Able to bear this no longer she had a heart to heart talk with her daughter-in-law. 'Estorhild, we are sisters now – each of us has had a child murdered. There is nought you can tell me that I have not felt myself.'

Estorhild's needle paused and she looked up. Her eyes were blank. She said nothing. What was there to say? But the thought was there – you compare yourself to me? You who never had a warm thought nor word in your life?

'At least you have the satisfaction of knowing Gytha's murderer is also dead,' coaxed Ragnhild.

Estorhild poked a different colour thread at the eye of the needle. 'It does not help.'

Ragnhild agreed with a sad shake of her head, a head that had aged rapidly over these last grief-filled months. 'Ja, I know. My thoughts were the same when Ethelred died. After wishing him dead for so long I thought . . .' she clicked her tongue and stared at her own dreadful memory. 'The pain will never heal for sure – but you must look to the future now. Unlike me, you still have a husband, you will have more babies.'

Callous, stupid woman, raged Estorhild inside, but she said calmly, 'How will that happen when he does not care to even look at me?'

'It is guilt that averts his eye, not revulsion. He blames himself and thinks you blame him too.'

'I do.' Estorhild's eye turned hard.

'You must not!' Ragnhild leaned over and pressed her arm. 'He loved Gytha as much as you did. He could not help himself against the power of the witch, but now her spell is truly broken . . .'

'At such bitter price.' Estorhild's voice barely altered its monotone.

'If you continue to think like that then the witch will have won! You must try to repair the gap between you – you do still love my son?'

Estorhild did not answer immediately, yet paused in her sewing to think about it. Had she ever really loved him? She forced herself to remember the good times – their wedding, the evening of Cnut's visit, the intimate conversations, his beard on her breasts – even whilst they were enjoying all this he had been going with that one. But yes, she could remember the warmth he had produced in her. Ragnhild was right, she should not blame Sigurd for the witch's sins, but oh, it was difficult not to. She responded to her mother-in-law's question. 'Yes . . . I think so.'

'Then you must make the first move.'

Estorhild swayed in apathy. 'Oh, I have not the heart.'

'You must! This rift is killing you both. I shall help you all I can. Tomorrow I will go and visit Ulf and stay for the night. It will give you time to mend things.'

Estorhild was beginning to yield. With a few more persuasive words from her mother-in-law she agreed to Ragnhild's plan. No mention was made of this to Sigurd, who went out in the morning, was absent all day as had become usual and came home for supper to find a different wife from the one of the last three months. He faltered under her smile of greeting and looked around the otherwise empty room.

'Your mother has gone to visit Eric and Ulf,' explained Estorhild.

'Oh.' He stood there lamely, fondling the dog which had come to greet him. His wife had changed her robe. Her hair was newly plaited and hung like a golden rope between her shoulder-blades. For once there was no hint of frost in her voice.

'Come, sit and eat.' She led him to the table, stood

behind his chair and waited until he sat upon it, then she too sat down.

'It looks good.' He complimented her on the meal and picked up a spoon to eat the broth.

Few words were exchanged other than mundanities about the food. Frequently he broke off lumps of bread, using the opportunity to snatch baffled glances at his wife. Estorhild provided him with a goblet of wine. She herself did not, as she usually did, take up her tapestry but remained beside him on the settle. There was a friendly awkwardness between them. They began to converse more easily, though discussed nothing of import. The wine was consumed. Sigurd toyed with the empty goblet. He felt his hand covered by light fingers and looked at Estorhild. She smiled at him. But what a miserable smile! Her lip quivered and tears bulged over her lower lids. She blinked, scattering them onto her cheeks. Sigurd put down his goblet and took her in his arms, envying her ability to weep, his own pain ravaging breast and mind. Neither of them mentioned Gytha, though both were of the same thought.

'I am sorry I have neglected you so long,' whispered Sigurd into her hair as her body racked with sobs.

Estorhild gave a huge sniff and wiped away the tears with the flat of her palms. 'Hush, speak not of the past.'

Sigurd began to warm towards her. She was still as beautiful as ever, even if that beauty was scarred by tragedy. It was impossible to live with this pain; he must make an effort to escape Una's clutches. He embraced his wife again. She returned his kiss. There was something frantic about the way they clawed at each other as if trying to recapture that which was buried too deeply. Estorhild broke away and began to undress. Sigurd followed suit. They came together. Sigurd looked deep into her eyes. 'Give me another child, Sigurd,' she breathed urgently.

314

Then something went wrong. He panicked, tried to enter her, but it proved impossible. Neither of them said a word, he just lay on top of her, masculinity demolished. Estorhild stared up into the smoke-filled roof wondering what had so revolted him. When he hoisted his body from her, she did not look at him for fear of seeing that revulsion in his face.

Sigurd got up and put on his clothes, then went out into the night. Estorhild had no more tears to give.

He was relieved to wake to his usual erection. On leaving his wife he had carved a huge phallus out of wood, had chanted and prayed over it and made offerings, then, fearing laughter, he had buried it.

Afterwards, he had slept in his carpentry room, ashamed to return to his wife, afraid to see the scorn in her eyes or even worse – pity. In the event, when he returned to the house there was neither, just a bland greeting and the offer of breakfast. This he ate, then went out hunting for the rest of the day.

When Ragnhild came home she brought Ulf and Eric back to cheer her son. In private conference with her daughter-in-law she asked how the reconciliation had gone. Out of shame, Estorhild lied and said things were more amicable between her and Sigurd now. She was glad to see Ulf and Eric not only for her own benefit, but in the hope that they might put her husband in a better frame of mind.

When Sigurd came home and saw four expectant faces turn towards him he reddened in anger. The bitch! Not only had she told his mother of his failure but his friends, too.

'Heill, Sigurd!' Eric remained in his seat to deliver a cuff of greeting. Ulf held up a hand too.

Sigurd remained aloof. 'Why do you come here?'

Eric became nonplussed and turned to Ragnhild for

315

explanation; none was provided. 'Why . . . are your friends no longer welcome?'

It dawned on Sigurd then that he had been so obsessed with his problem that he was inventing slight where there was none. 'Forgive me!' He returned Eric's slap with false heartiness, unhooked the bow and quiverful of arrows from his shoulder and removed his hat. ''Twas not my aim to vent my anger on you. I have just lost the mightiest pair of antlers you ever saw. Such a stag he was! I wounded him but where he went I cannot say. I have been chasing him all afternoon to no avail.' Unbuckling his sword, he leaned over to kiss his wife which pleased Ragnhild; she did not notice that he never once locked eyes with the woman he kissed. Seated amongst them he asked, 'And how are my friends?'

Conversation turned to Eric and Ulf. Both noticed that Sigurd's contribution was a little forced and tried to keep the tone light. When they all made ready for bed Estorhild was encouraged that Sigurd chose to lie beside her, but alas when she talked to him he pretended to be almost asleep. She rolled over and put her arm round him. 'Say that you still love me.'

His answer was faint. 'Of course I do.'

'Show me,' she murmured in a girlish voice. 'Last night I feared . . .'

'Hush! I am tired after galloping about the forest all day.'

How could she expect to test his virility with his friends lying in the next room? He shrugged away from her and no more was said, but he could not rid his mind of the pathetic little figure behind him. It took a long time for either of them to go to sleep.

When he woke, there it was straining against the coverlet. See! There is nought wrong with you, he told himself, relieved. All night you have lain here

316

worrying, and for what? Estorhild stirred and rolled against him. After the briefest of decisions he turned over to face her. She came awake, felt his ardour and welcomed him to her.

It was as if she were poison. No sooner had he touched her than he began to shrivel. Furious, he thumped the pillow at the side of her head, then threw off the covers, thrust his limbs into his clothes and went from the room.

His friends were yet asleep. He rode out of the enclosure with not a word to anyone. When he returned he was fully composed.

Ulf and Eric stayed for a week. During that week Sigurd made no further attempt at consummation, passing his time wrestling with the men, drinking, riding, hunting, anything that would tire him physically. On his friends' last evening the males were seated laughing and talking, sharpening arrows and adjusting bowstrings, Ragnhild was at her knitting, Estorhild ostensibly at her needlepoint. Unexpectedly, her voice broke into the male conversation. 'Sigurd, I would speak with you.'

He looked at her somewhat testily, arrow in hand. 'Speak, then.'

She inserted her needle into the tapestry and left it there, hands resting on her lap. 'Mayhap you would not wish your friends to hear what I have to say.'

He looked annoyed and anxious, but rose and indicated for her to follow him into the bed-closet. When the door separated them from the others he demanded, 'Well, what is it?'

Estorhild was calm. 'You know what it is.'

He did not hide his contempt. 'Are you a mare in heat that you have to drag me from my friends?'

She dropped the façade to volley his insult. 'If I were it would do me no good with a droop-wand like you for a husband!'

Sigurd was furious that her words might be audible

317

to his friends. 'There is nought wrong with me! I would defy any man to find passion for a miserable gimmer like you!'

Estorhild fought for control, kneading her fingers into her brow. 'I cannot live like this, Sigurd. I am only twenty-one years old yet you make me feel as though I am dead. I do not wish to feel like that any more. I want a husband who will love me and give me more children.'

His deep-set eyes abrased her. 'How easily you forget the one we had.'

She slapped his face, drawing a look of shock. 'I shall never forget! Nor shall I forget that it was your concubine who killed her!' A muscle twitched in her cheek as she awaited violent response.

But instead of retaliating he covered his head with his arms, cringing from his own recognition of the fact. *Una, Una!* The name reared up to haunt him.

'Even in death your witch weaves her spells – but I shall not let her kill me too!' Estorhild's diatribe ended though her breast continued to heave whilst she awaited his retaliation.

Sigurd's voice when it came was without emotion. 'So, you want to marry again? Go then, if you think that another man would look at one so undesirable. Divorce me now, call your witnesses and get it over with. I no longer care.' He appeared to have shrunk in size, his head bowed, chest concave.

Estorhild stared, granting him ample time in which to recant his loathing of her. There came no such word. Losing what feeling she had left for him, she opened the door. 'Let us go before them.'

Sigurd did not move. His wife took a step into the other room and announced to the three quizzical faces, 'I ask these good folk to witness that I divorce thee.'

In her shock, Ragnhild dropped the stitches

318

from her needle. 'On what grounds do you divorce my son?'

The young woman shrunk from explanation; how terrible to admit to one's own inadequacies. *No, no!* She forced aside self-guilt: *it is not your doing, put the fault where it rightly lies.* She blurted out the reason. 'On the grounds of impotence. He is unable to give me children to replace the one murdered by his woman, the one who still bewitches him. Therefore I shall take back my dowry and return to the house of my parents.'

Whereas Eric and Ulf hung their heads, Ragnhild was prepared to fight. She came out of her chair and took hold of her daughter-in-law's arm. 'You have given him no chance! Nor yourself, either. It is barely three months since your daughter was killed. These things take time – come, show your face, Sigurd, and let us talk about this.'

Her son emerged but was obviously too wounded to look at any of the witnesses. His voice was tired. 'Mother, let her go, I beg you. I would rather have no wife at all than one who is disloyal.'

Estorhild turned on him, no longer in awe of his power. 'You dare accuse me of that? When I have clung to your side even when you stank of your witch? When I served you without complaint in every manner that a wife should, when I welcomed your friends as mine own, raised you in the King's eyes – yea! 'Twas my hospitality which coaxed him into giving you the reeveship, make no mistake about that.' The whites of her eyes were red with anger. 'So do not dare talk to me of loyalty!'

After the embarrassed silence she recouped her dignity and turned to the other men. 'Could I prevail upon our former friendship and ask you to accompany me to my parents' home? I dare not ride alone, there are mean men about.'

'Nei, do not relegate our friendship to the past,

lady,' bemoaned Eric, playing with his tousled black beard. 'We would be glad to guard your journey, though it shall be with heavy hearts.'

Estorhild thanked him. 'I will be but a short time to pack.'

'At least wait until morning,' begged Ragnhild.

Her daughter-in-law took hold of her hand and delivered a last affectionate grip. 'I cannot bear to.' Serene in her decision, she picked up her little dog who had been whining as if he sensed her pain, then walked away.

'Will you grant him no chance?' Ragnhild wrung her hands and pleaded. 'Despite all I know he still cares for you.'

'Let her go, Mother.' Sigurd turned his back on all of them.

The old woman resigned herself. 'Then I must go and help her.' She followed Estorhild. 'Call two slaves to assist us.'

Ulf carried out her request and the thralls came running. Whilst Estorhild and her mother-in-law were gone there was awkwardness between the three men.

'Come, then!' Sigurd gave bitter cry and marched theatrically before them. 'Will you not make some jest about my broken tool?'

Both showed they felt it too delicate a matter to joke about. Eric ran a hand around his black chin and tried to bolster. 'It will come right in time.'

'It is well enough now!' Sigurd bent from the waist and tapped Eric's chest furiously. 'The only thing amiss is that I have an uncompromising shrew for a wife! She blames me for everything.'

'Nei, that cannot be true,' ventured Ulf.

In a trice Sigurd had veered his invective from Eric to Ulf, hissing into the fringed face, 'Do you say that I lie? Wouldst care to take on Estorhild? For you would be most welcome!'

'I am just sorry for both my friends,' muttered Ulf, and averted his eyes from the angry pair before him.

'Do not pity me!' Sigurd charged out. He was not present to see their departure with his wife, but another watched with great satisfaction.

Ecstatic though she might be over the mental destruction of her enemy, Black Mary was as terrified as any of her fellows under the new harsh regime. Sigurd had rarely beaten his thralls but he thrashed them most enthusiastically now, and not even children escaped his malice.

'Get thee to work!' Sigurd hurled a lump of wood at seven-year-old Murtagh, who had the misfortune to have just sneaked a moment to relax from his endless labours as the master came out of his carpentry room. 'I did not spare thy life to have it idled away!'

Murtagh ducked but the wood hit him on the shoulder. Immediately he shot to his feet and ran, not daring to stop and rub his injury until the master was inside the big house.

Wearing his permanent frown, Sigurd slammed the door behind him, then paused on seeing the visitor at his hearth. At the look in his eye Ragnhild hurried to explain, 'It is a messenger from the King. He comes to . . .'

'The man can speak for himself, can he not?' Sigurd brushed the wood-dust from his sleeves, took the cup of ale offered by his mother and came to rest by the hearth.

'I come to ask you to summon levies for the King's fyrd,' said the quietly-spoken visitor, holding his cup to be renewed with ale by Ragnhild. 'And to meet with him at the mouth of the Humbre in one week's time.'

Sigurd showed not one iota of interest. 'Very well, I shall send heralds out at once. I myself will set out tomorrow.'

'Do you not wish to know whom we go to fight?' asked the man.

Sigurd was blunt. 'Nei.'

'Well, I should like to know!' cut in Ragnhild as the messenger, faced with such rudeness, made to leave. 'He is my only son, I have more need of him here than has the King. Sigurd, he does not require you to go for another week!'

'Do not interfere,' ordered Sigurd. 'I go tomorrow and that is final.'

Ragnhild was not pleased, but told the visitor, 'If he is to go then have supper with us and tell me all about it.'

The man reseated himself by the fire. 'Thank you, mistress, but I cannot tarry. I have others to inform. The King gathers a fleet to sail on Norway.'

'Ah, he moves against Olaf at last, does he?' Ragnhild turned to her son but he made no comment. 'Why now? Olaf has been King of Norway for ten years.'

'He has gone too far.' The man was only repeating Cnut's angry reaction to the news. 'Not content to have stolen Norway he has made a pact with Onund Jacob of Sweden and the pair plan to take Denmark.' Since the death of Thorkell the Tall this was in the regency of Cnut's brother-in-law.

Ragnhild was more understanding. 'Then I suppose the King must have all the help he can.' She turned pensive. In this frame of mind her son was going to get himself killed. 'You will be taking Ulf and Eric with you?'

'I have enough men without them.' Sigurd did not want to see his friends, did not want to encounter the pity in their eyes, hence he had treated them with the same rudeness doled out to the King's messenger.

This attitude had successfully deterred their visits of late.

But Ragnhild needed them now. Saying nothing more, she dished out supper for the men then excused herself. In the privacy of shadows she whispered an urgent message to a servant then dispatched him in all haste to Eric's house.

It was late in the day but still light when Ragnhild's servant, having run all the way as instructed, arrived to find Eric and Ulf enjoying a cup of ale in the summer evening, relaxing on the grass amongst a collection of pecking fowl, ginger kittens and small girls. The moment Ulf heard the news of Sigurd's imminent departure he rose and gave instant response to the messenger. 'Tell Lord Sigurd that we prepare to join him and will be in Jorvik at first light.'

'Hold!' Eric put down his ale and struggled to his feet to halt the man before he could retrace his steps. 'I thought I heard you say that it was the Lady Ragnhild who asked for us.'

'That is so.' The messenger, still panting, was grateful for this opportunity to rest.

Eric nodded. 'There is no need to rush back if we do not leave until morning. Go into the house and catch your breath. My wife will give you refreshment before you leave.'

It was better treatment than Ragnhild's servant was accustomed to and he did not need to be told twice. When he had disappeared into the thatched cabin with tiny girls pulling him by the sleeves, Eric spoke to Ulf. 'Think carefully about this. It is not Sigurd who has asked us to go. He may not want us there – he has not been well-disposed towards us of late.'

'It makes no difference who has asked. In the mood he is in at present he is likely to get himself killed, and we as his friends should prevent that.' At Eric's mocking response, Ulf added, 'Yea, I know he has always been able to take care of himself, but this madness that he suffers now will lead him to rash deeds. He cares not whether he lives nor dies.' Whilst he and his friend were becoming more English in speech and habit, Sigurd had reverted to his viking ways.

Eric showed a reluctance to swap his comfortable life. 'I am a farmer now, grown used to the quiet life. What use would I be?'

Ulf curled his upper lip at the lame excuse. 'You are no farmer! You are a fat lazy troll who would sit drinking whilst his friend died!'

Eric rocked from side to side in an attempt to evade Ulf's persuasive eye. 'Sigurd is happy where there is danger, I am not. How would my wife run things without me?'

There came a rude laugh. 'The same way she does now! What work do you do around here? She and I do most of it. That is the least of our worries, we can always get extra thralls from Sigurd.' He growled his disgust at this lack of cooperation. 'You think it is a pleasure for me to go to Norway?' Whereas Sigurd fought to win prizes or even simply for the joy of fighting, Ulf's aggression was only brought about by personal slight or defence of his freedom; neither factor was relevant here. 'I have no wish to join foreign battles.'

Thwarted in his argument, Eric's swarthy black face resorted to pathos. 'But my little daughters, Ulf . . .' Of the five he had sired, only four lived.

Immune to such wheedling, Ulf's reply was firm. 'They shall be here to fetch and carry for you when you return. Come, fatman, sharpen your weapons. The morrow we ride for Jorvik.' And as usual when a decision had been made for him Eric was unable to resist.

Sigurd showed no gladness to see them when they rode into the yard at a very early hour, only mild surprise. 'I did not expect you to be here.'

'Nor I,' grumbled Eric, as both dismounted and hitched their reins to a pole. 'My trusty friend volunteered our services as your bodyguard.'

The recipient offered a nasty snort. 'Think you that I am no longer a man that I require nursemaids? Turn around and go home, the pair of you.' He lowered his eyes back to the whetstone on which he sharpened his blade.

Whilst Eric's eyes asked his comrade why they stood for this treatment, Ulf hunkered by Sigurd, resting forearms on knees, watching the whetstone move feveredly over the blade. 'I know you for a man, the man who saved my life. We come not to protect you from the enemy but from yourself. Your anger may cause you to be reckless. I would hate to see the one who saved my life die from a foolish mistake if I could prevent it.'

Sigurd gave nonchalant permission. 'Do as you will. I cannot stop you, but blame not me if you yourselves should die. I do not ask you to do this.' Blade honed to his satisfaction, he sheathed his sword and marched away across the enclosure.

'See, he does not need us,' said Eric, much relieved. 'Why do we not just go home?'

Ulf gave reply with his eyes, then set off for the house where Ragnhild had appeared in the doorway.

'Oh, I thank you most humbly for being so swift!' She took hold of Ulf's arm. There was no saucy jest today. 'Forgive me for not offering victuals but my son has already loaded his ship and given me his keys. He will not be long in his departure – where is he now?' She looked around, a worried look upon her forehead.

Ulf replied, 'He has left the yard, but surely he would say farewell to his mother before he sets sail?'

'I fear not,' sighed Ragnhild. 'He does not care about his mother nor anyone. Come! We must make

325

haste to the Staith – I trust you have come to sail with him?'

Ulf nodded. 'May I just crave a boon before we go? Eric's wife will need male help . . .'

'She will have everything she needs!' Ragnhild cut him off and urged the two of them to follow her. 'The gods protect you all and send you back safely, my boys. Now hurry before Sigurd is away!'

Ragnhild was correct in her assumption that Sigurd was about to depart. When they reached the Staith, both Ragnhild and Eric puffing and perspiring, the ship was almost ready to cast off. To a look of unconcern from Sigurd, Ulf jumped nimbly on board and held out his hand to pull Eric after him. 'You should have more respect than to leave your mother without a word,' he scolded, and when this was ignored he demanded, 'Well? Have you nought to say to any of us?'

Sigurd did not look at him, but responded in loud voice for those left behind on the wharf. 'I have only one message to leave: let any man take ought of mine whilst I am away . . .'

Eric, mopping his brow, tried to make a humorous interjection. 'With Ragnhild in charge? He would have to be a madman!'

Sigurd pressed his lips together, his blond hair lank as his spirit, and continued as if without interruption, 'Let him take so much as a cat, and he shall know my wrath.'

With this threat, the ship cast off for the Humbre.

From here the assembled northern fyrd sailed north for Denmark where they met up with the rest of the combined English and Danish fleet, and whence they pressed on into the mouth of the River Helge on the Baltic coast of Skane where, encountering the enemy, they grouped for battle.

Sigurd had never once rested; even in sleep his body

jerked and trembled. During the voyage Ulf had tried to inject some lightheartedness into his friend by persuading a novice to share a sleeping bag with Eric, just as they had done with Sigurd all those years ago, but their friend was not amused, intent only on the engagement. He was now busying himself by hauling down masts and lashing ships together to act as a platform for the fighting. The sun played upon the cornfield of his hair as he bent and bobbed and fidgeted.

'Just look at him!' bewailed Eric to Ulf. 'How do you expect me to keep apace of him when he dances around like a frog? It is a waste of time my being here.'

Ulf held the silent fear that Eric was probably right but merely shook his head and looked across the rivermouth at Onund's fleet. 'I just thank God that I am here and not on yonder side, for when Sigurd's anger makes itself felt . . .' He did not finish but sucked in his breath and shook his head again. Like Eric's, his stomach churned and he wished that he was far from here.

But it was too late to turn back for orders were being barked. Men swarmed over the ships erecting wattle screens to ward off the flights of enemy arrows. Cnut's rowers began to manoeuvre the ships nearer to their adversary while Onund began to question the wisdom of his alliance with Olaf, but such thoughts were luxury now. There came the *thrum* of a thousand bowstrings, the hiss of arrows launched high into the air; they arched, soared, descended . . . thudded into timber, flesh and bone! An answering shower of darts leapt quivering against the blue sky, soaring, falling, seeking heart and brow, others wasted on the choppy waters.

The rowers were moving their floating platforms closer together, spears were already hurtling through the air. Above the clangour Sigurd gave rent to his battle cry and unleashed a shooting-snake from each hand. The missiles were too numerous to tell if his own had found their target, but men were toppling into the sea. Cnut's rowers laid brawn into their oars. Prows corseted in iron lunged towards the foe, rammed home, tipped men into the drink. Upon those boiling waters ships collided, timbers groaned and scraped and bucked as in the grip of Orca, men roared and grappled with bearded axe, pulling Death into their bosom. Amid the deafening confusion friend lost friend. Sigurd, aware only of his target, yelled at the top of his voice. With axe and shield he launched himself into the foray, cleaving skull and sinew with his blade. Blind to humanity he hacked and hewed and rent men's flesh; sweat ran with blood down shrieking muscle whilst overhead wheeled the Choosers of the Slain, the Valkyries, ready to take the glorious fallen to their eternal battleground, and Sigurd hoped to be amongst them.

Suddenly, as if by power of Odin's axe, the tangled mass of butchery was split asunder. The enemy fell back in shoals, abandoning craft and weapons and diving into the waters. Hair flying like a banner, Sigurd urged his men to row after them, whilst he lanced the swimmers like fish until his King ordered the killing to cease. Then they stood upon the floating platforms, beating their shields and whooping in triumph as the ill-starred alliance of the Kings of Norway and Sweden was dashed against the rocks, their bloodied dross limping ashore.

Sigurd was eager to continue the attack, to harry and kill every last man. Performing an agile leap across the rafts to the King's ship, he exhorted Cnut to press home the advantage. But Cnut had not held his English throne by being impetuous. 'No! Olaf may be bloodied but a wounded rat is as dangerous as a boar and enough blood has been spilt today, on our own side too. We shall retire.'

'And allow Olaf's troops to regroup!' barked Sigurd in disbelief.

Cnut was firm. 'There are more subtle ways to skin a bear. Where is the merit in throwing myself into his jaws when I could easier be tempting him with honey? Besides, the king who has lost control of the sea has also lost his crown. I shall return to take it at my leisure. Come! Rest before we sail for Denmark.'

Unsated in his bloodlust, Sigurd continued to gripe, untying the ropes that bound his ship to the others and pushing it away with an oar. He was helping to lift the dead bodies of his enemies and roll them over the side and had just bent to grasp another pair of legs when he recognized their owner.

'Eric!' Aghast, he knelt down and touched his friend's breast where a gaping spear-wound had displayed a lung. For a moment he grieved, then his heart palpitated with a terrible thought and his eyes came up to search.

Relief caused a sigh. There was Ulf on a rowing bench supporting his weak chin on a palm. With a last haggard look at Eric, Sigurd went to the other man and touched his shoulder, only then becoming aware of the cuts and gashes on his own body, that felt as if under attack from a swarm of wasps.

'I forced him to come,' muttered Ulf, and moved his hand from chin to brow, pushing up his fringe. 'I should have known he was not fit.' He could think of nothing else to say and neither could Sigurd, who had told both his friends before the battle that if they died it would be their own faults.

They transported their dead friend back to Denmark, where they buried him and raised a stone in his honour. 'Though he will likely blow it out of the ground,' came Ulf's weak joke. Then he turned his face to the sky and made an oath. 'I shall never fight again.'

Sigurd put a comforting hand to his shoulder. 'Not even if I beat you at hnefatafl?'

'Not even in defence of my country,' swore Ulf. 'I am finished. Finished.'

Sigurd looked grim and indicated the flat Danish landscape. 'Why do we stay here, Ulf? If we are not to fight then we might as well go home. I am grown sick of Cnut's dalliance. I go to tell him that I will no longer waste my skills here.' He marched off to Court.

It was an indication of Cnut's friendship towards this angry warrior that he bothered to explain his intentions. 'Sit.' The monarch beckoned to a place beside his throne, and Sigurd did as he was commanded. 'You killed many foes in the battle, but not enough, I think.'

Sigurd's eyes questioned. After ten years amongst Lundeners the King had become much anglicized. Though Sigurd had begun to think of himself as English now, he often found it hard to interpret southern grammar. 'Did I not do you service, my lord?' He looked away.

Cnut's reply was astute. 'You know well enough my meaning. You killed not for me but for killing's sake. I could see it in your eyes. You were angry at your King for what you saw as cowardice.'

'Not so!'

'Then you took me for a fool – yes!' Cnut warded off another negation. 'You hated me for denying you the right to kill so now you withdraw your aid.'

Sigurd hung his head. His body heaved. 'It is not you I hate, but myself.' He rubbed his palms over his face.

Cnut spoke softly. 'I have been told about your bad fortune – your child being murdered and your wife divorcing you.'

Sigurd threw him a brief look of gratitude. 'I am

honoured that my King should interest himself in the affairs of his servants.'

'Not every one, just those whose ambitions might prove a threat to my crown.'

Sigurd reacted sharply. 'You cannot think that of me!'

Cnut smiled. 'A jest, my friend. If I had any doubts as to your loyalty you would have been dead long ago. We have shared much, you and I, since you came to warn me of Thorald. You have always been generous with your help and advice.'

'But you do not often take it.' The moment had passed; Sigurd was once again confident enough of his relationship with the King to voice his thoughts.

Cnut leaned forth and spoke earnestly, pointing a jewelled finger. 'If I had not prevented it you would have slain every man in Olaf's army and then been killed yourself. I have enough berserks in my pay but only a handful of men I can trust. I number you amongst those, Sigurd, I value your life even if you do not value it yourself. So let me explain why I stayed your hand: Olaf is still in possession of Norway but his support is not wholehearted. I can name many chieftains who, with only a little coaxing, can be bought over to our side. If I can win this battle from my fireside why get my feet wet? A little silver, a few titles – oh, and a little help from Christ – and Norway will be begging me to come and save her from that tyrant Olaf.'

Sigurd laughed, a softly mocking chuckle and shook his head.

Cnut laughed too. 'Yes, I know you do not truly share my faith, and in that I will call you a fool, for Christ is more powerful than you know.'

Sigurd was obstinate. 'The old gods protected us well enough in the past.'

'How well have they protected you, my friend?' Cnut touched a jewelled finger to yet another wound on Sigurd's brow. 'This God can win battles without even raising His sword – though I know you would say that that is half the fun.' The King smiled indulgence. 'Myself, I would sooner use my head than risk it being sliced off. That is why I intend to sail home for now and leave others to do the bargaining for me.'

Sigurd, misinterpreting the reason that the King had sent for him, looked aghast. 'You cannot mean to leave me here all winter!'

Cnut laughed. 'Be calm! Much as I admire your soldierly skills you are no ambassador. I have others more fitted to that duty.'

A relieved Sigurd rolled his eyes, then reverted to apathy. 'Then I too shall sail home.'

'Not in this mood you shall not,' came the royal command. 'You shall spend the winter with me in Lunden where I have plenty to occupy a troubled mind.' Cnut was wise enough to disguise his act of charity. 'Besides, I have an ulterior motive. Word has reached me of the death of my brother-in-law and friend Duke Richard of Normandy, and Robert rules in his place.'

Sigurd made a noise of understanding. 'He who is like a brother to Ethelred's sons.'

'Yes, so it seems that our truce with the Normans has come to an end. I have never been on good terms with him. I am afraid that he will take the opportunity of my absence to launch an attack on England, that is my real reason for wanting you in the south for a while.'

'I would advise you not to worry too greatly.' Sigurd was unmoved. 'Our people know you for a just King. Robert would get no help from within even when you are away. But,' he shrugged, 'I will lend you my arms for as long as you wish.' He withdrew on a bow.

When told that they would be spending winter in

Lunden, Ulf was none too pleased. 'We should really get the news of Eric's death to his wife as soon as possible.'

'It is I who have been ordered to stay in Lunden,' replied Sigurd. 'There is nought to prevent you from going home.'

Ulf would not hear of it. 'I remain by your side.'

Sigurd patted his hand. 'You are a good friend. I will be glad of your company. In truth. . .' It took courage to utter even to a friend. 'I am afraid to go home, Ulf.' He gave a bitter laugh. 'Is that not ridiculous? Sigurd Einarsson who is afraid of no man's sword, yet . . .'

Ulf waived the explanation. 'You do not have to give your reasons.'

Sigurd nodded, patted the other man again, then sighed. 'So, what do we do about Eric's widow? Send a messenger?'

'Nay, I would rather it came from my own lips,' replied Ulf. 'Whether she receives the news now or in the spring it will not bring Eric back.'

It turned out that Eric's widow was not to receive news of his death in the spring, either. Cnut, having been keeping an eye on Sigurd during the winter months in Lunden, was disturbed that all his efforts to bring the man out of his melancholy were ineffectual. Oh, Sigurd carried out his duties to the letter, but there was no enthusiasm in him. When the thaw arrived it might be expected that Sigurd would ask to be relieved and go home but when he failed to do so Cnut sent for him.

'You will be pleased to know that my envoys inform me that there is no imminent threat of attack from Normandy. Robert has not the strength to try his hand yet. So, you must be eager to return north.' The eagle eyes watched the other's reaction carefully. 'I thank you for all the work you have done for me these past months.'

Sigurd bowed his head and studied the lines on the palm of his hand. He and the King were alone; he felt able to speak honestly. 'There is nought to go home for. I might as well stay here if I can be of use to you, my lord – if you deplete your troops Duke Robert might decide to attack.'

'Maybe, maybe.' Cnut was silent for a while before disgressing to a more cheery topic. 'Oh, I have word that my plan seems to be working in Norway! The promise of a title has brought many chieftains over to our cause.'

'That is good.' Sigurd tried to show pleasure.

'There is also news that the coronation of the new Emperor of Rome will take place at Easter. I intend to go there and pay homage, and on my journey I will pay court to those whose territories bound the Great Road in the hope that my overtures will safe-guard passage for our pilgrims – and also for our tradeships!' He gave a statesmanlike grin. 'Mayhap I could even persuade them to reduce tolls – and one never knows, I may even be able to do something about Robert of Normandy while I am there. So! Instead of going home with your tail between your legs why not come with me? There is much excitement for a young man in Rome, they say.'

Sigurd was pensive. A voyage such as was pre-scribed might help to lift the veil of maudlin. 'If such is your will I shall come.'

Cnut heaved in his throne. 'Christ above! Why do I feel that you are the one to grant me favour?' Grappling with his frustration, he tried to put himself in his friend's shoes, saying quietly, 'You still hate yourself so much that you will not allow yourself to live. Well, if I am to bestow titles on those who mean nought to me should I not reward those whom I call friend? Let me grant you favour so that you may learn to love yourself a little more – as much as I do.' Cnut looked upon the other fondly. 'When we

return to England from Rome you will be my ealdorman.' This was the King's representative acting between monarch and people, a highly respected position in the shire. 'Ealdorman Aelfric of Eoforwicshire is dead from the bloody flux. You shall fill his
role, take care of my royal estate at Eoforwic,' he
used the city's English name, 'preside over the shire
courts and keep the peace.' He laid great emphasis
on the last word. 'I give you leave to build a house
at Earlsburh and a company of my housecarls to
guard it.'

'I am greatly honoured, my lord!' Sigurd's face
showed that the thanks were genuine. To be granted
leave to reside there was to announce one's importance to the whole city. For that moment a spark of
his old ambition was rekindled – there was chance of
an earldom yet!

'So, will you come to Rome with good heart and
join me in giving thanks to God for His help in the
fight for Norway?'

'Gladly, my King.'

'Good!' And for once Cnut appeared satisfied with
his friend's reaction.

When informed of Sigurd's new title Ulf was glad
for him too, and without objection agreed to accompany him on the pilgrimage to Rome in the hope that
it would heal their winter melancholy over Eric's
death.

The winds across the channel between England and
France blew icy cold and the pilgrims' ships had to
forge their way deep into the rivers of Aquitane
before they began to feel any change in the temperature. Once the warmth was felt, however, it was not
limited to the sunshine, for here Cnut was to achieve
one of his great aims: the friendship of the ruler of
Aquitane.

When their ships would go no further they changed
to horseback and no church along the way went

unvisited. At every one Ulf, like the King, paid penance for his role in the violence that had brought about Eric's death. Sigurd joined in these pious interludes, but hedged his bets by making secret offerings to the old gods. Despite Cnut's words he remained convinced that the move towards total Christianity would be his downfall. If he deserted Thor and Odin, how was he to win battles? This Jesus was meek, preached things unknown to Sigurd – it was all very well for Cnut to say he preferred to win wars with friendship, but sometimes one just had to fight.

The only fighting that took place in Rome was that in the circuses, between grotesque horned beasts whose skins were tough as mail. Sigurd was agog at this spectacle – and with all he had witnessed since his arrival that morning. 'Never have I known such an exciting place, Ulf!' was his enthusiastic verdict as he and the vast audience rose in applause at the bloody conclusion of the afternoon's performance and jostled their way from the amphitheatre. 'And the people – look, they are every colour under the sun! Black, brown, yellow . . .'

Ulf gave him a dig. 'People? You mean women! Your eyes have been everywhere. I am surprised you have not sampled any local flesh yet.' Immediately he realized he had said the wrong thing and quickly changed the subject. 'But I would not be surprised if you are loth to return to flat old Jorvik after this!' He spread his arm in an admiring gesture. Rome was a city that shouted grandeur from its seven hills. There were colossal Parian figures that had been visible from miles away as the pilgrims approached, shimmering in the Mediterranean sun – as indeed everything was wont to shimmer here. The houses were built of stone, gleaming white with huge pillars, porticos and domes. 'If I do succeed in dragging you back I can see what kind of house you will build at Earlsburh.'

Sigurd's long nose wrinkled in disagreement. 'It would look good but I wager it would be like an ice-palace to live in.'

Ulf noticed that his friend's gay mood had regressed and holding himself responsible for this with his careless remark, said, 'Well, let's go and find out!'

Cnut had arranged for his loyal retainer to have a room in the palace; Ulf as his friend would share the privilege. On admittance to the palace it was necessary for them to find a guide who would take them to the King. Once on his way along the marble corridors Sigurd regained some of his former buoyancy for there was none of the draughtiness he had expected. 'Why, I have to admit that I was wrong, Ulf. It is as warm as my own wooden house. How is it so?' As he moved along the network of passages he swivelled his head about in child-like awe, looking for fires, not understanding that the hot air blew from ducts throughout the royal residence. The splendour of the bronze equestrian statues which loomed up at every turn of the way, the painted women – and men – whom they encountered, the hospitality, all made him giddy, so too Ulf.

'So, you have changed your mind,' teased his friend after listening to numerous compliments about the palace. 'You think you would like to live here after all?'

Sigurd looked bemused as they toured the marble labyrinth. 'I am impressed, but . . . oh, how can I explain that which is lacking after I have praised it so highly? I do not know what it is.' The lack which he felt was the cosiness of shadows, for in every vaulted hall he felt as if on display against a glare of marble. 'I feel like one of those men.' He pointed to the frieze that graced each wall. 'Everyone is looking at me.'

Ulf mistook his meaning and snorted derision. 'Even here you think that you are the most important person in the world! These people prepare for the coronation of their Emperor – they have not time to stare at you!'

And Sigurd let the misunderstanding pass as they finally arrived at the quarters that had been designated to the King. Bowing on entry he presented himself to Cnut whilst Ulf waited in the background.

The King was tired from his travels but had a smile for his visitor. 'What think you to this splendour, my friend – was it worth the journey?'

'Forsooth it was, my lord, though I am probably too exhausted to fully appreciate it at present.' All of a sudden the only thing Sigurd craved was rest.

'I, too – so eat well then go to your bed and be fully refreshed to honour the Emperor tomorrow. Your quarters ajoin mine, the guide will show you the way – and Sigurd!' About to turn away, the other halted for the King to add, 'All will be well here, you will see.'

Sigurd was led to doubt the King's sentiment when made to endure hours of piety at the coronation, but after the prayers came feasting and entertainment on a scale that gave him back his zest for living, and he went to his bed much happier than he had done for many a month. He was even happier at the discovery that he was not to sleep alone. Yet there was hesitation too before he approached the couch on which lay a girl clothed in diaphanous gown and golden jewellery. 'I crave your pardon, lady.' His eyes scanned her body which could be seen clearly through the dress. 'I fear that I intrude upon you – I thought this to be my room.'

The girl's smile never wavered. She looked very foreign with dark hair and eyes, olive skin, but spoke in English. 'I am sent to please you, master.'

At the term of address Sigurd's face dropped. 'You are a slave?' His voice held total disbelief.

The girl affirmed, looking somewhat concerned at his expression. 'Am I not beautiful enough for you, master?'

Sigurd came to his senses. 'Ja, ja! I had just not expected . . . You are so richly-dressed for one so low.'

The smile returned and there was pride in her reply. 'That is because my lord is so rich and powerful. It is good to have such a master.'

Sigurd nodded and, thinking of his own thralls, learnt a valuable lesson. He must set about clothing them in a manner that reflected his new status. He dithered by the couch, looking down at her, wanting to touch but fearing Una's curse. The girl reached out for him. He took a pace backwards. 'I am not ready yet. Wait there.'

He left the room and stood for a while, biting his knuckle and wondering what to do. It occurred to him to go into the small room next door and confer with Ulf, but then what use would that woman-fearer be? He began to wander along the marbled corridor. By chance his feet led him past a tiny chapel. He paused for thought, backtracked and went through the fretwork doors. There were shadows here. Diffused candlelight shone through an iron grille speckling the feet of a Christ who dominated the tranquil room. There was no one else present. Sigurd knelt on a mat and asked for the help of the Christian God, begged that he might not go flaccid before he had even entered her. Then, loosening the thong of his purse, he took a handful of silver and laid it at the foot of the statue.

When he made his apprehensive return he thought for a moment that he had taken a wrong passage; on his bed was not one girl but half a dozen, all of equal beauty and clad in similar diaphanous robes.

The original girl peered from under her long lashes. 'My lord saw you leave, master, and thought that he had offended you by only offering one girl.'

Sigurd was even more confused; he had passed no one either on his way to the chapel nor on his return, he was too low a subject for the Emperor to trouble his mind over, so who was responsible for the favour? He stared at the collection of female flesh on the bed. They seemed not human; six heads but one smile. Where did he begin?

The girls giggled at his obvious dilemma and leapt up to pull him onto the satin couch. They plied him with figs which he refused, then began to strip off his clothes, one taking charge of his boots, whilst another unbuckled his belt and relieved him of his jewellery and yet another was pulling off his breeches. Whilst they made admiring remarks on his long blond hair, Sigurd's mind reeled with one thought: I cannot pleasure one, how am I expected to cope with six?

One of them kissed him full on the lips. In the time this took, her companions had shed their own flimsy garments. Naked, he was tugged into an ante-room where a deep mosaic bath awaited. The females escorted him down the steps and into the warm water, its ripples distorting the elaborate picture on the bottom. They began to wash and stroke him. A dozen hands slithered over his body, into his groin, tumescence formed, in a moment of panic that he was going to lose it, and so lose face, Sigurd grabbed one of the girls under her bottom and entered her. Beneath the water she wrapped her limbs around his torso and drew him into her. He ejaculated at once, grinding his chin into her shoulder and with an embarrassed laugh explained his poor performance. 'I am not used to such lavish attention!'

The girl smiled her permanent smile and uncoupled herself. 'I will fetch you something, master.' She waded towards the steps. He watched the water trickle down her haunches as she left the bath, then he too was led out by the girls who patted him dry, laid him on a couch and began to massage him with perfumed oils.

The friction produced warmth deep within his muscles. He closed his mind to all things past, concentrated only on what was happening to his body. The first girl reappeared with a silver cup from which she bade him drink. Sigurd refused, thinking it was wine or ale, which was the last thing he needed, but the girl was firm in a coaxing provocative way and to please her he tossed the contents down his throat.

They all tittered when he made a face and spat. 'By the gods! You give me piss to drink!'

The bearer of the cup retrieved it from his hand. 'No, master, it will bring you much happiness. Turn over and let us pleasure you.'

Still grimacing, Sigurd turned onto his belly and closed his eyes. One of the girls caught his long hair in a towel and rubbed it gently. Hands began to massage him, rubbing the oil into every crevasse of his body. Sinew by sinew, he relaxed, opened himself to the sensual experience. They talked in a low foreign murmur as they worshipped him. He became more and more aware of their hands: fingers stroked gently at his temples, gliding in circular motion round and around . . . palms lubricating his back, easing shoulder muscles, up his arms, round each of his fingernails, down between each digit, fingers locked with his fingers working oil into every battle-scarred muscle, up and down and round and in between, hands massaged his thighs and calves, ankles, heels, toes . . . A pause. He felt oil dribbled into the small of his back; fingertips worked it round and round, widening the circle, over his clenched buttocks, smoothing, relaxing. Fingertips traced a pattern around the hollows of his back, probed gently at the very base

341

of his spine, slid down the cleft of his buttocks . . .
He groaned.

Without a pause in their massage they turned him
over, anointed him with oil from temple to neck to
chest to belly to thigh, knees, shins, ankles, toes. Blood
began to pulsate through his body. Fingers crept into
his groin, around his genitals, cupping, stimulating,
worked up and down and round.

Relaxation was displaced by vigour and apprehension. Sigurd opened his eyes, dark slits of excitement.
Instantly the girls ceased their massaging. One of
them threw her leg astride him and impaled herself,
wriggling her flesh down around his. Sigurd arched
to meet her, expecting any minute to explode; but it
did not happen. The girl writhed and brought herself
to climax, fell away to be replaced by one of her
sisters. Whilst she coupled with him, her sisters ran
their lips and tongues about his body, breathed warm
breath in his ear.

His thoughts swirled as if he were in some dream.
When the next girl threw back her head and shouted
in ecstasy his confidence soared. The Christ had
listened! Before the third houri could straddle him he
had thrown her onto her back and thrust himself at
the perfumed flesh . . .

It was thus so all evening. He coupled with them
all and went with each again, and still he was not
spent. Exhausted, he lay back on the couch and paid
thanks to Christ: *You certainly deliver Your money's
worth, oh God. If anything You are a little too generous.* Amidst the ecstasy he thought he saw one of the
wall curtains move and the glimpse of a familiar face,
but was too tired to object. He tried to sleep, co-
cooned in female flesh, but the virile member proved
a distraction.

By morning it was still there. One of the girls laid
a drowsy hand over his groin, encountered the hard-
ness and obligingly opened herself to his sleepy at-

tentions. Even now it did not wilt. Jaded and extremely sore, he gave up trying and using her breast as a cushion, fell back asleep. When he woke again the girls were sitting up around him. Their eyes on his nether regions, they did not notice that his own had come open to watch them. They spoke in foreign tongue but it was obvious from the note of marvel in their tone just what they were discussing.

'I have never seen it last this long. Do not tell me we have to go through last night's performance again, it is too tiresome to fake at this time of morning. If he expects me to remedy it he had better wake soon. I promised Sophia I would put beads in her hair, she will be tearing it out thinking I am not coming – and I badly need to shave. Look at the state of my legs!' She ran a hand up and down them. 'The way young Priapus performs I shall be here for a week and they'll begin to look like his beard – oh hush, he awakes!'

Immediately all adopted their fixed smiles and became attentive to his needs. When they tried to lead him to the bath he groaned and instead they brought sponges to mop his fatigue.

He was still in bed when Ulf paid a visit. 'I was concerned.' Getting no response to his statement he approached the couch and looked down at Sigurd. 'When you did not come to the table I thought mayhap you had been slain in your bed.'

'You would not be far wrong.' Sigurd delivered a grin that Ulf had not seen for a long time and, rolling onto his back, presented the reason for his nonappearance.

'By Christ!' Ulf stared down at it.

'You may well praise His name for He is responsible.' Sigurd could not drag his head from the pillow. Still displaying the trophy, he gave Ulf the details of what had occurred last night. When the other showed disbelief he cried, 'I fool you not, my friend! I had

343

been with each of them at least twice and still I could not come, and when I woke there was I with this massive great shaft pulsing to be at them and the girls all sitting round discussing a remedy.' Sigurd pretended to cry, entreating with his hands. 'Ulf, what am I to do if it does not go down?'

Ulf sat on the edge of the couch and pondered over the dilemma. 'Hmm ... we could always tie a sail to it and float you home.'

At this point a girl entered, a different one from those of the night before. She did not speak but came towards Sigurd with a cup. 'Oh, be gone, woman!' With pained expression he waved her away, but she insisted on holding it to his lips until he drank it. As he did so his mind became alerted to the foul stuff he had consumed last night, and he wondered if that had anything to do with his predicament. The girl put aside the empty cup and disappeared for a while, during which time Ulf made more jokes at his friend's expense. The girl returned naked and without a thought for the spectator climbed onto the couch and mounted Sigurd. Ulf stood and watched the show. He had only to wait seconds.

This time semen flowed, burning, releasing. Sigurd closed his eyes and gave a beatific grin. Never had he been so glad to droop.

Ulf was unimpressed. 'What a liar!' He flicked a dismissive hand as he left. 'All night, says he – hah!'

In the afternoon Sigurd, Ulf and their friends accompanied the King on an expedition into the market to buy luxuries to take home with them. Cnut demurred the offer of transportation, preferring to go on foot through the narrow streets where he again illustrated his greatness by rubbing shoulders with beggars. A retinue of slaves followed behind to carry the purchases. Far from being lifted by the exotic music, the fun of haggling and the peacock he had bought,

Sigurd was toppled into a deep melancholia. He could not stop thinking about Gytha and the pointlessness of life. Depression sat upon his brow like a crown of thorns. Finally, he explained his disability to the King. 'I must return to my quarters, my lord, for I am like to die.'

Cnut seemed not to regard the malady as life-threatening, and whispered encouragement into the haggard face. 'Fret you not, it is but the drink you had last evening. It will lift soon.'

Sigurd lowered his gingery brows. 'How did . . . ?' Then probing that mischievous smile he remembered the face peering out from behind the wall curtain.

'My friend the Emperor is a very generous host, would you not say?' Cnut winked and before Sigurd could offer either rebuke or thanks, the King went on his route.

'I must be more careful what I drink whilst I am in Rome,' muttered Sigurd to Ulf who had remained at his shoulder. 'By the gods, I have never felt so bad in all my days. It will lift soon, sayeth the King; it had better – Ulf, take my knife lest I open my veins and do not give it back to me until I am mended . . . though I feel that I never shall be.'

However, his depression did ease and his physical problem appeared to have been remedied too. Whether by Christ or King he was unsure, but he was glad of the chance to prove to Ulf that he had been right all along: it was Estorhild who had caused it.

His was not the only success during their stay here. As had been his hope, Cnut had charmed the foreign rulers into giving safe access for English pilgrims and traders along the route to Rome. Spirits were high when they finally sailed home to England, and were boosted even higher with the news on landing that the opportunity had come to take Norway. As Cnut had prophesied, Olaf Haraldsson's most powerful enemies had been bought over.

'You cannot go home now!' the King urged Sigurd. 'We must spend the winter repairing our boats and strike as soon as possible. I did not take you for a man who would refuse the chance of a fight.'

Ulf, when told that they would not be going home after all, threw up his arms and swore. 'The King certainly knows how to manipulate you! All he must do is mention the word fight – do you not recall that I am sworn never to fight again after Eric's death? Did you not consider that I might just like to spend some time at the plough? When all is said and done we have been away for almost two years.' He caught the expression in Sigurd's eye. 'You are still afraid to go home, aren't you? I thought you were over Gytha's loss. You seemed much more cheerful of late.'

How could Sigurd explain to one who had never had a child? 'It is not so much that I am afraid to go home now. There is just something missing. Something that can never be replaced.'

'And what of your poor mother? Does she not care about you? You cannot spend the rest of your life in perpetual fight, Sigurd.'

The reply was stern. 'You are a farmer, Ulf, I am a soldier. Do not speak of things you know nought about. If you want to go home, then go.'

Ulf was exasperated. 'One last time I come with you! But I shall not fight, and the next time I set foot on English soil I swear I shall never leave it again – that is, if I ever manage to see its shores alive.'

Ulf was to be greatly relieved, for when Cnut's fleet landed in Norway they met with no opposition, only cheers. The tyrant Olaf had flown.

Cnut acknowledged the triumphant shouts of his men, whilst apologizing to Sigurd with a laugh. 'I am sorry to disappoint you – you were so looking forward to a battle. But it is as I told you. Battles can be won from one's fireside if one is clever.'

Sigurd shrugged. 'There will doubtless be others.' In the anti-climax he thought of Gytha. The pain was ever-present, but none could read it under that mask. Each man here must get on with his own life, and so must Sigurd; what was one man's grief to another?

On this note he returned with his crew to the ship. The fleet sailed up the Norwegian coast to spend winter in Nidaros where Cnut was hailed as King.

Chapter Fourteen

In 1029 the fleet sailed home to England, taking
hostages to ensure peace in Norway. Cnut's son,
Harthacnut, was left behind as King of Denmark and
one of his jarls, Hakon, as Regent of Norway. Sigurd
arrived in Jorvik with his title of ealdorman and a
ship full of exotic goods and captives. In the act
of unloading these on to the Staith he asked of
Ulf, 'What will you do now that Eric is dead? You
are welcome to live with me if you wish. I know my
mother would be pleased.'

Ulf refused. 'It is because of me that our friend
died. Now that I am finally home I must take care
of his wife and daughters. But I will stay with you
this eve whilst I get my land legs.' With the goods
loaded on to a wagon, he and Sigurd made for
Peseholme.

Not far from here, Murtagh was playing truant. It
was too fine an afternoon for a ten-year-old to sit
waiting for rats to creep out of hiding; he had instead
been hunting on the marshes with a net borrowed
from his master. His lord had been gone for three
years now – hopefully killed in battle – and it had
become much easier to sneak from under the old
lady's failing eye. Murtagh could have run away for
good had he wanted to and she probably would never
notice that he had gone. He had tried to convey this
in sign-language to his Aunt Mary but she refused
either to understand or to take the risk and he would
not leave her. She would doubtless be worried over

his absence now, but when she saw the brace of godwits that dangled from his fist she would not be so cross. Nearing home he hid the birds inside his ragged tunic lest the Lady Ragnhild confiscate them. It was then that he saw the wagon entering the gates and all his geniality collapsed into terror. From instinct he ran and hid behind a drinking trough, almost in tears so frightened was he.

Inside the enclosure a reunion was taking place between Sigurd and his mother, who appeared to have aged dramatically in his absence. Her posture was stooped, her hair completely white and her downy upper lip puckered as if she were in the constant act of sucking fruit. Yet the rest of her face was remarkably pink and healthy. 'You do well to catch me at home! I have been out for hours collecting ergot.' She patted the basket on her arm in which were the black fungus-like spurs that she had picked from shafts of grain.

'I do not know why you have to do this yourself at your age,' opined Sigurd as she mopped her brow with a rag.

'I will tell you why! If I let the wenches do it they'd be using it to abort themselves, and then where would we get our new supply of workers? By Odin, what is this you bring me?' Breaking with tradition, she reacted most favourably to the peacock and to the other gift her son had brought her – a set of opaque glass cups painted with animals. 'They are just the thing for a wedding feast!'

Sigurd's heavily-bearded jaw dropped. 'Mother, how many times must I tell you, I am finished with wives . . .'

Ragnhild bristled. 'Who said ought about thee? 'Tis my own wedding of which I speak.' When her son gawped at Ulf, she explained. 'You left me alone for so long that I had to find company.' Her voice became an exaggerated whisper. 'The poor fellow, he is not long a widower and needs a woman to take care of him. He cannot bear to be in the house where he lived with his first wife so I have said he shall live here.'

'The moment my back is turned she gets up to mischief.' Sigurd received a blow for his impudence.

'Rascal! Come, he is in the house.' Ragnhild ushered both men inside where they met her prospective husband, a handsome but unassuming man with the build and attributes of a poplar tree, bending easily to Ragnhild's whims. 'We did but wait for your return before we wed. Everything is prepared. Now that you are here the wedding can occur tomorrow.'

'Hold!' Sigurd laughed. 'Grant me time to have clothes made for so wondrous an occasion, for I cannot appear like this.'

'Quite so,' his mother agreed, though secretly thinking that under the dirt was a fine-looking man, who had at last grown into his hands and feet. 'But do not delay or I may be a widow before I am a wife.'

'That would surprise me not,' laughed Sigurd to Ulf when they were out of earshot. 'I would count it a miracle if the poor fellow outlived his wedding night. He is certainly not what you might call robust.'

'What?' Ulf sounded indignant for the victim of this criticism. 'He is a most noble man!'

Sigurd remained merry. 'Because he diverts Ragnhild's attention from you?'

Ulf reflected the humour. 'Any man who takes on Ragnhild has my full admiration. I wish the fellow luck; he shall need it.'

Ulf left the next day to give Eric's wife the sad news of her husband's demise, promising to return for Ragnhild's wedding. At his mother's carping insistence, Sigurd called for a sempstress and ordered an outfit to be made from the richest material she had, but even this was unacceptable to Ragnhild when she was presented with the finished article.

'What is the point of having the finest cloth then skimping on the breeches? Look, I can hardly nip an inch on either side of your thighs!'

'Have a care where you nip, Mother.' Sigurd jumped.

'They are no good! You must have three times as much cloth in them. What is the use of being made an ealdorman if you do not advertise your title?' And the sempstress was packed off to cut the cloth more generously.

There were other cuts to be made. Ragnhild insisted that half a foot be trimmed off Sigurd's hair. 'You are seven and twenty years old, a titled and wealthy noble; you must curb your boyish urge to play the Hun. What woman would marry a man whose hair is longer and more lustrous than her own?'

'I have said there will be no more wives.' Sigurd protected his crowning glory from her grasp. 'But I will trim it to a suitable length to appear at my beloved mother's wedding.' A ghoulish cry brought a curse from his lips. 'Before I take a blade to my hair I would sooner take it to that damned bird!' The peacock had woken him every morning since he came home, strutting amongst the fowl in the garth with its crowned head and fanned tail as if it were a king.

Only on the eve of the wedding did it give them some peace. Sigurd was to find out why at the feast: there it was on the table, complete with head and feathers, its tail fanned out in all its glory.

'Mother, I did not fetch it all this way just to eat!'

'Oh, pooh!' The wrinkled lips jutted out. 'You complained about it shrieking through the night – and does it not grace my table well?'

Sigurd gasped a laugh and turned to Grimkell, her mild-mannered husband. 'I trust you are well prepared for my mother's expensive tastes?'

Grimkell smiled and reached into his pouch. 'I have something here which may please her.'

'I doubt it,' murmured Sigurd to Ulf who hid his smile in a goblet.

Ragnhild showed the gift, a brooch, to all assembled. 'Such workmanship, such quality . . . of course, 'tis not as fine as the one my son gave me.'

Sigurd blew bubbles into his wine, drenching his beard and the front of his clothes. Dabbing at them, he laughed heartily, and realized that it was the first time he had done so since before Gytha's death. Feeling guilty, he rearranged his lips and thought deeply for a moment, thoughts that were only for his child. Since Rome, he had begun to think less and less of Estorhild and Una. Maybe this was the time to start a new life, try to dispel the pain that had haunted him so long.

This he began by having plans drawn up for his new house which the King had given him leave to build on the stretch of high ground that the English called Galmanhowe. But alas, before the builders could be instructed Sigurd was called to accompany Cnut's fyrd to Scotland, which was a persistent source of danger.

Naturally, he called upon the services of his friend.

'No,' came the blunt response from Ulf who did not even stop digging.

Sigurd frowned. 'What do you say?'

'I said no, I will not come with you. Have you lost your memory, Sigurd Einarsson?'

Sigurd pulled a face. 'Oh, I have not forgotten that you swore never to leave English soil again, but . . .'

'I meant it, Sigurd.' Ulf rammed his fork into the soil, unearthing another root. 'I will not come for you, nor even at the King's command.'

Sigurd grew pompous. 'I am your lord and I have

need of your services. If you refuse to fight I shall demand a fine!'

Ulf merely sneered. 'Your browbeating does not work with me, Smallaxe.'

Sigurd compressed his lips. 'Then I cannot rely on you ever again?'

Ulf drove his heel at the fork and answered tersely, 'If you refer to my sword, then no. But my friendship is yours forever and my prayers go with you for a safe return.'

And that was as much help as Sigurd was going to get. However, the outcome in Scotland was good. King Malcolm was finally made to pledge his obeisance, and the fyrd returned to England. With his wise administration and respect for law and order Cnut was now at the height of his powers, King of the North Sea, overlord of all those Scandinavians in Ireland and the northern isles, his rights of free passage extending to the Baltic, and Sigurd had taken part in all these triumphs.

His proud mother, as usual, barely gave him chance to get into the house before demanding to hear the tales of his latest exploits. She was not yet dressed from her bed for it was early, but pulled on her clothes whilst he listed his achievements, and beamed at his conclusion. 'Oh, to think that my son has shared in all the King's great deeds!'

Sigurd was for once relaxed and apparently happy as he held out his cup for another dash of ale from a sleepy Grimkell's pitcher. 'Do not let the King hear you speak of him thus; it has become almost a crime to do so. Oh yes, it is true,' he told the listeners. 'Cnut refuses to accept praise for these feats. He says that we should instead give glory to God. His modesty verges on obsession – do you know, he will go to extraordinary lengths to prove that he is not the powerful King we think he is. Oh, you would not believe it . . .'

'Tell us!' begged his mother, still dressing.

'Very well.' Sigurd leaned forward in his chair as if about to issue revelation. 'We had all been showering him with compliments one day, telling him he was lord of all the seas, when he grew most irritated and ordered us all down to the seashore. To prove to us how insignificant he is, he planted his throne at the edge of the incoming tide and commanded the waves to turn back, and when they kept on coming and were lapping round his ankles he cried with great delight, "Know all inhabitants of earth, that vain and trivial is the power of kings, nor is anyone worthy of the name King save Him Whose nod heaven and earth and sea obey under laws eternal!" ' Sigurd ended on a laugh, but then looked concerned. 'I begin to worry about him and trust that all his great deeds are not to be undone in madness. He will not even wear his crown now, but has placed it on the altar as tribute to One greater.'

'What a waste!' breathed Ragnhild.

'True – but anyway!' Sigurd changed the subject. 'There is enough here to occupy my thoughts. If the King is losing his mind he may just decide to withdraw his offer of a house in Earlsburh and make me follow his holy example by scorning riches, so I must get it built as quickly as I can.'

Ragnhild showed glee, but was to be discommoded by his next remark.

'You and Grimkell will no doubt enjoy having Peseholme all to yourselves.'

His mother could not believe this great insult. 'Live here, whilst you go off to live alongside Jarl Siward? Nei! We come with you!' She was balanced on a stool, one bare leg crossed over the other as she pulled a woollen stocking up to meet her knee-length breeches. Her skin was white and marbled with veins. 'Live here, indeed!'

Sigurd's heart fell; in one respect he would be glad

of the company but he hoped his mother would not be forever pestering him to take a wife. 'Then I must look for a tenant.'

'Look no further than your old heart-friend.' Stockings in place, Ragnhild tugged her dress down to cover them.

'Ulf?' Sigurd laughed and cupped his hand as if to exclude Grimkell from the conversation but only out of fun. 'Even though you are married you still try to tempt the beardless one near you. I know not whether he will leave the responsibilities he has made for himself.'

'Eric's widow? What is to prevent her and the children coming too?'

Sigurd agreed it was commonsense and early next morning rode out through the Forest of Galtres to speak to Ulf. He took a few men with him but rode some way ahead, wanting solitude; his heart was heavy for his dead child today. The dark wood compounded his mood and he was most glad when he came out of it to find Ulf in one of the fields about to begin spring ploughing, alone but for his team of oxen and a boy slave.

'Ah, I would welcome some help,' said Ulf by way of greeting, whilst thinking how gaunt his friend looked.

Sigurd dismounted. 'I come not to soil my hands but to bring a gift.'

Ulf examined him. 'I see none.'

'Only because it is far too large for me to carry. I come to offer you my house at Peseholme.'

Ulf looked impressed. 'Will not Ragnhild be aggrieved?'

'She does not want it – it is not good enough for her now.' Sigurd grinned.

The sunken eyes were cynical. 'I wondered why 'twas offered to me. What of your reeve, would it not make a fine home for him?'

'It would, that is why I offer it.'

Ulf looked at him sharply. 'Do I take this to mean that you offer me the reeveship again?'

'Yea.' After all this time Sigurd had now begun to use English pronunciation. 'My reeve has just fallen dead. I would sooner the post goes to my dearest friend. Will you not reconsider your past decision? Have not the years lent you wisdom to know it is not beyond your skills?'

Ulf glanced beyond him; a woman and four small girls were coming towards the men. 'I will have to ask the opinion of Eric's wife.'

Sigurd turned to watch the female's approach. 'She looks well. You must be taking good care of her.'

Ulf nodded and began to check that the oxen were correctly yoked to the iron plough. 'What else could I do when 'twas I who got her man killed?'

Sigurd turned back to look at him. 'Do not carry it all upon yourself. I am equally to blame. I am to blame for many things.' He paused for a while, watching Ulf run his hands over the oxen's quivering skins and under the harnesses to check for burrs. It made him hanker for a woman. Deep in thought, he eventually said, 'I have decided to liberate my thralls.'

Ulf gave no reaction. 'Shall you not require more hands for this wondrous new house of yours?'

Sigurd wrinkled his nose. 'I will keep those most recently acquired but the others are becoming a burden. They have found mates, had children – dozens of them. Their shrill voices, they grate upon my ear, remind me of . . .' He tightened the muscles of his jaw and was glad that Eric's widow chose that moment to arrive. He greeted her, said how well she looked and gave her the news about the reeveship. 'I would welcome your help in persuading our stubborn friend to accept. Do not worry that it will take him away from your land, for you and your daughters are welcome to use the house with him. Let another have

356

this hard work.' Eric's widow was quick to accept for Ulf and thanked their benefactor. Sigurd looked at the tray she carried which bore a flagon and a cake. 'You must have known that I am come.' He reached for the cake but she swerved away.

'Nay! Wouldst rob us of a good harvest? This is for the Earth Mother.'

'A thousand pardons, dame, but could I not steal a crumb?'

'If you would take my place behind the plough-share.' Ulf offered him the reins.

Sigurd declined and leaned against his horse to watch the ceremony. The cake was broken, a piece given to Ulf, some to the oxen, the lady herself ate a mouthful and the rest was crumbled over the earth to be ploughed in. Each partook of the flagon, the remainder being trickled over the oxen and the plough. 'Now all will be fertile,' said Eric's wife with satisfaction. When Ulf did not begin ploughing immediately she gave him a look that was worthy of Ragnhild, told him to 'Go to it!' then turned to Sigurd. 'Will you come back to the house and take meat with us?'

Sigurd agreed and together with the girls they went off, leaving Ulf to his work.

When Sigurd returned to Peseholme he assembled his thralls and told them of his decision. 'Those who have lived here for five years or more step forth.' When they did so he continued, 'You have worked hard, and so I have decided that you have earned the right to buy your freedom . . .'

'And just how does he think we'll do that?' Black Mary queried her nephew who clung terrified to her ragged skirts as Sigurd proceeded to explain.

'. . . I intend to grant each of you five acres of land. You shall continue to work for me during the day-time, some of you as house thralls, others in your separate trades, but in the evening and on every

Wodnesdaeg of the week you have my permission to work upon your own land and thus earn the money to buy your freedom.'

'Isn't he the generous one,' breathed Mary. 'Sure 'tis dead I'll be afore I can earn half the amount he'll ask for my freedom.' She was the last surviving woman of that Irish raid ten years ago and was almost thirty now. Only half the female population reached her age, and certainly not many of them were slaves! But if willpower could keep death at bay she had promised to outlive her captor. Grasping Murtagh's thin body, she hugged him into her side. He looked up at her, a question in his dark eyes – then reacted with fright as his name was mentioned.

'There is one whom I will never free.' Sigurd was looking straight at the boy who tried to camouflage himself with the drab skirts of his aunt. 'The one called Murtagh, son of the murderess, you are not worthy of freedom. You shall live as a dog for the rest of your life. That is all – be gone!' At their rapid dispersal, he went into the house.

Black Mary stared after him, unable to disguise her hatred. With one hand he gave her freedom, only to snatch it back with the other; how could she go and leave Murtagh? She looked down at the cowering little wretch and gripped him protectively. 'Ah, don't you worry, my darling. I'll not leave you, ever.'

The finished house was magnificent. Its gabled timbers encompassed a great hall with a door set into each of the long sides. Both inside and out the supporting pillars terminated in the heads of mythical beasts. There were carved panels: one depicting a continuous snake intertwining with itself, another of birds, serpents and animals biting each other. The walls were clad in gold-threaded tapestries and shields. Around these walls were elaborately carved benches, a table massive enough to accommodate all

Sigurd's friends and visitors, and a chair for himself that looked remarkably like a throne.

The kitchen was an entirely separate building, far grander than most citizens' houses, equipped with every possible artifact. There was a salthouse and an outbuilding where entrails and feathers could be removed without having to foul the kitchen. The house had an upper storey from where its lord and master could admire the view of the river through glass windows and where there was a bed with sumptuous mattresses, eiderdowns and curtains.

But there was no one to share his heart's dream; no wife to recline with him on embroidered cushions by the hearth on a winter's night; no child to listen spellbound to his tales of battle; only two old folk, a company of housecarls and the odd pedlar who drifted through.

Fortunately, Sigurd's position as ealdorman prevented a relapse into melancholy. If he was not required to serve on the King's witan then there was always some thief or adulterer to deal with at the shire court. Today the line of such cases before him had been longer than usual. When the time came to deal with the last perpetrator he had grown short-tempered and correspondingly imposed a heftier fine than he might otherwise have done.

Ulf, as his reeve, was there to aid him and, at the gasp of shock from the defendant, leaned to whisper in Sigurd's ear: 'My lord is a little harsh with his judgment today. The woman was only the wife of a churl, not a noble. A fine of a hundred shillings is excessive.'

Sigurd was unresponsive. 'Then it will teach him not to go stealing another man's wife.'

'Sigurd, do you wish to lose your reputation of fairness just because you are in a foul mood?'

'I am not in a bad mood! I am merely bored by these petty feuds that come before me time after time . . . oh, very well!' He looked into Ulf's reproving face and gave way. 'I grant that you are right – the fine is reduced to forty shillings!'

The defendant dropped to one knee clutching his hat. 'You are a fair and generous lord! I repent of my crime and submit to your judgment.'

'Repent of his crime!' scoffed Sigurd, as he and his friend rode home through town, saddlebags laden with the fines exacted. 'He'll be there before me next month charged with tupping someone else's wife.'

'How else would you come to own such wealth if not for men such as him?' joked Ulf. Sigurd was entitled to exact a portion of the fines for himself.

Laughingly Sigurd agreed, then asked as they were almost nigh to Earlsburh, 'Will you eat with us tonight?'

Ulf looked unsure. 'I have three executions to arrange – then there are those stolen cattle to trail . . .'

'Oh, stay. The condemned men will thank you for a few extra hours and so would I. My mother and Grimkell are not exactly the best of conversation fellows.'

'What about your housecarls?'

'They are fine as shoulder-comrades but their words are limited to tales of the battlefield.'

Ulf gave a rare laugh at this. 'You are a fine one to talk!'

Sigurd shook his head, looking misunderstood. 'Oh no, Ulf, I love to fight but I see no merit in talking about it.' He turned waspish. 'But if you do not wish to stay . . .'

'Of course I will stay, though if your mother begats any ribaldry . . .'

'I shall lock her up,' promised Sigurd as they reached Earlsburh.

Whilst they ate supper the conversation hung around the King's decision to send his illegitimate son Swein to rule Norway in place of Earl Hakon,

360

who had recently drowned. Aelgifu, the young man's mother who had insulted Sigurd all those years ago – a thing which he had never forgotten – had gone with him. 'A foolish decision,' Sigurd dubbed it, through a mouthful of warm, fresh bread. 'He is not the man his father is – none of them are. All that work Cnut did to retrieve Norway and it will soon be lost again, mark my words.'

Ulf was bitter. 'I was not aware that the King did all the work alone.'

Sigurd caught his drift. 'Yea, I know, 'tis hard to imagine that Eric's sacrifice will be for nought.'

'You do not know that that will be the case,' argued Grimkell.

Sigurd passed a condescending glance at Ulf; Grimkell was an old man with little experience of kings. 'I know Swein. He is weak. Olaf will see this as his chance to grab his crown back.'

'Why must you always be right?' asked a discordant Ulf, when news came to Jorvik that this was exactly what had happened.

Sigurd assumed an air of false modesty. 'I try so hard not to be, Ulf, I just cannot seem to help it.'

'I do not need to ask if you will go.'

'Just as soon as I gather a fleet.'

'You do not even like Swein,' put forth Ulf.

'I do not do it out of loyalty to Swein but to his father,' corrected Sigurd. 'Calm your worries, Ulf, I shall not get myself killed.'

'It will happen one day, my friend.' The hollow eyes looked unusually grave. 'But I pray that God be with you for a safe return.'

Whilst Olaf and his half-brother Harald advanced through the forests and mountains of Norway, Sigurd was at a huge gathering in Nidaros with all those whom Cnut had bribed to win back this country. If Olaf was allowed to return they were doomed – yet

361

theirs was not the only resistance; the peasants had no wish to return to Olaf's barbarous rule either. The army that met him at Stiklarstadir was vast: nearly fourteen and a half thousand men and Sigurd amongst them. Olaf with barely a third of these could not hope to win, but fought with valour on that bright sunny day in July with no thought of retreat.

Beneath the golden sun and blue sky Sigurd wielded his axe with the usual unfeeling precision, cutting down all around him, taking fathers, brothers, sons as if they were logs of wood. At the end of the day Olaf was dead and his fifteen-year-old brother Harald was compelled to escape with what remained of the army. Sigurd joined the triumphant chase across the green fields until all tired of the fun, whence he cheered and hooted after the fleeing Harald, little knowing that their paths would cross again in years to come.

During the next five years Sigurd devoted much of his time to one battle or another, however far afield. Battle was the one time he felt like the young man he was. What irony that only when embroiled in death could he himself feel alive. Knowing this, Ulf quashed the urge to lecture him, promising only to deputize in the ealdorman's absence.

'Ah, you are a good man, Ulf,' Sigurd thanked him, then offered a note of philosophy. 'Why is it that men such as you and I do not have sons? We would breed much finer rulers of Norway than that weakling of Cnut's.'

'I beg you not to be so outspoken, friend,' warned Ulf.

Sigurd did not care who overheard him. 'Well, it is true! I am only surprised that Swein has managed to hold on to his crown for so long. Have you heard the latest news from Norway? It is the strangest thing you will ever hear: the King whom they once called tyrant is now sanctified! They say that someone collected blood from Olaf's wounds after battle and that blood is now being used to cure the blind and maimed! The fools are now saying that they regret killing Olaf for he was a great ruler compared to Swein – well, they are not so foolish, for anyone would rule better than Swein – but someone is doing their best to oust him and Aelgifu by spreading gossip of their badness, and I fear they will be successful. For Cnut's sake I must go and help the wretch.'

But even Sigurd Einarsson was unable to counter the massive uprising that finally deposed Swein and put Olaf's son Magnus on the Norwegian throne; both he and the vanquished Swein were forced to flee to Denmark and seek refuge with Cnut's other son, Harthacnut, where Swein died some months later. No argument from Sigurd could induce Harthacnut to avenge his half-brother's death. Discouraged by the feebleness of Cnut's offspring, Sigurd remained only long enough to re-equip his fleet, then sailed home to Jorvik.

'I feel that I have let Cnut down,' he told Ulf, who coincidentally was there to greet his arrival at Earlsburh.

'No man can say that you did not do your best.' Ulf seemed preoccupied.

'That is true.' Sigurd handed the reins of his horse to a servant and began to walk towards the house. 'Well, come you in, friend, and have some wine with us.'

Ulf stopped him. 'I have just been in and must go for I have many duties to perform, but first . . . I have bad news to impart, friend.'

Alarmed, Sigurd grasped him. 'Is it Mother?'

'In a way – no, she is not dead!' Ulf frowned at himself for frightening his friend thus. 'It is Grimkell.'

Sigurd looked at first relieved, then sad. 'Poor

mother, I must go and comfort her. When did it happen?'

'Shortly after you left for Norway and . . . I fear that it has affected Ragnhild greatly. You may find her changed, Sigurd.'

Sigurd furrowed his brow. 'In what way?'

'You will see what I mean when you meet her.' Ulf seemed ill at ease.

The ealdorman ran a thoughtful hand over his mouth. 'Thank you for warning me. Must you go immediately?' All at once he was reluctant to go in.

'I fear so.' Ulf patted him before moving off. 'But I shall come over to visit just as soon as I catch these wretched poachers.'

Sigurd watched him leave, then rather hesitantly went into the house. Ulf had told him true: Ragnhild was nothing like the bombastic woman he had left behind several months ago, but had an air of vagueness about her. Over the coming weeks he was to witness more evidence of her malady. She had become forgetful, told Sigurd things that she had told him only a moment ago. Out of the blue she would take it upon herself to cook his supper as she had not done for years; though the result was often appalling he indulged her, for she was very old. Tonight, though, her ingredients were even less palatable. He spat out the mouthful of fish and rinsed his mouth with wine.

'Mother, art trying to kill us!'

Ragnhild lifted confused eyes from her own meal.

'Do not eat it!' Sigurd grabbed the platter of fish from under her nose and tipped it at the hearth. 'By the gods, that fish must be as old as I! Where did you buy it – and more importantly, when?'

The old Ragnhild returned, lips pursed with indignance. 'I bought it fresh this morn at the market. See!' She hoisted her gown and withdrew a fish from her breeches. 'There is nought wrong with that.'

Sigurd lost his patience. 'Mother, why do you carry a fish in your broks?'

''Tis the only place that robber Ethelred cannot get at it!' Ragnhild shoved the fish back, tugged her dress over it, then her face softened. 'I am sorry if my cooking does not please you, Einar.'

She mistook him for his father quite often these days; that was the chief reason why Sigurd was closeted in this bower away from the jibes of house-carls in the main hall – he was even reluctant to have his old friend Ulf witness his embarrassment. Sometimes, as now, he looked at his old mother slumped in her chair like a sack of corn and he hated her for making him feel old, too. He covered his eyes then shook his head. 'Your cooking is delicious, usually, but we have servants to do that.' He bellowed for one to bring fresh meat. 'Sit you there, Mother.'

A strong whiff of fish clung to the air. Before he sat down Sigurd lifted a cushion; his mother had taken to hiding food all about the house. The servant who witnessed this fun later shared it with the others. 'The Lady Ragnhild will have them both poisoned! The lord says we are to tell him if she cooks ought in future.'

Black Mary laughed, no more nor less than any of her peers, but the next evening when Sigurd came home it was she who waited on him in his private room. 'My lord,' she whispered on approaching, 'you asked to be informed if the Lady Ragnhild cooked your meal . . . I fear she would not be deterred.'

Sigurd proffered a tired nod and waved her away. She left, turning only to see her master embark on his meal, and when she returned to the slaves' abode she made sure that all were informed that Ragnhild had cooked supper.

Not an hour had passed before noises of excitement filled the yard. 'Fetch the physician! The dame is sick!'

The physician came and pronounced Ragnhild already dead. 'But what of the master?' Black Mary asked another, and was informed: 'Upon hearing that the lady had cooked supper he gave his platter to the dogs! When two of them fell dead he feared for his mother and sent for the physician, but too late.'

'Doest know what the lady put into the meal?' Mary tried not to sound anxious.

'Nay, it could have been ought. I myself have caught her making bread with lime. Holy Virgin, the master said she would poison them one day. A good thing he did not eat.'

Black Mary nodded and put an unconscious hand to her breast where the phial of poison had once been hidden. It had been too much to hope that she would kill both at one sitting. Would he guess that she and not his mother was to blame?

But Sigurd was blaming himself. 'If only I had stopped her,' he told the healer. ''Twas only in my wish not to offend her that I let her think I ate my own. When the dogs keeled over I sent for you as quick as I could . . .'

'Nay, you could not have known,' soothed the man of medicine. 'Eight and fifty is a great age, she would not have lived much longer. 'Twas very quick.'

This was the palliative employed by other friends, including the King, whose visit to the Earl of Northumbria coincided with Ragnhild's demise. 'Death comes to us all, my friend. I pray that mine own will be as swift.'

Sigurd nodded and directed Cnut to the place of honour in the great hall, seating himself opposite with the hearth between them. The housecarls were grouped along the benches, talking quietly amongst themselves and did not prove an intrusion. 'When one's mother dies it brings one's own death closer.' However domineering Ragnhild had been, she was his mother, and the sense of loneliness was acute. 'I

366

ask myself, who is to inherit all of this after me?' His arm swept the luxurious room then fell upon his lap.

Cnut looked into the crimson depths of his goblet. ''Tis as hard a decision when one has sons.'

'Yea, especially when each is as unworthy as the other,' came the warped reply.

Cnut was magnanimous. 'I shall forgive you that envious retort and pity your lack of heirs.'

Sigurd abhorred pity. 'You might have more sons than I but all are worthless. It is hard to credit that he who is lord of half the world would have such weak seed.'

Cnut gritted his teeth and rose to leave, offended not so much by the other's outspokenness, but the truth of his words.

'Oh, mighty one, forgive me!' The housecarls watched in apprehension as Sigurd reached the door before Cnut, barring his exit. 'You were correct, 'tis envy forms my words. I beg you to consider that my mother's death has robbed me of right mind. Come back and let me make amends.'

Cnut delayed his exit, his blue eyes piercing the other's. Sigurd tried again. 'My lord King . . .'

''Tis not as King that you offend me but as a man! Any man would take insult from such reference to his progeny.'

Sigurd gave a weary nod. 'And he would have right to do so. If you let fly your hand as my mouth let fly the words I would understand, my lord.' He presented his bearded chin for the blow.

Cnut glanced at the inquisitive housecarls who immediately looked away. ''Tis only you I would forgive for that insolence, Sigurd.'

'My lord King, I thank you.' Sigurd kneeled, grabbed Cnut's hand and pressed a fervent kiss to it. 'Whomsoever you name as your heir, then I shall follow him.'

'Harthacnut, as the son of my rightful queen, shall

reign after me.' Cnut managed a stiff smile. 'But I hope 'twill be many years yet.'

'I, too, lord.' Sigurd coaxed him back to the hearth, attempting humour. 'Er, tell me, have you yet written your Will?'

Cnut gave a genuine laugh. 'I have, but take care that your name is not erased from it after recent remarks about my offspring.'

'Oh, shame!' Enacting disappointment, Sigurd cowered like a dog. 'I did not include all your offspring – why, your daughter Gunnhild is extremely fair.'

The monarch cuffed him lightly. 'Well, you need not think I shall bequeath her to you. She is already claimed by a mightier suitor.'

'My heart is broken!' Sigurd waited for the King to take a chair then sat alongside. 'Who can be mightier than Sigurd Einarsson?'

'The Emperor of Rome asks that I give the hand of Gunnhild to his son, Henry, and in return he promises to surrender that land which he holds north of the Eider.'

It was an important coup and more than made up for the loss of Norway. Sigurd looked impressed. 'My salutations, oh lord.'

Cnut's reply bore a note of lament. 'It is unworthy, I know, but much as I dislike Robert of Normandy I would sooner it were he who was negotiating.' There had been no improvement in the relations between England and Normandy.

'Pooh, the man is an idiot!' Sigurd kicked at the hearth in an act of contempt.

'True, but he is the only ruler whom I have failed to be on good terms with and he is too close to home to ignore. One day he will attack.'

'Then let us attack him first,' came the cheerful proposition from Sigurd before he downed his wine.

Cnut gave a wishful nod and reached for his own goblet – but recoiled in dismay. There on a limb of the table was a hibernating moth, upon its back the head of Death.

Chapter Fifteen

November brought catastrophe. 'Oh, Ulf, the most terrible news!' An anguished Sigurd burst into the house at Peseholme, startling not only his friend but Eric's widow, her four little girls and a number of servants. 'The King is dead!' He took the role of emissary himself, the news too important to leave to others.

The occupants around the hearth gasped, Eric's widow mopped at her eyes with her apron though Sigurd witnessed no sign of a tear. 'When?' was all Ulf could say.

'Two days ago.' A shocked Sigurd took the place that had been made for him by the fire.

'Was there foul deed involved?' Ulf held out a goblet to be filled with wine then put it into Sigurd's hand.

'Nay.' Sigurd drank and stared into the fire. 'The King is to be buried at Wintanceaster – will you come there with me, Ulf?'

Ulf replied that of course he would, and some days later enacted his promise.

'What is to become of England now?' he enquired as the two braved a wall of November fog to row for Wintanceaster in the company of thirty housecarls.

His friend snorted, adding more moisture to his beard which was already well-dampened by mist. His mood of sadness had been tainted by the revelation that Cnut had not used his Will to grant an earldom to his old friend as Sigurd had hoped but had instead bequeathed land. 'Only the gods know that.'

'Will you be loyal to your promise to Cnut?'

'To support Harthacnut?' Sigurd was honest. 'I do not know, Ulf, for it would mean siding with his mother Queen Emma, a woman who was once married to Ethelred.'

'You surely cannot let old grudges tarnish your promise to the King?' said Ulf, chin buried into his mantle as he rowed. 'Besides, who else would you support?'

'Oh, I do not know. Perhaps we will find the answer when we get to Wintanceaster.'

They were not to hear anything definite until after Cnut's funeral when a witan was held, of which Sigurd was part. It appeared that Harthacnut had refused to leave Denmark for fear that someone would steal that throne. Harald Harefoot, son of Aelgifu, had been quick to stake his own claim.

Sigurd thought on this. Harald might be even less suited to the task than his brother, but he was a man who could be easily manipulated and in this Sigurd glimpsed for himself an earldom. His alliance was beginning to shift.

But many of the witan were against Harald, especially Earl Godwin. 'I promised Cnut that I would support Harthacnut and I cannot go back on my word.'

Sigurd damned his rival's holier than thou attitude, and proposed what he saw as logical action. 'But we must have a king and Harthacnut is trapped in Denmark!'

Earl Godwin merely laughed. 'Who else if not Harald – you?' Sigurd looked away under Godwin's chastizing gaze.

Leofric, Earl of Mercia and Cnut's other chief adviser, jumped in to alleviate the tense atmosphere between the two men. 'We do not have to make Harald King, only Regent until Harthacnut can safely leave Denmark.'

'That may be years,' said another. 'We need a king.'

'I find myself in favour of making Harald Regent,' said an archbishop, 'but I feel that it may be unwise to entrust him with the King's treasure chest.'

'Nor Queen Emma neither,' muttered Sigurd, but was condemned by Godwin who had appointed himself her protector.

'It is well-known that you bear a grudge against anyone who has any connection with Ethelred, however tenuous!'

A suggestion came from another member which received nods of approval. 'Perhaps if Earl Godwin were to take charge of both the queen and the treasure chest, he would feel more disposed towards making Harald Regent?'

Godwin's lower lip jutted out in thought, then he nodded. 'I am agreeable to the first suggestion but I cannot go back on my word to our dead King. He wished me to support Harthacnut and in all conscience I must do so.'

Without reaching full agreement the witan broke up and England was plunged into turmoil. The future of the country became a game of hnefatafl and Sigurd was unsure which way to move, kicking himself for antagonizing his rival in so petty a manner. Only an idiot would choose such a crucial time to oppose the powerful Godwin who ruled much of southern England – especially with him now in charge of the treasury – but perhaps the Earl of Wessex could be made to heed sense. He paraded his ideas before Ulf as they rowed home to Jorvik. 'If only Godwin can be won over from Emma I could find myself in a very strong position indeed.'

Ulf was uneasy. 'Do not tell me any more.'

His friend looked surprised. 'Why?'

'Just do as you must do,' said Ulf. 'I am a simple man and have no mind for politics. If I say I will support one lord then I support him.'

372

'And so do I!' objected Sigurd. 'But . . .'

'Just do as you must do,' repeated Ulf. 'But leave me out of it.'

And Sigurd decided that perhaps his friend was right. The fewer who knew of his plans the better.

Acting independently of his own overlord, Sigurd journeyed to Godwin's estate some weeks later with the intent of bridging the rift between them. As expected Godwin was none too receptive to his visitor but heard what Sigurd had to say.

Their meeting took place in the yard where Godwin watched a friendly sword-fight between his sons, the eldest Harold against the gawkier Tostig who looked about sixteen. Sigurd began by complimenting Godwin on their agility, and watched until the fight was over, whence he offered congratulations to the winner, Harold, and pleased the shamefaced Tostig by saying that it was a closely-fought match. 'I am certain you would give even a seasoned warrior like me a hard fight.'

'I thank you, my lord.' Tostig disposed of his sulk and bowed.

'Such gracious manners,' observed Sigurd to Godwin. 'And so handsome. Would that my daughter were still alive. She and your son would be of an age. Young Tostig here would make a most attractive son-in-law.'

The pimply Tostig, unaccustomed to such flattery, was easily won over and clung to Sigurd as the men walked towards the house in the hope of further compliments. Normally it was the more attractive Harold who received them. Sigurd, of course, had recognized this, and also the fact that Godwin had a soft spot for his uglier son. If he could win over the petulant Tostig he would be halfway to winning his father too. Harold did not need to be told that he was handsome, he already knew it. Sigurd put aside his dislike of Godwin and his sons to spend a few moments chatting with the young men, glad that they laughed at his jokes and hoping that Godwin could not see through his motives.

The earl appeared to be impressed by the attention paid to his sons, particularly Tostig for he was often overshadowed by his siblings, if not the eldest then it was the youngest. Eventually though, the hour forced him to dismiss them and bid Sigurd state his business. 'My sons appear to like you but I doubt that they are the reason for your visit.' He told a servant to pour them wine.

The ealdorman smiled. 'Delightful though they are, I must confess that it is to you I wish to speak, my lord, on a matter most urgent.' He tried to appear earnest, spreading his palm in a gesture of veneration. 'I understand your loyalty towards Queen Emma . . .'

'Do you?' Godwin drank from his goblet.

'I do, and I admire you for your steadfastness in the face of such opposition – most of the witan is determined that Harald Harefoot be King.' Sigurd, too, drank.

Godwin was firm. 'And I am of the mind that he will not.'

'Yea, I appreciate the debt you owe to our great Cnut, my lord. He did much for me, and I too am loth to go back on the promise I made to him, but have you thought that you would more easily retain your power under Harald? I have thought long on the dangers of waiting for Harthacnut to come forth. Whilst the country is without a proper king there is the threat from other sources.'

Godwin knew immediately that Sigurd referred to Ethelred's sons who were exiled when their mother married Cnut. 'You think that you can win me over by playing on my dislike of a return to Ethelred's line? Save your breath, Ealdorman Sigurd, I do not think that will come to pass. Now, if you would pardon me . . .'

And no amount of argument could dislodge Godwin from his views. However, before a defeated Sigurd left for Jorvik, Providence leapt to his aid: news arrived that Alfred, Emma's son by Ethelred, had landed in England ostensibly to visit his mother.

Immediately Sigurd revisited Godwin, telling him in urgent tone, 'There! Already they start to creep from under their rocks. Will you not change your mind and support Harald? What matter if it is the wrong son who fills the throne, he is still Cnut's son!'

The Earl was forced to agree and was already shouting orders to his men. 'We must prevent the Ætheling from reaching the Queen – will you ride with me?'

'It will be my pleasure!' replied Sigurd.

With Godwin at its head the party of soldiers rode out to intercept Alfred, easily dispersing the Normans who had accompanied him and putting the Ætheling under arrest. When this was done Godwin, eager to inform Harald of the small invasion, gave Sigurd command of the prisoner. 'Ealdorman Sigurd, I hand this usurper to your charge and ride to tell the King what has occurred. Treat him as you see fit.'

'I will, my lord, but what of the Queen? Should King Harald not also be told of her conspiracy to rob him of his throne?'

The Earl looked suitably grim. It was evident as he rode away that he had learnt where the key to his power lay. Pleased with himself, Sigurd watched Godwin's departure then gave orders of his own.

Encircled by housecarls, a quivering Alfred was transported to Sigurd's ship and taken on board. The young man, without friend to aid him, was terrified by the violence in the Norseman's eye, but held the cold stare bravely and demanded, 'What will you do with me?' The accent was French.

'I have not yet decided.' Sigurd crossed his arms.

Alfred clung to his own royalty. 'If you harm me I wouldst warn you of the consequences.'

The gingery moustache twitched. 'You think I care ought for the threat of Ethelred's spawn? If I kill you I should have every right; your father butchered my father, my brother and sisters too. I swore that I would see him dead and likewise all his kin. So far I have kept my vow.'

Alfred's wrists twisted to be free of his bonds. 'And like a coward you would slay a fettered man! Free me and I shall match your threat.' Sigurd's beard took on a firmer edge. He glared at Alfred and Alfred glared back uncowed. The youngster's eyes challenged as he mouthed deliberately, 'Oh, dunghill cock!'

Sigurd whipped out his knife, gripped Alfred's head beneath his left elbow and with his right hand gouged out each disrespectful eye whilst his victim screamed and gurgled and lashed his legs, then fainted.

When Sigurd let go, the mutilated Alfred fell to the deck.

One housecarl braver than most, observed with dismay, 'I fear you should not have done this, lord.' But when Sigurd turned on him still with knife in bloodstained hand he withheld further criticism.

So savage was the torture that Alfred died. Sigurd awaited repercussions for his impulsive act, but only Alfred's mother the Queen was there to mourn. With this opposition disposed of and the most powerful of Englishmen on his side, Harald Harefoot was crowned King and Emma was exiled to Bruges. His position fortified, Sigurd returned to Jorvik where life went on as before.

At Lammastide Ulf brought the dues he had collected from Sigurd's tenants, explaining the presence of the lamb that he carried under his arm. 'I am away to

St Peter's to have it blessed.' Setting the lamb down, he began to unfasten the pouch from his belt. 'But I thought I should bring this first or some thieving monk would filch it in the crowd.'

Sigurd made a grunt of aknowledgement. 'As if they don't take enough.' He resented giving his dues to the church – Peter's Pence on St Peter's Day, Ploughman's after Easter, tithe of young beasts at Whitsun, hardly a month went by without such extortion. 'You know, Ulf, I think I shall build a church at Osboldewic so as to retrieve some of the money I've paid. If it is on my property I should get dues.'

'Well, here are some to be going on with.' Ulf put his leather bag of cash into Sigurd's hand and accepted the offer of a seat and refreshment. They were the only occupants of the main hall, the housecarls in rough play outside on this hot August morn. Through the open door came oaths and the clanging of weapons.

Ulf appeared to have something to get off his chest. It was not long before Sigurd discovered what that was.

'I hear rumour that disturbs me. They say you did blind the Ætheling, and so viciously he died.' When Sigurd did not respond, Ulf looked him in the face. The hollows of his eyes gleamed with sweat. 'Is it true?'

'You are well aware of the blood-feud I have with Ethelred and his kin.' Sigurd's hair hung lank with the heat.

Ulf's bland visage changed to one of accusation. 'Yea, but to treat a lad so vicious . . .'

''Tis done, Ulf.' Sigurd's voice warned his friend not to press the recrimination.

But Ulf would not be bullied. 'These grudges of yours, they last too long, they shall destroy you.'

'Hah! You are a fine one to talk of grudges, you who almost drowned me once.'

377

'That was not grudge!' Ulf looked at him as if he were mad. 'I say my piece and then 'tis over, but you . . . 'Tis thirty-five years since your family was massacred – how long shall the feud prevail?'

'For as long as Ethelred's heirs lay claim to the English throne.' Sigurd rose and called for more drink. A terrier got in his way; he kicked it out of temper with Ulf. The dog yelped.

Ulf regarded him with wry mouth. 'And you will tell me now that that is the dog who pissed on your boots in 1026.'

Sigurd had to laugh, but reminded his accuser, 'I once told you that to a friend I am loyal unto death, but the reverse applies to my enemies. I had every right to kill him, Ulf.' He donned a pained expression. 'Besides, he insulted me . . . called me dunghill cock.'

Ulf shook his head and leaned his elbows on his knees. During the quiet interval Sigurd watched the lamb which bleated plaintively and eyed the lounging wolfhounds by the hearth. With the lack of conversation from Ulf, Sigurd felt that he was brooding over his friend's unchivalrous deed, but when he looked more carefully he thought there might be something else. Ulf appeared shifty and ill at ease. 'What is the trouble, my friend?'

'Trouble?' Ulf looked not at him but down into his cup. 'Why should there be trouble?' A glob of sweat trickled down his nose and hung on its tip.

Sigurd indicated the bag. 'If the money is short . . .'

'The dues are all paid!' The droplet flew off. 'Have I ever failed in my duties as reeve?'

'Nay, I did not mean to offend,' hurried Sigurd. 'But something is amiss, I can tell. It is not just this other business. I just fancied . . .' He spoke earnestly. 'You know you need never fear me, Ulf. If one of my tenants is being truculent . . .'

'Fear you? Hah! I have told you it is all there. Count it if you do not believe me!'

Sigurd threw the moneybag at the table with a curse. Alarmed, the lamb skittered across the wooden floor and stood baa-ing next to the huge dogs. One of them unfolded its great wiry frame and loped off to a quieter corner. The other lifted its head to nose the lamb, then flopped back unconcerned.

Ulf emptied his cup at one go and put it down. Standing, he clasped his hands behind his back and began to pace up and down the hall, trying to appear nonchalant but only making his manner more staged. The lamb tottered after him. He coughed, his back to Sigurd. 'Did you hear that Eric's wife is with child?'

After a moment's calculation, Sigurd frowned. 'But how can this be? Eric has been dead eight – nay, nine years!'

Ulf dealt a withering look over his shoulder.

'You mean . . .' Sigurd laughed aloud. 'Why, you *have* been taking care of her – Ulf you sly old woolf!' He slapped his knee and howled amusement. 'By the gods, you could give me no greater shock if you told me my mother was risen from the dead!'

Ulf turned on him, highly offended.

'Nay, nay, old friend I cast no slur!' Sigurd grabbed Ulf's upper arms. 'I think it is wonderful. 'Tis just that you have shown not the slightest inclination to take a wife . . . well, well, well.' He shook his head. 'This calls for a feast of celebration.'

At centre table was a great drinking horn that he used for ceremonial purposes and otherwise kept for ornament; even without the silver mounts it would have been most beautiful, ivory-coloured with smudges of grey and black – resembling marble or agate rather than horn. It held four quarts of ale and was often the source of competitions and after-dinner toastings. He grabbed it now to toast the auspicious news.

'Leave it till the child is born,' bade Ulf. 'I would not tempt the gods.' Still embarrassed, he edged on to the bench hardly able to look at Sigurd. 'You are not angry, then?'

Sigurd was nonplussed. 'Why should I be angry?'

Ulf examined his hands, constantly a-fidget. 'I am angry with myself. Eric was our friend, I feel I have betrayed him.'

The reply was uttered with amazement. 'By taking care of his widow?'

'By taking advantage of her. I had no intent . . . it just happened.'

'Ulf, you have lived with her for nine years. It is a miracle that it has not happened before. Come! Be not melancholy. I am so happy for you that I will even come to St Peter's to pray for a healthy child. When is it to be born?'

'Around Yule.' The rock-face grimaced. 'What sort of father would give a child such a bad start in life?' He picked up the lamb and rubbed its curly poll.

Sigurd thought of his dear Gytha and said gruffly, 'You will be a good father to this one just as you are to Eric's girls.'

Ulf looked gloomy and shook his head.

But his pessimism was groundless; in the depths of the winter solstice his wife – or Eric's wife, as he insisted on calling her – gave birth to the most robust of sons.

'A boy?' Sigurd showed disbelief when Ulf arrived with breathless news.

'Ja! And fists on him like a pair of hammers!' Ulf could not conceal his pride, lapsing into his old dialect.

'A son . . .' Sigurd remained mystified as to how this could happen. 'But we all had girls. Eric sired four daughters, I myself . . .'

'You think I did not have it in me?' Ulf delivered a pointed glare and thumped his own chest. 'It takes a man to get a man!'

Sigurd delivered a thump too, half in retribution but mostly in pleasure. 'You do not use it very often,

Ulf, but when you do it is certainly to good effect – my friend, I am most happy for you!' He grasped the other's arm, face sincere. 'Come, let us toast the child and then you must take me to see him.' A crafty twinkle lurked in the deep-set eye as he held the ceremonial horn for a slave to fill. 'I will not believe this till I witness it for myself!'

Sigurd was to have little acquaintance with Ulf's son throughout Asketil's babyhood. Less than a year after his birth came the news that Harthacnut had made a pact with Magnus of Norway that allowed him to leave Denmark without fear of losing it, and sail for England to claim his throne here. Apart from Harefoot, who awaited his homecoming with apprehension, Sigurd and Earl Godwin had most to lose, not only for their support of Harald but being responsible for the death of his other half-brother, Alfred. Much was the relief of all three when they heard that he had dropped anchor at Bruges to seek his mother's advice.

Prepared to fend off Harthacnut's attack, Sigurd was devastated when the sickly King Harald expired without heir, leaving the way open for his brother. As Harthacnut approached England with sixty-two warships, he and Godwin, hundreds of miles apart from each other, sought frantically for a way out of their predicament and both reached identical conclusions: when a group of the King's housecarls arrived to take Sigurd to Lunden for prosecution he, like his coaccused, had his speech and witnesses prepared.

'My lord king.' Sigurd performed an extremely low bow before the new monarch, his beard almost trailing the floor. 'I come to swear my loyalty and to pledge fifty fighting men with swords and axes and five thousand pounds in silver.'

'And this purports to compensate for my brother's death?' Harthacnut looked bitter. In contrast to his feelings for his other sibling Harald, he felt great kinship for his mother's sons by Ethelred and grieved deeply over Alfred's cruel treatment.

Sigurd was contrite, but it was all an act, as was the King's display of authority. Harthacnut had always been afraid of Sigurd, and the raddled cheeks spoke for themselves; their owner had needed much wine before having the courage to face these two lions. However, it paid to be diplomatic to one so unstable. 'My lord, nought can compensate for the death of a brother, but I swear I took no part in his death.'

Harthacnut stroked his chin and mused. 'Strange, Earl Godwin has also denied any part in it, and his gifts were even more generous than yours.'

'My lord, Earl Godwin is far wealthier than I. It is not out of guilt that I bring tribute but out of loyalty to your father Cnut who numbered me amongst his friends. He was a great king and . . .'

'Enough!' Harthacnut was tired of being judged on his father's reign. 'You try to deflect my thoughts from the murder of my brother.'

'Nay, my lord . . .'

'Earl Godwin doth tell that the last occasion he saw Alfred alive was in your company. He denies giving the order for him to be blinded.'

The response was swift. 'Lord, I deny this cruel deed also! When I took him captive I acted upon the orders of the King your brother Harald. What is a man to do against a King's demands? If you give me an order wouldst I not obey? Just as I must take orders from a jarl.' He glanced maliciously at Godwin who stood with his fellow-accused Bishop Lyfing of Weogornaceaster. 'But upon my oath I was not party to the Aetheling's mutilation. Forsooth, I was not even present. The last I saw of him he lived.'

Harthacnut's bloodshot eyes glared at him for long moments, their owner swaying. Sigurd remained in humble pose on one knee, head and shoulders bent, vowing that if he lived he would repay Cnut's son for making him grovel, whilst one by one his many friends, including the Earl of Northumbria, spoke on his behalf. None of the housecarls witness to the blinding made comment now, though it must have been one of them who had leaked the gossip to the King's ears.

Eventually, as he had done with Godwin, the King accepted the financial offering and gave only verbal punishment, except to Bishop Lyfing who was deprived of his see. To show Harald's supporters just how foolish they had been, Harthacnut ordered his brother's body to be disinterred from its tomb at Wintanceaster and thrown into the Temes.

'He is a madman!' complained Sigurd to his visitor, Ulf, who was glad to see him home unscathed though as ever his face did not reveal any emotion. 'He has caused havoc down south with his new taxes, the people are murdering his collectors and I cannot say I blame them – Murtagh!' He gave a roar which made the child on Ulf's lap jump. Asketil was three years old and in awe of his father's friend.

The cross-eyed slave appeared. 'Fetch us drink!' commanded Sigurd. Murtagh bowed and hurried to obey. Asketil pressed himself into his father's chest as Sigurd went on ranting about the King.

'I cannot believe it, Ulf! It is beyond belief that he is a son of our great Cnut. He must be some . . . some changeling put there by Loki – what is that?' He sprang forward, weapon at the ready, glaring across the room. 'Oh, 'tis the dog's tail.' He relaxed. 'I saw this thing curled around the chair-leg and thought it was a snake. I almost lopped it off.'

From the safety of his father's knee, little Asketil chanced a thoughtful remark. 'Would it hurt if you had?'

''Twould not hurt me.' Sigurd gave a laugh that frightened the boy into silence and the man returned to his pet topic. 'There he sits in his father's court with that runt of Ethelred's by his side . . .' Harthacnut showed great fondness for Edward '. . . how can I stand by and watch him destroy all that my friend Cnut has built – that I, Sigurd Einarsson, helped him to build!'

Murtagh arrived with the flagon and goblets, too slowly in Sigurd's opinion for when the thrall had put them down he jumped up and beat him viciously about the head with his fist. Asketil cowered. Murtagh ran. Ulf watched dispassionately and kept his ear available to his friend's grumblings as Sigurd flopped down, rolled up his sleeves to uncover the dragons and gulped his wine before starting again. ''Twould not surprise me if Harthacnut favoured Ethelred's cub as his heir!'

Despite this outburst he was surprised – outraged – when his prophesy came true. Within two years of his unworthy reign Harthacnut had fallen dead at a feast. Upon his exit the thrones of Denmark and England became vacant. Magnus of Norway lost no time in claiming the Scandinavian crown, enforcing the treaty made with Harthacnut. The witan, grasping this chance to be free of Danish kings, chose Edward who was crowned the next year. Sigurd's had been the only voice raised against the motion. The viking empire had started to crumble.

'Ulf, the world is surely gone mad!' Sigurd played with one of the intricately-carved bone strap-ends of his belt, face nonplussed. 'And Godwin maddest of them all. He who was so opposed to Ethelred's brats now plays Edward's shoulder-comrade. I ask you, what claim does he have?'

Ulf hoisted one shoulder and offered logic. 'Cnut's line is come to an end. Edward's father was once King of England . . .'

'Thirty years ago! By that yardstick I could lay claim myself for having once shared a whore with the

King's cousin! Magnus of Norway has as much right as Edward – why, the man doth hardly speak our language! Oh, how can it be that Cnut had such weak offspring?' He spun testily on Asketil, whose playful voice intruded on the serious debate. 'Such noise you do make, child! What game is this?'

Asketil had fashioned a red beard from a large fur glove which he gripped in his teeth, and danced like an elf, whacking a stick at the furniture. 'I am Eric the Red!' he put forth in deep voice.

'Well, if you do not cease you will be Eric with the red arse. I came in here for peace and quiet.' They sat in his ante-room. Warning heeded, Sigurd went back to griping. 'Maybe those simpletons in Lunden will accept him but I will die first!' He was too furious to notice that Ulf looked unwell; his friend was never ruddy of cheek and the slight change of pallor went undetected.

A quieter Asketil had climbed on to his father's lap. His hair was light, but not as blond as Sigurd's, and was cut like his father's, short at the neck, deep in the fringe. Ulf shifted under his featherweight and, unable to get comfortable, put Asketil back on his feet. After eyeing Sigurd with caution the five-year-old began to wander around the room, tracing his fingers over carvings on the furniture and licking a cluster of wooden grapes to see how they tasted. Sigurd proceeded to grumble. Asketil looked at Murtagh who hovered unobtrusively in a corner, as frozen as one of the carvings on the panelled walls. He felt sorry for the wretched creature, for he knew what it was to be afraid of Sigurd; even though the man had never beaten him as he did Murtagh, his voice alone could instil fear. Trailing his fingers round the walls, he encountered the dogs' leashes and unhooked them. Immediately the wolfhounds leapt to their feet and bounded over.

'Oh, see what you have done now!' Sigurd broke

off complaining about the King to rebuke Asketil again. 'They think they go hunting – down!' The huge dogs would not be subdued but pranced and fussed around Asketil, nudging him into attaching the leads to their studded collars. 'Ulf, can you not keep this boy of yours in check?'

'May I take them outside?' Asketil was looking at his father.

'You should not ask me, but their master.' Ulf winced and shifted in his seat; no one noticed.

Sigurd clicked his tongue and waved a permissive hand. 'So be it – but do not come crying if they pull you over.'

'Keep inside the burh,' warned Ulf as his son made for the door, almost invisible between the hounds. Asketil turned to give a smiling nod; his two front teeth were missing.

'Bring me a pot to piss in!' Sigurd shouted at Murtagh who hurried over and tried not to listen to the sound of running urine for his own bladder was fit to burst.

'He who can afford to piss on silver need not worry over church dues,' muttered Ulf, observing the fluted silver vessel being so abused. 'I eat from lesser bowls than that.'

'Then you may have it with pleasure!' Sigurd offered him the receptacle, laughed, then handed it back to Murtagh, his expression twisting. 'Oh, get out of my sight, black one!' The grateful slave dashed outside.

Ulf did not mind that the thrall received an occasional beating, but opposed this constant display of tyranny. 'Why do you keep him ever-present when he so annoys you?'

Sigurd looked confused. 'I know not. I just cannot bring myself to free him after what his mother did.'

'You could sell him.'

'Nay, for then he could gain freedom. Neither will

I kill him. It is small revenge on Una, I know, but it is all I have. She robbed me of my child, Ulf, but hers will not die so quickly.' He jerked his shoulders and returned to his former topic. 'This Edward, he knows nothing of northern folk. We could quite easily rip the country into separate kingdoms again.'

'With yourself as King of Jorvik?' Ulf knew his friend of old. 'Methinks Earl Siward would have words to say on that.' Since Cnut's death all the great earls had gathered power; Siward ran Northumbria as though he were King.

Sigurd was calmer now and grinned back. 'He and I are friends. I would not usurp him, but neither shall he live forever. He has but one son who is old enough to take over – and who knows when he might die? The earldom would better go to one with experience – where goest thou?' His friend had risen quickly and was making for the door.

'To chase my bowels!'

Sigurd laughed, but when a grey-faced Ulf limped back into the room, he voiced concern. 'What ails my friend?'

Ulf closed his eyes and eased himself onto a chair, pausing a while before answering. 'I have been losing blood.'

Sigurd leaned forward and touched the other's arm. 'How long?'

Ulf looked him in the eye for a span, then admitted, 'Some weeks. You must find yourself a new reeve, my friend. I am too weak to carry out the task properly.'

His friend came bolt upright. 'I will send for the physician.' But Ulf tugged him back into his seat.

'Nay, doest think I have not consulted one already? He gives me potions which have no effect. My fate is with God.'

Numbed, his friend leaned back. How often had he

387

saved Ulf's life in battle and how often had Ulf saved his? He could do nought now.

Ulf patted his hand, then rose as a cripple. 'I must go. I told Eric's wife I would not tarry long.'

Sigurd leapt up. 'You cannot go like this! I will have Murtagh take you on the wagon.'

Ulf made no complaint, unable to face even the short journey across town. Sigurd bellowed for the thrall who came running and was given instructions. Asketil came running too, not from choice but being compelled to follow the dogs who, at their master's shout bounded across the yard dragging the tiny boy with them and eventually pulling him off his feet. He let go of the leads, picked himself up and came towards his father, rubbing the torn knees of his leggings.

Ulf half-turned to Sigurd, avoiding his eyes. 'I will send for you,' was all he said.

The ealdorman did not wait to be summmoned but visited Ulf each day, and each day he saw his friend's health deteriorate until in November the end was close. So thin and gaunt was Ulf, so shallow his breath, that he barely raised the blanket which covered him. The pools in the rock-face had sunken to caverns. His wife lifted his head to try and feed him soup, but he refused saying he did not wish to prolong the agony. 'Is friend Sigurd here yet?' came his weak query as she laid his head back on the pillow.

'Not yet.' She handed the bowl to one of her daughters who melted into the shadows where her sisters observed with grave faces.

'Before he comes I have something to impart.'

'Save your breath for your friend,' urged his wife, patting him. 'I am content to sit here.'

'Nay, 'tis for you to hear now.'

His wife leaned forward but was irritated by the child who played nearby. 'Asketil, be quiet!' she uttered in low but stern tone to her son who had just leapt off the table with a howl.

But Asketil was away in his own private world killing pirates and did not hear her order above his own yells of excitement, nor the entreaties of his sisters. He clambered onto the table again, wielding an imaginary sword and bawling.

'I said, be quiet!' Mouth set in a determined line, the child's mother crossed the room and lashed out, knocking him from table to floor. 'How dare you make so much noise with your father lying ill?' At her raised voice, the girls hastily departed.

Asketil did not cry but, knowing that he deserved the punishment, looked so riddled with guilt that his mother gave him a rough kiss and cuddle before shoving him towards the door. 'Be gone and play outside.'

'It is too cold . . .'

'Go!'

'Let him play,' muttered Ulf. 'He does not bother me.'

His wife ignored the entreaty. 'Go!' When the child had slunk from the room she turned back to the bed. 'That boy!'

'It is that boy whom I wish to discuss,' murmured Ulf. 'When I die, Asketil must go to live with Sigurd.'

She reacted as he had known she would. 'You would give our son to a man such as him?'

'Do not speak of my friend in that manner.'

'But Ulf, he is so harsh. You have heard how he blinded the Aetheling just for staring at him.'

'You understand nothing, woman.' Ulf sounded weary.

'And he has no wife! What is Til to do for affection?'

'Sigurd will provide it.' Ulf rebuked the look of astonishment. 'I know him better than you. Believe

389

me, he will give the boy all that he gave to Gytha and more.'

'That was a long time ago! Why did his wife leave him if he was so kind? I have never seen him be generous to any of my children – oh, he brings gifts, yes, but never real affection.'

'You do not see that side of him because he dare not show it. A man who does not love cannot be hurt. But Asketil will draw it from his breast, I am sure of it. Heed not the tales of his cruelty, for to his friends he is steadfast. I know he will never lift a finger to Asketil, and will love him . . . and if I am mistaken, then you will not be so far away that Til cannot run home if he lacks a hug. Be not unkind. When I go you will have four daughters. Sigurd will have no one, no one in the world. Let me grant him this.'

Before she could argue further Sigurd arrived. He wondered why she behaved so coldly towards him, then put it down to melancholy over Ulf's condition. He sat by Ulf's bed and took his limp hand, surprising the woman with the unexpected show of tenderness. Face thoughtful, she left them. 'How are you today, my friend? You look better.'

'No time for lies,' responded Ulf. 'I have just told Eric's wife that I want Til to come and live with you when I die.'

Sigurd was so taken aback that he dropped his friend's hand.

'But I have had few dealings with boys!'

'Where you not a boy once? A boy with an axe almost as big as himself.' Ulf lifted a corner of his mouth, remembering their first encounter, then spoke as firmly as he was able. 'Cease your argument and listen. You are as bad as Eric's wife interrupting when I have so little time. There is no one else to whom I would entrust his care. You are my greatest friend and a brave warrior; who better to teach him the things that I have no time left to show?' He soothed the other's obvious misgivings. 'You will be good for each other. Let him be the son you never had.'

Now Sigurd understood the cool reception. 'The boy's mother is not pleased about this?'

'It must be expected for a mother to cling to her bairn, but she knows that she has not the skill to be a father as well as a mother.'

Sigurd thought of his own mother, often more brutal in her teachings than any male. After a while he gave Ulf his answer. 'I would be proud to call him mine.'

Grateful, Ulf required one more favour. 'Will you also take care of the lad's mother?'

Sigurd nodded. 'She may stay in this house all her days.'

Ulf thanked him and asked then if he would summon the child to his bedside. When a nervous Asketil appeared, Ulf explained, 'Your father is going away on a long journey. Sigurd here will be your *fostri*. You shall respect him and he will teach you the things you need to be a man.'

Asketil threw a stricken glance under his fringe at the visitor who had retreated in order to grant father and son privacy, then lisped through the gap in his teeth, 'I do not want to go.'

'Are you not always begging me to show you how to handle weapons? This man is a thousand times more equipped than I to turn you into a warrior.'

Asketil paused in his objection to show a flicker of interest. 'Shall I have a sword of my own?'

'Not until you are big enough to use it without cutting your own head off.'

Asketil hesitated, then whispered into the dying man's face, 'I don't want to go with him, he makes me afraid.'

Ulf whispered back, 'He frightens me too sometimes, but so long as you do not harm him he will not harm you.'

Asketil spread himself across his father's body and muttered into the jaundiced cheek, 'He shouts and roars.'

'So does your mother.' Ulf barely had strength to raise a smile. 'And she hits you twice as hard as Sigurd ever will.' His voice was failing. He pulled the child closer and spoke into his face. Asketil thought his breath foul. 'My son, my dear son, you will find him gruff and oft severe, but he will give you many things . . . though not perhaps as great as the gift that you can bestow on him. He has no one in this world. Whatever he does or says to you, I want you to promise that you will never withdraw your friendship nor your loyalty. I love that man with my life. Do this for me.'

Still unconvinced, Asketil raised his head, looked deep into the yellow eyes, then nodded.

'Good . . . now, let me see you take his hand.'

Asketil went towards Sigurd, looked up at him, then inserted his hand into the rough one.

Memories of Gytha flooded back. Sigurd wanted to push the hand away, it burnt such pain into his heart.

Asketil looked back at the bed. 'When will you return, Father?'

Ulf closed his eyes in sad exasperation that the boy had not grasped this. 'I shall never return. From here onwards you shall know Sigurd as your father.'

The little boy's eyes became round. 'Shall I never see Mother again, neither?'

Ulf was feeling much pain and shifted on his blood-stained mattress. 'Your mother will remain here. You will go and live in the house of your foster-father, but you can come and visit her whenever Sigurd will permit. Now . . . come here one last moment.' The child ran to him and after petting him Ulf whispered in his ear. Following a puzzled hesitation, Asketil scampered out of the house. In his absence

Ulf beckoned his friend to return to the bedside. 'Come, take my hand, shipmate, and let us say our goodbyes now.' The hand was accepted. 'I will leave the boy my weapons, but do not give them to him until he is old enough to respect them.' At Sigurd's nod he continued, 'Can I ask one last thing of you? I wish to be buried in St Cuthbert's. Will you raise a stone to me?'

Sigurd replied that he would be honoured. They remained in silence, holding hands until Asketil returned breathless and clutching a fistful of horsehair. 'Lay it here around my chin,' instructed his father. Sigurd looked on as the boy draped the hair about his father's face. How uncanny that in death those pain-filled eyes came the nearest Sigurd had ever seen them to merriment. 'I could not go without letting my friend see what I look like with a beard.'

Sigurd forced a hearty laugh, said, 'I shall see you on the morrow,' then abruptly he grabbed Asketil's hand and dragged him from the house, never looking back.

393

Chapter Sixteen

At the age of fifty-four, Ulf died and was buried in St Cuthbert's churchyard. Sigurd erected a stone in his honour, upon which he carved his own runic message: *Sigurd put up this stone to his heart-friend Ulf.* Asketil accompanied him to the burial and took the opportunity to say proper farewells to his mother and half-sisters which, because Sigurd had dragged him away so rudely from Ulf's deathbed, he had been unable to do before this. Afterwards the youngster was lifted onto the ealdorman's horse and taken back through alleyways awash with mud and straw to that big house he so feared.

There were few children of his own age in the burh, the inhabitants being mainly fighting men and their servants. Today, when he had just seen his father buried, this did not seem so vital to Asketil, for he did not feel like playing, but it would have been a comfort to have someone to talk to. He dared not talk to his fostri. Since bringing him here the man had shared but a dozen words with him.

On return from his father's burial, Asketil did not join Sigurd but remained outside. The man asked only once if he were coming in, and receiving a shake of head left the boy to his own devices, totally apathetic to his pain.

Needing occupation, Asketil wandered out of the enclosure and began to follow the perimeters of the burh which was enclosed by a ditch on three sides – the fourth being defended by the Use – and incorporated the south-west wall of the ancient Legionary Fortress. The traces of a Roman road cut through the centre. Within these bounds, apart from Sigurd's wooden mansion, were the great houses of the King, Earl and other nobles, plus the humbler abodes of their retainers, each with their own enclosing fence. Any other lad would have been proud to live here, but all Asketil could think of was his father in the cruel ground and the family he had left behind. He followed the ramparts right around their length, pushing through a herd of goats that stood in his track. A woman tending geese smiled at him. He did not return the compliment, but wandered on past the silent beehives and the well, past doe-eyed maidens flirting with soldiers, until he found himself back at the main gatehouse built of stone. Not knowing whether to go in or out, he rested on his heels and began to whittle a twig, assailed by loneliness and cold.

Another lonely soul tramped towards the burh. Murtagh's life was one of endless toil. He had been out all day ploughing his master's fields since daybreak, plodding up and down the furrows behind eight oxen. The boy who goaded the beasts found him dull company, for he had no conversation; that and the misaligned eyeball was why no woman would marry him. He wasn't right in the head. He was twenty-four years of age and had no wife, only a loving aunt to chase away the tormentors who called him dummy. Murtagh's naked feet were blue with the cutting November wind. It was pointless wrapping rags around them for they would only end up clogged with mud and hampering his straight ploughlines. It was now dusk and he was on his way home. He had completed the statutory acre for that day. But then there would be tomorrow and tomorrow and tomorrow . . .

Were it not for his aunt, who vowed to liberate

him, he would have laid down and died. Mary's indomitability amazed him. Without help, she had cultivated her five acres and from the sale of produce had bought her own freedom. That had been a day! She had taken Murtagh with her, as much to witness the look on the master's face as to witness the handing over of the money. His expression when she slapped the coins on his table and said that he no longer owned her! A little smile played around Murtagh's lips as he remembered, though it did not last, for his aunt was not really free, was she? She could not go and build a house on her land for what would Murtagh do without her? So she continued to live virtually as a slave. He felt such a hindrance, but at the same time he did not tell her to go, for without her he would have no one.

He came across the flat board that spanned the drainage ditch, through the gates and lifted his dispirited eyes as his name was called. A small boy came running towards him. It was Asketil, son of the one called Ulf. Murtagh wondered why the child was so interested in him. Whenever he came to visit Earlsburh he would seek out the thrall and tag along while Murtagh did his chores.

'How went your day, Murtagh?' Asketil looked up at him but did not smile as he usually did for he was too sad.

'No use talking to him,' said the one who walked behind the oxen alongside Murtagh. 'He's a dummy.'

Murtagh, of infinite patience, did not strike him.

'I know he cannot speak,' retorted Asketil.

'Who are you, then?' the ox-goader enquired of the gap-toothed child.

'My name is Asketil, *fostri* to Sigurd and I do not think it shows much charity to call him dummy.' Beneath the heavy fringe blue eyes glared their objection.

''Tis but a name, master,' muttered the ox-goader.

Even a little boy demanded respect if he was akin to Lord Sigurd. 'What else are we to call him if he does not speak?'

'You could call him by his proper name; 'twould be kinder.' Asketil looked up at Murtagh but did not know if the man looked back for his eyes were askew. Out of curiosity he asked, 'How do you plough true furrows when your eye is twisted?'

'It beats me.' The boy answered for Murtagh. 'But he does – you never seen such straight rows, straight as arrows. Hey ho! I must leave you now.' He gave the oxen a parting wallop as they reached the shippen and left them. Asketil followed the procession into the building where he sat in the lamplight to watch Murtagh feed and water the beasts. It was warmer here. He hunkered and went back to whittling his twig for a while, chatting to Murtagh who gave not the slightest sign of acknowledgement. The man looked so tired that Asketil put down his knife on the straw and jumped to his feet. 'Shall I help you? Show me what to do.' Murtagh ignored him. Asketil watched the slave rub a handful of straw over an ox's coat and made childish attempts to do likewise. When he looked up for assurance that he was doing it right the man was smiling. Encouraged, Asketil smiled back and put more vigour into his movements. It helped to take his mind off his loss. Black Mary entered then to tell her nephew that his meal was ready, biting back her intended greeting when she saw Asketil. She regarded him so viciously that he threw down the bundle of straw and hurried from the byre.

The woman checked to make sure he had gone, then turned back to Murtagh with a smile. 'That's another of them dead. The little swine's father was buried today – and without any help from me!' She gave a cackle of appreciation. The door was pushed open and she spun round with a guilty expression, but seeing it was only another slave she relaxed.

397

'May I share the jest?' asked the newcomer. 'Such a day have I had.'

'To be sure, there was no jest,' answered Mary. '′Twas only laughing I was because I felt merry.'

The other gave her a sour look. 'You are always laughing.' It grieved her to be kept in the dark as to Mary's amusement, made her feel that perhaps she was the butt of Mary's joke. 'What has a slave to laugh about?'

'I'm no slave.' Black Mary's face darkened. 'I stay here through choice.'

The other acquiesced. 'Still, you have little reason for humour I would have thought.' Faced with hostility, she withdrew, leaving the door ajar on purpose to let in the cold.

'Ah, if only she knew!' whispered Mary to her nephew, then laughed again. 'One by one they die, these sons of Satan. Christ is with us, Murtagh. I hope He can grant as painful a death to Lord Sigurd as He did to his friend, Ulf. I love to think o' the blood seeping out of him, killing him inch by inch.' She sobered and rubbed her arms to ward off the draught. 'But this child he's brought here to replace his dead brat . . . we cannot wait for Christ to act, I must snuff him out quickly as I did Gytha. What fun to watch that pain all over ag . . .' She broke off as Murtagh shook his head urgently, and turned to see Asketil.

The little boy did not know what to do. He had returned for his knife but hearing the cruel words about his father had made him forget about it. He started to back away. Black Mary took a step forward and he ran. Murtagh caught his aunt's arm as she made to follow and shook his head again more vigorously. She laid an anxious hand over his, staring into the crooked eyes. 'D'ye think he heard?'

Murtagh looked afraid and nodded.

'Oh, Sweet Jesus . . .' Black Mary hugged him fiercely. Murtagh would have continued to cling in desperation but she prized herself free. 'Murtagh, let go, *let go*! Your aunt must find sanctuary.' She made for the door, her nephew after her. 'Don't worry, 'tis safe I'll be in the church.' With these parting words she ran from the shippen across the enclosure then gathering her wits she slowed and forced herself to appear less guilty so as to get through the gates without attracting attention. Avoiding the main exit where there were more guards, she hurried for the one which opened onto the Great North Road. Every eye was upon her, or so she felt, as she clutched her cloak around her trembling body. It was well dark now, torches were lit. She looked straight ahead at the gate, praying that it would not be locked before she reached it. Five steps. Five miles. The two guards looked at her as she drew level with them. Her breath came in quick clouds. Her whole body pulsated, awaiting the order to stop. But why would they question a free woman whose comings and goings they were well accustomed to?

She was through the gate and into the road.

'Hey!' She froze and only just withheld a scream. Half-turning, she waited for the accusation. 'Be not long, we bar the gates soon.'

Her reply was tremulous, almost a laugh. 'Then I must run.' Given the excuse she fled towards the *porta principalis dextra*, that led into the city and salvation.

Since overhearing Black Mary's words, Asketil had been wavering outside the great timber door, watching and waiting for her to come after him. The look on her face had brought fear to his heart, but who would he tell when the man indoors frightened him too? He must go in some time, it was too dark and cold out here. Spotting Mary's exit he panicked and, applying both small hands to the iron handle, he twisted it this way and that before someone opened the door from the other side. He leapt past the servant into the grand hall full of men. They were quieter this eve in respect for Ulf's death, but their brutish appearance worried him, as much if not more than his foster-father, and he moved on quickly through the pall of wood smoke to Sigurd's private room.

The warrior was in his chair by the fire. Still brooding over his friend's death he did not look up but continued to mope over all the things that were going wrong in his life, from the monarchy down. Asketil chose not to sit with him, instead he wandered about the room, as ever intrigued by the carved panels. There was much bare wood still to be worked. Finding another knife he began to chip away at his own design.

The noise of grating permeated Sigurd's dejection. He looked up, witnessed the act of vandalism and with the silent swoop of an owl pounced on Asketil, knocking the blade from his hand. His foster-son cowered, expecting to be thrashed.

'Thou demon!' Sigurd pointed at the damaged panel. 'Is this how you repay your father's friend?'

'I thought the wall unfinished,' whimpered the boy. 'I tried only to help.'

Sigurd glared down into the wide blue eyes. The child was obviously terrified. Remembering only now that he was dealing with a five year old, his temper began to abate and he examined the panel more closely. What he had thought to be mere vandalism was in fact the crude beginnings of a snake.

'Well . . . I think you need a little more practice first.' Sigurd picked up the bone-handled knife, handed it back to the boy and in doing so rebuked himself. *Look at the child, the son of your friend entrusted to you and your first act is to frighten him half to death*! He struggled to make amends. 'Tomorrow I will teach you how to carve properly. Come by the fire, you are shivering.'

Even more wary now, Asketil took refuge in his heavy fringe, crouched beside Sigurd's chair. At home his inquisitive nature had always been given free rein and he would chatter all night if allowed but he was too unsure of himself here to ask questions of Sigurd. There were plenty he wanted to ask, but instead he gazed at the fire, darting the occasional furtive look at the man from beneath his fringe. Sigurd was not sure what to say, either. It was so long since he had enjoyed the company of a child. Regretting his harshness, he wanted to put Asketil at ease but could not remember how. Gytha had liked to hear the sagas; though too young to understand, she had been charmed by the sound of her father's voice.

'Once, there was a man called . . .' Sigurd noted the look of alarm on the boy's face at the unexpected intrusion, and offered an apologetic smile. 'I did not mean to frighten thee.'

Asketil cuddled his knees to his chest to ward off the shiver of apprehension and lied. 'I am not afraid. 'Twas only that you startled me. I was thinking of my father.'

Sigurd recognized the boy's misery and offered rough comfort. 'I, too, have been thinking of him. I knew Ulf for almost thirty years. 'Tis strange that he is no longer here. There will be many who mourn him.'

'But not everyone,' Asketil muttered into his knee-cap. Sigurd asked what he meant. 'I overheard that woman, Murtagh's mother . . .'

'Oh, you mean Black Mary,' nodded Sigurd. 'What of her?'

'She was laughing because my father died.' The child's voice held disbelief. To ward off tears he fixed his eyes to the smoke which spiralled to the roof.

401

Sigurd growled, 'She is a madwoman. I know not why I give her shelter. Tomorrow I will get rid of her then you shall not have to listen to her spiteful ramblings.'

Encouraged that his *fostri* would do this for him, Asketil shed one of the layers of dread. 'What does it mean to snuff a person out?'

'It is as you do to a candle-flame.' Sigurd performed a nipping motion. 'If it is said of a man, it means you kill him.'

'Who was Gytha?'

The man stiffened, his fingers curling round the arms of the chair. 'We do not speak of her.'

Curiosity overcame nervousness. 'Because she is dead?'

Sigurd nodded, feeling choked, and pretended that it was the fire which made him cough.

Quick to assess the mood, Asketil became bolder, staring up at the man who tried to avert his face. 'Who was she?'

After a long pause Sigurd gave brusque reply. 'She was my daughter.' He snatched up a goblet and drank.

Acquainted with the ealdorman's fierce reputation, Asketil looked perplexed. '*Fostri*, why does the woman who killed your daughter still live?'

'One does not live without a head.' Sigurd gulped down the wine, trying to wash away the dreadful last vision of Una.

'But she has her head.'

Sigurd frowned at him over the rim of the goblet, then lowered it. 'What is this you say?'

'The woman, Black Mary, she . . .'

Sigurd dropped the goblet, shot upwards and lifted the boy off his feet. 'What has been said?!'

Plunged back into terror, Asketil stammered, 'She has just told Murtagh she killed Gytha!'

Sigurd dropped him most rudely and kicked at the

hound that came to lap at the spilt wine. Asketil pelted off to cringe with the chastized dog. Buckling on his sword, Sigurd charged from the room, through the hall and raked the dark and peaceful courtyard with his eyes before yelling at the top of his voice. '*Mary!*' Heads went up in alarm, but no one came running. He seized a flare from its sheath and holding it before him ran to every dark corner. A woman came out of the darkness; Sigurd grabbed her. 'Where lurks Black Mary?'

'Mary? My lord, I have not seen her!'

Casting her aside he ran to the slaves' hut and burst in. The occupants reared back at the threat of fire from Sigurd's torch. Murtagh tried to hide behind fellow thralls. Sigurd threw the brand outside, hauled him to his feet and demanded to know where his aunt was. Murtagh offered only choking sounds as the man's grip tightened on his throat. He lifted his arm towards the main gate. Through the terror there was a hint of defiance. Sigurd pushed the wretch at the shivering knot of thralls, downing them like skittles and ran in the direction of the pointed finger. Clutching his throat, Murtagh jumped up and ran after him. There was no sign of the murderess.

Sigurd ran on to the main gates, where he accosted the guards. 'Has Black Mary passed this way?'

'Nay, my lord, she . . .' The guard broke off as Sigurd ran back towards the Conyngstrete exit. He hared through the gates and was about to continue down the King's Street when something made his head turn to the left. The Minster! Changing course he fought his way between the houses until he came to the open ground before the cathedral, its grandeur illuminated by flares – and there was Mary's fleeing figure almost at the great doors! Sigurd injected every ounce of effort into catching her before her fingers touched the handle, rage lending him speed. Black Mary flung a worried look over her shoulder, saw him and made the last few bounds for her life. He was within three yards of her. Frantic hands twisted and rived at the handle, the door came open, she flung herself inside and screamed at the top of her voice, '*Sanctuary!*'

Her pursuer burst into the Minster, weapon in hand, but it was too late. The sweet echoes of nocturne lingered on the air as a group of brethren foiled his attack. He teetered on the verge of murder, chest rising and falling with pent-up rage, sword upheld . . . but much as he reviled the Christian doctrine he dared not break the laws of sanctuary.

'Sheath your weapon!' One of the brethren stepped forth whilst the others closed ranks around a sobbing Mary. 'You are in the house of God.'

'That woman killed my daughter!' Enraged, Sigurd pointed his blade at them, trembling to be at her. Behind the protective curtain of robes Mary flinched and crossed herself.

'Then she must stand trial,' replied the brethren's spokesman, not a tremor in his voice. 'But you alone must not be her judge. She shall remain in God's protection for three days until she can appear at the wapentake. Now take your violent ways from this House!'

Thwarted, Sigurd glared at the canon for what felt like an age to Mary. Then still volatile, he rammed his blade into its sheath and barged out. Murtagh pressed himself into the dark corner waiting for his master to pass. Content that his aunt would be safe in the cathedral, he returned to Earlsburh before the gates were locked for the night.

When Sigurd bullied his way through the hall of curious soldiers and returned to his room it was empty of all but the dogs. Simmering with frustration, he flopped into his chair and threw one of his boots at the hound which snored unconscious of the drama.

He buried his head in his hands, killing Mary over and over again, until a sound made him lift his sharp gaze. Asketil stood holding his foster-father's boot. The man's chest heaved, he looked ready to collapse. 'I thought you were gone.'

'I was over there.' Asketil pointed in the direction in which the boot had been aimed. Despite the man's terrifying exit, there was something in his pose now that encouraged approach.

Sigurd just looked at him. 'Did I hit you?'

Asketil shook his head, was silent for a while, then asked, 'May I try your big boot on?' Given permission he donned it and admired the effect. 'Look, I can get both feet in.'

'You could get four feet in there if you had them,' replied Sigurd, at which Asketil pushed his hands inside the boot too, tried to hop around on all fours and fell over.

Sigurd raised half a smile, though inside his heart throbbed.

Asketil displayed his gums and held up the boot. ''Tis as big as a ship.' He began to collect various objects off the table and put them into the 'ship' to represent men, using spoons for oars.

Sigurd watched him, his fury gradually abating. 'I will carve you a real ship tomorr . . . ' He broke off, hearing Gytha say of the one he had made for her: *Duck. Duck. Duck.* He rubbed his face and head vigorously, itching to be at his daughter's true murderer and begging poor Una to forgive him. When he looked up again Asketil was craning his neck. 'What is it you look for?'

'I look to see if you have blood on your hands,' whispered the child.

Sigurd's nostrils flared. 'Not on mine, but there is much on Black Mary's.'

'Shall you kill her?'

'Yes,' was the blunt reply.

*

As ealdorman, it was Sigurd's duty to preside over legal assemblies, but because he was an interested party on this occasion his role was given to another, Ealdorman Gufrith. Sigurd felt no ire; the consequences would be the same whomsoever presided.

At the wapentake each party delivered their version of events before the twelve thegns. Asketil too was brought forward to recount what he had overheard. Black Mary, protected from Sigurd's wrath by a bishop, though not from his wrathful gaze, yelled out in her defence, 'The boy lies! Everyone knows my nephew is a mute – why would I speak to him when he cannot answer?'

Asketil's voice was almost inaudible but the thegns listened. 'I speak to him. It matters not that he cannot reply.'

'Mayhap that is the very reason why she confides in Murtagh!' Sigurd gesticulated at Mary. 'Because he cannot give away her murderous secrets!'

Black Mary fell to her knees and appealed to the listeners. 'My lords, doesn't everyone know the boy is a mischief-maker! He seeks revenge because he heard me speak of his own father. I spake only the truth but he did not wish to hear it.' She gabbled and supplicated. ''Tis a poor woman I am. What is my word against that of a lord? Yet I speak the truth. Ye cannot try me for the child Gytha's death, for her murderer lies dead already – by *his* hand!' She swivelled on her knees and pointed at Sigurd.

He remained steadfast. 'I confess that I killed the wrong person! The true murderer is there! Asketil is the son of an honourable man, I believe what he says.'

The ealdorman, thegns and bishop put their heads together, whilst Mary wrung her hands and prayed urgently for help from the Almighty.

Finally, Ealdorman Gufrith announced, 'The woman

shall be tried by ordeal. She shall be put into the snakepit . . . ' Mary let out a scream and tried to run but was arrested by guards and made to wait for the rest of the sentence. '. . . for two days and two nights. If she should come out alive then she shall be adjudged innocent.'

Asketil looked up at his foster-father as Black Mary was dragged spitting and kicking from the room. Ordering another to take the child home Sigurd followed the prisoner to the snakepit and watched her being lowered in. Verging on hibernation, the creatures barely reacted, but the mere sight of them had Mary paralyzed with fear. Her tormentor was like a snake himself, watching the event calmly with that cold dead eye of his. The brethren intoned for Almighty God to be her judge, whilst Mary huddled into a corner trying to keep away from the reptilian coils and darting one last beseeching glance at the circle of faces before the wattle lid cut out the light. With the lid made tight by boulders, the spectators turned and went home, Sigurd too. He wondered if the next two days would be as long for Black Mary as they would for him.

Mary could only guess that it was evening by the falling temperature and the sounds from above. Smells assailed her, cooking smells that made her belly ache, smells of animal dung and the smell of her own terror. Gradually the roll of wagonwheels diminished, curfew knelled. All day in the darkness she had been waiting for one of the snakes to inject its venom into her, unable to see or hear them, imagining those points entering her flesh, first here, then there. The waiting was almost as bad as the eventuality – she was now contemplating suicide by clasping a reptile to her breast. Her mind carried her fingers to those smooth coils: just one bite and her torment would be ended . . .

There came the sound of a rolling boulder. The lid was lifted and the outline of a man appeared against the midnight blue of the sky. Shivering from the cold, Mary tilted her eager face upwards, straining to see who it was. The outline made no noise. For a brief moment of joy she thought it was her nephew come to rescue her and she whispered urgently, 'Murtagh?'

Still there was no response. Then, 'You shall not escape,' murmured Ealdorman Sigurd, causing her to shrink against the mud wall. For hours she had held onto the contents of her bladder, unwilling to make her prison more foul; now terror robbed her of control. Like a wee child! she damned herself as the warmth flooded her bare feet. Sigurd poked a rod into the dark corners where the snakes lurked, hoping to provoke them to anger. There was barely a hiss.

Mary's voice quavered but her words were brave. 'They've not touched me yet!'

'It matters not.' Abruptly, the lid dropped.

Plunged back into solitude Black Mary answered his unspoken threat. 'Ye cannot go against the verdict! If I come out of here alive I am innocent. 'Tis the law! I am not a slave!'

There was no answer.

Some time during the murky hours before dawn the lid was lifted again. This time it was Murtagh come to bring her food and hot ale which he lowered on a string. By now her wet skirts compounded the bitter cold. Cupping her trembling hands around the jug she drank and felt the warmth travel to her belly. 'God bless ye, Murtagh! But away with you now. 'Tis punished ye'll be if you're caught.'

Murtagh indicated for her to eat and drink her fill, pushing the jug back down at her when she tried to return it still half-full. All the while she ate, his eyes swivelled and darted like a beast at a watering-hole.

Mary wondered how he had managed to get past the guards; probably with a bribe from Sigurd's wine stock, a ploy used by all his underlings. She blessed her nephew again and urged him to go. 'Don't fuss. Christ has protected me from the snakes so far, they will not touch me now.'

Two days later in the presence of witnesses, the lid was lifted from the pit. All stared down at the huddled form. At first glance the occupant appeared to be lifeless, then Mary lifted her pallid face, eyes slitted against the harsh light. Cramped of movement, she displayed her forearms to show the absence of bites.

'She is innocent,' announced Ealdorman Gufrith without drama. From his viewpoint at the back of the crowd Murtagh rejoiced at the words, but would the master heed them? A ladder was put down and a stinking Mary helped up it. Her eyes had not yet adjusted themselves but even a blind man could feel Sigurd's murderous intention. Though her limbs were weak Mary lunged through the crowd, throwing off her cloak to confuse them and fled.

'Stop the witch!' Sigurd made to pursue her, but Ealdorman Gufrith held on to his embroidered sleeve. 'She has been judged! You cannot take the law unto yourself.'

'A false judgment!' Sigurd hurled at him. 'She bewitched the snakes as she bewitched you.'

Gufrith withheld him more forcefully. 'You would not act thus if the jarl were here!' Their ruler was away up north.

'If he were here this murderess would be already dead!' Shaking off the man's grasp, Sigurd ran after Mary.

Ealdorman Gufrith shouted to his carls to pursue. A stricken Murtagh joined the chase. Once again Mary headed for the only place that could give her sanctuary but this time she had further to run and her limbs were as jelly. Along Steinngata she fled, cold feet stumbling along the paved Roman road that led to the Minster. Sigurd was gaining fast. She could scarcely breathe from exhaustion and terror. Mind crying out to God for salvation, she dared not turn, conserving every ounce of will into escaping. The Minster was in sight . . . her last sight. Still running, eyes focused clearly on his target, Sigurd hefted his weapon and with both hands clasped around its hilt hacked downwards through her neck and deep into her back.

Too late, his pursuers thudded up in clouds of white breath. There came the sound of a terrified steer. Murtagh flung himself at the mutilated body, mouth and face contorted with anguish, futile hands trying to staunch the blood that trickled between the gaps in the cobbles.

Ealdorman Gufrith was furious. 'I shall report this to my lord archbishop! You throw scorn upon my authority!'

The deep-set eyes showed unconcern: their owner flicked his blade and rammed it into its scabbard where the sheepskin lining wiped off Mary's blood. 'And I shall tell the archbishop what I told you. 'Twas a false judgment. Go to the archbishop if you must, but be warned – you may find yourself having to pay compensation for your dealings with a sorceress!' He was about to turn in disdain when he looked down again at the vile body and saw the pure loathing in Murtagh's twisted eyes. 'Do not even dare to contemplate it,' his thin lips warned. And Murtagh, utterly powerless, lowered his gaze as Sigurd walked away.

On return to his private room, he found Asketil waiting for the result of the ordeal. 'Is she dead?'

Looking down at the miniature Ulf, Sigurd began to lose the tautness in his shoulders. He nodded and calling for wine, flopped into his carved chair. Asketil sat frog-like on the cushion at his feet and rubbed his own legs in a gesture of satisfaction. 'Good. I am glad.'

His foster-father did not feel the need to elaborate on Mary's end. When the servant handed him the cup he took a long drink, wiped his moustache and announced, 'Never trust a woman, Til.'

Asketil wrinkled his brow. 'My mother is a woman.'

'Never trust a woman,' emphasized Sigurd, 'not even your mother.' He looked down at the boy. 'We shall have no need of them, you and I, in our new life together.'

Asketil clamped his lower lip between his eye-teeth and underwent thoughtful pause. 'Am I not permitted to see my mother, then?'

The reply was testy. 'Can your mother teach you how to carve, how to shoot an arrow, how to fight like I do?'

Asketil was thoughtful. 'Nay ... but yours is no breast upon which to lay my head, 'tis too hard.'

Sigurd was ready to bite again, when he considered the innocent words. Yes, his breast was hard, filled with bitterness. Mary's death had solved nothing, for now he knew that his execution of Una had been unjust. Never would he involve himself with a woman again ... but it was unfair to deny Asketil a mother. Sighing, he gave permission. 'Go to her if you must.'

'I do not need to go today,' lisped the boy. 'You promised to carve me a ship – is it finished yet?'

Duck, said Gytha. Sigurd flinched and shot from his chair. 'Come! I will show you. Let us forget about women for now.'

Ealdorman Gufrith had no such intention of forgetting. Whilst Mary's body was carted away by her stricken nephew, he himself went directly to the arch-bishop, who ordered the culprit to appear before him.

Sigurd, involved in a mock fight with Asketil, spat contemptuously at the messenger's feet. 'I am not at the beck and call of kirkmen.'

'Then he shall answer to the King!' rasped Arch-bishop Aelfric when given this reply, and redirected his messenger to Lunden where Sigurd's lawless activities were reported to King Edward. The following week Sigurd was ordered to appear at the palace. His ship undergoing repairs, he went there on horse-back.

When he entered, the King was listening to a min-strel playing his lyre. Sigurd had had few dealings with Edward, for the King chose not to venture North, but he had heard rumours of his piety. It was said that he could work miracles. Blind men had been cured by rinsing their eyes in the water Edward had washed in. Looking at him, Sigurd saw only the King's father Ethelred. Edward was a joyless man who divided his time between hunting and the religious observances. Some said that even at the hunt his devotion led him to having mass said before the killing began. It appeared that his character had been shaped by his exile in childhood. He had never forgiven his mother for her rejection of him when she married Cnut, and they were forever at odds with each other. Only a matter of weeks ago he had confiscated all her property. But then his pious side had come to the fore and he had repented and given it all back, even though he held her guilty for his unhappiness. Indeed it was said that he blamed all women, that was why he had not yet married. This was the only point with which Sigurd could identify, otherwise he detested that pious visage.

There was a less holy side to the King and Sigurd, with the arrogant way he paraded himself, was in danger of evoking this. Edward was well familiar with

Sigurd's part in his brother Alfred's death. He did not care for the way Harthacnut had been bought off, and he himself had hoped to revive the case when he became King. Unfortunately, like that other power-mad villain Godwin, this ealdorman was too strong and too popular in his region to be easily disposed of. If Sigurd remained in the North, Edward could tolerate him, but when his intransigence brought him down here, that was another matter. He cursed the Northmen. Why could not they handle their own affairs instead of littering his court with such offal?

He spoke at last, his accent most foreign to Sigurd's ears. 'It has come to my notice that you defied the judgment of Ealdorman Gufrith and carried out a death penalty yourself. Are you not aware that it is against the law to shed blood on the King's highway?'

Sigurd began tiredly, 'The woman had been my slave. She . . .'

'*Had* been your slave! But I am led to understand that she had bought her freedom!' This King would brook no impertinence as friend Cnut had done. 'You had no rights over her.'

Sigurd had grown used to having his own way. 'She was a witch! She killed my daughter and blamed another.'

'So you say! Yet she came through her ordeal.' The fate of one woman mattered not to Edward, but this display of recalcitrance did.

''Tis plain for an idiot to see that if the snakes did not bite her then she is surely a witch.'

This was enough to launch Edward into a rage. 'You call your King an idiot!'

Too late Sigurd showed respect. 'Not so, my lord, I simply . . .'

'Out! Out!' Edward's face took on the hue of claret. 'You are *nithing*, a man without honour! Your title

413

is forfeit, your lands are forfeit! I wish you out of my sight, out of my kingdom!' And he launched into an indecipherable string of French curses that resulted in Sigurd being ejected from the palace.

Venting his anger on the men who had accompanied him to Lunden, Sigurd ordered them to abandon their half-eaten meal and assemble at once for a return to Jorvik – 'And then let this so-called King try to oust me from there! I will soon show him how important he is in the north!'

His hungry foot-troops in tow, Sigurd was fifteen miles into his journey when the rearguard warned that a group of riders approached at a fast pace from behind. Sigurd reined in and ordered the troops to face the danger, then waited for the cloud of dust to come nearer. On seeing that one of the arrivals carried Edward's standard, he was even more prepared for a fight, and when the group of horsemen finally thundered up they were met with hostile words. 'If Edward has sent you to press for my exile you will have a fight on your hands!' roared Sigurd.

The leader of the party responded with similar heat. 'King Edward demands your presence at court. You are to come with us now!'

Sigurd replied on a laugh of disbelief. 'I have just come from there – he told me to get out!'

'Well, now he wishes to see you again,' said the other. 'He was told you had left Lunden and was most concerned that you be brought back. I would advise you strongly to come.'

Sigurd groaned and looked at his men. They were not on the best of terms with him after he had dragged them from their meal and not allowed them to stop for a rest since leaving Lunden. 'It is not fair to subject my men to a fight after they have marched so far,' he decided impudently. 'Otherwise you would not return to give the King my answer.'

Wondering what fate lay in store, he kicked his

horse into motion and led his band of grumbling men back to Lunden. Here he was granted no leave to join his weary followers at the table but taken in his dishevelled state before the King.

However, there was no sign of the raving lunatic who had dismissed him hours ago. This King spoke calmly. 'Come hither and stand before me, Sigurd Einarsson.'

Biting back a groan of frustration, Sigurd marched stiff-legged to the throne, bowed, then stood aloof and erect.

'I have decided to forgive you,' announced a po-faced Edward.

Ready for a fight, Sigurd could not have been more surprised and it showed on his face.

'It was uncharitable of me to forfeit your title and lands when you have lost so much already, namely your only child. I am not yet accustomed to the ways of northern men, forgot that they are by nature bluntly-spoken and took your words as personal affront when you were only voicing your anger at your child's murderer. Therefore, I will restore you to your former position.' He laced his hands as if in prayer and awaited Sigurd's reply. In the hours that had passed since his castigation, Edward had been advised by a wiser person than himself that his actions against the ealdorman might bring repercussions from the North. Knowing that he had not the support to deal with this at the moment he was forced to back down, but had drawn on his saintly reputation to camouflage the true reason – or so he thought.

Too dumbfounded to offer sarcasm, the ealdorman mouthed gratitude. 'I thank you, my lord.'

Edward inclined his saintly head. 'You will of course do penance for your blood-letting, and make redress to the family of the woman whom you killed.'

Sigurd nodded but had no intention of obeying, his

415

only intent being to get out of this room before he vomited at the piety.

'What is the King like?' pestered Asketil when his foster-father arrived home from Lunden. 'What did he say?'

'He is berserk!' Sigurd jumped down from his horse and threw the reins at Murtagh. 'He ordered me into exile for killing my daughter's murderer.'

Murtagh could not help an involuntary glance at the speaker. The little boy, too, looked shocked. 'When must you go – and where?'

'I go nowhere!' Dousing Murtagh's hopes, Sigurd pushed Asketil at the house where he hollered for food and drink. 'Within hours he had called me back to inform me that I was forgiven! You have never seen such piety. Forgiven? Addle!' By now Sigurd had worked out the true reason for Edward's retreat. 'He knew he had gone too far, that I am too strong for him. *Nithing*, he calls me! I tell you the man is not fit to rule. He flies into a rage for no reason at all.' Anger kept him perched uncomfortably on the edge of his chair.

Asketil sought verification. 'So you do not have to leave me?'

'Hah! I had no intention of leaving by that *kunta*'s yea or nay . . .' Sigurd focused upon the worried boy then and patted him. 'I will never leave you, Til.'

Asketil shuffled closer and leaned against his *fostri*'s knee, no longer afraid of these bouts of fury for never were they directed at him.

'Ah, but it is sad to see Cnut's kingdom fall to such a whelp.' The man sighed, then issued one last word of contempt before flopping back against his chair. 'Southerners!'

'Shall we play tables?' Asketil went to fetch the gaming board, setting it between the two of them. Sigurd cheered up, giving his kirtle an enthusiastic tug. 'A good idea! I have not played since . . . ah well, since many months ago.' During the game he noticed that the boy kept making wrong moves, and eventually pointed this out to him. 'I am dismayed that the son of Ulf should play so badly. You could have won there.'

'I know.' Asketil was placid. 'But Mother would never allow me to beat Father or he'd be in a temper for hours.'

'So you lost to me a-purpose?' Sigurd roared with laughter, forgetting all about the contretemps with the monarch. 'Ah, Til, you so amuse me! Would you do this on the battlefield so as not to offend your enemy?'

The little face remained solemn. 'What is it like to kill a man, *fostri*?'

'Oh, you will learn in time.' Sigurd calmed his bluster, though retained the fond expression.

'I wonder what it is like to be killed.' Asketil sucked thoughtfully on the ivory piece in his hand.

Sigurd tapped a positive finger on the board. 'You shall never know, for I will teach you all that has kept me alive these forty years.' Waiting for the boy to reset the pieces, he leaned back in his chair.

'Shall you teach me to read too?' Asketil shoved the figures around the squares.

'Have I not already?'

'Only the runes, not books. I wish to read in English for I am English.'

Sigurd retained his even temper, enjoying their conversation. 'I am English too but all the years I have lived I have never needed a book. The truth is for my head to hold and my tongue to tell.'

Asketil postponed the new game to rock back and forth on his buttocks. 'But if you die with word unspoken, who shall know? I should dearly love to have this skill, *fostri*.'

His foster-father conceded with a shrug. 'Then you

417

shall have it, for all the good it will do you. I will speak to the brethren.'

The boy smiled and made his first move. This time he did not allow himself to be defeated so easily. Several games later the pieces were dropped back into their box and Asketil sat cuddling his knees. 'Tell me a tale.'

Sigurd moistened his tongue with wine, and recounted the sagas handed down to him by his mother, uncle and numerous others. When he had exhausted many of these, he was then asked, 'How was the world begun?'

Sigurd looked at the water clock; it was past the usual hour at which Asketil went to bed, but he was enjoying himself too much to carp. 'It was made long, long ago.' Totally relaxed, he poured another glass of wine from the pitcher. 'Before it existed there was a great nothingness called Gunningagap. North of this was Niflheim, a place of many rivers that was dark and misty. South was the fiery kingdom of the giant Surt. The rivers of Niflheim froze and from the merging of ice and fire was born the giant Ymir whose left armpit sweated offspring . . .'

During the lengthy and riveting tale the boy never took his eyes from its narrator, thrilled by this sanguine account of the world's creation. At the end he made a sound of wonder and enjoyment, then wriggled and yawned. 'Where did you live whilst all this was going on, *fostri*?' He reacted innocently to Sigurd's look of affront. 'Well, I know you are very old now but you must only have been a babe then.'

'Thou little louse!' Sigurd laughed and cuffed him. 'To bed with you!' And he slung the boy over his shoulder to much squealing and jollity, up the staircase to bed.

That night he dreamed of Una, held her tight and told her of his sorrow at killing her. She laid her head upon his breast and whispered her forgiveness. Preparing to make love to her, he felt himself about to wake and took desperate hold so that she would emerge from the dream with him.

But when his eyes came open, she was not there.

Chapter Seventeen

The fitfulness of the King's mood was echoed in nature; in the year following his altercation with Sigurd the harvest failed and a great famine swept throughout the land. Peasants turned to charms and priests to mass, but Sigurd was a rich man, his barns full of grain, and neither he nor Asketil would perish. The child had become the most important person in Sigurd's life; never before had he found ought to match the rejuvenation he felt after a good battle, but he found it now in Til's company. The boy was much altered in appearance. His new front teeth had just begun to show, and with no mother in attendance to check on his hair, this had grown out of its pudding-basin style and was more like a girl's, though whenever he paid a visit to his old home he returned neatly shorn. In character, Asketil had many similarities with his natural father – he was brave and would fight other boys if he had cause, but he lacked Ulf's spiteful temper and preferred the academic life to that of the land or the battlefield. Due to the efforts of the brethren he was now able to read English, though he still loved the verbal accounts of his foster-father's travels.

There was just one thing that marred these tales. Sometimes, in the middle of them, Sigurd had noticed a cloud passing over the child's face, but had never been able to prise the reason from him.

'What is it, Til?' he begged one day, expecting to receive the same old answer, a dumb shake of the head. 'I wish you would tell me. Do these tales of mine bore you?'

'Oh, no!'

'What, then? Do they frighten you?' The change of expression was ever so slight but the man noticed it at once and knew he had hit upon the truth. 'Yes, I think they do! Why is that? Do tell me. I would not have you afraid.'

Asketil was hesitant, looking down at his bare toes. 'It is not the stories. I am . . . ' he bit his lip. 'I am just afraid that one day you will fall off the edge of the world and not return!'

Sigurd could not help but laugh. 'Oh, Til! The earth has no edge.'

Embarrassed, the boy objected. 'Everyone else says it has!'

'If it did I should have fallen off it years ago, the amount of travelling I have done. Nay, lad,' Sigurd put his arm around Asketil and squeezed. 'Believe me, the world goes on and on and on! Do not listen to the prattle of fools – they have never sailed the world like Sigurd Einarsson!'

Asketil grinned to show that he was pacified and in future would gain full enjoyment from his foster-father's tales. Indeed, these were many, for with the combination of his duties as ealdorman and his rest-less nature, Sigurd was away from home quite fre-quently and always had exciting things to relate about the places he had visited: the land of the walrus, the land where the sun never set and the land of wild men with red faces. The vastness of the world was lost upon one who had travelled no more than two miles in any direction, but Asketil yearned to see these places too. One day he would, said his *fostri*, who never failed to bring back some gift – a seashell, or a little charm made from amber – and on that special day when Asketil was allowed out of the burh to play with older boys he brought Sigurd a gift from his adventures, in exchange for all those he had received. The glossy horse chestnut had sat upon the table as ornament for many weeks before it had shrivelled and gone dull. Even then Sigurd had not thrown it away but tucked it safe inside his pouch: thus was the affection they had for each other.

The frequent absences did not worry Asketil unduly, for he was secure in his adoptive father's love and had now made many friends here. Diligent by nature, he made a point of asking everyone's name, became involved with the running of the household and learned how to do the most menial tasks, which Sigurd had never bothered to show him. He even managed to befriend Murtagh whom others tormented, and would follow the slave about the place chattering away for hours. Murtagh did not seem to mind; sometimes Asketil even made him smile, which was a feat no one else could perform, or indeed had even cared enough to try.

Another year passed. At the age of forty the confirmed misogynist King Edward married Earl Godwin's daughter. Sigurd's instant reaction was to joke about this with his old friend Ulf, but then he remembered that Ulf was long dead and the only person he had to share it with was Asketil. Though the boy was too young to grasp the full humour of it, this did not prevent Sigurd from musing.

'I wonder if it was Godwin who manipulated this, or whether Edward sees the marriage as a way of getting closer to his enemy so that he doth not have to stretch so far to plunge the dagger in.'

'Does the King want to kill Earl Godwin?' Asketil frowned.

'I spoke poetically, but yes, he would not shrink from bringing his enemy down. There has never been any goodwill between them. He will never forget Godwin's part in his brother's death nor mine nei ...' Sigurd broke off, aware that he had gone too far. He glanced at Asketil to see if his words had registered; they had.

'You killed the King's brother?' The boy was wide-eyed.

'You must not repeat that to anyone! But yes . . . I will admit it only to you, I had a hand in his death. He was a wicked man, Til, tried to seize the throne from its rightful heir. Something had to be done.'

Til nodded acceptance. 'But I am puzzled as to why King Edward allows you to go free. Indeed he acts with such charity towards you.'

'It is all pretence, as is my subservience to him. He dare not move against me, I am too strong. But believe me when he gets the chance he will take it.'

'Are you not afraid, that he hates you so?'

'I give not one jot for the King's opinion! In the time of the great Cnut it was a privilege to be invited to court, now it is a chore – nay, an embarrassment! You should see them all apeing Edward's mode of dress in order to curry favour with him. Why, one could almost forget that one is in England with their fancy talk and their arses on display!' – the French style of tunic was absurdly short – 'If that is what the English wear now I shall remain up here lest someone takes a fancy to my noble buttock. I wonder that Earl Godwin can bear it.'

Not unexpectedly, the obtrusion of the King's Norman friends was a continuous source of displeasure to Godwin, but he reminded himself that Edward was English and stayed loyally patient. Edward in turn hated this most powerful man, but was too weak to deny the earldoms which Godwin demanded for his sons and nephew, knowing that he could not rule without him. Between them, the hearty, pragmatic extrovert and the priggish weakling thwarted all invasions of English shores – though many tried their hand. The Norwegian King Magnus who, through his treaty with Harthacnut regarded England as his, was one such challenger. When news of this threat reached the North, Sigurd gave it mixed reception: he was English now, with a position of power, and the earldom he had long sought was within his reach. As strong as Godwin was, what if he failed to repulse Magnus and the Norwegians claimed victory? Sigurd might find himself with nought.

However, whilst Magnus plotted against England another would have his Norwegian throne: his ruthless Uncle Harald had allied himself with Swein Estridsson, Magnus' rival for the Danish crown. This helped to form Sigurd's decision; rather than bob up and down with the rest of Edward's fleet that waited off Sandwich to repel viking invaders, Sigurd decided to steal a march and join forces with Harald, so preventing Magnus from ever reaching England.

Asketil begged to be allowed to go too, but he was only nine and Sigurd forbade it. 'There will be fierce battles.' Even as he uttered the words, there came echoes from his own boyhood and the fleeting image of Thorald which he soon dismissed. 'If you would see the land of my blood let it be in peacetime. I shall take you, be patient.'

'But what if you are killed?' Asketil displayed no fear though it tingled his heart.

'I – the greatest warrior who ever lived? Such confidence you show in your teacher! I shall be back within the year.'

This was a mite optimistic, for things were not as straightforward as they might appear. Though Sigurd could not place him, the Harald in question was the one who, fifteen years ago, had escaped from the battlefield at Stiklestadir when Sigurd had helped defeat his brother Olaf, and had fled abroad. Now he was home from Byzantium, a rich man, famous for his harsh leadership. Like Sigurd he had a passion for battle and had fought in every corner of the world, but news had reached him that his nephew

Magnus was in possession of two kingdoms since the death of Harthacnut, and now he himself returned to stake his claim to the Norwegian crown.

Naturally, Magnus was not about to capitulate and so Harald, through sheer expediency, allied himself to Swein, his nephew's rival for the Danish crown. Predictably, huge losses resulted from this three-cornered battle and Harald decided to hold talks with Magnus to see if he had changed his attitude.

Sigurd was not privy to what went on in these talks, but was to discover that the alliance had changed; Magnus had agreed to give Harald half of Norway if he would turn coat against Swein and help protect Denmark. This put a different hue on things – for if Magnus won this round he could soon be attacking England. Instead, Magnus's death was to remedy all three men's problems: Harald took Norway, Swein claimed Denmark, and Sigurd Einarsson sailed home to the worst winter in living memory. Men, beasts, fish and fowl, all perished, and to compound the torture an earthquake was to follow, convincing Sigurd that it was the gods' disapproval of the way England was ruled by her King.

The gods were not alone in their anger. In this same year, 1048, Godwin and the monarch came to quarrelling about Edward's foreign favourites who were in danger of taking precedence over the English at court. During the next couple of years Sigurd watched the crumbling relationship with interest, eager for an opportunity to unseat the King.

Asketil, now almost come to manhood, had learnt most of his foster-father's skills – apart from the ability to swim. Only the strength was missing, but that would come in a few years and he was blessed with an agility that Sigurd at the ripe age of forty-eight could not recapture. The latter retained his muscularity, but his skin had lost its tautness and he had a slight paunch. His only advantage apart from

brute strength was a cunning born of many engage-
ments. This did not come easily to Asketil, who was
open and honest to the point of naivety. It would
have to be perforce instilled, and his tendency to
dream be curbed if he was to remain alive as long as
his mentor.

Discounting these weaknesses, Sigurd had much
pride in his son – for he was his son as surely as if
grown from his own loins. Asketil felt the bond too,
except when he visited his mother, who was always
quick to remind him of his true paternity when he
spoke so warmly of Sigurd. However, the memory of
Ulf had grown dim and secretly Asketil preferred his
life now with Sigurd. Their amity was the one un-
shakable thing in the turmoil that plagued England
at the moment.

On Asketil's twelfth birthday, Sigurd carried out
his promise to Ulf by giving the boy his father's
sword, though something made him cringe from re-
vealing its previous ownership, as if by mention of
Ulf's name the bond would be rent. It was petty, he
knew, and he begged his dead friend's forgiveness,
but his love for Asketil made him wary of ought that
might take the lad away.

In the six months that Asketil had owned the sword
he had put it to good practice, though the displays
were done more to please his benefactor than himself.
Possessing a weapon had seemed so important to him
at six years old; nowadays he derived much more
enjoyment from his books and music, but for Sigurd's
sake he was today once again involved in mock battle
in the yard.

After a good hour of parry and thrust in the hot
May sunshine, Sigurd felt the need to quench his
thirst. Requiring shade, he took a drink by the open
door watching Asketil who now larked with a boy of
his own age, a friendship made just recently. He
moved his eyes from Til to look around at the sum-

mer activities: women were cooking outdoors, others
tripped from well to animal trough, there were hides
stretched out on racks and bees flitting round the
hives. Unobserved by his lord, Murtagh took a rest
and watched the bees too. Their flight had become
more agitated and the hive throbbed with their hum
– suddenly those inside the hive began to hurl themselves through the exit, jostling to be free, a black
ribbon soaring up, up into the sky in their thousands,
wheeling and soaring in a dense mass . . . oh, how
Murtagh envied them.

To Sigurd they were just bees. About to drink from
his cup, he noticed over its rim that Asketil had passed
his sword to the other boy and now came loping
towards the house, fringe adhering to his brow. Sigurd gagged his annoyance for the time being, moved
aside as the boy entered and helped himself to a
drink. Asketil gasped relief, then sprawled on a pile
of cushions and opened a book lent to him by the
brethren.

Sigurd's voice was terse. 'Why did you give Aelred
your sword?'

'Because he asked for it,' came the artless reply.

'Wouldst you give your sword thus to an enemy?'

Asketil looked up from the page and smiled bewilderment. 'But Aelred is my friend.'

Sigurd compressed his bearded lips. 'You are sure
of this?'

'Has he not told me?' Asketil went back to reading.

The ealdorman was having difficulty in holding on
to his temper. 'Friendship speaks not in word but in
deed! I have had men call me friend who tried to kill
me. A true friend would not have taken your sword
but would have given their own. Whilst you sit idly
reading he could lop off thine head – heed me when
I instruct you!' When this drew the boy's attention,
he continued. 'You have had life too easy. You show
contempt for your weapon because you did not have

to earn it like I did. When you have been deprived of all your possessions and had to fight to get them back then will you cherish them. It is time you learnt this – Murtagh! Saddle two horses. And you, pick up your book and fetch it along.'

Earrings tinkling with each bad-humoured turn of his head, he took Asketil out of Earlsburh, along the Great North Road, through some wooden gates that spanned the highway and out into open country where they rode for many miles. Asketil dared not enquire whither they went. Finally Sigurd reined in his mount and took hold of the other horse's bridle. 'Get down.'

Book under one arm, Asketil did as he was told.

'Now, let us see how that book compares to a sword as a means of protection!' Sigurd wheeled away, towing the other's horse.

Asketil's lower jaw dropped and he made to follow. '*Fostri*! Where do you go?'

But the man kicked his mount into a gallop and rode out of sight.

Marooned in the sprawling acres of wasteland Asketil stood perplexed and ill-equipped. The weather was calm and the sky clear, there was no wind. He should have been glad, yet instead he felt threatened by the stillness of his environment, shifting nervously in his boots and waiting for his *fostri* to return.

He waited, and waited. The sun reached its apex and began to descend. Still Asketil had faith that his mentor would return and hence did not stray from his position. Only when it grew dark did his optimism fade. With the dying of evensong he knew that he was going into the night alone and wished he had used the day to search for a means to light a fire instead of reading his book. What use was a book in the dark? Raking about, he cleared a site on which to arrange clumps of dried grass. With no trees in the vicinity it was unlikely that he would find wood and even when he managed to produce a spark from two rocks and ignite the grass it soon fizzled out. Something screamed. A butterfly of panic tickled his gut; he ducked into a frightened ball, covering his head with his arms.

The barn owl hooted again. This time the boy recognized it for what it was and half emerged from his cramped position. Even so, he did not sleep. Throughout that long cool night, a night that lasted a hundred years, he grasped the little pendant that hung from a thong round his neck – a pair of writhing beasts carved from amber – rubbed their little elbows and knees, took comfort in their smooth familiarity.

Daylight came and drove away the evil spirits, but there was no Sigurd. Asketil stood, rubbed his dead buttocks, arched his back and looked around. Nothing had changed. Attacked by thirst and hunger he did as he had seen Murtagh do and uprooted some leaves of plantain. Unpalatable though they were to one accustomed to rich living, he ate them gladly. After some consideration he decided not to search for water; in doing so he might become completely lost. As it was, by remaining in the area in which Sigurd had left him he had a good chance of finding his route home. Heavy of limb and heart he picked up his book and followed the direction taken by Sigurd yesterday, reassured by the intermittent appearance of a hoofprint in a patch of dust. Stopping only to relieve himself he eventually completed the ten miles back to Jorvik. Passing through wooden gates he almost cried with relief as a familiar figure told him he was nearly home.

'Murtagh!' Unable to run he limped and hobbled as fast as he could to catch up with the slave who, though acknowledging his shout with a wave, continued on his way.

Wincing at the blisters on his heels Asketil finally drew alongside the man who had been working in the fields, judging by the hoe he carried over his shoulder. 'Do not walk so fast! My poor feet are howling.' Murtagh slowed but did not offer to carry the boy on his back as he had done in the past for he was too exhausted himself.

At the slave's questioning look Asketil told what had befallen him, eyes brimming with self-pity. 'I could not believe it! He left me there with no food, no shelter – no water, even! What did I do that was so bad? Lent the sword which he had given to me, that is all. He cares more about possessions than he does about folk.'

Murtagh bestowed a shrewd glance.

'Yes, you would know,' nodded the boy and took the weight of the book on his head for a while.

Earlsburh came into sight. Asketil slowed the pace to a crawl. 'Why do I come back here, Murtagh? 'Tis plain he does not want me . . . ' He made a swift decision. 'I shall go instead to my mother's house!' Without a goodbye he left Murtagh to proceed home. The downtrodden creature watched him with envy; how lucky is the little hog that he can pick and choose wheresoever he goes.

Night fell. Sigurd, alone in his private quarters except for the dogs and a cat, was beginning to feel concern. Had he been too optimistic in comparing Til to himself at twelve years old? He, coached by rough fighting men and a mother who could almost match them for toughness, would soon have made a shelter, fed himself and walked home the next day, but Til had never known hardship and in retrospect it was foolish to think that by throwing him into deep water he would naturally bob to the surface – he had employed this very method when trying to teach the boy to swim and Til had almost drowned. The noise from his men, drinking in the grand hall, grew irksome. Sigurd found his eyes perpetually flicking to the water clock, and he began to contemplate a search. He cursed himself as an ogre. What kind of guardian is it who abandons a child with no weapon, no sup of water even? Then he argued with himself – did I not do it for his own good? For I will not always be here to take care of him.

His thoughts moved to Ulf and how his old friend would react to the treatment of his son. Again he justified his actions: this was a foolish argument, for Ulf played hard himself – look at the way he had almost drowned Sigurd in Ireland. Memories took his thoughts away from Til for a while, memories of Ulf and Eric . . . and Una. Totally immersed, he remained unaware of another presence for some time. Then, through his thoughts, came the prickling realization that someone else was in the room. He had heard no door open but felt the intruder's presence without turning. Their stealth was tangible, making his body hair stand on end. He tensed for the attack, fingers inching from his lap towards the axe beside his chair, his ears picking out every footfall to gauge from which direction the attack would come. The intruder was mere feet away – Sigurd grabbed the handle of his axe and whirled from the chair to confront his assassin. A second before the heavy blade embedded itself in his brain Asketil ducked and threw aside his knife, a look of sheer horror on his face.

It could scarcely match the horror felt by Sigurd. In relief and anger he lashed out and sent the boy flying. 'Fool! You could be slain! Have you not listened to a thing I have told you? Never, never creep up behind me . . . ' He heaved a roaring sigh, bent his head, then laid down the axe and pulled the boy to his feet. 'I could have killed you – the only son I will ever have!'

Enveloped in a great odorous hug the boy's voice

431

was muffled. 'I waited for you to come and you did not.'

Sigurd clasped him, thumped his back, then held him at arm's length to see his face. 'I did not come because I wanted you to learn how to fend for yourself.' A thought struck him and he voiced it. 'Is this why you try to kill me?'

'Nay!' Til was aghast at the very suggestion. ''Twas merely a prank. I would never have harmed you.'

Sigurd nodded and closed his eyes; when he opened them again they were kind. 'And there you have learnt another valuable lesson. Never creep up on a man with a weapon that you do not intend to use – and never underestimate your *fostri*'s wits. I might seem ancient to you but my ears are keen and there is yet strength in my arm to tan your backside.'

Asketil rubbed his head and managed a sheepish smile. 'I know, I felt it.'

'I am sorry for the blow and also for leaving you yesterday.' Sigurd put an arm round the boy and led him to a seat. 'You must be hungry, I will call for meat.'

Asketil's tone was lighter. A moment ago Sigurd's bower was the most dangerous place on earth, now it was cosy with the glow of candlelight reflected in its wooden panels. 'Not for me, my belly is full.'

Sigurd looked impressed. 'So, you did manage to fend for yourself after all.'

The boy risked an impudent grin. 'Nay, I have been at my mother's house since dusk. She fed me well.'

Sigurd's laughter held a rebuke. 'Your mother will not always be there, Til, and neither will I. That is all I aimed to teach you yesterday.'

'I know.' Asketil settled upon a cushion and hugged his green-breeched knees, a frog on a lily pad. 'And I understand what you meant about the book. I see it all now, but I could not see it whilst I was shivering alone and afraid. My mother explained.'

'She did?' This was news to the man for he knew Ulf's widow resented losing her son to him.

'In her opinion your methods are too harsh.'

Sigurd conceded. 'She is right. I will not abandon you thus again.'

'You shall have no need to. I accept what you were trying to teach me and will show more respect for the things you have fought so hard to give me.'

'It is not just that, Til.' Sigurd laid a hand upon the fair head and rubbed. 'Yes, one day I shall die and you must be strong enough to keep the lands and riches I have won. However, it is not just possessions that you must respect but yourself. If my teachings seem harsh it is because you are so dear to me that I cannot bear to see others take advantage of you.'

Asketil felt rather stupid. 'They do not do that.'

'See! You do not even recognize it.'

'If you mean the sword that I lent to Aelred, he really is my friend, I swear it.'

'That is the nub, Til! You call every man friend, even the slaves. I have seen the way you help them with their chores.'

'Only Murtagh and he is my frie . . .'

'He is not your friend!' Sigurd was firm but not angry. 'He is a slave and twice your age. You think he would be friend to the son of the man who killed his mother and father and aunt? He takes your help to ease his burden, but ask him to protect you when your enemy lifts his weapon and he would as likely wield the sword himself.'

Asketil looked chastened. 'Why did you slay his parents, *fostri*?'

''Twas a long time ago. His father was killed in a raid we made upon Ireland while Murtagh was still in his mother's belly. Murtagh was born into captivity. He knows nothing else, you must not weep for him.'

Asketil thirsted for more. 'What of his mother?'

Sigurd could speak of Una now without experiencing pain – time and Asketil had both helped to ease it – but the wound of losing his child was as raw as the day it was inflicted. 'I thought that she poisoned my daughter and so I killed her.'

Asketil understood a lot more now. 'But it was really Black Mary.'

Sigurd inclined his head.

The boy wore a look of pity for the orphaned slave. 'Could you not treat him a little more kindly? After all, you killed his mother unjustly.'

Sigurd chuckled at this sentimentality, but would do almost anything to please the boy. 'Very well. I shall try not to beat him so much, though he tests my patience sorely at times.'

'It is terrible to be so wretched,' sighed Asketil, looking downcast.

His *fostri* tried to cheer the atmosphere. 'You will never have to know such wretchedness, Til . . . and there is something I kept from you. The sword, it was your father's.'

The weapon took on a new significance. 'It is? I did not recognize it. Why did you not tell me?'

'Because . . . ' The man dropped his chin to his breast. 'You will not understand this.' He shook his head a couple of times as if reluctant or unable to explain. 'Though I loved Ulf I did not want to remind myself that you had once had another father . . . for I covet that role myself.' The admission lured a warm smile from Asketil. Sigurd appeared to be embarrassed. 'Come, call for meat and drink! For even if you are not hungry I am. I have eaten barely a morsel for worrying over you, young rascal. Tell me, why did you not come straight home?'

Asketil went to call for a servant, then reseated himself. 'I was sad that you had done this to me so I went to my mother's house . . . but I grew bored listening to women's talk.'

434

Sigurd laughed. 'It is as I always told you, my son – what need have we of women?'

Asketil grinned back to show that he was beginning to agree with the philosophy. There was just one topic concerning women that he would wish to have explained. '*Fostri*, how did Murtagh get into his mother's belly?'

In 1051 Edward's Norman companions finally overstepped the mark. Spurred on by their insidious requests, Godwin's quarrel with the King erupted into mutiny. A fracas had taken place at Dover; a Norman count and his retinue had made overbearing demands and the local men sought to put them in their place, killing and wounding many. The Count complained to the King who ordered Godwin to sack the town. Godwin refused and knowing what the outcome of his rebellion would be, began to muster all his forces.

As ever, news was slow to reach the northern lands: when it did Sigurd called immediately upon his neighbour the jarl and asked what position they would take.

There was no prevarication from his leader. 'I owe nought to Godwin. We must stand loyal to the King.'

'But Godwin is more king than Edward,' argued Sigurd. 'Is it wise to oppose one so powerful?'

'Wise?' the grizzled warrior barked. 'There is nought wise about Englishman fighting Englishman. In war there is no winner – but the King is the King and we must stand with him. Leofric of Mercia is of like mind.'

Dwelling on it, Sigurd knew that there was no choice; much as he would like to see Edward deposed he would not sacrifice everything in its accomplishment. The majority of earls were on the side of Edward and for this reason only he too rode south to mass with the King's army, though it went against his code.

Powerful as Godwin was, he could not match these odds and damned his own miscalculation; he had counted upon the English hatred of Normans working to his advantage. Now instead of the rapid removal of the King it looked as if he might be in for a long war of attrition.

Good sense prevailed. The earls persuaded Edward to see that civil war would be catastrophic for England. Keen as he might be to destroy Godwin once and for all, the King was wise enough to agree and an arrangement was reached whereby hostages were taken and a witan would be held at Lunden in September when Godwin and his sons would appear to answer charges brought by the King. However, the threat of war was not totally averted; Godwin refused to come to Lunden without the King's promise of immunity. Confident of his own support, Edward retorted that if Godwin chose not to appear then he and his sons had five days to leave the country and in addition packed his wife – Godwin's sister – off to an abbey.

'So is there to be no war?' enquired Asketil, who had been somewhat apprehensive of his first time in battle.

Sigurd tousled his hair. 'Nay, Godwin has gone to Flanders and we, my son, return to Jorvik.' This they did and Sigurd was never so glad to reach home. 'I must be getting old. Though I would rather see Edward in Godwin's place I am not sorry we were robbed of a fight.'

'I thought you loved to battle, *fostri*,' teased the youth as they relaxed by the fire.

'Not with my own countrymen. I have too much to lose.'

'Is that why you sided with the King even though you hate him?'

Sigurd nodded. 'I trust that he will reward my loyalty when the earldom of Northumbria falls vacant – as I hope it shall before his memory of this favour is gone.'

Asketil spoke mischievously. 'The old jarl looks to have plenty of life in him yet.'

His foster-father rolled a warning eye. 'Speak thus often and you shall not enjoy the treat I had in mind.'

There was instant compunction. 'What is it?' When Sigurd remained tight-lipped Asketil craned forward. 'Oh, do tell, *fostri*!'

Sigurd gave in with a smile. 'Now that the dust has settled, I thought we might make that trip about which you have always harried my ear.'

'Norway!' Til danced to his feet. 'I shall go prepare straightaway!'

'Hold!' Sigurd laughed as his foster-son bolted for a chest and began to drag items from it. 'I do not intend to go before spring.'

'Oh, you tease me!' Asketil threw down the spare breeches he held. 'Why tell me now if you would make me wait so long?'

Sigurd was amused at the display of immaturity – the boy was almost fourteen and sometimes acted ten. ''Tis not that long, six months.'

'An age!' Asketil fell at Sigurd's feet. 'Why can we not go tomorrow? The weather is good.'

The ealdorman was easy. 'We could, but we should not be able to stay long afore winter comes.'

'It matters not! I hunger to sail. You keep promising and promising that I shall go to sea but that day never comes – why, you could be dead afore spring.'

'Oh, my thanks,' was the dry response.

'Please, please.' Asketil writhed and grovelled like a worm. When Sigurd merely grinned the boy rose and backed away. 'You are telling me we can go? You are, I can see it in your eyes.' Unchecked, he backed towards the door, hands still clasped in

437

prayer. 'I shall get my weapons together, yes? My sword, arrows . . .' His back was pressed to the door, he groped behind him for the handle.

Sigurd laughed, waved a permissive hand and the lad vanished like a puff of wind.

It took a little longer than Asketil might have wished to summon a crew and load victuals for the trip – partly because everyone thought it mad to go in autumn – but within the week he and Sigurd were out in the North Sea with two other ships for company, one a trader, the other bearing folk who went to visit their homeland and relatives. Sigurd thought this latter a good idea and when planning the trip had told Asketil that they would make for Vestfold and see if there were any of his own kin left alive, for he had not visited them in years.

Fizzing with excitement, Til gripped the mast and leaned starboards, swinging to and fro, his face alight. Although he could not swim, he was a good sailor. 'Is it not the best feeling in the world?' he entreated Murtagh, who had been brought along at Til's insistence. 'All my life I have longed to sail the ocean.' He inhaled loudly through his nostrils – 'Taste the wind!' – and grinned at Murtagh whose eyes, in spite of their obliquity, gleamed with a brilliance Til had never seen at home. Was it just the reflection of the waves or did Murtagh's soul take wing as did his own?

Notwithstanding his crooked eye, the man appeared quite handsome today, his black hair swept in the wind to reveal a different profile from that of the cowed beast of Earlsburh. Looking at him now, Asketil felt such affinity that he wanted to clasp his arm, swear oaths of kinship, but Sigurd would be livid. Instead he waited for Murtagh to turn and the instant he did Til caught the straighter of the two eyes and pierced it with his secret joy. *One day, when*

I am master of the estate I will free you. Whether the thought reached Murtagh's brain he could not tell, but it gave him pleasure to think it.

Murtagh's eyes smiled back in their crooked way, but he hoped that his own thoughts would not be conveyed. *You are my only friend, but if I thought that by killing you I would gain my freedom then I would do it.*

The good weather did not last. With but a day of their voyage left to go, the sky took on a sulphurous tint in the advent of an electric storm. Til first became aware of it when the noise of the wind ripping though the sail drew his eyes upwards. Yellow clouds like old bruises rumbled across the face of the world. Gulls shone luminous against the moody firmament. The wind began to wrench more insistently at the sail. Sigurd bawled orders for the mast to be lowered and himself checked that the cargo was secure. The other two ships alternately vanished and reappeared on the undulating water. The wind burgeoned to a gale, took hold of the ship whose rowers narrowed their eyes against the spray and held on for life, their mighty wave-stallion reduced to a twig on a pond. Thoroughly drenched, Asketil knelt and clung to the lowered mast, unable to open his eyes under the stinging onslaught. Murtagh had joined one of the oarsmen and fought to keep the ship on course. The god of thunder ranted and raged and whisked the sea with a truculent finger, the balers worked frenziedly against his tricks – and then a huge jade wall rose up before them, towered and plunged and crashed down upon the ship, raping its timbers. Asketil was wrenched from his position, washed away like a leaf in a stream. Sigurd's yell was ripped from his mouth by the gale as he made a lunge for the boy, missed and watched in horror as Til slithered helplessly along the planking. His son was going to drown.

Without thinking, Murtagh reached out and grasped

a handful of tunic as the boy floated past, locked his fingers tightly into it, dragged him back, held on, muscles straining, whilst others came to the rescue, then returned to his task without waiting for thanks.

The storm died. Battered and sodden, the men fought to keep the crippled ship afloat. The accompanying vessels had gone, whether sunk or merely blown off-course none could tell. There was land in the distance: not the land that should have been, for the gale had foiled their navigation, but it was clearly Norway and any land where they could make good the damage and dry out was welcome. Now that all was calm, Sigurd made a head-count and found that none were lost, not even the wretched Murtagh.

Asketil's first act was to thank the man who had saved his life and knowing how dear he himself was to his *fostri*, expected Sigurd to offer some reward. But Sigurd ignored the boy's rescuer and was bent only on castigating his foster-son. ''Twas madness to come in autumn! Why do I listen to thee?'

Asketil hung his head whilst the rebuke was issued, thinking, poor Murtagh, such a brave deed with no reward. When I am lord I will most definitely grant him freedom – and not only this, I shall make him my right arm.

'Boy, do I talk to myself?'

The bellow made Asketil jump.

'Thou art forever dreaming!' Sigurd's white face moved up and down with the sea, nausea compounding his fury. 'If you do not heed my rebuke how are you to learn?'

Asketil raised guilty eyes. 'I did heed, *fostri*. I wondered only . . . would it not be kind to offer Murtagh reward for saving my life?'

'Why should he expect reward?' snapped the tyrant. 'It is his duty to protect his master.'

'Nay, you foretold that he would not protect me!' Certain that he was in the right Asketil refused to be cowed. 'You said that when the moment came he would not be counted as a friend. Well, he hath proved you wrong, *fostri*.'

Sigurd was not going to allow a youth to get the better of him. 'He hath proved nought and he shall get no reward! Now come, make yourself useful, we are about to land.'

And what a land! All sense of injustice was forgotten. Asketil's mind soared with the spectacular rise of the mountains as the boat limped into the yawning chasm. To either side were sheer rock walls; in the aftermath of the tempest there was about them a fearsome grandeur, like a giant's palace, shades of black and grey and purple. Asketil bent over to peer into the sinister waters, and asked his *fostri*, 'Is it very deep?'

'The fjords have no bottom,' replied Sigurd, his belly calmer now. 'If you who cannot swim fall over we shall never see you again.'

In awe, Asketil gazed around him as the ship nosed deeper into the fjord, looking for a place to land. Gradually the sky began to clear and the sun came out – and oh, such a transformation! The sombre fjord glittered with diamonds, all oppression slid away and the mauve crags were now etched against vivid blue.

Asketil was enraptured. 'How could you bear ever to leave this country?'

'What do you see here?' asked Sigurd. 'Why do you think that there are more Norwegians in every other country in the world than there are in Norway? There is nought important enough to keep them here.'

Asketil could not believe the ignorance of this remark and threw his arm in sweeping gesture around the wonderful landscape, his mind already composing verse in its praise.

Sigurd laughed. 'Beauty cannot fill a man's pocket nor his belly. Yea, there are fish aplenty in the rivers, and birds and beasts – but travel the whole of this land and you will find it is long and skinny, and in the winter, fooh! You would not wish to live here, Til.'

Asketil was stubborn. 'I would.'

'You have not yet seen the winter.'

'Then let us stay and see it,' urged the boy.

'What! You think I risked life and limb in England just to end my life here?'

'It would not kill you,' teased Asketil, putting an arm around Sigurd's waist.

'You do not know the Norwegian winter.' The mere thought of those long depressing nights locked in one's cabin by snow and ice was bad enough. Only under an avalanche of begging and pleading from the boy did Sigurd give in. 'Oh . . . you can talk me into ought, you fiend! So be it – but we must find a place to live and use what is left of the good weather to gather supplies. By the gods I must be addled.'

Eventually the fjord opened up and they found a place to land. Whilst one group investigated the area the other hauled the ship out of water to inspect the damage. Still Asketil could not believe the magnificence of all this, and lay on his belly dreaming into the green glass of the fjord until Sigurd barked for him to stop idling and do some work. Yet even as he toiled the lad was composing verse, digressing only to ask, 'Why are the mountain tops white, *fostri*?'

'It is snow.'

'And not yet winter?'

'Even in summer it never goes. See what is yet to come? Now wilt thou stop this dreaming and get thee to work!'

Those early weeks of autumn were spent coasting around the fjords, each one different with new forests to explore and people to meet. To Sigurd this was of most import, for he derived no joy from lifeless rockpiles, classed each mountain the same. Asketil was more sensitive to how drastically the landscape changed from valley to valley and so too did the language – often he could barely understand what was said, but then as his attention usually drifted halfway through a conversation anyway, it hardly mattered. How he wished that he could live this amphibious life forever instead of returning to Jorvik. Alas, cities were what his fostri loved best, for they meant people.

Whilst the weather remained clement Sigurd decided to visit the capital Nidaros. To Asketil's relief they did not stop too long and went no further north than this but returned south again in preparation for the winter. Away from the city, Til relaxed and once again began to compose verse: to one side of the fjord the land was heavily wooded with lanky red trunks and branches that did not sprout until the very top of the tree – like a quiverful of arrows. To the other side were green pastures dotted with cabins. Around the next headland he pointed. 'Look! The mountains are on fire.' A shroud of smoke hid their pinnacles. Then Sigurd explained that it was only a cloud forgotten by the wind and impaled on points of arrows, and Til relaxed to marvel.

For hours they coasted effortlessly along without change in the weather until gradually the cloud increased, the land turned barren and there were no trees just a range of angry mountains – yes, even the mountains had personality, thought Til – jagged peaks that no snow could soften. To the foot of the slopes the land was drab with rocky outcrops, but even here he saw beauty for in the distance a gap had opened in the clouds and a heavenly light shone down on a glacier. Asketil thought it the most wonderful sight. After this the fjord opened into the sea and the motion of the ship increased. Sigurd began to look unwell. Murtagh, unaffected, hid a smirk as his lord vomited over the side and remained in this position until, an hour or so later, the pilot steered a quieter course and the turbulence eased.

After some nights camping under the stars they came to the place where Sigurd had lived as a boy and passed an enjoyable week with his kin. His aunt was now dead but her children were hale. With such a long absence there was a great deal to say to his cousins, and talk Sigurd did, far into the night. Asketil, normally the centre of his fostri's world, began to feel left out. The elders spoke over his head and when he tried to ask a question the tone of their answer made him feel a nuisance. So, after he had eaten tonight's meal, which to him looked like frog-spawn, he settled back to compose more verse.

It was a particularly eloquent attempt he decided, on mentally reciting it, and could not wait to find an audience. However when he tried to interrupt the conversation Sigurd waved him away. 'Later, Til. I am talking with my kin whom I have not seen since I was a lad. I will listen to your verse later.'

Asketil turned away. 'It does not matter.'

Sigurd knew this tone by now. 'Do not sulk. I have said I will listen to it later. What difference does an hour make to we who are always together?'

Asketil made for the door, head down. 'It does not matter, it was no good anyway.'

The look of martyrdom exasperated Sigurd. 'Oh, come and recite for us, then!'

Forgiveness was not one of Asketil's qualities. He stubbornly refused and crept off to find an audience in Murtagh.

Sigurd shook his head and laughed at his cousins. 'He is such a child sometimes. I do not know that I shall ever make a warrior of him. Oh, but he is the most precious thing to me! If ever I lost him I know that I should die.'

The next day they made for Oslo where they would spend the winter. Asketil draped his upper half over the stern, fascinated by the globs of jelly in the water. Whilst so involved, he did not notice the two ships which sneaked from a concealed waterway and began to follow. His companions were working at the oars and did not see them either. Only Asketil was in the right position to give warning, but as usual he was lost in a dream of his own. The ships began to close.

Luckily, just then Sigurd happened to turn and look back at Asketil, saw the ships and bellowed a warning that precipitated a furious increase in speed from his rowers, but the pirates had drawn too close to be so easily repulsed. With the ships almost clipping his tail, Sigurd urged the rowers on with curses and gesticulations. A viking prow was almost to his stern. Timbers collided, jolting men to the bone. Sigurd righted himself, hurled a lance and perforated one of the enemy, but even as he did so another grabbed the nearest victim, Asketil, and dragged him from one ship to the other.

Sigurd cried out to the rowers. 'Stop! They have taken my son! You must stop!'

But they were too worried for their own necks. Every muscle straining, their efforts pulled the ship away from its attackers. Sigurd yelled and lashed out at them but it did him no good. There was only one course of action. Without a thought for himself the ealdorman dived overboard and swam back to try and rescue his son.

Asketil struggled and kicked out at his captors, yelling, 'Save me, Father! Help! Help!'

Plunging through the cold waters, Sigurd cried out with his mind, *I'm coming, my son! I'm coming*! But to what was he coming? *You fool, you damned fool, you should have stayed with the ship! We could have returned to rescue Til, now you will both be captive.* But it was far too late to turn back. He was hooked from the water by a member of one crew, whilst the other ship rowed after the escaping craft. Dripping, he picked himself up from the deck and made a grab for Til, who clung to him in terror before they were ripped apart. 'Take your hands off him!' Sigurd yelled and wrestled with his captors, but was punched and kicked into submission. Preoccupied thus, he failed to see whether his own ship was captured. Only later when he and Asketil were taken to the chieftain's lair and the other pirate ship returned empty-handed did he know that it was safe. However much he cursed its crew for leaving him he nurtured the hope that they might return, and used this to calm Asketil's nervousness. 'Fear not, Til, they shall come and rescue us.'

The two were bound hand and foot, on a wide shelf of rock. Behind them was a pine forest, in front of them the fjord, but the shelf was raised so that all they could see of the ships were their masts. Sigurd was wringing wet. There was a fire nearby, around which the vikings sat, though it cast no warmth this far. In the dusk the surrounding mountains had once more become a giant's palace.

Til was too afraid to reply and could only look back at Sigurd with wide blue eyes. When he did find voice it was to condemn his own stupidity. 'I am most sorry. If I had not been dreaming . . .'

'Yea, *if*,' returned Sigurd, hair dripping. 'But knowing how you dream I should have been more alert.'

Til's voice quavered. 'If we are freed . . .'

'*When* we are freed,' corrected Sigurd. 'You will be the wiser.'

The chieftain, a handsome man, came to interrupt their exchange, damning his friends who had allowed the ship to escape. 'A rich haul we got for our efforts – an old man and a suckling.'

'Cut these bonds and I shall show thee what this old man can do,' warned Sigurd.

446

'Ah, a spark of life! I am most glad. I thought that I had wasted my time on a dotard but you shall make a slave after all.'

'Sigurd Einarsson is no man's thrall!'

The pirate threw up his arms in fake alarm, then relaxed into a laugh. ''Tis obvious I am meant to be impressed by the name. I regret I have never heard it.'

'Cut these ropes and I shall make sure you never forget it!'

The chieftain probed his lip. 'Mm, maybe I shall not waste you on thraldom after all. You would make better sport, you and the boy. 'Tis a long time since I saw the blood-eagle carved on a man's back.'

Purely for Til's benefit Sigurd became wary of invoking further punishment.

'Ah, he is quieter now!' The chieftain laughed and eyed Asketil. 'Doest know of this ceremony of which I speak?'

'Leave him be!' There was threat in Sigurd's voice. His heart had begun to thump.

'Nei, he should be forewarned of the honour that his father's show of spirit has earned for him.' The pirate bent down and spoke in cheerful manner to the shivering Asketil. 'Tomorrow when it is light I shall take my knife and run it down your spine, then I shall peel the flesh back and one by one prise your ribs up to give you wings . . .'

'Cease!' Red-faced, Sigurd rocked in his bonds.

'Then I shall lift out thy lungs . . .'

'Leave the lad alone! I consent to be your thrall and do whatever you wish.'

'Oh, I am most downhearted,' sulked the chieftain. 'I do not know if I care to accept your offer. Maybe I shall allow you to think about it until morning.' He left them and joined the circle by the fire.

Never had Asketil felt such terror. It encompassed his whole mind and body, took him out of his own control into a place that he had not known existed, where he could not tell if it were day or night, his only instinct being to run and run and run.

'Do not worry, Til, he is bluffing.' Sigurd looked at the youngster whose face was turned away. 'Til? Look at me.'

The voice carried Til out of that black pit and into the present, but it was some time before he could react.

Sigurd urged again. 'Til, look at me!'

There came a wet sniffle and a shuddering sigh. 'I cannot! I am too shamed.'

'Oh, Til . . .' groaned the man.

'I have shit myself.' Asketil sobbed quietly into his chest. 'Such a coward.'

'Nay, a man's bowels are nought to do with his heart. That demon would frighten any man – I am afraid, too.'

'But you do not soil your breeches!'

'Oh, you force me to say it – I have pissed myself but no one knows for I am drenched already!' It was a lie designed to give the boy heart.

Til gave a little laugh and turned his face slowly; it was wet with tears.

'That is better.' Sigurd laid warm eyes upon his son.

'You only say this to make me feel less shamed.' Til's nose was running; he gave a huge sniff and gulped. His legs felt like jelly.

The man nudged him with a shoulder. 'Does not your *fostri* always tell the truth? Now take heart. Before the morning we shall be freed.' Sigurd looked up as a young girl came through the dusk with food for the vikings.

The chieftain noticed him watching her and called, 'Ah, I see you are not too old that you would refuse this little virgin if I offered her to you! How would you like to taste that sweet flesh before you die?' He lifted the girl's rough garb; she wore nothing underneath but she remained a proud little thing, thought Sigurd before looking away. The viking laughed and shoved the girl from him. 'I regret, I am saving her to barter with the Arabs next summer. But you are welcome to dream if you wish.'

After feeding the pirates, the girl came across the rocks to sit near to the captives. This irritated Asketil; he did not want her laughing at his odour.

She did not laugh but, when her captors were engaged in conversation, edged her bottom nearer and whispered, 'My name is Mildryth.'

Immediately Til recognized the dialect and, momentarily forgetting his dilemma, turned to her with interest. 'You are from Northumbria?'

She nodded. 'I was on the shore collecting mussels when they came and took me in summer. My kin shall think I am dead. How did they take you?'

With four sisters of his own, Til was not awed by the girl as some youths might be, and he addressed her as an equal, telling her briefly of his capture and what was to happen in the morning.

Mildryth heard the tremble in his voice. 'Mark not his threat too strongly. The old pisspot puffs and blows like the whale but has no teeth. He says these things to frighten you. He has tried the same with me for months, threatening to ravish me, but I fear him not.'

'You are worth money to him,' said a worried Asketil, descending once more into the pit. 'I am not.'

With Til between them, Sigurd could not hear the words she spoke, but watched her like a hawk. When, briefly, their eyes met, he detected a twinkle of candour as if she were laughing at him. The eyes were round, ever so slightly protuberant and of a shade as close to violet as he had ever seen. No . . . not quite pure violet; in the light of the fire they were like purple agate with little flecks in them. Despite his mistrust of women, despite the fact that she had no breasts and her rump was flat, the purity of her smile was the most erotic thing he had ever seen; it made his flesh crawl. He was almost fifty years of age, had known all nationalities of women – voluptuous women – had thought that after Una he would never feel that way about a female again. Yet this twelve-year-old child held him captive and with one twitch of her lips gave him life. Mildryth blinked, her eyelids descending with the slow movement of a lizard; it turned his gut inside out.

Mildryth failed to recognize his lust, but noticed that he was wet from head to foot and rose to drape a blanket around his shoulders. He watched her hands, imagined them sliding down the front of his breeches. She moved away.

After serving Asketil in like manner, she tossed back her straggly fair hair and went off to her bed. The night was cold. Neither Sigurd nor Asketil slept, the former anticipating rescue, the boy in terror of the morning's ordeal.

But before birdsong came a whisper: 'Do not stir!' Asketil felt his bonds cut through and, with a quick rub of his wrists, turned to offer a look of gratitude to Mildryth. Sigurd gave no thanks but tapped Asketil on the elbow and beckoned. Shamed by the mess in his breeches, Til hesitated in getting to his feet but the thought of what would happen if he tarried soon changed his mind and he ran after Sigurd. Mildryth ran with them.

A shout went up – their escape had been heard! Asketil yelled out, already feeling that knife cutting its way down his spine, his lungs ripped out . . . he pelted with Sigurd down the rocky slope for the water but neither had an inkling of what he would do when he arrived, for how could two men handle a boat made for thirty? When Sigurd saw a canoe he dashed towards it, hoping that Til followed – and a screaming horde of warriors rose out of the darkness! His path blocked, Til screamed too, then realized with joy that they were his own friends come to rescue him! Apeing Sigurd, he grabbed an oar and used it to crack heads, much braver now behind numbers. Whilst the fight raged Mildryth ran for the ship to watch from a safe distance.

Another watched too, alert to see if Sigurd would be killed. There were weapons in the hull. Murtagh's fingers itched to use them – had already begun to reach for a spear – when Mildryth jumped aboard. He looked startled, then quick-wittedly handed the weapon to Mildryth who leapt back on to land where she jabbed at leg and groin and buttock. Her earlier comment had been prophetic; the pirate chieftain was all bluster and could not match Sigurd's ferocity. He was the first to die at his former captive's hand. One by one his men followed, and the remainder fled. Wasting no time to gather prizes, Sigurd pushed Asketil and Mildryth on board, called his men to oars and off they rowed into the night.

Chapter Eighteen

They rowed continuously until they knew that they were safe, then father and son collapsed into each other's arms and laughed hysterically with relief until Sigurd broke away. 'Pooh, Til! You are ripe as a midden in those broks. Let us see if we can find you some more.'

So glad was Asketil to escape unscathed, that he did not mind being made fun of and when a fresh pair of breeches was provided he cast his soiled ones overboard.

His father was now talking to the girl who had rescued them. 'Oh, Mildryth, you are a true friend!' Sigurd reached out to touch her, which proved uncomfortable for some reason and he drew back his hand, making do with a smile of thanks. 'How can we repay you?'

Mildryth shrugged. 'You can take me back to England, for I have no other means of getting home.'

'Oh, for sure if that is what you want – but we cannot go until the spring. First we must find a haven for the winter – and without delay, for those demons may come after us. Come! Man the oars, we head for Oslo!'

When they arrived, they found that the ruthless King Harald had also chosen to spend winter in the city he had founded, rather than in the northern capital. Having previous acquaintance with the Norwegian monarch, Sigurd paid homage and was invited to remain until spring at the home of one of his jarls.

The winter was fierce. Icicles hung over the doorway like sharks' teeth so that when one entered or left it was like walking in and out of a fish's mouth – at least this was Asketil's poetical view as he and Mildryth, heavily muffled in fur and equipped with snow-shoes, set out for a midday walk. The weather had made a turn for the better and today the icicles drip, drip, dripped on to both heads as the two passed beneath.

The girl bent to pick up one that had been knocked off. 'Shark's tooth?' She held the huge icicle aloft. 'Nay, 'tis an ice-giant's pezzle.' She turned to laugh at Asketil, but he had gone into one of his huffs and marched ahead. She threw down the icicle and lolloped to catch up, veering around a man who dragged his child on a sledge. 'Where shall we go?'

Asketil replied without looking at her, 'I thought I would go for a walk first then, on the way back I will buy gifts to take home to my mother and sisters.'

'I will help you choose.' Mildryth thought the youth was wonderful, which was obvious from the expression on her face.

Til could not help but be aware of her adoration and secretly enjoyed it, but in the perverse way that boys do he acted as if the younger child were a handicap. 'I do not need help. Besides, you have never met them so how will you know what they like?'

'I know more than any boy!' She wished he would not put on these untypical displays. Cooped up all winter she had got to know him well and recognized a good and compassionate soul. Why then did he pretend that he did not like her?

Insulted that she did not recognize his manhood, he spat, 'Oh, come if you must – but do not mention this to my father.' When the girl asked why, Asketil explained Sigurd's aversion to women and the reasons for this. 'I do not like to talk of my fondness for my kin in his presence.'

'What has it to do with him if you honour your family?' demanded Mildryth, then turned curious. 'Art sure about him not liking females? He treats me well enough.'

The youth looked confused; he had noticed that Sigurd did not speak of Mildryth with contempt even behind her back. 'Oh, I do not know . . . Stop dawdling! If you are coming for a walk then come.'

'Why are you cross with me today?'

At Mildryth's crestfallen visage Asketil felt mean and could not give proper response. If there was any answer at all it was that when he found himself being too nice to her he felt disloyal to Sigurd. 'I am not cross!'

'You sound it.'

'I am just cold with waiting for you, that is all.'

'Oh. I am sorry.' Mildryth tried to quicken her pace but kept rapping her ankles with the snowshoes.

With the aid of poles, they climbed up a slope, as high as their burning chests would allow, then sat overlooking the timber city, its fjord and the townsfolk in their sleighs who had come out to enjoy the sunshine. Occasionally there would be a muted thud as branches of pine shed their weight of melting snow. Apart from this it was silent. The air was fresh and spring not far away. Mildryth squeezed her knees and beamed. 'I love this place.'

This was unexpected. Asketil deigned to treat her with more respect. 'Are you not eager to go home?'

'Only so that I may show my kin I am alive. I cannot say I yearn for it and would as soon tarry here a while.'

Asketil decided to confide his own emotions. 'I wish we did not have to leave at all. I feel so much part of this country. The wrench will be terrible.'

Mildryth could not envisage a problem. 'Why do you not ask Lord Sigurd if you can stay?'

'He will not allow it. Even a city such as Oslo and a court like King Harald's is not enough for him.'

Mildryth peered from the fur hood. Her cheeks were pink and a dewdrop clung to her nosetip. 'But from what you have told me, he travels to many countries. Why does he set his base at Jorvik when he is wont to leave it so often?'

'Because, much as he loves to travel, Jorvik is his heart's home and always draws him back,' answered Til. 'Though how he could leave this in the first place shows blindness indeed.' Sharing this view, Mildryth wiped her nose on her cuff and snuggled up to him. Asketil edged his buttocks away and made to leave. 'It is getting too cold to sit here and there are yet those gifts to be found.'

Mildryth jumped up, stumbled and put out her hand to right herself. 'Ow! I have cut my finger.' She held her grazed knuckle under his nose. 'See, it bleeds!'

''Tis nought but a scratch, baby,' replied Asketil. But Mildryth grimaced in discomfort, moaning and groaning until the boy produced a rag. 'Oh here, tie this on.'

She looked disgusted. 'I do not want that snotty thing on me!'

'Then help yourself, ungrateful!' He shoved it back up his cuff.

Maintaining her wounded air, Mildryth followed him, regretting now that she had caused offence. However, before long her breezy manner helped to surmount his martyred look and they were soon talking again.

On the way down he came across a lump of wood and picked it up. She asked what he wanted with it. 'It is a gift for my father. Watch when I give it to him: he will feel and probe the shape until it tells him what to make of it.'

'How can wood talk?' scoffed Mildryth.

'I do not know, but that is what he will say.' At times Asketil felt encumbered by her presence, especially when she kept interfering with his gift-buying. However, she did have her uses; when he arrived back at the jarl's house with an armful of gifts and nowhere to hide them, it was Mildryth who took control, pretending to Lord Sigurd that she had bought them for her own family, and he did not think to ask where she had got the money.

The timbered hall was lively with other folk who played music and games. Sigurd had just been outsmarted at a board game by the jarl and was therefore pleased to turn his attention to the lump of wood that his foster-son presented. Asketil looked obliquely at Mildryth as if to say, see what he does. The old man's eyes lit up. 'Why, thank you, most kindly. It will be a good piece when it has dried out.' He sniffed the offering and ran his hands over it. 'Now, what does it say it will be?'

Mildryth sniggered. The man looked at her sharply, then at Asketil, and gave a laugh of recognition. 'My son makes jest of me, I think.' With wry smile, he put the lump of wood at the edge of the hearth. 'It shall speak to me later – in private.'

'Look!' Mildryth brought forth her injury for inspection. 'I have cut my hand.'

'Oh, most dreadful.' Sigurd peered at the graze which was now barely visible. 'And tell me, where have you been to get that?'

'Up a mountain looking down.' A blithe Mildryth disregarded nobler guests, assessing the contents of the table. 'You should have come with us, for the weather was not too cold.'

Sigurd eyed her as she collected food for herself and Asketil. 'Maybe I will come next time. Though it will not be long before we sail for home if the good weather keeps up. Murtagh! Stop idling there and feed these good people.'

456

Over the years Murtagh had learnt to keep all emotion from his face. It was impossible to tell the resentment he felt at his position, but Mildryth knew. Having been a thrall herself, she objected to the way Sigurd clouted him when he came running so dutifully. 'I am able enough to pick up food.' It was a blatant rebuke. 'Do not treat him so harsh.'

Asketil ducked as Sigurd's narrowed eyes challenged her. Mildryth did not flinch, but merely added in response to his previous statement. 'Til would like to stay here – ask him, he will tell you.'

The youth dealt a nudge for this interference. She rubbed her arm, scowled, then picked up the food he had knocked from her bread platter and thrust some of it at him.

Sigurd looked amused. 'I am well aware of my son's feelings on the matter, but he knows we cannot stay.'

Asketil's expression warned Mildryth not to press the theme. Returning his scowl she crammed her mouth with food and the meal was eaten without further reference to the topic. Afterwards the boy, having recovered from his upset, took out a small pipe which he had carved from a goose bone and drew from it a wavering tune.

Sigurd made a grimace of pain at a wrong note and covered his ears. 'It sounds like you castrate a mouse!' Others laughingly agreed.

Unoffended, Asketil laughed too. 'How do you castrate a mouse, Father?'

'With a very small knife, I should imagine, though I have never tried.' Sigurd grinned at the renewed laughter from the jarl's other guests.

Mildryth, imagining that her loved one was being made mock of, was rather cross. 'Play some more, I like it.' She thought Asketil very talented in the way he had carved such a minute instrument, besides all the other more practical things he made from tiny bones such as needles and pins.

But, 'Nay!' begged Lord Sigurd. 'Let us instead have some of Asketil's verse. That is gentler on the ear.'

This appeased Mildryth, for she could sit and listen to Asketil's poetry for hours. Neither she nor the boy noticed that throughout the recital Sigurd's eyes kept leaving the orator, drawn constantly to her rapt face.

Whilst Sigurd was away, much was happening in England. Without Godwin to keep him in check, King Edward began to invite more of his Norman friends to Court, and during that winter whilst Sigurd and Asketil tarried in Norway another of those friends enjoyed long private conversations with Edward: Duke William of Normandy.

The English, angered over the King's favouritism, sent word to Godwin that they would now support him if he wished to return. In triumph he came up the Temes with his son Harold to be fêted as a hero. With his Norman allies fled and national opinion against him, Edward had no option but to restore Godwin to his old position. No more would the English be subjected to foreign interference. Henceforth, Godwin was invincible.

It was to this encouraging state of affairs that Sigurd came home in 1052, totally besmitten with the girl he took with him. When, after a night under his roof, Mildryth said that she must go north and show her kin that she was alive, the man invented frantic excuses to keep her there. 'You do not need to rush away! I can easy send a messenger. Bide awhile with us – Asketil will welcome your company for I know he likes you as a sister.'

The boy was surprised at this, but now that his foster-father had by this quote apparently given permission for him to like Mildryth, he found that to do so was easy, and he now gave her a reassuring smile.

Totally devoted to Asketil, it took no persuasion other than that smile to make her stay. With her kin informed as to her well-being, she felt no need to see them at this moment, and so became a permanent member of the household, enjoying all the benefits that this entailed – fine clothes, a comfortable bed, good food. During that first year Til did indeed come to regard her as a sister. It was a long time since he had lived at the house of Ulf, but he held fond memories of being surrounded by women. When he was tiny his real sisters would dress him up in girls' clothing and do as they liked with him. It had not bothered Til, for while he was dressed like a girl they seemed to regard him as one and had exchanged women's secrets in front of him. Being with them all the time he had learnt more about the intimacies of women than those of a man – that is, until he had gone to live with his fostri – but it had stood him in good stead and he retained this easiness in Mildryth's presence, even though he was never secure enough to disclose his own secrets to her.

Outwardly, Sigurd tried to regard Mildryth as Asketil's sister too, though inside raged a conflict of passions. On the one hand he adored her chastity, on the other, it was this same virtue that made her so desirable. He did not detest her as he did other women, for she was unlike any other female. In spite of witnessing the most basic of pleasures between her captor and his slavewomen in Norway, Mildryth failed to descry Sigurd's longing and viewed his affection for her as that of a parent. Even now when she had reached womanhood and there came to her breast strange yearnings of her own, she did not grasp that Lord Sigurd wanted her in the same way that she wanted Asketil. Her feelings for the youth had begun to deepen. She thought about him all the time – even dreamt about him: vivid, unsettling dreams.

To her chagrin, the boy's attitude remained

unchanged – he was more intimate with Murtagh than with her. Mildryth had overheard him divulging all his private thoughts to the slave, confident that they could not be repeated. Interesting though it was to learn that he too had odd dreams, it was upsetting that her name was never mentioned. Nevertheless, she spent as much time as she could in his presence.

Sigurd, watching them this balmy afternoon from his window, saw Mildryth trying to teach Asketil how to dance. She was not making very much progress. He grinned to himself and wondered how long it would be before they fell to squabbling. It was not that they disliked each other – far from it – but that they were so different in character. They could not help but argue. Peeping round the edge of his window so they would not see him, he felt a surge of warmth for both of them. Mildryth, exasperated with Til's efforts, had begun to tease, imitating his clumsy method of dancing. She staggered about like a cripple. Muffling his laughter, Sigurd jerked his head back as Til looked towards the house; it would not do for the youth to know his humiliation was witnessed. When he peeped from the window again a black-faced Asketil had risen and was walking away. Oh, Til! Sigurd gave an inward sigh. After all the experiences you have had, when will you lose that childish trait? It does not befit a man to sulk. Maybe . . . maybe I should give the lad more responsibility, thought Sigurd; with Til behaving as he did the ealdorman had been wary of entrusting him with anything important but maybe that was just what the lad needed to make him grow up. Yes, that was what he would do. The reeve who had replaced Ulf was now too decrepit and needed to be replaced himself. Asketil would fill his shoes.

Glancing from the window again he saw Mildryth still engaged in her unalluring dance, following Til around Elrondyng, a pillar of the Roman Fortress.

Just as he was about to call to his foster-son another face appeared on the scene.

'Thou ungodly harlot!' A priest bore down on Mildryth, brandishing a stick which he proceeded to lay about her shoulders. 'How dare thee cavort in such a heathen manner on a feast-day!' And he used the stick to such violence that Mildryth howled and danced about even more and so earned herself further pain.

Sigurd gave a roar and was out of the house within seconds, but his intention was surplanted by Asketil.

'Enough!' The youngster intercepted the priest's attack, grabbed the stick and wrested it from him. 'She was wrong but has surely taken enough punishment now.'

'Give it back!' ordered the red-faced churchman.

'Nay!' Asketil was obstinate. 'I will not let you beat Mildryth again. There was no malice intended, she had just forgotten 'twas a holy day.'

'Then I will teach her never to forget again!' The priest tried to retrieve his weapon. 'Give it back or you will earn your own beating.' With Til holding the stick above his head the shorter man began to box the youngster's ears.

'The man wants his stick, Til!' Sigurd grabbed it with ease from Til's hand. 'You must give it to him.' And he brought the stick down upon the priest's head with such violence that it broke. The man's knees buckled but his punishment was not over. Sigurd used his fists and feet to drive Mildryth's attacker all the way back to his church where the whimpering priest bolted the door behind him, only then daring to offer retaliation. 'The archbishop shall hear of this!'

When a furious Sigurd returned to check on Mildryth's health he found her and Asketil barely able to keep straight faces. At first he was too angry to laugh with them. 'Let him dare to lay a hand on my folk again!' He reached out to Mildryth who sat where

461

she had fallen, and pulled her to her feet. 'Art bruised, my dear?'

She pushed her hair from her face. The action hurt her shoulders which had taken the brunt of the stick, but she did not complain. 'If I am, 'twill be my own fault and I am sorry if I have brought the wrath of the church down upon you both.'

'Pooh, it will be like a fart in the wind!' retorted Sigurd, and Asketil could no longer withhold his laughter. Mildryth's contrition gave way too and very soon all three were laughing at the memory of the priest's come-uppance. 'Oh, by the gods!' Sigurd gave one last laugh and shook his head. 'To think I was on my way here to offer you more responsibility and find you upsetting a priest!'

Asketil's merriment gave way to curiosity. 'What do you mean, *fostri*?'

'I thought that you were man enough to take on the position of reeve but now . . . I am sure of it!' He laughed again as relief flooded Til's cheeks.

'I thought I had spoilt my chances!' breathed the lad, grinning at Mildryth who looked delighted for him.

'And so you would have done if you had not grabbed that stick off him!' replied Sigurd. 'Doest think I care what fines the church might impose? But I care about this one here!' He put his arm around Mildryth but soon withdrew it for the touch of her always unnerved him. 'You have shown you are man enough to protect her and now I will reward you. From today you are my reeve with all the responsibilities it holds.'

Some of those responsibilities turned out to be less enjoyable than others. Whilst Asketil was happy to tour the city on a Sunday making sure that there was no illegal trading, and any laborious task such as collecting dues from the tenants on Sigurd's estates, he did not particularly like arranging executions, but to shirk these would be irresponsible and he took his role very seriously. Even though he had made a few mistakes, his foster-father had in general been very pleased with his handling of the more difficult duties.

Today, though, was less exacting. He was in charge of handing out the annual rations to the thralls. A table had been carried into the sunshine and Til sat behind it with a register. Mildryth crouched nearby with a large pair of scales and whatever amount Til read from the register she would weigh the corn or some other commodity and pour it into the thrall's sack.

Murtagh was last in line. When Mildryth had weighed out his twelve pounds of corn and tipped it into the sack that he held, Asketil scratched a last comment in the register and said, 'Right, that is done. You may go now, Mildryth.'

'Oh, that is too kind of you!'

Asketil looked suitably apologetic. 'Thank you for all your help.'

'That is more courteous!' She was about to shift the scales but Asketil interrupted.

'Murtagh will do that. Off with you and get some victuals, you must be hungry, I know I am.'

'Come with me, then.' She waited.

'I will be in shortly,' he answered, and when Mildryth went towards the house he made a sound of exasperation to Murtagh. 'Always she is at my side! I cannot have a moment's peace. I know just how you feel with Lord Sigurd at your back all the time. Come, let us find a quiet spot where we can both get some respite.' He and the thrall walked off together.

Mildryth had decided to eat her meal outside and took some for Asketil, too. However, when she came out he and Murtagh were disappearing over the brow of the slope which led to the river. Pressing her lips together, she bundled up the food in her apron and ran after them, ale slopping about in the jug she carried. They were too far ahead to notice her and she decided to leave it that way, allowing them to get settled amongst the trees on the riverbank before creeping up and hiding nearby in the long grass. Here, she eavesdropped whilst eating her meal, tutting occasionally at the private, one-sided conversation. What addle! Any resentment she might feel was certainly not against the mute for, being acquainted with his harrowing story, she shared Asketil's compassion. No, it was Asketil who annoyed her by his refusal to see how she felt. She brushed crumbs from her mouth, drank from the jug of ale and continued to listen; it seemed the only way she could get her own back on him for excluding her.

'How many years have you been a slave now, Murtagh?' Asketil was lying on his back, face to the late summer sun.

Murtagh cradled his arms.

'Since you were a babe, yes, I know, but how long is that now?' Murtagh shrugged.

'I would guess it is over thirty summers.'

What summer? thought the slave. My life has been one long winter. I have no wife, no children, no house, no kin. And all because of the tyrant Sigurd. The man you love so well and the one I hate with all of my being.

Asketil could not fail to notice the shadow of resentment and despair that had passed across Murtagh's face. 'Never was there a man who has been slave so long. It is unfair that my lord keeps you thus.' Mildryth pricked up her ears at this hint of insurrection. 'I have tried my best to gain you fairer treatment but it is more than I can do to persuade him to grant you your liberty. But one day, Murtagh, I will repay you for saving me from drowning, even if I have to go against my *fostri . . .*' He broke off, hearing a rustle.

Mildryth cursed herself for knocking over the ale jug and ducked, but Til was alert now.

'Come out and show yourself!' He had sprung to his feet, Murtagh too.

The maid, deciding to end her pretence on a note of flair, burst out from the long grass like a sprite. Asketil was half relieved it was only her, but still looked like one caught in the act. 'How long have you been there, Mildew? Hiding in the grass like a spittlebug!'

'What need have I to hide, Ant-hill?' Her manner was airy. She bobbed and preened and cocked her pretty head. 'I go wherever I choose.'

'Did you hear my words?' Asketil maintained his watch in case Sigurd discovered them and beat Murtagh for idling.

Mildryth decided to use what she had heard to torment him. 'I did indeed!'

At the impudent challenge in her eyes, he looked away and centred his nervousness on a cluster of toadstools, kicking each one down with a toe. 'You will not repeat them?'

'And why would I do that?' Mildryth's eyebrows lifted in wonder. 'Just because you prefer to tell your secrets to a slave . . .'

'Murtagh does not tell tales!' cut in Asketil. 'That is why I share them with him. Now please swear . . .'

'Do you think that just because you choose to exclude me from your secrets I am so petty as to run and tell tales to Lord Sigurd? That may be your way, Asketil, it is not mine.'

He looked into her flushed cheeks and felt guilty enough to offer reparation. 'I am sorry for having offended you, Mildryth. It is just that I have always spoken thus to Murtagh. It is a hard habit to break. He has been my friend for a long time. He saved my life . . .'

'And so did I!'

'I had not forgotten!' He looked defeated. 'Oh, how can I make amends?'

'I thought that I was your friend.' The girl looked downcast, milking every ounce of sympathy that she could.

'Why, so you are! Indeed you are like a sister, but there are things that a man can say to another man that he cannot say to his sister! Do you see? It is not because I do not like you. I do like you.'

Mildryth overlooked the fact that he viewed her as a sister and decided to cease her game. 'Very well, I forgive you!' She smiled and went to retrieve the uneaten food from her hiding place whilst Asketil breathed a sigh of relief and rolled his eyes at Murtagh who enjoyed a private grin.

They sat down again beside the river and Mildryth put the food before them, some apples, bread, nuts and honey cake. She herself had taken her fill but watched Asketil whilst he ate. It disconcerted him and he spoke to cover this. 'Do not let us eat the food you brought for yourself.'

She leaned forward to pick a crumb from his upper lip. 'I brought extra for you but you were too busy grumbling about Lord Sigurd.'

Asketil recognized it as simply her teasing. 'Thank heaven it was you who overheard us and not *fostri*.'

'Oh, I cannot think there is any great sin in what you said. You wish to free Murtagh in exchange for saving your life, that is a . . .'

'Quiet!' Asketil had just filled his mouth with bread and almost choked in his effort to swallow it, alarmed that a housecarl or someone might overhear. 'Have a care for my skin if not your own. You do not know how angry my father would be just at the mention of it.'

Mildryth showed unconcern. 'Old Nit-whiskers? I fear him not. He is like a kitten in my hands.'

'Huh! You are so sure of yourself. Well, just ask him to free Murtagh then you shall know.'

'Very well!' She made to jump up. 'If you dare not ask him to free Murtagh then I will.'

'Nay!' He grabbed hold of her to prevent her rising, but to her disappointment soon let go.

Again she dismissed his fear. 'Be calm, I shall not say you have a hand in this.'

'Do not be a fool, you will bring his anger down upon you!'

'Not I.' Her confidence stemmed from the knowledge that the ealdorman loved her as a daughter. She wished that Til would love her too, though in a very different way.

'I do not know why you think he will listen to you when he ignores all I have to say on the matter!' Much as he liked her, Asketil often felt jealous at the way she was favoured by Sigurd.

She swivelled her bottom and turned to Murtagh. 'I'll warrant if you could speak you would not forbid me to ask him.'

The man shook his dark head emphatically. He liked this young girl but would use her to his own ends if it meant freedom. A great observer, he had become aware of Lord Sigurd's feelings for her. He who had never lain with a woman knew unrequited passion when he saw it in another man's face.

'Mildryth, leave well alone!'

Laughing at Asketil's chariness, she jumped up before he could stop her and went off to find Sigurd.

'Oh, that girl will be the death of us! In heaven's name what are we to do?' Til demanded of Murtagh. And when the slave indicated that he must return to work, Til agreed. 'Yes, you are right, I will make myself busy too!' And the pair of them beat a hasty path back to the house.

The ealdorman was involved with artistic endeavours.

As usual there was no preamble to Mildryth's conversation. 'Why do you keep Murtagh as a slave so long?'

Sigurd blew on his carving, then turned a fond eye on her. 'Do not tell me you are ignorant, for nought is private in this gossip-hole.'

'I know that his aunt murdered your child but that was long, long ago . . .'

'Twas only yesterday, thought Sigurd. How meaningless is the death of one child to another.

'. . . surely he has paid for that with years of his life.'

'This is your opinion?' There was only the merest hint of sarcasm. He loved the way her violet eyes held his, unafraid. 'And tell me, Mildryth, why do you bother with one so low?'

'Do you not bother with me?' she asked. 'I, too, was once so low – and you were very nearly slave yourself, had I not rescued you.'

He laughed and patted her, then drew his hand away quickly and turned back to his work.

Mildryth performed a balancing act on a block of wood. 'Mind you do not twist your ankle,' warned Sigurd.

This reminded her. 'Have I shown you the bruise where Asketil's horse bit me?'

'I think perhaps you did.' The man smiled to himself. If he had seen the bruise once he had seen it twenty times. 'Have a sip from my cup, 'twill sweeten the misery.'

Mildryth drank the mead, but was persistent, leaning forward as she spoke. 'So what are you to do about Murtagh? It is not right that one man should own another. Come, my lord, do this for me who cut your bonds. When will you give him his freedom?'

Aroused by her nearness, the scent of her body, he did not turn. 'When? I have not said I shall free him yet.'

Mildryth bent forward, hands pressed between knees, and puckered her lips. 'You will.'

Of course he would. Just to look into her eyes was to be defeated. Mildryth had changed his whole life, melted the ice in his breast. Even Til, much as Sigurd loved him, could not get his fostri to do the things that she asked of him. Sigurd despaired of himself for being so malleable. When they learnt he was to free Murtagh everyone would think the tyrant had gone soft . . . and they would probably be right. He gave a private laugh, then contemplated his own re-action were he to free the hated one, and decided that Murtagh's fate meant nought to him any more. Maybe it was time to let the wretch go – all the others had gone – what use was he except as a reminder of Una? And Sigurd needed no reminding, for he had another very different love.

However, he refused to let Mildryth know that she had won so easily. 'I will think upon it. Now get you gone.'

He did not hear her leave and waited a good few minutes before turning. The spot where she had been was now unoccupied. Involuntarily, he wandered to the doorway to look for her, but instead saw Murtagh at his labours. He leaned there, watching and think-ing, remembering Asketil's words – 'How terrible to be so wretched.' Was he mistaken, or had the hate inside him really lessened? Whatever the truth, it went against the grain to let Murtagh go scot free. The man must be made to pay for his liberty. But how? Nearby was a pile of manure from the domestic animals. On impulse, he barked at Murtagh and the filthy creature came bounding over.

'The dungpile, it has grown too high . . .'

Relieved that the master's summons was not to be accompanied by punishment – Mildryth must not have broached the subject of his freedom after all –

Murtagh bowed and was already on his way to move the heap when Sigurd held up his hand.

'You shall take half of it for your own use. Take it away now for it offends me.'

Murtagh's face showed that he was not sure that he understood the command but, unable to question, bowed again and ran off to shovel the manure into a barrow. Sigurd watched the dungbeetle scuttle around his acquisition, and feeling content that he had pleased Mildryth, went back to work on the oaken chest that he was making for her.

Later, wearing an expression of anticipation, Murtagh showed Asketil and Mildryth the dungpile that was now transferred to the back of the slaves' hut.

Mildryth had expected to be shown something of great interest when the excited slave had waylaid them during their evening walk and dragged them round here. She turned up her nose. 'Looks like shite to me.'

Murtagh gave an inwards sigh at having to enact an explanation, but tried his best to show that Lord Sigurd had given him the dung.

Asketil sniggered. 'Your persuasion must have worked well, Mildryth, for my father to donate so generous a gift.'

Mildryth, who had boasted all afternoon that she had talked Lord Sigurd into freeing Murtagh, now felt slightly humiliated. But Murtagh was to change her mood, indicating with some impatience that the dung was to be sold and he to receive the proceeds.

The listeners understood at last. Mildryth gave a cry of delight. 'It worked, then!'

'I do not know how you can say that.' Much as he was glad for Murtagh, Asketil could not help feeling resentful at her small success. '*Fostri* has but given Murtagh the chance to earn himself a few pence, that is all. He has made no mention of freedom, has he?' He glanced at Murtagh who shook his head.

'He will do,' vouched Mildryth to the dubious slave. 'Mark my words, he would not have done this if he did not intend to free you. This is just the beginning. He does not want to free you at once because of his pride – it would make him look weak. He has decided to make it appear to others as if you have earned your own freedom. He thinks that you are unable to tell anyone that he gave you the dung.'

'Mildryth, you are too fanciful,' said Asketil.

'What will you wager on it?' she demanded. 'For I will go and enquire right now of his intentions.'

'I will wager nought,' replied Til. 'But if you are right, my congratulations will be genuine for it is something I have long tried to do and have failed miserably in my efforts. Go now for I too am eager to know – and good luck!'

Mildryth ran for the house. 'Take heart, Murtagh!'

When she returned it was with a skip of joy. 'Forsooth! Murtagh is to be freed. He is to be allowed every *Wodnesdaeg* to labour for himself and so buy his own freedom – though Lord Sigurd has not yet quoted the price, but I am sure it will be fair for I would not allow otherwise. Here! Let me contribute towards it.' She pulled up her dress and from a knot in her shift extricated another silver penny.

Although excited for his friend, Asketil objected. '*Fostri* gave you that!'

'To spend as I please,' retorted the girl. 'And it pleases me to spend it on Murtagh.' Sigurd was generous towards his young charges; there would soon be another penny to replace this one.

The thrall snatched it before Asketil could persuade her to change her mind. But the youth had been touched by her generosity, too, and not wanting to look mean fished amongst his clothes for a penny of his own which he gave to Murtagh. 'There! You have a good start towards freedom, my friend.'

When the coins were on his person Murtagh allowed

Asketil to grip his gnarled hand, and the trio enjoyed a clandestine smile.

'Murtagh!' Sigurd's voice penetrated their sojourn.

Mildryth gave a withering look. 'Oh, hark to him honking like a steg – make him wait.'

Murtagh actually grinned, but shook his head, jumped up and ran.

The price which Sigurd had put on Murtagh's freedom might be negligible to him, but for the slave it involved months of toil. The master had verified his intention of granting him Wednesdays off to pursue his own labours, and amongst other small enterprises Murtagh had taken to collecting reeds with which he made baskets, selling the finished items at the riverside market. The baskets were well-made but Murtagh with no voice to advertise them found it hard to attract custom. Many a soul-destroying hour did he pass on that riverbank without a single customer, until a kindly boat-builder, feeling pity for the man, called him over.

'It is poor business today, yes?'

Murtagh nodded.

The man, knowing that Ealdorman Sigurd's thrall was mute, did not expect a fuller response. 'I notice you watch me closely every week – you like boats?' A nod. 'Would you like to learn how to build one?' At Murtagh's rapid affirmation he smiled. 'Good, you can help me at the same time. My boy is sick and it is a devil of a job without someone to pass me the tools. If I show you which ones I need can you do it?'

Murtagh was eager to learn and for the rest of that afternoon he watched and helped in his small way, forgetting all about his baskets. At the end of the working day the man said, 'You have done a good job! If my boy is not recovered by next *Wodnesdaeg* you can help again – here! A penny for you.'

To Murtagh's disappointment his services were not required the following week for the man's usual helper had recovered, but then he had suffered many disappointments in his life, and he enjoyed watching the boatbuilding just the same whilst he sat waiting for folk to buy his baskets. Even when he did manage to sell any, the few coins they earned him made little impact on the bond payment. Mildryth and Asketil asked to be kept abreast of the progress he had made towards freedom, and when he showed them the pitiful amount he had earned from his hard work, they decided to help in its accrual by donating any money that Lord Sigurd might have given them. When snowdrops began to peep through the grass Asketil, who safeguarded the money, was able to announce that Murtagh needed only one more day's work to achieve his target. Both youngsters were delighted for him. Had they been able to read what was in his heart they would surely not have been.

Before the final contribution, Murtagh indicated for Asketil to return the money to him. The youth was quick to grasp his meaning. 'Yes, I understand that you wish to hand over your bond price in person, but I beg you to take care that it is not stolen at this late hour.' Watching Murtagh tuck the leather pouch down his shirt, he added, 'When you go to buy your freedom I would like to be present if I may – we have long been friends. Wait there a moment and let me show you what I have done!' He ran off to the house and returned a few moments later bearing a parchment. 'See! Your freedom awaits only Lord Sigurd's mark. I wrote it out myself.'

Murtagh took great interest in the manuscript, though of course he could not read one word of it.

'So, you must tell me when you have those last few pence, in order that I may witness the signing of your freedom,' begged Asketil, rolling up the manuscript.

Mildryth agreed. 'I too would like to be present.'

Murtagh nodded, but had no intention of complying with her desire, for he wanted neither of the youngsters there when he faced his captor. Later, when they asked if he had earned those last few precious pence, he lied and shook his head. For two days he hung on to it, desperate to be free but waiting for the youngsters to absent themselves. On Friday afternoon his opportunity came at last. Having just helped to serve the midday meal he was dismissed to work outside and some half an hour later saw Asketil and Mildryth leave the burh. Knowing that his master was often alone at this hour having a brief nap after eating, he put down his hoe and bent to grubble amongst the vegetable rows, unearthing an object which he transferred to the folds of his mantle. With the pouch of money in his black fist, he went across to the ealdorman's house. No one remarked upon the nervous manner in which he frequently patted his body.

There was no one else in the hall apart from the usual assortment of dogs which were too familiar with Murtagh to provide any obstacle. From his relaxed position Sigurd opened one eye to see who disturbed him. With as much dignity as his nervousness would permit, Murtagh emptied his coins on to the table and dropped his hands. Yawning, Sigurd pushed himself from his chair and flicked the silver pence this way and that in half-hearted manner, too dozy to wonder how Murtagh had got the money so quickly. Finding the manuscript that Asketil had drawn up, he dipped his quill into ink and added his mark. 'So, you are free ... though I have no doubt that you will expect me to grant you work and a roof over your head, hmm?' Handing over the document, he lifted a contemptuous eye to Murtagh's crooked one – then grunted in surprise as the bondsman punched him in the belly. Only when Murtagh snatched the manuscript, turned tail and fled did

Sigurd look down and see the hilt protruding from his tunic. The dogs slept on.

Asketil and Mildryth had not been far and now came back across the bridge over the ditch. The maid, wearing a garland of flowers in her hair, skipped way ahead and waved to Murtagh as he flew from the house, but he did not appear to notice. Asketil, too, shouted cheerily to him but the thrall, consumed with a mixture of revenge and terror, made for the river where he had hidden a small boat, painstakingly restored from a wreck with bits of wood, tar and nails that he had collected whilst watching his boat-builder friend over many months. Just as God had provided the rusty blade from the earth with which to kill the despot, so He had turned the tide in Murtagh's favour; the river was at an unusually low ebb and the grounded longboats, even with their shallow draughts, would have difficulty in following the smaller craft immediately, lending him a head start. Panting, he dragged it into the water and used his single oar to paddle towards freedom.

After pulling a face at his retreating back, Mildryth had gone on her way and now went inside the house. Sigurd was lying on the floor unconscious, his tunic soaked in blood and a dagger in his hand. Giving urgent cry for Til, she ran to the stricken man, knocked away the inquisitive hound that sniffed at the blood and knelt down beside him. Asketil rushed in. ''Twas Murtagh, I know it,' breathed the girl.

Til acted with remarkable authority, calling the housecarls from their games and sending a party of them after Murtagh whilst ordering the others to carry their lord to a makeshift bed in the anteroom, for it would be too traumatic to lift him up the stairs. Jolted into consciousness, Sigurd groaned then yelled and cursed. Mildryth rushed off to the kitchen where she grabbed an onion, chopped it into pieces and threw it into hot water, mashing and stirring purposefully to make a thin broth – all to the mystification of the servants. When she returned to the house Sigurd was white as snow and moaning.

'Where is the physician?' yelled Asketil.

'How do I know!' Mildryth hurried up to the bed trying not to spill the bowl of liquid.

'I thought you had gone to fetch him!' Asketil packed one of the servants off to do the job.

'I have no time to fart about with medicine men.' Mildryth lifted Sigurd's anguished head and tried to dribble a little of the soup down him. 'Drink, damn thee!' Impatient, she tipped the bowl at his lips, dousing his beard but managing to get him to swallow. After forcing another gulp upon him she thrust the bowl at a carl – 'Take that away!' – and bent to sniff the abdominal wound. There was no scent of onions. 'Well, it has not pierced his belly anyway – and if it had struck his heart he would be already dead. I think he shall live.'

'You are no doctor – what do you know?' yelled Til. All at once he had lost his air of authority when faced with the thought that his father could die.

But when the physician came hurrying in and his prognosis was exactly the same as Mildryth's, the youth's panic began to subside. Whilst the wound was being dressed, he asked one of the houscarls if Murtagh had been found, receiving a negative answer. 'Then keep searching!' he roared. The room was quickly vacated except for the two who were closest to Sigurd and the physician. When the latter had gone Asketil turned to the girl. 'How could he betray us like this, Mildryth?'

There was no look of retribution in her eye. 'I expect that I would have done the same, were I him.'

'But we contributed towards this!' He threw a hand at Sigurd's inert body. 'We helped Murtagh to raise the money. If *fostri* dies we shall be his murderers.'

'He shall not die.' Mildryth dragged a cushion to

the paillasse on which Sigurd lay. 'Sit you on that side of his bed and me on this, and together we will bring him through and make amends for any part we might have played.'

And this was how it was. For the next few days Sigurd meandered in and out of consciousness, too ill to be carried to his own bed. Asketil never left his side at all, except to relieve himself. Mildryth was constant too, mopping his pallid brow and applying more St John's Wort to his wound. During this intimate time Asketil, with nothing more to occupy his eyes, began to look upon her in a different light, noticing her little breasts and her dark blonde hair. Suddenly he was shocked to find himself no longer at ease with her.

Mildryth finished packing a new batch of 'Save' around the wound and looked up to offer encouragement to Asketil. 'It is healing well. There is no pus around it . . . what is the matter?' He had snatched his eyes away as if caught out.

'Nought! I am just tired.' He rubbed his eyes, shifted on the cushion and pressed his hand to the small of his back, looking extremely uncomfortable.

The wound attended to, she eased herself back on to her cushion. 'You ought to get some rest.'

Asketil remained loyal. 'Not until my lord wakes.' For something to do he poked at the nearby fire then coughed at the smoke it produced.

Mildryth eyed him for a while. Something had happened here; his approach towards her was different. She was not looking at a boy but a man.

For some moments he pretended not to notice, looking at the carved walls of the bower, anywhere except at her. In the end, though, he was forced to object. 'Why do you stare so?'

Unabashed, she replied with the candour of a thirteen year old: 'I like to look at you. I think you are most handsome.'

'Nay! Stop this teasing, Mildryth. I am not handsome.' But his tone sought confirmation.

'To me you are.' She had been right; the way he looked at her was not the way a man beholds his sister.

Breast pounding, he gazed into her eyes, then coloured as the invalid stirred. 'Hark, he wakes!'

Sigurd's eyelids came open. Two faces peered down at him, but not the face that had haunted him in his nightmares. 'Did you catch him?' It was not the voice of a tyrant but the croak of a frog.

Without the need to ask who Sigurd referred to, the boy shook his head. 'Nay, the carls scoured the town and a good many miles downriver – there were reports that he had made himself a boat, but he was not captured. Maybe he drowned.' The hopeful statement merged into an apology. 'I am most ashamed, *fostri*.'

Sigurd vented his rage and pain on Mildryth. 'This is all your doing, wench! In persuading me to free the devil you have made him think he is a man and . . .' he tried to rise on his elbows but was too weak.

An offended Mildryth rushed from the room. Asketil shot to his feet. 'That is unfair! How could she be aware of Murtagh's intention? She has sat here for days nursing you back to health.'

Sigurd was already regretting his impulsiveness and collapsed on his pillow. 'Call her back,' was his tired order. 'And I shall say I am sorry.'

But when Asketil relayed this to her, Mildryth refused to come. 'The miserable old bear can go rot! I am glad Murtagh escaped!'

'Then tell that to Lord Sigurd, not to me!' Asketil dragged her back to the bed where Sigurd made gruff apology.

'I am most sorry, my daughter. It was anger at myself which made me curse you. I was the one to free him and there is no one else to blame.' Asketil's face burned as he thought of the donation he had made to Murtagh's bond price. Sigurd was too ill and too concerned with Mildryth to notice. 'Do you forgive me?'

The maid looked stubborn. 'You are not the first to curse me.'

'But am I forgiven?' He made it sound as if it were important to him.

Mildryth played with her necklace of fish teeth for a while, then relented. 'Yes.'

Sigurd's anguish melted into contentment, then he gave a painful sigh. 'Ah . . . how long have I been lying thus? There are things to be done.'

Asketil assured him that everything was being attended to. 'Now that you are safe from death I shall go today and collect the tithes from Osboldewic.'

'Tell him to go the morrow,' urged Mildryth. 'See how his eyes droop, he has barely slept a wink during his vigil.'

Sigurd cut off the boy's objection. 'The lass is right,' he croaked. 'You do look wan. Go and sleep, both of you, until you are fully rested. The dues will wait – but instruct the men to keep searching for Murtagh. If he has drowned the body shall come up some time. I would see it for myself.'

After making him comfortable, the pair of them were about to leave him in peace when Sigurd called them back. 'Give me your hands.' When Asketil and Mildryth slipped their fingers into his he tried to squeeze them but found his own grip as weak as a babe's and had to convey his fondness in his tone. 'I give thee my most grateful thanks for thy tender mercies.' Each returned his warmth, but he wondered as he watched them leave if Mildryth knew just how intense were his feelings for her.

The next day found Sigurd mended enough to be lifted upstairs to the luxury of his own bed. Asketil, having caught up on his sleep, prepared to ride out and collect the dues from Osboldewic. Mildryth insisted on going, too. Though her company unnerved him he could give no good reason why she should not come, and so delayed his journey whilst her pony was saddled. Apart from the party of housecarls, several falcons accompanied them; these were released along the way in the Forest of Galtres.

'So that they may breed,' explained the youth, when Mildryth asked the reason, both watching the falcons soar into the tree-tops. 'We shall return in autumn to collect the young.'

'And will you train them?' Mildryth had discovered some hazelnuts left over from the winter store; she cracked one with her teeth like a mouse.

Asketil wanted to impress without appearing boastful. 'Well, it is mostly the duty of the falconer, but I have learned to handle them quite well.' Trying to assume modesty, he held out his hand. 'Spare a nut for me, Mildew.'

She threw one at his head, laughed as he ducked, then leaned over in her saddle to place one on his palm. 'Art thou capable of everything? You can read and write, you make poetry, carve wood and bone, play music, train falcons . . .'

Asketil disposed of the nutshell and ate its kernel. Was she teasing him? Perhaps he had sounded a braggart; it was important that she did not think so. 'I cannot swim and . . . I do not know if I could kill a man. Apart from that I am perfect.' He laughed as she pelted him with more nuts.

They rode on from shadowed wood to sunlit dell, to moor and common and back to forest. When they reached Osboldewic Asketil left the officer in charge of the housecarls to collect the dues, for he himself was thirsty. Whilst he drank from the well Mildryth asked to share his cup, staring at him over its rim with those unusual eyes of hers. It must have been the spring sunshine that caused it; Mildryth had one of her impish moods, coaxed and dragged him away across the pasture, back towards the forest with the excited proposition, 'Let's go hunt for brocks!'

'You must not go in there alone, it is dangerous! There might be boar and wolves!' Asketil's warning received only a giggle and she tore off. He was compelled to go, too. The woodland was silent but across the pasture could be heard the laughter and chat of housecarls. Asketil wondered if they were laughing at the way he had bounded after her like a puppy.

It did not take long for Mildryth to sniff out a badger sett. Pointing, she turned gleeful face on her companion. 'Stick your hand down there and see if Master Brock's at home.' Then she hoisted her shoulders and laughed, so clearly delighted to be free and alive. 'What shall we do next?'

Asketil could not take his eyes off her breathless, joyful face and pondered for a moment. 'Hast ever seen the nadder's dance?' When she shook her head he looked pleased at being able to enlighten her and with a gesture of invitation began to comb the scrubland. The object of his search took so long to find that Mildryth grew bored and was ready to head back for the village when Asketil said, 'Hush!' and pointed. 'Be still.'

She flopped onto her belly beside him resting on points of elbows, but could not see at first what had caught his interest. And then she saw it too.

The vipers coiled their bodies around each other in a sensuous dance, not just two or three but a writhing knot of them. Mildryth giggled. Asketil shushed her and both continued to watch as the male adders fought to press each other into submission. Mildryth whispered to her partner, 'It feels as though they have got inside my belly.'

Asketil nodded, experiencing at first a tickling

481

sensation in the pit of his abdomen and then intense heat. He looked at Mildryth. The pupils of her eyes had almost obscured the violet. An inner voice told him it was a mistake to have followed her here. Something was happening and he had no power to stop it. She laid her lips on his. He could not help himself, the frenzy of the reptiles drove them to a passion. They danced with the nadders, coiled and writhed and kissed . . .

No sooner than it was done he leapt up and ran away. Ashamed and angry too, Mildryth clutched her smock to her naked breast and yelled after him, 'Art frightened old Goatbeard will find out?' But he ran away and left her.

When Til came pelting red-faced across the meadow alone, and a dishevelled Mildryth followed soon after, the housecarls nudged and whispered amongst themselves. Neither the youth nor the girl spoke a word to each other on the way home.

Sigurd opened his eyes to see Asketil's flushed cheeks and gave a throaty laugh. 'I wager I can guess what you have been up to.'

The lad's heart leapt. 'I have only been to fetch the dues, that is all.'

'Nay, that is not all.' The wan face turned knowing. 'I can tell you have argued with our Mildryth again. Look at your cheeks, like apples. What has she said to make you so cross?' It was a shame that the youngsters he loved could not get along more peaceably.

Asketil said the first thing that came to his lips. 'She made fun of my beard.' His colour deepened; he had never lied to Sigurd.

'I do not know how she could say ought about that.' Sigurd applied a doddery touch to the fine hair on the youth's chin. ''Tis a grand effort – more than your father ever had. You must take after your mother.' He laughed, then winced. 'Aagh! This confounded wound. Where is Mildryth? 'Tis only she who hath the touch to make it better.' The youth said he did not know. 'Ah, she is a bold lass.' Sigurd warmed to his subject. 'Nought frightens her, not even this tyrant. She treats me like a bairn. Would that I were thirty years younger . . .' Wistful of face, he looked at the youth. 'Til, how old would you say I appear to others?' When Asketil shrugged, he pressed the point. 'What I mean is, would you say I was still comely to a woman's eye?'

The reply was obtuse. Til's mind was far away and his heart still pounded. 'I am not a woman so I cannot know.'

'Damn it, lad! I expect you to boost my confidence – it is Mildryth of whom I speak. If I hold my question for a few years until she is fifteen or so, doest think there is more chance of her accepting me?'

'Accepting you as a father?'

'You are looking for a tanned hide! Nay, I mean as a husband, man! Do not tell me you cannot see how I feel about her. I am sure it is evident to all.'

Asketil could not speak for renewed shock.

Sigurd misinterpreted the reason. 'Oh, I know you think I am an old lecher – but I prize her virtue most highly. I would never use her in that way, but would honour her as my wife. Come, she is like your sister – she must have told you of her feelings. Does she speak kindly of me?'

Asketil blushed to his hair-roots, unable to rid himself of the vision of the writhing snakes and the one between his legs that threatened to dance whenever he thought of her. Just when his heart had begun to calm, now it raced anew. He stammered a reply. 'She never says ought like that to me, *fostri*. I am not given leave to her thoughts. You must ask another wench. Rest now, *fostri*, I will leave you and return later when I have done my chores.' He beat a hasty departure.

*

He tried to avoid her but eventually Mildryth cornered him by the kitchen.

'Why do you run from me?' she entreated.

'I do not run!' He tried to brush past her but when his elbow made contact with her breast he shrank back. ''Tis just with *fostri* laid a-bed I have much more to do.'

'Liar!' She closed on him. ''Tis because of what happened between us.'

He pressed himself into the wall. 'I am most sorry about that, it will not happen again.'

'I want it to!' How blind he is, thought Mildryth.

'Nay! It cannot be.' He tried to unclamp her fingers from his arm.

'Why? I love thee!'

'I enjoin you not to say it!' The tempestuous nature of her lovemaking had scared him; even the touch of her hand was too much to bear. One by one he prised her digits off, one by one she pressed them back.

''Tis true.'

'It cannot be so!' He tried to deflect her attention by pointing at a gander which had broken into the vegetable patch. 'Look! The steg is causing havoc!' When this failed to work he whined like a cur. 'Let me go, Mildryth, I beg you.'

'Not until you say what keeps you from admitting your love for me – yea! You do love me, I know it.'

Unable to deny it to her face and totally frustrated, he pushed her. She fell but as he made to stride over her she grabbed his calf and held on.

'Mildryth!' In his efforts to be free he dragged her with him.

'Tell me!' When he still tried to escape she bit his leg.

'Aagh! Very well, it is because of *fostri*!'

She removed her teeth but still clung on. 'Because he hates all women, you mean?'

'Because he loves you and wants you for his wife.'

Stunned, she released his leg and turned her astonished face up to question.

Now that all was revealed Asketil delayed his escape. When she was too amazed to utter a word he gave a snort and nodded. 'Yea, I too was shocked. To the rest of the world he may regard you as a daughter but in truth he wants more than that. When you gain a few years he intends to ask you to wed him.'

Mildryth began to laugh.

'Cease!' Asketil told her, but she was helpless to stop, falling on to her side and giggling uncontrollably. 'Mildryth, have done!'

She could barely reply for laughing. 'Well, what else wouldst you expect when you tell me such a joke. The old tup!'

'You will not mock him!' Asketil hauled her to her feet. 'He is besmitten with you.'

Her laughter turned to defiance. 'As besmitten as you are?'

'Yea! Nay!' He reddened and let her go. 'I mean . . . Stop trying to trick me!'

An impulsive Mildryth embraced him. 'You can deny it all you please but I know.'

'Even if it were true, it cannot be!' Asketil tried to push her off. The merest proximity made him go hard and her mischievous smile told that she knew it. 'Lord Sigurd wants you as his wife and . . .'

'He will never have me! Think you I would choose to wed an old goat such as he when I have a handsome lad like you?'

'You do not have me! *Cannot* have me. I will never betray him.'

'But you have already.' Her eyes reminded him of this afternoon's lust.

'I did not mean it! You must never tell. It will break his heart. He thinks you chaste.'

485

She found his attitude incomprehensible. 'Why did you not tell him of our love when he broached the subject?'

'Mildryth, for the last time there can be no love between us! Much as I might want you – yea, you are right, it is useless to deny it, but I will not go against the man who has given me everything. Henceforth I shall revert to calling you sister.'

The girl became quieter, but just as resolute. 'There is no turning back, Til. You took my maidenhead and my heart. Lord Sigurd can yearn all he likes but they cannot be given again.'

He stared, desperate to kiss her. When she made the decision for him he returned her embrace with zeal, but then the intensity of her passion made him afraid and he pulled away, his lips still tingling from her assault. 'In Christ, I love thee dearly! But that must be the last time.'

Chapter Nineteen

Til kept his vow. After wrenching himself from her that day he never swayed from his determination, however much she might provoke him – and provoke him she did in the most diabolical method; not a day went by without some trick or other. He dared not take his eyes off her for fear what she would do next.

Mildryth took comfort in the fact that he was forever watching her – even today when he worked outside and she in here by the window. Oh, he pretended not to be but he was a bad actor. What could she frighten him with this afternoon? Her ingenuity and patience were beginning to run out. Why not just leave and be done with him, she asked herself. Because just as he could not take his eyes off her, she could not leave whilst there was a chance that he might change his mind.

As she paused in her embroidery to gaze through the window, a leper slumped outside the church that Earl Siward had raised in the burh to St Olaf. For a moment she did not notice him, still thinking of new ways to infuriate Til. When her eyes did focus on the unfortunate man she felt a surge of pity and wandered outside to exchange a few kind words. Never once was there thought for her own health. Mildryth regarded herself as invincible – besides, her mother had given succour to many such wretches in the past and had not been infected. Mildryth reckoned it was safe enough if one did not actually touch the infected person and could not understand how others could be so uncharitable towards them. However, by the time she reached the man her intentions were not wholly honourable. A grin tweaked her lips at the image of Til's reaction but she hid it as she bent and spoke to the leper.

Only half-involved with his arrow-making, Til watched in revulsion at the contrast between the pretty face and the disfigured one, but the revulsion was soon overwhelmed by surprise as Mildryth urged the ragged fellow to his feet and guided him into the compound. It was time to intervene; he threw down his implements and blocked her path before she arrived. Undeterred, Mildryth bade the leper, 'Wait a while, I shall fetch you drink,' and calmly proceeded to milk a goat which had recently given birth. The colostrum had been meant to aid the bed-ridden Sigurd's recovery, as Til excitedly pointed out.

'What am I to tell *fostri*?'

'Pooh! Tell him the goatsucker came in the night.' Mildryth removed the wooden bowl from beneath the teat and was about to offer it to the leper when the mischief in her eye intensified. 'Come where it is warmer, there is a breath of winter still left in the air.'

'You cannot take him in there!' but Til was forced to step aside as the leper threatened to brush against him. He gave a horrified look at his arm as though it were contaminated, then shadowed the pair inside.

'Sit you down.' Mildryth guided the leper to a bench by the hearth and sat by him. All other occupants gawped, then moved swiftly out of the house. Til gasped an oath, but was to be even further offended when Mildryth reached for Sigurd's personal goblet and pretended to give it to the leper.

She laughed and kicked up her legs with sheer glee at his cry of horror and instead left the leper's refreshments in the wooden bowl. Til remained to guard Sigurd's possessions against further outrage and when the miserable beggar eventually shuffled on his way some half an hour later with a bundle of victuals, he was furious with Mildryth. She seemed not in the least concerned, indeed she appeared to gloat at having distressed him to such a pitch.

'How could you use that poor wretch in your schemes against me?' His face was red from suppressed anger. It was all he could do to prevent himself shouting and waking the invalid.

Scorn was added to Mildryth's gleeful air. 'I did not hear him complaining! In fact he was delighted with my hospitality.'

'Nevertheless, you used him! And to fetch him into this house when *fostri* is already in his sickbed . . .'

'Lord Sigurd will not catch it through the walls, fool! 'Twas only in jest that I gave him Sigurd's cup, it never went anywhere near his lips. I did nought wrong but feed a poor leper whom no one else cares for.'

'Lies! You do not care for him, you only brought him in here because you knew it would anger me. To be so cruel in your sport . . .'

Mildryth's amusement was growing thin. 'If you care for him so deeply then why did you not offer succour?' She gave a curt nod at his blushing response. 'Do not lecture me, Til, for you are no saint yourself. Your anger is not for that man's sake but your own. You want me, but instead of being a man you prefer to act the martyr.'

Asketil dug his chin into his neck, nostrils flared. 'You think it merely acting that I refuse to go against my father? Well, you can tease and wheedle and damn me as a martyr as much as you like, I will never betray my *fostri*'s trust!'

And this continued to be his valiant reply whenever she played her tricks – which continued despite all objections. How could she purport to love him and make his life such a misery? Finally, he decided it was time to get his own back. Though not inherently devious he had a creative mind and a few moments was all it took to produce a trick that would stop her cruelty once and for all. It required meticulous arrangement to achieve its potential, but the very thought of it made Til chuckle to himself. Mildryth was greatly enamoured of the horse, Toki, that Sigurd had given her, but was irresponsible in her ownership. One evening when she left it tethered on the riverbank instead of fetching it into the yard, Til had his chance.

The next morning Mildryth was roused to consciousness by the worried youth. 'Did you leave Toki by the river last night?'

She rubbed her eyes. 'Oh . . . yes, I forgot . . .'

'Then come with me!' Til kept his voice low so as not to waken Sigurd. 'There has been a terrible mishap.' When the pair hurried outside Mildryth could see nothing, and Til pointed at the river. 'There!'

Mildryth, still half-asleep, could just make out a pair of horse's ears sticking out of the water.

Asketil tried to keep a straight face. 'It was a high tide last night. The horse must have been unable to free himself from the tether. What a terrible thing to happen . . .' He waited expectantly.

But Mildryth did not react. There was no scream, no frantic running about as he had assumed. She did not even raise a hand to cover her mouth, just stared at the river, her protuberant eyes filling with tears that spilled over to run down her cheeks.

Asketil felt dreadful. This was not the way he had imagined it at all! He chewed the inside of his cheek, watching her silent misery until he could bear it no longer. 'I am sorry! It is not your horse. I was just taking revenge for the tricks you played on me! It was silly and cruel and I feel wretched – look!' He left her and waded into the brown river until he was up to his chest.

'Have care!' came the nasal shout from Mildryth. 'You cannot swim!'

Asketil felt so mean that at this moment he did not care if he were swept away. However, he managed to keep his footing as he tugged at the ears – which were attached to poles in the mud – and waded back to her. 'Look, it was a trick!' Sopping, he brandished the ears before her. 'Your horse is safe in the laithe where he has been all night. These belong to one who was butchered – it took me an age to find the right colour!'

Angry now, she snatched the poles off him, threw them at the ground and stamped on them. 'I will never forgive you for this! You know how much I love my Toki.'

'And you know how much I love my *fostri* but it does not stop you playing your nasty tricks!' Asketil felt justifiable anger now. Why should she make him feel so rotten when she had dealt many more cruelties to him? 'You cannot take your own treatment!'

Pondering on this, Mildryth swallowed, then accepted what he had said. But her next words came as a shock. 'Very well. You have made it clear that you will not return my love. There is nought else for me to do but go back to my parents.'

Asketil panicked. 'You cannot! It will break *fostri*'s heart. Stay, I beg you.'

Her response was sardonic. 'For your sake or his?'

Asketil hung his head. Unsure of the answer, he posed another question; 'Will you forgive my trick, and promise not to inflict any more on me?' She nodded, not wholly convincing. 'Then I would like you to stay,' he told her.

Mildryth blew her nose and abandoned empty threats. 'So be it, I will remain,' she murmured, drawing a smile of relief. 'But only in the hope that the old man shall soon be dead and then you will be free to love me.'

Til's voice was agonized. 'Oh, never say that! He is my father, I love him.'

'Love him or nay,' replied Mildryth, 'he will die like we all have to die and on that day you will come to me.'

Unaware that Asketil shared his longing, Sigurd urged his belly to heal and allow him to begin his courtship as a man should. There came echoes of his wooing of Una all those years ago; the giving of gifts, the intense longing to hold her, the burning, the shuddering at her nearness . . . only one aspect differed: Una had known exactly what she was doing to him, but this child, this innocent, how could she know that just by lowering her lashes she caused untold torment? When he confided this to Asketil the youth blushed, partly from anger. Did *fostri* never consider that Mildryth could be attractive to another? Could he not see that Til was a man with appetites of his own? Apparently not. To Sigurd he was still a boy; it was infuriating.

'Ah, I have embarrassed the lad with my intimate talk.' Sigurd reached from the bed to place a fatherly hand on Asketil's knee, then leaned back on his pillow, his face showing that the movement had caused discomfort. 'I should not speak of your sister in this manner . . . 'tis just that I have no one else to whom I can open my heart, and I must share the feeling or I shall go mad. You have no inkling of what it is like to want a woman like this – though breathe not a word of it to Mildryth, I would not have her innocence sullied.' The invalid's face creased with a pain that was deeper than his wound. 'But oh, I could scream my love out loud whenever she enters the room. Er, Til, fetch me yon piece of chestnut! I have been lying a-bed too long and my fingers are itching for work.'

Asketil frowned at the incongruity of the request, but on turning saw Mildryth coming up the staircase. Ever the dutiful son, he brought the lump of wood and a knife to Sigurd then sat down again to watch Mildryth's antics. Again he marvelled at the old man's blindness. How could *fostri* believe her chaste? Just look at the brazen little puss making lewd actions whilst Sigurd's eyes were on his whittling. Yet whenever *fostri* chanced to look up at her there she was, chastity personified.

'You promised you would cease all your tricks and be decent!' he scolded later on following her downstairs. 'I have a mind to tell my lord that you are not all you appear to be.'

'But you dare not, for you are afraid of him,' she taunted.

'Not afraid! 'Tis because I love him that I protect him.'

Mildryth turned thoughtful, finger on chin, the most provocative sparkle in her eye. 'I have been giving this matter much thought. Mayhap I will do as he wants and wed him. It might be amusing to hear you call me Lady Mildryth and bow to my every whim.'

'I shall call you nought but strumpet! You tease him with your body and he cannot see it because he is too blind with love for you.'

'Blind with lust, you mean! How can an old goat make to wed a young maid? 'Tis unnatural.'

'You encourage him!'

'It amuses me.' Mildryth thrived on Til's display – at least it showed he cared.

'You should not treat him so when he loves you!'

'You treat me cruel when I love thee,' she retorted.

'It is not the same!'

'Why? You have admitted that you love me.'

'Because . . . because even if I do love you, I have done everything I can to discourage you.'

Her face held a pained kind of scorn. 'And that is not cruel enough?'

'Mildryth, you know that I have not a cruel bone in my body. Nay, do not bring up that business with the horse, you know it was only an attempt to make you see how I felt when you tormented me . . . and much good it did. I have told you a hundred times over why I cannot give in to your love. If you are hurt then I am hurt, too. Please, I beg you, do not make matters worse than they are already.'

She twirled decisively. 'I shall confront the old goat!'

'Nay! Please say nought for if he knows that I love you he will sacrifice his ambition to wed you, and if I were responsible for that I would die. After what he has suffered in the past he deserves a little happiness.'

Temper was brewing in her immature breast. 'You call it a little happiness when he would use me like . . .'

'Not *use* you! *Love* you. Now, cease this talk forever.' Til feigned an airiness of manner. 'If you utter one word to Lord Sigurd it will do you no good, for if you hurt him I will never talk to you again.' He stalked away.

Mildryth gritted her teeth, wanting to throw something at his retreating back, but not daring to call his bluff, for unwelcome though his words might be they were better than no words at all.

'Doest argue again?'

The girl spun, her face red from the duologue. Sigurd, frustrated at being the invalid – and wanting to be near Mildryth – had limped from his bed to imbibe fresh air, luckily too late to catch any word of the argument but able to tell even from a distance that it had been a hot exchange. 'What was the cause this time?'

Mildryth, fighting tears of anger, wanted to shout

– 'twas about thee as usual, old tup! Instead, she pretended to be wrenching weeds from a clump of herbs and mumbled, ''Twas nought to bother a sick man, just Til and his boyish ways.'

Sigurd leaned on his staff, incapable of bringing himself upright due to the abdominal wound, in this pose even more aware of the difference in their ages. Lately he had noted an alteration in her attitude towards him. She was not so light-hearted. Maybe it was because she had attained womanhood and thought she had to act the part, but he could not help feeling that she was still cross with him over his accusation that she was responsible for Murtagh's treachery. He was desperate to kiss the frown from her brow and tell her of his passion, but how could he, bent over like a cripple? *Heal, damn thee, heal!*

Time was of the essence to one who had become acutely conscious that the years were slipping away. The fact that he had lived to a ripe age made him one of an exclusive clan but he denied membership, for inside he felt like a youth again whenever he looked at her. One difference: the young Sigurd had never feared death – apart from all those years ago when Ulf's sword had pricked his throat; now he feared it, terrified it would claim him before he had the chance to make Mildryth his wife.

However, death was to claim another first. Before Sigurd was back on his feet, a messenger brought word from the south which Asketil in turn relayed to his foster-father. 'Earl Godwin is dead!'

Sigurd, bored from his inactivity, was interested only enough to ask, 'Who is King now?'

Asketil frowned, thinking the injury had affected Sigurd's brain. 'It is not the King who is dead, but Earl Godwin.'

'I heard you the first time.' Sigurd looked wry. 'And I ask who rules now – you do not think Edward is King of England, do you? Godwin has been monarch for years in all but the crown.'

Asketil nodded his understanding, then digressed for a moment. 'Does the King have sons?'

'Nay! He is too holy to get children.' It was a public joke that Edward's marriage was unconsummated. 'Besides, he would not even know where to put it – so, tell me, who rules now?'

Asketil returned to the pertinent topic. 'Naturally, Earl Godwin has bequeathed his title to his eldest son Harold.'

'Eldest or no, I am surprised that Edward did not arrange for Tostig to have the title. He has always been the King's favourite and Edward could do with a friend in that earldom. Harold is too much like his father to suit the King.' The old man looked sour. 'So . . . Godwin is dead at last. Would that it were news of Murtagh's death that you bring me. Has nought been heard of him?'

Asketil looked blank. 'Not one sighting, my lord. The search goes on but I think he must surely have drowned.'

'If he is ever brought to justice,' growled Sigurd, 'he will find that drowning is too merciful a death.'

Murtagh had known that he was going to drown for some time now. His little boat and paddle had been adequate for the Use but once into the wide yawn of the Humbre the current had taken control and it was all he could do to hang on, let alone steer the boat where he wanted to go. Now in the North Sea waves it was tossed about like a nutshell and it would not be long before it was swamped altogether. He had known all along, of course, that this would happen; it had been a futile hope that he could reach Ireland in his botched craft. But he had been forced to make the attempt or die in Jorvik for his murder of Lord Sigurd.

496

His oar gone, he clung to the sides of the boat, reliving that wonderful moment when he had plunged the knife in, his flight from Jorvik, the following days when he had not eaten nor slept nor even set foot on dry land for fear of being arrested. Even now he could scarcely believe that he had come this far. Well, his boat might be sinking but his mind could sail on. From listening to conversations he knew the route to Ireland like the back of his hand; he went there now.

Another wave swamped the boat. Murtagh had only a pair of desperate hands to scoop it back into the writhing sea. His actions became frantic as more and more water poured into the boat. His hands could not cope with it. This was the moment he had dreaded; the water was coming in faster than he could bale, the boat was tilting . . . 'Do not be afraid to die!' he heard his aunt and mother say. 'The tyrant is dead, you have avenged us; that is all that matters.' But Murtagh *was* afraid to die. In previous imagination the moment of death had always been a noble thing but now, as his boat sank under him and he was up to his neck in water, he discovered that it was not noble at all, it was terrifying and cold and inglorious. He did not want to be noble, he wanted to live.

Ice-cold waves lashed his face and swamped his mouth with brine. He spat and began to tread water, moving in a circle, looking frantically for the shore-line. He had planned to row close to the land on his journey up the east coast but the tide had thought otherwise. It was a long way to swim, but he had no choice and struck out for the land. I will not die! *You will*, said another more confident voice. No, no, no! He swam for all he was worth but the land got further away. He was being carried out to sea! Panic rose in his breast. God, help me! came his mental cry. His arms began to thrash without effect until he was utterly exhausted and had to give up. Wave after wave washed over his head, diluting his strength, implanting futility. All at once he became light-headed. The fear had left him. He watched the document that vouched his freedom drift out of the neck of his shirt and away on the swell, and he did not care. He was no longer afraid to die, welcomed the waves that closed over his head . . .

'Got him!'

Half-conscious, Murtagh barely felt himself plucked from death and the sea pummelled from his lungs. He came round on a bout of violent retching, heaved on to the slippery planking of a ship's deck, then turned on his back to look up at his rescuers . . . or may be they were his executioners. Eyes wary, he studied the circle of faces. Did they know who he was? Would they take him back to Jorvik?

'Ach!' One of them had seen his crooked eye. 'Look what bad luck we have brought on board. Let us throw him back, master!'

'Do not be so superstitious, Emain.' The man who had dragged Murtagh from the waves laughed and pulled him to his feet. 'Now, my friend, it is an odd place to choose for a swim! The current is treacherous round this point. How come we find you here?'

A thrill of recognition stung Murtagh's breast. The man addressed him not in Norse but in the language spoken by his Aunt Mary and his mother! The agony of his retching stomach was forgotten. Excitedly, he pointed at his mouth and shook his head to indicate that he was mute.

'Ah, you cannot speak.' The Irish merchant nodded, whilst his crew remained suspicious. 'But you hear what I say, I think?'

Murtagh nodded back, excited yet still nervous.

'There is little use in asking you what happened,' said the man, as one of his shipmates brought a cloak

498

to wrap around the dripping Murtagh. 'We came around the point to see you floundering in the waves. You must have fallen from a boat?'

A grateful Murtagh pulled the cloak around him and nodded.

'So you are a local fisherman, then?'

Murtagh shook his head.

The man grew tired. 'Look, I have no time to stand here guessing. My name is Diarmaid. I and my men are on our way back to Erin, but we could take you into the shore if . . .'

Murtagh shook his wet head more positively.

'You wish to come with us?' At the affirmative nod the man laughed. 'Oh, would that I were privy to your reasons!' A troubled look came to his eye and he voiced it. 'Hey, you are not an escaped slave, are you?'

Murtagh shook his head and was about to reach into his shirt when he remembered with a lurch that the manuscript had gone. At the other's mercy, he could only try to meet Diarmaid's eye, shake his head and hope that he looked convincing.

'As if you would tell me if you were,' responded the man, looking at Murtagh more closely. Murtagh shook his head again and crossed his heart.

'Then I can think of only one other reason why you would not wish to return to your home.' His inquisitor was grim. Murtagh's sore belly tensed again.

'You have an ugly wife!' Diarmaid uttered a high-pitched giggle and slapped Murtagh on the back. 'Come! We must delay no more. If you are to sail with us you must pull your weight.'

And Murtagh hurried to assist in any way he could, still unable to believe his luck whilst the rest of the crew grumbled over their bad fortune; the ship was bound to sink, they would never reach Ireland.

But, a few weeks later, reach it they did and, as if setting foot on that blessed soil was not enough, there was more luck in store for Murtagh.

'What will you do now?' asked the merchant as his crew unloaded the goods they had bartered in Jorvik, Murtagh assisting. When Murtagh shrugged and looked vague, Diarmaid added, 'However you choose to make your living you should do well. I am much impressed by your industry.' Murtagh nodded thanks, not only for the compliment but for his life. He could not convey this but the man seemed to understand the look in his eyes and extended his hand in friendship. 'No, I really mean it. I have never seen a man work so hard. Would you care to work for me?' Murtagh's crooked eyes lit up. He gasped his disbelief then nodded rapidly.

'Do not be so grateful,' joked another member of the crew who had, during their weeks at sea, come to like Murtagh. 'He does not pay very well.'

Grinning at the jest Diarmaid cuffed him. 'I pay well to those who earn it! There is one thing certain, I would never have to worry about him wasting my time chattering like someone else I could mention.' He turned back to Murtagh. 'You can start right now and can rest your head at my home until you are able to build a house of your own.'

A house of his own! It seemed like only yesterday that Murtagh had been thankful to escape with his life, now there were all sorts of opportunities opening up for him. At the age of thirty-four when life for some was over, life for Murtagh O' Cellaigh had just begun.

By the following summer, Sigurd had to accept that Murtagh would never be brought to justice and that he was most probably dead. Mind preoccupied with Mildryth, the ealdorman's thirst for vengeance began to dwindle and in the event of the latest news he forgot about the slave altogether. Earl Siward's eldest son was killed in battle with Macbeth. The other son was too young to rule if his father died and at long last Sigurd was given the hope that he was close to achieving the earldom for which he had hungered so long. With this in mind he enthused to Asketil, 'The time is nigh to ask Mildryth to be my wife! She would surely not refuse the chance to wed an earl. Where is the lovely lass? I can wait no more.'

Asketil felt a sudden attack of nausea. The moment he had been dreading had arrived but he had never truly envisaged just how dreadful he would feel on having to watch Mildryth betrothed to another. All through the winter he had suffered a kind of purgatory, being shut up in the house with her, praying for the spring when the weather would allow him to get out more and so avoid her . . . yet when spring had come and he was able to escape he felt such an intense emptiness that he did not know which was worse. So well did he hide this that no one knew of it except himself. Just how long he could continue was impossible to tell, for inside he grew sicker and sicker with the wanting of her. A voice broke into his thoughts and he jumped. 'What did you say, *fostri*?'

Sigurd clicked his tongue. 'I do not know what ails you these days! You walk about as if in a dream. I asked after Mildryth's whereabouts.'

Faced with her name, Asketil's reply was tart. 'How would I know? I have been listening to you for the last hour.'

Sigurd's hackles rose. 'Is it such a chore, then?'

'Nay, I did not mean that!' Til was often short with his mentor nowadays, angry both at Sigurd for robbing him of Mildryth and at himself for being so weak in not speaking out. 'Do you wish me to go fetch her?'

'It is obvious from your tone that it will be an irksome task!' retorted Sigurd.

'For the sake of Our Lord do you want her or not!' Asketil closed his eyes, prayed for patience then shook his head. 'Nay . . . I beg pardon, *fostri*.'

'Til,' Sigurd dropped the hostility and looked worried. 'What ails thee, lad? You have been showing these bouts of temper for months now.' Receiving no explanation he tried to work it out for himself. 'Doest think that I am wrong in asking to wed Mildryth because she is not yet fifteen and I am more than fifty? Or is it that you imagine she is placed more highly than yourself in my affections?' If so, then strike that from your mind.'

'It is not that,' cut in Til.

'You like her, do you not? I know you quarrel but all brothers and sisters do that and you seem to look warmly upon . . . upon her.' *Oh you dolt!* He cursed himself. *You blind fool!* In that moment of panic, he completely forgot where he was and what he had been talking of. On recovery, his heart gave urgent warning – *say nought! If it is not said it cannot be true.*

Asketil noted the stumble and looked at his foster-father. There was an expression in those eyes that he could not fathom, but as quickly as it appeared it was gone and Sigurd was covering his tracks.

'I think I know what worries thee. You fear that if Mildryth and I have sons they will come before you.' He gripped Asketil's shoulders, conveying sincerity into the youngster's eyes. 'It shall never happen. None shall come before my beloved Til who shall be my heir. I promise you here and now, it shall be written down for all to see.'

Til searched that expression, imagined those whiskery old lips kissing Mildryth, was on the verge of telling him . . . but how could he throw such a gesture of commitment back in Sigurd's face? The opportunity to confess had gone. He nodded his gratitude for the honour bestowed. 'I will try to rule as well as you have done, *fostri*.'

Sigurd heaved a private sigh of relief. 'I have every faith in you, my son – now come help me look for my bride.'

With Mildryth nowhere in sight they divided, the easier to find her. Asketil felt as if his head was about to burst open. *You must confess!* Nay, I cannot bring such hurt upon him. The pain will go away, it will. *Never,* said his heart. *Never, never.*

Sigurd found her, treading clothes in a tub, and was reproachful. 'Have I not said before, you ought not to be wasting yourself on menial tasks such as this!'

Mildryth disregarded his opinion and continued to slosh up and down in the tub. 'I like to earn my keep.' She was cool but not unpleasant.

'A lady hath no need to earn her keep.'

'I am not a lady.'

'Would you like to be?' Sigurd's heartbeat increased.

She held him with a bland expression as if she had no idea of his meaning. 'Fine chance there will be of that.'

'There could be.' His pulse raced even quicker. Now that the moment had come there was the fear of being rejected. Feeling like a youth beneath that violet stare he changed his mind – what a coward! 'Instead of treading clothes those pretty limbs should be more suitably employed . . .'

Like being wrapped around you, thought Mildryth. Did he think she was stupid that she could not guess the reason behind all the gifts? The oaken chest, the fine woollen clothes, the jewels.

'Come cheer me with a dance,' he coaxed.

'There is no music,' the girl pointed out, though she stopped marching up and down.

'That can soon be remedied. Til!' Sigurd looked

around, called again and spotted the youth. 'Fetch your pipes – Mildryth is to dance for us.'

Leaving neither with any option, Sigurd planted himself in the sunshine and waited to be entertained. A trail of wet footprints marked Mildryth's path to the dance area. Legs still bare, she poised waiting for Til to begin his tune, but when the music flowed she did not do it justice. Instead, she limped about in a most ungainly fashion, pretending that one leg was shorter than the other, then she mimicked the antics of a monkey, danced knock-kneed, bow-legged, jutted her neck like a chicken . . . Sigurd broke into laughter. The more she cavorted the louder he chuckled. Asketil tried not to show amusement – it was a gross insult upon his music – but he failed and was soon unable to blow into his pipes for laughing.

A teary-eyed Sigurd rebuked the girl. 'Yea, you spoke truly when you said there was fine chance of you being a lady, Mildryth! Enough of your teasing. Give us a proper dance.'

The haunting pipes gave voice again. This time Mildryth's interpretation of the music was more fitting. Enraptured by the graceful twirl of her limbs, Asketil closed his mind to his surroundings, forgetting Sigurd, forgetting everything except that lovely girl. Unable to consummate his passion in the flesh he made love to her through his music and she perceived it, returning his caresses in her dance.

There was no doubt in Sigurd's mind now. How flagrantly they coupled before his eyes and he was powerless to prevent it. *No, no, no,* his mind roared. *I love thee, Til, but I will not let this happen. She is mine.*

Both furious and enthralled, he could not take his eyes off her wraithe-like figure. Finally, able to bear it no longer he clapped his hands and shouted, 'Cease!' When music and dance came to a rude halt he addressed Mildryth. 'Your legs shall be dropping off, girl! Come sit here with me, I have something to say to thee – you too, Til.'

A breathless Mildryth joined the two men. Sigurd did not waste time – *could* not waste time. 'You know that the Earl has no suitable heir, Mildryth, and that I shall most likely inherit the title. Wouldst it pleasure thee to be the Earl's lady?'

Mildryth did not bat an eyelid, just gave a sideways glance at Til who was looking at his feet. 'You have said yourself I am no lady.'

The old man was firm. 'A mere jest – forget it. I ask you to be my wife, Mildryth.' The way she looked at Til for advice irked her suitor. 'I offer you a fortune – surely you do not need to think so hard. Perhaps my heir can persuade thee. Til, instruct your sister that I shall be a good loving husband. She shall want for nought.'

Nought save love, thought Mildryth. Speak up, she urged Til, tell him we adore each other.

But Til had no word of comfort. 'You should be grateful for such an honour, sister – as I am for the one which *fostri* has laid upon me.'

Her violet eyes bored into his, forcing him to look away. He does not mean it, she told herself. If you can hold on long enough the old man shall die and Til will be yours. Perhaps Sigurd would die before the Earl, both were old men. She could only pray that it would be so, but until then Sigurd must be fended off and the only way to keep both him and Asketil content was to make a promise. 'If you become Earl then I will wed you,' she announced.

Asketil wanted to vomit.

Sigurd's joy was tempered by the tone of her reply; it was as if she were saying only if he were Earl would she wed him. Nay, you are making difficulties where none occur, he told himself. The earldom is bound to be yours and so is Mildryth. A feeling of triumph filled his breast. 'I am greatly honoured, my dear! You will have a wedding feast such as no woman has had before – but one thing I must make clear and you are at liberty to withdraw your consent if it does not meet with your agreement, though I pray that you will not.' He gave a warm smile of entreaty. 'I have sworn that Asketil shall be my heir above all others; even if you and I have sons that shall still be so.'

'Til shall be your heir come what may,' came the soft confirmation. And if I have ought to do with it, thought Mildryth, he shall also be my husband.

Sigurd might have chosen his heir but the English people had not; they needed to ensure that the child-less Edward would not appoint a Norman as the next King of England and so the Bishop of Worcestor was sent abroad to look for survivors of Ethelred's line who had been exiled when Cnut came to power. He found such a one and brought him back to England, but barely had his feet touched land than he died, leaving the witan in a quandary.

However, the present King was as yet hale and England was relatively peaceful at the moment, there was no urgency to find an heir. Besides, mayhap they had already found one and did not know it; Edward had become increasingly glad to leave politics to Harold Godwinsson who was proving himself to be an even greater leader than his father.

In 1055 the old warrior Siward finally died, allow-ing the mantle of Earl to fall on to waiting shoulders. 'It has happened!' a jubilant Sigurd announced to Til, though the young man had already heard. 'My great-est ambition is achieved – the earldom is mine! And not only this, Til!' Excited as a child he grabbed the young man's arms and shook him with glee. 'I have Mildryth, too!' Unable to believe his luck he slapped a hand to his face. 'Oh, there are so many things to plan! What should I do first?'

Asketil was subdued. 'Perhaps it might be a kind gesture to offer your sympathies to Earl Siward's boy.'

'Why, naturally! I shall take the lad under my wing and treat him as if he were my own.' Sigurd pinched his chin and tried to look sombre. 'I must offer to arrange the funeral, too – though I would much rather be arranging a wedding! By the by, where is Mildryth? Has she heard the good news?'

'I think perhaps she has.' Asketil had been with her when they had heard the news. From the look on her face it had obviously been as big a shock to her as it had to him and when he had said he must go and see his foster-father she had made an excuse to rush off.

'Good!' Sigurd rubbed his hands. 'Well, Til, can you summon my thegns Rorik, Thorgerd, er . . . Edgar and Helgi. I must waste no time in arranging the funeral.'

Asketil obeyed.

Mildryth, hiding in the stable with her horse Toki, had more important things on her mind than a funeral. The old Earl's death-knell heralded her own wedding. 'Oh, how could I be so stupid as to promise to be his wife, Toki?' She rested her chin on the horse's withers. 'It was only an excuse to make Asketil jealous. I was sure that he would eventually give in to his feelings . . . but he has never wavered.' Just the thought of him brought tears to her eyes. He was friendly, loving – as a brother – he talked with her, played music for her, worked alongside her, and remained totally loyal to Sigurd.

She sighed and raised her wan face from the horse's shoulder. 'Oh well, I cannot stay hidden in here forever.' She had been here for a good hour or more. 'I should spend what time I have left with the man I love.' Patting the horse, she went into the sunlight.

The first thing she heard was the lyrical call of Til's

pan-pipes and, shading her eyes, she glimpsed him beneath the spread of an ancient chestnut. After doing his lord's bidding he had excused himself from the funeral arrangements and come out here to be alone in his melancholy and to lose himself in his music. Wandering over, Mildryth perched upon one of the massive branches that swept the ground. Un-acknowledged, she said nothing but watched him play. The sight of him made her want to cry again. Two years ago there had been little difference be-tween their heights but now at seventeen Til had grown a good six inches taller, his beard was more dense and the hands that held the pipes were those of a man used to hard work. The winter-brown of his hair was highlighted by the sun and tied back with a headband that Mildryth had woven for him. She watched his bearded lips kiss the pipes, his eyes closed, oblivious to her presence. The enjoyment of hearing him play was spoilt by an acute loneliness. She had the urge to cough and interrupt his flow, which she did with great exaggeration.

Til opened his eyes and stopped playing. A shadow crossed his face when he saw it was her. 'Hail, Mil-dew, I thought I was alone.'

'So did I.'

Her response was too cryptic for him to grasp, but before he could be enlightened a group of horsemen rode through the gates. Curious, Asketil pushed him-self from the tree and came out of its shade to investigate, Mildryth in tow. Strangers were always welcome for the news they brought. It transpired that the arrivals rode in advance of their master, Tostig Godwinsson – the new Earl of Northumbria.

At the proclamation, Mildryth could not help a gasp of relief and her whole deportment changed. I do not have to marry him, sang her heart! The bargain was that when he was Earl he would make me his lady – and he is not Earl! She wanted to hug

Til, but the expression on his face as he spun on her was totally different.

'God in heaven! Who will tell Lord Sigurd?'

'Not I!' Mildryth gave a cautious laugh and backed away, both of them envisaging the rage that the news would invoke, though nothing could mar her wonderful feeling of relief.

Til felt desperately sorry for his father. 'Oh, Mildryth, how long he has cherished this earldom and now to have it snatched away . . . he shall never have another chance at his age.'

It was evident from the grim faces of those around him and their rapid departures that none of them was keen to be the harbinger. Til stood resolute and took a deep breath. 'He will accept the news better from me.' Then Mildryth leapt forward in such a manner that made him shy away, demanding crossly, 'What foolery is this?'

The reprieval caused Mildryth to be playful. 'I merely wished to touch your head whilst it is still on those shoulders.'

'Poor jest!' scolded Til and, presenting his back to her, walked towards the house.

Mildryth did not care how rudely he behaved. The news had brought her hope, her only worry being Sigurd's violent reaction towards her loved one.

Sigurd glanced up from the table at which he sat as Asketil crunched his way across the layer of mussel shells and litter that had accumulated from recent meals, smiled welcome, but was soon back to discussing the funeral arrangements with his thegns. 'My Lord.' Asketil brought himself nearer the table. 'There is a herald arrived.'

'From whom?' The query showed only mild interest.

'He rides in advance . . . to announce the coming of the new Earl of Northumbria.'

The atmosphere underwent drastic change. Those who dared quickly removed themselves, on a crackle

509

of shell and a whisper of cloak, from the vicinity of impending wrath.

The room fell silent. Sigurd's only word as he stared at Til was, 'Whom?'

Asketil projected commiseration. 'It is Lord Tostig.'

'Tostig!' It was expectorated like an oath. 'For thirty years his father grabbed the King's favours from my hand and now his whelp does likewise!' Sigurd closed his eyes and leaned on the table. It was obvious why Edward had sent his favourite Godwinsson: so that he would have more control over his hitherto remote northern lands and at the same time take revenge on Sigurd whom he had always resented.

After a tense moment he stood abruptly, making all jump aside, including Asketil. The rage was evident to all and yet it was not unleashed. Sigurd left the room without a word. Asketil gathered his courage and trailed his foster-father to the bathhouse, hesitated a moment, then undressed and joined him in the nebulous interior. Sigurd made no murmur, just perched on the wooden boards looking at his feet, occasionally throwing a ladle of water upon the hot stones that hissed and bubbled like his own constrained fury.

'Tostig,' he uttered at length. 'The one I flattered as a youth to gain his father's alliance. It is most amusing really . . .' But he did not laugh. 'When does he come to take what is mine?'

'I am told he is yet at Tathaceaster, my lord. He will be here on the morrow.' Asketil wrung his hands. Did Sigurd have a violent reception in mind?

Whether he did or no, Asketil was not to hear it. Without lifting his eyes from the floor Sigurd told him bluntly, 'Go now.'

When Asketil was tardy in obeying the order, his father responded with forced patience. 'Go! I have much to think on and your presence distracts me.'

Til went to the door, hesitated and looked back.

'She will not wed me now.' The old man's delivery was so poignant that a lump came to Til's throat. He left the steam-filled room, towelled his body and dressed, his mind in conflict.

An anxious Mildryth was waiting nearby to learn the outcome. 'I heard no anger and feared that he had struck you dead.'

'I worry for him.' Til let his eyes linger on the hands that were clasped to her bosom. 'He just sits there.'

'There will be many would find that a relief,' said his partner, who felt as if she were walking on air.

'I'll wager you are one of them!' Til was peeved that she chose not to share his distress. 'Well, let me tell you that his sadness is not just because his title has been snatched away but that he fears you will refuse to wed him without his earldom.'

Always Lord Sigurd! raged Mildryth, and this drew the urge to hurt. It was the little sting of the wasp which lands, jabs and is off again. 'Why should he think I was only interested in his earldom? He has enough riches already for me.'

Til stared at her. 'You mean, you would wed him without the earldom if he asked?'

'Why should you care one way or another?' Fool! Mildryth damned herself. See what you are getting into.

Til made swift examination of his feelings. No, he warned himself, do not say it. If there is a chance yet for Sigurd you must not spoil it for him because of your own selfish needs. He tried to be convincing and his face took on what he hoped was a beam of pleasure, though it quavered at the edges. 'Of course I care! It will be just the tonic to ease the pain of losing his earldom.'

Mildryth could have screamed at his fanaticism – almost did so. Asketil could not fail to read her contempt and was again tetchy. 'You have me for a fool! You do not mean to wed him at all.'

'A fool? Yea, by God I have never known such a gurt one if thou think for a moment I would wed that old ram even if he were King!' She ran away to cry in private. When her hot tears dried she made a pact with herself. Tonight I will have one last try. If he does not see sense then tomorrow I will go. I will. *I will.*

When Sigurd finally emerged from the bathhouse he spoke few words to anyone for the rest of the day. What a fool the King had made of him by making Tostig Earl – and what a fool he had made of himself! Luckily everyone was keeping out of his way, including Mildryth. Only Asketil his loyal son was there to keep him company that evening. The hall was silent and Sigurd's whisper came like an echo. 'How can I face her, Til?'

Asketil tried to be kind. 'Just because you have been robbed of the earldom does not mean she will refuse to wed you. Why do you not ask her?'

'If I could find her,' came the ironic snort. 'She is avoiding me. Nay, she has already made her mind up.' He drank deeply from his goblet. 'God, I feel so tired and old and stupid!'

'Then go to bed.' Asketil reached out to pat him.

'Nay, I will not be able to sleep with all this on my mind,' grumbled Sigurd. 'And if that is not enough my belly plagues me too.'

Til rose. 'I will fetch you a sleeping draught.' Prone to a legacy of discomfort from Murtagh's knife, this was a remedy Sigurd often employed. 'You will feel much better in the morn.' God grant that *I* will, came the young man's dismal prayer.

Asketil was dreaming. A hundred snakes writhed about his body. One of them came slithering up his chest, its evil eyes fixed on his, its darting tongue heading straight for his own mouth. He yelled and tried to push it away but his arms were encased in coils. The snake raised its head and entered his screaming mouth. He woke, panting, and stared at the moon-dappled roof of Sigurd's chamber where he slept in a bed near to that of his fostri.

Something was wrong. For a moment there was befuddlement . . . then he looked down at his body where the cover had been removed. Mildryth's hair tickled his thigh. Startled, he sat up, knocking her head away and covering his body. 'In God's name, what of my lord!' Terrified that his exclamation had woken Sigurd he craned his neck to peep between the elaborate bed-curtains, but his mentor, courtesy of the herbal draught, slept as if dead. The moon shone so brightly through the window that the room appeared as if candlelit.

Mildryth rested her chin on his belly and deliberately put lewd interpretation on the remark. 'If he would have this he must go elsewhere.'

Asketil tried to wriggle up his bed. 'Have you no shame?'

'Shame?' She wriggled after him, breasts squashing into his ribs. 'To give the man I love what he desires?'

'I have never asked for this!' Once again Asketil's eyes darted at Sigurd's bed.

'Only because you are too prim. Let me show you how it would be if we two were wed.'

The more he squirmed against her the harder he became. 'You will not bring these vile tricks learned from other men and practise them on me! I shall not let you.' Oh do, please do, cried his body!

She released him and kneeled up, her voice stricken. 'I have been with no other man but thee. That which you term vile trick I do for love of Asketil – I have learned it from no one. How could you think it of me?'

'What am I to think?' He laid a protective but

insufficient hand over his groin. 'No other lass acts the way you do. From now on I forbid you to sleep near us. Whatever *fostri* says you must give him some excuse, for if he knew you were such a slut he would not wish to wed thee.'

She thumped him, but kept her voice to an angry whisper. 'Slut indeed I would be if I let that old pezzle within an inch of these lips – fie, I would sooner bite it off!' She tried to dislodge his hand. 'But thy sweet flesh . . .'

'Mildryth!' He put up a half-hearted attempt to stop her, wishing that his body could be as resolute as his mind, but when the struggle ended it was Mildryth who was victor. He let her do as she willed, using the despicable excuse that further objection might wake Sigurd. Never had he felt such ecstasy. Though he bit on his knuckle it was impossible in the end not to cry out. The old man snored on.

Mildryth's self-congratulation was not to last. She may have won the moment but when her flushed and joyous face raised itself to his, he turned his own away, his voice a cold hiss. 'You are the most debased creature on God's earth! To do such a thing when my father is in the room . . . my father who adores you. Well, tonight you have killed any fondness I had for you. I hate you, Mildryth. If you were the most beautiful woman in creation – which you are *not* – I would still refuse to wed you. You are contemptible.'

As his words had emerged so Mildryth's joy had frozen into an agonized grimace. Without a word from either of them, she rose and left the room. Asketil turned and pressed his belly into the mattress, listening to the pad of her bare feet as she fled down the stairs, his mind screaming for her to come back.

Chapter Twenty

In the morning she was gone. Sigurd was the first to miss her, for in his waking hours he had decided not to accept defeat; he would ask her to wed him even without the earldom. 'Why does our little lass not break her fast with us?'

Asketil's flesh crawled. The merest thought of last night was enough to send the blood pumping. 'She must have eaten earlier. What do you intend to do about Lord Tostig, *fostri*? And can I help?'

Sigurd was unusually pragmatic; the draught had granted him a decent night's rest. 'You can help by making copies of the proclamation about Tostig and get a man to deliver them around the shire.' He glanced at Asketil's face. 'You expected me to do more? Nay, there is nought I can do at present. I have grovelled to his father in the past, I shall have to do likewise again and bide my time. Tostig has no idea how to handle northerners; sooner or later one of them will kill him. I must simply ensure that he appoints me as his heir before then.' An ironic chuckle burst from his lips. 'The poor wretch! All that flattery I paid him as a youth has stood me in good stead. He treats me as an old friend on the rare occasions that I see him. Eat up, these herrings are delicious.'

After breakfast Asketil set upon his task with quill and ink whilst Sigurd had a meeting with his thegns. It was not until mid-morning, when the ealdorman plucked up the courage to face Mildryth and sent

515

Asketil to find her, that the young woman's departure was noted. At first it was thought that she had been abducted, for all her belongings plus her horse were left behind. Then Asketil searched the whole area, discovered from a guard that she had walked out of the gates of her own accord, and was left with the onerous task of having to tell Sigurd.

The jilted man displayed panic. 'I do not need to ask why – 'tis because I have lost my earldom! We must find her, tell her it will not be long before I have it in my grasp again. Damn! That usurper Tostig will be here any moment. Oh, Asketil, I feel I am torn in two. I do not know whether to stay and pamper him or run after her.'

Sigurd's discomposure was no less than Asketil's, who now made a move towards the stables. 'I can pursue Mildryth for you.' *For you, liar, for you!*

'Nay!' Sigurd made a decision. 'She is the more important of the two. I must go myself.'

'But Lord Tostig . . .'

'A shite on Godwin's get – you entertain him until I get back. I have more vital things to do than lick the boots of that little snot.' Sigurd shouted for his horse and moved quickly to the door with Asketil in tow.

Mildryth heard the thud of hooves upon the hardened track long before her pursuers came into view and was safely concealed in a thicket by the time they cantered past. Sigurd rode until it was evident that she could not possibly have come this far and with heavy heart ordered the party to double back in case they had missed her. Again Mildryth was forced to hide. This time she had the temerity to peep between the stalks of grass to see if Asketil was amongst the group. His absence hurt most cruelly. When the hoofbeats died away she did not emerge from her hiding place but lay there weeping and forlorn – though no less forlorn than Sigurd and Asketil.

The latter, having temporarily abandoned his scribblings due to lack of concentration, was rehearsing what he would say to Tostig, bowing and muttering to himself. It was all to no effect. When the Earl arrived with his wife on a tide of pomp Asketil, absorbed with daydreams of Mildryth, became tongue-tied and his stately welcome degenerated into nonsense. Tostig, now about thirty years of age and as unattractive a man as he had been a youth, was not impressed by the reception, demanding to know, 'Where is Ealdorman Sigurd?'

An ink-stained Til bowed again, eyes still rather vacant. 'He sends his regrets, my lord. Er . . . um . . . he had urgent business to pursue.'

'And his Earl takes second place, it would appear.' Tostig, after helping his wife down from her horse, whipped off his hat and hung it from his saddle-bow. 'In fact, so highly does he rate my office that he leaves a clod to greet me.'

Asketil, jerked rudely from his preoccupation, reddened with offence. 'My lord, I am second-in-command to the ealdorman!'

'Just get out of my way!' Tostig was dusty and aching from his horse-ride and in no mood to pander to the hurt ego of a seventeen year old. He elbowed Til aside and with his followers went towards the house he had inherited. 'Attend my mare – if you have the wits to manage that! And pay her respect, she is worth more than you!'

Asketil fumed at the discourteous treatment. Grabbing Tostig's hat from the saddle-bow he gouged two holes in it with his knife, rammed it over the mare's ears, bowed low to the animal and at the observers' laughter growled, 'Is that sufficient respect to pay her?' Given a choice he would have ignored the new Earl after this but Sigurd wanted him to be kept sweet and so, loyal to his mentor, he prepared for further insult and went into the Earl's residence.

And all the time he was putting up with Tostig's jibes he wondered whether Sigurd had found her, half of him desperately wanting this to be so, the other half praying he would never suffer the torment of her nearness again.

Why then was he so bitterly disappointed when Sigurd, broken and dejected, returned without her? Why did he instantly offer to abandon his writing and search the places that Sigurd had missed? It was madness; they were both of them better off without her.

Sigurd was of different mind and accepted the offer of help. 'I will gladly excuse you to go and search – but hold, before you go.' His voice held a tired irony. 'How went the meeting with our new Earl?'

'He hath no manners,' answered Til, scrawling a last word on the parchment with his quill.

Sigurd looked sharp. 'Did he insult you?'

'Yea, but I managed to bite my tongue for your sake.'

'Oh, you are a true friend.' The weary man patted him, causing an ink-blot to fall from his quill upon the parchment and ruin the whole thing. Asketil closed his eyes in frustration and gave up writing as Sigurd added, 'I will make it up to you, Til. He will not last long and you will be present to enjoy his downfall. Now, go and find our Mildryth, for I shall not rest until she is safe back here.'

The hunt was fruitless. Asketil visited every place he could think of, to no avail. 'I have searched everywhere,' he told Sigurd days later. 'She is not to be found.'

'Not everywhere,' replied his foster-father. 'We have yet to visit her kin. She will be there, I know it.' And so a northwards expedition was planned.

Sigurd, Asketil and the party of soldiers who were to accompany them were in the process of mounting their horses when one of Tostig's servants approached.

'My lord, the Earl has called a gemot for this afternoon and wishes for you and all your thegns to be present.'

Sigurd groaned, leaned on his saddle and looked across at Asketil. 'I cannot ignore the summons, for who knows what might be decided in my absence. Our trip will have to wait another day.' Dropping the horse's reins he went back towards the house. 'Be so good as to broadcast the message to my thegns, Til, and let us hear what our new Earl has to say.'

Tostig's first comment in the moot hall that afternoon was on the state of the earldom he had inherited. 'My lords, Earl Siward was a great man – in his day – but his skills as a warrior in foreign parts allowed him to overlook the state of law and order in his own domain . . . and he appears to have had little assistance from those under his rule.' He moved his eyes slowly around the assembly of nobles in an obvious rebuke. 'Since my arrival in Jorvik I have heard numerous reports of attacks on travellers by outlaws, yet I can find few records of the offenders being brought to justice. It appears, my lords, that you have been most slipshod. This lawlessness shall not continue. I demand a purge on these vermin. They are to be driven without quarter from their lairs to the gallows. Ealdorman Sigurd, I expect you to act upon this without delay.'

'Very good, my lord.' Sigurd forced himself to bow.

The rest of Tostig's speech was given to his proposals for the betterment of the shire. 'All pure addle!' opined Sigurd to Asketil when both were freed from this monotony an hour later. 'But it will be to our advantage in the long run. Given the rope Tostig will hang himself within two years at most.'

'If he does not hang the whole of Jorvik first,' replied Asketil, preparing to ride in pursuit of outlaws.

'Yea.' Sigurd's deeply-set eyes turned knowing.

'Methinks he will not stop at outlaws, neither. We shall have to have our wits about us, Til. Now, waste no time in rounding up those criminals. The sooner Tostig has his executions the sooner we can continue our search for Mildryth.'

Asketil was successful. A week later, with twenty perpetrators dangling from the gibbet, he and Sigurd were able to make their journey north.

Mildryth's parents quaked at the number of soldiers who arrived at their modest cottage, but when they heard that it was Lord Sigurd who came they threw open their doors and bade the mighty noble enter. 'My Lord, we are overcome that you honour us with your visit!' Mildryth's father bowed and backed inside before Sigurd. 'We have only humble fayre but everything we have is at your disposal. Sit, I beseech you.' He indicated the best seat by the hearth then began to drag a low table towards them. 'Mistress, fetch ale and meat for Ealdorman Sigurd and his friend. Daughter, feed the soldiers.'

At the mention of a daughter both Sigurd and Asketil looked round sharply, but it was a much older woman than Mildryth. Both turned back to accept cups of ale.

'It is too much to hope that Mildryth travels with you?' The woman wore a look of anticipation.

'She is not here, then?' Asketil glanced at Sigurd.

The woman frowned and tinkered with one of the cheap brooches that held her shoulderstraps. 'Why . . . I thought she lived with you, my lord.'

'And so she did until last week,' replied Asketil, then jumped in quickly to soothe the woman who had put a worried hand to her cheek. It was evident from which parent Mildryth had inherited her protuberant eyes, though her mother's were not such an unusual shade. 'Be not alarmed. We know that she left of her own accord and no harm has befallen her.

It is simply that she left without telling us of her destination and we hoped that she might be with you.'

Mildryth's parents looked at each other, then both presented blank faces to the visitors. 'I regret to say that she is not, my lord.' The woman resumed her task of hostess, placing trenchers of meat on the low table before the guests. 'We have had no news of her since she sent word to say that she lived with you. But, tell us, why would she leave so good a home? You have more to offer her than have we.' That was true. The only furniture here was the table at which they ate, and the benches around the walls. There were no hangings, other than the pots and pans that dangled from hooks. The floor was earthen and embedded with bones, litter and straw. Where Sigurd's great hall glowed with candles this was as dingy as the shack that housed his slaves. The occupants' garb was in great contrast, too. A disappointed Asketil, picking at his meal, fixed his downcast eyes to the man's boots; their leather was dark with age, crinkled and creased, showing every line of his toes.

Sigurd had been watching the couple's reaction to Til's words, and for the moment did not eat. 'If you are lying . . .'

'My lord, why would we lie!' Mildryth's father looked aggrieved. Out of respect he and his wife remained standing.

'Mayhap she asked you to,' replied Sigurd, eyes only leaving the man to stare at Mildryth's mother.

'How could she when we have not seen her?'

'Mayhap she told you to say that.'

'But what reason could she have?'

Sigurd decided to acquaint them with his intentions. 'It was my aim to wed Mildryth . . .'

Whilst the man portrayed disbelief that his little girl was now a woman, his wife voiced delight. 'My lord, this is an honour!'

'But I cannot wed her if she is missing. So if you know of her whereabouts I command you to tell me.'

'My lord, I beg you to believe me!' The man clasped his hands. 'If I were hiding Mildryth do you think that I would continue to do so after what you have just told me? The girl must be mad to throw away this opportunity! I swear that she is not here.'

'You swear to that on your lives?'

Without hesitation, the couple replied simultaneously: 'We swear!'

Sigurd issued instructions without taking his eyes off the couple. 'Til, go order the men to comb the area. If Mildryth is found within five miles of here, torch the house.'

The woman gasped and clutched her breast. Asketil stopped eating to look enquiringly at Sigurd, showing that he thought this a little harsh. Nevertheless, he did as he was told, then came back to finish his meal whilst the troops searched for Mildryth. In the interim Sigurd ate too, watched by the anxious parents.

An hour or so later, the soldiers returned without Mildryth, and much to her parents' relief Lord Sigurd prepared to leave. 'If she should come here after we depart, you must send word immediately.'

'We will, my lord!' The man's tunic was dark beneath the arms from his nervous wait. 'God speed you on your journey.' And he watched the party ride away, before muttering to his wife, 'No wonder she did not wish to wed him. He is old enough to be *my* father let alone hers, and if his treatment of us is any indication he would make her life a misery.'

She nodded ruefully and accompanied him back into the house. 'But I could whip her for endangering us like that. She must have known that he would threaten us.'

Mildryth's father was a loyal man. 'Yea, but she is our daughter. She came to us for help and we promised to give it.'

''Tis true.' The woman ballooned her flushed cheeks. 'I could not wed a man like that, neither – nor could I ever earn my living as an actor. I trust I will not have to go through that again. Do you think he will return?'

'If he does then he will get the same answer. And it will be no lie for she does not live here, does she?'

'No, indeed!' The woman turned a little cross. 'We do not see her for years on end then up she jumps, expects us to put our lives at risk, then tells us she is off to help others more needy. Who can be more needy than her own parents?'

Her husband was less judgmental. 'Mildryth is a good lass. She has made up her mind what life she will follow and we must support her. Lord Sigurd will never find out from us where she is.'

To all intents Mildryth had vanished off the face of the earth. Weeks later neither Sigurd nor his foster-son could eat nor sleep. For Asketil the loss was an ever-present knife in his heart but he could not voice this to Sigurd nor to anyone. His mother was dead now, his sisters married and moved to other parts. He felt totally alone in his pain, and likewise Sigurd whose own distress caused him to grasp at straws. 'Mayhap she has been captured by raiders again, Til, and taken to Norway! That is one place we have not searched.'

Til was not about to argue. Each time the mountainous fjords came into sight he had the strongest feeling that he was coming home . . . though for Sigurd home would always be Jorvik. 'Very well, I will arrange for the ship to be prepared,' he told his foster-father, knowing deep in his heart that they would not find Mildryth, because she did not wish to be found.

Finally came the acceptance that she was lost to both of them and in time the chronic pain eased, leaving just a weeping sore upon each breast. Sigurd, vastly aged and broken-hearted, looked at Til and wondered if he felt the same; but this could not be spoken. Indeed, after the decision had been made to abandon the hunt any mention of Mildryth had become taboo. Tonight, though, when the two were alone by the fire, Sigurd announced, 'This is madness. Much as it hurts me I cannot go on forever thinking she will come back. There is nought for me now save the earldom – for I will have that come what may.' His look of anguish retreated. 'But there is no need for you to share my misery, Til, and it is nigh time we found you a bride.'

'No!' Til, realizing that his swift refusal must look odd, qualified his negativity. 'I am not ready for marriage yet. Besides, did you not always tell me never to trust a woman?'

'Trust her, nay! But I did not mean for you to be celibate. A man cannot get his sons without a woman, and you will find it is a very enjoyable pursuit.' Sigurd waited for a tell-tale look in Til's eye, but none was evident.

Asketil thought about making love to someone other than Mildryth. What his foster-father said was right; he could not live like a monk – look how impossible it had been to resist what Mildryth offered. Having tasted that, he did not wish to abandon it altogether – his martyrdom did not stretch that far. But marriage? He could not face such a commitment yet. For answer he shrugged and muttered, 'We will see what comes along. Of more import is your quest for the earldom. I will help you all I can. Just tell me what to do.'

'Mmm,' Sigurd was thoughtful. 'There is nought much either of us can do whilst Tostig has his brother's support. We shall have to bide our time. As I have said before, if we give Tostig the rope he will hang himself within two years at the most. And what is an extra two years to one who has already waited over thirty?'

Asketil seemed uncertain. 'The townspeople appear to admire their new Earl. I have listened in the marketplace and have heard them praise him.'

Sigurd was unmoved. 'And quite rightly! For does he not rid them of vagabonds and robbers to give them safe travel? But somehow I do not think his executions will stop there. Wait and see.'

Asketil nodded, then in the gap that followed, re-submerged himself in thoughts of Mildryth.

Thankfully, as the year ended, Asketil was eventually able to go about his life without thinking of her every minute of the day – even if she did return to him in the loneliness of his bed. More of a hindrance was the attitude of Earl Tostig who, because of the initial nature of their meeting, appeared to have retained a permanent dislike of Asketil, never failing to grasp some opportunity to belittle him in Sigurd's eyes.

This made things difficult for Sigurd, who wanted to keep on good terms with Tostig out of self-interest. He tried to explain his apparent lack of support to Asketil after one unpleasant episode. 'It is not that I side with Tostig against you, Til! I am not thinking merely of myself when I say I want the earldom. You would benefit, too.'

'I know that.' Asketil did not appear concerned. 'Do not worry that the Earl upsets me. I can stand my ground with him.'

'Oh, you are a better man than him any day! Nay, I just do not want you to think me perfidious after all the loyalty you have shown me. So . . .' here he gave a smile. 'I have arranged consolation for you.'

Asketil looked interested. 'Judging by your face it must be something good.'

'Oh, she is.' Sigurd laughed as Til's jaw dropped, and he clapped the younger man on the back. 'Close your mouth! She will be here soon and you do not want her to think she is to wed a half-wit, do you?'

'I have no wish to wed anyone!' Asketil retained his pallor.

Sigurd did not appear to regard this as a handicap. 'You will when you see her!' That brought back memories. For a second he envisioned himself in Una's arms and his mother bursting in to tell him she had arranged a bride.

But Asketil's reaction was very different than his own had been towards Estorhild.

'Your daughter is very beautiful,' he said politely to the girl's parents when, dressed in their finery, they rolled up that afternoon in the garth. 'But I cannot wed her.'

'Til! What is this foolishness?' Sigurd gave a false laugh. 'These good people have not even climbed down from their wagon and you insult them.' Hurrying forth he assisted the bemused womenfolk from their wagon and into the house. 'I beg you to excuse my son! He is so nervous of wedlock that he does not know what he says – food, drink for these good people!' Whilst the servants hurried to comply, Asketil watched his foster-father try to repair the damage he himself had inflicted but could not feel sorry even for the intended bride who sat there blushing and uncomfortable. He even resented her – resented her for not being Mildryth.

Sigurd was coming towards him, a look of barely concealed anger on his face. 'Til,' he growled. 'You will go and apologise to these people at once and seat yourself next to your betrothed.'

Asketil set his jaw and hissed back, 'You should have given me more warning!'

'You make it sound as if I am asking you to wed a leper!' Sigurd was red in the face. 'Look at her, man! How often do you see a beauty like that?' The maid was fifteen, the same age that Mildryth had been when she left; she was blonde, creamy-skinned and voluptuous. 'Give me one good reason for not wanting her and I will send them all packing!'

Asketil fought for an excuse, but in doing so began to look more closely at his intended bride. Sigurd was right, of course. He could refuse to marry this one but his foster-father would not give up here and subsequent brides might not be so attractive.

'What are you saving yourself for, man?' hissed Sigurd.

How could Asketil tell him? Besides, it had been over a year since Mildryth had gone. She would never come back now . . . but he could dream.

When his foster-son remained dumb, Sigurd tried another tack. 'Or art thou one of those who prefers men?'

'Nay!' Asketil was wounded.

'Then answer me now yea or nay, will you humiliate me in front of these people?'

Asketil looked into Sigurd's face, then shook his head in relenting fashion. 'Nay, I will wed her, if you will forgive me for being an idiot.'

Sigurd was happy again. 'You are no idiot! It is natural that you are nervous. I remember acting the fool myself when I first met Estorhild. Come now, they are growing restless.' All smiles, he drew Til back to the group by the hearth who had been served with food but hardly touched it.

'My son has something to say to you.' Sigurd coaxed Asketil forth.

The young man cleared his throat and bowed to the embarrassed group, speaking mainly to the bride's father. 'I most humbly beg your forgiveness if, in my nervous state, I insulted you. If you are willing to overlook my rude manners I would like to ask for your daughter's hand.'

The man, a wealthy noble, rose and returned the bow first to Asketil then to Sigurd. From politeness, he tried to hide the fact that he had been grossly insulted by the reception but it showed in the coolly courteous reply. 'Forgiveness is granted . . . and I hope that you too will forgive us, Lord Sigurd, if we turn the offer down. I regret that our daughter does not find your son to her liking. She does not wish to be his bride and has expressed a desire to go home.'

Sigurd reacted as if struck in the face, murmuring lamely, 'Then she is at liberty to do so.'

Asketil was equally taken aback as the party left the house with only polite bows being exchanged. For the moment he was speechless, watching the servants remove the uneaten food and dismantle the table.

Sigurd was annoyed now. 'Let him find a better catch elsewhere! The rat – and you are not entirely blameless for my humiliation!' He stabbed a finger at Asketil. 'It will be a long time before I put myself in such a position again.'

'I pray you not to,' said Asketil. 'I would not have you humiliated on my behalf. If I find a woman whom I wish to wed then so be it, but until then I will grab my pleasure where I can.'

Sigurd grunted. 'Do not imagine I will let you use my concubines after the way you have just made me look.'

Asketil shrugged. 'I think that Earl Tostig will keep us both too busy for that.'

This was true and continued to be so for another year. The number of prosecutions at the shire courts remained high.

'Who would have imagined that there could be so many criminals in Eoforwicshire?' wondered Asketil.

'You will not hear me complain.' Sigurd, who took a percentage of the fines imposed, had seen his coffers bulge in the last two years.

'But others complain about you,' answered Til who, as his reeve, had to collect the fines. 'Before Tostig, you always enjoyed a reputation as a fair and just lord; now you are not always so fair in your imposition of penalties. I have heard many grumbles. Take care that in following his example you do not alienate yourself from your people.'

Sigurd was adamant. 'They will understand that my actions are only on Tostig's instructions. Once we get rid of him they will see again their fair and just lord – fair and just *earl*,' he corrected himself with a grin.

Asketil was dubious. 'Tostig remains in great favour.'

Sigurd only laughed and gave his usual reply. 'Watch and wait, oh faithless one.'

But Tostig went from strength to strength in the opinions of Jorvik's citizens. They had feared that on Siward's death King Malcolm would come warring down on them from Scotland, but lo and behold Tostig had succeeded in making a friend out of him! Four years after taking office he persuaded Malcolm to visit King Edward and the Archbishop of Jorvik. There had been no visit of a Scottish king for eighty years. The citizens were impressed, Sigurd less so.

'Four years,' he sighed heavily to Asketil. 'I must eat my words. I did not imagine I would have to wait so long. Indeed, I have to accept that I may never live to claim the earldom.'

'I never thought I would see the day!' cried Asketil, now a man of twenty-two and as yet unmarried though content enough to be so.

Sigurd laughed. 'Yea, you are right. Old as I am I would still take it if I had the chance, even unto the day I die.' He passed some moments in silence looking into the fire by which they both sat in the company of trusted housecarls. 'And I would still wed Mildryth if I could find her.'

An electric current rippled Til's body. Sigurd did not notice the look on his face but continued speaking.

'I often wonder where she is, and is she wed to another? She would be . . . oh, about nineteen or twenty years of age now.' He shook his head in confusion. 'You would think that to marry an ealdorman would be enough to someone of her background, but no, she had to wed an earl or nought. I used to get angry when I thought of the way she rejected me, leaving behind everything I had bought for her. But no more. No man died of rejection.' He glanced at Til who had made not a murmur, and was jolted into remembrance of his friend Ulf – not that Til shared many of his real father's features, it was just that sometimes he would tilt his head in a particular way and for that moment Sigurd would be transported back in time. Til moved and the likeness was gone. The older man gave a knowing smile. 'I think you had a soft spot for her yourself – more than was natural for a sister.'

Asketil displayed shock, but did not answer yea or nay.

Sigurd chuckled, not realizing the depth of Asketil's feeling for the girl – how could it have been as intense as his own? 'I thought so. 'Tis best she is gone, though I did not think so at the time. We might have come to blows over her and that would not do. Now we have both gotten over her.'

Asketil gave a weak smile and leaned on his knees, still unable to disclose his true love for Mildryth and the sacrifice he had made for Sigurd. Had he truly got over her loss? Not truly – for why had he still not found any woman to compare? Would he live his whole life relying on concubines for affection?

Both men's lives went on in similar fashion for another three years, having plenty to occupy them other than home matters, for ever since Tostig had come to power there had been war between England and Gruffydd ap Llewelyn, King of Gywnedd and Powys. In 1062, however, Tostig's brother Earl

Harold, virtual ruler of England, decided to bring the matter to a decisive close and called on Tostig's help. Whilst Harold sailed around the coast receiving hostages, Sigurd and Asketil as part of Tostig's army penetrated Gywnedd where, eventually, both of Godwin's sons met up and laid the country waste. In an attempt to stop the carnage, Gruffydd was killed by his own men and his head presented to Harold who finally partitioned Wales. Tostig, basking in his brother's glory, took his army back to Jorvik to be greeted as a hero. This constant adulation went to the Earl of Northumbria's head. He began to think that he could do anything and the people would accept it. In this supposition he called his ealdorman to a private meeting and told Sigurd that he intended to raise taxes. 'After all, I have done much for them during my seven years as Earl. By exterminating the robbers that plagued their highways I have in effect granted them more money in their purses, so it is only right that they contribute towards this service. The expense should not all be mine.'

Sigurd, leaning one elbow on the table before him, tapped a thoughtful finger to his mouth, saying nothing at the moment but inside enjoying a surge of optimism. The Earl was about to make a most serious error by equating hero-worship with financial reward; the citizens would think otherwise.

'You do not offer an opinion,' said Tostig.

'I am here but to do your bidding,' answered Sigurd, who had no wish to prevent anything that would detract from the Earl's popularity.

'Quite so,' nodded Tostig, and reached for a document. 'And I bid you to have copies of this posted around the shire – it is a list of the new taxes.' Before handing it to his ealdorman he read its contents aloud.

Sigurd could not help raising an eyebrow at the harshness of the taxes. 'They will be difficult to impose, but not impossible.' He took possession of the rolled manuscript.

Tostig smiled at the man whom he regarded as an old friend. 'I knew that I could rely on you, Sigurd, and I recognize that you as my collector will be faced with opposition, but you will be amply rewarded.'

Sigurd could barely contain himself as he rushed home to announce to Asketil, 'It has begun! Tostig has started to dig his own grave at last!' In excited tone he related to his foster-son all that the Earl had said, including the part about his own reward.

'But if you take a share of the taxes you are as bad as him,' Asketil pointed out.

'Nay! It is only right that I be paid for doing his dirty work.' Nothing could shake Sigurd's enthusiasm. 'And shall I not have to pay these taxes myself?'

'I hope the citizens will see it like that,' replied a worried Asketil.

Naturally there was a great deal of opposition to the harsh taxes. Shortly after the notices were posted, a deputation arrived, representing the thegns of the shire. Sigurd was sympathetic to their hardship but regretted that there was little he could do to help. 'Am I not in the same boat as yourselves?'

'But you have more oars,' was the cryptic reply from their spokesman, Rudolf. 'And you are the one responsible for the collection of these taxes. Could you not simply refuse to do so?'

'How can I go against the Earl?' Sigurd spread his hands in helpless gesture and looked around at the collection of faces. 'My lords, I do not agree with Tostig's impositions – I have told him this – but he has warned me of dire consequences if I do not comply. Still . . . for the sake of my friends I will try one last time to change his mind.'

The thegns left. Sigurd turned to grin at his foster-son, but Asketil showed disapproval. 'You have no intention of speaking to the Earl, have you?'

'Oh, do not be so pious, Til!' Sigurd delivered a friendly clout.

This infuriated Asketil. After all I have given up for you! he wanted to shout. But of course he did not.

'I shall not have to keep up the pretence for long,' opined Sigurd. 'The thegns themselves will remove him.'

But to Sigurd's annoyance this did not happen. Out of respect for the King who had appointed Tostig and for his past heroics, the northerners continued to tolerate their Earl and he went on to enjoy almost a decade in office.

During the past two or three years, Asketil's unquestioning loyalty towards his foster-father had begun to wane. Old age had changed Lord Sigurd. He might argue that it was all pretence but Asketil felt that in his waiting game he enjoyed too many of Tostig's favours. At the age of twenty-seven Asketil began to question his own future. Once, it had been a foregone conclusion that he would be Sigurd's heir – but heir of what? It was certainly no honour to inherit such ill-gotten harvest as Sigurd had reaped lately. In his disappointment with his father he thought more and more of the love he had sacrificed. He had been young and idealistic then; he would not do the same now. Oh, no. If Mildryth were here he would wed her tomorrow. Thoughts of her began to dominate his whole life. When he played music he saw her dancing, when he combed his horse's tail it was Mildryth's hair he touched. Who would have thought that after ten years the flame could be rekindled so easily? Nay, there was nought easy about it. It was ten times worse at this age, for the knowledge that his life was halfway through with nought to show for it begat a panic that made him physically sick.

This state of lethargy was bound to draw Sigurd's attention. 'Come with me on my hunting trip with

Tostig and the King,' he entreated, worried that his adopted son was going to go the way of Ulf, so thin and pale had he become. 'We will fatten you up with fresh meat – that will redden your cheeks.'

Asketil was stooped over a book as had become too much of a habit lately according to Sigurd. 'I have no desire to rub shoulders with one who has ruined this city – and have you not always maintained that you hate the King?'

'And so I do! But if I am given an opportunity to make Tostig look the fool before the King then I must snatch it. I thought you were sworn to help me?'

'I have tried to help you with my good advice but you refuse to take it.' Asketil lifted his eyes from the page and directed them at his foster-father. It was time to speak bluntly. 'Father, if you still crave the earldom then you must act now. I was in the marketplace today and I heard many complaints about your failure to protect the citizens from Tostig's abuse; they were not the first.'

'Oh, have I not heard them myself.' Sigurd flicked the air dismissively and began a leisurely walk up the hall that was empty but for the two of them. Sigurd himself would not have been in here had it not been for Til.

'Then heed them! Tostig is draining the town of its prosperity and its good humour – and you by association are just as guilty!'

The old man reached a table and, picking some grapes from a bowl, put several into his mouth. 'The people will eventually understand my strategy.'

Asketil banged his lectern to show frustration. 'Father, I beg you do something now!'

Sigurd peppered the floor with a shower of grape-pips. 'Kill the King's favourite and have the might of his fyrd down upon my shoulders? Nay, if there is one thing I have learnt in my life it is to be patient.'

'Patient or indifferent?' quothed Asketil. That there

534

was no responding fire proved to him that Sigurd had reached decrepitude at last. It was sad to witness after so great a career. 'Your thegns send constant petitions about the Earl's behaviour and you ignore them – worse! You allow Tostig to get away with murder.' Til's accusation was not metaphorical: if the Earl wanted someone's property he would kill for it. 'He has even robbed churches! Had he been a common man this alone would warrant the amputation of his hand, yet because he is an earl he gets away scot free.'

But the protestations fell upon deaf ears. Unperturbed, Sigurd retraced his steps back to the lectern, hands behind back. 'It would be unwise to make my move before I am sure that the people will follow me,' was his mild objection. 'Why, it would look as if I had instigated the rebellion and if it failed . . . Well, I should be the first to lose my head. The initiative must appear to come from the thegns.'

'Oh, be off on your hunting trip!' Asketil dismissed him and went back to crouching over his book, though he was in no mood to read now. 'I will remain here – you have much need of a friend to guard your interests.'

Chapter Twenty-one

Sigurd's interests were far from Til's mind as he maundered alone in Jorvik. Day after day he gazed into the future and saw nothing. In his increasingly restless state he came to see that the future was of his own making, and in this revelation he made his choice: he would search for Mildryth again. There was no logic to his actions – for had he not combed every possible place before? – but he followed his instincts regardless and rode north alone. Maybe her parents had been hiding her on his original visit. True, they had quaked when Sigurd threatened to torch their house unless they produced her, and their repudiations had obviously been genuine, but even if they had been truthful at that time Mildryth could have gone to them later. It was worth the journey.

Alas, Mildryth's aged parents repeated their denial. 'You must tell Lord Sigurd that we have not seen hide nor hair of her for years,' announced the man, looking rather apprehensive.

Asketil wore an air of disappointment. ''Tis not on Lord Sigurd's behalf that I come, but for myself.' His look told all.

Mildryth's mother was confused. 'Lord Sigurd is dead?'

Asketil shook his head. 'No, but he has resigned himself to the fact that he will not see Mildryth again. I, however, have not.' He risked taking them into his confidence. 'I have loved Mildryth for years – as she loved me . . .' He glanced at the woman, waiting for a nod of recognition that would tell him that Mildryth had been here, but the woman gave nothing away. Pessimism rising, he continued, 'But I could do nought against my foster-father. Lately, though, I have begun to see what a dreadful error I made in spurning her love. I have tried my hardest to love others but every attempt has failed. I have now realized that it is unfair, indeed cruel, of me to continue to deceive. If I could only find her I would wed her today . . .'

Asketil had a more human approach than Lord Sigurd's. Mildryth's father took pity on the forlorn man. 'You have come a long way for nought.' His voice was kind. 'There is little we can do save ask you to eat with us before your return journey.'

This drew forth a pledge. 'I will never return to Jorvik without her, even if it means that I must travel until the day I die, and if you have any notion of where she might be I beg you to tell me. I should be forever in your debt.' He made no move to accept the offer to go into the house.

Mildryth's mother looked from Asketil's beseeching eyes into those of her husband, which warned her not to speak. She took no notice and blurted, 'Mildryth has been here.'

'But the last occasion was many months ago!' said her father hastily at the spark of life in Til's eye. 'We did not send word to Lord Sigurd because she stayed only hours before leaving again, we know not where.'

'Do not be afraid of Lord Sigurd! I will tell him nought of this.' Where Sigurd would have punished them Asketil employed charm. 'I can see from your eye that you are a kind man and would not have me suffer . . .'

Mildryth's father cut him off. 'Forgive me, lord, I would tell you if it were in my power, but she would not disclose her whereabouts even to us.'

Til stared him in the eye, trying to guess if he was

being truthful and eventually looked away in despair. The man was lying but it was useless to employ force. Even when Sigurd had threatened to burn their house down Mildryth's parents had maintained their ignorance. They would protect her to the death. In a way Til admired this, but it did not help him. 'Is she well?' he asked lamely.

'She is of good health,' replied the mother.

'And tell me, is she . . . yea, it is foolish to ask.' Asketil shook his head and looked flummoxed. 'She must be wed for many years now.'

'Must be by now,' said the man.

'She wasn't the last time she was here,' corrected his wife to her husband's chagrin.

'Then I must hope that this is still the case.' Asketil stood there for a moment, looking uncertain what to do. 'Well, I will not find her standing here . . .' He looked to right and left.

Mildryth's old mother felt compassion and touched his arm. 'It is small help I know, but when she left us 'twas in a westerly direction.' She chose to ignore the sharp intake of breath from her husband.

When Til jumped up and made hasty departure the man chastised his wife. 'You've betrayed our lass!'

'Do not talk stupid! The young lord's besotted with her. Anyway, I only told him the direction she took when she left.'

'You might as well have told him where she bides! You know very well there's no house on that road for miles save that one. You should not have told him ought. You promised her!'

'Oh, go duck your head! You're as daft as her. We promised not to tell Lord Sigurd where she is but it isn't he who asks to wed her, is it? You heard him say that Mildryth loves him.'

'We have only his word for it! She never mentioned ought herself.'

'Well, if she doesn't want him then she can tell him

that, but I don't think she's going to throw away this chance he offers because it will be her last, you know! She does not get any younger.'

'She may be happy enough where she is,' he pointed out.

His wife scoffed. 'You know as well as I that she's not cut out for the life she's chosen. 'Tis a miracle she's lasted this long. For the sake of good sense I hope he does find her!'

Asketil travelled the westerly road for miles accosting every person he met to ask if they had seen her – she was, after all, very distinctive in her looks – but none could help him. Vowing not to give up he proceeded as far as he could before nightfall, hoping that there would be a roof over his head tonight, for so far he had not encountered one single dwelling. When he came across an abbey he pulled the bell-rope and waited in the autumnal evening until the grille in the door was slid aside, then turned to meet a pair of startled violet eyes.

She was almost twice the age that she had been on their last encounter but if her face had altered those eyes had not, and neither had Asketil, judging by the recognition in them. Mildryth took one look at the visitor and immediately slammed the door on the grille.

He emerged from his trance and began to kick and bang at the wood. 'Mildryth, open up! Open the door or I'll smash it down!'

The young woman leaned against it as if her feather-weight would prevent his violent entry, then exasperated at his noise she slid the grille open once more and hissed at him, 'Shut your damned noise or you'll bring the Abbess out!'

'Then open up and let me in!'

'I cannot! We are all female here, 'tis barred to menfolk – oh, hush then! I will come out to you!' Ensuring that she was unobserved she unbolted the gate and stepped into the road where she demanded, 'What business have you here?'

'Hah! I should ask that of you.' He made a stabbing gesture at her austere robes. 'What right has an unvirtuous wench like you to wear nun's garb?'

'Unvirtuous? Hah! Little chance I had to be unvirtuous with you! You treated me like a nun so I decided I might as well be one.'

'I'll warrant the sisters do not know what is in their midst! Maybe I should tell them.'

During the altercation Mildryth had edged closer so that now her nose was mere inches away from his. 'Why would you do that? You made it clear that you do not want me for any other purpose.'

He said the first idiotic thing that came into his head. 'But Lord Sigurd does and I am to take you back!'

He grabbed her, she struggled and brought her knee up to his groin. Yelling in agony he fell to the dust. Mildryth ran. When the nausea lifted she was gone. The next fifteen minutes were spent intermittently cursing her and rubbing at his injured parts. Blinking to clear his vision, he hoisted his throbbing body and looked around. 'I will not chase after thee! If you do not come back I shall bang on this door until all the sisters come out and inform them what you are!'

When she did not materialize, Til flopped back to the ground, rolling upon it, both angry and sore. Finally, when he had given up hope of ever seeing her again she came out of the sun, her long shadow falling across him, wary of eye and prepared for flight.

Til was sulking. 'Do not panic, my hands are occupied with my bruised plums.'

She laughed, ripped off her veil and sat beside him on a tussock. 'I shall soothe them.'

'Nay, be damned!' He careened away. 'You have done enough damage in one way or another.'

Mildryth was unrepentant, raking her fingers over her itching head. 'And I will do some more if you intend to drag me back to wed old Goatbeard.'

The man was quiet for a while, watching her rearrange her blonde hair, then admitted, 'I did not really come here to do that. I do not know what made me say it.' When Mildryth trained her eyes on him his stomach lurched. 'I miss you, Mildryth, and come to see if you will have me.'

She could not have been more surprised and consequently allowed him to hold the stage for the moment.

'I am grown sick of *fostri*'s games with Earl Tostig. He drives the people away from him, not only the common folk but his friends too.'

'And you?' Those magnificent eyes held his face.

He nodded. 'I regret to say he has lost much of my loyalty. He has always been harsh but never unjust to his followers; now he watches Tostig commit murder, rob his thegns of their land and does nought about it. At the beginning he said it was his plan to give Tostig the rope to hang himself, but for pity's sake that was ten years ago and by condoning these deeds he brings guilt upon himself. I have warned him that there are mutterings against him but he seems to care for nought these days . . . that is what you did when you left him.'

'Oh, 'tis all my fault!' riposted Mildryth, then after an angry interval mumbled, 'Is he over his infatuation?'

'Yea, but he is not the same.'

'So now that he no longer lusts after me you decide it is fair for you to try your hand.'

Til frowned. ''Twas not like that!'

Mildryth guessed how he had found her. 'I will have harsh words for my kin when next I see them.'

Til defended them. 'They did not tell me your whereabouts. 'Twas pure luck that I arrived here.'

She was subdued. 'Luck for whom?'

'For me, if you will forgive the cruel words I flung at you. I did not mean them. I was young then, thought I was acting nobly – towards Lord Sigurd, that is. But I am older now. I am halfway through my life and yet I do not seem to be alive. When you left you took my heart with you.'

Mildryth re-experienced her own pain. 'How long it has taken you to realize it.'

Asketil looked suitably rebuked. 'Yea, I admit I was a fool, but I come now to see if you will have me.'

She turned her nose to the sky. 'I do not know. I have grown used to this life.'

When he cocked a disbelieving eye she had to laugh and put an affectionate arm through his, totally forgiving. 'How are your privities?'

He looked rueful. 'No good for your purposes.'

She gave a mocking scold. 'Then why should I waste my time lingering with thee?'

He did not answer, just smiled into her eyes.

She returned his fondness for a while, studying him. He was more certain of himself now. 'You have changed,' she told him, and brushed the dust from his hair that still held its summer gold whilst the beard was dark.

He showed amusement. 'At one score years and seven? I should hope that I have. You yourself have not.'

'Oh, I have, Til, I have.' A wistful look came to her eye. 'When I said I had grown used to this life I was serious. Ten years is a long time . . .'

'It is a long time in a place like this for one such as you.' He nodded to indicate the abbey.

'Nay, it has been no hardship. Indeed, after the torment I suffered over you . . .'

'Oh, don't.' He cringed.

'Nay, I am saying nought against you, just telling

you that I needed a peaceful place where I could put my life to some good use. I have enjoyed helping folk . . .'

'There is another here whom you could help, Mildryth,' he said quietly.

She gave no answer but, after a further period of inspection she bade him stand. 'Come, we cannot sit here. I shall be discovered. Let us walk awhile if you can manage it.'

Wincing, he stood, banged his hat against his dusty clothes and after a few pained steps took on a more natural gait. As they walked with his horse tagging behind she asked him to tell her all that had happened since she had left; this took some time. They had walked a good few miles and it was growing dark. Asketil paused by a field where kine grazed on the stubble left behind after harvest, their dark shapes outlined in the disappearing sun. The pain was gone and so were all thoughts of loyalty to Sigurd. Without leave, he threw his arms round her, pressing the length of his body against hers. Released, the horse bent its head to graze whilst the lovers fell upon each other with searching tongues. Asketil gave freely of himself for the first time in his life, and in the final throes Mildryth gasped, 'Stay with me, Til, I beg you, stay!'

Til's chest rose and fell several times before he had breath to answer. Burying his face in her neck he swore, 'I will never leave you, dear one! We will be man and wife and never be parted again.'

Mildryth did not return to the abbey. Scorning wild animals, she and Asketil made a fire and passed a night of love that outmatched its flame. In the morning after Til had supplied breakfast he rolled up his blanket and tied it to his saddle.

Mildryth was puffy-eyed from lack of sleep and remained by the fire, for the morning was cool. 'Whither do you go now?'

'Jork.' He and others had started to abbreviate the name.

She jumped up, alarmed. 'You swore that you would never leave me!'

Til laughed, quick to allay her fears. 'But you shall come too, my wife.'

'Art thou mad! I shall never go back there!'

He took her in his arms. 'We have to go and face him, Mildryth; at least I do, for he will fret if he returns to discover me gone.'

Mildryth tried to restrain him by gripping his brown beard. 'In his anger he could kill you!'

'Ow! Mayhap . . .' He disentangled her fingers. 'But I must face him. I cannot live like an outlaw. Besides, he is an old man of three score years. Passions die.'

She was unconvinced. 'He was an old man ten years ago, and that did not stop him lusting after me.'

Til made soft reproach, brushing away a strand of blonde hair that obscured her eye. 'I do not think you realize how strongly he did feel for you, Mildryth. It was not mere lust. He genuinely intended to wed you. When you left he was like one demented, insisting on searching for you himself.'

'I know.' She nodded and reseated herself on the dry patch she had inhabited all night, for there was a heavy dew elsewhere.

Til rested on his heels. 'You saw him?'

'I hid and watched. My heart hoped that you would be the one to come after me.' Her eyes reflected sorrow. 'When you did not, I knew that all was lost and devoted my life to caring for the sick and unfortunate.'

Feeling responsible, he tried to tease a smile from her. 'I wager the nuns wondered what they had amongst them.'

Mildryth was slow to grasp that he jested. 'I did not take kindly to the restrictions, 'tis true, but I gave myself wholeheartedly to the life and was good at . . .'

'There was none more goodly than you, Mildryth.'
He stopped her words of defence with his fingers.
Like her own, his eyes were bleary but full of affection. 'I remember how you treated poor Murtagh
and . . .'

'Oh, you have changed your opinion of me since
last we met! Calling me slut or other vile insults.'

He was earnest. 'I meant none of it!'

Mildryth chuckled to show that she had only been
getting her own back. 'Well, you may have been right.
I could never boast chastity . . . but if slut I be, Til,
then 'tis your slut and no one else's. Only with you.'
She leaned forward to instigate a passionate kiss.

When they drew apart, she referred to the slave
again. 'I often wonder if Murtagh got away.'

'So do I,' admitted Asketil. ''Twould be nice to
think that he did – I feel no disloyalty in saying that
now.'

'Oh, Lord Sigurd must really have lost your love!'

'Nay, I still love him as a father.' His voice was
sincere. Then he noticed a shadow of doubt cloud
her eye, asked immediately, 'What is it, my dear?'
and cupped the point of her chin in his hands.

She rubbed her cheek against his fingers. ''Tis
nought.'

'No lies.' He was stern. 'If we are to spend our
lives together we must be honest with each other.'

Mildryth held back. 'You may be angry.'

'Never mind. I would have the truth all the same.'

Her violet eyes blinked as if to discourage tears.
'Then tell me true and I will ask no more: do you
take me back to Jorvik only to hand me over to the
father you adore? Was this all a ploy to lure me
back?' There was no need for answer. She could tell
by the look on his face that she had grossly insulted
him. 'Nay! I wish I had not asked and I beg you to
forgive me.' She gripped the hands that had fallen
from her cheeks.

'I have treated you badly in the past but I would ne'er do ought so shameful as that!' He tried to rise but she pulled him back to the wet grass.

'Yea, I know that! I was a fool to even think it. Come, rip out my tongue for its wicked slur on your character.' She thrust her pink tongue under his nose and wiggled it.

He pushed her, unamused – 'You still act the child!' – and lifted one buttock to feel at his damp leggings.

She came back, petting and pawing her way back to favour, just like the twelve year old he had met in Norway. 'Til, dear Til, 'twas only that I know how much you love the man and are willing to forego your own happiness for him. That was the only worry I had and you have dispelled it.'

Til had grown out of his boyhood tendency to act the martyr. He soon gave in to her persuasion and hugged her. 'Forsooth, I do love him, but he is headed down a dangerous road. Whatever I say I cannot deter him and besides, I have wasted enough of my youth. He will go mad when he hears of my love for you . . .'

'And mine for you,' Mildryth butted in.

'. . . but I owe him explanation and must go back.'

Mildryth tried to project a happier outcome. 'When he learns how much you tried to resist me he will not be so angry.'

Both knew that she was being over-optimistic. 'Nay, he will be furious,' corrected Til, 'and mayhap will never speak to me again. It will be terrible to lose his love and respect but even more terrible to live without you. Indeed, I can no longer live without you.' Unable to resist, he ran his hands over her one last time, then pulled her to her feet. 'Ugh, my broks are sodden! Come, jump up and let us make haste, for I fear that if I have too much time to think on it, I will revert to being the coward I was and will shirk my duty.' Mounted on the bay stallion, he put down a helping hand.

'You are no coward.' She hauled herself into position and leaned back against him. 'Just too noble for your own good. Sigurd's life is almost over; he has had his chances, and now you must take yours.'

'You understand that he will also disown me as his heir?'

'If I wished just for titles I would already be his wife. I care nought for any of it, soft fool, only for thee.'

Asketil grinned then kissed her ear, and with a click of his tongue spurred the horse homewards.

They reached Earlsburh some days later, arriving in the afternoon. Long before this, however, they were made aware that trouble was brewing. There was an air of unrest far outside the palisades and the sentinels on the gates were unusually keen to check the identity of those arriving. Sigurd had not yet returned from his hunting trip with Tostig and the King, which was both a relief and a disappoinment for Til who had primed himself for early confrontation. Once he and Mildryth had bathed and been given food he questioned a housecarl over the fraught atmosphere amongst the men of Earlsburh.

'Since you left, the mood against Earl Tostig has worsened,' replied the guard, unable to prevent his eyes from running over Mildryth who had arrived in nun's garb and was now dressed as a lady. 'If there should be an attack on his property the men fear we will not be able to withhold it.' The majority of bodyguards had gone hunting with their master.

Til assumed concern. 'Is the threat real?'

'Yea, there has been a gemot of the thegns – not just those of the city but many have come from miles away to attend. I pray that my lord Sigurd will soon return.'

Til was decisive. 'We must send immediate warning. There shall be no leave for any man, everyone must be . . .'

At this point a commotion went up from outside. It was too late – the attack had begun! Til grabbed his sword and ran outside. Instantaneously the house-carl with whom he had just been conversing fell dead, an arrow in his chest. Til looked round as Mildryth followed with spear aloft. 'Get back inside! I will not have you hurt.'

She pretended to comply, but when her beloved rushed into the fray she went too and hovered ready to sink her point of iron into any would-be assailant. Sigurd's teaching was not wasted; in spite of being outnumbered Til displayed great prowess. Inevitably, though, the depleted force of Earlsburh was overrun by the rebel thegns. Til fought until his right arm suffered a deep gash and he could no longer grip his sword. The thegns fell upon him. Mildryth charged at them but was tripped before her spear did any harm and bundled up with the other survivors.

Watching her manhandled, Til raged to be free but a swordpoint held him at bay. 'Kill me then, you cowards!' he yelled.

'We have no reason to kill one who has our respect,' grunted the owner of the weapon, Rudolf. 'We know that you spake in our favour to the tyrant – besides, you are a valuable hostage. Maybe now Lord Sigurd will listen to reason.'

'Fools! When he hears what you have done he will vent much savagery for your betrayal.'

'He has enjoyed enough of our loyalty,' came the joint response.

Til showed uncustomary harshness. 'This is what you call loyalty for his years of protection?'

'What protection did he offer against Earl Tostig?' demanded Rudolf. 'We gave him every chance to right his wrongs but he dismissed our petition!'

Til knew that everything the thegns said was valid, though out of faithfulness he argued Sigurd's case until they would no longer heed. One of them was in the process of making a declaration.

'From this moment Earl Tostig is an outlaw – death to all those who aid him!'

By means of travelling folk, news of the attack preceded any official messenger. When Tostig learnt of it he was furious, urging the King to ride for Lunden and gather support to overthrow the insurgents. Sigurd found it hard to conceal his delight. Telling the deposed Earl that he would go north and quell the trouble he made for home, assuming that on his arrival he would hear himself pronounced Tostig's successor. Such was his confidence that when he and his men attempted to pull into the riverbank at Jorvik and were repulsed by a horde, he laughed, thinking it was a case of mistaken identity. 'Hold, men, it is your Earl come to replace the tyrant Godwinsson!'

'Our earl is Morcar!' came the retort, along with a shower of missiles.

Incensed, Sigurd shouted orders for his crew to attack. He himself jumped from the prow into shallower waters and waded for the bank of Earlsburh, axe upraised. Another fear displaced the loss of his earldom now – Til was in that besieged city, maybe dead. He wished that he had brought more men for the thegns were greater in number. Nevertheless his housecarls were professional fighters; whilst they battled and splashed around the river he fought a path up the bank towards his own house, slicing and hacking with his axe. It was rash to detach himself from his bodyguards. Just as Asketil had been encircled and captured, so too was he – though not until many had fallen dead by his hand.

The men who pinioned his arms were well-known to him. 'A boon before you kill me, Helgi!' he cried to one of them. 'I would have news of my son. Tell me, is he dead?'

'We have no wish to kill you,' replied Helgi, breathless from the fight. 'You have served us well enough in times gone by, but you deserted us with Tostig. We have chosen our own Earl Morcar and you must depart. Call off your men before any more die.' The one-sided battle still continued on land and in the river.

Relieved as Sigurd was to keep his life, he remained anxious for Til and tried to wrench himself free. 'I will not go without news of my son!'

'He is safe,' came the answer, 'and under house arrest.'

'Then I would see him!' It was not a request.

Helgi's face consulted with his partners. The thegns' prime wish was to be rid of the old warrior. If they showed him Asketil, then maybe he would go peaceably. 'Call off your men and you shall see him!' came the instruction. A yell from Sigurd brought the bloody engagement to a halt. Whilst his surviving men were held at swordpoint, Helgi and two others led the old man, half-sodden and bound with ropes, into the hall.

The group of hostages, around thirty in all, were eating their midday meal as if everything were as normal, but there were indications of rough handling upon them. Sigurd gave a cry at the stained bandage on Til's arm as the young man rose to greet him. 'You told me he was safe!'

'He is not dead,' replied the informant calmly.

'But well he might be, for all the protection afforded by his sword arm now!' The arm hung uselessly by Til's side. He was obviously in great pain but smiled a welcome at his fostri. Sigurd tried to approach but found himself repressed. 'In the name of God, cannot I comfort him? What evil can I do with my army gone?'

Deciding it was no risk they untied him. Leaving a trail of wet footprints, he came at once to Til, who raised his good arm to encircle the old man.

'I have been well tended, *fostri*. The arm will heal.'

'Hmph!' responded Sigurd . . . then over the younger man's shoulder noticed another. Til felt him go rigid and knew that Mildryth had returned from her trip to fetch more ale. As the two men drew apart she came forth and set the pitcher on the table, a hesitant smile on her lips. Incredulity lit Sigurd's face as he beheld the young woman. 'Can it be . . . Mildryth! Mildryth, my sweet one, you have come back to us!'

Enveloped in the old man's hug, Mildryth could not see Til's face. She waited for his explanation, but Til could not bring himself to add to his father's disappointment. Without looking at Mildryth he felt her anger and hoped she would restrain any outburst.

All trace of failure gone, Sigurd was ecstatic, running his horny old fingers up and down her arms, poring over her face. She was very much a woman now but miraculously had retained that air of purity that had captured his heart. 'Oh, I cannot believe that I see you! Why did you leave me? Where have you been?'

'I have lived at an abbey for the last ten years.'

'As a nun?' He sounded hopeful, but then noticed that her eyes flickered towards Asketil and he too looked at his foster-son. The truth was there for all to read. He fought it most desperately, his grip tightening on Mildryth's arms.

Til noted the discomfort on her face. 'You are hurting her, *fostri*.'

Deafened by his emotions, Sigurd did not heed at once, staring into his foster-son's face. That treacherous face. When? When had it happened? He showed great reluctance to let her go but his captors had other ideas.

'You shall go now to the King,' said Helgi. 'And tell him that we will not have Tostig back.'

As Sigurd was removed his mind began to form plans. 'Would you drag me away already? Cannot I have Asketil and Mildryth to come with me?'

'Nay, they remain here as hostages to guard against your duplicity.'

'Then at least let us say our farewells! The lad's arm is so badly wounded that he could die before I set eyes on him again.' When this was allowed he hugged Asketil. *No, it cannot be, Til would never betray me. I am wrong, surely. My love for her misleads me.* He whispered into his foster-son's ear: 'I shall go to the palace and enlist the help of Earl Tostig – he does not know of my grudge against him. I will be back as soon as I can to rescue you. Farewell, my son.' Pulling away, he looked deep into Til's face. 'Look after my bride for me.' Til averted his eyes. There was no doubt in Sigurd's mind now. Aching, he grabbed Mildryth again, hugged her, then was compelled to leave.

When he was gone, Mildryth turned on her lover. 'Why did you not tell him? You were right to say you are a coward!'

'Then you will not want to be my wife.' It was delivered with comic pathos.

She tore at her hair – 'Aagh! You make me so mad!' – then hugged him. 'Whether I would or no I am left with no choice for I carry your child in my belly.'

Preoccupied with the bandage that was sticking to his wound, he dismissed this as fantasy. 'We have been together only days; it must be the quickest conception there has ever been.'

'Even so I know it to be true. Another month will tell you that I am right. That is why it was vital that Lord Sigurd be told about us.'

'He hath no need to be told.' The reply was flat.

Til stopped picking at the bandage and eyed her. 'He saw it by the way we looked at each other.'

Mildryth cringed. 'Art certain? He showed no anger – said he would come back to rescue you.'

Til used his good arm to pull her into his side, leaning his head against hers. 'Not to rescue me, dear one – to kill me.'

Sigurd abandoned the city to its new leaders and with his remaining housecarls sailed for Lunden, vowing that his exile would be temporary. Whilst he travelled down the coast, what had begun as a northern re-volt with two hundred thegns now developed into a general uprising. News of this had just reached the palace where an argument raged: Harold, Tostig's brother, sympathized with the thegns. 'They do not revolt without good reason.'

Tostig responded with spite. 'You use this excuse to fulfil your own grudge against me!'

Harold was of calmer disposition than either his brother or the King. 'I have no grudge – did I not support your right to the earldom of Northumbria?' Even if I knew you were unsuitable, he added privately.

'To get me out of your way!' Tostig spun from his brother and addressed himself to Edward. 'He knows I am your favourite and dreads that you will nomin-ate me as your heir when he would have the throne himself!'

The King recognized this to be true. Harold God-winsson was too much like his sire to find favour with Edward. But much as he liked Tostig he knew which of the brothers was the greater power – this was one of his reasons for despatching Tostig north out of harm's way – and he had not hung on to his position by being stupid. 'You are too impetuous, my friend, and tired from your hunting expedition.' The long thin face urged reason. 'Let us see what your brother can do first to quell the uprising.'

So Harold set out to meet the rebels at Northampton. Meanwhile Sigurd, having reached Lunden, laid low to rethink his position and also to hear the result of Harold's efforts. By the time Harold returned Sigurd was fully recuperated and dashed to the palace for enlightenment.

Godwinsson bore only an ultimatum: the rebels had been respectful but adamant. Under no circumstances would they have Tostig back as Earl. He had abused his position and unless the King dismissed his favourite, the northerners would attack the King himself. To press this point they had marched south and were now at Oxnaford.

Edward threw himself into a frenzy and ordered Harold to return north with his army and wipe out the offenders. 'They shall not tell me how to rule my kingdom!' He had turned crimson and appeared to be on the verge of apoplexy.

Harold did not fear the King's tantrums. 'My lord, they have a worthy case. One rash act could plunge the whole country into war.'

Standing amongst the collection of lesser nobles, Sigurd held back his opinion, listening to the King's ranting and Tostig's whines.

'My lord, he exaggerates!' said the deposed Earl. 'Let me take an army and I will soon put them down for their impudence against their King.'

Harold spoke again. 'If you grant my brother's wish, oh lord, then I must tell you that I cannot be party to the slaughter of fellow Englishmen.'

Edward's mouth was rimmed with spittle. 'You would disobey your monarch?'

Harold was polite. 'If he has been ill-advised by those who only have their own interest at heart.'

When Tostig began to abuse his brother, Sigurd decided it was time to come forth. 'If I might . . .'

'Be done!' roared the confused monarch. 'I will not listen to these squabbles. Tostig, you are most dear to me, you know that, but I cannot afford a war on behalf of one friend . . . I am compelled to do as those northern wretches ask and banish you. Nay, do not look at me like that! It gives me no pleasure. As soon as the trouble has died down perhaps you can return; until then the northern earldom must go to Morcar.'

'It is mine!' Sigurd could not help the exclamation. As all eyes turned to the old man he moderated his tone. 'My King, I have served Lord Tostig well and have aided each of the earls of Northumbria over fifty years. I know the people, know the country, I have brought many riches to your own coffers. If Earl Tostig is to be cruelly deposed,' he thought it prudent to keep on Tostig's side for the moment, 'let me serve in his proxy until it is right for him to return.'

'The people did not ask for you, they asked for Morcar.' Edward's bloodshot eyes focused on the man who had been a constant irritation since his own reign had begun, and thereby found a scapegoat for the current problems. 'I wonder why, if you lead them so well, do they not mention your name? I will tell you, Ealdorman Sigurd: it is because they recognize as I do that you are much to blame for many of their ills – more so than Earl Tostig. He was a stranger to the north and was ignorant of how to handle his thegns, but you know them well, should have advised him more carefully. It is therefore only right and proper that if I am to expel Lord Tostig then the cause of his downfall must go too – and go now.'

In all the years that Sigurd had nurtured his blood-feud with Ethelred's kin, never had he hated any of them as much as at this moment, but with his immediate expulsion there was no chance of redress. Mildryth – what would happen to her in his absence? The answer was unbearable. *Do not do it, Til, I beg you. Do not dare to take her.*

Whilst Tostig sought shelter with his wife's kinsman Baldwin, Count of Flanders, Sigurd made for Norway with one aim in mind: to prompt another great invasion of England. This time Ethelred's line would be totally annihilated – others would be made to pay, too.

Chapter Twenty-two

The news of both tyrants' exile was greeted with celebration in Jorvik, and no citizen was more glad than Mildryth whose prediction had been realized; she carried Til's child. They had wed immediately after their release by the thegns, eager to grasp every loving moment before Lord Sigurd came to take his revenge. Then the miracle had occurred: King Edward had banished his ealdorman and with him went the terror. Asketil had sworn fealty to the new Earl, Morcar, and in doing so had won for himself the position that Sigurd had forfeited. The young ealdorman and his wife continued to reside at Earlsburh where, in the absence of its previous owner, the house had lost its edge of danger. It was a happy place with much music and easy laughter. If, during this sociability a fight should break out due to an excess of ale, Asketil would not exact a fine as had the despot, but instead had the miscreants ejected until they had slept off their drunkenness. Only if Mildryth was insulted did he punish them, but few would insult the mistress of the house who was very popular around Jorvik for her acts of charity.

Yet Asketil's happiness was tinged, for was his residence here not just another betrayal of the man who had loved him? Mildryth tried to eliminate his guilt. 'You are a good leader! You hold the people's respect. Lord Sigurd deserved his fate.'

But his bond with Sigurd was too tightly knotted to be so easily shrugged off. 'If I were granted one wish,' he told Mildryth as she comforted him with a goblet of mead, 'it would be that my father would forgive me.'

But Sigurd was in no mood to forgive. On Christmas Eve whilst Asketil watched the sacred branch of mistletoe laid ceremoniously upon the high altar of the Minster, Sigurd was holed up in a Norwegian cabin, plotting war. On first arrival he had made for the house of King Harald at Oslo, but the monarch was at his palace in the capital Nidaros and so he had rowed back along the Oslofjord to spend winter with his kin. There could be no attack before summer anyway. Depressed and betrayed, he could not concentrate on the winter games, the songs, the riddles: all he saw was Asketil with Mildryth.

In England, King Edward's humiliation over Tostig had caused a seizure and more were to follow. In January 1066 Asketil returned from a visit to the palace with the news that the King was dead.

Mildryth, far advanced into her pregnancy, was instantly worried about a successor. 'Will Earl Tostig take his chance to return, and with him Lord Sigurd?'

'If he does he shall have a formidable opponent,' replied Til, eating the handful of raisins given to him by the cook – he had found Mildryth in the kitchen. 'Harold Godwinsson has been chosen as King.'

'Another Godwinsson.' His wife fingered her necklace of garnets, her apprehension shared by the cook. 'The northern men will not take kindly to it.'

Til was concerned about this too. 'Neither will the earls.' Rivalry between the families of Godwin and Leofric had been passed down to their heirs. 'Let us hope the disunity will not unleash an invasion from other sources – William of Normandy has a thirst for English ale. Still, Harold is a different kettle of fish from his brother. He will be a good King. Besides, has he not virtually ruled for the last ten years?'

'There is something else,' accused Mildryth. 'I can tell by your face.'

Til pretended that his mouth was too full for him to answer at the moment. Impatient of feature, Mildryth went to help a servant cram her mixture of lard, meat and blood into an intestinal membrane. When the sausage was made, she turned back to her husband. 'Well?'

Til was reluctant to worry her lest it harmed the child, but concluded that it was better to be truthful; there had been enough deceit with Sigurd. He used a fingernail to dislodge a raisin from his tooth. 'It is just that ... well, I heard tell of a dream that King Edward had before he died. In this vision he met two monks whom he had known in Normandy – both were long dead – and they told him that because of the wickedness of the earls and churchmen, God has cursed this country. They warn that devils will come through the land with fire and sword and war ...'

'Oh, hush! Do not tell me any more.' Mildryth had turned pale.

'Nay, I knew 'twould be wrong of me to worry you with such nonsense!' Til grabbed a stool and put it under her whilst the cook brought water. 'The King was likely raving, there is no truth in it. Whatever we might think of Godwinsson he is a great leader. He would not let England be overrun.'

Mildryth refused the cup of water, hugged her belly and prayed that he were right, but the seed of fear had been sown. She could not rid her mind of the omen.

The announcement that Harold was to be King met with resistance from the north, but the new monarch soon overcame this with a display of bravery. Without aid of arms he rode to Jorvik and offered himself to the mercy of the Northumbrians. A gemot of earldoms was held in the city. Til, having great admiration for Harold's audacity, supported his claim to the throne. The earls were convinced and pledged their swords, and the whole of England was behind Harold. This was just as well, for within ten days of his coronation there came a threatening message from William of Normandy who saw himself as a claimant to the throne, and the fyrd was put on alert.

When no attack came, the people dropped their caution and the celebration of Easter was as big as ever. But on the Tuesday night after the festival, a terrifying vision appeared in the sky – a ball of light with a long shimmering tail. Mildryth, ripe for birth, saw it as a portent of doom. Still nothing happened.

Catkin-bearers turned to leaf, pale-green buds with silvery hairs adorned the beeches, woodland came to life with fawn and fledgling, and in the early eve when badgers coaxed their cubs abroad, Mildryth's son was born – a child of the spring, a new beginning.

Almost at the moment of his birth, came news that Tostig's fleet had been spotted in the Humbre. Asketil thought it best to keep this from his wife when he was finally allowed in to see her, and this was not difficult for his thoughts were immediately centred on his firstborn son. 'Oh, see his hair!' He laughed and bent over his wife who held the babe in her arms. 'It is black as night. And his fingers – see the way they grip mine! Oh, he is wonderful.' After a few moments of admiration he remembered Mildryth's screams and lifted his face from the babe to show concern. 'Thank God your suffering is over. I could not have borne another second.'

Mildryth laughed, her face was radiant in the glow of candles that surrounded her bed. 'Nor I, neither.'

Til looked abashed and laughed too. 'What are we to call him?' He moved aside as the midwife brought a cup of warm milk and honey for the mother and, taking the baby, laid him in a crib nearby.

'That is for his father to say,' replied Mildryth, wondering why her hands trembled upon the cup while she felt so strong in spirit. 'But I rather like the name Elfin myself.'

'Yea, it suits him.' Asketil nodded and enquired of the midwife, 'Good mistress, what do you think to my son?'

The midwife, a plump woman with Slavic features, made ready to leave, tucking her mysterious bottles and potions into her bag. 'He is a good lad and caused no trouble coming into the world – but what a day to be born on! I wonder how far down the Humbre Lord Tostig has got. Have you heard, my lord?'

Asketil could have punched the woman for her stupidity. Mildryth's joyous expression had calcified and she dropped the cup, spilling milk over her bed. Throwing the empty vessel to the floor he clutched her arms. 'There is nought for thee to worry about! We do not even know if the reports are true.' A glare over his shoulder sent the midwife into retreat.

Mildryth was stricken. 'Is Lord Sigurd with Tostig?'

'We do not even know if the news of Tostig is true.' Asketil tried to sound calming.

But Mildryth was not to be calmed. What should have been a celebration was instead a day of terror. 'Why did you not tell me at once? And why do I lie here in bed when the man who would kill us may be at our door!' She flung back the covers and tried to get out of bed.

'Wife, you are too weak!' It took little effort from Asketil to prevent her from rising. In her mind she brimmed with energy but the moment her feet hit the ground her legs buckled and she fell back onto the bed.

'Fetch me my child!' She reached frantic arms for Elfin and when Asketil lifted him from the crib she clutched him to her breast, violet eyes almost popping out of her head with fear.

'Do you think I would let him hurt thee?' breathed

561

Til. 'The day is gone when I put my father above all, Mildryth. He shall not get within one inch of Jorvik. I was but waiting for our son to be born before joining Earl Morcar's army. We go to rout the invaders.'

'Nay!' Mildryth snatched at him with one hand. 'Do not leave us!'

'You will be safe enough here . . .'

'Nay, Til, do not leave us!' Mildryth burst into tears. Asketil had never seen her so emotional.

'Be calm!' He put his arms round her with the snuffling child in between them. 'I will not go with Morcar if you do not wish me to.'

'Do not go at all!' she begged him. 'Not even from this room. Lord Sigurd comes, I know he does!'

Try as he might to assuage this worry, Mildryth would not allow her husband to leave her side for hours, and even then he was only able to creep away when she fell asleep. But he made sure she was never alone during those next few days and was always at her bedside when she woke. This being so, her panic subsided, and good news was to herald her return to the world outside the bower where she had given birth.

'A messenger has just come with news of Earl Morcar's progress.' Asketil beamed at his wife. 'Tostig's force was cut to pieces – and my father's ship was not spotted amongst his fleet.'

Mildryth was only slightly pacified, shushing the crying babe whom she had never let out of her care for one moment. 'Did Tostig die?'

Til was less jubilant. 'Nay, he escaped northwards – but he has not enough ships to make another attack. You can sleep more easy now.'

'How can you say that when we do not know Lord Sigurd's whereabouts? I shall not sleep easy until he is dead.'

Whilst others rejoiced at Tostig's defeat, Mildryth retained her nervousness, convinced that any moment she would see Lord Sigurd's ship in the Use.

If only she had known, Lord Sigurd remained in exile. As usual the Norwegian winter had been endless, and Sigurd was almost out of his mind with boredom. The moment the ice began to melt he sailed for Nidaros and an audience with Harald Hardrada, launching with the grand announcement, 'I have come to offer my services in the war against England.'

Hardrada surveyed the visitor and saw a lean old man with leathery skin, thinning pate, tufts of white hair sprouting from ears and nose, and eyebrows that were almost two inches long. Apart from the boldness of his eye, Sigurd had changed a lot since their last encounter. The King regarded him with amusement. 'We are at war? Why did no one tell me?'

Sigurd hated this sort of conversation. Others had tried it with him, thinking that because he was old he was no longer a man; he had soon taught them otherwise. 'Do not try to pretend you are ignorant of the state of affairs in England, for I know that you have long had your eye on that prize. If ever there were time to grab it then that time is now, with all the squabbling that goes on between its earls – and if Earl Tostig has not sent word to you then 'twill not be long before he does so. With his army and mine to bolster your fleet you cannot fail against such disunity.'

'You do not offer your services unless there is glory in it for you,' cognized Hardrada, reaching for a drink. The goblet was engulfed by his huge hand. Despite the King being seated it was evident that he was a very large man with a voice to match.

Sigurd gave one of the reasons for joining Hardrada. 'I have never forgotten that Ethelred was responsible for my father's death and that Edward is part of that line. Fifty years ago I made a blood-oath not to rest until every one of my enemy's kin is dead.'

'If that is your only reason then you can rest easy.' Hardrada's normally severe brow was relaxed today; there was no hint of the ruthlessness that his enemies feared. 'Word arrived from England last week that Edward is buried; he perished in mid-winter.' Ringed fingers came up to wipe the long fair moustache.

Sigurd's face changed. 'Who reigns now?'

'My namesake Harold Godwinsson.'

Sigurd returned a grim nod, fixing his gaze to Hardrada's misaligned eyebrows. 'It does not surprise me – Godwin and his brood were yet another bane on my ambitions. All my life I have coveted the earldom of Northumbria and have been robbed by one means or another, whilst Godwin by virtue only of his smile was showered with titles.'

'Aha!' Hardrada did not need to be told more. 'The mud clears. You offer your help in return for Northumbria.' He chuckled. 'Unfortunately, Tostig has offered his services too. You cannot both be jarl, so why should I give preference to the older man?'

'Because I am the only one who knows how to keep your northern kingdom in order,' replied Sigurd. 'Tostig has been deposed by his own people for his treachery; not even his friends can trust him. On the other hand, if a man or a king does me one friendly deed he has my loyalty for life. Give me the earldom and I will pledge my sword and fifty men – more when we land on Northumbrian soil.'

'But what use have I for an old man's sword? And if all your men are as toothless as you . . .'

Sigurd retaliated for the blow to his pride. 'Draw your blade! King or no I will fight you now and you will see who wins!' It was a rash boast; Harald would likely kill him.

But the warrior belied his harsh reputation with a languid wave of his arm and merely laughed. 'I tease

you, Sigurd. You do not have to prove your manhood. That you remain alive at such a remarkable
age is proof enough of your cunning – and you are
right about Tostig: he is no leader. I shall make use
of his army and if he is still living after the battle, I
shall appease him with some other title. Northumbria
is yours.' He could not resist a further tease. 'If you
think you will survive to claim it.'

The old man replied with dignity. 'I have survived
six English kings and will outlive a seventh. Besides,
I do not merely go to claim my title, I have a little
bride awaiting me in Jork.'

This set Hardrada laughing. Not many were capable of amusing him but the Norwegian King had
always liked this old battle-scarred warrior. 'Then prepare for a summer wedding, my friend!'

The waiting had become unbearable.

'Dear Lord in Heaven, I feel that I am like to go
mad!' raged Mildryth to her husband as they made
a futile attempt to relax outside on this warm July
evening. 'Where is he?' She swiped at the hoverflies
that hung in the sultry air. 'Why does he not come,
if that is his intent?' Elfin started to wake and whimper. His mother began an agitated rocking of the
cradle.

Til was on edge, too. It was difficult not to be with
the thought that Sigurd could have joined Duke
William's force, but he tried to keep calm for Mildryth's sake. 'Why does he need to come at all when
the mere threat of him can ruin our happiness?'

It was a good choice of words. Mildryth frowned
at the truth of them, then exploded, 'Why, you are
right! What a fool I am to let that happen.' She gave
up trying to soothe Elfin and lifted him from cradle
to breast. 'From this eve I refuse to worry about him
again. After all, he could be dead! I must give myself
more to do. 'Tis all very well being the lady but an

idle mind breeds unwelcome thoughts.' She looked down at the guzzling babe and fingered his cheek. Asketil knew that her mind held the same thought as his; a thought too terrible to be spoken.

Whilst they sat on the bench and talked, birds flew in and out of the open hall to peck crumbs from the table. A combination of aromas wafted from the herb garden – sage, lemon balm, lavender. Starlings flocked in black clouds to their evening roost, all was as normal, yet throughout the nursing of her child Mildryth exhibited agitation. When Elfin had taken his fill she adjusted her clothes and got up. 'I think I will go and collect the last of the honey. The bees should all be home by now. Will you come, husband?'

The beekeeper was pleased to hand over his task to the mistress, and after doffing his cap went home to his wife. Before starting, Mildryth knelt within safe distance of the hive. 'See all the bees, Elfin? We must not go too near for they become angry if folk keep passing their door – that is why it faces away from the path. Now, lie quiet in the grass by your father and maybe you will learn.' She laid him down beside her husband.

Til had brought his flute. Spotting two friends, he called for them to enjoy a musical half-hour and interplayed with lute and lyre whilst Mildryth occupied her hands. Bringing a flame, she ignited some dried puff-ball fungus and wafted the smoke into the hive. Soon the buzzing went quiet and she was able to remove the honeycombs. 'The bees are not dead,' she reassured the child as if he could understand. 'They merely sleep.'

When the combs were all collected a more relaxed Mildryth and her husband went home, each enjoying a piece of sweet beebread. Their journey took them by a clump of goatsbeard, its creamy plumes jolting Mildryth back to her nervousness. *Lord Sigurd is not dead; he merely sleeps.*

Ever since the thaw, Hardrada's heralds had ridden through Norway bearing the iron arrow that was the symbol of war; each man who set eyes on it must join the King's army or be outlawed. Gathering an army was less of a problem than the weather. All summer Harald of Norway awaited a favourable wind; midway through August it came. Sigurd had become more and more crazed by the delay and was therefore one of the first to congregate off the mountainous island of Solund where Hardrada directed his magnificent fleet. All assembled, Harald of Norway left his son Magnus to rule and with his two hundred ships embarked for the Shetland Isles.

In England King Harold's fyrd had been in the same position for over two months, waiting for the Duke of Normandy's attack. It was becoming more and more difficult to feed the men from resources in that part of the country and now food was having to be brought in by packhorse from other shires. Moreover, the army had already completed the required service for that year and its members were eager to return home – what of their families, the harvest and the thousand jobs that needed to be done before winter? How long did the King intend to keep them here? Surely the Normans would not come now. The wind was against them and autumn just around the corner. Why could they not go home? Only a man of Harold Godwinsson's calibre could milk from them the last drop of loyalty: just a few more weeks until the danger was over . . .

The dragons came with the September gales, meeting with Tostig in the Tyne and rampaging down the east coast, their number risen to three hundred. Before steering inland, they attacked the village of Skarthaborg where, having lit a huge bonfire atop a mount, they pushed it down onto the roofs of the fishermen's houses.

Sigurd was impatient at Hardrada's boyish tricks. The town was of no significance; it was all a game and he resented the delay that kept him from his real goal, Jorvik. Whilst the boys romped the old man remained on his ship and brooded over Mildryth. Once the fun was over Hardrada urged his ten thousand men onwards, into the Humbre and on to Jorvik.

Asketil, Mildryth and their son had enjoyed a week's feasting at the home of one of his thegns who dwelt ten miles east of Jorvik, and now travelled home through the Forest of Galtres in the company of fifty soldiers. From the corner of his eye Til gauged the effect that the forest had upon his wife, but saw that her face was for once calm, and he smiled to himself. With autumn nigh the danger of attack from abroad had lessened and Mildryth had begun to relax. The trip had helped – and the new gown she wore. It was violet with wide embroidered cuffs of golden thread and a similar border around the hem. She wore gold in her hair too, a circlet encrusted with amethysts to hold her white veil in place. Asketil marvelled at how lovely she looked, and had to tell her. 'Wife, you are even lovelier than when you were a girl.'

Mildryth uttered a surprised laugh of pleasure that invoked chirrups of alarm from the trees. 'If that is so then it is because I am so happy – and you look almost handsome yourself today!'

He returned her air of gaiety, preening himself in comic fashion to show off his light green tunic encrusted with gold, the fur trimmings, and the embroidered cap that Mildryth had made for him. His horse pricked its ears at his laughter; the brass decorations on its harness jingled with the movement of its forelegs and the sword that hung from Til's waist tapped incessantly against its haunch; it was not his only weapon. Resting on his other hip was a quiverful of arrows and over his shoulder a bow. The soldiers were equally well-armed.

His wife retained her lightness of mood even when he stopped in the forest to allow his falconer to capture two young hawks from their tree-top nest. There was almost catastrophe when the man slipped in his descent and set Mildryth's heart pounding. But he managed to cling on, and with the gawky fledglings tucked into his saddlebag the party continued its homewards journey.

There was a further stop when they came to a village in order to take refreshment. Whilst hospitable peasants employed bellows to whip up a fire that would heat the food, Asketil took the babe from Mildryth, allowing her to dismount. She stretched and rubbed at the arm which had held Elfin, her other being employed with the rein. 'That child gets too heavy!'

'I told thee to bring a nurse but thou will not let anyone else have him,' replied Til, bending his knees. Accepting a cup of ale brought by a grubby-cheeked maiden he gave thanks and smiled.

'I would not trust anyone with him.' Mildryth took the child back, but laid him beside her on the grass when she sat down, and waited for the kotsetlan to bring food which they shortly did.

Whilst the travellers ate, the peasants' work continued, repairing thatches and fences damaged in the recent gales, the ploughing, the cutting of wood for the winter, the brewing of beer, the making of preserves. 'That is something I must get done.' Having enjoyed her fresh bread and meat flavoured with horseradish, Mildryth leaned back on her palms. 'I am tardy in my preparation for the winter this year.'

'You have had enough to contend with,' replied Til, looking fondly at the babe who gurgled in the grass. 'And there are plenty of servants to do your bidding at home – come, let us tarry no longer.' Supping the dregs of his cup, he got to his feet, shouting to the soldiers to make a move, and once again the procession set in motion, this time not stopping until they arrived at Jorvik.

The resounding thud of their horses' feet across the wooden bridge at Earlsburh caused both agitation and relief. 'My lord, thank God you are back!' A trusty servant ran up to grab the ealdorman's reins. 'We feared you might have met with accident!' When Asketil showed confusion he cried, 'Have you not heard? The King of Norway attacked Skarthaborg with ten thousand men this morning!'

Mildryth wondered why she was so shocked at the news of the invasion. Had she not been expecting it all year in one form or another? What difference that it was vikings and not Normans, as they had been led to believe? 'For sure Lord Sigurd is amongst the devils,' she breathed, clutching her baby.

Asketil showed impatience at her obsession, already deploying his troops. 'Mildryth, it matters not when there are ten thousand others who would slay us, too. Get those gates closed now!' This last command was for the soldiers.

'No . . . no, you are right! I do not think clearly. It is worry over Elfin's safety that does it.' She looked down at Elfin, then donned a practical air. 'I will do him no good by whimpering, but must prepare for a siege.' Not content with a passive role she ripped off her veil and gold circlet, anything that might hinder her, and rigging a sling across her breast for the baby she set to helping Asketil and others to reinforce the barricades. 'God help those poor folk out there – they have just repaired their houses after the gale and now another menace threatens to tear them down!'

'God help us all,' said her husband.

Word of the destruction of Skarthaborg had travelled and a small English fleet awaited the vikings in the Use, but when they saw the might of their foe they

570

put aside all thoughts of engagement and escaped up a tributary. Hardrada, pondering on his next move, consulted with Sigurd. 'You know these rivers well. Should we go on or follow them?'

Sigurd was flattered that the great Hardrada sought his wisdom. He spoke cautiously. 'It could be a trap. If we row on for Jorvik the English could sneak back out of their tributary and block our escape. Besides, the river is very narrow higher up. We should moor here at Richale where there is still room for our boats to turn round, and march the rest of the way.'

'So be it,' replied Hardrada, and ordered his trumpeter to sound the order to pull into the banks. 'We will pass the night here so that we are fresh for tomorrow's fight.'

By nightfall news of the invasion had reached the south. The next morning as the viking force began their march to Jorvik, Harold Godwinsson's army hurried northwards.

There had been little sleep in Jorvik. Once the barricades were secure there was nothing more to be done except wait and pray. Whilst her husband snatched a few precious hours' rest, Mildryth and her babe spent the night in vigil at the kirk of St Olaf where prayers were said and candles lit for the deliverance of the citizens from Hardrada. The church was crammed to the limit. Now in the morning only the women remained to pray, their menfolk assembling in the burh to go with Earl Morcar and challenge the viking invaders. Asketil was amongst them.

'If you go, I go!' announced Mildryth. 'Even with Elfin I can be of some use in passing you arrows. And if we are to die . . . let it be together.'

Asketil knew from experience that it was useless to argue with her but did so out of habit. 'Mildryth, you are a mother now. Your job is to safeguard our child.'

'Then you stay here and guard him too!'

'The Earl is no more than a lad. He has never been to war and needs every man he can get – and you know what folk will say if I do not go. They will have it that I support the enemy because my father is amongst them.'

'If they are stupid enough to think that, then let them. I care not!' Mildryth raked at a lock of hair that stuck to her lips and threw it back over her shoulder; the wind blew it back. 'And you have never been to war, neither! Harald of Norway has ten thousand men, you say, then he will wipe out any challenge like a horse's tail swats flies. At least if we stay in the burh we have more chance of keeping our lives. Lord Sigurd may be killed in the battle and even if Harald of Norway wins he will have no need for further violence when he enters Jorvik.'

Asketil gripped his head in torment, but there was nothing he could do against such a line of reasoning. Oh, yes, he could beat her into submission but the moment he left with Morcar this headstrong woman would follow. So, whilst the young Earl and his brother Edwin set off with their army to meet the vikings, he remained to guard Earlsburh, feeling like a traitor on two fronts.

Sigurd's old eyes were not as keen as they had once been; others saw Morcar's army before he did. Just over a mile outside the city at Fuleford both sides lined up to each other. The old viking peered at the row of blurred faces, seeking that of Asketil. Before he had found his son, the English attacked.

The land on which they fought lay between the river on the west and a dyke on the east that flanked a deep and watery marsh. Morcar saw that the Norse troops were thinnest on the latter side and by some fluke managed to beat them back. It was a dangerous moment. Hardrada saw his men retreating and feared he would be surrounded. He ordered a blast from the horn and unfurled his battle flag, a white standard with a black raven upon it. At the signal his army attacked with renewed vigour. The English broke and ran, to be slaughtered in the marsh.

It was a brief and bloody affair lasting only an hour. Despite his great age, Sigurd Einarsson emerged from it untouched, if a little out of breath, the only blood upon his face being that of the enemy. Less uplifting was the fact that Tostig lived too; Sigurd would no doubt have another fight on his hands when he claimed the earldom, but then he had come for much more than a title. Was Til amongst the dead? He looked but did not find him, and was soon called upon to go with Hardrada and Tostig into the city.

This time he was glad that there was no gratuitous destruction; Harald wanted his northern capital intact. The huge gates rolled open and the cheering horde milled through into the narrow streets. Hemmed in on either side by jubilant vikings, Sigurd made his way through the city to Earlsburh. It was good to be back in Jorvik again, though he noted that the city was as yet in a state of disrepair after the recent gales. Lopsided thatches hung almost to the ground, littering the street with rushes. Wattle fences leaned at an angle. Tentatively, the citizens came out to risk a peep at the conquering army. The faces along the route showed various expressions; servility, obstinance or merely blandness. Not one of them greeted Sigurd as a friend. It did not matter; their former ealdorman was too busy wondering how to get rid of Tostig.

The army sang its way along Conyngstrete. A look-out called from a wooden tower to Asketil, 'My lord! The city has fallen – Hardrada's army comes this way.'

If Asketil had nurtured any hope of success then it withered now. With the city surrendered there was little point in Earlsburh fighting on. He looked around at the tired, questioning faces of those under his command. 'I fear we must yield.'

'Til, you cannot!' Mildryth seized him. 'If Sigurd is amongst them . . .'

'It will mean death for myself.' Asketil finished her sentence. 'Yea, I am well aware of that, my love. But I cannot jeopardize the lives of hundreds just to save my own and besides, we do not know yet if my father comes or not.' He looked into Mildryth's face, agonizing over their parting. 'If I am to die . . .'

'Nay!' she raged.

'If I am to die I will do so alone. You will not argue this time, but will do as your husband tells you!' His placid brow was overtaken by fury. 'Go and hide with the bairn. Do not come out until you know it to be safe – do it, Mildryth!'

She knew well enough when not to argue and after the briefest of resistance, kissed him fiercely, grinding her lips on to his, gasped, 'I love thee!' then fled to the house with Elfin and looked for a place to hide.

But – 'How stupid!' she cried aloud. It was Lord Sigurd's house, he knew every hiding place there was. Nibbling her lip she glanced around, came to a decision, kissed the child and hid him. Then, belly churning, she sat down to wait.

Asketil ordered the guards to unbar the wooden gates. It was a celebrated bunch who confronted him – the famous Harald of Norway, Earl Tostig – but the only face to leap out was that of Lord Sigurd. The two men held each other with their eyes as all parties came together. Hardrada spoke to Tostig: 'You know all the foremost citizens of Jorvik. Show me their sons so that I may take them hostage.'

Tostig glanced at Sigurd. 'One such prominent son is here before you.' He indicated Asketil.

Hardrada turned to quiz the old man. 'How odd that he remained behind when his father was exiled.'

'It is a long tale.' Sigurd's legs ached from the march. He would have to find himself a horse.

'Then it will entertain us later, perhaps.' The King of Norway had business to attend. 'I will leave him in your hands.'

When the leader moved away Sigurd remained to glare at his foster-son. The tension became unbearable. Asketil could not decide whether to give up the sword in his hand or use it. In the event he threw it at the old man's feet.

Sigurd uttered nothing and walked towards the house. Til followed and was dismayed to see an apparently calm Mildryth at her embroidery by the hearth. She did not rise when they entered but assumed her most brazen attitude, hoping that Sigurd would not see her true fear.

Asketil displayed a mixture of pent-up fury and sadness. 'Why, Mildryth, why?'

The old man turned and fixed Til with pained eyes. 'I ask the same of thee, Til. Why, oh why, didst thou betray me?'

Asketil looked shamed, but Mildryth leapt to his defence. 'Blame not him! He tried for ten long years to escape the love we have for each other. 'Twas only by your own lust for power that you drove him into my arms! Even when your own thegns rose against you he defended your name.'

Sigurd looked at her, his eyes icy pools. 'And did you too defend your betrothed, Mildryth?'

'I was never your betrothed!'

'You swore to wed me!'

'Only so that I could be near my heart's desire!'

'You *will* be my wife!' he railed at her.

'How can that be when I am already wed to Asketil?' Her voice cracked, ending the display of bravado.

The words came as no shock at all, but he stared as if they had. Under that cruel scrutiny Mildryth was unable to maintain her act, her eyes wide with fear and her whole body trembling. It caused such a pang to gaze upon the loveliness that was lost to him that he turned away to pace the hall and with each step his wrath increased. Mildryth shuddered uncontrollably in Asketil's arms, both awaiting certain death. Suddenly they heard a faint wail; Lord Sigurd heard it too, but when he looked around there was no child present. He cocked his ear. The cry came again – from behind one of the false panels in the wall. Mildryth blanched as he advanced towards it, ear still cocked. She made an attempt to divert his murderous intentions from her child. 'Is the brave ealdorman afraid of a cat in his dotage?'

Oh, Mildryth . . . Asketil cursed her rashness as their captor paused and seemed about to attack her. Then the wail came again. Sigurd's ears were failing but he knew the location of every secret panel here, and one by one investigated them. Mildryth could bear the tension no longer. She dashed for Elfin's hidey-hole and reached inside, whilst Asketil grasped Sigurd from behind. There was a tussle. The old man wrested himself this way and that, raking Til's arm with his cloak-pin, furious to be at Mildryth who made for the door with her son. With one gigantic effort he broke loose, turned tables on Asketil and put the blade of his axe to the younger man's neck. 'Stop!'

Mildryth had reached the door but turned out of reflex, saw her husband with the axe at his throat and was forced to halt.

'Go!' Til choked on his words as the blade was pressed into his neck, though only deep enough to cut, not to kill.

Mildryth came back at once, her son bawling and squirming in her arms. Carefully, the ealdorman released Asketil and indicated for him to stand near to the woman and child. When this was done Sigurd beheld them for long threatening moments, axe at the ready. Then, step by trembling step, he came closer, fists tight around the shaft. Asketil held his breath, the axe was being lifted – he placed himself in front of Mildryth and his son, Sigurd's face was a mask of hate and betrayal, the axe-blade soared and fell . . . and embedded itself in a chair, slicing it clean in two. As the two pieces fell apart, Asketil released his trapped breath and a cowering Mildryth felt her bowels go to jelly. Elfin had stopped crying and turned his interest on his mother's beads.

Asketil took a few more calming breaths, then ventured, 'I knew you would not kill us, *fostri*.'

In his pain, Sigurd was unforgiving, shoved Til and Mildryth at the door. 'I spare you only that you may act as hostages against attack from Godwinsson!'

Asketil, more confident now, argued for his wife's safety. 'Give me as hostage but not Mildryth. You know how ruthless Harald of Norway can be.'

Sigurd totally ignored the plea and bullied both of them to the door with the shaft of his axe.

Asketil finally abandoned all kinship; guilt was displaced by anger. 'If you would see us dead be man enough to do it yourself and not leave it to another!'

But Sigurd would not be goaded. Neither Til nor his wife realized that for once in his adult life, the warrior did not know what to do.

In the evening, after making a treaty with its citizens that they should join forces with Hardrada when he attempted the conquest of all England, the invaders left the city with their hostages, crossed the marshy battlefield thick with corpses and went back to their ships at Richale.

The next four days were as a dream to Mildryth. She and Asketil and their fellow hostages were witness to a curious air of leisure amongst the vikings. It was as if Hardrada, having won Jorvik, believed that his battle was over. Sigurd could have enlightened them as to the reason; Tostig was to blame for this. He had promised Hardrada that more aid would arrive from his northern earldom and together they would make a strong contest for Harold Godwinsson who was doubtless on his way here by now. Sigurd himself was in a cleft stick. He had achieved none of the things he had set out to do. Tostig believed himself to be Earl of Northumbria again – well, that could soon be remedied, there was no hurry on that score . . . but what of Asketil and Mildryth? Why had he not killed them as he had fully intended? And just what was he going to do next? He had advised Hardrada that he had too few hostages with whom to barter and should take more. Harald had agreed and had sent a force into Jorvik to demand an extra five hundred. With the reply that these would be forthcoming, Hardrada seemed content to wait upon the day of delivery, Monday the twenty-fifth of September. Sigurd had felt it too long a wait, but he was not in command. The agreed meeting place was Stanfordbrycg, twelve miles from here and seven from Jorvik, which was easy to get to by both sides. Once again he found himself waiting, but waiting for what – Death? There was little else left now that he had lost both Mildryth and the man he had called son. He lifted dispirited eyes towards the group of hostages. On this pleasant Sunday eve Mildryth and Asketil sat with their babe under an oak tree constricted by ivy. With other sources of nectar gone its flowers were amass with bees. Birch and poplar had shed their leaves; others were turning to pink and orange. Sorrel grew here in abundance like spears of dried blood.

A priest who was amongst the hostages had just finished Mass, but prayers lived on in every heart. Mildryth, about to feed Elfin, caught Sigurd watching her. As she put the baby to her breast the old man looked away. 'Ah dear Til, I feel much sorrow for him.'

Believing that she referred to their son, Asketil brushed Elfin's cheek with a finger. 'Do not worry, I will ensure he comes to no harm.'

'Nay, I meant the old man.' Arms occupied with the babe she inclined her head towards Sigurd.

Til gasped. 'How can you pity one who nearly killed you?' Every last drop of respect for Sigurd had evaporated now.

She shook her head. 'I have had much time to dwell on it over the last few days. Remember his face – did you not witness the pain there? Much as we had hurt him he could not have killed us if his own life had depended on it – and if he had, then I would hold myself partly to blame. I led him on, allowed him to believe that I returned his love. You told me it was cruel but I was too young to see it then, I cared too much for my own appetites. Now I know how he must feel. He is old and will die soon. We must make our peace with him, Til.'

'Never!' vowed Asketil. 'By God, Mildryth, you have changed your tune – and how do you know that he will be the one to die and not us?'

'If we are to die then even more reason why we should repent of our sins against him.'

'*Our* sins?' Her husband was scandalized.

'Nay, I phrased it badly.' Mildryth dropped her head to kiss the suckling child, her voice low. 'The sin was all mine. I meant only that you should make peace with him before either of you dies.'

'I will never grant him peace! All my life I was loyal as a son. When I knew that he wanted you as his wife I tried most desperately not to love you, supported him through thick and thin in his fight for the earldom – and he calls me traitor, when he fights for the Norwegian against his own people! Well, I have done with him, Mildryth. If I am to die then there is

579

only one with whom I would share my last words.' He put his arm round her, squeezed and rubbed her fondly.

His vigour dislodged the child from her breast; Elfin complained loudly. Mildryth redirected his gaping mouth, then was quiet for a time whilst he took sustenance. When he lay bloated in her arms she came to a decision. 'You must do as you see fit, Til, but that man loved me once and I cannot go to my Maker without thanks for that at least.'

Expelling a sigh, Asketil took charge of the babe and let her go alone, watching the old man's face turn up to her as she stood before him. Through the rage came uncertainty as twenty years of memories filled his mind. But no, he swore to himself, I will not join her.

Sigurd was rubbing grease on the links of his byrnie to guard against rust. His peripheral vision had caught Mildryth's approach but when she arrived to stand before him he glanced up only once. Once was enough to make his heart bleed at her loveliness. Even in her desperate state she had combed her blonde hair – looked as pure and clean as ever.

Mildryth looked down at him. 'I have only short speech to make.' There was no edge to her voice, neither cold nor warm. 'I ask no forgiveness for wedding Asketil. I love him more than life itself and would do the same again if he asked me to . . . but I am much in your debt for all that you have given me in the past and must make amends. Right or wrong though either of us be in our actions, I know that I should not have tried so hard to come between Til and the father he loved. For that I am truly repentant, and I wish you only peace.' On her conclusion, she gazed for a while at the faded dragons on his arms, the working sinews making them writhe into life. When no response was forthcoming, she turned and walked back to her husband who did not scoff at her attempt at reconciliation but hugged and kissed her.

'You are a brave lass for trying,' he comforted. 'The ogre is not worth it.'

Sigurd rubbed furiously at his byrnie, never lifting his eyes from it. When this was done he polished his sword, then his axe, and every blade in his possession. In each polished surface shone Mildryth's face.

They slept on the ships, some remaining on land to guard the hostages. Sigurd was amongst these, though at midnight a younger man came to relieve him and told him to get some sleep. Little chance there is of that, thought Sigurd, with my old man's bladder and the thoughts that plague me, but he laid his head down anyway and must have drifted off at some point for when he woke it was dawn. For a time he lay there, wondering what this Monday morn held in store. Then, he stretched, pulled himself into a sitting position and finally got to his feet, passing a few more moments looking up at the sky. At least it was going to be a fine day.

Hundreds of miles away a wizened Irishman emerged from his bothy and looked up at that same sky. Murtagh O'Cellaigh stretched, and yawned, then moved away from the house before passing water. Whilst so engaged he looked at the sky again. It was going to be a fine day for ploughing. There was no dread attached to the thought; Murtagh's land-holding was but a crumb when compared with the huge expanses he had been forced to work for Lord Sigurd. And it was his own land! He would have ploughing over well before dusk, then he would set upon building a winter sty for the pig.

Having relieved himself, Murtagh enjoyed another few moments of idleness, running his crooked eye over the Irish landscape, for some strange reason thinking of Asketil and Mildryth. Had they grieved long over Lord Sigurd's death? Had they cursed his murderer? Murtagh did not really care. He had just celebrated his forty-seventh birthday. Who would have thought that the former slave would outlive his master?

'Father!' A small boy came running out of the house. Murtagh grinned and caught the child up in his arms.

'Mother says, food is on the table.' The black-haired child linked fond arms round his father's neck.

Murtagh nodded and, heading towards the house, carried his child in to breakfast.

Hardrada had finished breaking his own fast and ordered his trumpeters to signal for the men to disembark.

'Christ in Heaven!' objected the man next to Sigurd. 'This bread has not even touched my lips yet – does the King expect us to march on an empty belly?' Others joined his complaint. Sigurd ate little these days and was already preparing to depart, but sympathized with those who went hungry before going to find out Hardrada's plans for the day.

The King of Norway announced that he was to divide his army. 'One third of the men will look after the ships, the others will accompany me for the hostages.'

With fifty years experience of war Sigurd was a good military tactician. 'It would be unwise to so weaken your force, my lord.'

Hardrada was a clever strategist too, but the lack of resistance to his invasion had caused him to relax. 'I have decided.'

'What do you intend to do with the hostages you already have?' asked Sigurd.

'We will leave them here.'

Sigurd was uneasy. 'I would advise you to take them along in case of ambush.'

Tostig thought this wholly unnecessary, but this

time Hardrada gave credence to the old warrior's instinct. 'Bring them along and you will be responsible for keeping them in order.' He knew that Sigurd's adopted son was amongst the group, but the old man had not been keen to acquaint him with the reason and Harald was not particularly interested.

It was a warm morning, sun and blue sky adding depth to the autumn colours. The King was so sure the fighting was over that he and his men left their coats of mail behind, carrying helmets and shields, bows and arrows, swords and axes. Sigurd was not so blasé and wore his mail even though it caused discomfort. He took up a position behind the hostages, mounted on the horse he had taken from Earlsburh. The King, Tostig and other nobles rode at the head of the procession. All were merry except for the wretched captives and Sigurd, who brooded over Mildryth's words, as he had done all night. A child cried. Mildryth's child . . . Til's child. *Forgive them,* urged his heart. *Let Til have her; you are an old man and would soon make her a widow.* But when had Sigurd ever listened to his heart?

The army crossed a ploughed field, disturbing a flock of lapwings that wheeled and called overhead. Dust rose from the thousands of boots that tramped across the dry soil, parching throats. One hour passed, then another. Sun-warmed fruits perfumed the air, luring hungry hands to reach out and grab at branches, turning mouths red and purple. Sigurd was too consumed with thoughts to eat: thoughts of all the comrades who had died over the years, thoughts of Una and Estorhild, thoughts of his mother, thoughts of Gytha. His daughter would have been a woman of forty-four now! But for as long as he lived his mind would always see her as a three-year-old child.

The morning grew hotter and the destined river crossing was a most welcome sight. Stanfordbrycg was a village of some importance, for many roads converged here. On either side of the brown ribbon of water the land sloped gently upwards. Hardrada's soldiers, grateful that their march was over, relaxed around both ends of the wooden bridge in a disorderly heap, some on the Jorvik bank of the river in flat water meadows and some on the rising ground of the opposite edge. Sigurd ordered the hostages and his own company of men to halt, then dismounted and allowed his horse to bend its head over the river. His face glowed from the heat, but he kept on his mail and only removed his helmet. A thirsty Mildryth begged Asketil to fetch water for them both in his hat. She was famished, too, but unlikely to be fed by her captors, and would have gone hungry this morning also if Til had not found some mushrooms and fruit. She gulped from his hat before the water soaked in. Sigurd drank too, swearing at those whose boyish rompings clouded the river with mud. With their lewd songs and japes the young men were beginning to grate on his nerves, but it was impossible to get away from their mass. Thousands upon thousand lined the river, cooling their throbbing feet. Sigurd moved a little way back from the water and flopped to the ground.

All were in this leisurely, scattered pose when a look-out alerted the King that the new hostages were almost arrived; they were about a mile away and clearly visible atop the gentle hill on the road from Jorvik.

Hardrada had sharper eyes. 'These are no hostages but an army – see, the glint of weapons!' He called Tostig to him and asked who the arrivals could be.

'It will be my friends come to make their vows of obedience to you their King,' answered Tostig. As the army drew nearer, however, he had the dreadful realization that it was his brother, but did not give him away, saying only to Hardrada, 'My lord . . . I am mistaken. I think we shall have a fight on our hands.'

A curious Sigurd had wandered up to Hardrada's shoulder; the Norwegian dwarfed him. 'Do you know who he is, my lord?'

Hardrada narrowed his eyes. 'Whoever it is, he is obviously an important personage.'

'It is Harold Godwinsson.' Sigurd took malevolent delight in evening the score with Tostig for his revelation of Asketil's identity to Hardrada. 'I am surprised the Earl did not recognize his brother.'

At Tathaceaster Harold Godwinsson, having learnt of the battle of Fuleford and the capture of Jorvik, had wasted no time in going there. He had set out from Lunden with around three thousand housecarls and during the march his army had grown; at each village he had rallied men to him and last night he had done the same with the battered folk of Jorvik who now came to face Hardrada, not to surrender but to fight.

By now interest had spread and the Norse army was gathering form. Sigurd made ready for war. The King of Norway was asking Tostig's advice but the old man answered first. 'You have taken enough instruction from him! If we had not dallied for days we might have had our extra hostages and could make treaty. Where are Tostig's friends that he promised? We should have gone south whilst we had the upper hand.'

Tostig could not believe that his ealdorman had so turned against him, but ignored the slur for this moment. 'We must retreat to the ships and fight them there.'

Sigurd was against any retreat. 'We would be cut to pieces by their horse soldiers.'

Hardrada had already thought of this. 'We will have to make a stand and send messengers on the best horses to fetch the others here.'

Whilst the messengers rode for help, Tostig made a suggestion. 'We should try to barter, using the hostages already in our possession.' A look at Sigurd showed that he was attempting to get his own back.

Hardrada decreed this useless. 'There are too few to have any influence. We might as well kill them lest they aid the enemy from within.'

Sigurd tried to conceal his alarm. ''Tis a great waste to do that, they might come in useful later. Besides, we have not the time, the enemy are almost upon us.'

Hardrada conceded. 'Very well. Line them up over that side of the bridge – they will bear the brunt of English arrows.'

Sigurd faltered, but with the attack imminent he had his men round up the captives and shepherd them over the narrow wooden bridge. It was as he crossed it himself that he knew he was going to die today.

'What does he intend to do with us?' Mildryth asked her husband, covering Elfin to avoid him being elbowed by the terrified people around her – they were at the centre of the group.

Asketil guessed and spoke bitterly. 'We are to act as a shield. It is as I said before – he will not kill us himself, but wants others to do it.'

Mildryth gasped outrage and swivelled her head to look for Sigurd but could not see above the crowd of greasy heads. However, once the hostages were on the other side of the river their captors came amongst them, prodding them with spears and making them thin out into a line. Mildryth still looked around wildly for the old man who had brought them to this. There he was! Without warning she broke from the line and ran towards Sigurd. Til made a grab for her but missed and was forced to run after her. Norse voices called for them to stop or be killed but Mildryth reached her objective first.

'You cannot do this to Asketil and his son!' She

fell on her knees before him, babe in arms, and before Til had a chance to muzzle her gave the added cry, 'If one of us has to die for what we did to you then let it be me!'

'Take no heed!' Asketil reached for his wife's arm and pulled her to her feet. 'I want no woman and babe to die in my place.'

'Neither of you will die,' muttered a dispassionate Sigurd, and waved away the soldier who had chased the pair. His eyes were not on them now but on the approaching army. 'Take the child and go back to Jorvik.'

Both were too astounded to move at first, but as Sigurd turned his back Mildryth shouted after him, 'And that is all – after what you have put us through? No word for the loving son whom you treated so badly? And what of our fellow hostages? We will not go without them!'

Sigurd turned, looked her in the eye then gave both a hefty push. 'Be gone, I say!'

She took a pace after him but Til dragged her from the river and away up a slope. 'Mildryth, it is not in your power to save the entire world! Be just grateful that he hath spared us three.'

She closed her eyes and nodded acceptance, then looked back over her shoulder as they hurried to escape. 'Still, he could have made peace with you!'

'It requires no words to do that.' Asketil continued to put more distance between them and the battle that was to come. 'This is his way of saying all is forgiven.' When they were far enough away, he paused to look at her, gave a tight smile and pulled at his beard. 'It must have been your words last night that pricked his conscience. What did you say?'

Mildryth came to a halt and looked blank. 'Nought of substance . . . Are we to go home, then?' She noticed a fluffy seedhead clinging to his whiskers and teased it out.

'Not until I know the outcome.' Leaden-hearted, Asketil sought a place from which to observe the impending clash, found one and sat down with his wife. Quaking grass shivered in the breeze, sending waves across the field and bringing to Asketil an emptiness that he had not experienced since Ulf had died.

The main bulk of Hardrada's army was by now formed into a circle; many of the approaching Saxons were on horseback and Sigurd offered the wise advice that Hardrada should prepare for a mounted attack in case under Edward's influence the English had adopted the continental manner of warfare. He had taken up a position to the rear of the hostages just in front of the bridge. As ever when in battle, age had drained away, he was filled with youthful enthusiasm, keen to engage the enemy, and even more heartened now to see the English dismount – battle was to be in the good old hand-to-hand style to which he was accustomed. Archers took their positions. At the first warning *twang* of bowstrings the hostages scattered, but were not quick enough to escape the deadly rain. There were bursts of thistledown as a host of them fell, coated with the fluffy seeds. Watching from his hillock Asketil winced, experiencing the pain in his own breast. The air whistled with missiles – stones, arrows, javelins – and another batch of vikings fell dead and wounded.

With King Harold at their nucleus, the Saxon warriors presented a shield-wall; flanking them were the lightly-armed civilians, many of whom Sigurd had passed in the alleys of Jorvik; one day neighbours, the next enemies. The man beside him fell dead, a throwing-axe embedded in his brow. The byrnie-clad mass edged towards him, thump, thump, thumping shields, faint mumbles growing into one enormous chant – *'Holy Cross!'* Sigurd responded with customary boldness, ran out from the line, danced and

gyrated between the corpses, feinted with his axe –
'Come and get us!' Closer, closer, edged his foe,
ploughing through the water meadows, trampling
flowers and dead alike.

'Pig's snout!' yelled Sigurd. It was not an insult but
an instruction. A number of his men formed themselves into a wedge-shaped pack and edged forth to
try and break through the English shield-wall, the
man at the tip of the wedge intending to hack a
breech which would then be widened by others in the
wedge. But this time it did not work. Mounted skirm-
ishers rode out from the English line to encircle and
harass the pig's snout with throwing spears until
it crumbled and fell apart – and then the English
charged with sword and spear and battle-axe, mouths
yelling, eyes wild with hate and fear.

Under sheer weight of numbers the Norwegians
were forced to give ground, but did so by the inch,
trying to let those behind them get across the bridge
and form a shield-wall around the leaders. Hardrada
cursed himself for underestimating the strength of his
opponent and watched from his horse with growing
unease as the two sides clashed. Already the English
were pressing the vikings back towards the bridge –
that all-important bridge, for once the army had
crossed it the Norsemen were considerably disadvant-
aged.

The battle screamed on for hours. Men were disem-
bowelled, decapitated, destroyed, pushed backwards,
ever backwards . . . Asketil was on his feet now,
watching Sigurd's practised strokes hack through
English flesh and bone. The old man had the merry
air of a butcher at his trade, face alight with resolu-
tion, cleaving joints and steaks and tripes, but the
Norse wall around him was crumbling fast. Asketil
grew concerned and knew at once that Sigurd was
about to die. *I should have made peace with him: I
cannot let him die alone*. He turned a haggard face

on Mildryth, who guessed instinctively what he was about to do.

'Do not be a fool, Til!' With one arm, she fought to hold him back, riving at his tunic. 'Think of your son!'

'And what is my son to think of me if I watch my own father die and do nought? I have to help him, Mildryth.' He kissed her long and hard – 'God bless thee, lass!' – then wrenched himself away, pelted over silvery-green cushions of moss and exploding thistle-heads to where the meadow was slippery with gore. Mildryth had no second thoughts; she laid her baby amongst the ferns and chased after Til.

There were hundreds of weapons abandoned by the dead. Til paused only to grab a sword and raced headlong into the fray, lunging at the row of unsuspecting backs. Sigurd's muscles begged to let go of the heavy axe whose twelve-inch blade arched back and forth, keeping the English at bay. Groin and armpit burnt with sweat, noseguard chafed and rubbed flesh raw, spine and shoulder groaned for mercy, yet the foe demanded more – and then here was a shoulder-comrade whose blade slashed energetically to right and left! Not a word passed his lips when he saw it was his son but the joy was evident in his eye and in the renewed vigour of his fighting. The faded dragons on his arms gained new power, lifting the axe again and again, crunching, splintering, rejoicing in the battle frenzy.

A woman's scream rose above the grunts and snarls and roars, not a frightened cry for help but a scream of angry intent. Mildryth had picked up a spear, and used it to jab a passage towards her husband, caring not where it met the body, only that it did its job.

'Go back!' Sigurd and Asketil yelled almost in unison, but Mildryth came on, teeth bared – 'Demons! Villains!' The English could not know that she was not with the enemy and treated her as such.

'You must get her away, Til!' yelled Sigurd, maintaining his rhythmic axe-swing. 'The English shall beat us. If you do not fall in battle you shall both be killed as traitors. Get her back across the bridge and away to my ship, it is your only hope!'

'Mildryth can go but I will not leave you!' shouted his son – just as an English sword caught Mildryth on the arm. Red bloomed upon the material of her sleeve and she dropped her weapon to clasp her limb.

'Back! Back!' With Til occupied Sigurd beat a maniacal path to Mildryth, shielded her with his body whilst she recovered then with rampant axe gaining safe retreat piloted her towards the bridge. 'Take your husband and go, damn thee!'

'We cannot go!' cried Mildryth. 'I have left my baby over this side!'

'Then I will fetch him to you after the battle!' panted a wild-eyed Sigurd. 'He will be safe enough over there – but go! Go, I say!'

Til grabbed his wife and tried to jostle a way through the confusion on the bridge – every viking was attempting to get across at the same time, eager to join their fellows to regroup. Somehow, by pushing and shoving they eventually escaped from the stinking tangle of male flesh and found themselves on the other side where Hardrada waited to inflict a second wave of violence should the English break through.

Every viking was across the bridge now and streaming up the hill on the other side – all save one. Asketil marvelled how the old man could produce such berserk energy to maintain that deadly swing of blade. The bridge was the only feasible method of crossing the river, its waters too deep for men to wade across; the obstruction had to be removed. Ten, twenty, thirty men fell under that great curved blade; Sigurd was euphoric.

Upriver, an enterprising Englishman found a swilltub. Whilst his fellows risked their lives against the threshing axe, he devised an easier method of removing the obstacle. Dropping the tub into the water he jumped inside it and began to drift towards the bridge.

Imbued with such energy, Sigurd felt he could last forever. *Mildryth! Mildryth!* chanted his brain. He glanced over his shoulder to see if she and Til had got away, saw her blonde hair fluttering about her anxious face as she stood on the far bank, hypnotized by his brave performance. 'Get you gone!' he yelled, knowing that when the English broke his hold she would be trampled. 'Go!' But his voice was lost on the manic roar. He raised his axeblade one more time – then grunted, shivered from head to toe, lips pursed, eyebrows raised.

In the split second that the old warrior had removed his concentration from the battle, a swill-tub drifted underneath the bridge. With calm precision the Englishman inserted his vicious winged blade up through the chinks in the wooden planking and with one mighty lung of its ashen shaft, impaled the brave old man where he stood. Til cried out in horror and anguish, Mildryth too, their voices merging in the battle-madness. Sigurd hung there, balanced on tiptoe, the lance skewering bowels and belly, unable to fall, nor move. Then the look of indignance faded to opacity, his dead weight wrenched the spear from the Englishman's hold, there was the creak of splintering wood from the bridge as he went crashing down. Asketil, crouched in agony, felt the barbs rip through his own guts, turned and retched . . .

The English poured over the bridge in a wave of triumphant yelling, trampling the hero underfoot, and the battle continued on the other side – continued throughout the afternoon. Low in the sky, the sun lost its heat and cast long shadows, turning the struggling figures to giants. In adjacent pastures the lowing kine wended their way home, eager for the milkmaid's touch. Seeing his army dwindling to nought Hardrada went berserk and in a last burst of passion killed dozens before this great warrior, too, fell to an English arrow.

The battle came to a lull; it appeared that Harold Godwinsson was about to offer his brother peace – a desperate Asketil prayed that this were so, for on the far side of the river a baby cried. But the Norsemen were far too enraged to allow any quarter and at this precise moment reinforcements arrived from the ships. Breathless though they were from having run all the way in their mail, they waded into the quagmire of destruction. A weary Tostig picked up Hardrada's fallen standard and battle began anew.

Towards evening Tostig died, adding to the thick pile of carrion in the glistening meadow. With their leaders fallen the soldiers were honour-bound to avenge those who had given them protection, and so fought on. Now that Sigurd was dead, Asketil felt no commitment to either side and with Mildryth had removed himself to watch and listen to the carnage from afar. They held each other tight and wondered did the baby sleep or was he dead.

'Oh, God!' Mildryth's dusty face was streaked with tears, her wounded arm bound with a rag. She tore at her hair and rocked back and forth. 'Will this bloody battle never end?'

Hollow of heart and eye, Asketil could only hug her more tightly, staring through the failing light at the crumpled pile of bodies upon the bridge, one of which was his father.

The battle that had started in the morning ended at dusk, the pulverized ranks of Hardrada's army breaking away to flee the battlefield. They were hounded all the way back to their ships where some were drowned and others burnt to death. Under cover of darkness Asketil waded through the bloody malodorous fields where bloated flies escaped the evening chill in the cavities of those upon whom they had gorged throughout the day. Pausing on the bridge to kneel by Sigurd he touched his father's hair. The brow was icy, the eyes not sparkling in the night as were his own, but dull with grit. Amongst the litter of splintered shields and bent swords he picked up Sigurd's axe, distinctive with its fine tracery of coiled snakes upon the blade. A baby cried, reminding Til why he had come here. Using his palm to wipe away tears and mucus he crept on towards the English camp, hiding the axe before he arrived and following the sound of the ravenous Elfin.

He found the babe – in an Englishman's arms. The troops had come across the squalling infant and adopted him as mascot. They were not so well-disposed towards his father.

When Asketil did not return in what seemed like hours, Mildryth could wait no longer and, disturbing feasting vermin, hurried through the grisly meadow to find him. Thus, both were taken captive by the English, accused of fighting on the side of the enemy and threatened with death. But Harold Godwinsson was not a man to glory in unnecessary carnage. Acquainted with Asketil and Mildryth's sorry plight he allowed them to remain in his camp without fear until morning, when Hardrada's son Olav came to give himself up with the two young Earls of Orkney, who had escaped only because they had been left in charge of the ships. Instead of killing them, Harold extracted a promise that they would never attack England again and in return allowed them to take what ships they needed to get the survivors home.

Asketil, Mildryth and the baby were accorded the same mercy, but Til was to lose his rank, his house and land and be sent into exile. He considered it a small price to pay for their lives, but did however ask one more boon of Harold. 'Great King, can I prevail upon your kindness to lend me a horse so that I may carry my father's body home for burial in Jork?'

When informed who Til's father was, Harold breathed recognition. 'Ah, the mighty Sigurd. Would that he had fought on our side. We might have suffered fewer losses.'

'Would that he had never fought at all,' murmured Asketil. 'Then I would not be burying him today.'

Harold nodded. 'I will give you a wagon to transport your dead hero to Jorvik.'

Numbed by immense grief and the horrors they had seen, few words passed between Asketil and Mildryth as the wagon carried Sigurd to his final resting place. The moment they reached Jorvik Asketil gave a last order to his servants, telling them to dig a grave whilst he rushed off to buy a fitting headstone for such an heroic warrior.

As he and Mildryth knelt to pay their last respects he found the courage to smile. 'My father would think it amusing – here is the King thinking he does me great hurt by sending me into exile when all my life I have wanted to live elsewhere!'

A tearful Mildryth smiled too. 'We must hurry if we are not to be left behind.'

Til nodded and rose with purpose. One last grieving look at the stone cross, and he was on his way.

There was nothing to load upon the borrowed wagon, only themselves, the baby, and as much food as they could carry. A mood of urgency accompanied them all the way to Richale – would the ships be gone without them? But urgency could not lend speed to the heavy-limbed horse who insisted on going at his own pace. Following the route of the river, they passed a host of captured dragonships being rowed by the English back to Jorvik. The victors cheered and waved to them. They retained an air of reserve, looking straight ahead and earning curses from the insulted soldiers.

At Richale they feared that they were too late. The only occupants of the river were coot and waterhen. But Asketil's blood was up. 'We cannot be that far behind them!' he urged his despondent wife. 'Let us try to catch them up – we *must* catch them up or swim to our destination!'

Miles, they travelled along that riverbank. Elfin started to cry and even after being fed kept up his insistent wail until a despairing Mildryth rubbed her throbbing head and sighed, 'It is no good, Til! It will be dark soon. You must accept that they have gone. We can always return to Jorvik and find a ship to take us.'

'What fool would take us in autumn?' demanded her angry husband, venting his pique on the horse by whipping its fat rump, but failing to speed its gait. 'I shall never return to Jorvik, never!' – and then he rose in his seat and pointed excitedly. A serpent was just disappearing around the bend in the river! Cursing the horse Asketil jumped down and raced along the bank. More bowed sterns came into view, around two dozen in all – twenty-four ships out of three hundred! Til began to hail Olav and his pitiful survivors – 'Hey, wait for us!' – and ran, heedless of the briar and thistle that tore at his garters. The pilot of the last in line, a cargo ship, looked round, saw him and hauled into the bank to wait, whence Til made frantic summons at Mildryth to hurry with the wagon. It would prove useful for their new life, and King Harold could spare it.

When the cart was dismantled and stowed on board, the oarsmen coaxed their dragon to follow the pack. Sharing a look that was a mixture of relief, sorrow and excitement, Asketil and Mildryth were on their way, bound for the glorious fjords with their son Elfin who would beget a gentler breed of Norseman, leaving Jorvik to one who had loved it: Sigurd – the last viking.

Bibliography

P. Brent: The Viking Saga (Weidenfeld & Nicolson)

J. Bronsted: The Vikings (Penguin, 1960)

J. G. Campbell: The Viking World (Windward, 1989)

D. C. Douglas: William the Conqueror (Eyre and Spottiswood 1964)

C. E. Fell: Jorvikinga Saga (Cultural Resource Management, York, 1984)

G. N. Garmonsway, trans.: The Anglo-Saxon Chronicle (Dent, 1972)

R. Hall: The Viking Dig (Bodley Head, 1984)

W. O. Hassall: They Saw It Happen 55BC to 1485 (Basil Blackwell, Oxford, 1957)

C. Hole: English Custom and Usage (Batsford, 1941)

G. Jones: A History of the Vikings (Oxford University Press, 1984)

G. Jones: The Norse Atlantic Saga (Oxford University Press, 1964)

M. H. Kirkby: The Vikings (Phaidon, Oxford)

M. Magnusson: Viking Hammer of the North (Orbis, 1979)

A. V. B. Norman and D. Pottinger: English Weapons and Warfare 449 – 1660 (Trustees of the Wallace Collection, 1986)

R. I. Page: Life in Anglo-Saxon England (Batsford, 1970)

J. Simpson: Everyday Life in the Viking Age (Dorset, U.S., 1988)

A. Smythe: Scandinavian York and Dublin (Templekieran Press, Dublin)

F. Stenton: Anglo-Saxon England (Oxford University Press, 1971)

D. M. Wilson, ed.: The Northern World (Thames & Hudson, 1980)

R. Wordsworth: The Battle of Stamford Bridge and the Northern Campaign of 1066 (Privately printed)